A TANGLE OF THREADS

A TANGLE OF THREADS

THE SIMULACRUM · BOOK 2

Egathentale

Podium

Cover design by Podium Publishing

ISBN: 978-1-0394-1118-0

Published in 2022 by Podium Publishing, ULC
www.podiumaudio.com

A TANGLE
OF THREADS

PROLOGUE

"Where the hell is he?" bellowed the voice waking me from my dreams of stellar marvels.

It took me some time to reorient myself. I was still in the familiar not-new, not-dark not-room. I tried to turn towards the source of the voice, but then I remembered I had no head to turn. Or body. Instead, the pitch-black space surrounding me twisted around so that the incensed speaker was right in front of me.

It was a gruff, middle-aged man with a thick mustache. It was a dark, barren moon circling a purple gas giant around a pale blue star. It was both, but neither. It was weird.

Then he/it opened his/its mouth again and The Man came into focus, his features rapidly sharpening like I was looking at him through binoculars while adjusting the magnification.

"We need to find him! We are running out of time!"

"Calm down," the strangely familiar ocean of ruby chided him before it took the form of a businesslike young woman. "If we rush things, he will just hide even deeper and then jump out to ruin everything when we least expect it. You know how he operates."

"I... I'm not sure..." whispered The Boy, his image only faintly overlapping with alien skies endlessly raining molten glass.

"What are you not sure about?" growled The Man.

"I mean..." The Boy began, then hesitated for a moment. "I mean, he really isn't acting like himself."

"He has a point," The Girl chimed in with a tinkling voice.

"True," The Woman relented. "But then what do you propose?"

There was a long moment of silence before The Boy let out a strained cough.

"M-maybe we shouldn't do anything? I mean, just watch for now?"

"And how is that going to keep him from ruining our hard work?" The Man grumbled as he crossed his arms. I tried to do the same, but I didn't have any. Being disembodied sucks.

"It's worked out so far," The Girl chirped with a grin. "Didn't we all agree that this was one of the better scenarios we've put together in a while?"

"Yeah, but..." The Woman paused. "Well, I suppose you are right. Maybe he is trying to turn a new leaf?"

"Are you serious?" The Man said, incredulous. "I thought we made this scenario specifically to teach him a lesson. You know, because he's a prick and refused to change?"

"Maybe it worked?" The Woman stated with unusual uncertainty. "I mean, he got hit by the last layer of defenses, didn't he? Maybe he reflected on his actions because of it."

"Hehe—someone is unusually wishful today!" The Girl giggled, earning a scowl from The Woman, but before she could answer, the Man spoke up again.

"I will believe it when ******* turns his ******* inside out!"

And with that, he turned around. Or maybe the not-room turned around him? Either way, he left.

"W-wait! I'll help to look for him!" The Boy exclaimed, and they both evaporated, for lack of a better word.

"Should we go too?" The Girl asked, but The Woman only shook her head.

"No, we have better things to do."

So saying, the two of them also sublimated away in short order, leaving me all alone. Speaking of which, I had the feeling I had something better to do than listen to the vague discussions between… whatever these people were. After some thinking, I finally remembered. I was still sleeping, wasn't I?

Not right now, but yet still. It was hard to explain, but I was somehow still aware, and when I tried to remember where I left my body, the dark not-room around me was subsequently replaced with an actual dark room. My room.

I was still lying on my bed, covered to my neck with blankets. According to the clock on the nightstand, it was just a little after 7 a.m. It was usually around this time I took a shower before heading out. Not this time, of course, since, as far as I could tell, I was currently not inside my body, and thus it had no one to drive it through its morning routine.

It was about time I returned, I surmised. I'd rested long enough, though I couldn't tell exactly how long that was. Time was working weird in the not-dark not-rooms. However, I soon realized there was a minor problem: I had no idea how to get back into my body.

After a little thinking, I decided I would attempt the tried and true "spooky ghost" method. I floated above my unconscious body (though again, it felt more like the room was moving under me) and then I slowly lowered myself until I overlapped with it. For the first couple of seconds absolutely nothing happened, but then I noticed a strange, white glow coming from my head. My body's head, I mean, as "I" still didn't have one at the moment...

I tried to reach out towards it by reflex, and I could feel "something" reaching out, though it wasn't really a hand or a leg. It was weird, but since everything was weird, I figured it was probably normal. Anyways, once I "touched" that glow, I suddenly felt a strong suction drawing me in, and then abruptly (and quite unceremoniously) the world around me went black again.

CHAPTER 1

PART 1

I opened my eyes and exhaled. Well, it was more of a gasp, really. The breath escaping from my mouth felt heavy, almost like it had been trapped in my chest for months. After refreshing the insides of my lungs a couple times, I closed my eyes again and carefully massaged my temple. I had a feeling I'd had a weird dream just moments ago, but when I tried to recall what it was, it felt like dry sand slipping through my fingers. Something about rooms and heads and stars or something...

Anyways, after a few short minutes, I decided to stop being lazy and I sat up. Since my eyes were already adjusted to the darkness, I quickly found my clock and realized it was after 1 p.m. Had I slept in?

"That sounds subtly wrong," I muttered, trying to get my rusty brain to start working properly, and after a few seconds of prodding, it switched into gear.

Right. That made no sense because I never sleep in. As in, it is logically impossible, since I do not sleep. At all. In the past, I stayed awake for more than a month straight. But if so, then why was I sleeping in my bed and dreaming about star stuff?

The answer came to me with a flash of stinging pain in my abdomen. Right, I remembered. I'd poked my nose into a climactic fantasy battle and gotten an ice spike shoved into my stomach for my trouble. I cautiously rolled up my pajamas to check the damage. The injury wasn't particularly gory to begin with as far as I could remember, and I'd received magical emergency treatment, but something like that should've left a mark.

To my sincere surprise, all I found was a single patch of pink skin on my abs. I let out a soft "huh." Perhaps magical first aid was even better than I'd imagined. The spot was a little tender, but considering I'd had the equivalent of a spear stuck in there not too long ago, my recovery still blew all my expectations out of the water. I allowed myself a satisfied smile before it withered as a new question appeared in my head: I'd said "not too long ago," but for how long was I unconscious?

My first idea was to look the date up on my phone, but I couldn't find it in arm's reach. As such, I groggily threw off my blankets and put my legs down the side of the bed. For a moment, I felt a little lightheaded, probably because of the blood rushing to my head after lying down for too long, but I still rose to my feet without much of a problem.

First, I walked over to the window and opened the curtains, then after a few seconds of thinking, I threw open the windows, too. Fresh air never hurt anyone. Since now the room had better lighting conditions, I looked around again and finally found my phone on my desk. I turned it on, and while the battery was low, it seemed to be working, which was surprising after all the abuse I'd put it through that night.

Speaking of *that night*, what was the date again? That was the whole reason I had looked for my phone in the first place, wasn't it? After some fumbling, I opened up my calendar and grunted in surprise. It was October 15, meaning I'd been out cold for... let me see... three days? That wasn't too bad.

Still, it meant I hadn't showered in that long either. I decided to rectify the situation, which also provided me with a great opportunity to check the rest of my body for scars, so I picked up a clean set of clothes and headed for the bathroom.

My house was incredibly clean, as always. By the looks of it, my theoretical ninja maids had worked overtime even while I was unconscious. First, I headed for the toilet (for obvious reasons), then I stripped down to my underwear and stood in front of the bathroom mirror.

My face was smooth, without a hint of stubble, which wasn't surprising. I hadn't had to shave or cut my hair once since I woke up for the first time, so I figured this would be the case. It must've been because of the whole either-simulation-or-a-dream-or-whatever nature of this world, and while it brought my biology into question, I had to admit it was convenient. I checked my skin and found that, besides the already mentioned pink spot on my stomach, I had a couple of similarly coloured scars on my left calf and my left shoulder was a little bruised. Aside from these, I was completely fine. I did a few simple warm-up exercises, just to make sure my body was really all right. It was better to be on the safe side about those things.

First, I did a few squats, then I leaned forwards to touch my toes. I circled my waist, then my neck, and then stretched my three arms. Everything seemed to be in—

"Three arms...?"

I froze mid-stretch and slowly loosened my posture. I looked at my right hand. Yep, that was definitely one arm. Same on the other side. Two perfectly normal human arms with perfectly normal human hands topped with perfectly normal human fingers.

"So what the hell is *this*?"

I waved around my "third arm" or whatever, and the longer I did, the more squeamish I felt. I couldn't see it, either normally or through the mirror, but I was completely aware of its position, the same way I could feel where my normal hands were even with my eyes closed. When I moved it around, I could feel some wind resistance, and I could even faintly hear a whistling sound as it cut the air, though the latter part might've been just my imagination. More importantly, whatever it was, it didn't have any joints. In fact, it felt more like some kind of invisible tentacle than an actual human limb. It could also pass right through solid objects, such as my visible limbs. When I did that, it delivered a strange tingle to my skin, much like being jolted by a mild electric current.

After waving it around a little longer, I realized that either it could stretch a lot, or it didn't have a spot on my body it actually grew out from, as I could "touch" anything within a two-meter sphere around me. After a couple minutes, I stopped messing with it and groaned.

This was so typical.

When other people woke up after being asleep for too long, the worst they found was a bump or scar they couldn't remember. Me? I wake up with an extra bloody phantom limb! And the saddest part? This probably wouldn't even break the top five on my *weirdest stuff I experienced in the last two months* list.

Since it didn't feel like a pressing problem, I decided to temporarily ignore it and enter the shower, but then my ears picked up some sort of commotion coming from outside. I pulled my underwear back up—and just in time, too, as a moment later the bathroom door was thrown open with a bang.

"Leo!" came the panicked cry from the girl standing in the doorway. I let out another groan and frowned at her.

"What is it, princess?"

For a few long seconds, the familiar blonde girl only gaped repeatedly like a fish out of water. At last, after an embarrassingly long time, she let out one of her customary cutesy cries, covered her beet-red face with her hands, and hid behind the doorframe. The whole thing felt somewhat nostalgic; she rarely had these kinds of over-the-top reactions anymore. Anyways, at first I thought she might've run away, but a second later, she poked her head around the frame while sputtering at record speed.

"S-s-sorry! I wasn't peeping! It wasn't on purpose! I swear on the name of the house of Dracis! It was a completely honest accident and I..."

And so on and so forth, her motormouth kept making excuses without end.

"Did you find him?"

The question interrupted the princess. She glanced back and nodded twice. A moment later, the face of Judy, my dear deadpan research assistant, also appeared from behind the doorframe. She gave me an outwardly expressionless look-over, though from the way the corners of her eyes twitched and her cheeks got slightly flushed, I figured she was also somewhat flustered. After a long silence, she pointedly cleared her throat and flatly greeted me with, "Good morning, Chief."

"Back at you," I answered offhandedly as I directed my frown at her. "So, what exactly are you doing here?"

"We were looking for you," she answered immediately without averting her eyes.

"Y-yes!" The princess nodded repeatedly, and it only just registered with me that instead of her usual ringlets, she now wore her long hair loose. It was a refreshing look that suited her just as well. Then she started sputtering again.

"We went to your room to check your condition, but you were gone, and the window was open, so we thought you were kidnapped! I didn't barge in to peep; I was just worried! I swear!"

"You know, I'd have an easier time believing you if you would stop peeking through your fingers."

The princess blinked in incomprehension, but after a few seconds, she let out another cutesy yelp and disappeared once again behind the doorframe. I shook my head and returned my attention to the other girl, who in the meantime had come into the bathroom and was earnestly observing my abdomen.

"Does it hurt?" she asked, poking at the tender scar on my stomach. I let out a hiss, more in surprise than in pain, and she retracted her hand like she had touched fire.

"Only when you poke it," I answered, rubbing the spot.

"Sorry," she apologized flatly, but I knew her well enough to understand that she was genuinely regretful.

"Hey!" The princess once again poked her head through the door and she blindly reached out for Judy, as her other hand was firmly clamped over her eyes. After a few misses, she managed to grab hold of Judy's blouse and tugged on it. "No touching! We had an agreement!"

"What agreement?" I asked reflexively.

"You don't have to worry about that," my assistant answered just as quickly as she looked me over again, completely ignoring the other girl pulling on her, and asked, "Are you all right?"

"Mostly."

"Does it hurt anywhere?"

"As we already established, only when people poke me."

"So you don't need help washing yourself?"

"No, I'm fine."

"Are you sure?"

At this point, the princess grabbed hold of Judy with her other hand as well and tugged her hard. She lost her balance, and before I could do anything, they both tumbled backwards and fell on their butts by the door.

"Ow!" the princess whined while rubbing her hip, but then a moment later, she raised her hand and pointed an accusatory finger at my assistant. "Stop right there! You cannot offer such l-lewd services! It's against the agreement!"

"Lewd?" I asked while trying to raise only one of my eyebrows. It was harder than one would think. Anyways, was she talking about Judy's offer to help me wash myself? I'd say that was a fairly innocent thing to offer someone who'd recently gotten bitten by a monster, fallen off a roof, and then been skewered by an ice spear. But then again, the princess was always easily embarrassed, so maybe she'd read something into it.

Anyways, at this point, I rolled my eyes and said, "I would like to have a shower now, if you don't mind," and closed the door. I could hear some kind of scuffle from the other side, and the princess repeatedly complaining about some kind of agreement, but I decided to ignore them and whatever love-comedy antics they were up to, even if just for a little while.

PART 2

"How's the tea?"

"It's good, thank you," I answered before taking another sip from the cup in front of me. I savored the taste as I leaned back in my favourite comfy sofa in the living room, then breathed out in satisfaction and glanced at the young woman in a French maid outfit standing beside me. "By the way, what exactly are you doing here?"

"I'm looking after Lady Eleanor, naturally," Melinda, the princess's chambermaid, answered with a mild-mannered smile. "Meister von Fraenir decided it was improper for our lady to spend the night without supervision."

"I see." I nodded before turning my attention towards the lady in question. "Speaking of which, what are *you* doing here?"

"I'm here to look after you," the princess answered with a slight pout, like I'd just asked something stupid.

"So am I," Judy added, blowing on the teacup she held.

"Which reminds me, just how did you even get into my house?" The moment I asked the question, the princess immediately and pointedly averted her eyes. I gave her a scrutinizing look, which only made her act more forcedly nonchalant. "You know, when you act *that* innocent, it only makes you look more suspicious."

"H-huh?" She turned back to me with an astounded expression. "Really?"

"Yes. So, do you have something you want to tell me?"

After a bit of fidgeting, she gave me a pitiful smile.

"Ehehe… Y-you see, I might have been a little spooked at the time, so when we couldn't open the door, I… I broke the lock a little."

"You did what?" I raised my voice, and she immediately began waving her hands defensively.

"B-but we fixed it! I mean, Ammy fixed it! With magic! It's as good as new! No, it's even better!"

I kept frowning at her for a while, but in the end, I let out an exhausted breath and took another sip from my cup.

"Fine. I'll let that slide. I will also not ask how you can break a lock only a little, but I cannot ignore how you are still ignoring my original question. What are you doing inside my house on a school day?"

There was a short silence, but probably only because Judy was finishing up her tea. When she'd finished, she placed her cup on the table with a *clink* and pulled out her familiar pink smartphone. A moment later, my phone on the table let out a jaunty little tune, so I picked it right up, opened up the messaging app, and accepted the attachment.

"What's this?"

"My report. It will explain why we are here."

"Oh?" I quickly skimmed through the text file and nodded in approval. "You are diligent as ever."

"Of course." She nodded with the closest thing to a proud smile her face could produce and then added, "I want back pay."

"Back pay?"

"For the last three days."

"Still in sandwiches?"

She nodded, and I could only sigh at her eccentricities.

"Fine, my treat as usual. As for this," I paused and shook the phone in my hand while pointing at the screen. "Could you give me a moment?"

"Sure."

"So, let's see…" I glanced around the room for a second, then scrolled through the file while holding the phone close to my chest. "According to your report, after we left the purple zone, I collapsed. Angie applied healing magic to my wounds, but since I didn't regain consciousness, you took me home."

"Yes," the princess confirmed.

"Why not the hospital?"

"It would've been hard to explain where you got your injuries," Judy supplied the answer.

"Oh, and they were half-healed, too!" the princess added, desperate to contribute to the conversation. "It would've been impossible to explain those."

"I see," I said, then returned to the text. "So you took me home, where I was put to bed. I stayed unconscious until just this morning, and you two stayed over to watch over me."

"Indeed!" the princess declared proudly, for some reason.

"Did I really need guarding?"

"Yes," Judy stated emphatically. "Amelia said that the mages would suppress any information about what happened in the Restricted Space, but some people might still try to take advantage of the situation and try to kidnap you."

"You already said that when you barged in on me in the bathroom." When I mentioned that, the princess instantly flushed red to her ears, but I ignored her and continued, "Who would kidnap me? The Abyssals are gone, aren't they?"

"Not all of them," Judy stated, and it took me a moment to catch on to her meaning.

"Speaking of which, how's Snowy?"

The three women in the room sent meaningful glances at each other, immediately raising the warning flags in my head.

"Is she all right?"

"We don't know," Judy answered dryly. "After she woke up, she ran away, and we couldn't find her."

"Judy!" the princess hissed while glaring at my assistant, then whispered, "We agreed not to tell him yet!"

"I can hear you," I interjected, but I got totally ignored. Judy just shrugged.

"The Chief would find out in no time, anyway. I told you."

"But he is still injured! What if he tries to find her and gets into a stupidly dangerous situation again?" the blonde girl loudly whispered.

"I said, *I can hear you*," I told her again, this time a little more forcefully, but I was still ignored, so while they continued arguing, I simply closed my eyes and slipped into Far Sight.

My extrasensory ability, which I still didn't completely grasp due to my lack of understanding in regards to magic in this world, quickly found purchase on the red dot in the distance. After a split second, I could feel my vision blur, as if I was being dragged across space itself, through walls and everything, and after another split second, I found my disembodied consciousness in a small room.

It was a tidy place, a fairly high-class hotel bedroom by the looks of it. The curtains were closed, but I could still make out the shape of a human sleeping in a fetal position on the large bed. She had several blankets piled on her, so only her head could be seen, but it was obviously Snowy. Her pure white hair was hard to mistake. Her sleep was somewhat shallow, and she tossed and turned twice while I studied her. At first, I thought I might've woken her, but then I remembered that I could only observe things like this, without affecting them. Speaking of which, spying on a sleeping girl longer than absolutely necessary was rude, so with a flick of my mind (don't ask me how that worked; it just did), I was back in my body.

I opened my eyes and beheld the two girls in front of me, still glaring at each other. Well, okay, in Judy's case it was more of a tiny frown, but considering it was on her normally deadpan face, I judged it had about the same severity as the princess's scowl. I let out a long breath and reached for the teacup on the table, which had been refilled during my time out. I gave Melinda an appreciative nod, then took a sip and cleared my throat.

"She's fine for the time being, so don't worry, I won't rush out the door and get into any 'stupidly dangerous situations' just yet."

The princess twitched and gave me a skeptical look, ignoring the way I threw her words back at her, before muttering a similarly critical, "How do you know that?"

Before I could answer, Judy let out a satisfied huff and answered in my stead: "I told you he would figure it out in a moment."

"But why is he so certain about—?"

I cleared my throat again, this time a bit harder.

"Excuse me. I'm still in the room. Stop talking about me as if I'm not here." To my sincere surprise, not only the princess, but also Judy had fallen into a sheepish silence. I shook my head and continued with, "So you two have been keeping an eye on me because you thought she might try to kidnap me? Really?"

"Technically I was only keeping an eye on Eleanor," my assistant objected.

"Hey! What is that supposed to mean?" the princess flared up again and pointed an accusatory finger at the other girl. "If anything, I was the one who had to stop you from u-undressing him all the time!"

"I was only wiping his sweat," Judy retorted with the frown back on her face.

I let out a long sigh and gestured for the maid to get closer.

"Were they like this the whole time I was asleep?"

Melinda pondered that, then showed me one of her businesslike smiles and whispered, "Milady and Miss Judy actually get along very well." After a brief pause, she leaned a little closer and added, "I believe they are only expressing their relief this way."

"I see... I think."

She gave me another smile that felt maybe just a little bit mischievous. I'd never seen this side of her, though to be fair, I'd only met her a couple of times before. It was oddly refreshing. Anyways, I cleared my throat for the third time and waited for the two girls' attention to return to me.

"So, back to the report and what happened while I was out cold. Where are the others?"

"Amelia was only lightly injured, so she's already back at the School," Judy answered after sending one last pointed glance at the other girl. "The last time we talked, she said she was writing official reports about the incident."

"I see. Now that you mention injuries, what's my cover story?"

The two of them blanked out on me for a moment, but then the princess quickly spoke before Judy could answer, apparently still desperate to be a part of the conversation.

"We said you had the flu!" After noticing how loud she was, she toned her voice down a little and repeated, "We told them we had the flu."

"We?"

"You, me, Judy, Josh, and Angie," the princess spoke while counting on her fingers in a surprisingly cute display.

"So I was out, you two were keeping watch, Snowy is in hiding, and..." I scrolled through the text file before glancing up in surprise. "Angie is under house arrest?" The two nodded in unison. "By the mages?" They nodded again, and I let out a troubled breath. "Another thing to fix. Great. What about Josh?"

"You can ask him yourself," my assistant stated, earning a raised brow from me. She turned her phone towards me and added, "I messaged every-one that you got better. He said he's coming over."

I wanted to ask when, but then I remembered I had a better way to learn these things. I swiftly entered into the first stage of Far Sight, the radar mode in which I could sense the rough location of people I could observe. To my surprise, I found Josh's "dot" coming over at a very high speed, and when I got out of my trance, I could already recognize his moped's thrum.

I stood up at once and, walking through a crossfire of confused gazes, headed for the front door. I stood there for several long seconds, but just as the princess was about to ask me what the heck I was doing, I casually opened the door. Unsurprisingly, as per the unwritten laws of convenient timing, Josh was already standing in front of it, one hand raised, ready to knock.

I was planning to make this one of those amusing "how did you know" situations, but my intent flew out the window when I actually saw him. Josh was, frankly speaking, haggard. His short brown hair had a serious case of bed head and his wrinkled clothes suggested he'd just put on whatever was at hand. As far as I knew, he'd done just that. He also had black circles under his eyes, and as our gazes met, he let his arm down but his entire body tensed up like a piano wire about to snap. He took a deep breath, then said in a hoarse voice, "Leo, we need to talk."

I couldn't help but smile at his overly serious tone. I stood aside and gestured for him to enter.

"Yes, we do."

PART 3

There was a heavy silence in my living room. I was sitting in my comfy chair, and since the girls were still on the sofa, we brought in a wooden chair from the kitchen so Josh would have a place to sit. Once we all got comfortable (or at least as comfortable as we could get under the circumstances), I lightly cleared my throat to break the ice.

"So, I guess you want me to explain what the hell is going on, right?" I asked as cordially as I could.

"Yes." Josh nodded, but then his eyes seemed uncertain. He added, "If you are well enough to talk."

"Oh, I'm fit as a fiddle," I told him with a reassuring smile. "Thanks for the concern."

I was tempted to say he looked worse than I did, but I refrained. During that brief pause, he clasped his hands in his lap and said, "You told me that once I got *roped into this mess*, you would finally spill the beans. I think I am very much roped into..." He hesitated, looking for the right words, but in the end let out a feeble groan and settled on, "... into this weird-ass nightmare."

"Now, now," I soothed him with a raised hand. "It's not that bad."

Giving me a flat look, he crossed his arms.

"Dude. I got kidnapped from my own bathroom by a literal demon, I was tied up and gagged with invisible rope, then I was nearly dragged to literal hell until the people I thought were my friends showed up and turned out to be..." His mouthed worked soundlessly. Then he let out another groan. "The point is, my reality is literally falling apart, and you are telling me it's *not that bad*."

I ignored the barbs in his voice and answered as evenly as I could.

"First off, let me correct a few misconceptions: You were kidnapped by Abyssals, not demons."

"What's the difference?"

"I'll be damned if I know, but apparently there is one," I answered nonchalantly, which earned me another flat look. "Second, you were not going to be taken to literal hell, but the Abyss."

"Again, what's the difference?"

"Oh, I can actually answer that: Hell doesn't exist, but the Abyss does. It's something like a pocket dimension copy of this island, and it's a prison for the Abyssals. Kind of. Anyways"—I raised my voice before he could interrupt again—"as for your third misconception: the people who saved you are still very much your friends."

Josh twitched. He gave me a dubious look at first, but then slowly exhaled, and I could see the tension leaving his body like an overwound spring finally finding release. He closed his eyes for a moment and then gave me a look that was decidedly less dubious.

"I get it," he said softly. "I'm listening."

"Good!" I answered with a grin and leaned forward. "I'm glad we cleared that up. However..." I stood up at this point and gave a meaningful look to the maid by the couch. "Before we continue, since these are confidential matters that could land Josh in quite the pickle, I'd like to ask everyone not directly related to leave the house."

The clock ticked.

Melinda cleared her throat.

"I presume that refers to me," she said.

"Indeed," I answered.

"Wait!" the princess interrupted with a fierce glare. "Melinda has been my chambermaid since I was eight! She is completely trustworthy!"

I gave her my best imitation of Josh's brand of flat looks and shook my head.

"This is not about trustworthiness. While I'm sure she would not gossip about what I need to say, she is still part of the Dracis family."

"So am I!"

"Yes," I answered and raised my hands to indicate she should calm down. "However, you are the heiress. You can say no if, say, a nosy old butler tells you to expose everything said in this room. She can't."

The princess opened her mouth to reply, but before she could say anything, the maid took a step towards the door before she turned on her heels and gave us a small bow.

"I understand. I shall return to the mansion and tell Meister von Fraenir about your recovery."

I gave her a small smile and an appreciative nod in return. "Thank you for your cooperation and give my greetings to the old man."

Melinda returned the nod and then faced the princess. "Milady, I shall go ahead. I'll make sure your dinner will be ready by the time you return."

"Y-yes," the princess answered, seemingly dazed by the maid's decisiveness. I waited for Melinda to grab her bag and leave, and only let out my pent-up breath after I heard the door click shut.

"Well, that's one down," I said as I stood up.

"One down?" Judy repeated, looking over us and pointing at the princess. "Do you want her to leave too?"

"What?" the blonde girl snapped back. "If anyone should leave, it's you!"

"Hush," I interrupted them while gesturing for them to be quiet. Then I walked up to Josh and whispered, "Could you stand up for a moment? I need the chair."

"Um... sure?" he responded a touch uncertainly as he got to his feet.

I grabbed said chair and, while being followed by three pairs of skeptical eyes, I moved it to the corner of the room. In said corner, just under the ceiling, floated a small, softly glowing green eyeball. Well, not a physical one—that would have been creepy—but more of a magical... something. I was still not certain of the terminology, but I'd seen enough magic lately to recognize the glow. It was apparently another unique ability, as others weren't able to see magic, at least not in the way I could. Either way, the stupid thing had been bothering me for a while, but I couldn't do anything about it while Melinda was around. Call me paranoid, but I decided to start playing my cards close to my chest. The fewer people knew about my unusual abilities, the better, especially since even I didn't know how they worked.

But I digress. At this point, I positioned the chair just under the curiously swiveling translucent eyeball, then using another of my currently still unexplored abilities, I took a deep breath and extended two fingers before I made a quick cutting motion through the eye. There was a numbing tingle on my skin when I made contact, then it faded as my fingers passed through the eyeball, and as they did so, it disintegrated into green smoke. Then that dissipated too, leaving no trace behind. I let out another breath and got off the chair, returning it to Josh, who was giving me a weird look.

He wasn't the only one, as the princess was looking around the room with a strange expression on her face.

"What did you do?" she asked, fidgeting. "I got goosebumps all of a sudden."

"Still hush," I repeated, and she slapped her hand over her mouth. I gestured for everyone to stay put, then I left the living room to systematically check every part of the house, which took about ten minutes. The results were two more green magical eyeball things, seven tiny balls of blue fire, and something that looked like three oscillating white rings turning around each other like a gyroscope. After I got rid of them all, I returned to the living room and fell back onto my comfy chair with a tired sigh.

After a few seconds of awkward silence, the princess (who, for some reason, was still covering her mouth) asked the question that seemed to be on everyone's mind: "What were you doing just now?"

I shrugged. "I just dispelled some magical surveillance. Or at least I guess that's what they were."

"Wait, since when can you do that? And how?"

I raised my palms once again, and after she quieted down, I used them to point at my increasingly confused friend on the chair next to us.

"We'll discuss this in detail, but I think we should get Josh up to speed first." For a moment, she looked like she might object, but then she glanced over to Josh and nodded. Leaning forward, I clapped my hands to punctuate the change of topic. "Now then, here's the CliffsNotes version of this whole mess." I glanced at Judy, then added, "You may interrupt if I miss something."

"Mm," Judy mumbled with a nod while she fished her phone out of her pocket and began poking at it.

"What about me?" the princess interrupted with an indignant frown, but I simply ignored her. "Hey, don't you ignore me!"

I let out a short sigh and nodded towards her with, "Naturally, you can do that, too."

Elly puffed up her cheeks in an admittedly adorable display that didn't really fit her age while mumbling something about not being an afterthought, but by that time, I'd returned my attention to Josh.

"So, let's start at the beginning, shall we? First off, as you might've noticed, there's a bunch of supernatural stuff in this world. You didn't notice it, because there is a masquerade in effect."

"Masquerade?" Josh interrupted as he masterfully raised a single eyebrow.

Damn, he made it look so easy.

Anyways, back to the exposition: "Simply put, the supernatural power blocs are trying to keep a low profile because of various reasons. These power blocs are the Magi, the Celestials, the Draconians, and the Abyssals, along with a few minor factions. In detail: The Celestials are definitely-not-angels with a bad reputation for manipulating people. Then we have the Magi, who are bureaucratic magical researcher types who keep the other factions from running amok. Next are the Draconians, who are aristocratic dragon people with more money than common sense."

"Hey!" At this point, the princess interrupted me with a scowl that was completely ruined by her still-puffed cheeks, so I smoothly ignored her once again.

"Now where was I? Oh, right. The Abyssals. Who are definitely-not-demons exiled into the Abyss which, as I previously explained, is not hell. Any questions so far?"

Josh's hand shot up like we were in school, but he caught himself halfway and crossed his arms again.

"I have one. Draconians can turn into lizard-people, right?"

"It's called the *draconic form*," the princess interjected, pouting.

Josh uncertainly glanced up at her and then back to me. "What she said."

"Right. They get scales and horns and tails and the whole package."

"Like I did that night," Josh muttered before his eyebrows joined into a frown. "Does that mean that I am a… Draconian too?"

"Right, that's a good question!" Elly interrupted again, and now that she'd stopped puffing her cheeks, I could take her seriously. "I wanted to ask about that too!"

"No, it's a bit more complicated," I said. "Let's leave that for a little later. First, we have to discuss how this all relates to you."

"I suppose," Josh conceded.

"So, first off, I suppose you already know this, but for clarity's sake: The princess is a Draconian, along with her family and the maid who just vacated the premises. Angie is a Celestial, as you probably already guessed from the wings and all, while the class rep is a Magi. As for Snowy, by process of elimination, she is obviously an Abyssal."

"And you are?" Josh interrupted me once again.

"I am Leonard Dunning," I answered reflexively, earning a skeptical look from my friend.

"I know that. I was asking which of these... what did you call them, *power blokes*? Anyways, which one do you belong to?"

I paused for a moment, ignoring the princess's intrigued looks, and theatrically rolled my eyes.

"Damned if I know," I answered with a bit of self-derision. "You of all people should know better than to ask something like that."

"What do you...?" he began, but then realization dawned. "Right, I forgot about your... erm... condition." He sheepishly scratched the back of his neck, only to realize what he was doing and hastily crossed his arms in front of his chest again.

"Condition?" the princess echoed him with a raised eyebrow of her own.

I quickly brushed her off by muttering, "It's irrelevant for now, I'll tell you later."

"You will?" This time the surprised question came from my assistant, but now it was her turn to be ignored.

"Anyways!" I raised my voice to get the discussion back on track. "You're probably wondering why all of these supernatural people are crowding around you, right? The reason is a prophecy. Or rather, a bunch of vague prophecies that probably apply to you."

"Right, you told me there was more than one," Elly murmured, looking at me at least as attentively as Josh.

"Yes, it's as I told you. Each of the factions has a prophecy about Josh. In no particular order: The Draconians have a prophecy about a human restoring the old bloodline, meaning it would allow them to be more like dragons with all the benefits. The Celestials' prophecy is about their dear leader from a few thousand years ago being reincarnated as a human, coming back and ushering in a new golden age for them. The Abyssals' prophecy, on the other hand, is about a human who can absorb the power of the Abyss, and in doing so would allow their own dear leader to come back and wage war on the rest of the world again. As for the mages... well, I haven't asked the class rep yet, so I don't know, but I would bet they have something similar too."

"A moment," Judy interjected, and a few seconds later my phone jingled. I glanced at it and then told her with my eyes how she should continue the explanation while I read it. She didn't seem too thrilled by the idea (or maybe she just couldn't read eyes), so in the end, I had to do it myself.

"So," I began after skimming through the text, "according to what my taciturn assistant discovered from some really old documents in the Dracis library, although they didn't say anything about the mages' prophecy beyond the fact that it *exists*, we know that the Knights-with-the-long-name who are the sworn enemies of the Draconians also have a prophecy. It's about a young man who would pull out some very elaborately named magical sword from some equally magical stone and then go and beat down all the bad, bad dragons. Kinda clichéd, if you ask me, but if that is what's written there, then that's the prophecy."

I put down my phone, only to notice that Josh had raised his hand again. I gave him the go, so he let it down and asked, "So... you're saying all five of those are about me?"

I involuntarily raised my brows derisively at the question, then I quickly forced my face into neutral gear and chided myself for being insensitive. It should be laudable that Josh could keep up with the conversation so far without freaking out on us; I shouldn't fault him for not yet realizing just how absolutely bonkers this world was. That said, I cleared my throat and answered, "Yes."

"All of them!?" the princess exclaimed. "You mean, all of those are really about him?"

"Yes," I repeated.

"But... they contradict each other!"

"Obviously," I answered with a shrug.

"So... um..." Elly stammered. "Okay, so how does that work?"

"Well," I began, focusing on Josh again, "in practice, it means all the prophecies are practically meaningless." Looking at their confused expressions, I steepled my fingers in my best "all-knowing mastermind" impression. "Listen. If there was only one prophecy, then we would have a problem. Prophecies, by nature, tend to throw free will right out the window. If that happened, I would be already working on breaking said prophecy to pieces just on principle." I raised a hand and slowly opened it. "However, thankfully we have five prophecies, and at least four of them are contradictory. Based on the track record, I guess we can probably go five out of five. This means that for one of them to be true, four have to be wrong." Saying so, I closed my hand in a way that only my index finger remained outstretched. "That means that any single prophecy has an eighty percent chance of being wrong. At that point, either one of them is as good as complete bunk."

"But..." the princess stammered again as she looked at me with a weird expression. "But wouldn't that mean that our prophecy... it's wrong?"

"Wrong? No, not necessary." I told her, which for some reason seemed to immediately reassure her. "Now, when you think of prophecies, you think of ironclad predictions of the future, right? What if we look at them differently? What if all of those prophecies are just possibilities, and depending on your choices, you can fulfill or avoid any of them?"

"Ah!" came a soft exclamation from my assistant. Then she stated, "They are routes."

"*Routes?*" Josh repeated after her, a question mark proverbially hanging over his head, but I waved it away.

"It's not important, just terminology Judy and I use," I sent a meaningful look at my assistant, but she was too busy taking notes and didn't react. "So, this actually ties into a previous question. Josh, remember how you turned Draconian that night?"

My friend shuddered and answered, "How could I forget..."

"Yes, but can you do it now?"

Josh furrowed his brows, then shook his head.

Elly raised a hand. "I have a better question. How did it happen in the first place?"

"All right, let me explain from the beginning," I said, resuming my mastermind pose. "We are clear on the prophecies, right?"

Everyone nodded.

"We are also clear on all of them being bunk, right?"

I got another, less enthusiastic nod this time.

"However it also means they all have the *potential* to be true, right?" This time I only got confused looks, so I put extra emphasis on my words. "What I'm saying is that if we presume that Josh can fulfill any of those prophecies, it means he must have the *prerequisites* to fulfill each one separately. Out of all of them, the one that I could confirm for sure was the Abyssal one. According to Snowy, on your first meeting, you showed a reaction when you made physical contact."

Josh visibly twitched at the mention of *physical contact*, but he remained calm enough to ask, "What does that mean?"

"Well, for a start, the Abyssal prophecy said that their own," I made air quotes with my fingers, "*chosen one* will absorb the power of the Abyss. According to Snowy, that's what happened on your first exchange of bodily fluids. Now, that got me thinking, and while I never had the opportunity to confirm it until the incident, my hunch was right." I paused again, this time not for dramatic effect but to take a huge breath, and then pointed at Josh. "The thing that makes you special is that you can *absorb* the powers of others. This is the reason why you can fulfill all of their prophecies: so long as you have someone belonging to the supernatural guys next to you supplying you with some kind of bodily fluid, you can become one of them, even if temporarily."

"Combat transformation?" my assistant asked as she glanced up from her notes.

"We'll discuss that later."

"Wait, let me see if I get this straight," Josh interjected. "So I turned into a human dragon because… ?"

"Because you were given some of the princess's blood."

"So I need to drink their blood to… transform?"

I stifled a snort and shook my head. "You weren't paying attention. Remember how I told you that Snowy knew you were their chosen one by kissing you?"

"So saliva works too?" Josh blurted out, earning him a nod from me.

"Apparently, though, you probably need a lot more. You didn't transform on the street when you first met Snowy, right?"

"Right, but… what exactly do you mean by *'a lot more'*?"

"Probably a French kiss."

"A… French kiss?"

"Yeah, a vigorous one." Seeing that Josh's ears were getting redder by the second, I couldn't help but want to tease him a bit. "So, for example, if you want to get some fancy angel wings and a halo, all you have to do is get Angie, and then—"

"Stop!" Josh exclaimed. His breathing was strangely ragged. "You keep saying *probably, probably*. Does that mean you don't know for sure? Why is it me? Why did all of this happen to me in particular? Why aren't you telling me that?"

"Well, we never had the chance to actually experiment with your ability to transform, so I don't actually know yet, but—" I began, but then I noticed the severity of the looks everyone was giving me. "What?"

"Leo," Josh spoke in a quiet but unusually hard voice. "You didn't really know, did you? You didn't even know if this… this *transformation* would be permanent or not, and yet you *gave* me Elly's blood?"

"Well, excuse me!" I raised my voice in response to his accusing tone. "We were in a tight spot, and if I didn't do that, Snowy would be dead right now. Hell, we might all be dead!"

My words hit Josh like a bucket of cold water and he awkwardly averted his gaze, but then he looked back up. "Speaking of which, how's Lili? I haven't seen her since that night."

"She is fine," I told him offhandedly. "She seemed a little rattled, but safe. I'll go and visit her today after we—"

"Hold on a second!" Elly interrupted me while leaning forward, hands planted firmly on the coffee table between us. "I already asked this, but how do you know that? You just woke up! Not to mention, you promised you wouldn't go after her!"

"No," I chided her, "I promised I won't do anything *stupidly dangerous*."

"But—"

"As for how I know, it's a secret, but if you really, really want to know, I can tell you after we finished discussing things with Josh."

"You will?" Judy inquired incredulously from behind her phone.

"Yes." She gave me a weird look, but I refused to elaborate. Instead, I turned back to Josh and inquired, "Any further questions?"

PART 4

As it turned out, Josh had many questions, most of which were still about the very basics of the supernatural part of this wonderful, weird, and horribly inconsistent world we lived in, and I tried to answer them all to the best of my ability. Before we knew it, the sun was already near the horizon, though it didn't seem to bother the others.

"So, as I said, I'll get Snowy today, and then we'll look into getting Angie out of house arrest tomorrow. I may ask for your help with the latter, you would probably have a better chance persuading the class rep." I finished recounting my plans to Josh. Maybe it was all too much for him to take in at once, but he actually looked visibly worse than when he first arrived, to the point where I worried about his health.

He kept staring at me with a difficult expression, and in the end, he let out an audible groan and massaged his temple while tentatively asking, "So, what should I do?"

I glanced back at him and told him the first thing that came to mind.

"Get a good night's sleep. You look bad."

"That's not what I meant," he responded with a critical look. "You explained a lot of things to me, and you told me what you're planning to do, but I still have no idea what *I'm* supposed to do! Angels, demons, dragons, prophecies—I don't know what to do with any of this crap!"

I shrugged. "Let's start here, then. First, go home, take a hot bath, get some shut-eye. The Abyssals are out of town, the Mages are neutral, the Draconians won't bother you because of the princess, and the Celestials are..." I paused for a moment and peeked at Judy. She noticed my gaze, and after a moment she shook her head, so I let out a small sigh and told Josh, "The Celestials are none the wiser for the moment. You should be safe. Go home, calm down, and sleep. Meanwhile, I'll try to get everyone together tomorrow and we'll come up with a plan together, okay?"

Josh still looked wary, but ultimately he hung his head and told me,

"Fine. I really feel like crap, to be honest." He looked up and added, "Leo... can I trust you to keep me in the loop?"

"Of course. You are the center of the loop. It would be impossible to keep you out at this point."

Josh let out a derisive chuckle. "You are not making me feel any better, man."

"But a good night's sleep will."

"I suppose..." With that, he wearily stood up from his chair and stretched. I followed suit and walked over to him. After a moment of thinking, he seemed to reach some kind of decision and offered me a hand. "I didn't actually thank you for saving my skin back there. Thanks."

"You're welcome," I told him as I accepted the offered hand and shook it. "I'll have your back in the future as well."

"That's... Huh." My friend raised a surprised eyebrow and let out a dry chuckle. "You know, that's actually very reassuring."

I couldn't help but smile at his response.

"Thanks for the vote of confidence." After saying so, I waved for the girls to remain seated (not that it seemed like they wanted to go anywhere) and I led Josh to the entrance of the house. Once we were outside, and I made sure there were no magical eyeballs peeping on us, I patted him on the shoulder and told him, "Don't worry, things are not as complicated as they first seem."

He didn't answer at first, but then he looked behind me as if to check if the girls were in earshot before he asked, "Leo, why didn't you tell me about this ahead of time?"

"I had my reasons," I told him, then I shook my head and added, "You probably wouldn't have believed me, anyway."

"I might have," he answered with a huff. "It would've at least prepared me."

"Trust me, Josh, I knew about this for two weeks, and I still wasn't prepared."

My words got a surprised frown out of my friend, and he looked me over with dubious eyes.

"Did you just say *two weeks*?"

"Yup."

"And you figured all of this crazy stuff out in just *two weeks*?"

"What can I say? I've been busy. I also had Judy to help me." As I said that, I glanced back into the house and then my shoulders sank. "Speaking of which, I have to sit down and talk with her. The princess too."

"About what?"

I debated whether I should tell him, but considering the cat would be out of the bag very soon, I decided to come clean.

"About our relationship and stuff."

Hearing my mumbling, the corners of Josh's lips finally rose a little. He shook his head. "You know what? I'm glad that, even when my entire world turns upside down, there is at least one fixed point that never changes."

"Me?" I ventured a guess.

"You." Josh nodded, and added, "And your womanizing."

I was tempted to punch my smirking friend on the shoulder, but considering how exhausted he looked, it could keel him over, so I just pointedly shut the door on him, earning me a displeased "Hey!" from the other side. I didn't care though, as I turned on my heel and marched back into the living room, where my assistant and the princess were sitting still like mannequins. For a moment I thought they might have overheard what I was saying to Josh, but then again, the princess was way too calm for that. Ultimately, I walked over to my usual comfy chair and sat down with a quiet sigh.

"So," I said, slightly awkward, "it's just the three of us now."

"Yes," Judy nodded and then raised her phone. "Chief, about the prophecies being routes—"

"Not now, Dormouse," I interrupted her, causing her to twitch.

The princess raised a curious eyebrow. "Dormouse?"

My assistant shot her a slight squint (translation: bone-chilling glare), which she subsequently aimed at me.

"Chief, I thought we agreed you wouldn't call me that in public."

"We are not in public," I told her flatly while I gestured for her to calm down. It didn't work right away, but then she softly clicked her tongue, which I decided to interpret as her taking a step back. I took a deep breath in turn and looked the two girls in the eye (though not at the same time; that would've been hard) before I spoke up again. "Since it's just the three of us, I wanted to have a serious talk with you two."

The princess inaudibly swallowed before she linked her fingers in her lap and insecurely asked, "About... what happened at the school?"

I shook my head.

"No, it's about the three of us." The moment I said that, the air suddenly became heavier in the room, so I lightly cleared my throat. "You know, I just went through a near-death experience, right? I... would like to say it opened my eyes to certain things, but the truth of the matter is that I've been aware of our ambiguous relationship for a while."

"You mean our love triangle," Judy stated expressionlessly, earning a small gasp from the princess and a silent chuckle from me.

"Exactly."

My assistant tilted her head to the side and, with some actually perceptible concern in her voice, asked, "Chief, are you all right?"

"Yes. Why?"

"You are unusually..." She paused while looking for the right word, then uttered, "... blunt."

I gave her a wry smile. "As I said, while my near-death experience didn't give me any sort of last-second revelation, it did put some things into perspective." I once again paused, partially to change my posture, but mostly just to steel my nerves. "Listen. Things are going to get hectic from now on. We have to deal with Josh and his prophecies, resolve any lingering issues with Snowy and Angie, and I can guarantee that there is going to be some fallout after the incident at the school. Having our ambiguous love-triangle situation on top of that is just too much, so I want to break the ice and resolve it for good."

"W-w-wait! This is too sudden!" the princess raised her voice in protest, so I turned towards her first.

"Elly?"

The previously blushing princess went deadly pale.

"What?" I asked.

"Whenever you call me by name, something big happens! I'm not prepared!"

"Calm down, calm down. I just want you to answer a simple question: Do you remember what you told me on the rooftop a while ago?"

She cautiously nodded.

"Have your feelings changed?"

There was a long moment of silence before she sharply inhaled and sputtered, "No! If anything, I like you even more!"

As if only just realizing what she said, her face contorted and she immediately hid it in her hands. She couldn't see it, but I gave her a toothy smile and said, "I'm glad to hear that," which made her shudder like someone poked her side.

"So, Judy?"

I turned to my assistant, and to my surprise, she also twitched (a little).

"Correct me if I am wrong, but based on aaaaaaaall the clues you've been giving me since pretty much the first day we met, can I venture a guess and say that there is a slight chance that you might like me too?"

Judy looked me in the eye for a few seconds, then she let out a decidedly defeated sigh, only to snap back into a determined expression.

"Yes, Chief, I like you," she told me with a firm voice and a teensy blush. "A lot."

"I'm glad to hear that," I told her with a smile just as toothy as the one I gave to the princess before I closed my eyes and took a huge breath.

Now came the hard part.

I calmed my nerves and slowly exhaled, and then I stated, "I'm also glad we are on the same page. I also like both of you."

"You do?" Elly blurted with a frankly incredulous expression peeking through her fingers.

"Of course. Why else would I spend so much time with you two? The truth is, through all our misadventures since this school term started, I grew to like both of you for different reasons. I didn't want to move our relationship forward because I wanted to make sure things could work out between us, and I hoped we could transition into a relationship without too much drama. However, with how things are developing right now, I don't think I can pussyfoot around any longer." I was also getting really annoyed by the others thinking I was either a Casanova-wannabe or some dense idiot, but I didn't spell that out for them. "So, after some thinking, I decided it would be best if we actually made things official." I flashed them my winningest smile and finally asked, "So, would you like to go out with me?"

The silence that followed my question was deafening, and the two girls in front of me were slowly alternating their glances between me and each other. Finally, Judy broke the ice.

"Chief… which one of us were you asking?"

I gave her a look that implied it was a silly question and answered, "Both of you."

"Both of us?" Elly exclaimed so loud it almost hurt my ears, while Judy only looked at me uncomprehendingly for a second before there was a glint in her eyes.

"Chief, are you aiming for a harem?"

"No, just you two."

"So an OTT?"

"Erm… Maybe? What does that stand for?"

"*One true threesome,*" Judy stated, earning another exclamation from the princess before she slouched down like a puppet with its strings cut.

"Well, not really. What I'm thinking of is more along the line of a subtype of the polyamorous type 8 triang relationship with a platonic link in the triangle."

"So… you did your research," Judy noted, and I instantly responded with an unabashed nod.

"Yep. This isn't something anyone could just come up with on the fly, much less attempt, but if it's you two, I think it would work out. It would also be a lot of fun." I stopped for a beat, and then lowered my voice and added, "Also, you know what kind of world we live in, right? If this can work anywhere, it's here! We even have precedents already!" I tried to appear as confident as I could, and then asked the big question, "So, what is your answer?"

Judy gave me a very, very flat look and told me, "Chief, that—"

"That could actually work!"

Whatever she wanted to say, it was forcefully erased by the princess's sudden exclamation as she jumped to her feet with sparkling eyes.

"Why didn't I think of it before!"

"Whoa, princess! Calm down—"

The blonde girl rushed over to my side and grabbed my hand.

"Leo, listen! There is actually an old tradition in the Dracis family, where the head of the family can have multiple lovers! It's to uphold the bloodline, but if I asked Dad, I'm sure he would allow it!" All of a sudden, she sat down on the armrest of my comfy chair and linked her arm with mine. "I never really considered it before, but this way I could be the official wife, and Judy could be the concubine! Everyone wins!"

"Hey!" my assistant exclaimed as she also walked over and grabbed hold of my other arm. "What makes you think I will let you be the official wife?"

The princess leaned forward and smirked at Judy.

"Of course I will be the main wife! It's my family's rules!"

"Chief, Eleanor is trying to use her family influence to get ahead. It's cheating. Do something."

"No, it's not!" Elly protested with a huff. "This is the best way!"

"I don't like it," Judy said with a barely noticeable pout while holding on to my arm even harder. "If you want us to go with your plan, I'll let you be the concubine."

"Leo! Judy is being obstinate! Do something!"

I glanced at the two girls dragging me back and forth and let out a small groan. Well, I supposed that's as far as avoiding *love triangle shenanigans* went, huh? Oh well, it was my decision to do it this way, so it was my responsibility to deal with situations like these. That said, I smoothly disentangled my arms and grabbed both girls by their waists, abruptly pulling them towards me until they ended up practically sitting on my lap.

"So," I told them with a smile I hoped wasn't too impish, "I gather you are fine with my suggestion?"

The two of them looked at each other for a few seconds, seemingly engaging in that weird, girls-only communication that seemed to be able to get complex ideas across using eyebrow movement and small grimaces, until Judy finally exhaled and told me, "It's the prisoner's dilemma all over again."

"That's right," the princess added. "With the super-something of the coin, right?"

"No, it's the other half, though it still has nothing to do with the actual prisoner's dilemma," Judy grumbled under her breath, and I couldn't help but grin at her. She rolled her eyes at my expression, but after a long moment of consideration, she softly said, "I would be lying if I said I wasn't expecting something like this to happen, but so long as it's just the three of us, it's not a terrible solution to the problem."

"Right." The princess nodded.

"I think we can give it a try, at the very least."

"All right then," I spoke with palpable relief. Now that this ordeal was behind me, and I went ahead and used my already in-position hands to pull the two even closer into a bear hug. "Let's all get along, shall we?"

"Sure," Judy said with barely reddened cheeks, then after a moment she turned towards the other girl. "First things first, we should figure out a rotation."

"A what?" the blonde girl asked while cocking her head to the side.

"A rotation for when we can have the Chief all to ourselves, and when we should share him."

"Oh!" Elly's eyes sparkled as she nodded. "Great idea. What about the cooking?"

"We should schedule that too."

"Today is mine!" the princess exclaimed, much to my assistant's disapproval.

"No, I will cook today," Judy stated unusually empathically. "The Chief is recovering, so he needs something simple."

"Hey! I can make simple dishes too!"

I glanced between the two bickering girls sitting on my lap, and I couldn't help but feel that I might've bitten off more than I could chew... but at the same time, I felt that if I forced myself to pick one or the other, I would've regretted it in the long run. My life was already messed up beyond belief, so this polyamory or polygamy or whatever situation didn't even feel like that big a deal.

More importantly, though, while I felt tired, mentally exhausted, and just a touch famished, I was also strangely content. Giddy, even. As such, I simply let my lips curl into a smile that I hoped wasn't too dopey and continued to hug both my girlfriends until they figured out their *rotation* and whatnot. That was one dilemma successfully solved. I only hoped everything else would proceed this smoothly as well.

CHAPTER 2

PART 1

"You have what?" the princess shouted in a quite unladylike manner as she jumped to her feet and slapped the tabletop, prompting me to quickly grab the drinks before she would flood everything with them. I breathed out a sigh of relief as I managed to do so in the very last moment, then I glanced up at the wide-eyed girl standing on the opposite side of the dinner table.

"Careful," I told her as I set the glasses back down, then after a moment I added, "It's not such a big deal," but she only shook her head in response.

"No, this isn't something you can just trivialize like that!" she exclaimed, and I let out another tired breath and gestured for her to sit back down.

Now, for a bit of an explanation, we had to turn back the sands of time for about... ten minutes or so? Anyways, since my new girlfriends (damn, that still sounded weird, no matter how many times I repeated it) couldn't agree on who should make dinner, by process of elimination, they both did. This explained the fact that we had two different kinds of broths, mashed potatoes, some kind of fruit salad, a plateful of toast, and homemade waffles. Even if we considered that there were three of us, the amount of food on the table was daunting. As for where they even got the ingredients for all of this, that was one of the seven mysteries of my kitchen.

Anyways, once we sat down around the table, I decided to let the princess in on one of my little skeletons in the closet, namely my amnesia. She was my girlfriend after all (still weird), so it was only proper to let her know about some of my secrets, and this was one of the less weird ones. Which once again made me realize how messed up my life was, so I was trying to ignore it by filling my stomach, which she rudely interrupted. Hence, we were back in the present, where I rubbed my temple with one hand while grabbing a toast with another.

"I'm not trivializing anything. I had it even before we first met, and I learned to work around it. In other words, it's not that big a deal."

"How can you say that?" she continued to protest while leaning closer, her hands still on the tabletop. "And why didn't you tell me about this before?"

"It's complicated, so I kept it a secret," I answered between bites. "In fact, you are only the third person in the know."

The blonde girl's eyes narrowed in suspicion as she took a sneaky glance at my assistant, who was quietly eating her broth on my right.

"Who are the others?"

"Judy and Josh," I answered honestly.

"A—!" she began while she pointed an accusatory finger at me, but then her enthusiasm wilted in a matter of moments and her exclamation ended in a soft "… ha?" Then she shook her head and leaned closer, to the point where she was practically on top of the food in the middle of the table, and asked, "I kind of expected Judy, but Josh, too?"

"He was the first," I answered while I extended my arm and pushed her back with an index finger. "If you keep doing that, the end of your hair is going to get into the soup."

She let out a soft "Oh" and sat back down, only to give me a weird look a moment later.

"Why didn't you tell the others about it?"

"I told you, it's complicated."

"But you told me?"

Now it was my turn to give her a weird look, and since she didn't seem to get the message, I told her, "It's because we are going out now."

"Oh, right," she muttered with an absentminded voice, then her cheeks flushed as her lips curved up in a dopey smile and she began to giggle.

"Chief, she is creeping me out," my dear assistant stated with her usual deadpan voice, which was quite an achievement considering her cheeks were so full of waffles, she looked like a hamster. Unexpectedly, the princess didn't react to her words; instead she had a weird, dreamy look in her eyes. I looked between my two girlfriends (nope, still weird), and for a moment I couldn't decide which of them was the stranger. But then again, people in glass houses shouldn't call other people weirdoes or something. (I never got that saying, by the way. Who lives in glass houses? And why would they throw rocks? Language is weird.)

Anyways, I exploited the fleeting lull in the conversation to empty my mug, and by the time I put it down, the princess got over her momentary stupor and shook her head.

"Wait, don't try to sweet-talk me!"

"I didn't," I answered her protest with one of my own, and she honest-to-goodness huffed.

"You think I wouldn't be on to you after all this time?" she asked with a cocky grin. "Whenever you want to dodge a question, you say something to embarrass me. However, it's not going to work anymore!" Saying so, she pointed a challenging finger at me. I don't know how I knew it was a challenging one and not an accusative one, I just did. "Since I'm your girl… friend… now…"

Aaaaaand she got exactly that far before her voice trailed off, an almost translucent blush conquered her face, and her mouth twisted into a dopey smile… again.

"Chief. Eleanor is broken. We should return her to the shop while we still have the warranty on her," Judy spoke up, then added, "No need to fix her, just ask for our money back."

"Hush, Dormouse," I chided my assistant. "She's just not used to the situation yet. Remember how much she used to freak out whenever I teased her in the past? She got over that too. I'm sure if we give her a little time, she'll be fine."

Judy looked over the princess, then shrugged and continued eating her fruit salad. In the meantime, Elly wiped the smile off her face and scowled at me.

"Oh, that brings back some memories," I muttered, earning me a curiously raised eyebrow from both girls, so I hastily added, "It's been a while since you glared at me like that. It brings back memories."

The princess let out a huff and averted her face with a pout.

"And whose fault was that?"

"You can't fault me. It's in a man's nature to tease girls."

"No, Chief, that's just your nature," my assistant retorted between bites.

"Right, it's all because you are a flirt!" Suddenly the princess's eyes opened a fraction wider and her brows knit together in a frown as her gaze returned to me. "Now that you mention it, no more flirting!"

"Pardon?" I asked reflexively, taken more than a little aback.

"I said, no more flirting," Elly repeated with a look that was even more intense than usual. "Since we are in a relationship…" She paused, and while I was half-expecting that she would start giggling again, she only closed her eyes for a moment, took a huge breath, and continued, "… since we are in a relationship, you cannot flirt with other girls anymore!"

"I never flirted with anyone other than you," I answered emphatically, which, to my sincerest surprise, drew a reaction out of the other girl.

"I knew it!" Judy exclaimed… well, no, in her case it was more like *said a bit more forcefully*, but the effect was the same. Semantics aside, she continued by stating, "So you *were* aware that you were flirting with Eleanor."

"Well, in retrospect…" I muttered while scrutinizing the far corner of the room. Because it was interesting. There was no other reason. I was most definitely not avoiding her gaze at all.

"He was flirting with you too!" the other girl exclaimed as she pointed at my assistant with a fork in hand.

"That's a given," Judy answered, completely deadpan as usual.

"What is that supposed to mean?"

"It means it's only a problem when he flirts with other girls."

"That's right!" the princess agreed, completely ignoring the fact that Judy probably meant said category included her as well, and she faced me again. "There you go, we are both in agreement! You are no longer allowed to flirt and tease girls."

I let out a small sigh and faced her accusatory fork (that had somehow collected half a kiwi).

"Fine, fine. So what you are saying is I am only allowed to tease *you* from now on, my princess."

"That's..." Elly gave me a classic deer-in-the-headlights look.

"Say no more! I promise that, from now on, I will dedicate my whole being to teasing you!"

"Don't do that!" she riposted while she was getting red up to her ears again.

"But I have to! You just told me that it's my nature, and therefore I must tease someone. Since you are the only one I can tease, it is only logical that I will—"

"What about her?" she interrupted me while gesturing at my assistant. I also glanced over, and for a moment our eyes met. We held eye contact for a second, then Judy put down her own fork and let out a small sigh that sounded weirdly exasperated.

"I guess I have no choice," she uttered in a defeated voice. "Since you asked me directly, I will oblige and tease you too. Are you happy now?"

"No! That's not what I was asking for!"

"Too late," Judy said before she turned to me and asked, "Chief, since you are awake now, would you mind if I stayed over?"

The question raised a brow on my end, especially since it felt like a bit of a non sequitur, but in the end I nodded. We had a lot of things to discuss regarding the past three days, the state of the Celestial Hub, and some other things as well, so I was already inclined to ask her to stay.

"Very well. We need to *explore* a lot of things," Judy told me with a weird emphasis on the word *explore*, but I just nodded. "For example, we need to document your scars. I want to *observe* your body. From up close."

Again, there was some weird emphasis on certain words, and I finally figured out where she was going with this, so I gave her a knowing smile and told her, "Sure, you can look as much as you want."

"Can I touch too?"

"Only if you promise you won't poke too hard. I'm sensitive."

"I know. I will be very gentle for your first… examination."

"Now that you put it like that, I am getting a little shy," I told her with fake modesty.

"I want to see all of you, but I guess we can do it in the dark for the first time."

I wanted to point out that the innuendo no longer worked with that, but all of a sudden there was a loud creak coming from the other side of the table. We both looked over and found the princess gripping her fork so hard it was being bent out of shape.

"Leooooo…" she growled in a weird voice, but before I could answer, she jumped to her feet. No, correction: she jumped right over the table and towards me with a weird battle cry saying, "LEWDING IS PROHIBITED!"

Before I knew it, I too was on my feet and, using my finely honed girl-catching reflexes (which was a skill I still couldn't believe I had to develop), I grabbed the irate girl under her arms with a deft motion that surprised even me, then I spun her around to disperse the momentum. This part made me a little dizzy, but by some miracle I somehow managed to land my butt right back on my chair with a faint thud, followed by another soft sound as the princess landed on my lap.

After a long moment of silence, during which I admired the fact that I somehow managed to do all that without turning over the table, or even disturbing the dishes too much, I let out a pent-up breath and asked, "What does *lewding* even mean?"

"Was that really the first question that you should ask in this situation?" my disgruntled assistant inquired while getting out from under the table. I was tempted to ask just what she was doing under there, but then she sat down like it never happened, so I decided to ignore her and focus on the beet-red girl on my lap.

"What was that all about?"

"Shut up," she answered while averting her eyes. "You two are jerks."

"Now, now," I reflexively patted the head of the sulking girl. "We were just teasing you. We even told you we were going to do it."

"That's…" she began, but then fell silent. I let out a sigh and looked over at my assistant, only to find her frowning back at me.

"Is there something you would like to say, Dormouse?" I asked cautiously.

"She tried to attack us, and you are now rewarding her. You are spoiling her, Chief."

"I'm not," I answered indignantly. "Not to mention, I am pretty sure that wasn't an attack, just another one of her embarrassed reactions. She didn't mean harm, right, princess?" The girl on my lap nodded wordlessly. "You see?"

Judy's expression didn't change an iota.

"Playing favourites already?" she asked with thinly veiled irritation.

"Most definitely not," I answered in kind.

"That's not how it looks like from here," came the instantaneous answer, prompting me to roll my eyes and gesture with my free hand.

"Then come over here."

There was zero hesitation as my dear assistant stood up, walked over, and pushed the princess to the side with her butt so that she could also sit on my lap. For some reason, I was getting a distinct sense of déjà vu…

"Are you happy now?" I asked with a smile I hoped was dry enough to soak up oceans, but then Judy honest-to-goodness raised a finger to her lips like she was deep in thought before she lowered her head.

"Head pat," she stated. A small tinge of red on her cheeks told me she was less calm than what she showed on the surface. Since I didn't respond right away, she repeated, "I demand a head pat."

I rolled my eyes again and used my free hand to tussle her hair a little.

"We should've done this in the first place," Elly grumbled, earning a questioning look in the process.

"We should have done what? Head pats?"

"No!" The blonde girl puffed her cheeks. Then she exhaled and said, "I mean, I'm not saying I'm against it. It feels really nice and comfortable, and it makes my heart beat harder, and… um…" She paused, probably realizing she'd gone off topic, and then came back with, "I wanted to say we should've sat like this from the beginning. I sat on the other side so we could eat face-to-face, but then Judy sat down next to you. Then I realized I wanted to sit next to you too."

"Then… why didn't you just come over?"

"Because it would've made it look like I was following Judy's lead, and I didn't want to be second in line."

For a while, I could only stare at the girl in disbelief.

"Don't tell me we are going to be dealing with this kind of nonsense from now on?"

"It's your fault," Judy told me while she reached over and grabbed a toast.

"Yeah," Elly agreed while trying, and failing, to reach her plate while still sitting on my lap.

I couldn't help but shake my head. My girlfriends (nope, still not used to it) were on the same wavelength at the weirdest of times, but I had to grant it to them, they were right. I chose this outcome, so I had to live with the consequences. We still had a lot of kinks to hammer out, though. For example, how the heck was I supposed to have dinner like this?

PART 2

"Repeat after me!" the princess demanded with a severe look while standing on my front porch, her extended finger pointing at me in a very princess-like pose. "*NO*," she stressed the word, then her finger moved over to my dear assistant standing right next to me with her arm awkwardly entwined in mine, "*LEWDING!*"

Both of us gave her a flat look, and Judy voiced my thoughts by telling her, "Lewding is still not a word."

"I don't care," my other girlfriend huffed. "I want you to promise me you won't get up to anything while I'm away."

"So it's fine when you're around?" I asked in a very innocent voice that was completely genuine and in no way mischievous.

"Yes! I mean, no! No lewd things are allowed yet!" the flustered girl replied with a pout.

"She said *yet*," Judy stated with a strange light in her eyes.

That didn't go unnoticed by the princess, who grabbed hold of my assistant and leaned closer to whisper, "We will discuss this later, you hear me? Between the two of us. As girls. Understood?"

I had no idea what she was referring to (maybe some "girl thing," as Josh would put it), nor did I know if my assistant understood, but she gave the princess a shrug, which Elly conveniently accepted as a sign of agreement.

"Good." She turned to me and poked me in the chest. "As for you, Leo: You are still recuperating, so go and rest. Don't go outside. Don't move too much. Do *not* do any... activity that requires you to move your body a lot." She paused, then repeated her words with extra emphasis: "Any. Such. Activity."

I gave my girlfriend a wry look and sighed.

"I got it. We won't tear our off clothes and jump into the bed the moment you leave, I promise."

Elly's ears went crimson again, which of course didn't secretly amuse me or give me any kind of satisfaction, but she quickly overcame her embarrassment and mumbled something along the lines of, "So long as you understand."

It was around this time that her limo rounded the corner, and after some final farewells and a peck on the cheek, my girlfriend left the premises, leaving me alone with my girlfriend.

… Yeah, I know, this is confusing, but this was the bed I made, so now I had to lie in it. That aside, Judy and I closed the door behind us, and I immediately exhaled.

"All right, it's just the two of us now," I said and glanced down at the girl still holding on to my arm. "You know what that means, right?"

"We tear off each other's clothes and jump into the bed?"

I gave my dear assistant a flat look and said, "I am going to flick your forehead now."

She only blinked at my statement, so I proceeded to do just as I said, earning me a frown and an unenthusiastic "ow."

"Chief, that hurt," she told me while rubbing her forehead, but I scoffed at her protests.

"No it didn't, I barely touched you. Not to mention, even if it did, you would've deserved it. Now stop messing around and please get your notes."

My assistant let go of my arm with what I presumed to be mock reluctance before she clicked her tongue and mumbled, "Spoilsport." Still, in just a few seconds, she bounced back and we both took up our customary places in the living room. She sat on the sofa with her phone in hand, while I paced up and down all around the place.

It was at this point when I took a huge breath and tried to clear my head from unimportant thoughts as much as I could. After I felt adequately prepared, I gestured for Judy to pay attention.

"Let's not beat around the bush. The events at the school last Sunday were a disaster, and I believe we are to blame for it." I paused to see if Judy would like to add something, but she was only looking at me expectantly, so I continued, "The writing was on the wall, yet we… No, *I* ignored it all. One mistake and we could have ended up with one of our friends dying."

"You almost died yourself," Judy told me with a hint of disapproval, and I could only nod.

"Yes, unfortunately. I have nothing to say in my defense. I messed up, and I paid the price," I told her while placing my hand on the still tender scar on my stomach. "In retrospect, I missed many opportunities to prevent what happened that night. I should have interrogated Snowy better, or looked into Crowey's movements after I learned that he was out for my blood, but I guess I just didn't take the situation seriously enough." I paused to let my words sink in before I finished with, "That changes now."

The expression on Judy's face somehow felt conflicted, and I had a feeling she wanted to say something, but then she just closed her eyes, and when she opened them, she was back to normal and simply asked, "How so?"

"First, we have to expand our intelligence network. We've been wasting the potential of the Celestial Hub. We only used it as a source of background information. We need to start using it to monitor the movements of the other factions. We need to know if something is about to happen so we can prepare."

"Sounds reasonable."

"I'm glad you agree. By the way, I want to leave that part to you. I have other plans."

"Such as?"

I paused. In fact, I even stopped pacing up and down for a moment before I told her, "Judy, I'm a mess. I have all kinds of powers, but I have no idea how to use them effectively. Hell, I almost died that night, multiple times, because I kept forgetting about my various abilities at critical moments. I need training. I need to learn how to deal with whatever supernatural nastiness the world will throw at us next."

"If that happens, do you plan to get involved again?"

"Only if necessary," I answered uncertainly, but then I steeled my voice and added, "No—chances are, I will have to. We have already established that this world is running on the conventions of some kind of 'supernatural-battle-harem-school-life-comedy' genre. I'm afraid what we have seen is just the tip of the iceberg of the 'supernatural battle' part, and I need to be able to hold my own when the next crisis jumps out from around the corner."

Judy pursed her lips almost imperceptibly, but she only wrote a few more notes. When she finished, she asked, "Which power did you forget about? Your Far Sight?"

"Actually…" I paused again, then I shook my head and began pacing once more. "Actually, open up the file on my powers. I have a lot of new entries."

"Oh?" Judy voiced curiously before she began to furiously poke at her phone. Then she gave me the go-ahead.

"Okay, so my Far Sight is a given, no changes there. I also told you about my ability to see magic. I can apparently also see through magic, such as camouflage, and I can disrupt magic by cutting it with my fingers."

"I got all that," Judy informed me.

"All right. First off, I have precognitive reflexes."

"Didn't we test that already?" she inquired while glancing up at me.

I shook my head.

"There might be some kind of condition to it, such as only reacting to actual danger or intention to harm me. Either way, it was thanks to it that I could survive against Brang and the Chimera."

"Who's Brang?"

"The leader of the Faun. The one with the spear."

"You mean the one you growled at?"

That remark made me freeze for a moment before I told her, "Actually, that's another thing. Apparently, I can fluently speak Faunish, and started doing it without me realizing it was a different language at first. It might be just that I already knew it from before my amnesia, or it could be another power or ability. Maybe I have one of those convenient magical translation suites common in stories where someone travels to another world."

My assistant gave me a strange look, then she gestured for me to come closer. I did so, and after a few seconds of poking her phone, she showed the screen to me.

"What does this say?" she asked.

I took a close look at the symbols on the screen, but I only shook my head.

"I don't know. What is this?"

"Traditional Chinese," she said as she returned to the phone, and after some more screen-prodding, she turned it my way again. "What about this?"

"*Si vis amari, ama...* Is that Latin?"

"Yes. Do you know what it means?"

"No."

For some reason, she clicked her tongue as if I'd spoiled another of her jokes before she returned to her phone, this time for more than a minute, before she showed it to me again. Even at a glance, I recognized the familiar interface of the Celestial Hub, which earned my assistant a curiously raised brow, but she urged me to read on.

"... *Incident at twelve and ten under zone of school Magi...* No, wait, it's *inside the territory of the Magi*, I think, and..." My voice trailed off as I focused more closely on the screen. "Judy, what language is this?"

"Celestial Script," my assistant answered without missing a beat. "It's a type of magical cipher only Celestials can read. I thought you told MoroseMoose to organize the classified reports because you couldn't read them, either."

"Well, I can. Apparently." I squinted at the letters, which were some-what hazy on a second look, and asked, "What does it look like to you?"

Judy paused, then said, "Like angular hieroglyphs. What do *you* see?"

"Normal letters. Though if I look at it really hard, I can see the words kinda… shimmer and move around? It's hard to explain."

Both of us fell silent.

"So," I asked tentatively, "you said it's like a magical cipher? So does this fall under seeing through magic or understanding languages I have no business understanding?"

"Which is the weirder?"

"The latter."

"Then it's that," she told me with a kind of unwarranted sagely wisdom that made me shake my head.

"Doesn't really matter right now, but we are going to test this to hell and back later. For now, let's focus on my other new abilities."

"Roger," Judy answered as she closed the browser and returned to her notes. "So far, we have Far Sight, Magic Perception, Anti-Magic Swipes, Spidey-Sense—"

"Okay, stop! I will talk to you about the other names too, but that last one is just blatant copyright infringement!"

She clicked her tongue again.

"Fine, I will call it 'Chief-Sense,' then."

"That's… only marginally better."

My complaints fell on deaf ears as she continued, "Then we have Maybe Magic, Maybe Mundane Multilingualism. Anything else?"

I… just let it go.

"Yes. I can also teleport now."

My previously pouting assistant's expression took a 180-degree turn in a split second.

"Really?"

Instead of answering right away, I took a deep breath and tried to remember how I did it. I had a feeling the process was incredibly complex, but somehow it also felt intuitive, like riding a bike, and after a moment or two of fiddling in the proverbial saddle, I could feel my surroundings blur for a moment before my vision returned to normalcy and I found myself standing behind the sofa. I let out the aforementioned breath, and then quietly placed my palm on the top of Judy's head.

My dear assistant flinched, then she slowly looked over her shoulder and said, "That's new," in a deadpan voice made hilarious by her decidedly not deadpan expression. The whole thing was worth it just for that. I stifled a small chuckle and walked around the sofa to be face-to-face with her again.

"Yes, it's new. I just discovered it during my Dominance with Brang."

"Another new term. What's a 'Dominance'?"

"A kind of ritualistic magical duel fought with apparitions. More on that later," I told her before I began pacing again. "So, I obviously haven't done any controlled experiments, but as far as I can tell, I do not have too many limitations on this one. Using it is like my Far Sight—a little disorienting, but not particularly straining at short distances. I do not know how far I can teleport, but based on my experiences during my chase with the Chimera, I was moving anywhere between two to five meters without any issues. Anything more than that, and it became much harder and made me lightheaded." I halted for a moment and asked something that bothered me a little. "Hey, Judy? How does this look from the outside? Did I just disappear? Did it make a noise?"

She was still in something of a daze, but she quickly shook her head. "First you blurred, like you were out of focus, then you were gone. There was no sound accompanying it."

"Is that so? So it's stealthy as well. We are probably going to focus on testing the limits of this ability, because I think this has the most potential utility both in and outside of combat, but before that, there's one more thing." I extended my hand towards her, palm pointing up. "First, do you see this?"

Judy gave me a funny look, but then she squinted at my hand and observed it from multiple angles. At long last, she shook her head.

"I don't know. Am I supposed to see something other than your hand?"

"So you can't see it, huh?" I mused as I made my brand-new phantom tendril limb thing wriggle a bit. For a second or two I pondered how I could explain it to her, but eventually I decided to be blunt. "You see, after I woke up today, I found myself with a phantom limb of some sort. It feels something like a… tentacle, I guess?"

"Tentacle? Really?" Judy asked with a critical frown.

"Hey, I don't like it, either," I protested. "Thing is, I can't seem to do anything with it because it's completely intangible."

"So it's like a *real* phantom limb," Judy told me expressionlessly, and it was my turn to return her critical look.

"Yes, Judy. It's like that."

"So you can't use it to grab things? Or touch things? Or do tentacle-things with it?"

"No, no, and I don't even know what you mean by the third one," I grumbled as I waved my phantom limb around. "Look, if I try to use it to grab, say, my mug, it just—"

I got this far in my sentence. As I attempted to demonstrate my point and swipe my invisible appendage across my beloved *I <3 Coffee* mug sitting on the coffee table, my vision suddenly blurred. It was kind of like when I entered Far Sight, except about a thousand times more nauseating. I instinctively staggered back and my knees nearly buckled, but Judy caught me first.

"What happened? Are you all right?" she asked in a worried voice which, considering her temperament, could be probably translated to mild panic for anyone else.

"Yes, I just…" I began, but I had no idea how to finish that sentence. What exactly had happened? I shook my head and regained my balance. "Judy, I want to try something. Catch me if I keel over."

"Chief, you can't be serious," my assistant answered with the same worried voice, but then she added, "There is no way I can support you. You are too big."

"You'll manage," I told her offhandedly as I slowly extended my phantom limb towards the mug. Initially I only touched its surface, but there was no reaction. I tried it a few more times, and then I decided to go, for lack of a better word, deeper. It was like when I extended my consciousness towards a dot during Far Sight. In fact, maybe it was exactly the same? Maybe I'd been extending this "phantom limb" all this time? Questions for later.

I focused on the mug. As I did so, and my appendage reached *deeper*, I was once again assaulted by violent nausea. I clenched my teeth and endured. Then, just as tunnel vision was about to set in, something weird happened.

Okay, something *even weirder* happened.

The mug, for lack of a better word, divided, but it didn't. It was the same mug, but when I looked at it, there were countless other beverage containers overlaid on it. Tiny porcelain ones, large metal ones, wide-mouthed ones, and cylindrical ones. Some with or without handles, and all with countless colour variations. The longer I looked, the worse the nausea became, but I soldiered on, ignoring the voice of the girl in the process of steadily losing her composure at my side.

As I looked even *deeper*, I realized that the different mugs weren't overlaying each other, but they were… it was hard to explain, but if I were to use an analogy, I'd say they were like leaves on a gigantic tree, except instead of looking at them one by one, I was trying to look at all the leaves on an entire branch at the same time while looking at them individually at the same time. Does that make sense? I wasn't even sure I understood my own analogy, but I had no better words to describe what was going on. Then, as I reached even deeper, the nausea morphed into a terrible, terrible headache. A headache that seemed to permeate my entire being. A very… *familiar* headache.

I'm going to be honest: I panicked. I could deal with pain, but that *headache* was something else entirely. I tried to retract my phantom limb, but it felt like... like I'd stretched it too far? It passed through too many small holes? It got entangled with other branches full of different leaves? It made no logical sense, but something told me that I was in danger, so I pulled with all my might, and after a few tugs, my phantom limb dislodged. Then, just as abruptly as it came, the headache disappeared along with the tunnel vision and the overlapping mugs, and I could simultaneously feel my legs wave the white flag as they surrendered to gravity. I probably would have face-planted on my coffee table if not for Judy's intervention.

When my brain started working again, I found myself on my hands and knees, hyperventilating, and my stomach threatening to spread my dinner all over the carpet. I quickly got my bodily functions under control, and once my ears stopped ringing and my eyes started focusing, I realized that Judy was holding on to my waist with all her might.

"Dormouse?" I whispered.

"Chief, are you all right?" She held me like she was afraid I was going to run away.

"I... I'm fine," I answered through clenched teeth.

"What happened?" my assistant let me go and sidled over to look me in the eye. "You said you would try something, then it looked like you had a seizure. Do you have any idea how scared I was?"

"Sorry, sorry," I weakly told her as I sat down on the floor and took several deep breaths. "I don't think I was supposed to do that. Or rather, I don't think I was supposed to be *able* to do that..."

"Do what?"

I glanced between her and my beloved mug still sitting on the table without any sign of it being disturbed, let alone being overlapped by every single mug in existence, and at last I weakly muttered, "Something that was against the rules of this world."

PART 3

"Are you sure you're all right now?" my girlfriend inquired somewhere nearby while I rested on my sofa. I say "somewhere" because at the moment, I had a damp towel draped over my head while I lay on my back, my legs dangling off the side. It wasn't the most dignified of displays, but I still felt a little lightheaded, so I didn't really care.

I'll be frank here: this most recent stunt of mine left me feeling weak, sick, and more than a little freaked out. It was that headache, that infernal pain that felt like it permeated every cell in my body. It was something I could have lived without ever experiencing again, but apparently I wasn't so lucky. Right now it was gone, but that didn't mean I was fine; my eyes still hurt, my vision was messy, with colours and lights bleeding into one another, and my stomach churned. Now granted, this all felt like nothing compared to the headache itself, but it was bad enough to land me in my current situation with the cool towel and all.

I let out a long sigh and raised a hand to gesture in the general direction from where I last heard Judy's voice.

"Dormouse, please come—" I got that far before my waving palm made contact with something soft, eliciting a surprised noise from my girlfriend. I quickly pulled back. "Judy, what did I touch just now?"

There was a long moment of silence before she answered with a question of her own. "Do you really want me to tell you?"

"Depends. Would doing so result in comedic shenanigans followed by awkward sexual tension?"

"Most likely."

"Then I don't want to know. I'm not in the mood for either of those," I told her as firmly as I could under the circumstances.

After that, there were a few more seconds of heavy silence in the air (which, I assure you, didn't contain even one iota of awkward sexual tension) until Judy said, "Why did you call for me?"

"Right, that," I mumbled while I tried to clear my thoughts. "While I'm recuperating, I thought we should continue our discussion about my powers." I could hear some rustling nearby, and I was reasonably sure it was Judy getting her phone ready as usual. I waited for her to finish before I continued, "So, ignoring the names you gave them, I have two extra-sensory abilities, I can teleport short distances, I can understand languages I didn't know about, I can engage in ritualistic magic combat humans weren't supposed to be able to do, and on top of all that, I've got a phantom limb that does something that results in… well, let's just say it felt like the entire world whacked me over the head for even trying it. Are we clear on that?"

"Yes," Judy answered while her fingers never stopped tapping on her phone.

"Now, correct me if I'm wrong, but these abilities seem pretty much all over the place."

"Not all of them," my assistant countered. "Your Far Sight and Chief-Sense can be interpreted as psychic abilities."

First, I wanted to roll my eyes at her names, but then I realized that it would've been a pretty silly thing to do, considering my eyes were still covered by a towel. As such, I simply said, "I'm still not convinced those even exist."

"Says the person with the ability to teleport around like it's normal."

"Mystic apples and magical oranges," I grumbled back. "Speaking of which though, my teleportation could be magic. As in, the run-of-the-mill kind that others can use. Do you have anything on that?"

"Why are you asking me?"

"Hey, you are the girl with the photographic memory. Who else am I supposed to ask?"

My assistant may or may not have mumbled something about me being a total, unrepentant slave driver, but ultimately she launched into an explanation, anyway.

"We don't have much to go on, as usual. I have a few fragments from the Dracis library and some basic information from the Celestial Hub. First question: From where do you draw your power?"

"Pardon?"

"Let me reiterate: Where is the energy used by your abilities coming from?"

For a moment I hesitated between upholding my carefully cultivated faux image as a smart person or revealing my confusion, but eventually curiosity won me over and I admitted, "I don't even understand the question. I don't... *draw* anything from anywhere."

I could swear I heard my girlfriend huff in self-satisfaction, which I graciously ignored as I waited for her to enlighten me.

"As we all know," she began, and I was once again tempted to roll my hidden eyes at the clichéd delivery, "the people of magical persuasion living in this world have three methods of using magic."

"Vocal, kinetic, and harmonic magic," I added, but I only got silence in return. "What?"

"I shook my head," my deadpan girlfriend answered, eliciting a small groan from me.

"This is like our phone talks all over again," I whispered in a voice that wasn't the slightest bit exasperated, I swear, before I asked the most important question: "Why did you shake your head? I thought those were the three basic spellcasting methods and whatnot."

"Yes, Chief, but that wasn't what I asked about."

I wanted to protest, but then I thought back on her choice of words, so I only said, "Please do elaborate."

My assistant once again let out a self-satisfied noise that I continued to ignore.

"Those three are the ways to use magic. The source of that magic is different. It's the difference between a power tool and the thing that powers that tool. For the sake of analogy, let's say that each of the magical races is a handyman who has to get through a locked door with their tools. Draconians draw power from their blood, which acts as a huge, heavy-duty battery that can supply their huge drills and saws, but once they run out of charge, it takes a considerable amount of time to recharge it. Abyssals are similar, but their battery is smaller and they use it like a camera flash; they have an intermediary to store power, then they channel it into a capacitor, which allows them to power big tools they would be otherwise unable to use, but only briefly. Knights seem to also use batteries, except they use magical weapons to store power, and they are useless without them. The Magi use the power grid instead. By tapping into these rivers of power they call 'ley lines,' they can keep casting spells as long as they please, but once they are unplugged, they can't do anything. Finally, the Celestials have an internal battery too, but it's small, so they use it for powering a Wi-Fi to hack the door instead." There was a brief pause, then she innocently asked, "Which one would describe you the best?"

"Before I answer that, would you tell me how long it took you to prepare all those analogies?"

"No," she bluntly answered, and as much as I wanted to shake my head in response, I thought better of it and moved on.

"To be honest, neither of them. When I use Far Sight or when I teleport, I do not draw power or expend it anywhere. It's more like… it's like taking a breath or moving a limb. It's natural."

"And that's," my dear assistant began, then stopped for a beat for what I presumed to be a dramatic pause, "why your powers are different from the rest."

"That's not exactly news," I grumbled.

"You know, Chief, while I understand why you would leave this type of research to me, you should at least read up on some basic magic theory on the Celestial Hub. That way you'd understand how bizarre your abilities are."

"I know already. It doesn't mean they are psychic powers, though."

"We cannot exclude the possibility," Judy answered, and her insistence made me wonder if she had spent too much time with the class rep. However, before I could question her about it, her tone took an abrupt turn as she told me, "While I would really love to find out for sure, for the short-term, I believe it's more important that you realize that your abilities are strange by local standards. I would even go as far as to call them outside-context. I don't think the others have seen you teleport, but you still drew attention to yourself with your other powers."

"Yeah, yeah, I know…" I answered, slightly downhearted. "I think my ability to see and dispel magic is already out of the bag. Angie knows it, plus the others have seen it when I untied Josh and when I used it against Crowey. Twice."

"I gather that's why you used it so openly to destroy the surveillance in the room."

"Huh? I mean… Yeah, that's exactly why I did so."

After a fairly long pause, Judy simply said, "That didn't sound convincing."

It was at this point where I got fed up with not being able to visually express my displeasure at her jabs, so I took the lukewarm towel off my head and gingerly opened my eyes. Looking into any bright light still stung, but otherwise I was fine, so I tried to sit up and, to my surprise, I found my dizziness almost completely gone. I blinked a few times, and once I was sure I was fine, I looked at my girlfriend sitting on my favourite comfy chair and I promptly rolled my eyes.

"Come on, Dormouse. You can't expect me to think of everything all the time. I don't have your amazing memory. I tend to forget things."

Instead of giving me an immediate counter like I was expecting, my comment seemed to have triggered something in Judy, as her expression darkened. After a few seconds of weird silence, she quietly put her phone away and let out a shallow breath, though her face remained as strangely stern as before.

"Chief, I think we need to talk about the meta for a moment."

"You mean, about the prophecies being routes? I remember you mentioning—"

"No, not that," she interrupted me, much to my surprise, and then she warned me, "Do not get sidetracked, or we might forget to talk about it."

"Um… Okay, I don't know what you mean, but it sounds serious, so I'm listening."

Judy nodded, then dropped her bombshell: "Chief, I think we are being affected by the narrative." I blinked at her and wanted to say it was obvious, but she didn't give me an opportunity, as she continued, "Do you remember what you said not too long ago? How you kept forgetting about your abilities during the incident at the school and you almost died because of it?"

"Yes," I nodded, a little uncertain of what she was getting at. "I…" I wanted to say I reflected on it, but I couldn't really remember when I did that. I felt like I did that. I also reflected on a lot of other things, but I couldn't really recall any of them. As I tried, I felt the cold sweat running down my back. "Now that I think back, things could have been done so much better. I just… I guess I got caught up in the heat of the moment, and—"

"Are you sure? Are you sure it was just that? Do you remember your Far Sight?"

"Well, of course I do."

"It's a big deal, isn't it?"

"Er… Yes, it is."

"So why did you never use it after our first date and before the fight between Neige and Eleanor?"

That gave me a pause.

"I… I think I just didn't want to think about it? As in, I didn't want magic to be real, so I…" The more I thought about it, the less sense it made.

"Chief." My assistant spoke in a soft voice, as if to soften the coup de grace. "You keep telling me how great my memory is, but… I never really thought about it, either. I knew about it, but I never *thought* about it. Do you know what I mean?"

By this point, the cold sweat on my back was running in rivers as I answered, "Our thoughts are being censored?"

"I think it's not so direct." Judy shook her head. "If it was the same kind of perception masking, like how the others don't find the placeholders' behaviour strange, we wouldn't have even be able to notice the discrepancy."

"So it's more like misdirection," I ventured.

"Not just that," Judy told me in a grave voice. "I believe we are affected in multiple ways. For example, I looked at our old notes. I had a lot of time to do that while you were unconscious, and I found that we had all the clues to put together the fact that there were supernatural elements here, right around the time when we went on our date in the amusement park, even without your Far Sight being revealed."

"Yet we didn't," I said, mostly just to keep the conversation rolling.

"Correct," Judy continued with a nod. "We also never paid much attention to your reaction to Sebastian and Noir."

"Who?"

"Crowey."

"Ah, right…" I nodded, but then I slightly tilted my head to the side. "What do you mean by *reaction*?"

"Chief, think about it for a moment."

I did just that. How did I react to those two? Well, when I first met the old butler, I… antagonized him for some reason. No, actually, there was a reason. When I first looked at him, I felt really irritated. Same with Crowey.

"I could have been just subconsciously responding to their power," I told Judy with a frown. "They are both big shots, and with all those extra-sensory abilities, it's not unlikely that I was simply perceiving them as a threat."

"And you provoke people who you think pose a threat to you?"

"I... have poor impulse control?"

"Chief, I'm serious."

I let out a groan and threw up my hands.

"Okay, so let's presume that the reason why I was immediately irritated by them had nothing to do with the fact that they were both pompous authority figures, but there was some kind of other underlying reason. Now what?"

"I don't know," Judy said with a shake of her head. "We don't know enough of the narrative that exists to be sure."

"*If* there is a narrative in the first place."

Judy gave me a look like I just got an elementary math problem completely wrong.

"Chief, it's abundantly clear there is a narrative, and it's subtly steering us. Remember our discussion during the school incident? The whole thing was set up in a way that the authorities couldn't intervene to force us to act."

I took a deep breath and answered, "Let me be the devil's advocate for a moment. We already know that this was a plan by Crowey, and he timed it in a way to make sure he wouldn't have been interrupted by the authorities."

"Yes, it was planned by him," Judy told me with a shallow nod, "and it was executed by Neige. We both saw it happen, but we did nothing to stop it."

"We just talked about that. I just didn't take the situation seriously, and—"

"Don't try to rationalize it," my girlfriend warned me. "You are better than that."

I wanted to retort, but then I closed my mouth and thought about it for a moment, and as I did so, my mind began churning like an active volcano.

I knew about Brang's mission to assassinate me, and while I looked into Fauns, I never made any countermeasures. I was aware of Snowy's weird behaviour, her use of magic on school grounds, and I even knew they were leaving soon, but I never connected the dots. On the day of the incident, I had no reason to fight the Chimera, yet I wasted a lot of time trying to kill it, as if doing so was required to save Josh. Then there was the question of me forgetting to use my powers to their fullest. Even if I just recognized them, I used both my precognition and my teleportation very extensively against Brang, yet I repeatedly forgot to utilize them during the incident.

The more I thought about it, the more I felt like Judy was on to something.

"I think you are right. Not only that, this is a huge freaking deal and it was entirely in my blind spot," I finally told her with a weak smile. "Good catch."

"Thank you," she answered with a small smile of her own. "This is why you hired me."

"Indeed," I said as I crossed my arms. "So, if we follow the logic behind what you discovered, where does it lead us?"

"The Narrative is rigid," Judy began. "It requires certain things to happen, and if our actions go against them, it creates blind spots and situations to make us follow the script."

"And that takes us back to the prophecies," I said with a frown. "Your hypothesis was that they are routes, right? Like in a game?"

My girlfriend nodded. "We don't have enough information to know for sure, but that was the most obvious parallel that came to mind. Joshua is the protagonist. Each female member of the group has a prophecy that revolves around him. It's too much for a coincidence."

"From a meta-perspective, it's obviously not one," I continued where she left off. "If we combine that with the idea that each of the prophecies is 'predicting' a possible future Josh's choices could lead to..."

"It is likely that they are not predictions, but pre-written scenarios being foreshadowed," this time Judy continued my thoughts. "In that case, I believe we must be on the Neige scenario."

That remark made my brows skyrocket, and I immediately uttered a stern "No," surprising my girlfriend.

"No?" she asked back, and I could only furrow my brows in answer.

"Honestly... I don't know why, but I have this really strong feeling that Snowy..." I paused to collect my thoughts. "I don't know where I heard this or why it feels so obvious, but I think Snowy doesn't have a route, so to speak. In fact, I feel like the school incident didn't go the way it was 'supposed' to go, either. I mean... I can't really explain. It just feels like it has something to do with Snowy and Josh saving her, and Crowey getting his face burned off, and the Chimera, and..." I fell silent again. Then I let out an annoyed groan and declared, "I don't really know why myself, but it feels like I have this hazy idea that we might have... no, we *definitely* went off the rails. Am I making any sense?"

Judy only looked at me curiously, then she simply shrugged and said, "Not much, but I'm already used to it." She gave me a tiny little smirk.

"Ouch, that hurt," I responded, imitating her flat tone.

"You'll get used to it."

I allowed myself a slightly hollow chuckle in response, then asked, "So, what should we do now that we are aware that at any given moment some kind of ethereal force could sneakily tweak our perceptions and priorities to uphold some form of narrative flow?"

"Panic?" Judy replied with a completely serious face.

"Nah. That didn't work before, and probably won't work now."

"Fall into an existential crisis and cry ourselves to sleep?"

"That's so last season, we need something better."

"I got it," Judy stated emphatically as she raised a hand up high. "We take a ton of notes, scrutinize our every action and reaction, and then try to figure out this Narrative and how to beat it?"

I gave her a wide smile and a thumbs-up.

"That's more like it!"

For a few seconds we stayed in the exact same poses until we pretty much just deflated. Heavy topics concerning the meta always took a lot out of me, and this was no exception. As I thought about just how many ways this world could find to casually terrify me, my eyes landed on the clock on the wall and I noticed with a start that it was already after 7 p.m.

"Speaking of Snowy," I spoke up, maybe just a wee bit too loud, to clear some of the heavy atmosphere in the room, "it's getting late. I should go and talk to her right about now."

"Are you sure you're well enough for that?" Judy asked with a tinge of worry in her voice. "You look pale."

"All the more reason to go out and get some fresh air," I answered with a toothy smile. "Not to mention, it'll help me digest this discussion."

It looked like she would protest at first, but in the end she almost imperceptibly shook her head.

"Take care," she said. She stood up and took out her phone. "I'll write down what we discussed and make some backups."

At first I almost nodded and left her to her devices, but then I recalled something and I stopped mid-stretch to tell her, "Could you turn on the water heater in the ground floor bathroom? Also, please prepare some hot cocoa and light snacks while I'm away. I think Snowy will appreciate them."

My girlfriend shot me a glance, then she put her phone back away with a simple "Sure."

"Thanks, Dormouse. You're the best."

This time she only responded with a knowing nod as she exited the living room. Meanwhile, I limbered up my legs, just to make sure I completely recovered, and then headed up to my room. First things first, I took my phone off the charger and checked it for new messages. I had a missed call from Josh, but it was from before he came over, so I dismissed it.

I also had a text message from Angie asking about my health, so I sent her a message to explain that I was fine, and I also asked her about her situation.

I also got several messages from the class rep, half of them inquiring about my condition, the other half apologizing about not being able to visit me while also complaining about being buried under a mountain of paper-work, which may or may not have been the end result of the stunts I pulled off a few nights ago. I sent her a short apology, pocketed my phone, and headed for my wardrobe.

My indoor clothes were fine as they were, as I'd just put on a fresh set after I'd taken a shower, but the weather outside was already flirting with winter, so I looked for a coat to keep me warm. On a cursory examination, I had two black long coats, three black trench coats, something that looked like an honest-to-goodness duster (also black; figures), and last but not least, a black dress coat with embroidered lapels and fancy metallic buttons. I'd never worn the last one, by the way.

Okay, so, my default wardrobe was more than a little monotonous. Deciding on a trench coat, I put it on with practiced motions. It fit me like a glove and was comfortable as usual. I also picked up my spare keys for the front door (my main key was still with Judy), and after making sure I got everything I needed, I walked downstairs.

"Chief?" Judy, who just came out of the kitchen with an apron over her clothes, called out to me the moment I got to the living room and gestured me over. "Lean forward."

I gave her a quizzical eyebrow-raise, but complied. She then stood on her tippy-toes and started combing my hair with her fingers. Once she found my mug satisfying enough, she proceeded to straighten my collar and tug at my sleeves before she took a step back and gave me a full look-over.

She nodded to herself and told me, "All right, now I can let you out into the public without you embarrassing me."

This time I rewarded her with an unsubtle eye-roll and grumbled, "What are you, my mother?"

"No, I'm your girlfriend."

I looked for a good retort, but after a while I just shrugged a shoulder in defeat and said, "True enough," before I beamed a smile at her and added, "Thanks, Dormouse."

"You are welcome." There was a brief pause, after which Judy asked, "So?"

"So what?" I asked back reflexively, earning me a displeased pout from my girlfriend.

"Aren't you supposed to say something here? Or better yet, do something?"

"I'm… drawing a blank here. What do you mean?"

Instead of answering my question, Judy's shoulders drooped and she let out a clearly disappointed sigh, which made me twitch just by how overt it was, then she told me, "You are still horrible at reading the mood."

I raised my hand and awkwardly scratched my chin with a tentative "Sorry" on the tip of my tongue, but then she gestured for me to lean forward again, and when I did so, she planted a quick peck on my cheek.

"Stay safe," she said to me, and I couldn't help but chuckle.

"Will do," I answered with a completely plain and normal smile as I headed for the front door, only to stop as Judy called out one more time.

"When should I expect you back?"

I thought about that for a long moment before I replied, "Snowy doesn't seem to be too far away based on Far Sight. I'm also going to experiment with my teleportation on the way there; I might even discover something new. Either way, I should get there quick, but then I'll have a talk with Snowy, and as for the return trip, if we catch a taxi… Let's say two hours, give or take thirty minutes."

"Okay. Give me a call when you are on your way back."

I gave my unusually fussy girlfriend a slightly exasperated glance and waved her goodbye.

The cool mid-autumn air felt pleasant, and the evening sky was scenic as usual. I reflexively made my way towards the usual intersection, and a casual glance showed me that things hadn't changed much since the first day I woke up and walked down these roads. Things were still squeaky clean even after close to two months, and while the number of placeholders and cars had increased over time, it wasn't drastic enough to warrant surprise.

Maybe that was the reason why I pretty much immediately noticed that I was being shadowed by not one, not two, but three sneaky individuals. Well, at the very least I was sure they thought they were sneaky; however, not only were they very conspicuous in their actions, but all three were glowing with magic as well, so I could probably have seen them even in complete darkness.

Now, in their defense, they had no way of knowing that I could see magic, or that their stereotypical sneaking made them stick out like sore thumbs, or that I was a really observant guy whose attention no small detail could ever hope to escape. Then I rounded a corner, and I bumped into someone because I wasn't paying attention. In fact, I bumped into three people. Three *familiar* people.

"Hey, watch where ya goi—" the big guy in the middle, followed by a tall and a short one, began to grumble, but then he looked at me and his lips curled into a huge grin. "HA! Look, guys, it's him! I found 'im!"

I blinked in surprise, but then buried my face in one hand while raising the other to halt the goldfish poop gang in their tracks.

"Stop!" I told them in a stern voice and then after taking a deep breath, I looked the three in the eye. "Okay, listen up, guys. I'm in a hurry. I promised my girlfriend—"

"Which one? The blonde or the brunette?" the short one interjected.

Shooting him a scathing glare, I said, "The brunette one, but it doesn't matter. I promised her I'd do something and get home ASAP, so I don't have the time to waste on you." I gave each one of them a separate warning glare, and continued with, "So, here's what we are going to do: You are going to tell me your new naming scheme, I will make fun of you, and then you'll leave me alone. Deal?"

"Why do you have to make fun of us?" the tall one nasally protested. "You're mean!"

"Yea! Ya're a bully!" seconded the short one, but I ignored them and scowled at the pompadoured leader in the middle.

The guy gave me a weird look in return, but then he cleared his throat and said, "I am ProTony." I must have given him a weird look without me noticing, as he immediately became flustered and added, "Like, it's a combination of 'proton' and 'Tony.'"

"So, you're going with particles this time." I nodded, slightly frustrated. "That means the small guy is something-something electron, and you two are attracted to each other, but the tall one is the neutron who keeps your group stable and unable to act on your attraction. Insert joke about unresolved sexual tension here, yada-yada. Am I right so far?"

"What? No! I mean, yes on the particles but no on everything else!" ProTony protested, but I simply ignored him.

"Whatever. I've done my part, I made fun of you. Now go lick your imaginary wounds and let me get going on my way."

The three of them looked between each other for a few seconds, then their shoulders drooped in unison and they shuffled aside to allow me to pass, and when I did so, the tall one muttered something about me being a "real mean bully" or something. I didn't care though. I kept walking without looking back, and after I was sure I was out of earshot, I let out a tired groan. Okay, fine, I did care a tiny bit. I mean, this was these poor guys' whole thing, so I felt a little bad for ignoring their raison d'etre like that, but come on! There was a time and place for everything, and this was neither one nor the other.

But speaking of place, I quickly used Far Sight to see which way I was supposed to go to get to Snowy's hidey-hole. While it was convenient to be able to tell her general direction, it wasn't exactly a GPS navigation system; I didn't know the exact location, nor how to get there. Still, it was better than nothing, so I closed my eyes for a moment and focused on the red dot on the edge of my vision. With now practiced motions (if you can call them that), I extended my consciousness towards the dot, and after a short moment I (or rather, my point of view) was inside the dark hotel room I saw earlier. Apparently Snowy hadn't left the place.

With that, I once again had a rough idea of the direction where I was supposed to be going, so I looked for a quiet back alley where I could get out of the sight of my unwanted shadows just long enough for me to start teleporting. Of course, the suburbs had none of those, so I took a small detour towards the shopping district, where I was reasonably sure I could find some abandoned backstreet. It took me about ten minutes to get there and about five more to find a suitably secluded place, but once I was certain no one was looking at me, I hurriedly got ready to teleport. I was just about to start when I abruptly stopped myself.

As for why... I had a weird feeling. Or rather, the weird part was that it was a familiar feeling. Now, I'm the first to admit that I never really thought about the mechanics of my teleportation when in the heat of the situation back at the school, but since I wasn't under any serious time constraints just then, I allowed my senses to dwell on the process, and I noticed something peculiar. When I initiated my teleportation, for a very short time I became distinctly aware of literally everything in my environment in a bubble of about ten meters in diameter around me. That wasn't the weird part. I mean, yes, it was weird, but it was somehow intuitive. However, the part that surprised me was how similar the feeling was to something else I'd felt just a few minutes before.

I closed my eyes again and quickly brought forth my Far Sight one more time. First, I focused on Snowy, and in a moment I was in the hotel room. Then I focused on Judy, and after a quick shift of the world around me, I was looking at her washing the dishes at my place. I made a mental note to tell her that the theoretical ninja maids would take care of them, but that was for another time. For now, I focused on Snowy again, and I was in the hotel room for the third time.

"It's the same," I whispered in utter astonishment.

I looked around and focused on the interior of the place. I could perceive the furniture. I could perceive the walls. I could perceive the *things behind the walls*. As for the distance, it was in a bubble roughly ten meters in diameter centered on the girl huddled under the blankets on the bed.

Coincidence? There was no way this could be one.

I only hesitated for a moment. I glanced at the mouth of the alleyway between the buildings, and I didn't see any of my stalkers, so I inhaled a huge breath and closed my eyes again. Then I was back in the hotel room again. Another moment later, *I was in the hotel room, period.*

There was no fanfare, no headache. Only a tiny bit of dizziness that lasted for a few short seconds. In the literal blink of an eye, I found myself teleported across a vast distance the same way I had teleported a few meters to appear behind Judy not so long ago. Now, common sense told me that both of those were patently impossible and freaky, but my finely honed uncommon sense then told me that the whole *being able to freely teleport to any place I can see with Far Sight* was an absolute bullshit ability of epic proportions cut way above the rest.

Anyways, I spent a few seconds forcefully calming myself. Then I remembered that I'd stopped breathing, so I softly exhaled the lungful of air I took back in the alley. When I did that, Snowy shuddered in the bed and timidly poked her head out from under the bedsheets.

"Leo?" she asked with a weak, uncertain voice, and now that I could see her, I had to conclude that the rings under her eyes gave Josh a run for his money in the haggard department.

"Hi, Snowy," I answered her with a smile. I expected her to freak out, but instead she returned the gesture ever so feebly.

"I didn't think it would be so soon," she stated while her smile fell into a heartbreakingly pitiful grimace. "I didn't think I would be seeing things after not sleeping for just a few days."

"You haven't slept for days?" I asked as concern tugged my brows up, but she didn't react.

"I'm sorry, Leo," she muttered almost deliriously as a steadily rising stream of tears rolled down her cheeks. "I'm so sorry."

"It's fine," I told her while I took a few steps towards her. "It wasn't your fault. I know you were forced by your brother."

Snowy kept looking me in the eye with a distorted expression, then laughed ruefully.

"Even in my delusions, you are so nice to me. You... were... so nice..." As she continued, her voice became a stuttering mess drowned out by soft sobs. "I didn't want to... I didn't... want to hurt you... I didn't want to kill you!" She finally cried just as I reached the edge of her bed, at which point I sat down. The sudden bounce in the mattress prompted her to stop with a blank look on her face. The abrupt change in her expression was a little startling, but to be honest, I was just relieved she stopped sobbing. Hesitating, I raised my hand and tried to wipe away her tears. At first she flinched back a little, but then her eyes opened wide.

"You… touched me."

"Yes, I did. Do you have a handkerchief or something here? Some tissues? Your nose is running."

She ignored my question and instead reached out and poked my shoulder. She blinked a few times, then timidly asked, "Are you… haunting me?"

I gave her a long, critical look, but since she didn't seem to get it, I just rolled my eyes and used the corner of her bed sheet to wipe her nose.

"Do I look like a ghost to you?"

"But… but I saw it!" she exclaimed, startling me for a moment. "You collapsed outside the school! And there was so much blood!"

"Well, I got better," I replied with what I hoped was a soothing smile.

"But… but… but… why are you here?"

She was getting a little hysterical, so I placed my hand on her head and softly rustled her hair. Head pats had already worked once that day, and they didn't fail me this time, either, as she immediately quieted down.

"I'm here to take you home," I told her reassuringly.

"To… the Abyss?" she asked tentatively, and I shook my head.

"Don't be silly," I told her, rubbing her head a little harder. "I meant my place, obviously. Judy should be preparing the bath and making you a nice cup of hot cocoa as we speak. So, do you wanna come with me?"

The white-haired girl stared at me with wide-open eyes for a second, and before I could even react to it, she threw herself at me so hard, she almost pushed me off the edge of the bed. Her slender arms caught me like a vice as she hugged me and began to bawl into my chest.

"Whoa! Easy there, easy…" I soothed her to no avail, and no matter how much I rubbed her head and back, she didn't stop crying and holding on to me like she was afraid I would disappear in a puff of smoke. After a few minutes, I let out a sigh and gave up. I wasn't in a hurry, anyway. In fact, with my newest discovery, I doubted I'd be late to anywhere ever again, but that was beside the point, so for the time being I decided to indulge her and let her get all of it out of her system.

CHAPTER 3

PART 1

"Are you all right now?" I asked the nervously fidgeting girl sitting on the edge of the bed while I was in the process of wiping the front of my coat with a bathroom towel. She gave me a nod so insecure she might as well have shaken her head, but I didn't say that out loud, lest it prompt Snowy to grab me again and start sobbing for another ten minutes.

Speaking of time, I quickly checked my phone and noted that it was almost 8 p.m. I'd promised Judy we'd be back in two hours, so while we weren't late, that didn't mean I shouldn't hurry things up a bit. Anyways, the silence in the room was getting a little heavy, so I put my phone away, put down the towel, and then put on a smile as I nonchalantly asked, "Hey, Snowy? Where exactly is this place?"

She glanced up at me with eyes that couldn't tell whether I was serious or not, then said, "It's the... *a* hotel near the docks. I think it has a name, but I can't remember."

"Really?"

My casual question somehow made her visibly flinch and she quickly averted her eyes while whispering, "I... I knew I couldn't stay in the room brother rented, so when I ran away, I just looked for a place to stay and picked the first hotel I could find."

"Is that so?" I responded noncommittally while making sure that my clothes were in order, but then I raised a single brow as I remembered the most obvious question, "Speaking of which, why did you run away?"

The girl on the bed only bit her lip for a while. In fact, it took her so long to answer that I almost asked her again, but then she blurted out, "I'm from the Abyss."

"Yes. Everyone knows that. So what?"

She took a deep breath, then looked me in the eye.

"Leo, I... I hurt you. At the time, I even thought I killed you. You can say it was because of brother's orders, but it doesn't change the fact that I, an Abyssal, hurt someone. And on the grounds of a School too. The Magi only tolerated my presence because brother was here. Without him around, and after breaking the laws like that, they would hunt me down for sure."

"Well, they can try," I told her with a smile I hoped was decently reassuring, "but then they would have to deal with me and our friends."

"I know," Snowy answered with a small smile that didn't touch her eyes. "But at the time I thought you were dead. Do you think the others would've protected me like that?"

"Sure," I answered with all the baseless confidence in the world. "They are your friends, and they all knew you were under mind control or whatever. They would've helped you out without batting an eye."

"If you say so…" she said weakly and lowered her head. I could totally see her sobbing in a second, so as a preventative measure I swiftly sat down beside her.

"Come on, Snowy!" I told her while I reached my arm around her and patted her shoulder. "Do you think we went out of our way to rescue you and Josh just to abandon you at the finish line? Is that the kind of people you think we are?" She shook her head without saying anything, and I couldn't help but grin at her even if she couldn't see it.

I was just about to continue my pep talk, but then she slowly turned her head back to me and asked, in a mousy voice, "How's Josh doing?"

"Oh, him?" I mumbled as I wiped the grin off my face and replaced it with a very dignified pondering expression that was in no way taken aback or dopey for a moment. "All things considered, I'd say he is doing fine. He was a little rattled by the whole kidnapping thing, and he is still a bit freaked out about the supernatural, but he should settle down after a good night of sleep." I paused, then playfully added, "He was also worried about you, you know?"

"Really?"

Seeing the girl perk up made me chuckle.

"Yeah. I told him you were fine."

"I'm glad…" she began, but then she curiously tilted her head to the side and asked, "How did you know I was all right?" She blinked, as if she'd just realized something, then continued with, "And how did you even find me?"

I raised a finger to my mouth. "That's one of my little secrets. It might or might not be revealed in due time."

She didn't seem to appreciate the answer, so I did what I always do in situations like this and switched topics like a pro.

"Anyways, you should be able to talk with Josh tomorrow. We already agreed to have a tactical meeting with everyone to discuss the situation, so you two can catch up before that. Or after. Or during. I don't think anyone would mind either way." Snowy only looked at me funny, so I patted her on the shoulder again and stood up, pulling her along. "Before all that though, let's go home. You look like you could use a good night's sleep."

She gave me a sheepish nod as I stepped forth and took a look around the place.

"First of all, let's gather your stuff."

"Stuff?" she repeated after me a touch uncertainly as she followed my example and looked around as well, as if searching for something.

"Yeah. Clothes, bags, that kind of thing," I answered offhandedly, but instead of moving to gather her belongings, she kept looking at me like I'd said something weird. "What? Don't tell me you don't have anything."

"All my luggage was taken back to the Abyss." She stated it like it was obvious.

"When? Before the incident at school?"

She nodded.

"So you have no clothes?"

That earned me a head shake this time.

"No toothbrush? Favourite mug? Plushy?"

Shake, shake, and shake again.

"What about a purse?"

"I don't have one. All my belongings were managed by brother, and he took back my money and the fake ID last Saturday."

"Wait." I raised a hand to make her stop. "You say you have no money on you? At all?"

She shook her head for the umpteenth time, and I could only gawk at her.

"Then how did you pay for this room?"

Snowy gave me another strange look, then finally muttered, "I didn't. I… was in a hurry at the time, so I kind of… seduced the receptionist and she let me stay for free."

"Wait, you did what? You seduced…" I began, and then paused with my mouth still open as my brows slowly descended into a frown before I continued, "Did you just say 'she'?"

Snowy nervously nodded, and for a moment I had so many questions I couldn't decide what to ask first. Eventually I decided on none, and instead I let my palm cover my face as I exhaled an exasperated groan, followed by, "You know what? I don't even want to know. Okay, so you have no money, no ID, and we need to get you some clothes. On the bright side, that means you don't have any luggage, so moving in should be easy peasy. Silver linings, am I right?"

"Er… Yes?" The girl at my side spoke timidly, but my mind had already leaped to logistics.

First things first, we should call a taxi. Since it was just the two of us with no baggage, I figured it wouldn't cost that much. Not that it would matter; I still had a bad habit of keeping way more cash than necessary on hand. I reached into my coat's inner pocket and took out my phone. I decided to first look for a local taxi service, then I would call Judy to tell her we were coming. I couldn't wait to see the look on her face when I told her my teleporting ability got even more bullshit... and it was at this exact moment when my hand stopped typing into the search bar of my phone's browser as a realization hit me like lightning out of a clear blue sky.

"Snowy, come over here for a moment." I hastily put my phone away. "I want to try something."

She stepped closer, and I held out a hand. She glanced at it and gave me a skeptical look, but obediently grasped it. From the outside, it might've looked like we were shaking hands. In fact, it looked exactly like that. I should know, as I was looking at us from the above and a little to the right using Far Sight.

Now, here's what this was all about: I could teleport. When I did that, I could take all my clothes with me, and even miscellaneous items, such as a certain borrowed spear. So, if I could take inanimate objects along for the ride, could I do the same with a person? Or was there a limitation, like in that movie where an AI could only send organic matter back in time? And if there was, was the limitation as easily circumvented as covering a metallic endoskeleton with organic tissue? But wait, I was getting ahead of myself again.

First, I had to see if it was even possible before I started thinking about ways to exploit it. As such, I closed my eyes and focused on the area around us using Far Sight on Snowy, as it allowed me to see myself in the process. First test: I tried to teleport to the other side of the room. The moment I did that, I could see my body become hazy and somewhat transparent, but Snowy stayed the same. I sharply exhaled, and my body immediately regained its solidity. That made me blink in surprise, breaking my concentration, and the Far Sight with it. So, teleportation can be canceled. That was good to know.

"What happened?" came the flabbergasted question from the girl in front of me.

"Oh, that?" I said nonchalantly. "I'm just experimenting with something. Just humour me for a second."

"But... you were transparent," Snowy said, squeezing my hand. "Are you...?"

"Please tell me you are not going to ask, *Are you really a ghost?*"

She twitched and averted her eyes.

"I won't."

I let out a sigh and closed my eyes again, repeating the early steps of the previous experiment. What went wrong? Well, my first guess was that I used my ability as usual, but that was for transporting myself. So, what if I had to consciously try to take Snowy along? This time I tried that, and after taking a deep breath, I triggered my teleportation ability again. The change was readily apparent from the first moment, as I could feel a tug that was resisting my efforts to move. That resistance came from the hand clasped around Snowy's, unsurprisingly. I let out the breath I was holding and told her, "Don't move."

Then I stepped closer to her and hugged her. She stiffened, but when she realized I wasn't doing anything else, she relaxed and leaned on my chest. With that, it was time for the third experiment, and as they say, the third time's the charm.

Well, except in this case, as I failed to teleport once again.

Now, here's the thing: I got a glimpse of it on the second try, and this time I had a very strong and distinct sense that I could do it—I could take someone along for the ride, I was just missing something. I tried a few more times, sometimes holding Snowy closer, or holding on to different all-ages rating compatible parts of her anatomy, but nothing seemed to work. Credit where credit's due, Snowy was a real trooper, as she put up with all my unreasonable demands without any complaints.

I was just about to give up on the whole endeavour when something came to my attention. Well, that might have been a bit misleading, as it was always on my mind ever since my dangerous stunt this afternoon, but I was ignoring it exactly for that reason. At the end of the day, I was getting desperate enough for results to start incorporating my phantom limb into the equation.

Now, this wasn't just me blindly grasping for straws and hoping for the best. I had a distinct feeling that my new appendage and the thing reaching out towards my Far Sight dots were similar, if not the same thing. Because of this, it was not far-fetched to think that, considering that I could already find a synergy between my Far Sight and my as-of-yet unnamed teleportation ability, there could be something similar to discover here as well.

As such, I slowly stretched out my phantom tendril thingie, and wrapped it around Snowy's waist, making sure it only brushed the surface, lest I would be treated to the images of infinite overlapping Snowys followed by my favourite just-kill-me-already brand of headache. Fortunately, nothing of the sort happened. I took another deep breath, then I snugly held on to my test subject with all three of my arms before I crossed my proverbial fingers and triggered teleportation again.

There was the tugging sensation once again, but to my surprise, it felt entirely manageable this time around. If I had to make an analogy, it felt like that until now I was trying to lift a grocery bag from the floor using only my pinky finger, while now I was using both my hands. It was such an obvious difference it made me wonder why I'd bothered trying to do it the other way around.

Anyways, when I opened my eyes, we were in the same room, only a few meters to the right.

"It worked!" I exclaimed, startling the girl in my arms.

"What? What happened?"

"You didn't see it?" I asked incredulously as I glanced down at her.

"My eyes were closed," she told me, earning her a curious look, so she shyly clarified, "It felt comfortable…"

That was unusually forthcoming of her, and also a bit embarrassing, so I quickly cleared my throat and flashed a toothy smile to ease the mood in the room.

"Never mind then. As for what happened… Let's just say you are going to learn about one of my secrets sooner than anticipated." That line earned me another quizzical look, but I ignored it for the time being and let go of her. "So, just to be clear: You have nothing of importance here, right?" I waited for Snowy to shake her head again, then I continued, "That means we can leave right now if we wanted to, right?" This time there was a brief pause, but after a short while she nodded in the affirmative. "Great, now give me a second."

Saying so, I took out my phone and quickly dialed my dearest assistant. As I did that, I also quickly entered into Far Sight and my vision arrived back at my living room just as she was entering from the kitchen with her mug in hand. Perfect. A moment later her ringtone sounded (which was the theme song from some obscure anime about a blonde robot girl), and I watched on as she skillfully took out, unlocked, and answered her phone using only one hand with a single smooth motion.

"Chief?" she spoke in an echoing voice that resulted from hearing her through the phone and my Far Sight at the same time. A little spooky, but cool.

"Hi, Dormouse. I found Snowy," I told her in a chipper voice.

"Good. Is she all right?"

"Yeah, she's fine," I answered, absentmindedly reaching out to pat the subject of our conversation, an endeavour complicated by the fact that my eyes were closed and I was looking at someone else a couple kilometers away. Anyways, I continued with, "She's got panda-eyes, but is otherwise okay. Some shut-eye should fix that."

"I see. When can I expect you—?"

"Wait," I interrupted her as a new idea brought a smile to my face. "First put down the mug."

I could see her glance around the room, then she looked up (which was not at all where my point of view was located, by the way) and asked, "Are you Far Seeing me right now?"

"Yup," I answered while I gently pulled Snowy to my side again, and then wrapped my phantom limb around her waist.

In the meantime, Judy let out a small sigh and obediently placed her mug on top of the usual coffee table.

"There, are you happy now?"

"Tremendously," I answered while ignoring the confused fidgeting of Snowy at my side. "Now say what you wanted to say before."

"Why?"

"Come on, Judy! It's going to be funny, I promise."

My girlfriend rolled her eyes. Then she uttered, "When can I expect you back home?"

"In a moment."

I ended the call and was about to put my phone away, when another idea struck me. I turned on the camera app. My preparations complete, I told Snowy, "Stay calm. This might be a little strange at first, but it should be safe."

Entering back into Far Sight, I focused back on Judy. Then once I was sure everything was in order, I used my teleportation ability to appear in my living room.

This time the tugging sensation was pronounced, but not particularly bad. In a literal blink of an eye (plus some mild nausea), we were standing right in front of Judy.

The moment we appeared, I snapped a photo of my astonished assistant and said, "We're back."

For a moment Judy kept blinking at me with eyes wide open, then she cleared her throat and simply asked, "How is this funny?"

"What are you talking about? It's hilarious! Look." I tried to show her the photo I took, but when I looked at it, I couldn't help but burst out laughing myself. "Look, look! Your expression!"

My assistant frowned at me and then gestured at the white-haired girl clinging to me while glancing around the room like a rabbit that just got placed in an unfamiliar pen.

"I'm happy to see that you are enjoying yourself, but don't you think there is something more important to do right now?"

I glanced down at Snowy, who looked petrified.

"You are correct. Hey, Snowy?" I called out to her, and she gave me that classic deer-in-the-headlights look in return.

"Wha...? How did we...?"

"I will explain shortly, but first... You also think that Judy's expression is priceless on this picture, right?"

She looked at the screen I pushed in front of her, but after a few seconds of staring at it, she only shook her head.

"I... I don't see what you mean. I don't know what's going on—"

"What? But look! She looks so freaked out!" I retorted while pointing at the screen in my hand. "Look, you can see that her eyes are slightly wider than usual! And here, her mouth is a little open, which means she is shocked! On top of that, can you see how the tips of her ears are a little flushed? It means she is flustered and doesn't know what to say! It's so silly, it's downright adorable!"

"Chief!" Judy exclaimed while the tips of her ears turned red.

See, I told you that's how it is.

Anyways, she grabbed hold of me and told me, "Stop trying to embarrass me and let go of Neige already."

"I'm not trying to embarrass you, I just find your over-the-top reactions really cute," I answered while casually removing my hand from Snowy's waist.

"It wasn't over the top, or cute," my assistant denied with a tiny pout that didn't help her case.

"It was. Look, we have evidence. Right, Snowy?"

The other girl, apparently still confused by the situation, once again looked at the image on my phone and ultimately shook her head.

"I don't think Judy's expression is any different from usual."

"Really? You can't see it?" I asked back incredulously while I looked at the photo myself. "Huh. I guess you had to be there to get it."

"She was there, and you are just being obnoxious at this point," Judy fumed while she grabbed hold of Snowy and pulled her away. Then she added, "Also, we are going to have a talk about your prank later, just the two of us. Prepare yourself."

I gave her a flat look and muttered, "Well, that was ominous."

"E-excuse me?" came a sudden interjection from Snowy, who was finally getting to the point where she didn't look like she wanted to jump and hide under the sofa. "Are we in Leo's house?"

"Yes," I answered with a grin.

"But... we were in the hotel just now..."

"I said we would be home in a moment, didn't I? It's a neat trick, right?"

Snowy blinked again, apparently still confused, but before she could ask another question, my assistant grabbed hold of her again.

"Stop confusing the poor girl even worse than you've already done with your entry." She sent me another subdued glare. "Speaking of which, I can't believe you revealed another of your abilities just for a joke. We just talked about this."

"I didn't just do it for a joke," I pointed out with a huff. "It was also an experiment that opened up some brand-new possibilities, and on top of that, it helped me get Snowy home ASAP. The surprise photo was just icing on the cake."

Judy locked eyes with me, but when it became obvious I wouldn't show even a hint of remorse, she rolled her eyes and grumbled something along the lines of, "You are incorrigible."

"No, I'm not," I replied with a chuckle. "I'm Leonard Dunning, here to perform my boyfriendly duty of teasing my girlfriend without having to hold back."

My dear assistant gave me a sideways look, followed by a defeated sigh and the line, "This relationship is already off to a rocky start. Sometimes I wonder why I put up with your antics."

"Because you love me a bunch?" I asked with a cheeky smile, and Judy returned the gesture with another roll of her eyes.

"Against my better judgment."

I let out a mirthful little chuckle, but before I could continue, I noticed Snowy tapping on my upper arm, so I turned a curious glance at her.

"S-sorry, I didn't mean to interrupt, but… did you say 'girlfriend'?"

"Yup," I answered with a toothy grin.

She glanced over at Judy next, and after a long sigh and acting like this was the most bothersome thing in the world, my girlfriend stated, "We are going out."

"Really?" For some reason, this seemed to perk up our Abyssal guest. She grabbed hold of Judy's hand with both of her own. "Congratulations!"

"Thanks?" I answered, feeling a little awkward by her enthusiasm. Judy shared my sentiment, as she only gave her a nod.

In the meantime, Snowy leaned closer and asked my assistant in a whisper that I probably wasn't supposed to be able to hear, but I did anyway.

"Since when? And who confessed first? Wait, no, first tell me how Eleanor took it. Was she mad?"

My girlfriend let out a tired sigh, and she pulled on the other girl once again while saying, "The bath is ready, so let's go there first. I will tell you the details there."

With that, the two of them left without saying even a "see ya later," leaving me all alone in the living room. I let out a long breath and wandered over to my favourite comfy chair.

So, what did I learn just now? I could teleport long distances with others in tow, I had poor impulse control, and I was going to be scolded by my girlfriend for revealing the former because of the latter. That said, I took another look at Judy's dumbfounded face on my phone, and could barely hold back my chuckles long enough to save it into my backup folder.

"Still worth it," I whispered as I serenely glanced up at the stairs leading to the first floor, a serenity that not even the shouts of *"You and Eleanor are both going out with him?"* coming from there could break.

PART 2

"Is she asleep?" Judy asked me the moment I reached the bottom of the stairs, without even looking up from her phone.

"Yes," I answered lightly as I walked over and sat down beside her on the couch.

After Snowy took a quick bath, we realized she had no clothes to change into, so I lent her a shirt while Judy procured a set of brand-new underwear from somewhere (and when I asked her about it, she said she was carrying it around just in case, whatever the hell that meant). Now, I'm pretty damn tall, so Snowy was always petite to me (just like the other girls, now that I thought about it), but when she was wearing my comparatively circus-tent-sized shirt, she looked positively tiny. Anyways, after we explained to her how our new polyamorous relationship came to be, a conversation in which she was weirdly invested for some reason, I decided to lend her one of the empty rooms in the house for the time being, and she went to sleep pretty much the moment she hit the bed.

But back to the present: After I sat down beside her, Judy put her phone aside and turned to me with a serious expression.

"Chief, let's talk."

I closed my eyes for a moment. Ever since that morning, I could see something was eating at her. Some of the throwaway jabs made it clear she wasn't in a good mood. I had a sneaking suspicion about what she wanted to discuss, so I prepared myself and gave her the go.

"Sure."

My assistant took a deep breath, then began with, "Let's start with your new ability. You said you can teleport to anyone you can see with Far Sight?"

I was a little surprised by her opening topic, but I quickly collected myself. Maybe she was trying to ease me into it? Either way, there was no point in pondering her thought process at the moment.

"Pretty much, yes," I replied in a neutral voice.

"And you used Neige to test it?"

"Indeed."

"Even though we agreed that you would be more careful about revealing your abilities."

I expected this line of criticism, but since I had time to think about it, I was prepared with a rebuttal.

"Yeah. I mean, I had to test it somehow, and considering it was Snowy, I thought it was safe to use her as the guinea pig." I glanced up the stairs, making sure her "dot" was still where I left her, then I continued with, "She was sleep deprived and pretty shaken at the time, so I figured it wouldn't hurt if I could take her home in an instant. Win-win."

"That sounds like post hoc rationalization to me," Judy grumbled, but I dismissed her objection with a shrug.

"Well, it's done, and there's no point crying over spilled milk." My girlfriend seemed less than satisfied by my words, so I hastily added, "Okay, then how about this: I had this idea for a while, but how about some misdirection?" That earned me a curious look, so I told her, "Since people are bound to be interested in my abilities, why don't we tell them some consistent false info? Like for example, let's tell Snowy that it was some kind of emergency-escape skill that teleported me back to my house?"

"According to my knowledge, teleportation spells are very complicated and take a lot of time and resources to set up."

"Perfect," I said with a smirk. "I had to mess around a bit to get it working, so we can say I was preparing it."

"That... could theoretically work," Judy conceded.

"Yeah. I think we can do the same for my other abilities too. Make them think there are some limitations to them. Then I'll use them consistently with their expectations, and one of them might turn out to be a great ace in the hole during the next life-or-death situation."

Judy gave me a flat look.

"I would prefer it if you tried to avoid such situations, if possible."

"Yeah, yeah, naturally," I answered while thinking about the next thing. "So, for my magic vision, we can call that a unique ability of some kind."

"What kind?"

"Well..." I paused for a moment, then I tentatively said, "Psychic?"

"Psychic," Judy repeated after me.

"Hey, don't look at me like that! You were the one who insisted on it just this morning! Not to mention, it's already something the class rep suspects, so we might as well keep rolling with it. In fact, it's pretty much the only thing we can use. I remember Crowey once said that I had no mana whatsoever, so I can't really claim to be a hedge wizard or the like."

"He said that. He also said that his plan was flawless and we stood no chance against him."

"Just villain dialoging," I rebutted. "Seriously though, I'm inclined to believe him on the mana part. He said it to Brang while I spied on him; there was no reason for him to lie there."

"Very well," Judy conceded the point after writing down a few more lines. "So, what is your cover for your abilities again?"

"Well..." I began, and the discussion didn't stop for a good twenty minutes.

At the end of it, Judy set her phone down. "So, just to summarize: You have no mana because you are psychic. You can see and dispel magic because of that. Your precognitive reflexes should be hidden, so we explain them by saying you..." She paused and theatrically glanced at her phone, "*know kung fu.*"

"Well, maybe not kung fu, but some kind of martial art. Let's be vague about it."

"As always," my assistant nodded, then continued. "The information gained through Far Sight should be explained by you being an information trader on the side, and your teleportation is a..." She trailed off, probably just to annoy me, considering her memory.

"It's a secret artifact that can only be used once every seventy-two hours," I said a little begrudgingly.

"Yes." She nodded. Then she looked up at me and said, "So according to your cover story, you are a psychic anti-magic martial artist with an unknown intelligence network, equipped with a rare reusable teleportation artifact." She glanced down at her phone, then back at me, then at her phone again, and finally asked, "How is this supposed to bring less attention to you, again?"

"Oh, come on!" I threw my hands up in protest. "We both know this is the best we've got."

"Indeed. Since you've already dug yourself into this hole, we must work around it."

"Ouch," I muttered flatly. "You're grumpier than usual."

It was supposed to be a throwaway comment, but Judy gave me a sharp look, followed by, "Then maybe you should think about your actions a bit more."

"Is this still about my abilities? Are you still mad at me because I revealed them to Snowy?"

Now her glare was positively withering, and she only said, "Among other things."

That made me stop in my tracks. I felt like I'd somehow stepped on a landmine, and I had a feeling it was the one I'd known was right in front of me for a while now, but at present, I had no choice but to bite the bullet and ask, "Could you be a little more specific? I think I'm missing something."

I received another frown from my assistant, then she pointedly put down her phone and changed her posture on the couch so she would face me more directly.

"Yes, Chief, you are."

Seeing how the atmosphere in the room took a sudden turn to the serious, I involuntarily swallowed.

"You see, I'm fine with our current relationship."

I blinked at her in surprise. I expected some kind of bombshell to fall considering how serious she looked, but that was quite ordinary. Deceptively so. As such, I couldn't help but hesitantly say, "I'm glad to hear that, but—"

"But," she interrupted, "I'm not fine with how *you* are treating it." I must've looked supremely baffled, as she shook her head. "Chief, I knew what kind of world we live in. I also knew where your repeated *interactions* with Eleanor would lead. I tried my best to be more aggressive, so that we could enter into a monogamous relationship before things got more complicated with Eleanor, but I've prepared myself for an outcome like this from the very beginning. It's not my preferred result, but I could see things potentially turning out much more *crowded*, so to speak, so I accepted the compromise."

"I see," I muttered, somewhat humbled by the way she spelled things out for me, but she ignored me and continued completely unabated.

"However, I don't think you are taking this relationship seriously enough." Judy paused, and I was tempted to look away from her intense stare, but I forced myself to stay still. Then she softened. "Leo, tell me honestly: did you decide on this polyamorous relationship because it was the path of least resistance?"

"I... would be lying if I said it didn't factor into my thought process," I admitted, my voice sounding a little bitter even to myself.

"Chief, I love you. Eleanor loves you too. But do you actually love either of us? Have you ever said the word out loud?" Judy asked, her voice ever so slightly wavering with every word. "I'm willing to compromise, to put in the effort necessary to make this work, to make this something more than just a convenient way to avoid romantic tension between the three of us. Even now, I'm taking this relationship seriously." Judy paused for a moment, and her voice became very heavy as she asked, "Can I count on you to do that same?"

I tried to formulate an answer, but I couldn't. It didn't matter though, as my silence was condemning enough. Judy looked at me for a few long seconds, and the fact that she didn't seem like she expected an answer right away made it both relieving and humiliating at the same time.

At last, my assistant stood up and took a step back.

"It's getting late," she told me flatly while glancing at the clock. "I should go home, or Dad will worry." Grabbing her coat, she said, "Let's… continue this discussion tomorrow."

Then she left, as if escaping the oppressive silence, without saying anything else. Not that it mattered, as I was still in a bit of a guilt-induced stupor. For several silent minutes, I sat where she left me while holding my head in my palm, listening to the ticking of the clock on the wall of the lonely living room as I got my wayward thoughts in order.

Leaning back on the couch cushions with a self-deprecating groan, I stared at the ceiling, closed my eyes, and retreated into my mind for a much-needed self-reflection session.

As much as I hated to admit it, Judy had hit the nail on the head. Hard. So hard, in fact, that I was still reeling back from it. Hindsight is always twenty-twenty, but in this case, it was doubly embarrassing, as I more or less spelled this out to the girls when I asked them out. I told them I was taking drastic measures because I was expecting future troubles and I didn't want our love triangle to interfere. That was as good as admitting that I considered our love triangle bothersome and I wanted to exchange it for a less troublesome relationship. Not because I liked them, or because I wanted to be with them. In short, I made the choice for the wrong reasons. Judy could see that from the get-go, but the princess was simply too excited to notice.

After a moment of thinking, I stood up and headed towards the kitchen. I decided to make myself a big mug of tea, as doing menial tasks like that often helped me think more clearly.

As I did so, I began to ponder: if I entered into this relationship for the wrong reasons, then what were the right reasons? Let's discard all the external factors about harem narratives and annoying/comedic love-triangle situations. The first question was: did I like Judy and Elly?

The answer to that was a resounding yes. Judy was my assistant, my closest confidante, and we were practically always on the same wavelength.

I loved spending time with her, I loved talking with her, I loved how amusing her expressions were once you figured out how to read her, and I loved both her serious and cute sides.

As for the princess, I always had a lot of fun teasing her, and as much as she denied it, I'm sure she didn't hate it. I loved her awkwardness, I loved her cuteness peeking through her façade of confidence, and I loved how nice and sociable she was behind all those verbal thorns.

The teaspoon in my hand stopped midway in the air, sugar trickling into the mug, as my brows furrowed with a small yet alarming realization. Yes, there were many things I loved about both my girlfriends, but... did I love *them*? The answer should have been obvious, yet...

"Do I?" I wondered aloud as I finally put the spoon into my mug.

I mean, I obviously liked them both, a lot, but as for *love*? I wasn't so sure. Not that I had much experience in the subject, amnesia and all, but wasn't love supposed to be... I don't know. More intense? People always say it's like a yearning, or a burning sensation, but I couldn't say I'd ever felt that. I couldn't remember feeling lovestruck or exceptionally giddy when they were around me, nor did I recall suffering heartache when I hadn't seen them for a few days. Sure, I'd lately often felt strangely content when I was in their company, but wasn't love supposed to be more passionate than that?

I shook my head and took a sip from my mug. It was still missing something, so I went over to the cupboard and took out a jar of honey I saved for occasions like this. But back to the topic at hand: I actually didn't know how intense love was supposed to feel. Realizing that, I decided to look at the problem from another angle: did I want to stay with them in a relationship, potentially for the rest of my life? I thought long and hard about it, but for a slightly peculiar reason: I was immediately 100 percent certain I wanted to do that, and it made me wonder why that conclusion came to me so readily.

I mean, I'd just spent the last couple of minutes hesitating about whether my feelings would qualify as love or not, but if they asked me if I would like to get married and settle down tomorrow, I would probably say yes on the spot. Did that make sense?

I picked up my mug with a small sigh and left the kitchen. I walked up the stairs, making extra sure to stay very quiet as I walked past the room where Snowy was sleeping. At last, I entered my room and carefully closed the door, then sat down in front of my PC and placed the mug on the desk. I exhaled a pent-up breath.

So, what was my conclusion?

I liked them as people and wanted to have them close to me. In other words, I wanted this relationship, whether I was clear on the whole "love" thing or not.

Moreover, Judy was right. A relationship required compromise, effort, and sincerity. A relationship like ours required all three in droves. However, I was no longer hesitant about it.

Compromise? The two of them were already making the biggest one by agreeing with my selfishness, so it was only fair that I would follow suit.

Effort? I'm the man who never sleeps. If I would need to sacrifice those extra hours to make this work, it would be a small price to pay.

Sincerity?... Well, okay, maybe I didn't have the cleanest track record when it comes to that, but if it's about our relationship, I was more than willing to compromise with my habits and make the effort to be more sincere. For a start, I really had to start using the damn L-word more often, even if I wasn't entirely sure about the exact nature of my feelings yet.

With my mind finally clear, my enthusiasm renewed, and my computer booted, I took a sip from my mug and chuckled to myself, then opened my personal folder and created a new file titled, *Operation: OTT.*

Hey, it might not have been perfectly accurate, but it sure as hell was snappier than "a semi-platonic subtype of the polyamorous Type 8 Triangular Relationship"...

PART 3

I was right in the middle of finishing up my comprehensive and airtight explanation as Admin to cover my conspicuous absence from the Hub over the past few days when a guitar solo interrupted me. I blinked in surprise as I took my headset off and reached out towards my phone without paying much attention to the caller ID.

"Hello? Leonard speaking."

"Leo, please let us in," came the answer from a familiar voice, and I couldn't help but frown at the request.

"Class rep? What do you mean *let us in*? Where are you?"

"At your front door," she answered in a decidedly impatient voice. "We've been banging on it for minutes now."

"Really?" I mumbled as I turned off the power metal song still blaring from my headphones and sneakily checked the time. It was a little after 8 a.m., but it was still fairly dark outside. Wow, morning already.

"Weird, I didn't hear you," I told her. "I'll be down with you in a moment."

I put down the phone before she could answer and quickly finished up my excuse on the Hub. I locked up my machine and hid away my notes, making sure all the incriminating evidence was out of sight. Then I skipped down the stairs and opened the front door.

"Hi—" I began my welcome with a bright smile, which then turned into a surprised one as I finished, "Angie is here too?"

Right. The class rep had said "we," but I hadn't expected Angie to be the one with her. They were both dressed casually, which in Angie's case consisted of a grey turtleneck sweater with some kind of woven pattern on the chest under a light jacket, jeans, and a beanie, while the class rep was dressed in a white long coat that didn't let me see the rest of her clothes, a plaid scarf plus a pair of white mufflers on her head. More importantly though, they were followed by two floating eyeballs similar to the ones I'd dispatched the day before, except these were blue. Lovely.

"Hi, Leo," Angie returned the greeting with a smile considerably more upbeat than what I expected under the circumstances. "Are you all right? How are your injuries?"

"I'm fine, fit as a fiddle," I answered while checking her over. "How about you? I was told you were under house arrest."

"I..." she began, but then the class rep cut her off.

"I convinced my grandfather to put her under my custody. Now, would you please let us in? It's cold out here."

"Sure," I began, but then I frowned and raised my hand to stop them in their tracks. There was something I thought about yesterday after I dispelled all the surveillance, but I didn't have the opportunity to try it because, well, I already dispelled all the surveillance. I wanted to try it right away, but then I reflected on Judy's words from the day before, and decided to be a little less overt. As such, I told them, "One at a time."

The two girls looked at me funny, but then the class rep stepped forward, followed by the blue eyeball floating a little over and behind her head. I waited for it to get closer, then as she crossed the doorstep, I casually extended a hand as if welcoming her in. From that hand, I extended my phantom limb, and with a quick and nimble lash, it sliced right through the magical eyeball. To my deepest satisfaction, the effect was exactly the same as if I'd done it with my fingers. I'm not going to lie, as skeptical as I was about this phantom limb, it was slowly turning me around. This thing was *handy*.

Anyways, I did the exact same thing with Angie and her unwanted stalker, and then I closed the door behind them.

"What was that about?" asked the Celestial girl as she took off her beanie, her long auburn hair falling freely on her shoulders instead of her usual, tidy ponytail. This look suited her as well, though I couldn't help but wonder: the princess started to wear her hair in its natural waves instead of her drills, and now it was Angie who changed her hair. Maybe it was significant? I mean, their hair was significant to begin with, so changing it should be, too. Speaking of which, I glanced over to the class rep, and after she removed her muffler, I noticed that her long forelock was also left unbraided and she simply tucked it behind her ear. Yup, three for three. Definitely not a coincidence.

Anyways, I shelved this under *Write This Down in the Notes Later* while I shrugged my shoulder and told Angie, "Just a bit of precaution, nothing for you to worry about."

She still looked at me funny, but then shrugged with a nonchalant *If you say so*, and hung up her coat. In the meantime, the class rep peeked at me over her foggy glasses, as if waiting for me to say something.

I decided to bite.

"So, to what do I owe the pleasure of your early visit?"

"I'm glad you asked," Amelia huffed and crossed her arms in front of her chest. "Do you know how much paperwork I had to fill out to cover your back? Do you have any idea how many people I had to lie to about the Chimera? And, when you finally wake up, you couldn't even bother to call me!"

"Right," Angie agreed, crossing her own arms to mirror the class rep's pose. "You didn't even tell me there would be a gathering today. I only learned about it because Josh told me on the phone!"

"Okay, okay!" I raised my hands defensively in the face of their combined assault. "First off, I sent you a text message. You told me you were busy, so I didn't call you back." The class rep huffed in reply, an unusual reaction from her for sure, but I ignored it for the time being and turned to the other girl. "As for you, as far as I knew, you were under house arrest, so of course I wouldn't invite you *openly* like that."

"Openly?" Ammy asked with a raised brow, and since her glasses finally cleared up, I could see the suspicious glint in her eyes. "What do you mean by that?"

"Well, I would've smuggled her out without prior notice, obviously," I told her with a wink, which made both of them freeze up for a moment. "What?"

"Do you have any idea how much trouble that would have caused?" the class rep exclaimed. "If you did that, we would be lucky if we would be only put under twenty-four/seven surveillance! Do you want to live with a scrying spell over your head and your house filled with recorder orbs for the rest of your life!?"

I gave her a long, hard look, but since she seemed to be entirely serious, I tentatively asked, "Was that a trick question?"

"No!" she yelled, startling both me and Angie in the process. Then her shoulders slouched like she'd just given up on something. She looked back up and readjusted her glasses before she told me, "Seriously, Leo, you need to lie low."

"Please elaborate," I told her as I gestured for them to follow me to the living room.

"First off, if someone other than me tries to contact you from the School, don't answer. Next, stay indoors and don't wander outside, especially not after dark. We don't know how many allies the Abyssals left behind, so you might be in danger. And speaking of Abyssals"—she pushed her glasses up the bridge of her nose—"don't go out to look for Neige."

She might've misunderstood my expression as she once again stressed, "I'm serious. She is on the top of the School's most wanted list right now. If you tried to look for her, even if you found her, you would just lead others to her at the same time, and it would also make things more difficult for you, too. Just give me a few more days, and I should be able to convince my grandfather to let me handle her. Then we can work something out."

"Well, I would like to promise that, but there's this tiny little problem with—"

"Leo," she interrupted and gestured to Angie. "We both think this is for the best. Promise us you won't look for Neige. Now."

"Yes, this is important," Angie agreed, nodding.

I looked at the two concerned girls in turn, then I groaned aloud. "You know what? Fine." I put a hand on my heart and raised the other like I was taking an oath. "I hereby solemnly promise that I will, under no circumstances, go outside and look for Snowy. Are you happy now?"

"Good enough," the class rep stated, though based on her expression, she was far from satisfied.

"All right. So, remember that tiny little problem with your request that you didn't let me explain?"

The two of them shared a meaningful glance, but before they could say anything, as per the unwritten rules of comedic timing, a door burst open on the next floor up, so I turned towards the stairs and yelled, "Good morning!"

Soft steps approached, and then Snowy came into view at the top of the stairwell.

"Goo mowning," she replied, stifling a yawn and rubbing her eyes with the long sleeve of my oversized shirt, which reached down below her knees.

That, combined with her bed head, made the Abyssal look pretty comical, though I obviously didn't laugh at her. Only smiled. She was still a little groggy, as she didn't register the two flabbergasted girls behind me, and simply asked, "Weers de toiled?"

"Second door on the left, the paper's in the holder on the wall."

"Thanks," Snowy muttered while she pattered away in a pair of never-used kitten-slippers that were about five sizes too big for her. None of us said anything until the door clicked shut behind her, at which point the class rep turned towards me with mechanical motions.

"What was that?"

Her voice so flat it would've given my dear assistant a run for her money.

"Snowy, obviously?" I answered with my most innocent smile.

"But you said—" she began, but then Angie interrupted her.

"I get it!" she exclaimed as she did that thing where you drop your closed fist into your open palm. "You said you won't look for her because you'd already found her! I see what you did there."

"Thank you, thank you. It's nice to have a perceptive audience," I tried to pass it off as a joke, but Amelia closed in on me all the same.

"Leoooo…" she growled, grasping my shirt and pulling me down to her eye level. "Are you doing this on purpose? Do you *want* to make my life more difficult? Are you an assassin hired to kill me by burying me under a *mountain of paperwork?*"

"Easy there, easy…" I took her hands and peeled them off my clothes. "You are waaaay too high-strung. You're not even acting like yourself anymore."

"And whose fault is that?" she hissed.

"Guys, don't fight!" Angie interjected. "Ammy, look at the bright side! This means Neige is all right, and we don't have to look for her! Leo is all right, too! Everyone is all right!"

"Yeah, listen to her," I agreed with the enthusiastic Celestial. "Everyone is fine and safe. What else could you ask for?"

Amelia gave me a withering look in return, but after a while she simply walked over to the couch while murmuring, "A good night's sleep, for a start."

"Huh," I chuckled as she sat down. "That seems to be a common problem nowadays."

In the meantime, the other girl came to my side and asked, "Hey, Leo? How did you find Snowy?"

"I have my ways," I answered offhandedly.

"Oh, come on, don't be a tease!" The overly spirited Celestial poked me in the side, but my lips remained sealed, so she just puffed her cheeks and grumbled, "Fine, keep your secrets… But can you at least tell me if you have any snacks?"

I glanced at her, and she flashed me a toothy smile that made me chuckle again.

"The cookies are in the big cupboard on the left. You can find some instant cocoa in the drawers of the large cabinet. Milk's in the fridge."

"Yay," she exclaimed with her usual childlike enthusiasm, and she headed right for the kitchen, only to stop midway and ask, "Ammy, do you want anything? Leo's treat!"

While the two of them discussed what to plunder from my pantry, I noticed a series of knocks coming from the main entrance. I walked over, and to my sincerest surprise, I found the princess standing on my front porch. She was also very red. I mean, not in the usual, embarrassed way, but in that she wore a bright red peacoat, red boots, and red mufflers. Hell, on closer look, she even had some lipstick and even some eyeliner on. The moment our eyes met she beamed a brilliant smile and greeted me with a passionate, "Good morning, Leo!"

"Um… yeah," I answered in a daze. "You are early."

"Yes! Melinda told me that in a new relationship, it's best to start the day by greeting the one you love with all your heart in the morning! Did you like it?"

"I sure did," I told her with a smile while I gestured for her to enter. "Come in, it's cold outside."

Giggling, Elly came in. Once she was beside me, I suddenly recalled one of my entries in my OTT file. I did a lot of research on how to do it properly, and this was a good opportunity to put the theory into practice, so I waited for her to take off her outerwear while I come up next to her and softly said, "By the way, Elly?"

She tensed up for a moment, probably because I called her by name, and then when she turned back to me, I lightly raised her chin and leaned closer so that our faces were in line, then I planted a kiss on her lips. It was a chaste one, but for some reason I could still feel my cheeks burning. Elly locked up with a deer-in-a-headlight stare, so I added, "Good morning to you, too."

For a moment, she froze, her face a deep shade of crimson, then her lips slowly parted into a familiar dopey smile, and she gave me a giant hug, muttering something about how *"it worked!"*

"Oh, what do we have here?" came an intrigued question.

I glanced over my shoulder to see Angie peeking around the corner.

The princess stiffened, then she let go of my waist and cleared her throat before she casually said, "O-oh? He-hello, Angie. I-I wasn't expecting to see you... here..."

I was honestly impressed. Sure, she stuttered, her face was red as a tomato, and her smile was more than a little strained, but she managed to say all that without any cutesy exclamations or running away. My princess had come a long way, hadn't she?

Anyways, Elly quickly peeled herself out of the rest of her winter wear and hung it all up in the closet, where she quietly noted the number of coats already there. As a fellow victim of missing-the-obvious, I empathized with her a lot, and when she was ready, I offered her my arm. At first she didn't seem to know what I was doing, but then the proverbial light bulb lit up over her head and she immediately clamped on to me. Like that, we entered the living room, much to the apparent joy of a certain Celestial with an entire cookie jar in one hand.

"See, I told you!" she exclaimed from beside Amelia while gesturing towards us with her free hand.

"Well, I'll be damned," the girl with the glasses whispered.

Elly giggled at their reaction, holding on to my arm even tighter, then said in (what I hoped to be) a mock haughty tone, "Just what could you find so hard to believe, if I may ask?"

The other girls looked at each other, then shrugged. However, before they could say anything, a new voice entered the fray as Snowy, dressed in her (washed and dried) clothes from the day before, yet for some inexplicable reason still wearing the oversized pair of kitten-slippers, pattered down the stairs in a hurry.

"S-sorry I didn't greet you before! Good morning!" she sputtered towards the girls on the sofa without sparing us a single glance. On closer look, I had to conclude she must've been in quite a hurry to get downstairs, as she still had some toothpaste on her chin. After some more apologizing, her eyes finally came our way, and when she noticed my girlfriend, she put on a strained smile and told her, "Um... good morning, and... congratulations?"

The princess raised her hand to her mouth and let out one of those cheesy laughs stuck-up high-class ladies used in period dramas, so I guess (read: *hoped*) she was still doing the whole fake haughty shtick.

I was just about to interject when someone knocked on my front door. Again.

"Ugh, let go for a moment," I told Elly and disentangled our arms. She gave me an abandoned puppy look. I rolled my eyes and told her, "Don't worry, I'll be back in a moment."

With that, I turned around to answer the door, but I still caught Angie grabbing her hand and dragging her towards the couch, probably for an impromptu interrogation session, while the class rep gestured for Snowy to do the same. Anyways, I momentarily put the situation in the living room off my mind as I opened the front door once again. There was a fifty-fifty chance by now, so I was prepared, but I still twitched a little when I was face-to-face with Judy wearing a puffy winter coat and an honest-to-goodness ushanka with the earflaps down.

"Morning, Chief," she stated in her usual voice, as if yesterday's discussion didn't happen. I knew better, of course, so I waited for her to continue, but all she asked was, "Is Eleanor here already?"

"Yes. How'd you know?"

"I saw her limousine down the street."

"Figures," I muttered, then I stood aside to invite her in. She gave me an appreciative nod and entered.

So far things were fairly normal, but then she took her winter hat off and said, "Chief, about yesterday—"

I didn't let her finish, but instead I used the same motions as with the princess not too long ago to quickly lean down and plant a small peck on her half-open mouth. To my astonishment, the look on her face was a mirror image of Elly's.

… Well, maybe not on the surface level, but functionally.

Anyways, I let out a dry cough. "I took what you said to heart yesterday, about effort and taking things seriously, and… well, that's my answer."

I waited for her to react, but instead she just kept staring at me like she was seeing a ghost, so I poked her and asked, "Any comments?"

My question (or the poke, one or the other) finally snapped her out of it, and after she lightly cleared her throat and got her expression back to her baseline, my girlfriend said, "Chief, that was low. You can't just take a girl's first kiss without warning."

"The princess didn't mind," I retorted, which only earned me a huff.

"It's because she has low standards," she said before she raised her face and closed her eyes and told me, "Now give it back."

For a second or two I honest-to-goodness froze. This was unexpected. I was just about to feel awkward when suddenly a blonde head popped between us.

"What are you doing?" Elly exclaimed, probably voicing the thoughts of the peanut gallery in the back, but then her next words probably only plunged them into even deeper confusion as she said, "That's not fair! If she is getting a second good morning kiss, I want one too!"

Saying so, she also closed her eyes and puckered her lips in anticipation.

And then, as the unwritten rules of comedic timing dictate, the door behind me opened, followed by the words, "I'm letting myself… in?"

It was probably because of the whole commotion that I never noticed the sound of his moped, but when I turned around, I could see a much more presentable Joshua standing in the doorway, cautiously eyeing me and the two girls in front of him.

He scratched the back of his head and sheepishly asked, "Is this the wrong time?"

I looked at him, then at three in the back, and finally the two girls in front, and I let out the groan to end all groans.

Nothing for it.

"You, get in here already and close the door. You three, stop gawking and get back to the living room. As for you two…"

When they realized I was addressing them, my girlfriends stopped puckering their mouths and looked at me questioningly.

I sighed. "Rock, paper, scissors—best out of three, the winner gets their kiss first. Are we clear? Go!"

CHAPTER 4

"So, are we all done?" I inquired using my most diplomatic voice as my eyes swept over the usual suspects crowding around the single table in my living room. At the moment, due to the limited number of comfortable real-estate where three people could sit side by side at the same time, I was seated on my couch instead of my usual comfy chair, with one girlfriend on each side. My question thankfully made the rest finally stop gossiping in the open, so I let out a long breath and continued with, "I didn't think we would be having this gathering so early in the morning, but since we are all here already, I suppose we might as well talk about the most pressing issues we are facing at the moment. Are you fine with that?"

I took the momentary silence as a form of agreement, and I was just about to outline said issues when the class rep harrumphed.

"Give it up, Leo," she said sullenly. "You can't just try to sweep this elephant under the rug and expect us to ignore it."

"Seconded," Angie chimed in with a raised hand.

"Thirded," came the next blow from Josh. I glanced at Snowy by his side, actually expecting her to go "fourthed" or the like, but instead she shrank back and refused to meet my eyes.

Still, that was three against one, so I couldn't just ignore them.

"Could you please tell me what you mean by 'this elephant'?" I asked as I turned back to the class rep again, and she actually began to menacingly adjust her glasses in return, much to my sincerest bafflement. I mean… how do you even do that? Damned if I knew, but she did it, and I certainly felt menaced as she pointed sternly.

"This! We mean this! What else could we mean?"

I followed her pointed finger with my eyes, which led me to a certain blonde dragon girl blissfully hugging my left arm with a giant smile plastered on her face, apparently completely unaware of the fact that she was in the center of attention.

"First off, calling her an elephant is just plain rude, so shame on you," came my answer with the most innocent expression I could manage. "Secondly, I don't see the problem. She's been like that ever since we started going out."

Ammy seemed to be on the verge of exploding with a mixture of irritation and incomprehension, but before she could do so, Josh put in, "Leo, you told us you are going out with her *and* Judy. Both. At the same time. You cannot just expect us to accept that without an explanation."

"But there is nothing to explain!" I voiced my own irritation maybe just a wee bit too loudly, so I toned it back and continued, "We are going out. It's like when you date one girl, except it's two. It's very simple, really."

"You don't *simply* go out with two girls at once," Josh countered.

"Yeah, I'm totally with Josh on this one!" Angie agreed with him. But then she added, "It's actually really impressive! Leo, you're a real player!"

She even gave me a giant thumbs-up, stopping not only me but also the rest of the group in our tracks. To be honest, I wasn't expecting to find an ally in the group like that, but I decided it wasn't proper to look the gift horse in the mouth, so I returned the gesture with a "Thanks!" She giggled.

Unfortunately, peace didn't last long.

Ammy slammed her palm on the coffee table, startling all of us, and stared daggers at me.

"Leo," she began, then she took a deep breath to collect herself and sat up straight again, continuing in a calmer but no less thorny voice, "when I told you to make up your mind and stop leading Judy and Elly by the nose, this wasn't what I meant."

"Right," Josh agreed with a nod. "How did you even get them to agree to something like this?"

"Yeah, tell us!" Angie rejoined the fray with her trademark enthusiasm.

Feeling like I was getting backed into a corner, I did the most reasonable thing and hastily deflected the question.

"You guys are blowing this way out of proportion, right, Judy?" I glanced to my other girlfriend sitting on my right, her fingers clasping my hand, and, to my surprise, I found her spacing out. She tapped her lips, her cheeks flushed. Since she didn't respond, I squeezed her hand a little, which finally earned me a small shudder and a couple of surprised blinks.

For a moment I was afraid I'd squeezed too hard, but after blinking a few more times, she squeezed back and cleared her throat, then she said, "Sorry, I wasn't paying attention. What were we talking about?"

"Your relationship with Leo," Snowy interjected, apparently waiting for the right moment to enter the conversation, but then she shrank back just as fast without saying anything else.

"Oh, that?" She looked up at me, a mischievous glint in her eyes. "We had little choice. While the chief has numerous outstanding qualities, unfortunately being a born womanizer is one of them. Because of this, at least two of us are needed to keep his impulses under control. It's for the good of all the girls at school."

"Hey!" I protested as I lightly poked her in the side with my elbow. "Could you please not paint your boyfriend as some sort of predator?"

She gave me a flat look before she poked me back, then she stated, "Hush, Chief. I'm doing a thing here."

"I don't care. You're making me look bad!"

"That's the point," she insisted. "I'm in the process of lowering your perceived fitness as a potential mate. It's to prevent the foundation of a harem."

"I told you, I don't want one!"

"Then you shouldn't mind," she said, like it was the most logical thing in the world.

"But I do mind because it's slander!"

"Right!" To my greatest surprise, the one coming to my rescue was the girl clinging to my other arm. "Leo already promised he won't flirt anymore. Why don't you trust him?"

"It's not about trust, it's about this world's…" Judy began, but then she noticed the disapproving look I directed her way, so she quickly said, "This is not about flirting, and I don't expect you to understand yet. If you have nothing to add, please go back to daydreaming."

Well, I wanted her to change the subject, but I didn't think she would be *this* blunt about it. Fortunately, Elly only chuckled, then gave my assistant a huge grin. "Are you jealous because I got the first kiss twice?"

"No, I'm not," Judy told her in a flat voice, though the tiny twitch in the corner of her mouth belied her calm. "You got the first kiss; that just means I will be getting the next of his firsts."

"Wait, what?" I tried to cut in, but I was ignored by the suddenly beet-red blonde girl.

"Ho-hold on! That's not how this works! It's also too early! And even when appropriate, we should at least have another round of rock-paper-scissors to decide that!"

"Objection!" Judy, well, objected with a frown. "You cannot decide important things like that on the outcome of a game."

"Then what? Do you have anything better?" Elly responded, at this point completely ignoring not only the original subject, but everyone else in the room as well.

So I returned the favor by ignoring them both, instead telling Ammy, "Could we please stop talking about my love life? As you can see, it tends to derail things."

She gave me a contemplative look, and ultimately she relaxed and muttered a flat, "Fine."

"Wait!" Angie interjected with a raised hand. "At least tell us how you convinced them! Pretty please?"

I furrowed my brow. "Why do you want to know?"

"For future reference."

"What is that supposed to mean?" came the very good question from Josh, accompanied by one of those curiously raised single eyebrows he was so good at.

"Donn warry aboot eet," Angie answered with a weird fake accent. I had no idea what that was supposed to be, but Josh rolled his eyes with a stifled snicker, so I figured it was another of their weird childhood friend inside jokes.

Anyways, since there was no need for any kind of complicated cover story here, I simply told her, "As I said, I didn't convince them. I told them it was an option, and they agreed. Simple as that."

"Seriously? Just like that?"

I gave her a nod, which made the Celestial girl fall deep in thought. Josh, on the other hand, still appeared more than just a little skeptical.

"Listen, Leo, I'm not saying you're lying," he said in a tone that implied I was, "but do you really think we are just going to accept that Judy and Elly would agree to something so weird so easily?"

I was just about to answer, but then the princess suddenly declared, "We are in agreement!"

I tried to imitate Josh's eyebrow thing, but since she didn't seem to get the clue, I voiced the question even though I was sure the answer was going to be tiresome.

"What are you talking about?"

"Weren't you paying attention, Chief?" came another question in place of an answer, this time from Judy. "We agreed that rock-paper-scissors is not an adequate way to decide on 'first times,' so we are going to compete in collecting femininity points. The one who gathers more will be the one who gets the next 'first time.'"

"That's right!" Elly agreed with a nod as she stood up, dragging me halfway along as she was still holding my hand. "The first challenge is making the best breakfast!"

In the meantime, Judy also stood up, completely pulling me out of my seat in the process. Then she said, "Let's go!" her usual deadpan coloured by just a hint of fighting spirit. As for me, I simply rolled my eyes and sat back down, pulling my unsuspecting girlfriends along with a firm tug. After all three of us had landed back on the couch with a soft thud, I squeezed their hands hard to get their attention.

"We are in the middle of a meeting, and at this rate we are never going to get to the actual point! You can do whatever contest you want later, but for now, please behave yourselves," I chided them, then I turned back to Josh with a rueful smile. "As for your question, I rest my case."

Josh opened and closed his mouth several times, apparently looking for, and failing to find, the right words, but at last he simply mumbled, "Point taken."

"Fine," the princess also agreed at my side, albeit reluctantly. "We are going to make breakfast after it's over then."

"At this rate, it'll be lunch, but whatever… Now then!" I raised my voice to get everyone's attention. I wanted to clap once for emphasis, but the two girls were holding on to my hands like vices, so I had to settle with just a verbal demarcation. "So, now that we have finally put my new relationship behind us, can we please focus for a while and talk about the actual matters of importance?"

The gang shared some strange looks, then Ammy said, "I still have a lot of questions, but I grant it to you that we have more pressing problems to talk about just now."

"Finally!" I exclaimed with a slightly exaggerated sigh towards the heavens, then I quickly put on my business face as I looked at each member of the gang in turn. "So, before we start in earnest, let's make one thing clear: what we are about to discuss here is super-confidential. We all have our circumstances, but as far as trouble is concerned, Josh is in the deepest, and I don't want to make things worse by a leak."

"Well, gosh! That's reassuring!" Joshua complained.

The class rep leaned forward. "Is it that serious?"

"Yes," I told her. "I trust you guys, and I don't think any of you would tattle, but we are talking about actual, status-quo shaking things here, so we cannot be careful enough."

Amelia kept frowning hard, as if she was weighing her options. Suddenly she stood up, and after some whispering and hand waving, she snatched a familiar silver staff topped by a fist-sized emerald right out of thin air.

Seeing how everyone was startled out of their skin, I asked, "Ammy, what exactly are you doing?" before things would escalate.

She set the staff down with a small, metallic *tink* and gave me a look like I'd just asked something supremely silly.

"I'm going to search the house for surveillance. Angie, Neige, you help too. I'm going to start with—"

"Wait!" I raised my voice to stop her before she could gather momentum. "I already did that."

She froze in the middle of striking some kind of weird pose. She blinked at me, then she straightened her posture with a questioning expression.

"You probably misunderstood me," she began, gesturing with her free hand as if she was holding a small ball. "When I said 'surveillance,' I didn't mean mundane ones but spells like recorder orbs and—"

"Yes, yes, I know. I already got rid of all of them."

"You did?" she asked, and after I nodded, the large staff blinked away. After a few short moments of fidgeting, she sat down. "Right. I should've known. You wouldn't bring Neige here if the place was… But are you sure you got them all?"

"Positive," I told her, and for some inexplicable reason that made her slump her shoulders and let out a gigantic sigh, so I added, "Relax, class rep. You're acting so high-strung, you're making the piano wires jealous."

She snapped, "And whose fault is…?" Then, taking a deep breath, she continued with, "You know what? It doesn't matter. If you say the house is clean, I believe you. So, what are we going to talk about that requires secrecy?"

"I'm glad you asked," I spoke with a small smile. Things were finally moving along. "First things first, let's talk about prophecies."

"Prophecies?" Ammy repeated after me with a strange expression.

"Yeah. Do you have any? I mean, not *you* in particular, but the Magi?"

"We do not," she answered in an almost mechanical fashion. "Prophecies are for the small-minded and those who do not understand the laws of magic, nature, and causality."

"That's kinda rude to the others in the room, but not really what I wanted to know," I stated, but then I paused as Judy began fiddling with something by my side. I glanced over, and she was poking her phone with a single finger. Since her other hand was still holding mine, this resulted in her dragging my arm left and right.

I closed my eyes and simply asked, "Really, Dormouse? Really?"

She gave me a conflicted look, then she moved her hand over so that now she was holding the phone with two fingers on her occupied hand instead.

"Better?" she asked in such a natural, matter-of-fact manner that I was tempted to believe she wasn't doing it just for attention.

"Fine, whatever," I conceded, then I turned back to the class rep, who was once again adjusting her glasses at me in an implausibly menacing fashion.

"Sorry about that," I said. "Where were we? Oh, right, the prophecies. Or lack thereof. Anyways, I wanted to ask if anything comes to mind about a theoretical individual who may or may not fulfill a very specific role or may or may not provide some sort of crucial benefit to the magi in a way that may or may not remind you of some kind of larger-than-life prophesized hero?"

Based on her facial expression, Ammy really wanted to give me a piece of her mind, but instead she intoned, "As I just said, we do not have *prophecies* on principle, but if we are talking about someone special, there is always the Conduit of the Grimoire."

"Really now?" I asked while taking a sneak peek at Judy, who was indeed taking notes, albeit in a highly awkward position. Well, it was her fault for being stubborn and refusing to let go of my hand, so I didn't feel even a smidgen of pity for her. I also moved my hand a little, but only because it was getting a little uncomfortable, and I definitely didn't put it in her lap so she would have an easier time. No sirree. But back to the discussion at hand: "Could you tell me about this Conduit guy?"

"I really don't see how any of this has anything to do with… anything."

"Trust me, it's relevant," I told her with my most mysterious smile.

She gave me another critical look. "Fine. The Conduit of the Grimoire is an unofficial position that's been vacant in the Assembly for close to a thousand years. The Grimoire of the Last Truth is an ancient recorder crystal that grants its user knowledge of the grand magicks from before the Fall. Grandfather once told me that if we could find someone with the aptitude to draw the power and knowledge from the Grimoire, the Magi could easily banish the three Winged Races and safeguard humanity for the rest of time."

"I see…" I whispered while nodding to myself. I'd already looked into Ammy's background (only a little though, nothing invasive), so I knew that her grandfather was a famous scholar and authority figure in Magi circles. If that was to be believed, it meant he was most likely the sagely wizard mentor type, which in turn meant it was probably fine to take his words at face value. Anyways, I flashed another smile at her and declared, "Well, it's Josh."

"What's Josh?" she shot back, brows furrowed.

"Your conduit or whatever. Right, Josh?"

My friend gave me a harrowed look and simply dropped his shoulders in resignation.

"You tell me."

"Right, and that's what I'm telling you."

"But," Snowy spoke up again, and at first she seemed like she wanted to shrink back once more, but after our eyes met, she nervously continued with, "Wasn't Josh the Herald of the Emperor?"

"The what now?" That question came from the confused Celestial in the middle of the group. "I thought he was a candidate for being the reincarnated Deus?"

"Indeed," I told them with a small chuckle. "Let me introduce you to Joshua Bernstein, the reviver of the dragon bloodlines, the usherer of emperors, the reincarnation of dear leaders, the puller of magical swords, and as we just learned, the conduit of crystal books."

I had the urge to count that off on my fingers while I said it, but my hands being occupied, I had to content myself with speaking.

Snowy asked the obvious.

"All… at the same time?"

"Yup!" I answered with a grin.

"Leo, are actually you serious?" the class rep said, her ferocious eyes boring into my skull.

"Um, yeah?"

"You aren't joking."

"Of course it's not a joke," I told her with mild exasperation.

"I wish it was," Josh added on with an equally exhausted look.

Ammy looked at each of us in turn, and after she finally seemed certain we weren't pulling her leg, she leaned back in her seat, took off her glasses, and massaged her nose.

She put her glasses back on. "I think I get it why you said we had to keep this confidential. Can you tell me the details?"

"Oh, can I?" Elly piped up. "Come on—let me, let me!"

Well, I'd already given a lot of expositions lately; it was only fair to let someone else have a turn. I gave my girlfriend a nod.

"All right!" The princess puffed up her already generous chest, then she started with, "So, as far as I could follow Leo's explanation yesterday, each of the Old-Blooded Races, plus the accursed Knights, have a prophecy. Josh has a special ability that allows him to absorb the essences of the Old-Blooded and temporarily gain their powers. The prophecies are kind of contradictory, but he can fulfill any of them because of his power, and Leo thought that if there were already four of them about him, the Magi should have something similar too, which is what you just described." She glanced up at me with an uncertain expression and asked, "Did I say it right?"

"Um…" I hesitated, then nodded. "Yes. It was a very concise, but mostly accurate explanation. Thanks."

Elly giggled at my response and then proceeded to hug my arm again with a satisfied grin. To be honest, my arm was getting a little numb by this point, but I didn't have the heart to ask her to let go.

"That's it in a nutshell," I told Ammy.

"Really?" This time the question came from Snowy. "Brother said Joshua was the Herald, but I didn't think he was all those other things too…"

"I know, right?" Angie added on with a flabbergasted expression. "And that bit about essences… was that how he turned Draconian for a while when we confronted Neige's brother?"

"Exactly!" Elly declared. "It's quite obvious in retrospect, really."

"Leo, are you certain about this?" Ammy asked.

"About ninety-five percent sure."

"Seriously?" she spoke in a low voice. She glanced over to Josh, her eyes softening in concern, but then she quickly became deadly serious again. "I have a hard time believing this. Since when did you know about it? And how did you even find out about it?"

"A bit of knowledge, lots of legwork, and just a hint of outside-the-box thinking," I replied very modestly.

She still looked skeptical, but then Angie said, "Leo is an information broker," in a really helpful tone. Well, at least she might have thought she was helping, but as for me, I wanted to palm my face.

"Wait, what?" Amelia looked back and forth between the Celestial girl and yours truly so fast, I was afraid she'd strain her neck. "Are you really?"

"Something like that," I answered noncommittally, earning me some strange looks from the whole gang… well, except for my girlfriends, who were too busy taking notes and giggling to themselves, respectively.

"I shouldn't even be surprised anymore…" Ammy grumbled. "Well. Let's say I grant you all of your points about Josh. I won't question your sources or how you figured all of it out on your own. But I do need to know—what does this actually mean for us?"

I took a deep breath.

"It means that Josh has a giant bullseye on his back that'll put us all in danger if we don't deal with it ASAP."

"Hey!" the bullseye protested, but I dismissed him with a wave of my… well, I wanted to say *hand*, but it ended up being a shrug.

"Listen, Josh. As much as I don't like it either, it's true. You are vitally important for each and every supernatural power bloc to reach its ultimate goal. In the best-case scenario, they will try to use you to fulfill their prophecies, like Crowey attempted last week. In the worst-case scenario, they will try to get rid of you so that you wouldn't fulfill someone else's prophecy."

"Great," my friend grumbled. "All this supernatural shit just keeps getting worse by the minute."

"Which is why we're going to do something about it. First, we have to make sure people won't find out how important you are before we set some countermeasures. Elly?"

"Hm? Yes?"

My girlfriend glanced up at me with the equivalent of a giant question mark over her head, her head tilted to the side for added effect.

Cute as a button, if a little distracting.

I cleared my throat.

"Your family knew that Josh was special, right? That's why they allowed you to come here."

"Umm… My dad obviously didn't know he was *this* special, but yes."

"Do you have an idea of how much they know?"

"Um, well…" She hesitated, probably weighing whether she should say it in public, especially in front of the subject of the discussion, but then she gave me a determined look and continued. "My family puts a lot of importance on the purity of our bloodline. The two main ways of preserving it are by either marrying into the mainline of another draconic family or by finding a human with no supernatural heritage." She must've noticed my curiosity, as she quickly clarified, "If one of us mates with a pure human, the child is almost guaranteed to be a pure Draconian and maintain the purity of the bloodline."

"Apparently genetics work differently for giant lizards," my other girlfriend grumbled on my other side, but I let her words go and instead focused on the actual topic.

"Let me guess. Josh is a 'pure human'?"

"Um," she nodded while pointedly avoiding looking his way. "Father tested him when we were young. He said he was more than just suitable as a mate, so when I asked him to let me meet him again, he allowed it. We only figured he might be more important and related to the prophecy after Neige—"

"Now wait just a moment!" Josh interrupted us with a frankly scary look on him. "You can't just skim over this! What's this about 'mates'? And being tested when we were young? Could you please explain this right now before I freak out again?"

"Easy there," I soothed him. "There is absolutely no need to freak out, it's not even that big a deal. Well, not anymore, at least."

"Then you should have no trouble explaining it," my friend grumbled with a look that told me he was already sick and tired of this whole situation. I didn't blame him.

I peeked at Elly, and after a few seconds of conflict clearly visible on her face, she gave me a nod. I took a deep breath, and after exhaling it, I turned back to my friend.

"Very well. In a nutshell: you and the princess met as kids and played together for a short while. During that time, her family checked you for compatibility, and since you qualified, they allowed her to come here and meet you again."

"Wait, hold on!" Josh stopped me with a raised palm. "We played together as kids? When?" He paused for a moment while squinting at the blonde girl at my side, then his eyes lit up with recognition. "You were... Elly, are you Milady?!"

My girlfriend twitched and gave him a faint smile.

"Wow... I mean... Wow!" Josh muttered, seemingly lost in thought.

"At least he finally recognizes you," I told Elly, accompanied by a reassuring squeeze of the hand, but then our moment was interrupted.

"How was I supposed to recognize her without you guys saying anything?" Josh burst out. "She looks completely different now!"

"Really?" I asked, intrigued.

"Yes," Josh answered with a peeved huff, crossing his arms. "She was a total tomboy. She had pigtails, she was always wearing shorts, and every day she would drag me around the park until I thought I was going to die! Hell, I still have a hard time believing they are the same person! Why didn't you just tell me?" He fell silent. Then he narrowed his eyes again. "Was it because of that whole 'mate' business?"

"Kinda," I answered. "Do you remember anything significant related to the 'Milady' in your memories?"

"Significant? We were kids, what kind of significance..." His eyes went wide. Then he timidly asked, "Was it... the promise?"

"Yep, it was the promise," I told him in a chipper voice.

"Uh, crap..." Josh muttered while massaging his forehead. "Now I feel like a jerk. This day just keeps getting better and better."

"What are you talking about? What promise?" Ammy inquired, suspicious.

"Seconded," Angie chimed in as loudly as usual. "You can't just say that and not explain it. It's against the rules!"

My first reaction was to ask just what kind of rules she was talking about, but I refrained and instead said, "Josh and Elly made a childhood promise that they would get married when they grow up."

"Seriously?" the Celestial girl asked with wide eyes, and the princess nodded in the affirmative. Angie whistled, then turned her attention back to me. "Wow, Leo. You are not only dating two girls at once, you even seduced Josh's fiancée. I can't decide if I'm appalled or impressed!"

"I did not seduce anyone!" I objected.

"She is not my fiancée!" came an equally vehement protest from my friend. "We were, like, six years old! You can't make life decisions at that age! I mean, I'm sorry I didn't recognize you and all, but how was I supposed to remember you, let alone a promise like that, when you deliberately didn't tell me we already knew each other?"

"I'm... it's fine. Water under the bridge." Elly spoke with a strained smile, but then she glanced up at me, and said smile immediately turned into a genuine one as she threw herself at my shoulder and hugged my arm even tighter. "It all turned out fine in the end, so I'm good."

I sneakily rolled my eyes then let out a dry cough to get everyone's attention.

"Why don't you two have a good long talk about this, but later? We somehow ended up talking about my relationship again, so how about we return to the actually important topic instead?"

"Fine by me," Josh honest-to-goodness pouted, followed by a string of barely audible PG-13 curses interspersed with the words *supernatural, marriage,* and *fiancée.* I, naturally, completely ignored him and continued where we left off.

"Great. So, in conclusion, while Elly's family knows Josh is special, they don't know the details, and they only vaguely suspect that he might be important in the grand scheme of things. Snowy?"

"Y-yes?" the resident Abyssal yelped like I'd pinched her.

"I know that you and Crowey know about Josh, but what about the other Abyssals?"

"They shouldn't know?" she replied a tad uncertainly. "I-I mean, we only found him because... Uh... You know?"

"The kiss?"

Instead of answering, she awkwardly nodded. Hilariously enough, Josh immediately turned red to the tip of his ears at the mere mention of said kiss.

"So it's safe to assume that the other Abyssals don't know about it. Well, unless Crowey tells them," I corrected myself, but Snowy shook her head.

"Brother won't tell anyone."

"Are you sure?"

She gave me an emphatic nod.

"I think she's right," Ammy interjected with a solemn expression. "Lords of the Abyss love their intrigue and keeping their little secrets for political gains. Everyone knows that."

"That's right," Snowy agreed with unusual eagerness. "After what happened last weekend, brother lost a lot of prestige. He will need time to reaffirm his position and keep the vassals in line. He won't have the chance to come over here, and he'll never spread the news about the Herald until he can. It would be as good as asking the other lords to steal Josh from under his nose." Snowy abruptly paused as she glanced at my still flushed friend, and then she hastily added, "No-not that you are under his nose anymore! I will... we will make sure you are protected, right?" She looked around, and in a mousy voice she repeated, "R-right?"

"Hm." I mused for a moment while the others all told Josh they would make sure he would be okay, which would have been pretty heartwarming, except it was getting in the way of actually discussing *how* we would do so, so I cleared my throat and asked, "In your opinion, how long would it take for him to move again?"

Snowy fell silent before answering my question.

"He was injured, I'm no longer under his control, and he lost a Chimera. Considering all that, I would say, at least two months, possibly more depending on the vassals' reaction."

"That's good to know. Thanks, Snowy."

"You are welcome," she replied with a demure smile.

"Okay, so just to recap," I raised my voice again to gain everyone's attention. "The Dracis family only knows something is up with Josh because of Snowy and Crowey showing interest in him. Crowey knows Josh is a big deal, but he won't tell anyone. As for the Magi..."

I sent Ammy a pointed look.

After a shallow sigh, she followed up my words with, "We also knew that an Abyssal showing interest in Joshua wasn't coincidental, but it wasn't until the kidnapping that Grandfather started paying attention to him."

"Do you think he can figure out how important he is?"

"I don't know," she admitted. "I don't know how much he knows, but once he shows interest in someone, Grandfather is usually very meticulous."

"Well, that might be a problem," I mused, and for a short time, the living room fell silent. I was deep in thought putting together a rudimentary action plan, when my concentration was interrupted by a certain hyperactive girl going "Uhh..." while staring at me.

"Yes, Angie?"

"Aren't you going to ask me?"

"About what?" I replied, my brows furrowed.

"About how much the Celestials know about Josh!"

"No," I told her, then after a beat I added, "It's not like you could tell me anything new."

"Come on, Leo!" she protested in a childish voice. "I'm no longer the secretive gal I used to be! Now that my cover is blown, I will tell you whatever you want!"

"Really?" I queried with a curiously raised brow, and to my surprise,

I felt like I did it really well. Who knows? Maybe one of these days I will catch up to Josh and usurp his position of the group's number one single-eyebrow-raiser!

Jokes aside, Angie gave me a determined nod and repeated, "Whatever you want!"

"Okay," I said, her words accidentally triggering my slightly more mischievous side, "What are your three sizes?"

She gave me a weird look, then her cheeks flushed and she stated, "Whatever you want, with some exceptions…"

I shook my head and said, "You see, that's what I—ouch?" I blinked for a moment, then I looked at my side, where Judy was pinching my arm. "Dormouse, what exactly are you doing?"

She looked me in the eye and responded with an ever so slightly petulant, "No flirting."

"I'm not flirting!" I objected with the righteous indignation of the mostly innocent. "I only teased her a little! Am I not even allowed to do that?"

My girlfriend seemed to honest-to-goodness ponder on my entirely rhetorical question for a good five seconds before she concluded, "In moderation, and not in front of us."

"Oh, how gracious of you."

"You are welcome," she answered before she returned to her phone, apparently considering the discussion over.

I shook my head and resumed the previous conversation by saying, "Okay, since I'm apparently no longer allowed to pester you girls while my girlfriends are around, I'll be blunt: Angie, when I said you cannot tell me anything, I meant about Celestial intelligence in particular." Since both Angie and Ammy seemed less than satisfied by my words, I hastily clarified. "I looked into this, you know? There are hundreds of people the Celestials are keeping an eye on because they could be, theoretically, the second coming of their dear leader. If anything, after the recent events, Josh would be lower on the priority list than before because of his involvement with the supernatural powers that be."

"That sounds unlikely," Ammy told me skeptically.

"Well, Josh being the multi-messiah of several supernatural races is also unlikely, but here we are all the same," I answered in a tone that might've been a smidge flippant, but they didn't seem to mind.

"I suppose," she conceded, followed by Angie doing the same.

Of course, there was a tiny little detail I didn't disclose, namely that I was so confident about this particular point because of my direct access to the Celestial Hub. In fact, I was the one who sneakily pushed Josh's name down the priority list of candidates. But explaining that to the gang would've been possibly more annoying than the whole prophecy ordeal was.

"In conclusion," I said, to rerail the conversation, "we are not in dire straits just yet. The Knights with the ridiculously long name might be a rogue element, but considering we haven't seen them skulking around yet, I think we are safe to assume they don't know about Josh, either. However, that doesn't mean we can sit on our laurels. We need to prepare for the inevitable chaos when the powers that be figure out Josh's potential and start targeting him."

"Is it really inevitable?" Josh interjected with a conflicted expression. "I mean, can't I just… I dunno… maybe, hide? Change my identity, that kind of stuff?"

I gave my naïve friend a measuring look. Poor, poor Josh. He had no idea. Being the chosen one, the hero, and most importantly, the protagonist, meant that the "plot" was going to find him no matter what. Who has heard of a protagonist that decided he would exit the story and nothing happened to him afterwards? I mean, I get that the 'refusal of the call' was an integral part of the hero's journey, but I doubt any 'hero' has ever succeeded doing so in the history of ever. Of course I couldn't just tell him all this as directly as that, so I resorted to a more roundabout way to convince him.

"It's not so easy," I told him sternly, to get the point across. "Let's say you run away. What happens to your family? Do you think Crowey, or the others, wouldn't use them against you?"

"Then… what if my parents also—"

"How are you going to explain this to them? Hey, Mom, Dad? I am a multi-prophesized chosen one sought after by all sorts of supernatural people. Could you please change your names, leave your current lives behind, and run away and hide somewhere with me?"

"Okay, I get it!" Josh yielded with a sour face. "It wouldn't work. You don't have to be a dick about it."

"I wasn't a dick about it… Well, okay, maybe a little bit, but you have to understand your situation is not something you can run away from."

"Then what?"

"I'm glad you asked!" I answered with my best Machiavellian smile. "We have to consider our priorities. First and foremost, we have to protect ourselves. I propose three things for that. One: we need to be more vigilant in the future and deal with potential threats ahead of time. Two: we need to set up a rapid response system so that we can, well, respond at the first sight of trouble. And finally, three: training. In particular, Josh needs training in self-defense and with his new powers."

"Do I have to?" my friend whined, but I shot a scowl his way, and he wisely fell silent.

"That means we have to test Josh's powers," I continued. "We've got to work out all sorts of things, like his power levels, transformations, durations, et cetera. This will require a lot of experimentation and testing. I will prepare a place where we can do so in private, but for the 'essences,' I will have to ask for your help."

"Actually," Ammy spoke up with a serious look, "you and Elly both mentioned 'essences.' What are those?"

"Well, that's another thing we have to find out, but so far it seems like they are like a trigger that makes Josh transform."

"Yes, but *what* are they?"

"Bodily fluids," my assistant chimed in. "Blood works, for sure. Saliva should, as well. Other fluids are untested as of now."

"Ew!" Angie grimaced.

"When the time comes," I continued, refusing to acknowledge that bit of nothing Angie had added to the conversation, "I might ask you girls to provide some of the aforementioned essences during testing and training. It might be a bit annoying, but it's probably the most important part when it comes to keeping Josh safe and prepared. Does anyone have anything to add?"

"Actually," Ammy spoke up, one finger pushing her glasses up on the bridge of her nose. "You are forgetting an option."

"Which is?"

"The Assembly," she replied solemnly. "You seem to be labouring under the impression that we have to keep Joshua safe on our own. Since he was nearly kidnapped by the Abyssals, our School is obligated by the laws of the Assembly, article seventeen to be exact, to provide shelter and support for him."

"True..." I agreed, if only tentatively. "However, doing so would immediately impose on Josh. I mean, at this rate you are pretty much just sneakily recruiting him."

"I'm not," Ammy retorted. "I just want him to be safe."

"So do I. That's why I think it is more important to keep a low profile right now. I mean, if it was about protection, then going to Elly's family would've been my first pick, but doing so would put us right on a collision course with the Knights. I presume going to the Magi would lead to a similar conclusion, and to be frank with you, I don't want to trigger any kind of response from the less savory supernatural folks until I'm sure we are prepared to deal with them." I paused for a second as my gaze swept over the others, then stopped as it met Josh's conflicted expression, so I hastily added, "Don't take me wrong, Josh. If you decide you wanted to join Ammy's club, I won't stop you. I will even help you out to the best of my ability. However, I do not think you are informed enough to make that decision yet."

"Well…" my friend mumbled, then his voice became stronger as he said, "I suppose you are right. I mean, Elly's place didn't exactly give me the best first impression, either…"

"Sebastian?" I asked offhandedly, and Josh immediately agreed with a groan.

"Yeah, that guy! He keeps telling me he will hunt me! He was already scary before, but after I learned all this crap, I wouldn't want to be in the same postal code as him!"

"Tell me about it," I strongly agreed, earning me a classic frown from my related girlfriend, but before she could object, Josh continued, robbing her of the opportunity.

"I think Leo is right. I still don't know enough about this supernatural tangle to come to a decision."

"All the more reason for you to at least talk with Grandfather," Ammy countered. After a second, she looked at me and added, "Speaking of which, Leo…"

"Yes?"

"We need to tell Grandfather about Neige," she told me in a tone that didn't leave much room for argument.

I still tried, though.

"Do we really have to?"

"Yes. I already told Grandfather about her circumstances. If we go there together, we should be able to convince him of her innocence, or at the very least we could make sure she wouldn't be exiled, or worse. The longer we wait, the more likely it is that she will be treated like a fugitive."

I glanced over to Snowy to get her input, and after she finally realized I was waiting for her, she timidly said, "I think we should. I mean… I don't want to cause you any more trouble than I already have."

"It's all right," Josh attempted to reassure her. "Let's just go and talk to Ammy's grandpa, and while we are at it, I will see these Mage guys for myself. Two birds with one stone. I mean, what's the worst that could happen?"

"Aaaand now you jinxed it," said Angie, holding her head.

"What? I did what?"

"You jinxed it. You totally did," she repeated, her voice brimming with so much exasperation, I was pretty sure she was acting.

"I'm just being optimistic! Since when is that a crime? Not to mention, it's not like this whole mess could get much worse."

"Argh! You are doing it again!"

I shook my head at the bickering childhood friends and focused my attention on the class rep, who was in the middle of giving the two of them a classic *I'm too tired for this* expression.

"Hey, Ammy?" I waited for her to look my way, then I said, "How about we all go and visit your grandfather together?"

"When?" she asked back with an expression that wasn't nearly as relieved or pleased as I expected.

"After breakfast," I told her offhandedly.

"Does that mean the meeting is over?" Judy cut in with the question that had seemed to be on the tip of her tongue for a while now.

"Is it?" the princess followed suit with Angie-like enthusiasm.

I subtly rolled my eyes at them and said, "We're going to talk while we eat as well, but sure, go ahead."

The moment I gave them the green light, they both released my (at this point a bit numb and considerably sweaty) palms and stood up, but instead of heading for the kitchen right away, they faced each other and theatrically shook their hands.

"Let the best girlfriend win!" Elly exclaimed, followed by an affirmative grunt from my assistant, and then they both marched out of the living room in lockstep.

I followed them with my eyes, making sure my mild amusement was hidden behind an expression of disapproval, but when I turned back to everyone else, I found Ammy looking at me the exact same way.

"What? Is there something on my face?" I asked in an attempt to lighten her mood, but her frown only deepened.

"I think you are a bad influence on them," she told me about as bluntly as an anvil dropped from the third floor.

"Oh, come on! They've always been like that! And didn't we agree to leave my relationship alone?"

Ammy continued to give me a dissatisfied scowl, so I followed my usual modus operandi and looked for some way to change the topic, which I found in the form of the timid Abyssal girl sitting in the crossfire of the still bickering childhood friends (who, by the way, somehow went from jinxes to arguing about famous last lines in movies. Go figure).

Anyways, now that my hands were free, I gestured to get her attention and softly asked, "Hey, Snowy? You all right?"

For a moment, her eyes were uncertain, but then she said, "I'm... just a little nervous. I mean, I know that you are going to be with me, but...

we are going to meet one of the arch-mages of the Assembly. I know he is Amelia's grandfather, but I'm still a little worried."

"Wait, your grandfather is an arch-mage?" The question popped out of my mouth, earning me a critical look from Ammy.

"I thought you already knew. Didn't you say you were an 'information broker'?"

"Never mind that," I deflected like a pro as I quickly recalled what little I remembered about the Magi's power structure. "Normal" mages were in Schools, doing research and stuff. Each of the schools was headed by an arch-mage, and the oldest and most powerful arch-mages formed the Assembly, the closest thing they had to a governing body. In retrospect, I should've expected this; the class rep was a "main character," and I already knew that her grandfather was a big shot in the school, so I should've figured out that he wasn't just your run-of-the-mill mage. Hindsight, as always, was twenty-twenty.

Nevertheless, I didn't let the embarrassment I felt over discovering another blind spot show on my face, but turned back to Snowy and told her, "Don't worry about it, I'm sure he isn't a bad guy. I mean, what's the worst he could do to you?"

Snowy was about to reply, when all of a sudden, the arguing pair of childhood friends fell silent. Angie gaped at me with a frankly comical expression, then turned back to Josh and yelled, "See what you've done? Now even Leo is doing it! We are soooo jinxed right now!"

We shared a glance with my friend and then we both rolled our eyes at the same time. I leaned back on the couch and exhaled a long breath, closed my eyes, and proceeded to ignore all the bickering, the foreboding sounds of breakfast preparations from the kitchen, and the ominous feeling that my day was about to get even more tiresome once we visit the School...

CHAPTER 5

PART 1

In the end, I was right. I know that doesn't really narrow things down, as I am right about a lot of things, but this time in particular, I was extra right about how our breakfast would turn out to be our lunch in the end. Furthermore, what started out to be just another stunt by my girlfriends sneakily escalated into *The Calamity Lunch Version 2.0: Electric Boogaloo*.

Well, fine, perhaps I'm being slightly overly dramatic here. It wasn't *as* disastrous as the last time, but it was still a pain in the neck. As they say, too many cooks spoil the broth, and that idiom has rarely been as fitting as in this case. For some inexplicable reason, Angie, Snowy, and even Josh followed after my girlfriends, ostensibly to help with their impromptu competition, yet their meddling somehow resulted in a full course meal that got finished way outside of the "breakfast" time frame and consisted of a bunch of heavy dishes that did not complement each other in the slightest. While I could get into the extravagant nature of those dishes and even ponder where their exotic ingredients came from, I'd rather not go down that rabbit hole right now.

At the end of the meal, which may or may not have concluded with a swift and merciless scolding, Judy and Elly solemnly declared that the results were a draw and promised they wouldn't get carried away like that in the future.

"It's decided then! We are going on a group date on Sunday!" Elly declared with a fist pump while obviously getting carried away.

"You are making a scene," I chided her, prompting her to glance back at me over her shoulder with an apologetic smile, so I hastily added, "Pay attention while walking."

She blinked at me in surprise, but then she obediently turned back and continued whatever dastardly date plans she was in the process of hatching with the help of my dearest assistant while we walked.

Wait. Does this require some context? I suppose it does.

So, after we had our fill of our over-the-top lunch and shared some more much-needed exposition with Josh, I finally decided to stop delaying the inevitable. Thus, our little fellowship set out on a decidedly less-than-epic journey to meet the fabled arch-wizard of Blue Cherry High.

Damn, my life is weird…

Anyways, in a great display of self-organizing chaos, our group naturally formed into three lines. On the forefront were Snowy and Angie, with Josh pushing his moped between them as they shared even more vital information about the terrible dangers of the world of the supernatural masquerade, interspersed with random arguments about *Trucy the Werewolf Huntress* and some other shows I knew little about. In other words, business as usual.

Right behind them walked my two girlfriends, their discussion filled with a weird mixture of secretive harmony and sudden competitive outbursts. Also business as usual.

By process of elimination, that left me trailing behind them all with an especially sullen class rep at my side. Also, while I know the rule of three kind of demands it… no, that wasn't business as usual. I'm not even going to pretend it was. That said, this configuration meant that we had pretty much occupied the whole sidewalk, making me acutely aware of something quite unusual… or rather, it was very normal, but because it was, it was not.

Okay, I'll stop beating around the bush: it was the placeholder population. When I told Elly to keep it down because she was drawing attention, I actually meant it. For maybe the first time since I could remember, the placeholders paid attention to us. No, back up—they were actually there, on the street! I mean, I think I've already noted that the number of placeholders walking around and doing their business was increasing over time, but this early afternoon, I felt like we'd crossed some threshold. Now the streets felt lived in. There was still not a speck of dust on the road or a stray candy wrapper on the grass, so it still wasn't super-authentic, but it was definitely more than it had been just days before.

I couldn't help but wonder—was this supposed to be the natural progression of this world? Judy and I had discussed this before, and she even had a theory that perhaps the world was a kind of simulation. It was supposed to run while the placeholders gathered "character" before the actual action or game or experiment or whatever this world was designed for started. It was a somewhat elegant explanation of the rudimentary behaviour patterns of the placeholders and their slow yet steady improvement on that front. Of course, it also presupposed that the world was designed, or at the very least had some intent behind it, something of which I still wasn't 100 percent certain.

As I was having these thoughts, I couldn't help but shake my head in irritation. There was still so little I knew about this world—or dream or simulation or whatever—and unfortunately, it seemed like any earnest research would have to be put on hold once again, at least until I could make sure our lives weren't threatened by the plot. Speaking of which, I reminded myself for the umpteenth time to pay attention to my own thought processes to catch any signs of narrative meddling in action. Regrettably, knowing that my own thoughts could be sneakily tweaked by an unseen force was not particularly comforting, and paying attention to every stray brain wave only made the stress worse.

"Haaahhh..."

And then the girl with the glasses by my side started letting out dramatic sighs like that! For a while, I debated whether I should ask her about it or play dumb and avoid a potential landmine, but by this point I had a feeling she was doing it just to get me to ask. In the end, I let out a shallow breath of my own and decided to bite it.

"Why the long face?" I asked tentatively, only for her to turn towards me with a frown.

"I still don't understand how you figured it all out!" Ammy complained, earning a confused look from me.

"You mean, about Josh? Didn't I already tell you?"

"It still makes no sense," she grumbled as she put her hands into her coat pockets. "If these prophecies were secret, then how do you know about them? Don't tell me it's *I'm an information broker* again..."

"Nah, I just asked." She didn't seem convinced, so I explained, "Elly told me about the prophecy on her own. Then when I talked with Angie, we talked about their hallowed leader and their prophecy came up. Then I asked Snowy if Abyssals had something similar the next time we talked."

"Yeah, I wanted to ask about that, too!" she interjected while her brows somehow descended even farther. "How did you even know Angeline was a Celestial? And for how long?"

I couldn't give an immediate answer this time, as it involved some meta-logic, so I shrugged and deflected with a noncommittal, "It was fairly obvious."

"What do you mean 'fairly obvious'?" Ammy hissed at me. "I've known her since middle school, and I never even suspected her!"

At this point the words *She is called ANGELine!* were on the tip of my tongue, but with inhuman effort, I managed to swallow them back. Instead I told her, "That just shows that I'm exceptionally good when it comes to deduction."

"Sure, just dodge the question," Ammy grumbled and rolled her eyes at me. "You are being *exceptionally good* at that, too. In fact, you are being too exceptional at too many things."

"Am I?" I asked back just a little uncertainly, which earned me a sudden, but by no means unexpected, harrumph.

"Do I have to spell it out?" I nodded, so she wearily explained, "Just to list the most glaring ones: You fought a Faun general and won. You fought a Chimera and killed it. You faced a Lord of the Abyss, and you lived to tell the tale. On top of that, you have the money and the looks, your background is simultaneously too normal and yet mysterious, and while you are dangerously knowledgeable about all the Old-Blooded Clans, you do not belong to any of them."

"W-well," I stammered, "to be fair, I can't really do anything about the looks department, but thanks for the compliment."

"And there you are—grabbing on to the most insignificant thing to change the direction of the conversation. I'm not even mad right now, only disappointed."

"Ouch, class rep. That hurt. Mentally. Also, you are waaay more grouchy than usual."

"I think I said this before, but just to reiterate… Whose fault do you think that is?" She paused, apparently waiting for me to say something, but when I remained silent, she shook her head. "Let me stress this one more time: You killed a Chimera. Those are supposed to be so rare, they are more or less legendary at this point, and even Grandfather would've had a tough time facing one. Do you have any idea how much effort it took me to sort that mess out?"

"Hey, I didn't do it to cause you trouble!" I protested. "Also, it was a team effort. I can distinctly remember a certain girl's golem thingie contributing quite a bit of help. Not to mention, I wasn't the one who brought the bloody thing over. If you want to blame someone for all that happened, blame Crowey, not me. "

"Fine, you're right," she admitted with a voice that said she was still quite cranky. "But you being right doesn't change the fact that I still have mountains of paperwork to deal with when I get home today, and about half of it is because you—"

"Okay, time out! You keep saying that, but why are you doing paperwork in the first place?"

Instead of answering me, she gave me one of those classic uncomprehending looks you'd give when someone asked you which cereal flavour was your favourite mode of transportation, so I quickly reiterated, "I mean, why are *you*, in particular, doing paperwork? You are what? Sixteen?"

"So are you," she retorted with another frown, but I dismissed that with a wave.

"Seventeen on paper, but it doesn't matter. We are talking about you. I'm sure you have other people at the School who could deal with paperwork, so why are you doing it?"

This time, the look she gave me was a bit more pensive, even hesitant, but after a quick glance at the front of our little procession, she gestured for me to come closer.

"Before I tell you the details, I have a quick question for you. Do you know what happened at Cardiff?"

"Cardiff?" I repeated. Naturally, I knew what she was talking about, as it was the notorious "Cardhouse incident" that was, among other things, my primary cover as Admin over at the Celestial Hub. "Well, unless this is a trick question, the main thing that comes to mind is the incident when the Celestials tried to infiltrate a School and got caught red-handed. That was about three or so months ago, right?"

Amelia's face slackened in surprise, apparently not expecting me to actually answer her question, but then her expression recovered.

"Correct," she stated. Then she added, "I'll be damned. Maybe you are an informant after all…"

"That's neither here nor there. Back to the original question—what does the Cardiff incident have to do with paperwork?"

"More or less everything," she told me with a tired groan. "Before Cardiff, a lot of the more mundane operations of the Schools were done by normal humans. The Celestials used this hole in our security to plant spies in our administration. Not only that, they have been doing it for at least two generations."

"Yeah, they're sly like that. Almost disturbingly so," I spoke carelessly, earning me an approving grunt from Ammy.

"They are," she said, taking another sneaky peek at a certain overly enthusiastic girl, who was in the process of trying to convince Snowy to read some romance book about a friendly wight or something, like she didn't have a care in the world. Anyways, Ammy soon turned back to me and said, "So, as per the usual habit of the Assembly, they quickly threw the baby out with the bathwater and created a new law. Now, sensitive documents can only be handled by Magi directly related to the leadership of the School in question."

"And that's you," I guessed.

"Indeed," she answered with a mixture of exhaustion and indignation. "Since I'm Grandfather's only blood relative, I have to do literally all the important accounting in the School, which includes documenting such things as, let's say, someone killing a Chimera on School grounds."

"I get it, geez!" I rolled my eyes at her pointed words. "Would you have preferred if I'd let it eat someone?"

"No!" she said, aghast. "Do you have any idea how much paperwork *that* would have caused?"

I blinked at her response, unable to decide whether she was serious or not, but since her expression didn't lighten, I cautiously told her, "Class rep, I think you *really* need a break. I can't help but feel that doing all that accounting might've ever so slightly, maybe, partially, mostly or at the very least totally, consumed your entire thought process."

"And whose fault do you think—?"

"Yes, yes, it's my fault," I hastily admitted lest she start on another tirade.

Ammy huffed. Fortunately, we were a stone's throw away from the school's main gates. Seeing that, she only gave me a flat glance, and then jogged to get to the front of the group, leaving me all alone at the back. Not for long, though. My two girlfriends decelerated and fell in line beside me.

"We are going on a date this Sunday," Judy informed me.

"Just the two of you? Oh well, have fun."

"Of course not," Elly countered with a small frown. "It's all three of us."

"I know, I was kidding," I stressed before rolling my eyes. "However, could we discuss this *after* we talk with the Magi? You know, just in case things get messy and there's no time for any dates at all?"

"True," Judy said in a decidedly disapproving tone. "You have already tempted fate, so it's far from impossible."

"Oh, please. Don't tell me you're secretly superstitious."

"It's not about superstition, Chief," my dear assistant explained. "As far as we know, tempting fate like that might have very real consequences. I believe you even mentioned that things like the 'rules of comedic and dramatic timing' were actual, tangible things."

"Well, I suppose I did…" I spoke carefully while thinking hard about how to explain myself. "However, you see, Josh has already done it, right? Therefore, if jinxing is a thing and something bad happens because of it, it'll be his fault, and me following his example will have little significance. However, if jinxing is not a thing, then it doesn't matter if I do it, too, as nothing will happen either way. See, it's quite logical."

"That sounds like ad hoc rationalization to me," Judy grumbled flatly.

"Rubbish! I am always the model of a rational mind."

"Is it a scale model?"

"Of course. If it wasn't, it wouldn't fit into my head."

"I see. I learn something new every day."

"What are you talking about?" Elly interjected with a confused expression.

"Nothing serious," I reassured her while I glanced up the hill towards the school gates. My brows furrowed. "Jokes and jinxes aside, what should I be expecting once we're in the School? What's Ammy's grandpa like?"

"I don't think I ever met him," Judy stated, returning to her usual expression. "I think he might've given a speech at the opening ceremony, but my memories from back then are a little vague."

"Wait, hold on," I spoke up in a hurry. "So, he's actually the headmaster of the school, as well? I mean, I knew he was the head of *the School*, but not the school."

"That was confusing," Elly said while grimacing, and I couldn't help but agree. Just whose bright idea was it to call the hub of a magical secret society operating under a school "the School"?

"Anyways, I didn't even go to the opening ceremony, so I don't think I've ever seen the guy."

"You have seriously never met Lord Endymonion before?" Elly asked in a somewhat baffled voice, but she wasn't nearly as surprised as I was.

"Lord Endymonion? Really?"

"Yes, that's his name," she told me like it was really obvious. "I've known him since I was a kid. Our family had to pay him a visit every time we came to Critias."

"Figures. But why 'Lord'?"

"All the arch-mages of the Assembly are called lords," Judy answered my question immediately while giving me a look saying *That's common knowledge! Didn't you read any of the reports I gave you?*

"Oh, right," I spoke while scratching my chin. "It totally slipped my mind."

It was at this very moment that we reached the gates, which promptly opened, cutting our already less than fruitful discussion short. At first, I thought it was automatic, but then from behind the gap, my eyes met with those of Armband Guy.

He looked exactly the same as usual; his black hair cropped short, his small, round glasses sitting high on his hawkish nose, his cheeks sullen and giving him a gaunt appearance, and he was wearing his uniform as impeccably as ever, with a bright red band on his right arm. He looked us over before his eyes landed on Ammy.

"Hello, Pascal," she greeted him, and the guy returned it with a small nod. "Please inform Grandfather we are going to visit him."

"I see you found the Abyssal," he said with a disinterested voice. "I suppose you want to talk with him about her."

"Yes, among other things." Ammy nodded, at which point Armband Guy gestured for us to come through the gates before he hastily closed them behind us.

After doing so, he faced our group again and simply said, "You know the way."

"Yes," the class rep nodded, and Pascal returned to his duty of... standing by the gates. Weird.

Anyways, we waited for Josh to park his moped under the roof of the bicycle storage area, then once he was back, Ammy gestured for us to follow her. After a few steps, I carefully sidled up next to her and asked, "What's that guy's deal?"

"Pascal's?" she asked back, and I gave her a nod. "What do you mean? He's the same as usual."

"I get it, but... is he actually a student? I mean, classes are still in, and he's just standing out there like that."

"He takes his student council duties very seriously."

"That wasn't what I was..." I began, but then I shook my head. "You know what? Never mind."

Ammy looked at me funny, but before she could ask, I pulled the brakes so that I ended up next to Judy again. I told her in a whisper, "Raise Armband Guy from placeholder to a possible side character."

"Way ahead of you," she answered and showed me her phone.

"Good," I told her with a nod, then I followed after Ammy towards our destination, which seemed to be the entrance to the school's basement.

"This way," she told us as she stopped right in front of the fairly mundane metal doors. "The staff might be a little jumpy after what happened on Sunday, so don't touch anything, don't be too loud, and don't bother anyone we meet. Are we clear on that, everyone? Leo?"

"Hey!" I raised my voice in indignation. "Why am I singled out?"

"You know why," the class rep told me while doing that thing where she adjusted her glasses for emphasis. Before I could argue the point, she turned around and opened the door with a metallic *clank*.

Silently swallowing the injustice of being unfairly maligned, I followed behind the others into the secret base of the local supernatural superpower.

PART 2

"I'm not gonna lie, I feel a little underwhelmed. Am I the only one who feels underwhelmed?"

Ammy let out a small groan and asked, through clenched teeth, "Fine, I'll bite. Why are you underwhelmed?"

"Well..." I gestured towards the smooth white metal walls of the spacious, well-lit elevator in which we were currently standing. "For a start, we just kind of walked up to the lift. It was right by the basement entrance, too. It wasn't even hidden behind a fake wall or anything. It was just there."

"Why would you hide an elevator when people are using it every day?"

"She's got a point there," the princess noted by my side.

"But… why is it a lift in the first place? And a totally normal one, too! I thought we were going to use a teleportation circle or something."

"Yeah." This time Josh was the one who spoke up, taking my side for once. "Using an ordinary elevator to meet a wizard totally takes the sense of adventure out of it."

"The proper term is arch-mage, not wizard," Ammy countered politely. Then she readjusted her glasses and told me in a much less polite fashion, "Do you think teleport arrays grow on trees? Setting one up would use up half of our quarterly budget! Not to mention, some of the people working down there, who cannot use mana, would not be able to move between the School and the surface without help. Do you think we have the manpower to have a senior Magi on transportation duty when an 'ordinary elevator' does the job just as well for a fraction of the cost?"

"Fine, I get it! Geez!" I cut in with a groan. But then I remembered something, and I asked, using a slightly more diplomatic tone, "Just for the record, is teleportation really that costly?"

"Of course it is," Ammy scoffed. "Do you think breaking space itself and mending it afterwards is easy? You need a lot of rare reagents to create the arrays, then you would need two senior Magi to link them, and then whenever you would want to use them, you would need to use more valuable reagents. Why do you think only Grandfather uses one to go back and forth between here and Glasgow for the Assembly meetings?"

"Well, I didn't know that, that's why I asked," I defended myself, and to my surprise, the class rep seemed to take a proverbial step back in reaction.

"You are right, I suppose."

"I have another question, though," I told her, and she looked up at me attentively, so I inquired, "In theory, let's say that someone I knew had an artifact that could teleport them and other people they are in contact with to a predetermined location, no matter where they are. Is that a big deal?"

"A big deal?" Ammy asked back with eyes wide open. "An artifact? You mean an object with an array on it? Is it single-use?"

"Let's say it is," I muttered uncertainly, earning me an irritated scowl in the process.

"What do you mean, *let's say it*—? You know what, I don't even care. Now, to answer your question, even if it was just a single-use item, it would probably cause an uproar big enough to get not only the Assembly, but even the Celestials and the NSRS involved."

"The what now?"

"The Non-causative Science Research Society," Judy helpfully added.

"Father calls them 'the nerds,'" came the next, slightly less helpful, addendum from my other girlfriend.

"Hey, we call them that, too!" Angie said next, though her addition was decidedly less useful to the conversation.

Anyways, I turned to Judy and told her, "Thank you. Also, *ixnay onyay ethay eleportationtay artifactyay.*"

At first, she gave me a weird look, but then there was a sudden spark of recognition in her eyes, and she quickly took out her phone to follow my instructions.

"Was that pig latin?" Josh asked with a critically raised eyebrow, but before I could answer, the elevator shuddered to a halt. I had no idea whether it was slow, or we were going really deep, but considering I could feel my ears popping, my bet was on the latter.

Either way, once the lift door opened, I found myself staring down a long corridor with walls made of tightly packed stones, kind of like a castle wall. On the other hand, the floor and domed ceiling looked like they were made of solid white marble, and the whole place was evenly lit by a series of amorphous crystals glowing with a gentle blue light set in what at first glance looked like wrought iron torch sconces. On either side, I could see several large, elaborately designed wooden doors with huge brass handles, most of them closed, and while I couldn't see anybody, based on the faint noises I could hear, I was sure there were quite a few people down here.

"Now we're talking." Josh took the words right out of my mouth, so all I could do was to nod in agreement.

Sure, the place was still way too pristine to feel like an authentic ancient subterranean vault, but with the glowing crystals and the torch sconces, at least we finally had *some* ambience.

"You guys are weird," Angie murmured.

"A few more things: keep your voices down, don't make a ruckus, and turn off your phones before we enter Grandfather's study." Ammy stepped out of the elevator and gestured for us to follow, and we somehow formed into a line as we walked down the corridor. Honestly speaking, I was still a little bit underwhelmed. I mean, this was supposed to be the headquarters of the de facto supernatural big boss of the island, and it wasn't even a smidgen as grandiose as, say, the Dracis mansion. Even the security seemed pretty lame, as there were only two of those green eye orb things on opposite ends of the hallway.

While I was paying attention to those, I didn't notice Judy coming up to me right until she grabbed my sleeve and tugged.

"Hm? Yes?"

She gestured for me to lean closer, so I did just that.

"Chief, I would like to add one more entry to Amelia's warnings," she whispered conspiratorially. "We are in the heart of Magi territory, and we are about to meet the most important Magi on the island. We already discussed your 'impulse control' problem before, so please try to dial it back and do not pick a fight with an arch-mage of the Assembly in his home territory."

"Oh, come on, Dormouse!" I whispered back after a quick roll of the eyes. "I'm not *that* irresponsible. Maybe if I was alone, sure, but I wouldn't drag you guys into a conflict like that even if I wasn't aware of the problem, and now that I am conscious of it, I'll be sure to play nice."

"Good to know," my assistant told me, yet somehow I had a feeling I still didn't have her full confidence.

I couldn't explain myself any further, as we reached the biggest, heaviest door at the end of the hallway, and Ammy promptly knocked on it three times. After a long moment, I noticed a bunch of glowing white lines reminiscent of circuitry cascading across the surface of the wood. A blink of an eye later, the two wings of the door slowly, steadily, and soundlessly swung open.

Next to me, Josh gulped. I gave him a reassuring pat on the back. Surprisingly enough, Snowy, who I thought would be the most nervous out of everyone present, had a determined expression on her face.

Once the door was more than half open, I could finally take a good look inside. When I did so, I couldn't help but find the place familiar. An octagonal room with a high ceiling, walls covered in bookcases and lit by blue crystals, and a single, heavy-looking mahogany desk in the back. On top of said desk, there were several towers of white office paper, along with an assortment of writing utensils and an honest-to-goodness old-timey typewriter. Aside from the one we entered, there was another entrance on our right, nearly lost between the bookcases, while the opposing wall on the left had a large cabinet with glass doors. I was half expecting the musty scent of history in the air, but contrary to the fact that the books inside seemed old enough, all I could smell was a strange mixture of ink and some kind of sweet, possibly alcoholic fragrance.

Now, to be perfectly blunt, I'd seen this room before, specifically when I was checking up on the class rep with my Far Sight, but I'd never connected the dots, probably because the occupant of this room never struck me as the grandfatherly type. Speaking of which…

"Come in! No reason to be shy," came the deep yet whimsical voice of an elderly man who, as we shuffled in, dramatically turned around in the huge, padded swivel chair behind the desk (which, by the way, didn't fit the theme of the rest of the study at all).

In general, he looked the same as I remembered from my Far Sight. Our friendly neighbourhood arch-mage was a lean old man with a bushy yet inexplicably well-kept beard and a pair of equally abundant eyebrows on a high forehead. He was also dressed in a baggy black robe, yet under it I could see a fairly ordinary brown business suit that even had a tie. And, just to make his garb even more eclectic, he also wore a white Panama hat on top of all that. I mean, I get the rest, but who the hell wears a hat indoors? For some reason, that outfit wound me right up, and I was just about to give the man a snappy remark when I caught myself and hastily closed my mouth.

I blinked twice while looking at the arch-mage and used the couple of seconds of silence, during which the rest of the group entered the study, to observe him a bit more closely. His face... well, he had a kind of grandfatherly smile. A big, friendly, eminently punchable grandfatherly smile that made me want to give that smug sod a piece of my mind and...

God damn, I really do have an impulse control problem around important people who could kick my ass in a second! What the actual bloody hell?

I closed my eyes, lest I get even more wound up by the sight of the old man, after which I took a deep breath, held it in for a second, and slowly exhaled. Feeling marginally more collected, I opened my eyes again. By then the whole gang was already inside the study, and I could just barely catch the old geezer mutter something under his breath, at which point practically every surface in the room flashed with the familiar circuitry-like patterns, the doors thudded shut behind us, and the lights rose in intensity.

"Whoa," I heard Josh mutter under his breath, but I ignored him in favor of something weird I noticed.

I couldn't see it before, but now that the lighting conditions had significantly improved, I could tell that one of the old man's eyes was red. As in, not the actual iris, but the sclera around it, as if he had some nasty infection or got the blood vessels in his eye ruptured. The other eye seemed fine, but it was weird enough that I decided to ask about it later.

In the meantime, the arch-mage lightly cleared his throat as he looked over us all, until his eyes fell on Snowy.

"And so we meet again," he spoke in a pleasant voice that still made my skin crawl. I gritted my teeth and only moved half a step closer to the Abyssal girl, just in case. He didn't seem to mind, as he continued by telling her, "You have caused us quite the headache, young lady."

"I'm sorry, sir," Snowy answered, her head down.

"I am certain you are," Lord Grandpa told her with a calculated smile, but then he glanced over us and let out a small chuckle. "Oh, but where did I leave my manners? I am known as Lord Amadeus Endymonion, head of the Timaeus School of Conjuration and Alteration."

"Amadeus?" the surprised question slipped out of my mouth before I could stop it, and the old guy shot me a questioning look.

"Is there a problem?"

"None at all," I answered with a chipper voice that was only a tiny bit strained. "Absolutely nothing. Please ignore me, like I'm not even here."

Lord Grandpa gave me a long, hard look, then his lips curved into a pleasant smile. He let out a series of mirthful chuckles into his closed fist.

"I am afraid ignoring a young man of your accomplishments would paint me in a bad light, but for now I shall do as you wish," he told me in particular before he turned back to Snowy. "First, I believe we must discuss what to do with you."

"About that." Ammy took a step forwards. "I already talked with you about this, but Neige was not in control of her own actions. Also, as you can see, she came here of her own free will. I still believe she poses no harm to anyone."

"Yes, yes," the arch-mage repeated as he flashed a decidedly grandfatherly smile at his granddaughter. "You have already convinced me of that. However, I am afraid things are not so simple." Saying so, he reached out towards the seemingly haphazardly placed papers on the far corner of his desk, and after picking one up, he pointedly looked it over before returning his attention to us. "Not simple at all. I understand you were forced into being an accomplice of your brother by an artificial contract geas. Is that correct?"

"Y-yes," Snowy stammered as his attention returned to her.

"That would certainly invoke article ninety-four. No individual, be they a member of the Winged Races or human, shall be held responsible for the actions they were compelled to commit via the use of magical mind-alteration. Furthermore, coming here shows good faith in the fair judgment of the Magi."

"Indeed," Ammy spoke up with a serious expression. "Since you are the local representative of the Assembly, I would like to—"

"Hold on, dear child of mine," Lord Grandpa cut her short while flicking the paper in his grip. "As I have already told you, the situation is far from simple. While these are indeed extenuating factors, we cannot forget about the actual victims of this incident."

After saying so, he lazily looked Joshua over, as if trying to memorize his every feature, then to my abject horror, he proceeded to do the same to me. Ugh. Thankfully his gaze returned to Josh just before I would have no longer been able to hold my distaste from spilling out of my mouth, and he asked him, "Tell me, young man, as the victim of this attempted abduction, do you not blame your kidnapper?"

It was at this point I had just about enough with the old man's tone, and I was about to cut in with indignation, but somehow Josh managed to be a split second faster.

"Of course I do," he answered with a quiet yet firm voice. "Of course I blame him. But Lili… I mean, Neige was innocent. If anything, she was a victim, just like I was."

"Oh?" The old man's face practically lit up with a mirthful smile that strangely didn't reach his eyes. "How very unexpected. It is an answer that belongs to a generous heart. I wonder if your friend also agrees?" Saying so, he returned his attention to me. "If I am not mistaken, you suffered some quite grievous injuries at the hands of the lady of the Abyss. Am I right to assume you also hold no hard feelings towards her, young man?"

"The name's Leonard," I answered with a growl before I even knew it. "Also, no, I naturally do not blame her for something that she had no bloody control over."

For a moment the old geezer's face froze, but then his expression quickly returned to his previous grandfatherly visage as he let out a deep laugh that somehow made him look even more annoying than before. Meanwhile, I took several deep breaths to get my temper back under control, with only marginal success.

"You were right, my dear child," he spoke to Ammy once he stopped chuckling. "Your friend is truly a strange young man." I could distinctly feel that he was stressing the words *young man*, but I was still in the middle of my breathing exercise, so I managed to stay calm and not react. Well, aside from a death glare, but that was to be expected at this point. Anyways, he continued by saying, "So you two hold no ill feelings towards the Lady of House Inanna. Very commendable. Not many youths your age would be able to set aside their enmity so easily after such a traumatic event. However…"

The old man had the gall to pause for dramatic effect, but I was in no mood to deal with his verbal bollocks.

I rolled my eyes. "However?"

The geezer once again gave me an intrigued look. Then he told us—or rather, given that he was looking me dead in the eye, maybe just me in particular—

"Unfortunately, before the Lord of Inanna left for his domain in the

Abyss, he thoroughly erased any and all traces he left on the records of the mundane authorities. Said records naturally included all kinds of identifications related to both him and the young lady over there." He paused again, giving me yet another one of those really annoying genial smiles, and concluded with, "I am afraid she currently has no identity in the outside world. I believe I do not have to explain the implications of such matters to your generation."

I could hear rustling behind me, and that just made me realize that somehow I'd ended up standing about one step ahead of the others, with them clustered behind me. I couldn't remember moving forward, so… were they the ones who moved behind me? It was a question for later, I decided, and I chose to move the conversation along by asking, "We understand. So, what is your angle?"

"Angle?" he repeated after me. "What a curious choice of words. Very well, I shall cut to the bone of the pleasantries and share with you the offer I prepared in advance, one which I believe shall prove quite beneficial for all of us."

"Go on," I urged him cautiously, and the old man lifted another paper from his pile.

"As I am sure you are all aware, it is well within my right to grant you asylum." He glanced behind me, presumably at Josh. "This naturally applies to you as well, young man. As a victim of Abyssal violence, you are more than qualified to seek the protection of the Assembly." He paused to flash another jolly smile. "We can not only guarantee the safety of both you and your kin, but it might also serve as a once-in-a-lifetime opportunity, as well. So long as you cooperate with us, I can promise you not only security, but a chance to enter into the ranks of our School with the backing of a lord of the Assembly."

"What's the catch?" I cut in before Josh could be cajoled into a careless answer.

"The catch? What could you possibly mean?" the annoying geezer asked with an expression that said he was deeply hurt by my question. Yeah, I wish he was.

"You know exactly what I mean. There is no such thing as a free lunch in this world."

"True enough," the arch-mage admitted, his façade of jovial benevolence finally showing a small crack as he frowned at me. "As a token of goodwill, I shall be honest with you. In order to protect your friend from any future Abyssal incursions, he will need to be kept under strict supervision. Furthermore, we believe the reason behind his kidnapping was far from a random act of malevolence perpetrated by the Lord of Inanna, so we might need to subject him to certain nonintrusive tests." He abruptly glanced past me again, and based on the sharp gasp coming from behind me, he was probably looking at Snowy. Strangely enough, before I even knew it, I took half a step to the side, so that I was looking him in the eye again.

By this point, I could see that the old man was getting irritated under the guise of his gentle smile, but I didn't really mind. Anyways, after softly clearing his throat, he said, "Of course, if the young Lady of House Inanna would provide us with a proper explanation behind their unusual actions, such tests might be wholly unnecessary. Speaking of which, I naturally extend the same offer and courtesy to the young Mister Bernstein, as well." There was a long moment of silence in the room, during which the old man's countenance became decidedly less cordial, until he lightly cleared his throat and began, in a slightly strained voice, "Believe me when I say this: most of your peers would sacrifice much more than the small compromise I ask in compensation. It is also worth mentioning that, while the young lady might belong to one of the ruling families of the Abyss, by their very nature, the denizens of her realm do not condone open treachery, and needless to say, her current situation would definitely qualify as that. As such, I believe it is in your best interest to consider my offer well, for her fate may be truly harrowing once her brother returns and—"

"Aaaaand you just cocked it up," I said, eliciting a series of stifled gasps from the peanut gallery behind my back and a somewhat comical expression from the old man in front of me.

"Pardon?" he asked with an uncertain voice, and I couldn't help but scoff at him.

"You heard me right. You fucked up," I told him bluntly as I casually pocketed my hands and continued to give him a glare. "For a moment, I almost considered your offer, but then you just had to take that extra bloody step and use some backhanded threats like that."

"Young man, this is no way to talk to your elders."

I cut him short with a chortle and a slow shake of my head.

"Yeah, sure. I'm sooooo sorry for being rude to you, gramps. Because that is the main issue here, right?" I asked, my lips drawing back in a smile that didn't feel like one at all. "Let's just ignore all the double-talk. Supervision? Nonintrusive testing? Small compromises? Do we really look like idiots to you? No, wait, don't answer that. I don't care."

"Young man, if I were in your place, I would be careful with my words..." the old guy spoke in a low tone, and as he did, the air around him suffused with an eerie white glow.

The others behind me rustled, fidgeting. As for me…

"I told you, the name is Leonard." I pointedly locked eyes with the man and we both fell silent as we competed with each other's gaze.

The silent struggle lasted for about five seconds. In the end, the old man let out a single, derisive laugh, his previous grandfatherly mannerism all but gone as he told me, "Very well, *Leonard*." He stressed my name as his lips parted in a menacing smile, and for a moment I felt like I was facing Sebastian. Even more surprisingly, that somehow made me feel slightly less irritated. I couldn't really ponder on the reason behind that, as he continued, "No matter what I may or may not think of you, I believe you are forgetting your place. I have already explained my offer. Now it's their turn to make their choice. Not yours."

"That would be true if you actually gave them a choice," I countered.

"Truly?" he asked back with a curiously raised eyebrow.

"Indeed. If the only two options given were 'live in peace as a guinea pig under our thumb' and 'face a constant threat of death,' no one would ever pick the latter. Unfortunately for you, there are other choices out there."

"Such as?" he inquired with a somewhat amused expression. "House Dracis? True, with their influence, creating a new identity for the young lady would be easy, but are you certain they would help you? The price the pride of the dragon demands for its support is not something anyone can pay."

"Who talked about them?" I retorted with a shake of my head.

"If not the Dracis, then who do you have in mind? Who else out there could shelter them from harm? Do you believe you can do it all on your own?"

"Sure," I answered offhandedly. He gave me an odd look, so I added, "I'm pretty resourceful."

The old man's eyes opened wide, and he raised a hand to stifle a laugh.

"Yes, I was told so," he finally said after he finished chuckling. Then he fell silent for a few seconds, during which the ambient magical light around him subsided. He appeared to be in deep thought for a while longer, then he abruptly put the paper in his hand down and glanced behind me, calling out, "Amelia?"

"Yes, Grandfather?" the class rep replied with a somewhat unsteady voice. I really hoped it wasn't because she was shaking with anger over my behaviour, but I knew better. An Ammy-sized scolding was coming.

Meanwhile, the old arch-wizard's face was once again set in a grandfatherly smile as he told her, "Be a dear and show your friends around the School. It has been so long since we've had visitors. I am sure the others will be more than happy to show off the fruits of their research to a group of receptive minds." He paused for a beat, his eyes flickering between Josh and Snowy, or at least so I presumed, then he added, "As for you two, I wish to apologize for my forceful approach earlier. Please take your time and carefully consider your options. If you ever find yourself in trouble, my offer of asylum remains open for the both of you."

"I'll think about it," Josh muttered, his voice strangely weak.

I was just about to follow them out, when the owner of the study addressed me.

"As for my young friend, Leonard… Would you mind keeping me company until your friends return?" He gave me a huge, toothy smile that looked entirely wrong on his wrinkled face. "I believe we need to discuss some things, just the two of us."

Surprised by the sudden proposal, I glanced over my shoulder to see what the others would say and found them clustered around the door, all deathly pale, even the class rep. Elly and Snowy stood on their guard in the front, while Josh, Judy, and Angie were huddled together behind them.

I had a faint idea of what was going on, so after a short moment of hesitation, I flashed them a reassuring smile and told them, "Go on ahead, guys. You don't need to rush, either. I'll be right here."

"Are you sure?" Elly asked back, a drop of sweat rolling down the bridge of her nose.

"Yeah. Have fun," I answered with another carefree smile. The group seemed less than enthusiastic about leaving, but Ammy took the helm and hastily herded them out of the study across the slowly opening doors. Once outside, said doors immediately reversed their direction. I caught a few worried glances from the other side before the doors closed with a distinct thud.

I released a long breath and faced the old man behind the desk. His grin had grown positively devious. Not one to be outdone, I gave him an irreverent smirk of my own and asked, "Time for the real negotiations to start, Lord Amadeus?"

"Indeed it is," he answered with a sly glint in his eye, "Leonard Blackcloak."

PART 3

"Blackcloak?" I repeated the arch-mage's words after an uncomfortably long pause.

"Indeed," he smiled mirthfully as he slowly stood up from his seat. "I wonder why you look so surprised."

"Well, it wasn't something I expected to hear from you," I admitted, eliciting a self-satisfied chuckle from the old man.

"Truly? I believe your name is on the lips of countless people right now," he told me as he walked over to the cabinet on the left with leisurely steps. "You might be currently unaware, but you are quickly becoming a household name in the world of mystics." At this point the old man fell silent as his hand gently tapped on the side of the cabinet, which then flashed with the now-familiar patterns before swiftly opening, revealing an entire smorgasbord of liquors and spirits. "But before we start, can I interest you in a drink?" Saying so, he picked out a small, round bottle and showed it to me. "This is one of my latest acquisitions. It is an herbal liquor called Unicum. It is said to be a great digestif."

"I'm technically a minor," I answered him as bluntly as the broad side of an axe.

He chuckled.

"Technically? A truly peculiar choice of words once again. But alas, it would be uncouth for me to leave the laws of the mundane world unobserved. I shall put some of this away so that we may enjoy it in the future while reminiscing about this day," he mused as he poured the dark, thick liquid into an elaborately designed shot glass before sealing the bottle and closing the cabinet. Then he strolled back to the desk, glass in hand. After taking a sip, he asked, "What shall we discuss first?"

I could only stifle a groan in response. The old man managed to grab the reins of the conversation right from the start, and I had no choice but to ask the obvious question to get it moving.

"I want to hear about this 'Blackcloak' thing first," I told him, and he immediately beamed at me with the countenance of a fox who'd just gotten a mouse to walk into its mouth.

"A truly amusing story," he replied between sips from his glass. "Believe it or not, the title itself comes from none other than the Lord of Inanna himself."

"Really?" I frowned at the unexpected answer.

"Indeed. As they say, no denizen of the Abyss can overcome their heritage—they have all the deviousness of Celestials and the pride of dragons."

"That's kinda racist, but go on," I interjected, but my words didn't seem to faze the old man.

"Unlikely as it might have been at the time, the young Lord of House Inanna came to me on his own, and he paid a substantial price to secure his own welfare on my lands. He wove a beautiful tapestry of cooperation and peace, but I naturally knew that he would have a dagger hidden behind his back." He took another sip, then continued with a shameless smile. "I knew he would cause trouble, but curiosity won me over. Once you are my age, you will understand that there are not many things that can interest an old man, so I was not going to miss this opportunity to see something unusual. Of course, the materials he generously provided for research were a substantial boon in and of itself, so I reckoned I would not turn a loss even if he attempted to do something extravagantly unwise."

"Does trying to open a gate to the Abyss right on top of your School count as that?" I interjected, earning me another supremely grating chuckle.

"Indeed it does!" the old man agreed and downed the last of his drink. "His plan was by no means the work of a genius, but his preparations were thorough and careful. Of course, I also made my countermeasures in the shadows. It was a game I truly enjoyed, but to my eternal shame, I completely misread the game board. I thought he would try to break into my School, so I set an elegant collection of traps for him, if I do say so myself. Not in my wildest dreams did I imagine he would completely ignore it in favor of kidnapping a seemingly ordinary young student. A serious blunder by any measure, I would say."

"Yeah, a 'blunder.' I bet that's what the French called the Battle of Agincourt, too, but it doesn't make it any less of an abject cock-up," I answered his non-question, but instead of getting angry, the old geezer's smile only widened.

"Harsh words, but not unreasonable." After saying so, suddenly the arch-mage's eyes narrowed into a squint, which was actually a little bit unsettling, with his one red eye and everything. "However, in that moment of blunder, a group of youngsters presented themselves. My own granddaughter, a member of House Dracis, an undercover Celestial, and a pair of mundane youths, all working together as one. And on the forefront of this extraordinary gang was none other than you, Leonard."

The way he slowly drew out my name sent shivers down my spine, but I didn't let it show on my face.

"That's all jolly fine, but what does it have to do with this 'Blackcloak' business?"

"Everything," he answered me with a mysterious glint in his still narrowed eyes. "As I have told you, the denizens of the Abyss are ruled by their stubborn pride as much as their ancestors were, and none more so than the Lords themselves. Come on, lad—put yourself in his shoes for but a moment! Imagine you craft a most elaborate plan in order to gain both prestige and a profit for yourself, yet at the last moment, all your preparations are brought to naught by children! Not only that, but you lose a rare beast, your sister, and your very dignity to them in the process! What would you do?"

"Is… this a trick question?"

"No, I am quite serious," the old man told me, though his weird grin made the validity of his statement a little questionable. "Go on, share your thoughts!"

For a few long seconds, I only gave the expectant old man a wry look. Then I let out a tired breath and resigned myself to fall into his pace once again.

"Fine, let me think. So, I got beaten by a group of high schoolers, all my plans are FUBAR, and the rest of the Abyss is watching me for signs of weakness. I suppose the first step is damage control."

"Such as?"

"I would either make the loss seem less significant than it was or hide it altogether. Since you told me I somehow became a 'household name' or whatever, I guess it wasn't the latter. In fact, it almost seems like…" I paused for a moment as I realized something, and for a moment I almost forgot to breathe. "Please don't tell me he did what I think he's done?"

"Oh, I am afraid you are most likely correct in your deduction," Lord Punchable told me, his face plastered with a shit-eating grin. "He must have also realized that he couldn't keep his failure a secret for long, so he did something unexpected and told a new story. It was a tale where he was lured into a devious trap, devised by his treacherous sister, the heiress of the venerated Dracis family, the genius granddaughter of my humble self, an operative of the Celestial intelligence, and led by a certain Leonard Blackcloak, the Chimera Slayer. Quite an illustrious title, I might add."

"Oh, you've got to be shitting me!" I exclaimed, but the old man only chuckled at my frustration.

"I am afraid not. News like this travels fast among the mystics, and when such news comes directly from the mouth of a Lord of the Abyss and his loyal retainers, it does so even faster. It is actually quite ingenious, would you not agree? With just a few rumors, the Lord of Inanna turned his shameful defeat into a daring escape from the grasp of his traitorous sister and her alliance of powerful accomplices."

I took a few seconds to bury my head in my palm. Then, after I felt reasonably calm, I simply stated, "I swear, next time I see that son of a bitch, I'll beat him to within an inch of his life!"

"Oh my!" The annoying arch-mage shook his head with an amused expression. "No wonder people think highly of you. Few would dare to threaten a Lord of the Abyss like that, even behind closed doors." He paused, perhaps to see if I would find some more colourful expletives to express my distaste, but since I was silent, he crossed his fingers on the table and said, "Exaggeration aside, I believe the rumors about you are still just that—truth magnified by design. They could not exist without a kernel of truth, and you *have* killed a Chimera, have you not?"

"Well, yes," I grudgingly admitted. "But I didn't do it alone, and it sure as hell wasn't a walk in the park."

"I would be quite troubled if it was," Gramps stated with a small laugh in his voice. "However, the fact that you did is not only remarkable in and of itself, your actions on that peculiar night not only foiled a plan of the Abyss, but you also helped our School avoid humiliation. For this, I would sincerely thank you."

"You are welcome," I dourly said, though he didn't seem to mind.

"However, as thankful as I am, there are some things I find hard to overlook." Saying so, he casually reached into the pile of papers and produced yet another sheet, without even looking. By now, I was fairly certain those pages didn't have anything to do with any of this and he only waved them around for showmanship. Anyways, he continued, "A remarkable young man like you should have been known to me, would you not agree? Yet here you are—one day a mundane student with an unusual group of friends, and the next day a fabled Chimera Slayer and the sworn enemy of a Lord of the Abyss. Yet, when I attempted to look into your history, I found nothing. Average parents. Average grades. Average interests. A truly average person, who is at the same time a hero. How curious. So, I let my curiosity get the better of me once again, and I inquired about you from my granddaughter and your Celestial friend. You know what they said? Smart. Daring. Strong. Reliable. A born leader. Calm under pressure. A real—"

"Could we skip the part where you try to butter me up and get to the damn point?"

"The point, my young friend, is that I found you interesting even before we first met. But now..." He didn't finish his sentence. Instead, he pulled out a drawer and picked up a large manila envelope.

"You see, young Leonard, this was something I prepared ahead of time, but I was not sure whether I should give it to you. I could not be sure whether I could trust the rumors about you. Whether I could trust you. But alas, the curiosity of an old man, once ignited, is hard to quench." The old guy grinned at me again and placed the envelope on the desk. "Please consider this as a small token of my appreciation, and maybe a something of an investment."

I eyed the packet. "What's in it?"

The arch-mage's lips widened even further, like a fisherman who'd just got a huge catch on his hook, which made me quite uncomfortable, considering I was the fish in this analogy.

"I was told you wished to protect the peace of this city in general and the lives of your friends in particular. In this envelope, you will find a number of leads that might point you towards potential threats to that peace. What you do with them is entirely up to your discretion."

"So, your idea of a 'token of appreciation' is giving me leads to supernatural trouble so that I'll have to deal with it instead of you?"

"Indeed."

"And you expect me to just take it?"

"Can you afford not to?"

For a second or five, I stared daggers at the old man, but his friendly, grandfatherly smile never wavered. I was still hesitant, but then he tilted his head to the side like a curious cocker spaniel. I let out a long and pained groan and reached for the envelope.

"Crafty son of a bitch."

"Now, now. There is no reason to lose your guise of civility," he told me with another chuckle that made me want to roll up the package in my hand and stuff it down his throat. But then his expression finally lost the grin and he told me, "You might also consider this a test. I have a feeling that you and I should be able to enter into a mutually beneficial relationship, but I want to see your talents firsthand. Who knows? Maybe one day we may even work together as equals?"

"I sincerely doubt that will ever happen," I hissed through clenched teeth as I took a step towards the door.

"We shall see. For the time being, I shall keep a close eye on you."

Hearing those words, I stopped mid step and whipped my head around to give the man a glare.

"So long as you keep those eyes out of my home," I told him in a voice so cold it surprised even me. Even more surprisingly, the old man's smile twitched, which he tried to cover up with an embarrassed cough.

"Duly noted," he awkwardly told me. In the meantime I reached the door, and he quickly added, "I shall open the way."

"Don't stand up, I'll let myself out," I told him.

"I do not actually have to—" he began, but then I placed my hand on the entrance and pushed.

It didn't seem to work at first, so I tried again, harder, and when I did, I could feel a familiar, numbing buzz at the fingertips, following which the door clicked and swung right open. The strange part was that, unlike before, only one wing of the door moved. For a moment, I was afraid I'd broken something, so I glanced back at the old man, but he was only looking at me with a wooden smile. I hastily grunted something that could, under certain circumstances, be interpreted as a goodbye, then carefully closed the door behind me.

It was only after I was sure that the door stayed closed that I let out a long breath in relief. It didn't last long, though, as the irritation crept back the moment I glanced at the manila package in my hand.

I stared at it for a couple of seconds, my frustration growing until I finally burst out with a subdued, "Damn."

I was pissed. No, I was more than pissed. I was totally, irrationally enraged. The old sod led me by the nose through practically the entire discussion, if you could call it that, and he even tossed some extra work on my shoulders with an excuse of it being a "test"! Test, my bloody arse! I had more than enough problems on my plate! I came here to fix some of them, not to get even more heaped on me! Bollocks!

Meanwhile, as I quietly fumed and my fingers gripping the envelope went white, the lift door down the hallway opened. To my sincerest surprise, I found the rest of my little band of misfits on the other side. I naturally attempted to walk over to them, but before I could even take two steps, I was practically tackled by a certain blonde dragon girl.

"Leo! Are you all right!? Are you hurt anywhere?"

"I wasn't, until you head-butted my spleen," I grumbled, massaging my stomach.

"Sorry, but that's beside the point!" she told me while she frantically patted me down, and before I knew it, a certain Celestial girl also joined the fray.

"Let me look at him! I'm better at this!"

She grabbed hold of my wrist and began humming, which was the straw that broke the proverbial camel's back.

"Would you just calm down and let me go already?" I growled as I snatched my wrist out of Angie's grasp. "What's wrong with all of you?"

"Chief, are you sure you are all right?" Judy joined in, prompting me to groan in exasperation.

"Of course I'm fine."

"Good, then please lean forward a bit."

"Um, sure?" I replied somewhat suspiciously, and when I did so, my girlfriend suddenly caught hold of my ear and twisted it.

Now, to be perfectly honest, as with most of her attempts at physical violence, Judy somehow managed to accomplish that without hurting me in the slightest, but I felt obliged by the situation, so I gave her a confused "Ouch?"

"Chief, what did I tell you about picking a fight with an arch-mage of the Assembly in the middle of his School?"

"I didn't pick a fight!" I protested. "I was only looking out for Josh and Snowy."

"That doesn't change the fact that you made him angry."

"Right!" Angie piled on, grabbing my wrist again. "I was more scared for our lives than when we met that Chimera for the first time!"

"It was hard to breathe, like there was a mountain on my chest," Snowy agreed, her face still pale.

"Snowy's brother had something similar going on, but I would face him a hundred times over meeting Ammy's grandpa ever again," said Josh.

"Grandfather is not *that* scary," the class rep cut in to defend her elder. "Actually, I've never seen him act like that before. He must've magnified his presence and pressure."

"But why?" Joshua spoke up again with a truly perplexed voice. "Why did he want to scare us?"

"I think he only wanted to scare one of us," Ammy said, giving me a flat stare.

"I'm sorry, but I have absolutely no idea what you guys are talking about," I told them honestly, earning me several confused glances.

"How could you not feel it?" Elly put her hand on my forehead to take my temperature. "I could feel my skin tingle from the moment we stepped in the study, and it only got worse over time."

"Still doesn't ring a bell," I told them, then glanced down at the Celestial girl and asked, "How long are you going to keep doing that? Could we at least get going?"

"Um, sure." Angie let go of my wrist and told everyone, "He's fine. I think."

"Good," Judy spoke in a flat voice and tried to twist my ear again, so I rolled my eyes and straightened myself. She tried to stand on her tiptoes to keep holding on to me, but once it became obvious she wouldn't be able to once I started walking, she grudgingly let go and added, "Don't think you have escaped, mister. Once we are back home, you better get ready for an earful."

"Yes," my other girlfriend enthusiastically agreed and grabbed hold of my arm as usual. "We can't take you anywhere without you causing a scene! I will not let you go until..." Her worlds trailed off as she noticed the large envelope in my hand. "What's that?"

"This?" I asked innocently, then gestured towards the lift. "I will tell you on the way up. We should really get going."

"Oh, *now* you are in a hurry," the class rep fumed, scowling. "Could it be that Mister *I'm not affected by the presence of an arch-mage* is getting a little jittery?"

"Nah," I answered offhandedly as I began walking, practically dragging Elly along. "I just want to get as far away from the School grounds as possible before your grandpa realizes I probably broke his door."

"I see," Ammy answered absentmindedly at first, but then her eyes widened in shock. "Wait, you did WHAT?"

"No time to explain, just get in the lift." I gestured for her, and she quickly walked after us, all the while loudly explaining how hard she was going to kick my butt for giving her even more paperwork to deal with. What could I say? She really, really needed to take a break from doing administrative work.

CHAPTER 6

PART 1

Waving, my dear assistant said, "Bye!" with a rare sense of enthusiasm in her voice.

"I'm not leaving yet!" my other girlfriend retorted while still clinging to my arm, an act which normally made walking difficult, yet in this case, it actually helped with my balance, so I didn't really mind. Anyways, Elly gave my other girlfriend a classic type-C glare and stated, "We are still not at our mansion!"

"Bye-bye. Take care," Judy continued her (fairly) passionate waving, undaunted by her words.

"I told you, I'm not letting go until we are at the gates!"

"Buh-bye."

"Leooo! Judy is bullying me," my clingier girlfriend apparently gave up on the idea of a direct confrontation, and instead she pleaded with me by employing the tried-and-true puppy-eyes strategy. I would be lying if I said it had no effect on me, but I didn't let it show on my face. I mean, it's not like she was cute or anything.

"Stop it, you two," I chided them, then tried to raise my arm to poke them in the forehead (my usual last resort), but since one of my hands was occupied by the princess, and the other held several fairly heavy paper bags, I wisely decided against the idea and instead chose to divert their attention by telling them, "You are weirding out poor Snowy with your act."

"Are we?" my assistant questioned back, but before I could repeat myself, she sent what I presumed to be an inquisitive glance at the girl in question.

"U-um... I'm fine, not weirded out at all, I think..." Snowy told us with an awkward expression while peeking out from behind the gigantic white bear plushy she was holding. More on that later.

"See?" Judy turned back to me with a triumphant... well, I wanted to say *smirk*, but it was more of a twitch at the corners of her lips, really.

"Snowy is just too polite to tell you," I countered in mild exasperation.

"If you say so," my dearest assistant gave a noncommittal answer, but a moment later she faced Elly again and told her, in a voice that was even more monotonous than usual, "Oh look. We arrived. What a shame."

The girl holding my arm sent her another, obviously ineffective glare, but ultimately, she let out a disappointed sound as we came to a halt in front of the familiar gates of her family mansion. She finally let go of me… only to grab my arm again a moment later and began rubbing her cheek on my upper arm.

"What exactly are you doing right now?" I asked incredulously while trying to keep my balance.

"I'm stockpiling some leonium for the rest of the day."

"Okay… do I even want to know just what the heck this 'leonium' is?" I inquired, my incredulity level raised a notch.

"You wouldn't get it, Chief," Judy told me, gingerly tugging at the blonde dragon girl's coat. "It's an inside joke."

"Since when do you two have inside jokes?" came my next question, which incidentally also signaled the maxing out of my incredulity-o-meter.

"Don't sweat the small stuff." My assistant gave me this nonanswer as she finally got Elly to let me go. Well, okay, technically the princess let go of me on her own, completely independent of Judy's usual limp-wristed efforts, but the latter still seemed satisfied with the results.

"Oh fine," my draconic girlfriend grumbled before she unceremoniously pushed the large paper bag into the hands of my unprepared other girl-friend, and then she faced me with upturned, expectant eyes.

"Goodbye kiss?" she asked in a voice that was both shy and coquettish. I have no idea how she managed, but it wasn't as if common sense had a really firm grip on her in the first place, so I just filed it under *Yup, just as you would expect from our princess* and tossed it into one of the dusty corners of my brain.

In any case, the moment she said that, I leaned down and put a small peck on her lips, my decisiveness apparently surprising her. It couldn't be helped, though. Knowing my luck, if I would have hesitated for even a moment, it was guaranteed that a certain annoying butler would have shown up to "accidentally" witness me getting intimate with his young lady/charge/possible great-great-granddaughter, and then proceed to complicate my life even further.

After a second of shock, Elly giggled and tried to hug me again, only for Judy to drag her back with slightly more ardor, and not a moment too soon, as my knack to predict (and avoid) rom-com situations was once again validated by the aforementioned butler showing up out of nowhere and opening the gates with one of those tiny single-button remotes.

I had to smile. I mean, a dragon opening a gate with a remote control-ler. How silly is that?

But back to Elly: when she noticed him, the princess let out a disap-pointed grumble and finally stopped trying to glomp me. I was glad she had at least that much common sense, though I had a sneaking suspicion it wasn't because she was aware that our relationship should be kept low profile, but because she was shy in front of good old Sebastian. Speaking of the devil, by now the butler had walked up to us, his hands behind his back and his posture ramrod straight.

"Welcome back, milady, Miss Sennoma, and…" Getting to my name, Sebastian pulled a face like he'd just bitten into a lemon. Then he casually ignored me and focused on the white-haired girl behind me. "What a surprise. I thought young Miss Inanna was missing."

"Yep, she was. Past tense. She's with me now," I cheerfully told the annoying bastard. "By the way, I'm happy to see you too, old man."

"The sentiment is not at all mutual," he answered with a small twitch in the corner of his eye. "What precisely are you doing here?"

"I escorted the princess home, as a gentleman should. Got a problem with it?"

"Not with that, but with you," Sebastian said, and I had to hand it to him—he didn't beat around the bush. "Your very presence around the Dracis mansion offends my sensibilities."

"Really?" I answered with a toothy grin that probably didn't look like a glower. *Probably.* "I don't know why, but that just makes me want to stick around more. Maybe I should move closer? Are there any vacant lots around here?"

"If there were, expect it to be burned to the ground before you could even think about purchasing it."

"Aw, that's not good. I didn't know there was an arsonist on the loose. Maybe I should move even closer. Like, move *in* with you. For safety."

The butler theatrically shivered at my words and bitterly said, "Your jokes are getting worse over time."

"I'm not joking," I told the old lizard with a toothy grin. "Hey, Elly? What would you say if I tried to move in with you?"

"H-huh?" The princess shot me a classic deer-in-the-headlights look. Then her cheeks flushed in a familiar shade of crimson, which I just realized I'd been missing a little, and she stammered, "Y-you can't! I have to ask my parents first!"

"Milady, please don't encourage his juvenile behaviour," Sebastian mumbled while massaging his temple, somehow completely missing how weirdly she was acting. Though then again, this was pretty much how she acted all the time until just a couple weeks ago, so maybe he was already used to it?

Either way, I let out a small chuckle and told her, "Nah, maybe later. We should get going before it gets dark. See you tomorrow, Elly!"

"Um, yeah! Bye!" she returned my goodbyes with a timid wave.

Meanwhile, the old lizard shook his head and, to my surprise, directly addressed my other girlfriend.

"Miss Sennoma, please keep him on a short leash."

"Working on it," my assistant answered with a nod, making my eyes slowly narrow into suspicious slits, but she didn't seem to notice (or care), so I quit it and instead waved at the lonely dragon girl tragically staring after us from the other side of the gates. Honestly, while Elly was getting a little too clingy lately, now that she wasn't hanging on my arm, I kinda missed her warmth. Not much, just a little. A tiny bit. At any rate, once we were a fair bit away from the mansion, I finally addressed the proverbial elephant in the room.

"Hey, Dormouse?" I said to my dearest assistant, and she gave me a questioning look in return. "Just wondering. Since when are you on such good terms with the old butler?"

"Good terms? I believe we are simply familiar due to him observing me whenever I browsed the Dracis library." She momentarily paused, then she gave me a suspiciously innocent look and asked, "Why do you ask? Could it be that you are jealous?"

"What? No!" I denied.

"Oh?" Judy's expression fell, and she muttered, "That's a shame."

"You... want me to be jealous?" I asked suspiciously, and my girlfriend nodded in return. "Why?"

"My vast research on relationships tells me jealousy is one of the signs of a passionate relationship."

"Okay, first off, get better sources, as that is just silly. Secondly, I'd like to let you know that I'd rather jump off a bridge than even *consider* being jealous of that old coot."

Judy gave me a weird look, and it seemed like she wanted to say something, but she just clicked her tongue and muttered "spoilsport" under her breath, at which I promptly shook my head, rolled my eyes, and extended my free hand towards her.

My dear assistant looked at me funny for a moment, and then she asked, "Are you asking me to take Eleanor's place?"

"What? No," I grumbled, gesturing again. "I want you to give me the bags you are carrying."

"Oh," she said in a soft and overly disappointed tone, followed by a melodramatic sigh. "For a moment, I thought my subtle insinuations finally made you realize our relationship is lacking intimacy. How silly of me. In the future, I will strive to rid myself of such naïve thoughts."

"You call that subtle?" I asked with raised brows, but my girlfriend kept sighing so hard it sounded like she had some kind of respiratory problem, so I let out a groan of my own and relented. "Fine, I get it! Do you really want to link arms that much?"

"A little," she answered shamelessly, earning yet another eye roll, at which she huffed and then added, "Chief, skinship is really important in a relationship. It's how you build up familiarity towards the more intimate acts between a couple, such as—"

"Fine, I get it!" I finally admitted defeat. "Once we get home, you have my permission to snuggle or whatever, just stop talking about this in front of Snowy! Are you happy now?"

"Yay," she... well, not exactly *exclaimed*, as she was still deadpan as usual, but I took it as such, after which she finally gave me the bags.

And so I continued on our merry way again, except four bags heavier.

Said bags, by the way, all contained clothes. After our not at all frantic exit from the school grounds (which earned me a particularly disapproving look from Armband Guy on the way out), we decided that since we were already outside, we should take care of a few problems.

First and foremost, following Snowy's lead, we returned to the high-class hotel where she and her brother were staying during their excursion from the Abyss. Now, while getting into the already vacated hotel room required some convincing, a bit of bribery, and a metric crapload of refuge in audacity, we actually managed to gain entry after a talk with the manager's manager. While all of the incriminating evidence of Crowey's presence had been scrubbed, they thankfully didn't bother to bring back all of Snowy's clothes with them to the Abyss when they left. Unfortunately, while we could gather a few changes' worth, including her school uniform, most of them were of the skimpy variety she was wearing the first time we met. Needless to say, I was not going to let her run around in those during the winter, so after we finished packing what we could, our next stop was the local shopping street, where I proceeded to buy my new housemate several new outfits, even though she was fighting against it tooth and nail.

Oh, right, speaking of housemates... Since according to the others, I had totally screwed up Snowy's chances of getting proper asylum at the Magi headquarters, and since I was already living alone, I was unanimously delegated by the gang to take care of Snowy, which naturally included providing shelter, as well. Truth be told, that was my plan from the beginning, but getting the responsibility dumped on me like that was still frustrating.

In the end, I may have overdone it a little, as I not only bought her clothes, but an electric toothbrush, a set of combs and hairbrushes, new school supplies, several pairs of footwear, multiple warm jackets and other assorted winter wear, and a giant polar bear plushy, the last of which was specifically recommended by Josh. Naturally, I had to carry most of these by myself.

Hence the paper bags.

The impromptu shopping spree ended just a little after 5 p.m., and while it wasn't especially late yet, the others in general, and Josh in particular, complained that they'd been mentally drained by the day's events. So we decided to head home. This meant that I got grouped in with my girlfriends and Snowy, while Josh, Ammy, and Angie went the other way. They were still discussing the finer points of the supernatural masquerade using analogies from the oft-referenced show about a teenage werewolf hunter, the irony of which wasn't lost on me at all.

Anyways, after we escorted the princess home, we headed straight to my house and arrived without any interruptions along the way. Once inside, I finally put down the bags, hung my usual black coat on the hangers by the entrance, and rolled my stinging shoulders. Thankfully, I'd had the good sense to leave the thermostat turned up, so the temperature in the living room was quite balmy. Speaking of which, by the time I entered there, Judy had disappeared somewhere (the toilet, I presumed) while Snowy was awkwardly standing by the sofa, alternating between looking at me with an expression that said she wanted to say something and then burying her head into the back of her plushy. It was a little weird, even by her standards, but I decided not to ask her just yet and instead let her collect her wits while I absentmindedly sorted the bags into two piles of roughly equal weight.

Unfortunately, she didn't manage to do so under a minute, and since the silence was getting a little uncomfortable, I decided to lightly clear my throat to get her attention. Snowy winced, but instead of taking the opportunity to voice whatever was gnawing at her, she just hid behind her plushy again as if it somehow made her invisible. My patience slipping, I grabbed the bags again and told her, "I'll bring these to your room, and then we can—"

"I-I will get a job!" Snowy suddenly declared.

"That… was a bit of a non sequitur," I told her with a frown.

"I mean…" she stammered for a moment, then finally explained, "I will get a job and pay you back. For all of this. Rent, too."

"Oh, so that's what you meant!" I reacted with just a hint of bemusement as I moved closer to her. "Don't worry about it. I'm in no need of money, and as for rent, I have this whole house all to myself, anyway, so one more person staying here won't even be an inconvenience. At least this way those empty rooms will finally have some use."

"But I…"

"Come on, Snowy, no need to be reserved," I told her with an ever so slightly amused smile, then I gestured for her to follow after me. "Let's go up. You still need to unpack all of these, don't you?"

I didn't give her the chance to answer but headed up the stairs, and while at first she only gave me a conflicted look, by the time I was halfway up, she quickly caught up with me, and she was standing by my side when I opened the door to the guest room next to mine.

The insides were honestly pretty plain. Spartan, even. Squeaky clean, too—no doubt due to the tireless efforts of the loyal invisible ninja maids. In terms of dimensions, it was exactly the same as my room, though it looked bigger at first glance because it only had a normal-sized bed, a small desk, a single wardrobe, and a commode. As for the colour palette, the walls were pure white and the furniture a dark brown that was just barely on this side of black.

In short, it wasn't a room that screamed "girly," but that was something that could be fixed with time. Maybe I could get her some new wallpaper? Oh, and some less bland bedsheets. Plus one of those cat-shaped wall clocks with the swinging tail. I'd always found them amusing, but such a clock would've looked weird in my room. One would fit in here, once we'd done some remodeling.

"This is going to be your room," I told Snowy after I put down the bags. "Let's unpack your stuff."

"Okay…" she replied a tad uncertainly. First, she put down her plushy on the bed, then she looked around like it was a completely new environment, even though she'd slept here the night before. In fact, she was staring at every nook and cranny so intently, it kind of disturbed me.

"So, what are you waiting for?" I asked her once my patience ran out, again, but she only shook her head.

"Just a moment. I'm… trying to commit the room to memory."

I'm not going to lie; if someone had invented a machine that turned skepticism into electricity, my eyes would've been able to power half the damn island.

"You are committing what to memory, again?" I asked, just to make sure I heard it right.

"The room," Snowy answered while still scrutinizing the place as if she were performing a crime scene investigation in a detective show. "I'm trying to make sure I'll remember where all the furniture and items are."

"Okay… I'll bite," I told her. "Would you please tell me *why* you are memorizing the layout of the room?"

"Um..." She hesitated, then for some mysterious and slightly foreboding reason, she appeared to be steeling her nerves before she answered, "It's so that when I leave, I can make sure I would leave it in the same condition as it is now."

I gave her a long, hard look. Was she being serious? If her clenched fists and earnest gaze were any indication, she wasn't joking.

I allowed my brows to ever so slowly furrow into the mother of all disapproving frowns, which seemed to finally take her sincere, if misguided, fervor down a notch.

"Snowy," I raised my voice, making her shudder, but I didn't really care at this moment. "You are being really obnoxious right now." She only hung her head at my scolding, so I disapprovingly shook mine and continued, with added emphasis: "You didn't even unpack your things yet, and you are already planning on how you should make the room look when you leave? Are you serious?"

"But... I told you, I don't want to impose on you, so once I find a job, I will rent a room and—"

"Snowy!" I interrupted her sternly, but I quickly toned it back and added, "Please look at me when I'm talking to you."

For a couple of seconds, she didn't react to my request. Then she snuck a peek at me, and when she realized I wasn't glaring at her or anything, she finally relaxed a little and looked me in the eye.

"Good," I told her before I raised my right hand and set it on the crown of her head, eliciting a surprised yelp and a confused look from her. "I'm going to say this one more time, so please listen closely. Can you do that?" I waited for her to nod, and I ruffled her hair a little in endorsement. "Great. So, let me stress this once and for all: You are not imposing on anyone. From this moment onwards, this is your room. I'm not renting it to you, I'm not letting you stay. I'm giving it to you. Everything in it is yours; you can do with it whatever you want. You can stay as long as you want. I won't ask for rent, I won't throw you out, and while you can leave if you want, I won't hear anything more about finding any kind of job. You are going to go to school like us, and you are going to have a fun and memorable school life with the rest of us, whether you like it or not. Are we clear on that?"

I tried to make my voice a little more playful by the end, since Snowy was looking at me like she'd just found a white raven or an honest politician. Contrary to my best efforts, she just kept intently staring at me with those large, innocent, and slightly disquieting eyes of hers, so, as my last desperate move, I rustled her hair again. That finally got a reaction out of her, as she blinked at me with what I presumed to be disbelief.

"I can… stay here as long as I want," she said instead of asking, earning her another head pat.

"Yup, that's what I just said."

"And you'll take care of me?"

This time it was a proper question, and after a moment of thinking, I nodded.

"Sure."

"But… why?" she finally asked the pivotal question, and I could only awkwardly scratch the base of my neck with my free hand.

"Do you want me to be perfectly honest?" I asked back, and she immediately nodded, so I told her, "It's because I feel responsible for your current situation."

"You do?" she asked, her voice practically dripping with incredulity.

"Yeah," I mumbled a little sheepishly. "I mean, think about it. I knew you were doing something fishy back at the school, and I knew Crowey was up to no good, but I never pursued either of those obvious issues. If I had, I might've gotten ahead of him, and then the kidnapping wouldn't have happened, and then you wouldn't have thrown an icicle at me, and then you wouldn't be in trouble with the Magi."

"That makes no sense!" Snowy suddenly and vehemently objected against my assertions, tears springing to her eyes. "None of that was your fault! You didn't do anything wrong!"

"Not directly, maybe, but I am still guilty of inaction," I answered her softly as I continued to rub her head. "So, this time I decided to make sure that a certain awkward girl with a bad habit of daylighting as a cheesy seductress wouldn't do something stupid out of desperation. Something I could easily prevent by providing her shelter, sustenance, and maybe just a bit of security. Hence, here we are."

I flashed another optimistic smile at her as I waited for her next words, but those never came. Instead she sniffled hard, and before I could offer her a tissue, she tackled me, her arms clamping around my ribcage like a giant vice and pushing all the air out of my lungs.

"Whoa, easy there, Snowy. I—"

"So that's where you are!" my assistant said as she entered the room with the worst timing ever while carrying a tray with several mugs on it. "I brought some hot cocoa and…" Her words trailed off as she beheld Snowy clinging to me, and she added, in a dangerously flat voice, "Am I intruding?"

I promptly rolled my eyes at her and gestured for her to put down the tray and help me with calming the sniffling girl hugging me so hard I had trouble breathing. Just where did she even hide all that strength in that tiny frame of hers, anyway?

Nevertheless, after a few short minutes of coaxing, during which Snowy also clamped down on my flabbergasted assistant (which served her right, if you ask me), we finally ended up all sitting on the bed, with the Abyssal girl in the middle, and each of us holding our own mugs.

Speaking of which, I still had my trusty *I <3 Coffee* mug and Judy had her usual *I <3 My Boss* one, which left Snowy with a generic white one from the kitchen cupboard. It bothered me a little, so I made a mental note to get her a matching one. Maybe for her birthday?

Actually, that reminded me of something, and I decided to ask it before something inexplicably wacky derailed our conversation once again.

"Say, Snowy?" I addressed the girl adorably blowing on her hot cocoa.

"Yes?" she responded after a quick sniffle.

"As I recall, Ammy's grandpa said you have no ID right now. As in, not just that you don't have papers, but that you don't exist on any registers. Is that true?"

She gave me a questioning look, probably wondering where the question came from, but after a short while, she nodded in the affirmative.

"We really need to fix that if you want to stay over," I told her before taking a sip from the mug in my hand to collect my thoughts, "Or rather, considering I kinda already took responsibility for it in front of Lord Grandpa, *I* have to fix that."

"You reap what you sow," Judy spoke like she just said something really profound, but then she cocked her head to the side and added, "Also, did you just call the local arch-mage *Lord Grandpa?*"

"I sure did," I answered her with an irreverent smirk, but then I shifted my attention back to the other girl. "I was wondering where you got your papers when you and your brother came out of the Abyss in the first place. Did you go to a government office?"

"Um..." Snowy hesitated, unsure. "I don't know," she finally admitted and averted her eyes. "After we arrived, we went to the hotel right away, and then brother left the next morning. When he came back, he just handed me the cards. I know he talked with someone, but I don't think he was a government official."

"If that's how quickly he got them, I can pretty much guarantee he didn't go through the legal channels. Maybe he contacted some kind of document forger?" I ventured the guess, but she only hung her head even more in response.

"I don't know," she repeated apologetically. "I really don't know. Brother didn't tell me anything that wasn't strictly necessary to accomplish the tasks he gave me. I don't even know who he—" Suddenly, her face lit up with some kind of revelation. "Wait, I have an idea! Uncle Brang was with him, so he should..." she began, but then her sudden enthusiasm quickly wilted. "Oh, right. He went back... Sorry, I didn't think it through."

"Nah, don't sweat it," I told her with a reassuring pat on the back.

"Right," Judy readily agreed with me, patting Snowy's head, too. "Despite how silly he usually acts, Leo's actually really resourceful. He'll figure something out."

"Yep. Listen to Judy, and don't worry about a thing. I only asked in case you knew a shortcut or something. But I will do something about your situation, no matter what."

"I'm sorry for troubling you again," she muttered, prompting me to rub her back even harder.

"Come on, Snowy! How many times do I have to tell you to stop apologizing for every tiny little thing?"

"Sorry," she said reflexively, but then she raised a hand to her mouth and looked at me apologetically.

I chuckled. "We have a long way to go, huh?" I directed a question at my girlfriend, who just shrugged and began to rustle the supremely embarrassed Abyssal girl's hair with renewed vigor. I let out another chuckle and then took another sip from my mug, thinking that this kind of peaceful atmosphere wasn't half bad at all.

PART 2

"Let's get started," I spoke solemnly after sitting down on my padded swivel chair in front of the PC. Once Snowy calmed down, I told her to get familiar with her room and to put her new clothes away. Afterwards, Judy and I left the premises and went to my room for a much-needed discussion about all the recent developments. I took my usual spot right away.

"Before we begin," my girlfriend suddenly spoke up as she sat down on my bed, "it's imperative that you sit over here."

"Why?" I inquired while practicing my single-eyebrow-raising skill. "Do you want to use the computer?"

Judy shook her head, but instead of clarifying what she wanted, she mechanically patted the space next to her.

"You... want me to sit next to you," I stated rather than asked, and she immediately nodded in the affirmative. "You just want to cuddle, don't you?"

"That's correct," she confirmed my suspicion with a shameless nod, then added, "You already gave me permission."

"Yes, but… don't you think this should be a little higher on our priority list?" I picked up a certain manila envelope and waved it.

"We can do both. Judybot is powered by a state-of-the-art dual-core processor, so she is good at multitasking."

"I can't decide what disturbs me the most—the fact that you still beat the dead horse about the robot thing, that you talk about yourself in the third person, or that you think that a dual-core processor is state of the art."

When I said that, my girlfriend stopped patting the bed beside her and her eyes narrowed into a small frown.

"Chief, stop nitpicking already and come over, or I will be forced to take drastic measures."

"Such as…?"

"I will go over and sit in your lap."

I gave my unusually intense girlfriend a baffled look, then I tentatively asked, "And that is supposed to be a threat because…?"

At this point, Judy let out a grunt of displeasure and stood up, but instead of unexpectedly hopping on my lap as I expected, she deftly snatched the envelope right out of my hand and sat back down on the bed with an unmistakably pouting expression.

"There. Now you either come here, or I won't let you read this."

"Are you seriously blackmailing me into cuddling right now?" She only gave me a rather severe glare (by her standards) in return, so I quickly raised my hands in surrender. "Okay, I get it. I'm already moving."

So saying, I quickly got to my feet and sat down on the spot she was patting before. A split second later, Judy swiftly entwined our arms while simultaneously depositing the envelope back into my lap. Unfortunately, her mood already seemed to be quite sour, as she kept pouting at me with undaunted vigor. I thought this was the perfect moment to change the subject, but my plan was torpedoed when my girlfriend kicked my shin.

"You are still so bad at reading the mood, I don't even know why I'm trying," she grumbled sulkily, her words punctuated by another entirely harmless kick. "You said you would put in more effort."

"I do!" I protested, if a little weakly.

"Then why does it take an entire song and dance routine to get you to act like a proper boyfriend?"

"Fine, I get it," I told her with a sigh, but since she was still pouting, I decided to be a little assertive for a change, so I disentangled our arms and, before she could complain, I reached around and put my hand on her waist, then pulled her so close, our thighs touched.

Judy blinked at me in surprise, then she sharply exhaled through her nose in a way I could interpret either as a stifled chuckle or a derisive snort, and leaned even closer to rest her head against my shoulder.

"That's a start," she said, her voice still containing a tiny bit of sulkiness, so I leaned down and planted a small kiss on her forehead. It was a weird sensation. My extended research on romance told me that these kinds of interactions should be firing me up and getting my heart to beat faster, but while I did feel a kind of cozy warmth in the pit of my stomach, the situation felt oddly calming instead.

Anyways, I let my girlfriend snuggle me to her heart's content for about two minutes before I picked the envelope up from my lap and asked her, "Can we get started?"

Judy glanced up at me. After a moment of thinking, she replied, "Five more minutes."

"Oh, come on, Dormouse! Didn't you say you can multitask?"

"Yes, but that was before I realized that high-level cuddling algorithms use up way more processing power than I expected."

"That's just silly talk. You don't need algorithms for cuddling; it's entirely analog!"

"I... don't know enough about computers to come up with a snappy answer to that. Now I feel sad," my girlfriend said in a tone that was anything but sad.

"Oh, fine!" I gave up with a small sigh. "Would hugging for five minutes cancel it out?"

"Yes, but then I will be back at the baseline, so... ten minutes?"

I didn't answer her. Instead I just pulled her even closer, and then I did nothing for ten minutes, which I didn't enjoy at all, and I definitely didn't have anything silly like warm, fuzzy feels in the pit of my stomach. Anyways, once the allocated snuggling time was over, I tapped my fingers on Judy's waist to get her attention, following which I removed my hand so that I could actually open the package.

"Time's up! Let's take a look," I said as I carefully pried the seal on the back of the envelope open. I was paying very close attention to what I was doing, with extra focus on any magical tomfoolery the infuriating old man might have put on it. My disposition might've been infectious, as Judy also stared unblinking at the object in my hand while holding her breath.

Then the envelope finally opened and... nothing happened.

I'd be lying if I said it wasn't a bit of a letdown, but I quickly dismissed any such thoughts as I reached inside and carefully pulled out the contents. What we found was... considerably more mundane than what I expected, and based on the small frown on my girlfriend's brows, she shared my sentiment.

In total, there were a couple of standard A4 pages filled with words, a map of what I quickly recognized as Timaeus and its surroundings with several bright red circles drawn on it with a permanent marker, and four honest-to-goodness Polaroid photographs.

After skimming through everything in my hands, I turned to my assistant.

"What do you think?"

Judy visibly pondered for a moment before she replied, "Very noir."

"I know, right?" I agreed with a smidgen of my previous excitement returning to my voice.

The "leads" in my hand looked like the standard package any self-respecting hard-boiled private detective would be guaranteed to receive on a cold and stormy evening to kick off a noir murder mystery of some sort.

The trope would've been perfect, except for a small but glaring flaw: In a noir detective story, the person kicking off the plot by delivering the leads was supposed to be a pretty femme fatale walking into my office. Instead, all I got was a grating old wizard, and I was the one who had to walk into *his* office to boot!

But then again, maybe that was for the best. We already had too many pretty girls around these parts. We really didn't need another one, especially now that I was in a relationship and could get into trouble for messing around with femmes fatales.

I lightly shook my head to clear it of such miscellaneous thoughts and turned my attention to the papers in my hands in order to study them a wee bit more closely. Apparently, Judy had memorized the contents already, but she quietly waited for me to finish while she rested against my shoulder. It took me about five more minutes to reach the end of it, at which point I separated the clues into three groups and said, "We have three leads."

"Mm," Judy agreed, nodding against my shoulder. "The research society, the monster sightings, and the unknown swordswoman."

This time it was my turn to nod as I put down two of the bundles and focused on the first lead.

"Let's start with this one," I proposed. "According to this, the Non-causative Science Research Society has increased their presence on Critias during the past two weeks. At least one new research base, location unknown. An unknown number of operatives; estimations range between ten and twenty. Possible connections to both the Abyss and the Celestials. Combat forces numbering in the hundreds. Also..." I studied a certain paragraph again, just to make sure I'd read it right, "… they have giant robots with drill hands. Apparently those are a thing now."

"That's what it says," Judy confirmed my reading with a slightly bemused voice, then quickly added, "I don't understand this lead."

"Me neither," I agreed with a frown.

There were three huge issues with this particular "clue." First off, it was way too vague but at the same time way too confident. It made hard claims, but then it failed to back them up with any numbers or sources. Sure, the way it was written made it look like a legitimate compilation of reports and intel, but I was fairly sure it wasn't, due to issue number two: I knew better. Or rather, the Celestial Hub knew better, and since I was sneakily perusing their intelligence network, it meant I had up-to-date information on the Research Society. Granted, I hadn't paid them much attention in the past, but that didn't mean I wasn't keeping tabs on them… or rather, I had one of the anons on the site keeping track for me. I'm a busy man; I can't do everything myself.

Anyways, the third and biggest issue still remained: What was I supposed to do with this information? Was I supposed to contact them? To gather information about them? To fight them? How? Or was this part of his test, to see if I was really an information broker and could find out more for the old man? Wait, no, that couldn't be. I'd only told Ammy about it today, and he should not know about my cover yet. What else could it be? Was it just a straight up warning about them? There wasn't a single word on those pages about the NSRS actually posing a threat to me or Josh, only that they existed and that they were allegedly mustering their forces. As far as I knew, they could've been planning a company picnic or all-out war. Both possibilities had about the same weight.

"Could it be that the School simply has a poor information agency?" I ventured, but my assistant shook her head.

"The other leads should answer that question."

"True." I put down the papers and reached for the next bunch. "Let's verify the parts about the Research Society on the Hub, just to be safe. I don't think we can do much more on that front right now, so let's move on."

"Mm," Judy agreed as she also focused on the second lead.

To summarize, it was a compilation of eyewitness accounts, rumors, and what looked like police report excerpts, all pertaining to the sightings of some kind of large cryptid animal roaming the streets of Timaeus at night and wreaking havoc on butcher shops.

"There are no timestamps," I noted after skimming through the page again and settling on one witness testimony. "Three pairs of eyes. Sound familiar?"

"The Chimera," Judy confirmed my suspicion. "Another one?"

"Maybe," I wondered aloud as I thought about it. Giving me this particular lead made a bit more sense, if a twisted kind of one. After all, I'd recently had the title of "Chimera Slayer" stapled on to me against my wishes, so the old geezer telling me about another monster wandering the neighbourhood was at least somewhat logical. Anyways, I carefully read the descriptions given by the witnesses and tried to put together a mental image of the creature.

Six eyes, four legs, a doglike head without ears, thin fur, a long tail. That did vaguely remind me of the second form the Chimera transformed into when it was chasing me around the school building, but there were two things that still bothered me. First off, there were no casualties recorded after these sightings. Not even an injury. That was weird enough, considering the temper of the thing I "fought," air quotes intended, but I was also somewhat baffled by the size of the creature. Or rather, sizes, as the witnesses couldn't agree on just how big this thing was. Some claimed it was the size of a person, while others put it more in the stray cat range.

"Either there are multiple Chimeras running around, or this one can change its size," Judy pointed out.

I shook my head.

"The one in the school obeyed the laws of thermodynamics when it transformed, at least to some degree, so it's probably not the latter. As for multiple Chimeras of different sizes..." A new idea formed, and I quickly bounced it off my assistant. "Listen, Judy, I know this might sound silly, but I think this could be the first Chimera's arm." She gave me an intrigued look, so I quickly explained myself. "You see, when I was holding its attention in the courtyard, it bit off one of its limbs. It's possible that while we were busy with Crowey, the arm grew legs and escaped, and then went into hiding after the main body got liquified."

"Are Chimeras proliferous?"

"I have no frickin' idea, but the size roughly matches, and I've seen it grow new heads in the span of minutes. I see no reason why a part of it couldn't grow limbs to scurry away."

"How do you explain the conflicting reports on its size?"

"Maybe it grew?" I responded with an uncertain shrug. "Either that, or it tore off smaller pieces of itself, and then those grew legs. I'll be damned if I knew."

"That's troubling." Judy frowned. "What are we going to do about it?"

That simple question threw a bucket of cold water on my enthusiasm. Discussing the ways freakish shapeshifting monsters reproduced was somewhat intriguing; discussing ways to deal with said monstrosities was a whole lot less so.

"Honestly, I don't think we can do much about it now," I gave my answer after ruminating on it for a short while. "It's not something the guys on the Hub can help with, and unless we organize a search party and comb the streets, I doubt we would stumble upon this bugger. I say we just tell the others to be vigilant at night and hope it doesn't have a vengeful streak and try to find me instead."

"If it really is a piece of the old Chimera and not a brand-new one," Judy started, glancing over the final pile of papers, "what about the last one?"

"That... might be trouble." I picked up the last lead and pointed at the words under one of the Polaroids. "It says, 'an unknown swordswoman.'"

"A Knight?"

"It's about time one of them showed up, so that's the most obvious possibility, yes," I answered, inspecting the photo.

It was a somewhat grainy picture of a young woman, probably in her mid-twenties by the looks of it, standing on a pier. I figured it must've been taken on one of the docks around the island, and recently. But back to the subject of the pictures. Multiple photos from multiple angles revealed she had short, black, or at the very least very dark, hair in a pixie cut, with a single, bright red streak in it. That meant she was probably important; after all, the uniqueness of one's hairdo seemed to closely correspond to the narrative importance of people around these parts.

She was also wearing a dark blue pantsuit with her sleeves and the bottoms of her trousers fanning out, and a pair of large sunglasses (even though the weather on the pictures was quite cloudy) to complete the '90s *no-nonsense corporate career woman* look. What went against said look was a certain long object wrapped in bright purple cloth and Buddhist prayer beads slung by leather straps over her shoulders.

I spent some more time studying the images, after which I let out an irritated sigh.

"This is fishy as all hell," I stated, then waited to see if Judy would have something to add, but since she only looked at me expectantly, I elaborated. "Let's put the written reports aside for a moment. Look at these photos. Do you see the problem I'm seeing?"

Judy followed my finger and gave them a good long look, then she posited, "They are made with an instant camera."

"Exactly," I nodded with approval. "These aren't screenshots from a security camera feed or long-distance photographs with a telescopic lens. Someone actually had to get up to the face of this woman with a bulky

Polaroid camera and had to take several photos of her, yet at the same time all they know about her is that she is an 'unknown swordswoman.' Look." I picked the accompanying papers up again and pointed at various parts in turn. "*Name unknown, affiliation unknown, didn't make contact with School officials, destination unknown...* According to this 'lead,' they had no idea who she is, where she's from, and what she's doing on the island, yet they just happened to have a dedicated paparazzi on the docks to take multiple photos of her even though the only strange part about her is the thing on her back, and we don't even know if it's a sword for sure. This makes no sense."

"I'd like to say maybe they took pictures of her by coincidence, but I don't think those exist anymore," Judy answered my musings with her own. "If they didn't know who she is, they would have no reason to take the photos. If they knew ahead of time and prepared for her arrival, then the lead you were given is a lie."

"Which one do you think is more likely?"

My dear assistant fell silent for a moment as she pondered, then said, "I think the latter. In fact, I believe it's reasonable to assume that all of the leads are either incomplete or purposefully misleading."

"My thoughts exactly," I agreed with a frown. "We already discussed the Research Society one. This one is also obviously fishy. I wonder if the Chimera sightings lead also has more than meets the eye?"

"At this point, I would bet on it."

I grunted in agreement, after which we both fell silent for a few long minutes as we reorganized our thoughts. Or at the very least that's what I was doing, and I was hoping Judy found the time to do so as well while she continued snuggling. Anyways, I ultimately let out a heavy breath and stated, "We need to be even more vigilant. It's obvious the old man is up to something."

"Maybe you shouldn't have picked a fight with him," my girlfriend replied with a flat voice, then added, "Speaking of which, I don't think I have scolded you enough."

"Not now, Dormouse," I soothed her by grabbing her by the waist again. "We have more important things to do now."

"I think making sure you stop making enemies out of the most power-ful people on the island is plenty important."

"About that... Remember how I joked about having poor impulse con-trol? I think there's more to it." My girlfriend once again gave me a look that said *go on*, so I did just that. "I told you I had felt irrationally irritable around Crowey and Sebastian in the past, right? I had the same reaction when meeting with the old man today. Furthermore, I was acutely aware of it, but my temper still got the better of me, and to be frank with you, I don't like it."

"So, you *have* reflected on your actions? That's a first."

"Ha-ha. Very funny," I grumbled, followed by a precisely timed roll of my eyes.

"Do you think it was the narrative influence? Can you describe it?" Judy inquired as she finally let go of me and took out her phone to take notes.

"Before that, I have a separate theory." She glanced up at me with a questioning frown urging me on, so I told her, "You see, you guys were talking about some kind of pressure emanating from the old guy, right? The thing I didn't feel at all. What if the two are related?"

"So you posit that, instead of feeling a psychological pressure, you get a hair trigger from the presence of powerful supernatural entities?"

"I think so," I confirmed with a nod. "The rate at which I was getting angry at the old man corresponded pretty well with the rate the rest of you got pushed back. As for the second point of data, I had a similar reaction whenever I met with Sebastian in the past, but ever since he stopped actively threatening me, I don't really feel especially irritable around him."

"You are still at each other's throats all the time."

"That is neither here nor there. Just because I don't get supernaturally short-tempered around him doesn't mean he stopped being annoying. Anyways, the point is that the source of my irrational irritation might not be the Narrative trying to screw with my head, just my unique way of dealing with magical influence."

"Possible," Judy relented with a conflicted look. "We should ask Sebastian to help test it."

"I guess we should, though I doubt he will be cooperative. But speaking of testing…" I paused for a moment as I considered how I should break it to her, but finally just said, "Listen, Judy, I think we should put our research into the mechanics of the world on hold, at least until we make sure everyone is safe."

"I agree."

"Well, I… Wait, did you just agree?"

"Yes," Judy nodded with a determined glint in her eyes. "As much as I hate to admit it, staying alive is more important than research."

"That's a peculiar way to put it…" I mumbled, but she didn't seem to care about my half-hearted objection to her choice of words.

"So, what are we going to do instead?"

"I'm glad you asked," I answered as I tried to stand up to pace, as I usually did during our discussions, but she didn't let me, so I resigned myself to the fate of continued cuddling. "First, we have to figure out the 'plot,' so to speak. Whether we are dealing with routes or arcs, think we can conclude that with Josh's exposure to the supernatural parts of the setting, the preambles, are over."

"I concur," Judy agreed. "If we presume a route structure, things should start happening around either Angeline, Amelia, or Neige. The Eleanor route is most likely off the table, since you snatched her up."

"It wasn't exactly my original intention to do so, but yes, you are correct. However, if it's an arc-based structure, we might see some completely different developments."

"Such as these plot hooks?" Judy gestured at the pages laid out next to us. I shook my head.

"Nah. Lord Grandpa gave these to me, so they are probably supposed to be side plots or background events. We should keep an eye on unusual things happening around Josh, and then, once we got a handle on the plot, then we can start coming up with countermeasures."

"Or we could play into it if it is beneficial," Judy proposed, and I gave her an ambivalent grunt in return. I mean, it could happen, but I doubted it.

"For now, let's try to solve the homework Lord Grandpa gave us. While we know these 'leads' are fishy, we have to figure out exactly how fishy they are. The Hub should help with the Research Society and the swordswoman. As for the possible Chimera, should we ask the Dracis for support?"

"Sebastian is always concerned about the family's safety, so I think he will cooperate, so long as you don't pick another fight with him."

"I won't make any promises."

Judy gave me a flat look, but then she wisely decided not to retort, and instead she continued with, "Should we also tell them about the alleged Knight?"

"No," I replied immediately. "We don't even know if she is hostile, let alone one of the Knights. First, we should make contact and determine where she stands. If she is not a Knight, siccing Sebastian on them could cause an incident. If she is a Knight and she poses a threat to Elly and her family…"

I purposefully didn't finish my sentence. Not for dramatic effect, but because of the realization that I really didn't know what I would do. I mean, I didn't want to fight per se. I had a strong inkling that this was a world where supernatural battles were common, but I'd had my fill of those during the last weekend. If at all possible, I would've preferred if someone else did something about her. Like, say, Josh. I mean, he was the designated hero, so it was about damn time he did something heroic, and based on my memories of his capabilities as a pseudo-Draconian during the school incident, he should be more than capable to do so.

Speaking of Josh, that reminded me of another issue.

"The Hub has a list of emergency safe houses for Celestial operatives, right?"

Judy gave me a tentative nod.

"Next time you are up, please look into them and how we can appropriate one, preferably a spacious one that we could use as a hidden training ground."

"I already have two in mind," my girlfriend replied with a somewhat conflicted expression. "But wouldn't taking a physical property like that be risky? We might get found out."

"We'll figure that out. Maybe we can fake some reports saying that the Magi found the place and keep it under surveillance or something. Be creative, and I'll back you up with the authority of Admin."

"I'll try." Judy sounded less than enthusiastic, but she still proceeded to type a small novella into her notes.

"We should get it ready by the weekend, Sunday at the latest. The sooner we can get Josh to act like a proper battle-ready, hot-blooded shounen protagonist, the better."

"I think he wouldn't be happy to hear your plans. Also, don't plan anything on Sunday. We are going to have our first proper date then."

"Oh, right," I muttered as I recalled my girlfriends' earlier declaration, then I quickly added, "Let's try to set things up by Saturday so we can relax on Sunday then."

"That's the plan."

"Great. Speaking of plans, here's a rudimentary one: We double-check all the leads on the Hub. Then we'll contact Sebastian about the Chimera. Then we secure a secret hideout where we can train Josh and learn about everyone's abilities in a controlled environment. Finally, we should make contact with the swordswoman to see who she is and what she's after." I paused, as I suddenly had the distinct impression I was forgetting something really obvious, but then the gears in my head finally clicked and I hastily added, "Of course, Snowy's paperwork should come before all that. I don't want the police or some government agency with an on-the-nose acronym to get involved. As ridiculous as it may sound, at this point I feel more confident about dealing with the supernatural authorities than the mundane ones. To give you an example, I have no idea how I could get Snowy legally out of a jail."

"You can do it illegally?" Judy inquired, glancing up from her phone with an expression that was half intrigued and half exasperated.

"Well, yeah. I mean, I can just teleport in and teleport her out, right? It would make her a fugitive, though, and that would put a damper on our school life adventures."

"Oh, that," she muttered flatly.

"That indeed," I answered with a toothy smile. "Now then, I think my first priority should be finding someone who can forge some new papers for Snowy."

"Do you actually know someone like that?"

"Well, no, I don't..." I answered with a slightly mischievous smirk. "But I happen to know a guy who does."

CHAPTER 7

PART 1

I shivered for a moment after the longest, and second most nauseating, teleportation experience I had since I'd discovered this new ability of mine. Unlike the previous occasions, when I only felt the world blur for a blindingly fast second, this time the process felt like swimming through molasses. It wasn't as bad as when I tried to teleport outside of my "range" while running away from the Chimera, but it was a close second. There didn't seem to be other complications, though, so I quickly focused my attention on getting my churning stomach under control, an endeavour not helped by the thick, musty stink of excrement, sweat, and blood in the air.

While I steadied my breathing, my eyes adjusted to the dimness of the environment, and I had to conclude that the place was just as oppressively dreary as I had seen it through my Far Sight, though that didn't prepare me for the stench. I was, for lack of better descriptors, inside a *dungeon*. Not the fantasy kind, with labyrinthine tunnels and goblins and treasure chests, but the bona fide medieval kind.

On my left and right, I could see a worn (yet inexplicably clean) cobblestone corridor running so long, I could not see either end under the poor lighting conditions. In fact, the only light sources I could find were the ancient-looking doors made of metal bars set into the stone walls at regular intervals, though I had a feeling their enchantment-light was something only I could see. A soft purple glow seeped through the dark, fetid, and quite malodorous place, and it didn't help the eeriness factor one bit. To be honest, just then I wouldn't have been surprised if someone started screaming from the top of their lungs and shaking a bunch of chains just for the sake of ambience.

Anyways, in case the description doesn't make it abundantly clear, let me spell it out right here and now: I was currently inside the high-security jails of House Inanna. Well, "high-security" by medieval standards, as there were no cameras or even magical surveillance of any kind in sight. Or guard posts. Or guards, for that matter...

On second look, the whole place looked downright primitive and about as secure as a padlock made of papier-mâché, but hey, maybe they had a good reason for locking up their prisoners in a musty old dungeon instead of a state-of-the-art detention center. I mean, besides being anachronistic for kicks. You can never know.

At any rate, since I managed to get my nausea under control, I decided to put the motivations of the local non-demons aside, and focused on the actual reason behind my unannounced visit to this fine establishment. I crept towards the closest cell door and peered through the bars. It was about as grim as you would expect from a stereotypical old-school prison cell, with nothing but a stone floor, a bed seemingly made of random planks, and a single bucket in the corner. After taking in the scenery (and ignoring the bucket's contents), I focused my attention on the bed, or rather, the huge shape resting there under a thin, brown sheet.

"[*Greetings to you, scout-general,*]" I spoke in a series of familiar guttural grunts that made my throat tingle with effort. The moment I did so, the body under the sheets shuddered and I could see a head slowly turn in the darkness, topped by a curiously swiveling sheep-like ear. After a tense silence, the rest of his body started to move as well, as the large Faun slowly sat up and let his sorry excuse for a blanket fall aside.

To be perfectly honest, I expected Brang to be in bad shape, but he seemed to be mostly fine. He'd exchanged his armour for a pair of glowing violet shackles on his wrists, but otherwise he was no worse for wear. Said bindings were connected by a slightly translucent chain that reminded me of the one they'd used to tie up Josh, except this one was actively pulsing with magic or whatever. His softly glowing eyes scanned the cell before finally settling on me on the other side of the bars. He cocked his head to the side in a familiar and very human gesture, belying the fact that he was a huge half-ram-person built like a proverbial brick shithouse.

"[How curious,]" he whispered in a deep, raspy voice that still managed to boom like he was talking into a tube. "[I never thought my mind would start playing such tricks on me after only a few meager days. This is quite distressing.]"

I gave the Faun a long, skeptical look, but since he didn't seem to get the clue, I let out a tired breath and told him, "[Alas, you would not be capable of repudiating your connection with your snow-haired mistress even if you endeavoured to do so.]"

"[Truly?]" he replied with a guarded tone, his thick brows furrowed in confusion.

"[Verily. Your words upon laying eyes on me were as like to hers as her countenance is to a mirror's reflection,]" I muttered, once again annoyed by the verbose Faun language.

Brang let out a curious sound as he stood up and took a slightly unstable step towards me, his gaze fixed on me.

"[Is that thou truly, Leonard Blackcloak?]"

"[In both flesh and bone,]" I replied with a small sigh, then hastily added, "[Though before we share words, I would request that you cease to address me by that title, as it incurs untold amounts of embarrassment.]"

"[It is thee, indeed,]" he concluded, flashing me one of those huge, toothy smiles that made me instinctively want to take a step back. "[Thy visit is unexpected, but in no way an unpleasant surprise. Courtesy would dictate that I invite you in, but I fear I have misplaced the key."]

I couldn't help but smile in amusement at his words.

"[I'm glad to see your spirit suffered little in your captivity. Speaking of such, I have come here to inquire about a matter regarding the-one-whose-name-means-snow."]

At this point I paused to clear my throat, mostly to mask my aggravation at the Faun language's continued inability to express nicknames.

Brang's ears flicked back in apprehension.

"[Is the heiress safe?]"

"[Naturally. While the events have inflicted a great toll on her, she-whose-name-is-snow presently rests under my protection in my abode.]"

"[Is that so?]" Brang whispered in relief. "[My words mean no offense, yet while thy promise in front of the gate to our land eased my fears, I am nevertheless greatly relieved that the Wingless Lords have not discovered the heiress.]"

"[As a matter of fact, they have... but only in the case that your words refer to the leeches-of-the-lines-of-power,]" I answered, only to nearly roll my eyes. How my original words—"the mages"—turned into *that* by the time they left my mouth was a mystery.

The Faun's eyes widened, then grew confused. "[They have?]"

"[Yes. We did not wish for her to live as a runaway, therefore we informed their house of learning, and they have placed her in my care. She shall live with me for the future which is foreseen, and I shall shelter her as her patron.]"

"[Truly?]" he uttered incredulously, so I gave him an emphatic nod. He fell silent. Then his shoulders seemed to lose some of their tension as he told me, "[I have lived for many seasons, yet I've never heard of such a thing. I can't help but wonder in what manner thou hast accomplished this.]"

"[It is a long and intricate tale; I can tell you that with the utmost confidence.]"

"[Is that so? Then I believe it is a wonderful coincidence that I have no pressing matters that could come between me and listening to thy telling!]"

"[That may be, but before we discuss my less-than-illustrious exploits, I ask you to enlighten me about the reason behind your current predicament.]"

The Faun raised a single questioning brow (which annoyed me a little, as even he was better at it than I), so I continued with, "[To speak my words with pure honesty, when I embarked on this meeting, I expected not to find you in the bowels of the earth. How did you come to be in this place?]"

"[Aye, thy question is justified. The Chasm of Desolation is not a place one would, or indeed could, enter without good reason.]" Brang blinked and gave me a strange look. "[Speaking of such, I cannot help but wonder about thy presence before me at this very moment. Truly curious.]"

"[Tell me your tale, and I may even let you witness my ways firsthand,]" I answered with a not at all cocky grin, earning me an amused snort from the Faun.

He stroked his beard and said, "[As fair a trade as any, I suppose. Indeed, my tale be not long. It started on the night we last met. Upon our return from the world above, the uproar following my liege's defeat shook House Inanna to the core. Since I was the only officer of the Faun Inanna present, my liege and the elders of the House required my accounting of the events that night. My chronicle of the incident was thorough and true, thus I was immediately found guilty of dereliction of duty, and treason of the highest order. In short order, I was stripped of my rank among the Faun Inanna and then cast into the Chasm of Desolation, as is tradition.]"

"[Please restrain your beasts of burden!]" I interrupted him with yet another badly mangled translation, but I barreled through with, "[Correct me if I am mistaken, but according to rumors, your liege has laid the blame his failure of epic proportions upon my and my comrades' undeserving shoulders. Could it be that you have become yet another scapegoat in his schemes?]"

"[While it is not my place to criticize the actions of my liege, alas, I can do little to deny thine accusations. Indeed, I may have been cast aside, but such is the price of failure among my kin. At the very least, my brood siblings have escaped the same fate.]"

"[Hardly something I should call linings made of silver,]" I grumbled. "[How long will your sentence last?]"

"[That be a peculiar question to ask,]" he told me, once again petting his beard. "[I believe it would be accurate to say it shall last until the candle of my life is snuffed out, which shall happen rather sooner than later. Last I have heard from my wardens, my public execution shall commence within the week.]"

It took me several seconds to actually digest Brang's words, then I exclaimed, "[You must be excreting me!]" I blinked once in surprise then once more in exasperation. But I heroically suppressed my annoyance and said, "[Very well. While I admit that my reasons behind seeking you out were for my benefit, I will not permit you to suffer the indignity of death over the pettiness of a craven liege! You need but ask, and I shall extract you from this hole, or whatever you call it!]"

Brang gave me a strange look and, to my utter shock and confusion, he shook his head.

"[I appreciate thine offer, but while my liege indeed placed the burden of guilt upon me in excess proportion, he was not mistaken in his assessment of the nature of my crimes. I not only granted thee opportunity to interfere with his plans, but thou did so with mine own weapon. Such actions indeed be a dereliction of duty, and I did so knowing that I might receive due punishment for them.]"

"[Bovine excrement!]" I exclaimed. "[Did we not already conclude that it was only your liege's twisted scheme that placed the blame upon you? You attempted to stop me, and I overcame you in the Rites of Dominance, earning the right to wield your weapon. None of it was your willful doing.]"

"[It might be so...]" Brang muttered with a difficult expression, but after a short while he pursed his lips into a thin line and then said, "[Alas, he is my liege still. His verdict spoken, his words become my law.]"

I was about to object again, but then I stopped myself and took a deep breath instead. As I recalled, the Fauns were something of an honour-bound warrior culture, or at the very least Brang was a blatant example of a "proud warrior race guy," and yes, that was an actual character archetype. Trope semantics aside, I had already run into this problem the last time I met this guy and tried to convince him to let me go. Back then, I managed to twist his code of honour just a little bit to give myself a fighting chance, and considering how dour and uncooperative he was right now, I concluded I'd probably have to do it again. Thankfully, this time I already had a good idea in mind.

As such, I let out a provocative huff and directed a serious gaze at him.

"[Very well, then. In that case, could you please enlighten me as to this question: if my memory serves me well, you told me you are no longer a scout-general of the Faun of House Inanna?]"

"[Aye,]" Brang readily agreed.

"[Please advise me if my words ring untrue, but would that not mean that the-one-whose-hair-is-the-colour-of-crows has dismissed you from his service?]"

"[A Faun's service to the House never ends, not even in death,]" the big guy gave me an answer that sounded like some kind of recited dogma with a somewhat guarded voice, as if he were already aware that I was about to try to twist his honour code.

"[A truly admirable trait, but you must have misunderstood my words. I did not claim he dismissed your service to the *House Inanna*, but to himself.]"

"[I understand thy words, yet...]" he furrowed his brows, seemingly deep in thought, "[I believe I can see what thou attempts to say. Stripped of my rank and role by the liege, I no longer need to serve *him*. Yet, as one of the Faun Inanna, I shall forever serve the House, and he *is* the head of the House Inanna.]"

"[But not the House itself,]" I countered with a little more confidence once I was sure I had a foot in the door. "[As such, even if the craven one casts you aside, would serving another member of the House not uphold your obligations?]"

"[Aye, it would...]" Brang muttered with a really conflicted expression, as if he couldn't believe the words coming out of his mouth.

"[It is quite reasonable, is it not? Since he no longer requires your services, I see no reason why you should not acquire a new master within the House Inanna.]"

Brang fell silent for quite a while after this, visibly wavering, then he said, "[While thy words are not entirely composed of sophistry, I fail to see how such an act would improve my prospects. No vassal of House Inanna would shelter one such as I against the wishes of the liege.]"

"[When have my words ever referred to a vassal?]" I asked with a knowing grin.

The ex-general tilted his head.

"[You mean the young heiress, do you not?]"

"[Indeed I do,]" I answered, my smile growing even wider. "[Were you to return to her side, you would still serve her house, would you not? And should the crow-haired-one still wish to hold sway over your fate, he would need to order the one you serve, and she would certainly not allow you to meet an early demise at his hands.]"

"[Art thou certain of thy words?]"

"[As certain as I am of the sun that rises on the east and rests on the west,]" I said waxing poetic, though to be honest, most of it was just the Faun language using flowery words to interpret my meaning.

"[Hm.]" Brang grunted and the soft glow in his eyes dimmed to a pinprick, probably as he thought really, really hard. I didn't know why he did it, as the answer was really obvious to me, but I was not an honour-bound warrior race guy, so I had no idea exactly how much mental anguish he could be under at the moment. My guess was *a lot*, by the way. At long last, the light literally returned to his eyes and he muttered, "[Tell me, dost thou know of the heiress's curse of obedience?]"

"[Naturally,]" I answered with a nod. "[It was already removed by the efforts of her own hands and the support of my comrade.]"

"[Truly?]" I nodded at his surprised question, but then his shoulders slouched again and he told me, "[Alas, while it fills me with joy to know the heiress no longer labours under the yoke of the head of the House...]" He paused for a moment, and after patting his beard a bit more, he let out a rumbling breath. "[This is no decision that should be reached on a whim. I shall contemplate its ramifications to—]"

"[Brang,]" I spoke sternly. The huge Faun shuddered like I just hit him on the head with a hammer. Since this was the first time I'd used his name, I was afraid I might've unwittingly stepped on a random supernatural social faux pas landmine, but since he only kept staring at me expectantly, I cleared my throat and told him, "[I was under the impression that time was a commodity of which you had very little in your possession. Are you certain that spending it on such frivolous pondering is wise?]" I didn't really get any reaction out of him, so I hastily added, "[Especially when your mistress requires your service.]"

The ex-general studied me in silence, but then his huge shoulders slouched.

"[Aye, Blackcloak. Thy words are like honeyed venom, but they ring true all the same.]"

"[I take offense at such slander!]" I objected. "[Furthermore, I already requested for you to stop referring to me by such a title!]"

Brang's smile only widened at my vehement protests, but the movement of his ears told me he was at least a little agitated.

"[Indeed, thou hast done so. Now, might I inquire about thy method of allowing my flight from this room?]" his eyes wandered the cell before his gaze returned to me. "[While I admit the quiet of this pit of darkness is soothing, and the food my wardens provide is not the worst I have ever consumed, if I were to leave my present accommodations, under no circumstances would I mind doing so with haste.]"

"[The meaning of your words has not escaped me,]" I grumbled as I took a step towards the door, and I was just about to touch the bars to see if poking them with my anti-magic finger thing had any effect when I froze in my tracks and an admittedly mischievous smile formed on my lips.

Actually, if I was here already, why didn't I cause some extra headache to Crowey and his posse? I mean, breaking the door would be neat, but when I tried to imagine how hopping mad they would be to figure out how Brang disappeared from his cell without any trace, I decided to use a slightly more subtle approach. However, before I did so, I had to ask one last question.

"[Before I proceed to let you out of your cage, might I ask if you have any unfinished business in the Abyss?]"

"[Unfinished business?]" Brang muttered, then he chuckled. "[Aye, I have.]"

"[You do?]" I replied with a raised brow. I really only asked to be polite before I took him out of the Abyss. This was a surprise.

"[My spear lies in the hands of my brood siblings. If I am to serve my heiress once more, it is only natural that I should recover it first.]"

"[I see…]" I mumbled with a resigned sigh. I extended my hand towards him through the bars of the door. "[Is it within your means to recover your weapon once I let you out of this cell?]" The Faun gave me such a huge nod, it looked like he wanted to head-butt me through the bars. I once again restrained my primal instincts telling me to step back and instead gestured for him to step closer. "[If so, then hold on to my hand.]"

"[Aye,]" Brang agreed with unusual enthusiasm, and in retrospect I realized it was probably because he mistook my outstretched hand for a hot-blooded manly gesture of brotherhood or something.

In any case, he grabbed hold of my forearm with a grip that was just firm enough to be only slightly painful. Making sure not to flinch, I swiftly extended my phantom limb from my hand, slipped it through the bars, and wrapped it around the huge Faun's waist.

He gave me a weird look, as I didn't grasp his forearm back—partially because his shackles were in the way, but mostly because even with my finger extended, my phantom limb was just barely long enough to get a proper hold of him.

For a second, I wondered if I should ask him to step closer, but I wiggled my invisible tendril a bit more until I was sure he was secured for transport. At last, I activated my Far Sight and initiated a tiny teleportation, just enough to get the big guy out of the cell. One unceremonious moment later, I stood in the corridor with a very confused Faun.

"[There,]" I told him with a reassuring grin, but he didn't react, instead his ears and eyes were twitching all over the place.

"[What manner of trickery is this?]" he gasped.

I shrugged.

"[I told you I would release you from your captivity, did I not?]" I asked, then took a look at his shackles. "[Now that I speak of granting you freedom, I believe it is best I remove your bindings as well.]"

Although he looked at me funny, instead of bombarding me with questions, Brang simply extended his hands and gave me a small nod, as if to urge me to go ahead. Considering I still hadn't done enough experiments on the dispelling capabilities of my phantom limb, I decided to try looping it around the ethereal chain connecting the two manacles and yanking on it.

With a metallic *tink* and a brilliant flash, the manacles disintegrated into purple dust. The metal cuffs followed suit, scattering iron dust around the corridor.

Brang let out a pent-up breath and massaged his wrists with a somewhat sheepish expression.

"[Forgive me for being presumptuous, but might I ask thee to explain how thou accomplished such a feat?]"

"[It was but one of my less common abilities. Once you enter into the service of the-one-whose-name-is-snow, you shall have many opportunities to see it again.]"

"[Truly? How intriguing, to see something new and unexpected at my age.]"

He readily accepted my explanation, so I let out a silent, relieved sigh. In retrospect, I knew nothing about how the magic of those manacles actually worked. I could have just as easily triggered a self-destruct sequence to free him. Fortunately, everything turned out fine, so I decided not to dwell on it.

"[Are you going to be able to leave this place on your own, or do you require further assistance?]" I asked my towering companion.

"[Nay, I may be old and disgraced, yet I, Brang Shadowfeet, already have all I need to carve a path for myself.]"

"[I am... uh... most certainly glad to hear that. I shall find you once you have recovered your weapon and whatever other business you may wish to attend to before leaving.]"

"[Truly? Should we not agree on a site of meeting?]" the Faun inquired with a somewhat skeptical expression.

"[Worry not. I have found you once, I shall find you again.]"

Brang considered that, then he let out a subdued chortle as he turned around and raised his hand in a lazy wave. A familiar cloud enveloped his whole body and distorted his silhouette. His outlines melted into the darkness of the hallway, and only then did I let out a bottled-up sigh.

Right. I hadn't asked him about the document forger, but I figured I'd have plenty of opportunities to do so once I brought him over.

Speaking of which, now I had a brand-new reason to establish a secret base. While Brang was surprisingly amicable, I didn't want him living in my house, too. I mean, letting Snowy stay over was one thing. A giant half-ram muscle-bound warrior doing the same was something else entirely.

Anyways, I closed my eyes. *Should I go home or stick around and use Far Sight to keep an eye on Brang?* I wondered. Various red dots filled my vision, and one in particular caught my mind's eye. *Hello, you.* I hadn't been paying much attention to that one lately, and now that I did, an impish smile crossed my face.

Brang'll be fine, and I've got no reason to go home in a hurry… And since I'm here already, why not cause a little mayhem? My smile deepened with just a hint of malice as I disappeared from the prison without a sound.

PART 2

"Hi, Dormouse, I'm home!" I loudly announced as I arrived back in my room while simultaneously clamping on to a certain deadpan girl's waist from behind. I didn't know whether it was the voice or the sudden physical contact, but Judy immediately let out an uncharacteristic (if admittedly pretty gosh darn cute) *Eep!* sound, followed by a moment of silence.

"Chiiiief?" my assistant asked in a flat yet somehow still threatening voice and glanced over her shoulder. "Could you stop doing that? Do you want to give me a heart attack?"

"Oh, please! You complained that I wasn't acting like a proper boy-friend, so the first thing I did after coming home was to embrace you, and yet this is the reaction I get? I'm hurt."

"No, you are not." Saying so, Judy deftly turned around while still in my embrace so that we were face-to-face. Or rather, face to neck due to the height difference, but I decided it was a semantic question worth ignoring. There was something slightly harder to ignore happening at the same time, though. Due to our close proximity, I was once again reminded of the fact that while Judy might not have had the glamorous proportions of Elly or the sheer bust size of a certain class rep, she sure as hell wasn't flat, either, as the soft sensation on my abdomen readily testified. That, combined with her upturned eyes, made me smile wryly back at her.

"You are in high spirits," she noted.

"Does it really look like that?" I asked back.

"Yes." My dear girlfriend nodded. Then her brows ever so slightly fur-rowed. "Where have you been?"

"Didn't I tell you?"

Judy shook her head.

"No. We were talking about doing something about Neige's missing papers, then you said *I happen to know a guy who does* something. After that, you stared at the wall for a few seconds, then you told me, *I have to go now, I will be back in a moment,* and then you stood up and disappeared."

"That was a terrible impression of me," I grumbled.

"Really? I think it was highly accurate."

I wanted to ask *Since when do I sound like a posh British aristocrat?* but seeing her completely serious expression, I decided not to press the issue, lest the discussion would get derailed into oblivion, so I gave a noncommittal, "If you say so," and called it a day.

"So, where did you go?" Judy inquired again.

I let her go and went over to my bed, then gestured for her to sit with me.

"Okay, listen to this! It all started with using Far Sight on Brang," I told her with a mischievous smirk as I took a seat.

"Wait. Brang was the Faun," Judy stated.

"Yes," I answered with a small nod, though I quickly realized it was a statement instead of a question.

"The Faun who returned to the Abyss with the rest," she stated again, brows slowly slanting down into an angry frown I couldn't really understand. Still, I nodded in the affirmative, at which point her expression went even more deadpan than usual. Then she raised a hand for a somewhat clumsy facepalm and groaned. "Chief, please tell me you didn't actually teleport into the Abyss."

"Um... I actually did..."

"The actual Abyss. Where Neige came from."

"Yes. Is there another one?"

Judy apparently didn't find my comment amusing, as she kept staring deadpan daggers at me.

"Chief," she suddenly started, then just as abruptly paused, only to finally grumble, "do you ever think *anything* through before doing it?"

"Excuse me?" I asked back, a little baffled by her reaction.

"You still don't understand. How can you can be so smart and yet so careless at the same time?"

"Okay... let's say I admit that I am a bit of an idiot and I have absolutely no idea what you are going on about right now. Would you please explain it to me like I'm five?"

Judy gave me a withering look (once again, by her standards) and crossed her arms.

"Very well. I will walk you through this one. Where did you go?"

"Um... to meet Brang?" I reiterated, and she gestured for me to continue, so I ventured, "To the Abyss?"

"Yes," she said with a stern nod. "What is the defining characteristic of the Abyss?"

"It's full of Abyssals?" I guessed, still a little lost. Since that didn't seem to be the answer she was looking for, I continued with, "It's a prison? For the Abyssals?"

"Close enough," she relented. "What keeps them there?"

"The barrier," I answered reflexively.

"Yes, the impenetrable barrier designed to keep the Abyssals sealed inside. Do you start to see the issue yet?"

"I... um... It's only *mostly* impenetrable," I protested somewhat feebly. "I mean, I got in without too much problem."

"But you didn't know that ahead of time," she once again stated with 100 percent certainty, and while I wanted to protest, I really couldn't, as she was correct. Judy let out a tired breath and added, "Furthermore, even if you knew you could enter with your teleportation ability, there was no way for you to know you could come back. Am I right?"

"Well... yes, you are right," I admitted, averting my eyes.

"Did you consider this before you teleported there?"

"No."

"Do you understand now why I am angry with you?"

"Kinda."

For a few seconds, there was a heavy silence between us, but thankfully it didn't last too long, as Judy once again raised her hand to her forehead.

"Chief, I suspected this much in the past, but this incident made it certain: You lack even a semblance of risk assessment. You jump into action on a whim without first measuring the possible negative consequences. For example, imagine that you could teleport into the Abyss, but the barrier did what it was designed for and stopped you on the way out. What would you have done then, trapped in there? You had no money, no way to contact us, no connections over there, and one of the Lords absolutely hates you with a passion. Did you think about how you could've been hunted, captured, or worse? Did you think about how that would've affected the rest of us? Did you even consider how it would affect me if you suddenly disappeared with no way to contact you?"

"I... I'm sorry," I apologized before I even knew it. I was thinking about multiple ways to refute her while she spoke, but in the end, I couldn't say any of my excuses. "I suppose I really didn't think this through. At all." At this point, I glanced back at her and tried to give her a winning smile while saying, "But on the bright side, things turned out fine, and we even learned that I can enter and exit the Abyss at will."

"Yes, but what about the next time? Or the time after that? If you don't think things through and keep jumping into possible danger like that, it's only a question of time before things don't turn out so well, and then what? Chief, you have only one life. You can't risk it like that."

"Yeah, but… what am I supposed to do? I'm not a supercomputer that can predict the outcomes of my every action."

"That's why, from now on, every time you make a decision, you must turn it in for me to approve. In triplicate."

That comment immediately made me raise a clumsy eyebrow.

"Are we still having a serious discussion? I could swear that a moment ago, we were having a serious discussion. Did I miss a page? Is this still on?"

My girlfriend gave me an unsubtle roll of the eye and promptly sat down beside me.

"Yes, we are still having a serious discussion. I just know that if I don't lighten the mood every once in a while, you're going to throw in a non sequitur to do so, and it will completely derail the conversation for the foreseeable future."

"I wouldn't…" I began but then stopped myself. "Actually, now that I think about it, I probably would. Huh. It appears you know me better than even I do."

"Naturally." Judy nodded as she sidled closer to me. Then her expression became serious again. "I just want you to be aware of the fact that you are an irredeemable hothead who doesn't think anything through, and because of that he ends up in ridiculous situations. Like almost voluntarily trapping himself in our local underworld. Or having two girlfriends."

"I get it, I get it! Geez!" I moaned with a bit of theatrical flair.

"I'm glad to hear it," Judy responded with a nod and an expression that didn't seem confident in me at all. "So, what did you do in the Abyss?"

"Oh, right, I haven't told you that yet, have I?" I mused very thoughtfully, which definitely wasn't a ploy to buy me some time to gather my wits and figure out how to break the news to her.

"You haven't."

"Soooo… I told you that I went to see Brang, right?"

"Yes. I reckon it was because Neige mentioned him earlier today."

"That's right. I went to the Abyss to learn the identity of the document forger they used the last time."

Judy gave me a blank look, followed by a defeated sigh.

I frowned. "What? What's the problem?"

"Chief, we have the Celestial Hub at our fingertips. If you'd give me half an hour, I could've gotten you three of those."

"Yes, but if those guys are connected to the Celestials. It would leave a trace," I countered. "If we used one of their contacts, some hyperactive overachiever on the site might wonder where we learned of them, and even if they couldn't trace things back to us in particular, they might think there's a leak in the Hub and become more vigilant in the future."

Judy gave me a slightly skeptical look, but she soon relented with a reserved, "That makes sense. So much so that I think it's just another one of your post hoc rationalizations."

"Hey! I do consider things carefully... from time to time."

"You sure do," she replied with a voice made extremely biting by the lack of overt sarcasm, then she continued with, "So, did you learn where we can find a forger?"

"Erm, actually..." I stuttered for a moment, so I cleared my throat and spoke in a slightly more audible tone. "Actually, you know how Crowey put the blame on us for his colossal failure? Well, as it turns out, Brang was also made into a fall guy, and when I met him, he was locked up in this really old-school dungeon."

"The kind with goblins and treasure chests?"

"Nah, the medieval kind."

"Oh. The kind with chains, metal bars, and buckets then."

"Precisely!"

"So?"

"Weeeell..." I began while absentmindedly scratching the back of my neck. "You see, he got screwed over by Crowey and was about to be executed, and as we all know, the enemy of my enemy is my friend, so we had a long talk, and then..."

"And then you helped him break out of prison," Judy finished my line for me.

"Yup, though only a little. I just got him out of his cell; he said he could take care of the rest."

My girlfriend gave me another one of those really critical looks of hers, then she let out a small breath, presumably either in defeat or disappointment.

"So in short, you used your as-of-yet not fully tested teleportation ability to go into the Abyss to talk with a demonic-looking Faun who already tried to kill you, and you set him free."

"Yes, that is more or less accurate... except I wouldn't call Brang *demonic*, per se. I mean, he is big and kinda rammy, plus he has glowy eyes, and he lives in not-hell with the not-demons, and I'm going to shut up now before I dig myself even deeper."

My dear assistant shook her head again, and although the tiny twitch in the corner of her mouth didn't escape my notice, a moment later she was looking at me sternly once again.

"Did you at least get the identity of the forger out of him?"

"Well..."

Judy's eyes once again shone with naked skepticism.

"You forgot."

"Not really. I was just a little distracted by the whole jailbreak business." Judy didn't take that excuse well, so I hastily added, "Not to mention, it doesn't really matter, because we already agreed that I'd get him out of the Abyss and he would join us. After that, I can even get him to show me where to go in person."

"So. You hired the Faun who tried to kill you just a few days ago," Judy stated with a voice so flat it could be faxed.

"Technically, I only convinced him that it is in his best interest to swear allegiance to Snowy instead of her brother."

Over the span of several seconds, my assistant's gaze transformed from critical to resigned.

"Please tell me he isn't going to live in your house, too."

"Hell no!" I answered. "I mean, I like the guy, but there is no way he can fit in here."

"So?"

"I was thinking about having him live in our future secret base," I answered confidently. "After all, I need someone I can Far See to be present there so that I could teleport to the site. He can also guard the place against intruders, and he would have a roof over his head. Everyone wins."

"Another post hoc rationalization?"

"No, I... Wait, why was that a question?"

"Because I can't tell."

"Then how am I supposed to know? Didn't we already establish that you know me better than I do?"

"Now that you mention it, I suppose I do," Judy concluded with a nod. Then her eyes quickly narrowed in suspicion as she added, "And that's why I know you are not telling me something and trying to change the subject."

"Wait, really?" I blurted out in surprise. "I mean... I don't know what you are talking about."

"Come on, Chief, just say it. I promise I won't be too mad."

"That means you're still going to be a little mad."

"Oh?" Judy gave me a triumphant look. "So it is something I would be mad about! I knew it."

"I... walked right into that one, didn't I?"

"Splendidly," she agreed with a nod. "So, you were saying?"

"I'm not sure I want to anymore."

Judy didn't say anything. Instead she reached out and gently pinched my two cheeks and began ineffectually tugging at them. I let her do so for a few seconds while getting increasingly baffled, but when I couldn't take it anymore, I asked, "Okay, so, I know you are doing a *thing* now, but for the life of me, I cannot figure out what it is."

"I'm pulling your cheeks," she stated as if it was self-evident.

"Yes, I get that part," I grumbled. "I just don't get why."

"My research says it's a form of playful punishment that is also a sign of affection, particularly between couples."

"Really?" I wondered aloud, and on second thought, I did recall something similar, though the image that came to mind involved stretching the cheeks instead of, well, whatever she was doing at the moment. "I suppose there might really be something like that, but isn't that usually done to the girls?"

"That's sexist, and now you should be ashamed of your horrid male chauvinist ways," Judy stated with a deadpan voice as she continued to pinch my cheeks without actually causing even the mildest discomfort.

"Okay, at this rate, we are getting nowhere fast," I told her, quirking a smile, but then I raised my hands to her face and pinched her cheeks in turn. "See, I think this is how you are supposed to do it." Saying so, I very carefully stretched her cheeks a little, earning me a small frown.

"So I just have to put more strength into it," she concluded, somehow, and then she leaned in close.

Now, I would like to point out that by now I'd realized we were evoking a situation that would lead to either an awkward conclusion or a bucketload of sexual tension, but before I could do something about it, Judy put too much strength into her arms and not enough into her fingers, which led to her losing her grip on my face and then on her own balance as she fell forwards. Since I had my hands up at her face, which wasn't exactly the best body part to grab to stop someone's tumble, and since I knew that if I tried to lower my hands, it was guaranteed to lead to some embarrassing breast-related shenanigans, I wisely decided to open my arms instead and catch Judy in a bear hug.

She let out a soft, if quite obviously distressed sound, then she looked up from my chest with a strange expression on her face and asked, "What just happened?"

"Well, if I had to guess—" I began, but then the mysterious, yet at this point practically tangible forces of dramatic timing reared their ugly heads once again as a certain Abyssal girl opened my door without even knocking.

"Leo, I wanted to ask if—" Snowy stuck her head through the gap, but then her words came to an abrupt halt as she noticed us on the bed. "Am... am I intruding?"

I closed my eyes for a moment, stifling an annoyed chuckle, then gestured for her to stay.

"Nah, you aren't," I calmly told Snowy while letting go of Judy. But once we both sat down properly, I took my girlfriend by the waist again and pulled her a little closer, then said, "We are just being close, like usual."

"I see that," the flushed girl responded with an awkward smile.

"You said you wanted to ask something?" I quickly prompted her before we could lapse into a tense silence.

"Oh, you are right," my new housemate exclaimed with eyes wide open. "I want something clarified."

"I'm listening."

"So... Uh... You said I can have everything in the room, right?"

"Yes, that's what I said," I confirmed with a nod, wondering at her constant fidgeting.

"When you said *everything*, did you mean... all of it?"

"That's the definition of the word, yes."

"Really? Great!" she beamed in genuine delight, but then she quickly toned it back to her previous, slightly embarrassed expression. "I-I mean, thanks for the clarification! I'll go now and let you... um... be close? B-bye!"

With that, Snowy abruptly pulled her head back and shut the door with slightly more vigor than strictly necessary, leaving us in a strange silence.

"So, what do you think that was?" I cautiously asked to break the delicate atmosphere in the room.

"Very embarrassing," came the blunt answer from my ever so slightly flushed girlfriend.

"Really?" I reacted with measured incredulity. "I was a little surprised, but I wouldn't say it was *that* embarrassing."

"And that fills me with a profound sense of worry for our future," Judy grumbled, but then a moment later she glanced up at me and said, "Also, you still didn't tell me what else you did in the Abyss."

"Oh, fine," I grumbled. "It wasn't even *that* big a deal."

"Then you should have no reason to keep it from me," she countered, earning a defeated groan from me in the process.

"Okay, so here it is in a nutshell: I was already in the Abyss, right? So, after I parted with Brang, I realized if I was in the neighbourhood, I might as well pay a visit to Crowey."

"Please tell me you didn't do what I think you did..."

"Unfortunately I don't know what you think about, so I'll just tell you what happened. I spied on him for a while, and when the opportunity presented itself, I used my teleportation ability to sneak into his study just as he was leaving, and I made a bit of a mess there."

"Such as?" Judy asked, though the small twitch in the corner of her left eye told me she wasn't sure she wanted to hear the answer.

"Nothing serious. I mixed up a few of his parchments in the drawers, arranged the paperclips on his desk to look like a giant penis, wrote him a letter in fake blood, drew mustaches on the paintings in the room, that kind of stuff. Just harmless pranks."

The skepticism in Judy's disapproving stare was palpable.

"Chief, did you honestly think I would skim over the part with the fake blood?"

"Well, no, but it was worth a try," I answered with fake sheepishness.

"Where did you get the fake blood? And more importantly, what did you write?"

"Crowey had some... or at the very least, I really hope it wasn't real blood... but with him, you can never know. As for the contents of the letter..." I paused for a moment, mostly just to tease the cautiously expectant girl by my side, then went on and said, "Well, I figured causing some headache to the guy would help us in the long run, so I wrote him a very loquacious letter filled to the brim with ye-olde-English. You know, full of 'thy' and 'thou' and the like? Kinda how the Faun talk, but even more obnoxious."

"I understand, but what did you *actually* write?" Judy prompted me, obviously getting a little impatient.

"Oh, just more prank stuff about how his security was crap and that our assassins could end his life whenever we wanted but decided not to because he is so pathetic that keeping him as a Lord is better for us so that his place couldn't be taken by someone actually competent. Oh, and I made fun of his face and called him a nincompoop."

"You keep saying *'us'*..." Judy implied a question, though her tone told me she once again wasn't certain she wanted to know.

"Ah, that's the best part! I signed the letter in Celestial Script. Or at least I think I did. You know, even I don't really understand my knack for languages, right? Anyway, I wrote some random gibberish, though it probably won't matter, as the important bit is that he'll think it was done by the Celestials. Put all of that together, and I'm pretty sure he'll freak out for a while, focus on tightening his security, and hopefully delay his inevitable comeback. So, what do you think?"

With a really withering look, Judy delivered the silent treatment for several seconds. Then she let out a sharp breath and declared, with perfect seriousness, "You are making me think I need to produce those triplicate forms."

"Oh, come on, Dormouse!" I complained, but my pleas fell on deaf ears.

"I'm serious. You need to learn how to rein in your troublemaking impulses." As she said that she reached into her pocket and took out her phone. "I'll start by setting a few rules. Rule number one: *If it would make Judy angry at you, don't do it.*"

"Wait, are you actually writing those down?"

"Rule number two: *If it would make Judy annoyed, don't do it.*"

"You are serious…"

"Rule number three: *If it would cause a scandal between the supernatural powers, don't do it.*"

"Okay, just how many of these rules do you want to make?"

She thoughtfully tapped her chin, then stated, "About two hundred and twenty-one." Seeing my flabbergasted reaction, Judy gave me her version of a small smile and added, "Don't worry, we can discuss them all today. I already called my mother earlier and told her I'll be sleeping over at a friend's house."

"Hold on!" I objected with a raised hand. "You're telling me your parents agreed to let you stay over at my place, just like that?"

"Technically I am staying with Neige tonight. You just happen to live in the same house," she told me with a neutral expression that I was 200 percent sure had an impish grin hidden behind it. Then she casually raised her phone again and continued.

"Rule number four: *If it would—*"

As they say, desperate times call for desperate measures, and so I did the first thing that came to mind and grabbed hold of my assistant, much to her shock and surprise, and with a small heave, I placed her on my lap while declaring, "Oh, look at the time! It's cuddle-o-clock. We almost missed it! How about we continue this conversation *never?*"

Judy was quite flustered at first, then seemingly annoyed as she looked back over her shoulder and stared me in the eye. But when I flashed her my most winningest smile that has ever been smiled in the history of winning smiles, she looked as if she resigned herself and leaned back against my chest with a small shrug and an understated *"Fine."*

And that, ladies and gentlemen, was how I managed to avert disaster once again. Yay me.

However, just as I was about to congratulate myself, Judy whispered while typing, "Six in the evening is cuddle-o-clock. Noted."

And that, ladies and gentlemen, was how I managed to accidentally invent sanctioned daily cuddling time. Yay me?

CROWEY

"I want results!"

The strained, high-pitched roar of the wounded man echoed in the large, crowded bedroom, only to be immediately followed by a series of painful, wheezing coughs. None of the ten or so people in the room dared to utter a single word until the man in the bed finished.

They were all dressed in fine, if slightly eclectic, clothes ranging from modern suits to what looked like Victorian Era costumes. The only thing they wore in common were pale countenances filled with disbelief and uncertainty.

At last, a middle-aged man stepped forward. He was wearing what looked like a grey navy officer's uniform, with several black stripes on its sleeves. He had long, dark brown hair that reached down his back, and upon approaching the bedside, he bowed and respectfully told its occupant, "My liege, please calm down. Your previous injuries haven't completely healed yet, and you've also been poisoned. Losing your temper so will only hinder your recovery."

The man on the bed, the Lord of the Abyss, head of House Inanna, Noire Irdu Inanna—also colloquially known as Crowey or "that dick"—turned his withering glare towards the man.

"I wouldn't be losing my temper if I wasn't surrounded by incompetent buffoons," he seethed through clenched teeth, his voice rising until it reached a crescendo. "So *why* are you standing around my bed like a pack of vultures instead of looking for whoever is responsible for this… bullshit…!"

Crowey choked up at the end, seized by another violent coughing fit that turned his face purple. Or rather only one side, as the other was still wrapped up in layers of bandages covering the burns he suffered less than a week before.

At long last, his seizure abated, and after heaving several times, he croaked out, "Did you discover how they got into my study without any of your guards noticing a thing?"

"My deepest apologies, my liege, but we found no trace of the intruders," the middle-aged man answered with an apologetic bow. "None of the guards or servants noticed any intruders. The wards around the room are undisturbed, and neither the seals nor the locks show any kind of tampering. As for the insides of the study, we are currently unable to investigate in earnest. Lady Audra strongly insisted that no one should enter until the last traces of the Udug Blood Amalgam are neutralized by her men. The process may take days."

"Marvelous," Crowey scoffed. "And who is in charge of that damn letter?"

There was a long moment of pause before a young woman hurriedly stepped forward, like she just realized she'd been called. She had a youthful face with an upturned nose supporting a pair of round, thick-rimmed glasses, which was further emphasized by her outfit. She was dressed in a vampire cosplayer's wet dream with a fur coat on top. More significantly, however, her straight, shoulder-length hair was pitch-black on one side and a pinkish blonde on the other, meaning she was probably important in some way.

"It is also my responsibility, my lord," she stated in a low voice.

"Then speak," Crowey growled.

"Yes, sir, certainly," the woman sputtered, then she cleared her throat. "My men are still compiling the results of our test, but allow me to share with you our preliminary findings." She reached into her fur coat, slipping her hand just past her generous cleavage, and produced a folded paper.

"First, our experts have ascertained that the source of the Udug Blood Amalgam on the letter was the bottle our lord kept in the hidden compartment inside his desk. The beguilement, misdirection, and security wards have all been removed without any trace. We've also discovered that the culprit used our lord's fountain pen to write the letter. We've sealed all of these items for the time being. Based on the suffusion of the Blood Amalgam within the room, we estimate that the culprit wrote the letter last evening, between five and six o'clock."

"That's curious," interjected an older, grey-haired woman.

"What did you say, matron?" The middle-aged man gestured for her to continue.

"I find the circumstances surrounding the Blood Amalgam truly curious. It was a secret only our lord knew about, was it not? And it was hidden in a compartment impossible to find by chance."

"You mean to say that the culprit broke into our liege's study with the express purpose of using the Blood Amalgam?"

"Is there any other way to interpret this incident?" the woman responded with a disinterested shrug. "They must have already known not only where to find the poison, but also how to access it. There's no other way to explain what happened."

"True." The man in the navy uniform nodded. "Which would mean that this was a message. It was intended to show us they have infiltrated our estate so thoroughly, they are privy to even our most well-kept secrets."

"That would certainly agree with the contents of the letter," the busty woman agreed. "Maybe the two were supposed to reinforce each other?"

After some contemplation, the old woman nodded. "That is indeed likely. It would certainly fit the Celestials' modus operandi."

"Right!" exclaimed an old man with a big bushy beard. "What did that accursed script say at the end of the letter, anyway?"

"It's… please give me a moment… it was here somewhere…" The young woman rummaged through her pockets, slipping her hands around until she produced yet another piece of paper, which she quickly unfolded. "Yes, here it is." She theatrically cleared her throat and said, "After making sure the Blood Amalgam on the paper was properly sealed, we showed the final line to several of our experts on Celestial Script, including some of our collaborators. According to their assessments, the last line, which appears where the signature traditionally is signed, was written in an unusually complex, archaic dialect of High Celestial Script. After meeting with some difficulties during the translation process, our experts concluded that it was most likely an actual signature, consisting of four overlapping Sub-Scripts, most likely titles of the—"

"We don't need the history lesson, just tell us what it said," Crowey growled.

"Yes, my lord!" she hastily answered as she raised the paper to her eyes again. "The first part says, *The Second True Archon, Prince of the Blade and Sovereign of the Spear.*"

"'Archon'?" the man with the navy uniform repeated after her. "That isn't a rank amongst the Celestials."

"Not anymore, it's not," the old woman replied almost absentmindedly. "It hasn't been for centuries, if not for millennia. Not ever since the Celestials came to worship their false god."

"I can't make sense of this," the old man grumbled. "What about the rest?"

"The second part is a little vague, and our experts came up with multiple possible translations. The most likely one says, *A Conspiracy of Ravens.*"

"Conspiracy?" Crowey asked, baffled.

After some hesitation, a younger man sporting a crew cut and medieval cloth armour explained, "My lord, I believe it is not meant in the literal sense. It refers to the peculiar way a group of ravens is called."

"They call them a conspiracy?" the bushy bearded man asked skeptically.

"I believe so, yes."

"Huh. Learn something new every day."

"I'm glad to hear that, but we are still not any closer to the solution of this riddle," the long-haired man told his colleague with a disapproving frown.

"Let us hear the rest, maybe context can help," the old woman urged, and the dual-haired woman complied.

"Yes, matron. The third part was translated as *The One Who Rejects Your Reality and Substitutes His Own*."

The whole group fell silent.

"What the hell does that mean?" Crowey burst out, followed by a short but vicious coughing fit.

"I believe it's a quotation, my lord," the younger man answered confidently, but when everyone in the room gave him skeptical looks, he sheepishly added, "It's... from a human television show, I think."

"I thought it was from a parody cartoon on the internet," the busty woman added uncertainly.

"It's actually from an old low-budget movie, my dears," the old woman revealed with a nonchalant expression.

"Really? Matron is truly knowledgeable," the bearded man nodded repeatedly in approval, only to flinch when Crowey once again opened his mouth.

"Who the hell cares where that goddamn quote comes from? Can any of you bastards tell me *why* an assassin would sign his letter with one? Can you tell me that? No? Then shut up!"

After sitting through another coughing fit, the people in the room stayed true to their lord's command and remained completely silent, right until the man on the bed asked, in a slightly less sneering tone, "What's the last part?"

"I... I believe that it still requires some proofreading, so maybe your lordship should..."

"Tell me. Now."

Resigned, the busty woman said, "Yes... The last part is very complex, so this is certainly not the final translation—and our experts were sure there is some kind of hidden nuance or reference behind it, so..."

"Get on with it," the bearded man grumbled.

"Yes. Please just tell us as it is," the man in the navy suit agreed.

"Er... It says... *The One and Only True God of Grilled Cheese*..."

The whole room fell silent once again.

Crowey let out a sound halfway between a groan and gurgle. "I am surrounded by imbeciles..." He glared at each vassal in turn. "Do any of you have anything to say that wouldn't make me want to drown each and every one of you in a spoonful of vinegar?"

"Aaah!" the bearded man exclaimed as a shit-eating grin spread on his face. "Actually, my lord, I have good news!"

"Do you now?" the bedridden man scoffed.

"Yes, my lord! I didn't have the opportunity to report this until now, but we successfully tracked down the escaped convict and his cohorts! Warmaster Redmane has boxed them in within the servant quarters of the old armoury building. It's only a question of time before your loyal Fauns weed out the traitors from their midst!"

"At last, some actual competence," Crowey grumbled, though his expression lightened upon hearing the news, only for it to darken again a moment later. "Have you discovered how he escaped from the Hole?"

"No, my liege," the middle-aged man answered apologetically. "While we found the trail of the traitorous Faun after he left the prison, we couldn't determine how he escaped his cell or his bindings."

"Continue to investigate," Crowey ordered, paying no attention to the messenger quietly slipping into the room. "I want to know how he escaped. If you can find out how he did it, I might even be gracious enough not to have your inept guards skinned alive."

"I will do so," the man in the navy uniform nodded and then glanced towards the back of the room, where the bearded man was in the process of chasing out the messenger. "Is something the matter?"

"No," the other man denied quite suspiciously but quickly cracked under the pressure of so many gazes directed at him. He confessed, "My liege, I received... bad news."

"Clarify," the man in the bed demanded with an icy glare.

"Y-Yes. Er... I just informed you about the impending capture of the traitorous Fauns?"

"You did."

"Well, you see... they are gone."

"Has Redmane killed them all?"

"Er... No, my lord. I didn't mean that figuratively. They are *literally gone*. Like, at one moment they were inside the barricaded quarters, with no way in or out, and then a few seconds later, poof, they were all gone."

"You cannot be serious," the old woman muttered.

"I am," the bearded man huffed. "Even the 'poof' part. It's exactly what the messenger said."

"I—" the young woman tried to interrupt him, only to be interrupted by a quiet yet inescapable voice.

"Get out," Crowey whispered, and the air around him roiled with a black miasma.

"My liege, if you continue to use your powers, your injuries will—"

"I said, get out of my sight, you MISERABLE, USELESS SIMPLE-TONS!"

The man's voice swept through the space, and as it did so, the entire group backed out of the room, some more desperately than others. Soon the only person left was the bedridden Crowey, who was glaring at the closed doors with bloodshot eyes.

He lowered his eyes, only for his gaze to stop on the folded paper on the floor, no doubt left behind during his vassals' hasty retreat. Wincing, he made a few delicate gestures, and the paper fluttered up like it was hit by a gust of wind and drifted down on the bedsheets. Reaching out a shaky hand, he unfolded it and took a look at its contents.

"Second True Archon," he muttered as his fingers traced the words. "Sovereign of the Spear. Conspiracy of Ravens…"

He repeated the last translation a few more times, then his eyes opened wide as he muttered, in near delirium, "The note here says *conspiracy* means a *flock*. This note says the second part loosely means black birds. What if it isn't *ravens* but *crows*? Then that would make it a flock of crows, a…"

Suddenly the bedridden Abyssal Lord's eyes flared up with a colourless light that blasted the piece of paper, along with most of his bedding and the other end of the room, into shreds.

He howled, "A MURDER OF CROWS! CROWS! THAT MOTHERFU—!"

And that, ladies and gentlemen, was the point when I decided I'd spied on Crowey long enough for the day. I hoped this wouldn't bite me in the ass later (though I was fairly certain it would) and returned home with a sigh and an unexpected craving for grilled cheese sandwiches.

CHAPTER 8

PART 1

I stifled a yawn, which came more out of habit than actual sleepiness, and stretched my back as well for good measure. I was sitting in front of my PC at a little after 7 a.m. It was still quite dark outside my window, and the only source of room lighting was the harsh blue light of the computer screen. I made sure to move my joints, which were understandably stiff after sitting still for hours, as quietly as possible before I returned to the task at hand.

At the moment, I was organizing my older notes about my closest associates, plus making some updates in light of recent events. Actually, there were quite a lot of those that needed to be done. For example, the class rep had turned into a totally different kind of character after the incident, though I could probably chalk up the change in her behaviour to stress. Evidently, the people around me weren't static, and while that was somewhat reassuring to know (lest I once again get stuck in existential ponderings about narrative influences, consciousnesses, and other cheerful stuff like that), honestly, I would've preferred if she hadn't become so snarky. Why she had a bone to pick with me in particular, who knows, but for the time being, I decided to humour her.

Once I finished annotating Ammy's section, my eyes scanned through the pages again and stopped at Angie's entry. She... didn't change much, did she? Her behaviour was more or less exactly the same as before. Not even her house arrest and parole put a damper on her enthusiasm. Maybe she was a natural airhead like that? I mean, in a good way, not in a dumb way.

That aside, the other entry that caught my interest was Elly's. When I read through my old description of her, from even before we learned about the supernatural and her being a dragon-girl and whatnot, I couldn't help but chuckle. She used to freak out a lot, didn't she?

I kept reading, inserting addendums every here and there until I stopped at a very specific word. Near the end of her entry, there was a bolded *Tsundere?* written there, question mark included. That word hit me with nostalgia. The princess used to be so tense around me, with occasional outbursts of either aggression or affection, but lately all I was getting was the latter. That sounded somewhat familiar, so I minimized the text file and opened my browser instead. After a quick search, I found exactly what I was looking for, exactly where I expected it to be.

According to the trusty old site about tropes I'd been frequenting since day one, a *tsundere* was an archetype where someone starts out aloof and irritable—either because of a conflict of interest or being unable to deal with their attraction to another person—but then once those have weathered out, they become sweet and affectionate.

Is it just me, or does that description fit Elly to a T? According to the site, that would mean she was currently in her *deredere* phase.

"Deredere? Really?" I whispered, shaking my head in profound disapproval. Just who made up this terminology? Why couldn't these things have simple names for once?

Anyways, now I was back to thinking in meta-terms, much to my chagrin. The change in her behaviour more or less coincided with a tsundere's character arc, at least according to my sources. So… did she mellow out because she was *"designed"* by something or someone to be a *tsundere*, or is it that she had a prideful and tomboyish personality that led her to follow the arc of the archetype on her own?

I mean, I don't think I've ever heard her being… what was it again? *Tsuntsun*, I think?… irritable. Anyhow, the point I was trying to make was that she was fairly *deredere* towards Josh from the get-go and only showed her thorny side to me. If I look at it that way, could it be that she wasn't supposed to be a tsundere, but I turned her into one by my unwitting interference? A kinda scary thought.

Still, it was a distinct possibility.

I went back to the text file, and was about to write in my newest insights, when I glanced up to the previous entries, and my brows furrowed in response. At first, I tried to ignore the idea that had just reared its ugly head, but I couldn't, so I quickly read through the class rep's entry one more time, and by the end, cold sweat trickled down my back.

The rep… couldn't have turned into a tsundere, right? I mean, sure, she'd been pretty snarky with me lately, and had been talking with me way more than usual to deliver her barbs, but that didn't mean she was hiding her *dere* with that… right?

Oh damn, I really hoped she wasn't. Otherwise Judy would turn my life into an embarrassing mess with her anti-harem countermeasures. I mean, even more than she already did.

Right at that moment, as if somehow detecting I was thinking about her, a certain deadpan girl made a small sound as she turned under the blankets. I held my breath for a moment, only exhaling after I was sure her breathing was slow and steady once again, and then it came out as a sigh.

Yes, that's right: Judy wasn't kidding about staying over. Furthermore, once she was exhausted by our usual discussion about the day's events, the world we lived in, and random trivia about shellfish biology (don't ask why), she declared that, since I wasn't using my bed anyway, she would sleep there. Furthermore, she would do so in only her underwear! Well, that plus one of my unused shirts, à la Snowy, but really, it's almost the same. In fact, in some circles, that kind of getup would be considered even more erotic, so I really had to wonder if she was trying to tempt me.

No, scratch that. I was about 95 percent sure she was, what with all the weird sighs she made when she tucked herself into my bed. Ultimately nothing happened between us, partially because we'd promised Elly there would be no "lewding" yet, and mostly because Snowy was in the next room. Knowing our luck, she would've interrupted us once again. Since, according to Judy, even being seen during our chaste tussling was considered supremely embarrassing, she really didn't want to get seen doing something considerably less chaste. As such, she settled for a good night kiss.

Anyway, once I was sure she was still sleeping soundly, I turned back to my PC, only to immediately stop and listen. Since I was already paying attention to Judy's breathing, my ears were still perked. Without that, I doubt I would've noticed the barely audible shuffling sounds coming from downstairs. I listened closer.

Whiff, whuff, swish, swoosh.

Was that... sweeping?

But who? Snowy?

Using the radar mode of my Far Sight, I found that she wasn't in the room next door, but downstairs. Now, I was sure there were many reasonable explanations why she was up and about so early in the morning. I didn't want to overreact or anything, so I used my teleportation ability to move to the stairs with a quick hop.

Once there, I carefully inched forwards, and once I got a clear view of the living room, I almost fell over in shock and surprise, nearly exclaiming *There* are *ninja maids!* in the process. Fortunately (for my dignity), I managed to avoid doing both, as once my eyes adjusted to the lighting, I finally realized what, or rather *who,* I was looking at.

"Snowy?" I asked incredulously, prompting the contently humming girl to twirl around in surprise.

"Oh? Good morning, Leo!" she greeted me with unusual enthusiasm as she waved at me with a feather duster.

I gave her a nod in greeting and I quickly walked down the stairs so that I could take a better look at her. Let's not beat around the bush, though. Even from the top of the stairs, I could tell that Snowy was wearing a full black-and-white French maid outfit, complete with a frilly headpiece, a half-apron, and white stockings. I walked up, looked her over one more time, and couldn't help but ask the single most obvious question in the history of ever.

"So… what exactly are you doing?"

"I'm cleaning!" she answered me proudly.

"I can see that, but…"

Upstairs, my door creaked open, and a certain straight-faced girl walked towards the stairwell, rubbing one eye with the hem of my half-open shirt.

Judy halted at the top of the stairs, pretty much exactly where I'd been standing a few seconds before, and rubbed her eye again with a weird expression.

"Fetish?" she asked with an infuriatingly innocent tone, prompting me to face-palm.

"No! Also, please put on some clothes!"

My assistant glanced down at her quite exposed appearance, then hurriedly disappeared into my room.

With a sigh, I turned back towards the other girl complicating my life at the moment, and found her quite flushed. I was pretty sure she had some kind of weird misunderstanding running through her head, so I gestured for her to sit down.

"Take a seat. I'll make some tea and—"

"Wait, let me!" she interrupted me, and before I could say anything else, she rushed into the kitchen.

Giving up that fight, I took a seat on my usual comfy chair and waited. The first to come back was Judy, who walked down the stairs wearing her clothes from the day before. She apparently hadn't been to the bathroom yet, as her hair was slightly disheveled. Once she arrived downstairs, she glanced around the living room, then quickly made her way over to my side.

"What was that about?" she asked with a somewhat skeptical look in her eyes.

I shrugged.

"Don't know, either."

I was just about to add *Let's ask her when she's back*, when Snowy showed up with a tray, making my words redundant. Walking gracefully yet ramrod straight, she came over to us and set it on the coffee table in front of me, revealing not only the expected mugs, but also an honest-to-goodness porcelain teapot I didn't even know I'd had. More curiously, though, there were only two mugs present.

"Where's yours?" I asked, but Snowy only shook her head.

"I'm not supposed to drink at the same time you do," she responded once again like she was sharing common knowledge. I awarded her my most skeptical look, but she didn't appear to notice, so after a small groan, I got up, walked into the kitchen, and brought her mug over.

"Now sit down," I told her while placing hers next to the rest of the mugs, and even though she appeared hesitant at first, she did follow my instructions and took a seat on the couch. Judy also followed suit, sitting down beside her while showing obvious interest in her costume. Speaking of which, I lightly cleared my throat to get her attention, and then asked, "So, why are you acting like a maid?"

The Abyssal girl tilted her head to the side in a very familiar fashion (so familiar, in fact, that I wondered if she'd learned it from Brang or the other way around).

"I... I wasn't supposed to? But... I thought I was supposed to serve as one to pay my rent."

"What? No! And didn't we already discuss this 'rent' business to death?"

"But... but then why did you give me all those maid outfits?" she asked as if I was somehow betraying her expectations.

"When did I ever do that?"

"You said everything in the room was mine," Snowy responded with a pout.

"So?" I asked back.

"The wardrobe was full of maid outfits."

"It was?" I exclaimed as my brows rose with apprehension. After a moment of thinking, I told the girls, "Give me a second," following which I hurried up the stairs, only to return a few seconds later with a confused frown. "Well, I'll be damned. It really is full of maid outfits."

"So you do have a secret fetish?" Judy interjected a question that would've undoubtedly earned her a quick forehead flick if she was within arm's reach, but since she wasn't, I could only give her a harrowing look. Which she naturally ignored.

"No, it's not," I voiced my denial aloud before her imagination would run wild. In the meantime, I also gave the mystery of the wardrobe some thought and decided to venture a guess.

"Say, Judy, correct me if I'm wrong, but didn't you say Melinda was staying over to take care of Elly while I was unconscious?"

"Yes," she responded while sneakily filling her mug with tea.

"And she was staying in Snowy's current room, right?"

"I believe so, yes."

"So, what conclusion can we draw from that?"

Judy raised a thoughtful finger to her lips. "You asked her to leave her uniform behind so that you could indulge in your fetish?"

"Stop that!" I reprimanded her. "Also, come closer."

"Why?"

"So I can flick your forehead."

"I graciously refuse your invitation." She took a sip from her mug.

I shook my head and grabbed my own mug, after which I directed my attention at the Abyssal girl fidgeting beside her.

"Now that we established where the maid uniforms likely came from, could you tell me why you are wearing one?"

At first Snowy gave me a blank stare. Then, in a reserved voice, she said, "I… I thought you gave them to me because you wanted me to work here. You said you didn't want me to find a job to pay for the rent, so I thought you meant this."

"Just how did you come to that conclusion?" came my next incredulous question. "And why did you just put on these clothes without asking?"

Snowy fell silent, but then she grabbed the hem of her frilly skirt and said, "I… I actually like cleaning."

"You do?"

"Yes." She nodded with the same kind of adorably misplaced determination she normally reserved for discussing apple pies. "I liked to help the servants back home, ever since I was little. They were nice, and they gave me sweets when no one was looking."

"Really?"

"Yes," she answered with a huge nod. "Brother didn't like when I did it, though, so it was a secret."

"So let me see if I get this straight," I began as I massaged my temple. "You liked to help the maids at home, so now that you had a chance, you conveniently misunderstood my gestures so that you could dress up like one?"

"I… always thought maid uniforms were cute," Snowy mumbled with downcast eyes.

I took a deep breath. "I grant you that this maid outfit suits you so well, it's kind of disconcerting. However, as we've already established, I didn't know it was in your room, and it probably belongs to Elly's chambermaid to begin with. As such, I think we should ask her whether she wants them back before you get too attached to them."

"Okay," Snowy agreed, though based on her expression, she wasn't particularly enthusiastic about the idea.

"Now, I'm not saying you're not allowed to wear one, or to clean up in the living room, or to pretend to be a maid in general, if that's what you want. This is going to be your home as much as mine for the foreseeable future, so it's perfectly fine to indulge in your hobbies here."

"It's not really a hobby," she protested ineffectually, made all the more comical by the care with which she was straightening her apron while saying so. "I just don't want to be a freeloader, so I thought I would help in any way I can."

"That's commendable, and I have no problem with that, but you don't have to constantly worry about earning your rent like that. Just do what you want, okay, Judy?" I finished by throwing the ball into my assistant's court, hoping she could help me convince her.

"The Chief is right," she readily agreed with me and extended a hand to ruffle Snowy's hair, careful not to disturb her headdress. "You should do what you like. If you want to dress up as a maid, the Chief will definitely support you for the sake of his—"

"If you say 'fetish' one more time, I swear to God I will cancel today's cuddling quota!" I interrupted her with a raised voice and an exasperated glare.

"I was going to say, *peace of mind*," my girlfriend corrected herself while acting suspiciously innocent once again.

I shook my head at her and faced Snowy again, saying, "In short, if you really want to help out around the house, I'm definitely not going to stop you, you just don't have to be all subservient about it. Unless you really want to role-play as a maid. As I said, I'm not going to judge." With that said, I filled my mug again and told her, with a knowing smile, "Also, after breakfast, we are going on a little trip."

"We are?" Judy asked on the side, and I responded with a big old nod.

"Yeah. We are going to look at some real estate," I began, then I flashed another smile at Snowy and then added, in my best effort to sound mysterious, "Plus, there will be a nice surprise for you."

"Surprise?" Snowy asked with another Brang-esque tilt of the head. "What kind of surprise?"

"It wouldn't be one if I told you," I told her jokingly, already imagining how she would react once I reunited her with a certain someone...

PART 2

"All right, let's try it again!" I exclaimed while readjusting my grip on the metal shaft in my hands. "When I give you the signal, turn the knob!"

"Sir, yes sir!" Snowy responded with mountains of enthusiasm ineffectually hiding behind her professional words.

"Ready?" I called out while flexing my muscles, then I began turning the crank sticking out of the front of the large, antiquated generator. Once I felt like I'd built up enough momentum, I gave it one last push and yelled out, "Go!"

"Roger!" came the similarly spirited reply from my helper as she turned the ignition knob once, twice, and on the third try, the old (yet inexplicably pristine) machine came to life with a stutter. Then there was a slow yet steady ramp-up of the engine, followed by the magical sight of all the decades-old light bulbs in their wall sockets coming to life, filling the otherwise drab environment with enough light to make our flashlights pointless.

"I can't believe it actually worked!" I exclaimed in exhilaration as I did a small fist pump. "They sure as hell knew how to make things last back in those days, right?"

"They sure did!" Snowy readily agreed, grinning a feisty smile that made me want to pinch her cheek.

Judy, on the other hand, gave me a noncommittal shrug. She walked over, and I gave her a curious look, but she didn't respond in any way. So I ventured a guess.

"Are you still mad at me because I left you two here for five minutes when I went home to get gas?"

"No," she replied and kicked my shin.

"Your words and your actions are sending mixed messages."

"It's just your imagination," she deadpanned again, followed by yet another entirely harmless kick.

Since she didn't seem to want to engage in any kind of constructive dialog, I proceeded to ignore the aggressively sulking girl by my side and instead turned to Snowy, who was currently looking at me with expectant puppy-eyes. I looked her in the eyes, raised a fist at chest level, and after a tense moment, I flashed a toothy smile and gave her a thumbs-up.

"You can go and explore now," I told her, and her eyes gave off an excited sparkle as she turned on her heel and rushed up the stairs leading to the upper level of our new prospective secret base.

"It's unsafe to leave a young girl to run around in a bomb shelter all alone," Judy grumbled by my side, but I only shrugged in response.

"Unsafe? Come on, Dormouse! She's easily the single most dangerous thing in this entire complex! In fact, now that you mention it, I almost feel a little insecure since she left."

"Then let's follow after her," Judy immediately decided, grabbed my arm, and began to desperately try to drag me along. It wasn't as if there was anything else to be done in the generator room now, so I simply allowed her to haul me away. When we reached the top of the stairs, I could finally see the large, domed central area all lit up, and I couldn't help but whistle in approval.

We stood inside the bowels of a decommissioned bomb shelter in the mountains a couple kilometers north of Timaeus. After narrowing down our options last night, we decided on the last of the three candidates for our secret base, the most impressive site of them all.

According to what I read, this shelter was built more than forty years ago, though, considering the nature of this world, that only meant the place's design looked old. It was impeccably clean, of course, and everything was in working order. The thing that made this particular shelter special was that it was designed to house high-ranking military personnel and their families when the early detection sirens went off in a nearby secret radar base.

Thus, the whole complex was specifically designed to allow just a handful of people to weather a nuclear fallout scenario, and to do so in relative comfort. The dark grey concrete corridors and the green, solid steel blast doors made the place feel sturdy and secure. Its bare utilitarian plainness gave it a strange charm.

Only a couple hundred meters away from a highway, the main entrance was easily accessible, and as for security (or lack thereof), it had only a flimsy padlock at the front entrance. We easily got rid of the lock by first freezing it via Abyssal magic, and then I simply smashed it up with a rock. It didn't shatter like they do in the movies, but it still gave way in just a couple swings.

Anyways, once inside, we found a gently sloping hallway with an arched ceiling ending in a large central hall. Smaller chambers formed a ring around the hall, and a staircase led up into the already mentioned generator room. Seeing the place now, in a more well-lit condition, I was beginning to understand Snowy's uncharacteristic excitement for a "secret base." When you combined that word with actual, military-grade constructions like this, it certainly tickled one's sense of adventure. So I decided to follow in her footsteps and began to explore the insides of the underground shelter with renewed vigor.

"Leo, look what I found!" the Abyssal girl excitedly called out the moment she noticed us, gesturing. "That door leads to a kitchen. There's no water, but it has utensils and everything else. There are a lot of showers over there, and I found some toilets too, but look here!"

Following her instructions, we entered a side chamber, which turned out to be a large room filled with rows of metal framed bunks already made up with white bedding. By my estimate, about fifty people could be comfortably housed here, a number which matched my intel on the place.

When I looked around, I couldn't help but nod with satisfaction. While the beds looked somewhat flimsy, and the lack of water was an issue, with some effort, I was sure this place could be renovated so that Brang could live here and the rooms could be used for storage and training.

The site only had two major issues. First off, it was originally one of the Celestials' secret safe houses. They had sneakily removed from the registers and altered most of the written records, presumably so that the mundane authorities wouldn't try to reclaim it and turn it into a novelty amusement park or something. On the other hand, this meant that the Celestials were still very much aware of it. Hell, *we* learned about its location because of the Celestial Hub. I already had a few plans in mind to have them abandon this place, along with a few red herrings to make things harder to trace, but that plan was a work in progress.

The other significant problem was the fact that, while it was close to a highway, and thus accessible by using Critias's needlessly fancy public transportation system, the shelter was still way outside of Timaeus's city borders—far from the suburbs where our merry little band of magical misfits lived. This, of course, meant that getting here and back wasn't only time consuming but highly conspicuous, especially since I was about 101 percent sure we were still under at least loose surveillance.

Now granted, this was a problem with a readily available solution, and one I had already discussed with Judy. By stationing someone with a "red dot" over here, I could move unhindered between this place and my home, or anywhere else for that matter. I could also take people with me on the trip, although that would mean I'd need to reveal my teleportation ability to them. The cat was already out of the bag with Snowy, and Brang would inevitably learn about it too, but if at all possible, I wanted to keep it a secret from the others. At least for the time being.

Of course, the option to have the whole group conspicuously take a bus ride to the back end of nowhere for every training session was still open, but that was an even less than ideal solution. For the time being, I decided to stop worrying about the transportation of my friends and have a round of brainstorming about it with Judy later. Maybe we could create a fake teleportation circle between this place and my home, and tell them it was only usable by me plus one person at a time? It was an idea worth considering, but for the moment I shelved it and focused on another, closely related issue: the transportation of material goods.

I hadn't experimented nearly enough with the limits of my teleportation ability when it came to the volume or nature of inanimate matter I could take along with me for the ride, but I already knew that small things were no problem. Clothes, bags, cans filled with gasoline—practically anything I could pick up and carry was fair game. That opened up a lot of possibilities regarding supplying this prospective secret base of ours, but it also limited them. For example, bringing food, water, gas, and other amenities over should be no problem, but things like furniture were out of the picture.

Still, after I measured all the pros and cons of the site, I concluded that there was no way I could find a more suitable secret base than this, so I turned towards Judy and told her, "Honey, I think this is the place for us."

At first she gave me a weird look, but then she blinked in realization and asked, "Are you doing a newlywed thing now?"

"Well, I was, but now you spoiled it."

"You can't expect me to react to every one of your non sequiturs on the spot," she pouted. But then she abruptly added, "Say your line again."

"What's the point now?" I heaved a melodramatic sigh.

"I want to do a newlywed thing, too."

"Which one?"

"The one where I ask what you want to have first: dinner, bath, or—"

"That's a terrible cliché and you should feel bad for keeping it alive. Shame on you," I interrupted her, earning me a click of the tongue and a brand-new sulky *"spoilsport"* to add to my steadily growing collection. I ignored both with practiced grace and instead waved for my other companion, who was crouching to inspect something on the ground, to come over. "Hey, Snowy! We decided to make this our secret base!"

"Really?" the Abyssal girl jumped up, dusted off her long white coat, then pattered over with a curious expression. "This place is amazing! I can't believe they could make it without any mystic arts!"

"It probably wasn't easy, but that's military engineers for you." I glanced over the place again, silently agreeing with Snowy. Then I asked her, "Do you remember that I promised you a surprise?"

"Yes," she nodded. "Was it the base?"

"No-no-no. I promised a surprise to *you*, not something surprising in general."

"Chief, are you thinking what I think you are thinking?"

"Depends," I replied with a smile. "Are you thinking that I'm thinking about bringing Snowy's surprise over?"

"So it's a yes," Judy spoke with resignation as she stepped away from me. "I'll be over here, just in case."

"Come on, Dormouse. I told you he's perfectly safe," I protested, but my assistant only took another step back, so I gave up on persuading her.

"Who are you talking about?" Snowy inquired, her interest piqued.

"Your surprise," I answered with a (hopefully) mysterious smile. "But it won't be a surprise if you watch. Close your eyes for a moment."

"Okay."

To my surprise, she didn't ask a question or make a complaint, but slipped her hands up over her eyes. I was a little taken aback by her reaction but, stifling an amused chuckle, I closed my own eyes in preparation for Far Sight. (To be honest, I didn't really *need* to do that anymore. But it did help with the nausea, which was useful.) Anyhow, I focused on Brang's dot—but what I saw there made my brows furrow against my will.

"This might take a bit longer than expected," I told the girls with an ever so slightly annoyed voice. "Don't go anywhere."

With that, I used my teleportation ability to break through the mostly impenetrable barrier and headed into the bowels of the Abyss.

That… sounds way more epic than what actually happened.

One stomach-turning moment later, I found myself standing in a large room. At first glance, it looked surprisingly similar to the bunks in the shelter I'd just left, except that the large wooden beds inside were piled into makeshift barricades in front of the only entrance and the windows. Manning those barricades stood seven large, imposing Fauns. At least half of them had their own "red dots" at the edge of my senses, so these guys must have been the same group I'd encountered during the incident at the School.

However, unlike that time, now all of them wore armour. It reminded me of the segmented armour Roman legionnaires were using, except it wasn't made of metal, but some dark green material with a matte surface. And one familiar Faun with an equally familiar spear stood dressed in a similar fashion, except he appeared downright majestic.

His armour plates all had elaborate, baroque silver filigree on them, their fine detail creating an interesting contrast with his hulking frame. A cape hung from his shoulders, adorned with silver embroidery surrounding a large crest. It was in the shape of a rounded shield encircled by stylized flames and featuring a lightly dressed woman with one feathery and one leathery wing spread wide open, as if ready to take off into the skies.

Now, I would've loved to spend some time analyzing the symbolism behind said crest, but the angry yells coming from the outside reminded me that I came here for a reason, so I hastily cleared my throat. It might have been too soft, as the Faun in front of me didn't react at all, so I raised my voice and called out to the conspicuous guy in the middle.

"[Brang.]"

He flinched in surprise, though not as much as the rest of the group did, who were overreacting about as much as you would expect a bunch of tense, muscle-bound warriors to do when someone appeared behind them.

Brang turned towards me with his usual toothy grin that showed up all his ivories and said, "[Blackcloak. Thou art a sight for sore eyes in our hour of need.]"

I awarded the anachronistically chill Faun a tired sigh and told him, "[I insist that we shall, nay, we *must* cease to rendezvous under circumstances such as this. Also, I once again request you remedy your habit of addressing me by that moniker.]"

Brang cocked his head a little, then casually leaned on his spear and patted his beard. "[Names are a sacred thing, my friend,]" he said in a forlorn voice. "[It's unbecoming of thee to deny thine.]"

"[Howsomever, it is not my—]" I began, only to be interrupted by another series of furious roars coming from the outside, followed by a large impact on the door. The barricade lurched dangerously forward. I swallowed back my original retort and told him, "[We shall discuss this at a later opportunity. For the current moment, I would not so humbly request that you enlighten me about the nature of the present predicament you and your kin are facing.]"

"[Aye. In but a moment, I shall endeavour to do so.]"

Brang gestured, and like a well-oiled machine, the wary group dispersed and began to man and reinforce the makeshift barricades. Meanwhile, the big Faun strolled over.

"[Where shall I begin the telling of the events that lead to the unfortunate reality before thine eyes? After our ways parted inside the Chasm of Desolation, I ventured forth from my captivity to recover this weapon of mine, just as we agreed upon]." Saying so, he lightly tapped on his spear for emphasis. "[Thus, I sought out my brood siblings, and by means of the gifts I received from the heiress, I was able to reach their abode without being perceived by my captors. Upon our meeting, I shared the contents of our agreement with them. Suspecting that we might require additional hands during our flight from the Abyss, as overpowering the guards at the Well of Power Inanna is no simple feat, I offered them the same terms you have conferred to me, which they readily accepted.]"

I gave the Faun a good, hard look, but since he didn't seem to get the clue just from that, I subsequently palmed my face and told him, through clenched teeth, "[While I applaud your forethought, the gesture was absolutely unnecessary, bordering on outright detrimental.]" I paused for a moment to calm my nerves, and once I did so, I groaned aloud and added, "[Alas, you shall scarcely mind my dissatisfaction, as it is likely my fault that I have failed to clarify our avenue of departure.]"

Brang furrowed his brows, but before he could say anything, the main barricade lurched again. He glanced at it, then shrugged it like it was only a minor nuisance.

"[Where was I? Aye, my discussion with my fellows.]" He gave a nod to no one in particular. "[Upon attaining our covenant, we all embarked towards the armoury of the Faun Inanna so that we would adorn ourselves with arms fit for swearing new fealty, as it is tradition. For reasons unbeknownst to all, let alone us, the head of House Inanna thou likens to black birds of carrion burst with rage during our preparations, rallying all the forces of the house and its vassals, and in their frantic pursuit of a threat unknown, they regrettably discovered the vacant state of my cell. Upon attempting to send the Faun Inanna to discover my whereabouts, they instead exposed the gathering of my brood siblings. The rest thou canst readily see with thine eyes.]"

"[Aye, that I can,]" I grumbled. "[What is the number of foes you face?]"

"[Just about two hundred or so retainers of House Inanna, and roughly a dozen of my brethren loyal to the head of the house.]"

"[You appear to be remarkably serene considering the odds you and your kin face.]"

"[How can I not be so?]" the ex-general responded with a self-assured smirk. "[Thou hast made thine entry into our midst? Doubtless thou hast a way to depart from this location.]"

I was about to award the Faun a skeptical look, but those didn't seem to work on him, so instead I told him, "[It would do you good not to trust my prudence as such in the future, else you shall be sorely disappointed in me and your judgment of character both.]"

"[Mayhap, yet thy mention of the future speaks otherwise.]"

He won that round.

I shrugged. "[So be it. I admit I do possess the means to deliver you from your predicament.]"

Brang flashed another toothy smile that I didn't need any kind of magical language ability to understand meant *I knew it.*

Ignoring his smug expression, I bellowed, ["All of you! Gather round!"]

The Fauns seemed to be surprised by my unexpected outburst, yet for some reason (perhaps Faun military training) they stopped manning the barricades and formed a more or less tidy line in front of me. Now that I could see them side by side, I realized they were all significantly shorter than Brang. That, of course, didn't mean they were *short* short, as they had a couple inches on me, and what with their bulk and armour and weapons, they looked formidable.

Out of the six smaller Fauns, five had ram-like heads like Brang, with horns of various lengths and curls, while the last and shortest one had an elongated, gaunt face, a pair of triangular ears, and a misshapen nose. He reminded me of a wolf or a German shepherd, and his unique appearance left a fairly deep impression on me.

A ram-Faun glanced over to Brang and tried to sneakily ask, "[Hey, Elder? Is this really that Blackcloak fellow you talked about?]"

I am going to be honest here: for a moment I was so taken aback by the fact that the Faun language could be used without all the purple prose that I even forgot to glare at the guy. In my stead, Bang told him, "[Thy manners are once again deficient, young Karukk.]"

"[Sorry, I just expected someone… bigger?]" he mumbled after looking me over. "[Is he really Lady Neige's servant?]"

"[Nay, he—]" Brang began speaking, but I cut him off.

"[First and foremost, I would advise you to take your hackneyed words and insert them up your excrement hole. Secondly, she-whose-name-is-snow is my beneficiary, so no, I am most certainly not. Third of all, if you refuse to cease speaking about me in the third person, I shall let you have an honourable final standoff against the retainers of your craven liege whilst the rest of us shall have a nice dinner in your memory. Did I make myself clear, or shall we continue to have this discussion until your crude barriers fail you?]"

The offending Faun blinked at me, then he hastily said, "[My apologies, Sir Blackcloak.]"

"[For the love of all that may be holy, why can't you folk cease referring to me by such titles?]" I exploded.

Brang, the Chief offender, chuckled.

"[Cease your merriment, ex-general! It is the fault of none other than you that such a moniker exists on the first place, and I shall share a piece of my mind with you about it once your current predicament be resolved.]" That comment finally made him stop grinning, and with that, I also calmed down a little, so I continued with a slightly less infuriated voice, "[Before all else, let me ask you one last time. Are you all ready to leave the employ of he-whose-hair-is-the-colour-of-crows?]"

The younger Fauns glanced at each other. They all nodded and replied in some variation of "aye."

"[Very well. Under a less calamitous state of affairs, I would have likely interrogated you further, but since your barriers might fall at any moment, I shall trust the judgment of your former general and reunite you with your heiress. To do so, I only require one act from you all.]"

The barricade in the back lurched again from an impact so heavy, it reverberated in my guts, splintering the massive wooden door and shoving the pile of beds back.

"[Excrement. I believe that shall be our cue to leave this place posthaste. Close your eyes, cover them with your hands, and don't open them until I instruct you so,]" I gave my rushed commands, and to their credit, the Faun quickly followed them without any further backtalk.

Once I was sure all of them had their vision completely blocked, I stepped up to the first one of them. He happened to be the wolfish guy. Without further ado, I placed a hand on his chest—which made him flinch in surprise—wrapped my phantom limb around him, and connected my Far Sight to Judy.

The world twisted around me, and both the Faun and I reappeared inside the abandoned bomb shelter. My assistant gasped, but I was gone. The second I confirmed my passenger arrived safe and sound, I headed back for the second guy. A few blinks later, Brang was the last Faun in the room as a muscular arm reached through the cracked open door. I had no idea if its owner managed to get in, as I grabbed Brang and left at once.

Finished with my last ferry trip, my legs almost gave out on me. I stumbled over to a nearby bed and pretty much fell on my butt. The motion sickness accompanying teleportation was already magnitudes worse than usual, but teleporting so rapidly and so many times in a row got me to the point where I was amazed I hadn't emptied my stomach yet. In fact, I was about to heave when a certain deadpan girl (who, by the way, looked considerably less poker-faced than usual) grabbed my hand and whispered, "Chief, care to explain what's going on?"

My stomach roiled.

"It's... kind of a long story..." I gasped.

Judy seemed to be less than satisfied by my answer, but once she saw how sick I was, she gave up on drilling me any further, and instead began rubbing my back in circles. It didn't help much, but I appreciated the sentiment all the same.

In the meantime, another voice joined the fray as Snowy innocently asked, "Can I open my eyes now?"

Snowy was standing right where I'd left her, hands still covering her eyes. That was weird enough, but due to a freak coincidence, the seven Fauns I'd just delivered from the Abyss were standing right in front of her, also covering their eyes. The sight was surreal, to say the least.

"Sure, you can open them," I told Snowy. Then, in Faunish, I released the Fauns, as well.

Brang blinked in disbelief as he realized he was in a completely different place. But he didn't have much time to be thunderstruck, as a certain white-haired girl came barreling towards him in a full-body tackle. He dumped his spear and extended his hands towards her.

"Uncle Brang!" Snowy exclaimed with childlike joy as she jumped into the arms of the grinning burly Faun.

"Tiny heir. Be careful," Brang chided her, but took her under the arms and swung her around like a kid. Then he settled her on his broad shoulder.

So, there they stood, a giant muscle-bound warrior with a white-haired girl perched on his shoulder. That image reminded me of something I've seen on the net once, but I couldn't really remember, so it couldn't have been that important.

While the touching reunion went on, the other Fauns recovered from their initial shock and took in their environment, which for some reason made Judy even more skittish than before. She looked like she wanted to hide behind me, a prospect made somewhat difficult by the fact that I was sitting on a bed.

"What exactly are you doing?" I asked her with a critically raised brow, but she only huffed in return.

"That's my question," she finally declared after some more nudging. "Didn't we recently discuss that you should consider your actions a little more carefully?"

"We did," I readily admitted.

"Then what is a herd of angry goat people doing here?"

"Angry?" I asked with genuine confusion before I glanced over at the group of Fauns huddled together behind Brang and Snowy. I tried to listen to their conversation.

"They aren't angry," I told my assistant.

"Then why are they growling?"

"They aren't. They are discussing how they can sense that they are underground, yet the ventilation of the area is still very good, and they are simultaneously praising the architect who designed this place and wondering how they got here. Oh, and one of them is complaining that he forgot his favourite knife in the Abyss. Nobody's angry."

"Are… they really saying all that?" Judy glanced between me and the Fauns with increasingly incredulous eyes.

"Yes, and more."

After a long moment, Judy let out a small groan and said, "The Faun language is weird."

"Tell me about it!" I agreed.

A shadow crossed my face. Brang was towering over me. The girl on his shoulder leapt off, and before I knew what happened, an impact hit my chest. Smiling brilliantly, the culprit clasped her arms around my neck.

"Easy there," I told her. "I'm delicate."

"Thank you, Leo!" Snowy exclaimed. "I love the present! It's the best one ever!"

For a moment, I was completely taken aback by her innocent elation, and if I wasn't currently holding her in my arms, I probably would've patted her on the head, but since I was, I made do with just giving her my warmest smile and telling her, "You're welcome."

She let out a happy little giggle and tried to hug my neck, but since I was still a little out of it, I decided to politely peel her away and tell her, "I think Introductions are in order, plus we should show your new retainers around our base."

"My retainers?" Snowy asked, her angelic smile giving way to a confused one.

"Leave old liege. Serve you now. Long story," Brang summed things up nicely.

"I get it," Snowy responded, only to tack on a less confident "… or maybe not?" at the end.

"I'll explain," I told her. "But first…" I paused for a moment and turned to Judy. "Could you help me get up, please? My legs are a little wobbly just now. Too many round-trips with passengers."

Instead of answering, my dearest assistant linked her arm with mine and helped me to my feet. She didn't let go even after I was upright, which I didn't really mind, though I suspected that she was trying to use me as a shield so she wouldn't need to interact with the Fauns.

Speaking of which, once I was nominally stable, I raised my voice to say, "[Hear me, warriors of the Faun Inanna! You shall now discuss the terms of your fealty with your new liege, and once we have done so, you shall be allowed to make your inquiries. All queries shall be answered. Let us head forth to the next chamber!]"

The Fauns gave me puzzled looks until Brang added, "[Have thy ears fallen aslumber?]" Then he casually picked up Snowy again and headed towards the only exit.

Without further prompting, the rest of the Fauns followed suit. I was about to do so as well, but then I noticed the curious glint in my girlfriend's eyes.

"What did you do?" she asked while eyeing the group trickling out of the room.

"I told them that we should go to the central chamber so that they can swear loyalty to Snowy and then we can explain what's going on."

"And you said all that with just a few growls?"

"Yes," I answered with a nod. "Is there a problem?"

"No." Judy shook her head as she led me out of the room, muttering, "The Faun language is really, really, *really* weird…"

CHAPTER 9

PART 1

Standing before the Dracis mansion, Elly peeked left and right. "I'm outside the gates now. Where are you?"

"Move a little farther to the right," I instructed her through the phone while observing her with Far Sight. "Farther. Farther. Just a liiiiittle farther…"

She inched forward step by step (an admittedly amusing sight, as she was just a trench coat away from looking like a highly visible spy fresh from a Saturday morning cartoon), until I was sure she was hidden from casual observers by the thick hedge surrounding the estate. Then I tightened my grip on Judy's waist, and we both appeared right behind her.

The princess was still scanning the perimeter, so I quickly cut the line, put my phone away, and by the time she turned around, I was already flashing my most suave smile.

"Good evening, princess."

Elly still held her phone up, and she kept it there as she proceeded to blink at me with a weird mixture of surprise and confusion.

"Why were you hiding?" she asked as she awkwardly put her phone away.

"We weren't really hiding per se," I answered ambiguously, only to get elbowed in the side by Judy for my trouble.

"I told you—no more ad hoc excuses," she warned me and slipped out of my embrace.

"It wasn't an excuse! We weren't actually hiding," I said, only to get shot down by a withering scowl (by Judy standards, of course).

"Hush, Chief. After your recent track record, I am afraid even asking about the weather would cause you to make an international incident," my assistant replied with an exasperated pout.

"International incident?" Elly cut in with a curiously raised brow as she sidled up to the two of us.

"It's kind of a long story," I sheepishly told her, lest I incur even more of Judy's wrath.

"We will tell you later," Judy said and gestured towards the estate gates. "Let's go inside first, or you will catch a cold."

I blinked in honest surprise at her words. I mean, not the part about

Elly catching a cold. I'd asked her to go outside on short notice, so she was dressed only in her indoor clothes, and considering how it was late in the afternoon and how chilly the autumn weather had been lately, I wholeheartedly agreed that she should get inside. The part that confused me was Judy's insistence that *we* should do so, as well. Technically, the only reason why we were here on the first place was because I might have forgotten that, for us to get home from our secret base, I needed to have someone at home to teleport to.

Now, to be perfectly honest, the princess wasn't exactly on the top of my list of target-candidates, but a quick Far Sight peek at each member of our circle of friends revealed that their homes were filled with those creepy eyeball surveillance orb thingies. Well, except for the class rep's, but she was just about to have a shower, so she was out of the question—and no, I didn't actually tell the shower thing to Judy. She was cross enough already without some kind of misunderstanding about me peeking on girls. That would only throw more wood on my funeral pyre.

But, putting my metaphorical self-immolation aside, I considered what I'd observed of the Dracis estate via Far Sight. House Dracis wasn't under much surveillance, so the only thing we had to avoid while teleporting in was the ever vigilant eyes of the mansion's staff, especially a certain butler. As such, we left Snowy in the secret base, both so that she could continue her reunion with her "Uncle Brang" and so that they could work out the kinks in their new contract or fealty or whatever.

Hence the current situation.

Now, I'm not going to lie—I was about 90 percent sure that the moment we arrived back in the neighbourhood, Judy would grab me by the hand, drag me to my room, and spend an hour scolding me about my recent life decisions. To be fair, I did regret some of them, but I had a feeling the things she was most upset about weren't amongst them. I didn't regret, for example, bringing Brang and company over. Nor did I regret the pranks I played on Crowey, even if they kind of, let's say, *got out of hand?*

Of course, I'd told Judy everything I'd learned about Crowey's situation (and tantrum) through Far Sight… which was one of the things I regretted a tiny little bit. I mean, what she didn't know about, she couldn't reprimand me about, right? Granted, I would've told her about it eventually, but doing so right after she'd chewed me out for recruiting a squad of Faun might not have been one of my brighter ideas.

I had to admit, though, her concerns were valid. What exactly do you feed giant half-goat warriors? Cheeseburgers? I had no clue nor where to source it—but I needed to find out and soon. Before dinnertime, preferably.

Anywho, back to the present.

Judy was gesturing for us through the gates. I gave her a slightly hesitant look and asked, "Do we have some business here?"

"I do," she responded with a nod. "I want to talk to Mister von Fraenir and discuss your new recruits before it leads to some kind of enormous misunderstanding with the Dracis household."

"Recruits?" Elly asked, confused. She had somehow snuck over to my side, as if waiting for an opportunity to grab me.

"Another long story," I answered her, and then I let out a shallow breath and gave an affirmative nod to my other girlfriend, and began walking towards the gates with heavy steps.

"Wait!" the princess exclaimed as she excitedly followed after me. "Are you staying for dinner? I will go tell Melinda to prepare two extra servings!"

"I… don't think so?" I answered with more than a slight uncertainty. "We are just going to have a short talk with Sebastian."

"Not *we*," Judy interjected. "I want to sit down with him and explain our situation. Just the two of us. Without a certain someone picking a fight and causing another incident."

"I—" I wanted to defend myself, but in the end, all I could do was to swallow my flimsy rebuttal. I mean, while I was sure if I tried really, really hard, I could probably stop myself from verbally sparring with the old lizard, I couldn't guarantee it. Why did that old man always get under my skin? Frustrating. I mean, it wasn't my fault… or was it? Still, letting my temper get the best of me to the point where my girlfriend was outright disappointed in me honestly stung a lot.

In the meantime, Elly must have come to a conclusion of some kind, as she happily skipped ahead to the mansion entrance, saying, "All right! I will tell the staff we are having guests!"

"Call Mister von Fraenir, too," Judy stressed.

Elly theatrically rolled her eyes. "Come on, Judy! I'm not deaf, I heard it already."

Then, with a giggle, she disappeared through a large wooden door, leaving the two of us alone in the mansion's lavish foyer. I might have mentioned this before, but damn, the Dracis knew how to do interior decoration. What they didn't know was the word *restraint*. All the opulent golden foil, polished hardwood, and baroque filigree made the place feel suffocating.

Speaking of suffocation, for a few seconds there was a really heavy silence in the air between Judy and I, so I hastily cleared my throat and asked, "So, you think should we stay for dinner?"

She glanced up at me, her expression somewhere between "sulky" and "angry." Then she shrugged and said, "We might as well. The cook here can probably do better than grilled cheese."

"Oh, come on!" I raised my voice in protest. "I told you, I didn't actually write that!"

"Then what did you write?" she asked back, not at all swayed by my sincere assertion.

I groaned aloud, then I leaned forward and continued in a strained whisper, "I told you already! I wrote the Archon thing because I thought it would make the Celestial connection more believable if they managed to translate it somehow. The rest was supposed to be pure gibberish! How the hell was I supposed to know they would be able to read not one, but *four* different lines out of it? I'm totally innocent—a victim of circumstance!"

"Sure you are."

"Come on, Dormouse!" I objected again, and as much as I hate to admit it, it came out as a bit of a whine. "Please believe me!"

She gave me a long, hard look, after which her frown finally eased off a little.

"Very well, Chief. Let's say I will, against my better judgment, believe you. Can you explain what happened?"

I let out a relieved breath, following which I fell silent for a moment to collect my thoughts.

"I'd be lying if I said I have a concrete answer, but... I have three hypotheses off the top of my head."

"Three?" Judy raised a single brow, which finally erased the last traces of that awful glare from her face, to my utmost relief.

"Yes," I answered with an emphatic nod. "They are, from most to least mundane, as follows: My first option is that the actual translators messed up. I honestly thought I was writing complete gobbledygook, but it is possible that they have read into it something that wasn't actually there."

"The lines were too complex for that," Judy denied my explanation on the spot, but I gestured for her to let me continue.

"I know, but I have two possible explanations. Wither their *'experts'* were so desperate for answers, they completely fudged the translation, or they realized that it was meaningless, and so they translated it more 'liberally' in order to have an answer to present to the angry, bedridden Abyssal Lord."

"Whom you poisoned."

"On accident!" I protested again, only for her to shake her head.

"The one about crows is still too much on the nose," Judy stated after some consideration.

"True," I granted her. "But that's where my second hypothesis comes into the picture. Do you remember when we discussed my language skills and how weird Celestial Script was? Like, how the syntax felt like it was constantly shifting when I wasn't paying full attention?"

"Yes," Judy nodded. Then she frowned again. Thankfully this time it was the thoughtful kind of frown, not the disdainful one she'd been using until very recently. "You think the words you wrote rearranged themselves between the time you wrote them and when they translated them?"

"You once again prove you know me better than I do myself." I quirked a smile. "Yes, that's what I think. Or more precisely, I think there might have been some patterns in the gibberish I wrote based on my state of mind at the time. Like, I was thinking of Crowey, so I might have written something about crows in there. Then I was thinking about snappy words to add, which would explain the quote and the bits about being a true god of whatever."

"And the grilled cheese part?"

I shrugged. "Well, I might have been a little peckish…"

She looked me in the eye, as if to see if I were serious, but then she finally let her shoulders slacken and said, "So, you are saying that it is the unusual syntax of the Celestial Script that is at fault. It's a little convenient."

"Well… I still have my third hypothesis." I took a deep breath and told her with a forced smile, "It's your favourite, too. Narrative influence."

That earned me a curiously raised brow. "At which point?"

"Take your pick," I answered with exasperation masked by nonchalance. "It might have been influencing my choice of words, or changing the words on the paper itself, or influencing the translators. The depressing possibilities are endless!"

"That's strange." Judy raised a finger to her chin in contemplation. "Which part?"

"The one where you only acknowledge the possibility of narrative influence when it lets you avoid the consequences of your actions," she answered with a poker face even more deadpan than usual, but before I could voice my just protestations, she shook her head and added, "Nevertheless, you've made your point, and I have to admit that there were exonerating circumstances following your latest misdemeanors. For the time being, I will acquit you of your crimes against common sense and annul your prohibition of cuddling."

"Wait, since when was that prohibited?"

My dear assistant magnificently ignored my entirely valid question, and instead she glanced at her phone and told me, "Since it was postponed due to the previous prohibition, cuddle-o-clock will be rescheduled for after dinner."

I gave Judy a flat look. "So, I didn't actually convince you. You just wanted an excuse to move on so we could cuddle later."

"I can neither confirm nor deny such accusations without my attorney present."

"Wait, I'm confused now. Weren't you playing judge just a moment ago?"

"Chief, don't be silly. Judges and attorneys are not the same thing."

"I know, but—"

Our little—and at this point, practically customary—exchange of the banter ball would have continued unabated, if not for a nearby door swinging open. Out walked Sebastian and Melinda wearing their usual garb, with Sebastian opting for an actual, I-shit-you-not, monocle to complete his look, while Melinda had her long, blonde braids behind her back as usual.

"Good evening," Judy greeted them like they were close associates… which, considering how she had way more contact with them than I did due to her frequent visits to the Dracis Library, was likely on the mark.

In response, Melinda honest-to-goodness curtsied, while the old butler only glanced over us with a slight nod. "Good evening, Miss Sennoma. And you."

An appropriate retort was on the tip of my tongue, but a quick glance at my finally placated assistant made me swallow it back down, and instead I greeted them with a curt, "Evening."

That earned me an odd look from Sebastian, but before he could get started, Judy stepped forward and addressed him, "I wish to speak with you in private, if you have the time."

Now it was her turn to get a peculiar look from the old butler. In the end, he lightly shrugged.

"If it is important, I can open up some time in my schedule for the evening," he said. Then, glancing at me, he asked, "Should we head to my office or the library?"

"The library. I feel more comfortable there."

"Very well." He nodded, and to be honest, it kind of irked me how polite he was with her, as opposed to his usual abrasive attitude towards me.

Before I could not dwell on old Sebastian's rudeness, the blonde maid dipped a curtsy.

"Lady Eleanor informed me that you will be staying for dinner. I was told to lead you to her room until then."

"Okay," I answered a little uncertainly, but before I knew it, Judy was already walking out of the foyer behind the butler, so I had little choice but to follow after my own guide. The two of us started walking down some familiar corridors—though to be honest, I wasn't sure I had been in them before. Perhaps the whole huge mansion was a maze of similar hallways.

I was just about to get lost in my thoughts when Melinda yanked me out of my contemplations.

"I have been informed that milady and you are currently dating. Congratulations."

For a second or two, I could only stare at the maid in flabbergasted silence, and then I tentatively answered, "Thanks, though I would probably feel better about it if you didn't look like you wanted to stab me."

"I have no idea what you are talking about," she continued with a wooden smile while simultaneously staring daggers at me. "Could it be your inner guilt manifesting? Is there anything related to your relationship with milady that would make you think I would want to repeatedly stab you in cold blood?"

"Oookay, that was too graphic for my comfort." Hesitating, I looked around, then gestured for her to follow me to a nearby nook. "I have a feeling you really want to tell me something. So how about we stop here for a while and discuss it before it explodes into our faces?"

The blonde maid gave me a skeptical look, but then followed after me and faced me with a disapproving frown.

"Very well. Since you seem to be receptive, I will get to the point straightaway. Are you also dating Miss Sennoma?"

I had a feeling it was about something like this.

"Yes, things turned out like that," I told her.

"Are you intending to keep up this relationship?"

"Well, yes, that's the plan."

Melinda gave me another critical look, then she let out a tired breath and began, with a firm yet somewhat helpless voice, "I will be honest with you. I was well aware that milady would one day find a partner. I hoped, from the bottom of my heart, that she would find a special someone who loved her back, instead of being forced into a bleak political marriage. For a while, I hoped that someone would be you, but…"

"Hold on," I cut in with raised hands. "I do like her a lot, you know? I wouldn't be going out with her otherwise."

"Then why are you also dating another girl?"

"I told you, it just turned out that way!" I explained aloud, only to tone my voice back to a whisper as I continued, "Also, it's not like I am dating the two of them separately; all three of us are technically in the same, big relationship."

Melinda frowned. "All three of you are in a single relationship? How does that work?"

"I can't really tell you, since I am also pretty new to this, but so far, it just does." I paused for a moment to look for further arguments, and then I added, "Actually, Elly said the Dracis family had something similar going on, with multiple wives or whatnot."

"A practice like that exists, yes… But it is for the head of the family only."

"And the princess is going to be that when the current head retires, right?"

"Yes?" Melinda nodded with an expression that said she had a hard time believing she was agreeing with me.

"Then there is no problem, is there?"

The chambermaid fell silent for a long time, then said, "So, you are trying to use our traditions to benefit yourself in this strange relationship."

"I deny your accusation, and if anything, it was the princess who decided to invoke it to resolve our love triangle."

"I see." She once again fell silent for a moment, then said, "However, have you thought about this: if you grant this precedent to milady, aren't you afraid that it will open the door to allow her to take another mistress?"

"Mistress?" I mumbled, but then I shook my head. "Well, no. I mean, she was already very accommodating in the resolution of our current relationship, so if she *really* insisted, I don't think I would have the gall to object, especially since I am the guy who already has two girlfriends at the moment."

"Really?" Melinda suddenly perked up.

"Um... yes?" I replied uncertainly, at which point the maid gave me an uncharacteristically enthusiastic nod, only to finally realize she was acting weird, so she unashamedly cleared her throat and tried to act all prim and proper again, which incidentally only made her even more suspicious.

"I see. If you have put so much thought into your relationship with milady, and you are willing to compromise to that extent, I believe I have no objection to your liaison."

With that, she ended the conversation right there and gestured for me to follow her and exited the nook with a new spring in her steps. I had a very, very bad feeling about this, but I decided not to confront the suspicious maid right now and instead ask Elly about it in a roundabout way.

Anyways, as we continued on our way, I suddenly recalled something else that nearly slipped my mind.

"Melinda, I have a quick question?"

"Yes, sir?"

That almost made me stumble.

"Sir?"

"Would you prefer if I addressed you as 'young master' instead? Or, considering the circumstances, 'future young master'?"

"I... have no idea whether you are making fun of me right now or not, and frankly, I don't think I really want to know. Instead, can you just tell me if you left any of your uniforms over at my place?"

The chambermaid paused thoughtfully for a moment, then she admitted, "I believe I might have indeed left a pair of spare uniforms in your guest room. If they are in the way, I will arrange with the family chauffeur to fetch them home."

"Well, I was actually curious if you would be willing to sell them."

Melinda paused again, for what seemed like the umpteenth time in our short discussion, and then she pointedly took a step away from me.

"I never thought my future young master had such an interest. I believe I must be vigilant in the future."

"No, I don't, and no, you won't, and stop backing away from me and listen to what I am saying!"

In the end, I had to spend the entire trip to Elly's room attempting to resolve the misunderstanding before the whole estate concluded I had a maid fetish.

Seriously, why did all the women in my life have to be so bloody difficult?

PART 2

"We have arrived, future young master," Melinda stated, still staying two extra steps away from me.

"Yes, I figured," I answered with my own brand of deadpan while subtly pointing at the mahogany door with a large brass plaque bearing the words *Eleanor Dracis* on it in cursive letters.

"I will call you when dinner is ready to be served."

After saying so, she dipped a curt curtsy, turned on her heel, and walked down the corridor where we came from. I followed her with my eyes until she was out of sight, and only then did I let out an absolutely exasperated sigh. While I had a lot to dwell on following this encounter, I decided not to do so, and instead I did a quick Far Sight roll-call. It was a habit I decided to develop, just so I would be prepared in case the dreaded "Narrative" reared its ugly head again.

Soon I found that the class rep had finished showering and was now doing homework (or more paperwork, one or the other) at her desk. Josh and Angie were sitting on the latter's couch and watching some really old, B-grade, black-and-white monster movie while munching on popcorn and laughing their heads off. Snowy was sitting in a big circle on the floor with the Fauns, fervently discussing bodyguard rotations. Judy sat at a table with the old butler in a quite poorly lit room, while Elly was... well, she was stiffly sitting on her bed on the other side of this here door.

Since that meant no one else needed my immediate attention, I resolved myself and lightly knocked.

"Come in!" came the instant response from the other side, so I naturally obliged and opened the door.

The chamber on the other side was quite… err… let's go with *eclectic*. If this was the first time I'd laid eyes on Elly's room, I probably would have frozen in my tracks, but since I'd seen the place through Far Sight, I was mentally prepared. As for a description… where do I even begin?

Let's start with the general layout. Since the room was naturally part of the mansion, at its base it had the same kind of marble floor and dark hardwood wall paneling as the rest of the building. The rich architecture was further reinforced by a vaulted ceiling covered in baroque stucco decorations and huge, elaborate windows partially hidden by elegant black curtains. All white and intricately ornamented, the furniture had golden highlights on the edges and the handles, and the centerpiece of the room was definitely the giant, king-sized bed in the middle. In summary, it really did feel like I'd just stepped into the bedroom of a true princess.

Unfortunately, things didn't stop there. Now, while I am the first to admit that I am not above considering animal plushies cute, or finding them even cuter when they are arranged in a girl's room, there is something to be said about the effect not scaling well when it came to the kind of numbers I was facing at the moment. We weren't talking about a couple of plushies, or even dozens, but *hundreds* of the adorable little buggers, in various colours, sizes, and designs. All neatly arranged. All staring at me. Like I'd just walked onto the set of a schlocky horror movie. Chilling.

This would have been weird enough, but that wasn't all! On top of all this, as if to make the place even more anachronistic, the walls were plastered with posters. Now, for a teenage girl, no matter how well bred, having posters on her walls was nothing unusual. Well, I might have agreed with that assessment if they were, oh, I don't know… let's say some pop stars, or celebrities, or maybe even a handsome sports star or something. Usual, dare I say stereotypical, teenage girl stuff.

It probably doesn't take a genius to figure out that no, the faces staring at me from her walls didn't belong to the members of the latest dreamy boy band. In fact, all of them featured various groups of leather clad, long-haired, bearded men, occasionally with elaborate props in tow, posing in front of epic landscapes filled with thunderstorms, volcanoes, dark forests, mythical animals—or all of the above at the same time. In case my brief description wasn't enough, let me spell it out: Elly's walls were covered by dozens of different, carefully framed promotional posters from actual metal bands, and to make it even weirder, most were autographed.

So, let's put all of this together. An opulent room that looked like an actual royal suite, its furniture all but buried under a mountain of plushies, and snarling power metal bands covering the walls. If this was my first time seeing this, it would have easily taken me a minute to gather my wits, but due to my previous inoculation, I just let out a flat "huh" instead and closed the door behind me.

In the meantime, the princess demurely walked up to me and said, "Welcome to my room. It's… the first time I've invited a boy in here."

Now, this was the thing that *actually* had me freeze up to gather my wits. This scene playing out was a trope in certain romance narratives, but unfortunately I hadn't really done any research into that genre lately (being more focused on the whole "battle-shounen shenanigans" thing, because surviving's kinda important), so I had no idea which direction the trope would take us.

Let's be cautious, I decided, and answered with a noncommittal, "I'm honoured?"

Elly let out a delighted giggle and clamped on to my arm like it was the most natural thing to do. Then she began to pull me towards her bed while asking, "So, what do you think?"

I had to ponder for a moment to figure out just what she was asking about, but since we'd only talked about her room so far, I ventured a guess and tentatively answered, "Your room certainly has strong character," in my most diplomatic voice.

She smiled at my response. Meanwhile, we had reached her bedside and both sat down, and to my eternal shame, it was only at this crucial moment that I realized that I kind of just came to her place on autopilot because I was "requested," but I didn't actually have anything to talk about. Since I already had enough awkward silences, I grasped for possible conversation starters and blurted out the first thing that caught my eyes.

"Just where did you get so many plushies?"

"You like them?" she asked back, and after a moment of hesitation, I answered with a not at all confident nod that made her smile all the same. "Dad buys me one whenever he goes on a business trip or visits one of the branch families, and they've piled up over the years."

"Really? He must travel a lot."

"He does," she told me while, for some reason, proudly puffing up her chest. "That bunny over there is what he brought me this week." I followed her pointing finger towards a large, blue rabbit sitting on her cabinet in the corner. After a few moments of silence, she added, "Believe it or not, I actually have more plushies back in Vienna."

"You have a mansion in Vienna, too?" I asked, just to move the conversation away from plush animals.

"Yes." Elly nodded, then wiggled to free the hand clasped around my arm and counted off on her fingers in a familiar yet absolutely adorable display. "We have a big mansion like this in Vienna; one in Stockholm; a mountain villa near Sofia; and smaller mansions in Lisbon, Warsaw, and Berlin."

"Really? That's a lot of European real estate," I mused aloud, though it was something I was already aware of due to my research.

"We also have about thirty safe houses around the rest of the world, but Europe is the ancestral land of the Dracis family," Elly answered with a smug little smile that made me want to pinch her cheeks. Just a little.

I restrained the urge and said, "That's a lot of safe houses."

To my shock and surprise, the previously giddy smile disappeared from my girlfriend's face, only to be replaced by a seething, angry scowl.

"It cannot be helped," she said, her voice dour. "We can never be too vigilant against the accursed Knights."

"Oh right, those guys," I mumbled, still recovering from the sudden mood whiplash.

"Yes, them," Elly gave me an intense nod, as if I'd just said something really profound, and she also apparently took it as a prompt to yell, "I can't wait until every last one of them have been erased from the face of this planet!"

"Whoa, there!" I grabbed her hand and began soothing her. "No need to get that loud. It's not like they can hear you." Elly let out a huff, and after a second or two, I cautiously asked her, "I don't think they have been particularly active as of late, though."

"Right, but that just means they must be scheming something," she hissed. "Just like the last time."

I looked at the princess for a solid five seconds, debating whether I should ask or not, but in the end, curiosity got better of me.

"I feel like there is a personal story here. Do you want to talk about it?"

To my surprise, Elly jumped to her feet and declared, "Very well, if you insist, I will tell you the story of my everlasting grudge!"

"I'm not insisting *that* much," I whispered, but my mumbles fell on deaf ears as the princess crossed her arms (which, incidentally, put extra emphasis on her chest). I wisely decided to just sit back and enjoy the show.

"It all started a long-long time ago!" Elly began. "Our ancestors, after centuries of grueling battles and sacrifices, managed to claim all the accursed Knights' dragon-slaying weapons."

"Question!" I raised my hand like we were in school, and the princess immediately froze up with a perplexed expression. Since she didn't say anything, I took it as permission, so I asked, "I was just wondering, are there other kinds?"

"Um… yes, I think?" Elly muttered, obviously knocked out of her groove just as she was getting into it. "I mean, we are holding on to the last dragon-slaying weapon here, so for there to still be Knights, they must have other kinds of weapons." After saying that, she went deathly pale and all but threw herself at me, clasping my hands in her own. "Wait, that was supposed to be a secret!"

"Which part?"

"The part about the dragon-slaying spear in Sebastian's office."

I gave my girlfriend a long, hard look, just to make sure she wasn't pulling my leg, but after a short while, I told her, "Princess, you are terrible at keeping secrets."

"I know!" she agreed, and her pale face went beet-red in an instant. "I… I mean… Please don't tell anyone!"

"Don't worry, I won't," I reassured her while squeezing her hand back. "So, I figure you wanted to tell me the story of how your family snatched that spear."

"We didn't snatch it!" she pouted. Then she let go of me and stood, stuck out her chest, and proudly declared, "They attacked us first, and Father beat them up, so it's technically a spoil of war."

"You are also spoiling the ending," I reminded her, at which point she let out a small "Ah."

"Right, I should start from the beginning," she said, nodding, and began. "This happened about five years ago. Back then, we were living in Berlin, and I was going to a private elementary school there."

"Was this before or after you met Josh?"

"After. So, I told you that the accursed Knights like to lay low before they strike, right? It was just like that back then. The business was great, the Knights hadn't caused any trouble in years, and I made a lot of friends in school, so Father decided to stay in place for a little longer instead of moving to the next estate as usual. So, my parents booked an entire floor of this large boat restaurant on the Spree for their wedding anniversary."

"A boat restaurant? They have those in Berlin?"

"Yes!" Elly's solemn façade melted as she grinned at me. "It was on this large barge, and the food was really great. The sight of the river was also really romantic at night! Oh—I know! We should have our anniversary there, too! I mean… if they actually rebuilt the place after the battle."

"You are both thinking too far ahead *and* spoiling your story again."

"Oh, right. Sorry… Where was I?"

"Your parents booking an entire restaurant."

"Okay," she nodded and forced herself into a semblance of solemnity. "As I was saying, our family went to the restaurant on the boat, with only minimal security. The Knights had been waiting for an opportunity like that for years, and just when they finished serving the hors d'oeuvres, they attacked. At first, they created a diversion by causing an explosion nearby, and when we were distracted, they attacked us from behind like the cowards they are! Some of them were disguised as part of the staff of the restaurant, so it was complete chaos! Then one of the bastards sneaked up behind my mother and stabbed her in the side!"

"Oh…" That took me aback. "That must've been terrible."

"Well, I was a little scared for her at the time, but Mom is really tough, you know? So what does she do when she gets stabbed by the last remaining dragon-slayer spear? She grabbed the guy dressed in a tin can and punched him so hard, he flew across two tables! Then Father noticed what happened, and he let out this *amazing* roar as he dashed over, grabbed the guy, and hurled him right into the river! He flew for about thirty meters! It was so cool!"

"Okay, time out!" I raised my hands in T. "What kind of story is this? I thought you were going to share with me the dramatic experience that made you hate the Knights so much, and instead it devolved into you bragging about your parents!"

"I'm not bragging!" she retorted with a pout. "It was really traumatic! And I hate them because they stabbed my mom, so I'm still on topic!"

"Fine," I grumbled. "So, what happened after that?"

"After that?" Elly blinked at me, then said, "Well, Father and Sebastian beat up all the accursed Knights and we got the spear."

"That's the end of it? Where's the climax?"

"It was when my father threw the Knight into the river. Weren't you listening?"

I gave the blonde dragon girl my most critical look.

"So, in summary, you hate the Knights because they tried, and failed, to assassinate your mother." I hesitated, but I decided to ask, anyways, "Speaking of which, I guess she survived the ordeal?"

"Of course. I told you, Mom's tough," Elly emphasized her words like she was stating the obvious.

"So, if the Knights only scared you a little by completely botching an assassination that they had been planning for years, then what was the point of this story again?"

"It was… um… well… It still contributed to my dislike of the accursed Knights! And it also explains why Mom's in a wheelchair."

"Whoa, hold on!" I raised my hands in a T again. "This is the first time I've heard of this."

"Really?" Elly looked up, apparently in honest surprise, but then she grinned and said, "Oh, right! I haven't introduced you to her yet! We should do that today!"

"Do we have to?" I mumbled dispiritedly, but she only continued to grin at me, so I decided to change the subject. "So, you said she was stabbed in the side, right? Why is she in a wheelchair?"

"Because it was a dragon-slaying weapon," the princess answered as if it was completely self-evident. "Those are dangerous because they stop us from regenerating."

"Regenerating? Since when can you do that?"

"I could always do that."

"Then what happened when you sprained your ankle?"

Elly blinked at me. "Well, to regenerate, we have to assume our draconic form. That's why dragon-slaying weapons are dangerous; they make us unable to transform properly."

"Yes, I think I get that, but then why didn't you transform after you got home after hurting your ankle?"

"I…" she began, but then she gave me an odd look and said, "Actually… why didn't I do that?"

I was surprised by this new information. Could it be that whatever narrative influence was messing with me also did the same with the others? For example, to make sure the supernatural masquerade didn't get out of the bag early, it might have made Elly conveniently forget that she could transform.

Or my girlfriend was just a natural airhead. One or the other.

Since the princess looked like she was getting more confused the more she thought about her past actions (a sentiment I was really familiar with), I decided to change the topic by reaching out and gently pulling her into my lap. At first, she was a little startled by my sudden action, but she snuggled up to me.

"Are you sure you are a dragon girl and not a cat?" I whispered to myself.

She glanced up at me with a curious *"Hm?"*

"Nothing. I'm just thinking aloud."

There was a comfortable silence, but then the princess suddenly threw me a curveball and said, "We were joking about it, but… I really do hate the Knights, you know?"

"I figure it's not just because they hurt your mother," I ventured, and she nodded in return.

"No. I mean, I really hate that particular guy that stabbed her, but he's just the tip of the iceberg." As she said that, she twisted in my lap so that she could look at me properly before she continued, "I really hate them because our entire lives revolve around them. They're not a huge threat, not anymore, but they are a constant one. We always have to be on the move, never staying at one place for long. All the family businesses have to be run in secret. Whatever we do, we always have to be on the lookout for them and live under their menace." She paused, then with a slightly shaking voice, she said, "And… since we are dating, they might start targeting you. Or even Judy!"

"Easy there, princess. I am not worried about them, to be honest. I have enough people out for my blood already, so if they want to join the club, they'll need to draw a number first."

"That's not a good thing!" she protested. "In fact, adding them as an extra threat makes it even worse!"

"Now, now. It's not *that* bad. Not to mention, do you think I wouldn't get involved if they showed up, even if we weren't going out?"

Elly wrinkled her brows thoughtfully, then she answered, "Yes, you would. You would probably antagonize them to the point where they'd even forget about us for a while."

"See? That means there is no problem here."

"No, that's exactly the problem!" she retorted with a scowl. "How are we supposed to have a peaceful anniversary dinner on the Spree if you keep antagonizing everyone?"

"You really want to have a dinner there, don't you?"

"But only so that I can throw a Knight into the water like dad did. I have been training in martial arts just for that!"

"Easy, easy," I playfully chided her with a smile. "If we actually get to the point where we'd have a dinner like that, I probably would have already taken care of the Knights, so there's no need to worry your pretty head over it." I patted her on the head for emphasis. The feeling was a little different from when I did that to Snowy, and the way she delightedly rubbed her crown against my palm once again reminded me of a cat.

We stayed like this for a few minutes, in a strange yet comfortable silence. Maybe it was because of the cozy atmosphere, or our previous mention of hypothetical anniversaries, but I as I held my slightly less troublesome girlfriend (which, considering I was talking about an easily excitable rich ex-tsundere dragon girl, spoke volumes about Judy), I couldn't help but wonder about the future.

I still had to figure out what made this world tick, but that was something of a long-term goal currently on hold due to a need to establish our place in the supernatural hierarchy before we got swallowed up by it. Once we did that, I figured Judy and I would return to our previous cycle of theory-crafting and experimentation, but that wasn't going to put bread on the table. At the moment, I was fine due to my mysterious allowance and the money on my bank account, but neither of those were stable or infinite.

I had no idea how long it would take us to figure out the secret behind this world we lived in. It could take months or decades, and I had no long-term plans for the worst-case scenario. Also, it wasn't like once I finished settling the Faun and training Josh to take up his mantle as the hero that there would be no further distractions down the road.

Granted, all of this wasn't a really pressing issue at the moment, since I still had two years of high school left. But what if we couldn't reach a conclusion in our research before that was over? At that point, I would have to start thinking about higher education or finding work to support two girls at the same time. Though again, it's not like they needed support, per se. Judy was smart, both academically and in general, and I was pretty sure that she would do very well for herself in the future, while the princess was… well, an almost quite literal *princess*. If anything, she would be the one supporting me. Would that make me a trophy husband? A question for later, I concluded, and instead I focused on said girl grinning on my lap.

"Hey, Elly?" I called out to her, which apparently startled her a little.

"Yes? Is there a problem? Am I heavy?"

"No, you're not. I just wanted to ask something."

"Really?" For some mysterious reason, she was suspiciously delighted by my answer, but I decided not to dwell on it and instead asked the question on my mind.

"I was just wondering… do you have any plans?"

"Plans for what?" she asked, raising her brows.

"For the future. For example, what do you want to do once you graduate high school?"

"Oh, that… Actually, I probably won't graduate. Not like you do, at least. I never really attended school until recently, anyway, and once we leave the island, I will have my private tutors prepare me for the graduation exam, and that will be it."

"So… you won't go to university?"

"Almost certainly not," she answered, shrugging. "I will most likely take some business classes and then start working with Father."

"Really? So you want to take over the family business?"

"To be honest, I don't really *want* to, but I have to." She probably realized she sounded a little bleak there, so she hastily added, "Don't take me wrong! It's not a bad job or a hard one. Dad barely has to make any business decisions, and most of the work is taken care of by the accountants and managers."

"I see."

"What about you? Are you going to go to college?"

I blinked at the girl on my lap, eagerly awaiting my answer like it was something really significant, so after a moment of thinking, I honestly said, "I don't really know yet." She gave me an odd look, so I decided to elaborate. "To be perfectly frank with you, the reason why I asked you was because I just realized that *I* don't really have any plans for the future. I mean, I am currently bogged down with the Magi, and the Abyssals, and Snowy's situation…"

"Now that you mention it, did you manage to get her new papers?"

"There is some progress, but no, not yet." I heaved a sigh. "So, as I was saying, currently I am too busy averting whatever immediate disaster is heading our way to think about long-term plans."

"You can always work with us! In fact, once we get married, it is best that you work in the family business. It's safer that way."

I let out another sigh that may or may not have had a small chuckle hidden in it.

"You're putting the cart before the horse again."

The princess let out a soft giggle, though as to why I had no idea, and said, "So you have no dreams for the future? That's a little sad."

"Well, plans and dreams are not the same thing, but you are technically correct… Speaking of which, do you have any dreams yourself?"

To my surprise (and secret delight), the girl on my lap suddenly reddened to the tip of her ears and turned her head away in a very princess-like fashion.

"I… have nothing in particular," she told me, crossing her arms and refusing to look my way.

I poked her cheek.

"Come on, princess! You know if you act like that, it only confirms that you have something to hide."

"No, I don't," she responded while turning her head away, so I switched sides and continued to poke her other cheek. "Stop that! You probably don't even want to hear it!"

"You say I don't want to hear that thing that according to you doesn't even exist?"

Elly pouted for a while, then softly said, "It's silly."

"I'm not going to laugh," I promised at once.

When she heard that, she glanced at me again, and after looking each other in the eye for a while, she raised her right hand towards me.

"Pinky swear," she demanded, rather than asked. I decided to be nice and play along with her peculiar request. After entwining our pinkies and shaking fingers three times, she declared, "Since I was little, I've wanted to be a singer."

"A singer," I repeated after her. "Like, a pop star or something?"

"No, not that kind!" Elly jumped off my lap and walked over to the nearest wall. "Do you know Dragon Prodigy?"

She pointed at the large poster behind her. It featured five burly, long-haired men clad in black leather grimacing in the forefront, surrounding a young, pale-skinned brunette in the middle wearing an elaborate gothic dress. A giant blue mountain and two red dragons provided the background. As she said, the poster had the words *Dragon Prodigy* written in a font that resembled molten rocks. After a few seconds spent scrutinizing the image, I gave Elly a tentative nod.

"I was actually the backing vocalist for Janis in their last two albums," she stated, puffing up her chest again.

For a moment, I was kind of flabbergasted, and all I could ask was a confused, "That was you?"

Now it was my girlfriend's turn to look confused, as she asked back, "You listen to them?"

To be honest, it wasn't like I was some kind of metalhead or anything. In fact, I only learned about the existence of this band, along with many others also featured on Elly's wall, after being shocked by them on my first Far Sight visit into her room a few weeks back. I'd say that the eclectic image of the room left a deep impression on me, and so I immediately searched for them on the internet. They were in a genre called "gothic symphonic power metal," a phrase needing several paragraphs to explain, so I won't attempt to do so here. Even more shockingly, their music was actually pretty good. Because of this, whenever I was working on the research notes, administering the Hub, or just browsing at night, I had their discography running in a loop in the background.

So, after some deliberation, I told the princess, "You could say I am familiar with them, yes."

Beaming, she went on with extra gusto.

"You see, I've always wanted to be a singer in a band, like Janis! I told you I took music classes, right? I've been doing so ever since I was little, and a few years ago, when Father and I visited the recording studio, they let me do some backup for Janis. They were super-nice, and when they finished recording, they said my voice was great and it complemented the album, so they convinced Dad to let me sing in the rest of the songs they were recording, too!"

"Sooo… doesn't that mean that you're already a singer?" I pointed out.

Elly's smile withered into a disappointed pout.

"It's not the same. My name couldn't be put on the credits, so I had to use a pseudonym. I'm not allowed to appear on stage, because the accursed Knights might recognize me, and then what's the point?"

"You could still sing."

"Yes, but… the whole point of being a metal singer is the live performance! The lights, the crowd, the atmosphere—I want to do that! Being a backup singer who only appears on the studio albums is no fun."

While I was pretty sure that what she'd just said was a little disrespectful to backup singers everywhere, seeing her eyes go from sparkling in excitement to abject dejection over and over again made me decide not to file a complaint, for the time being. Instead I stood up and told her, "So, it's back to the Knights being a nuisance again, huh?"

"Yes!" Elly vehemently agreed with me. "They are the worst!"

"Yeah, they are," I muttered as I looked at the poster again. In my mind's eye, I tried imagining how Elly would look in that group, in that dress. Then I imagined how she would look on the stage while performing—the crowd, loud and lively, singing along with the chorus. In my mind, the only way I could imagine her was with an enormous, gorgeous, elated smile. Then I looked at the girl who was sighing in melancholy, and before I knew it, there was a new little *desire* born in me. It was whispering, planning, and scheming, with only one goal in mind: to make that smile a reality. Of course, to do so I would have to deal with a certain Order of Knights, but considering they were openly antagonizing my girl and her family, it was only a matter of time before I'd collide with them, anyway.

For the time being, I shut it away in one of the recesses of my mind and returned to the conversation at hand. Elly looked a little depressed after our discussion, so in order to improve her mood, some flattery seemed necessary.

"But still, you actually sang for a big band like that? That's still really impressive. I knew you had an amazing singing voice, but this means the professionals recognized it, too."

"I told you, I've been practicing since I was little," she told me with a smug little smile that suited her much better.

"I know, but I'm still happy for you. Even if it's just a baby step, it still means you have a foot in the industry. Who knows? You might even get your chance once the Knights are out of the picture."

"The Knights? Out of the picture?" She pondered that then shook her head. "Probably not in our lifetime. They're like cockroaches."

"You can never know," I told her with a wink. "Think of it this way: if you could go back in time and tell yourself that you'd come to this island and not only become friends with a Celestial, a Magi, and an Abyssal, but you'd also enter into a relationship with yours truly, your younger self would've probably said it was impossible, too, and yet here we are."

The princess looked at me funny for a moment, but let her shoulders slouch and said, "When you put it like that, our situation seems even weirder... And you forgot to mention the part where we only got together because you sabotaged my attempts to get close to Josh."

"I didn't sabotage anything," I answered with a slight huff. "I told you, I was a victim of circumstances, and then things just kind of snowballed from there."

"Yes, yes," she agreed with her mouth, but her eyes told me she wasn't listening to a word I was saying. A moment later, she crept closer, then suddenly glommed me while proclaiming, "Things worked out great in the end, so everything's fine."

"That's just the hormones talking," I muttered, at which point she pinched my side. Unlike Judy's valiant yet harmless efforts at inflicting physical violence, this one stung, but I decided to bear with it and not to react in any way.

"You are terrible at reading the mood," she sulked yet didn't show the slightest intention of letting go of me.

"Yeah, Judy tells me that a lot, too."

"Then you should—"

Someone loudly knocked on the door, and Elly all but leaped away from me as if I was made of burning lava or something, and let out a relieved sigh when she saw that the door was still closed. She checked her clothes (as if something would be out of place), and after a second or so, she called out, "Enter."

"Please pardon the intrusion," echoed two voices as a pair of familiar French maids entered the room. They were the... twins, maybe? The ones with the bubble cuts. I'd never gotten their names. Anyways, they bowed in unison, and the one on the left said, "Milady, your mother is requesting your presence."

"Right now?"

"Yes. It is quite urgent," the other maid with the exact same face and voice answered.

"If it's important..." the princess mumbled as she glanced between me and the duo, visibly hesitating, but at last she sighed and told me, "I'll be back in a minute."

"No need to rush," I spoke with a smile. "I'm not going anywhere."

She returned the gesture, and then the three of them left. The maids didn't even say goodbye or anything. To my surprise, less than thirty seconds later, just as I was about to sit back down on the bed and wait for Elly to return, someone knocked on the door again. At first, I was a little apprehensive, but then they knocked again, so I raised my voice and said, "Yes?"

Without further ado, the door swung open and Melinda entered the room, prim and proper as always, and she told me, "Future young master, the head of the household is requesting your presence."

For a moment, I could only stare at the chambermaid in disbelief, then I finally asked, "Right now?"

"Yes. It is quite urgent," she told me with a nod.

"Did you rehearse this ahead of time?"

Melinda didn't seem to get it.

"What are you referring to?"

"Never mind." I dismissed the topic with a wave of my hand. "Do I really have to go, though? Shouldn't we wait for Elly to come back?"

"I believe it's in future young master's best interest to do so."

I shook my head in resignation and started walking.

"All right then, let's get this over with. Please lead the way."

"Yes, future young master," Melinda agreed with a bow as she held the door open for me.

"Also, please stop calling me that."

"Yes, future young master," she repeated with a straight face.

"Are you doing this just to annoy me?"

"Yes, future young master."

At this point, I simply gave up on having a proper talk with her and instead just gestured for her to go ahead. Thus, unexpectedly enough, I was on my way to meet my possible future father-in-law for the first time... A man who was apparently capable of throwing grown men in plate armour over a distance of thirty meters.

How come Judy's father with his shotgun suddenly seemed quaint?

CHILDHOOD FRIENDS

It was already dark outside, and with the lights turned off, the only thing illuminating Joshua's living room was the old CRT television in front of the couch, a relic of the rapidly shifting technological landscape of the island. The place looked fairly ordinary even under the less-than-ideal lighting conditions. The white walls appeared light blue due to the light of the screen, and they were covered in numerous family photos, cheap landscape paintings, and other assorted decorations, giving it a cozy, middle-class atmosphere. There were only two people in the room, sitting on the previously mentioned couch, both of them cross-legged and facing each other.

The one on the left side was obviously Josh himself. He appeared to be in considerably better shape than before, the circles under his eyes all but gone, and he was dressed in a dark green tracksuit for some reason. On the other side of the couch sat Angie. She looked inexplicably more intense than usual, but with her hair done up in pigtails, which made her look even more childish, completely ruining the serious impression she was trying to project. To further complicate the image, she also wore a tracksuit, just like Josh's except it was bright yellow.

The two of them looked each other in the eye for a long moment, right until Josh gulped and asked, "What about zombies?"

"Beeep-beeep!" the Celestial girl exclaimed, crossing her arms in an *X* shape. "No zombies!"

"Oh, come on!" Josh threw his hands up in mock outrage. "There are no zombies, either?"

"Nope! Neither the magical nor the run-of-the-mill kind."

"What is the run-of-the-mill kind?" Josh inquired with a masterfully raised single brow of supreme incredulity.

"Oh, you know, the infectious type. The kind you get from a virus. Or a plague. Or parasites. Or some kind of fungus." She thoughtfully raised a finger to her lips and added, "Now that I think about it, there are a lot of different kinds of zombies, aren't there?"

"Yeah, and that's why I'm surprised none of them are real," Josh grumbled, apparently really disappointed by the fact that there were no ravenous undead hordes craving for the flesh and brains of the living out there in this great wide world. Then his eyes lit up.

"What about mummies? Are those real?"

"Well, yes," Angie answered, visibly perplexed for a moment. "You can see them in museums and stuff."

"No, I mean the living kind! The kind covered in bandages and walking around with their arms stretched out, like this," he said as he pantomimed a stereotypical mummy, all the while still sitting in place. "You know? The Boris Karloff kind!"

"Oh, you mean *that* kind of mummy!" Angie exclaimed in revelation, only to shake her head right afterwards. "Nope, those don't exist, either."

"Seriously?" Josh huffed. "Man, none of the classics exists. No zombies, no mummies, no vampires, no werewolves..."

"I told you, vampires do exist. Kinda."

"But those are not *real* vampires!" Josh protested. "Instead we have..." He reached down beside the couch and picked up a notebook, one of his school ones by the look of it, and turned it around so that he could see the hastily scrawled lines on its last pages. "... 'Celestials,' 'Abyssals,' 'Draconians,' and 'Fauns.'"

"Among other things," Angie agreed. Apparently, the two of them had been discussing the various kinds of supernatural folk inhabiting this world, and based on her expression, she was already tired of the topic.

"I still don't understand why they are called that, though. Why don't we just call a rabbit a rabbit and call them angels and demons and were-beasts and whatnot?"

"That's just what we're called," the girl on the couch answered with a shrug. "And do I look like an angel to you?"

"Actually, you do," Josh answered with perfect sincerity.

"Really?" Angie blinked at him as her cheeks subtly flushed.

"Yeah, with the wings and all? Total angel," he continued while still gazing at the notebook, none the wiser about the Celestial girl's reaction. "Hey, I have another question? Elly's 'Draconian,' right?"

"Uh... Yes, she is?" Angie answered a little uncertainly. "I thought we covered that."

"Yeah, but I'm curious. Draconians are descendants of dragons, right? That means that dragons are real, right? I mean, *actual* dragons. The big, flying, fire-breathing kind."

"Are there any other?" she asked back with a befuddled expression.

"After learning that vampires are body-snatching smoke monsters, I wouldn't be surprised if it turned out dragons were giant radioactive space fleas from the Neptune or something. Oh, speaking of which, do we have aliens?"

"Not that I know of. Also, there are no more dragons anymore. They just kind of... died out, I guess?"

"Seriously? Man, this sucks. We don't even have dragons."

"You shouldn't miss them too much," Angie griped, obviously still a little upset about Joshua abandoning the previous thread of conversation, then she added, "They were total jerks."

"At least the Draconians are nice enough," Josh responded absentmindedly, but then a second later, he added, "Well, most of them. Elly's butler still gives me the creeps. Now that I think about it, I haven't met with other Draconians, have I?"

"I think the maids working there are also like that," Angie mumbled while reaching behind the couch and recovering an open bag of chips. "Oh? There're still some tortilla chips left. Want some?"

Josh only shook his head. Then he asked, "So, this might sound like a silly question, but... Elly's parents are also Draconian, right?"

Angie gave him a skeptical look at first, but she nodded.

"And Lili's parents should be Abyssals, right?"

"Yes, that's how genetics work," she answered with a tiny, puzzled frown. Then she reached out with an impish grin while saying, "Weren't you paying attention during sex ed? Do we need to discuss the birds and the bees again?"

"No, I was paying attention," Josh huffed and swept away Angie's hand poking him in the side. "I was asking because I was curious if... you know?"

"I know?"

"Shouldn't you?"

Angie slowly cocked her head to the side and finally she asked, "Okay, I'm officially confused right now. What were we talking about?"

"Your parents, obviously." Since she still looked perplexed, Josh forcefully cleared his throat and clarified, "I mean, if you're a Celestial, then logically it would follow that they have to be Celestials as well, am I right?"

"Well, I suppose they should be," she answered after a moment of hesitation.

"You suppose?" Josh retorted with a skeptical look in his eyes.

"Yeah," Angie answered, this time visibly bewildered by Josh's insistence.

"Have you never asked them?"

"How was I supposed to ask my..." the Celestial girl grumbled, but then halfway through the sentence, her eyes opened wide in revelation, she raised her right fist, and then she theatrically dropped it into her palm. "Ah, I get it now! You're not talking about my parents, but Mum and Dad!"

Now it was Josh's turn to furrow his brows in puzzlement.

"Wait a moment, now I'm the one who's getting confused. Aren't those the same thing?"

"No-no! You see, Mum and Dad aren't my biological parents."

"You're adopted?" Josh exclaimed with the subtlety of a battle tank sneaking through a china shop, but Angie only shrugged.

"Duh, of course I am," the Celestial girl answered with a less than subtle roll of her eyes. "Didn't I already tell you that a long time ago?"

"Really? How long are we talking about?" Josh asked back with the lack of tact that was, at this point, more or less expected of him.

"In elementary school," she replied, her brows furrowed in suspicion. "Don't tell me you really forgot…"

"Of course I have!" Josh immediately countered with, of all possible things, an indignant voice.

"Are you serious? Man, I knew you are a total scatterbrain, but come on!" Angie exclaimed with a pout.

"I'm not! If anything, you probably never told me, and now you're just trying to make me feel like an idiot." Josh crossed his arms and scowled at his childhood friend.

"It's not particularly hard to do that! And I don't even look like my mum or dad, so if you paid even a tiiiiiiny little bit of attention, you could've realized it on your own."

"Am I supposed to pay attention to *everything*?"

"Yes, you should. Or at least to the important things. Like me," she answered, pointing at herself.

"Whatever," Josh grumbled, probably realizing he didn't have a leg to stand on, and afterwards they both stayed silent for several seconds.

It looked like the situation would soon develop into an awkward silence, but then, as if the previous argument never happened, Josh asked, "Are there any orcs?"

Angie glanced up at him in surprise, but after a split second, she answered, "Nope," without a shred of her previous sulkiness.

"No orcs, either? Damn," Josh whispered with the kind of gravitas usually reserved for strategists getting their plans foiled in period dramas. "How about elves, then? I mean, the Tolkien kind, not the Keebler ones."

"No elves, either." Angie tilted her head and asked, "By the by, are we seriously going through all the fantasy races now?"

"Hey, you call them fantasy races, but a week ago I would have thought that Celestials were one, and yet here I am, talking to one of them."

"Lucky you," she replied with a smug little grin, but Josh only rolled his eyes at her.

"I really hoped elves were real, though," he mumbled, prompting Angie to lean in closer.

"Why?" she inquired, her eyes narrowed in suspicion.

Naturally, Joshua completely disregarded the change in her expression before he said, "Elves are supposed to be super-pretty, right?" without a shred of delicacy or self-awareness.

"Depending on the source, yes..." Angie, surprisingly enough, agreed on the spot, but then she added, "Don't we have enough pretty girls in our group, though?"

"Nah, you can never have enough pretty girls," he answered with a toothy grin.

"So, you like elves, huh?" she grumbled. "Well, I'm sorry you are not satisfied with us lowly non-elves, but if I were you, I wouldn't hold my breath for a nonexistent elf transfer student to fall into your lap."

For a moment, Joshua looked quite surprised by her sulky outburst, but then he let out a small chortle and told her, "You know, I'm pretty sure that even if an elfin girl did appear in the school, Leo would wrap them around his little finger in a day or two." Angie gave him a curious look, which he finally noticed for a change, so he hastily continued, "I mean, think about it—Judy entered into our group, and a few weeks later, she ended up as his girlfriend. Then Elly transferred, and she ended up the same way. Then Lili transferred, and she now lives in his house. If there was another transfer student at this point, I'm pretty sure Leo would sink his talons into her in no time."

"Now that you mention it, I guess you're right," Angie answered in cautious agreement. Then she asked, "Hey, speaking of, do you think their arrangement will work out?"

"I've no idea." Josh scratched his chin. "I mean, I'm one of your unpopular guys, so getting along with one girl is already beyond me. Two at the same time? I can't even imagine."

"Booo! You're already getting along with a girl right now!" Angie exclaimed while sending a kick towards him.

"Ow! Hey, stop that!" It took a few seconds for Angie to stop play-kicking him, at which point he told her, "You're not a girl, you are Angie! There's a big difference!"

Whatever that difference was, it still resulted in her redoubling her efforts to kick him off the couch. At last, after several minutes of struggle, which left the couch cushions scattered all over the floor, they both returned to their previous cross-legged positions, heaving from the exertion.

Once again, it looked like they were on the brink of an awkward silence, but then Josh suddenly cleared his throat and he sat up straight.

"So…" he spoke up between two heaves, "… how about goblins? I'm fine with either the low-level monster or the high-level banker kind."

"Nope," Angie answered with an almost triumphant grin. "There are no goblins of any variety."

"Seriously? What kind of unreality is this?" Joshua burst out as if he'd just experienced the worst injustice in the universe. "How about trolls, then? Are they real?"

"Nope again," Angie responded with a tinkling voice, apparently enjoying her childhood friend's faux anguish.

"Oh, come on! No trolls, either? This sucks! None of the cool monsters are real!"

"Since when are trolls considered cool?"

"Silence, you heretic!" Josh retorted quite rudely, but Angie only giggled, indicating that it might have been some sort of inside joke between the two.

"Well, if you are looking for monsters, Chimeras are real," she suggested after she finished chuckling.

"Chimera…? Oh, right, that half-crocodile, half-gorilla, half-bear thing."

"I think it was more like half-bear, half-crocodile, and half-gorilla."

"Is there a difference?" he asked incredulously.

"Obviously," Angie replied with a firm nod.

"If you say so," Josh relented with a nonchalant shrug. "I wasn't paying it much attention at the time, but I don't think it was a cool monster-movie monster but more of a scary horror-movie monster."

"Is there a difference?" she asked incredulously.

"Obviously," Josh replied with a firm nod.

"If you say so." This time it was Angie's turn to shrug. "Leo said it was regenerating like a troll, though."

"Reeeally?" Josh enunciated like he was a detective who'd just found a crucial clue. He rubbed his chin in a thoughtful manner to complete the look. "Then I suppose they are a little cool, just by association."

"Cool or not, I don't want to fight another one," Angie said with a shudder. "Those things are really, really scary."

"Oh, right. You guys also fought it," Joshua said as if it was something that slipped his mind. "Leo's been hogging all the glory for himself, so I almost forgot."

"But I don't think he wanted to fight it, either. Or 'hog the glory.' Remember how mad he looked when he said that Ammy's grandfather called him 'Chimera Slayer'?"

"Yeah, I guess you're right." Josh gave a shrug, then silently mouthed something like *being called Chimera slayer is a little cool, though*—a sentiment he was so wrong about, he definitely deserved a smack with a slipper.

"Of course. I am always right, except when not." Angie grinned, oblivious to his silent words. Soon she noticed that Joshua seemed to be a little down, so she called out to him, saying, "Hey, pal, what's eatin' ya?" using some kind of forced accent.

Josh sighed. "I'm just a little worried. This whole Chimera-talk kinda reminded me of what happened on the weekend."

"Yeah, it was rough."

"It was," Josh nodded, then he continued with, "And do you remember how Leo was talking about figuring out how my transformation thing works? And how I'm supposed to train to use it? It's like he's expecting something like that to happen again, and that I'll have to fight."

"He didn't seem to be *just* expecting it, he looked dead sure about it."

"I know, right?" Josh agreed quite vehemently. "That's why I'm worried! I don't even know if I can do that transformation thing again, and yet he already wants me to fight against... hell, I don't even know what! Nor do I want to know. Like, what am I supposed to do if another Chimera shows up and wants to eat my spleen?"

"Hey, let's be realistic!" Angie raised her voice in encouragement. "The bad guys could show up whether you learn how to do your transformation thingie or not. In that case, wouldn't it be better to learn about it, just to be on the safe side? I mean, even if you can't fight, you can use your powers to run away!"

"Yeah, but that would make me a coward, especially if everyone else is fighting. How am I supposed to look any of you guys in the eye if you get injured while I ran away?"

"Hey, it's no biggie. I'm bad at fighting, too! If someone wanted to punch me, I'd run away..."

"Yeah, but you're the medic," Josh countered. "The medic is not supposed to be on the front line, so it makes perfect sense for you to retreat when an enemy is in melee range. Haven't you played any tactical RPGs?"

"I think you're ever so slightly overthinking this. Also, your analogy is weird," Angie told her childhood friend with a deadpan look that was more at home on Judy's face.

"I suppose." Josh shrugged. "But then there are all of those prophecies, that 'chosen one' business. It's a lot of pressure." He paused, then continued with a hopeful, "But then again, maybe that whole transformation thing was just a fluke, and we are *all* overthinking this whole situation." He finished his sentence with a dry chuckle.

Angie softly asked him, "Should we try it out, then?"

His eyes popped wide open. Blinking, he processed her words. "You mean, try… the transformation?"

"Mm-hmm." Angie nodded twice, probably for emphasis.

"You mean… like… right now?"

"Mm-hmm," Angie hummed again, though the nod following it was slightly less firm than the previous one.

"But… you have to cut yourself for that, right?"

"Not necessarily," Angie replied, her face getting more and more flushed. "You remember the original way Leo talked about?"

"You mean… er… you mean, kissing?" Josh mumbled, reddening.

Angie nodded, this time somewhat hesitantly. Meanwhile, Joshua awkwardly averted his eyes and said, "Are you sure about that? I mean… shouldn't your first kiss be with someone special?"

The bashful expression on the Celestial girl's face melted away like a snowball in a furnace, revealing an irritated scowl underneath it.

"It wouldn't be my first kiss," she stated with the bluntness of a falling anvil with *ACME* written on it.

"It… wouldn't?"

"No, of course not," she huffed, her expression growing sulky.

"Really? Wow! Who was the lucky recipient?" Joshua inquired with a provocative grin, which was covered up less than a second later by a pillow Angie smashed into his face so hard, he nearly lost his balance and fell off the couch. "Hey! Ouch! Stop that! What's your problem?"

"It was you, you inconsiderate jerk!" Angie exclaimed, her words punctuated by another smack with the pillow.

"What was I? You're not making any sense!" Josh complained while trying to protect his face with his forearms.

"My first kiss, you idiot!"

"Wait, what?" He froze up, only to get smacked so hard in the face, he did fall off the couch, right onto a strategically placed stray cushion on the floor. He didn't seem to mind, though, as he sat up and asked her, "When?"

"Back in elementary school, you dunderhead!" she declared, throwing the pillow at his face.

"Seriously?… Hey! Ow! Stop it already!"

Saying so, Josh picked up the same fluffy projectile and then promptly returned it to the sender. And thus followed the world's most intense pillow fight, which ended with them both panting and the cushions scattered all over the place once again.

After a while, Josh climbed back on the couch, his hair and clothes disheveled but otherwise no worse for wear.

"So… now that we resolved that… what are we going to do now?"

"Well, we are obviously not going to kiss after all that," Angie declared with a pout, one pigtail undone and springing free.

"Hey, don't look at me like it was my weird idea!" Josh protested, earning him a wounded glare.

"It's not weird, and you're still horrible for forgetting our—"

"Yeah, I sure am," Josh huffed. "I guess we're not going to have any kind of constructive discussion for the rest of the evening."

"Not likely," Angie answered, still pouting with the power of a thousand exploding suns.

"Okay, then I suppose we'd better return to our crappy horror movie marathon."

"That's the first sensible thing you've said in a while!" Angie declared, her sulking instantly replaced by an excited smile as she reached behind the couch again, and after some rummaging, she picked up a brand-new bag of chips. While she opened it and put it on her lap, Josh walked over to the TV, or to be more precise, the large VHS player under it, and looked over the videos on the shelf underneath.

"Let me see…" He rummaged through the movies, only to abruptly stop in his tracks and glance over his shoulder at the disheveled girl eating chips on the sofa. "Hey, Angie?"

"Hmph?" she grunted.

"Are leprechauns real?"

The Celestial girl swallowed the contents of her mouth and answered with an upbeat, "Nope."

"Really?" Josh mumbled as he put a VHS tape into the player. "Good riddance. Leprechauns are lame, anyway."

CHAPTER 10

PART 1

I'd just left the princess's room, and I was once again simultaneously amazed and annoyed by the sheer size of the Dracis estate. Was that irritatingly polite chambermaid leading me through the scenic route on purpose? Well, at least doing so gave me ample time to gather my wits. As such, I let the backdrop of the samey corridors become a kind of visual white noise, and I quietly retreated into my thoughts as my legs followed after Melinda.

So, I was about to meet with Elly's father. Considering all the crazy things I've seen and done as of late, that was not supposed to make me nervous, yet here I was, wracking my head over what to do. To be frank, the reasons for that were many and wide-branching, so let's start with the most mundane.

First and most obviously, I was steadily walking towards a *trope*. I didn't know the exact name of it, but I was pretty sure that the whole *boyfriend's first meeting with Dad* was something of a staple situation in romantic comedies designed to lead to the dreaded *shenanigans* I always preferred to avoid. Now, granted, in retrospect, I'd already passed through a round of that due to Judy's father, with his oft-mentioned shotgun, but he was fairly insignificant in the grand scheme of things. The man I was about to meet, on the other hand, was one of the most influential people on the island, both in terms of the supernatural politics and how much he could affect my future prospects if I got on his bad side which, given the nature of the aforementioned trope, was a very distinct possibility.

Actually, scratch that. The biggest problem was not his reaction to me, but the other way around. Due to time restraints, I still hadn't gotten around to test my hypothesis whether I was reacting badly to magical pressure, or if Judy's assumption of some sort of narrative influence was more on the nose. Not that it made a huge difference at the moment, as no matter the underlying reason, I was sure meeting with the head of the Dracis household would result in my nerves getting touched again, whether I liked it or not.

Because of all this, I had already begun mentally preparing myself for the meeting, and the best way to do it was to stay calm, steel my nerves, and make a game plan that would hopefully survive the encounter with the opponent. I took a deep breath and did just that.

So. What were my goals? First, I had to make a good impression, or if that were impossible, I had to avoid making a bad one. There were two obstacles: the trope and my unstable temper around powerful people. The latter I could do little about, other than fortifying my concentration and practicing my best diplomatic smile, and as for the former, I had a few ideas.

First and foremost, I had to figure out how to get into the good graces of Daddy Dracis. I didn't know much about his personality, but based on a few of Elly's stray comments and my observations, I could make a few inferences. For a start, he was a doting parent and a family man. He obviously spoiled the princess quite a bit; he went as far as to let her enroll in a public school just on the off-chance that she could woo a guy she'd met a few years before. He was also almost guaranteed to be at least as much, if not even more, hostile towards the Knights-with-the-unnecessarily-long-name as his daughter. That opened two avenues of approach: I could either flatter his family, or I could voice my eternal hatred towards the Knights. In fact, why not both?

Once I had my foot in the door, I would have to improvise based on the situation and whatever archetype Elly's father slotted into. Normally I didn't like to consider the people around me on simplistic narrative terms like that, but succeeding in my first impressions here was quite crucial, so I decided to suspend my rule for the time being. My guess was that he would be some iteration of a stereotypical aristocrat, just like how the princess was most likely supposed to be an example of the haughty *oujo* archetype until I kind of derailed her personality into a ditzy tsundere (for the better, I would say, as I liked her clumsy antics a lot. But I might be biased in that regard). In that case, I should expect some political talk regarding the supernatural folk, plus topics concerning wealth, influence, and traditional values. I was pretty bad with the last one, but if it came to money and influence, I think I had at least some spare change to bring to the table.

All things considered, while I wasn't 100 percent satisfied with my mental preparations, I felt significantly less tense by the time Melinda stopped in front of a lavishly decorated double door.

"We have arrived, future young master," she stated with the utmost seriousness.

"I figured," I told her, though this time I had no brass plaque to cheekily point at.

The chambermaid knocked twice on the door and announced, "The guest has arrived."

After a moment, there was a muffled *"Enter"* coming from the other side, and she opened the door. Very. Slowly. Probably for dramatic effect.

But damn, she was so slow, I wanted to help her push, but I restrained myself and waited for her to finish. At last, she gave me a quick nod and walked in, so I followed right after her, and what I found on the other side was just a tiny bit unexpected.

Let's start with the description of the room, shall we? It was big but not enormous, about one size larger than Elly's bedroom, but nowhere near as spacious as the parlor. Speaking of the parlor, in broad strokes, the place was similar. It also had a large, cozy hearth in the back, which also served as the sole source of light in the room, dressing everything in a soft, orange glow.

Before the fireplace stood four large, black leather sofas arranged around a glass-topped wrought iron coffee table (which, incidentally, had the same elaborate dragon-shaped legs as the one in the parlor), and all of these were standing on a huge, extremely intricate (and presumably equally costly) Persian rug. I kind of wondered if it was even safe to have such a fancy carpet so close to the hearth, but I decided not to dwell on the firesafety of the place, as I had more pressing issues to worry about.

I glanced around and noted that, on one side of the room, stuffed animal heads and antlered skulls decorated the wall, while the other side had a series of racks featuring dozens of weapons, from elaborately ornamented cavalry sabers and simple winged spears to muskets and hunting rifles.

I didn't spend a lot of time admiring those, either, as my attention was quickly drawn to the man rising from one of the sofas. He was big, but not enormous, with wide shoulders and a physique that was closer to "heavy," like an aging bodybuilder who had put on some weight. He wore a fairly simple ensemble consisting of brown trousers, a white long sleeve shirt, a brown waistcoat, and one of those strings with a large green gem around his neck.

What are they called? *Bolo ties?* Something like that.

Anyway, his hair was the same golden colour as his daughter's, and he had tidily cropped yet prominent sideburns that gave him a slightly wild look. That, combined with his wide jaw and large, flat nose, he reminded me of a lion, an image probably invoked due to all the hunting trophies surrounding him. As for his actual age, based on his features, I would've said somewhere in his early thirties, though considering that Draconians could apparently live up to three hundred years, he could have been eighty years old for all I knew.

When our eyes met, his lips slowly parted in a... welcoming smile? I guess that was the intent behind it, but it was pretty strained. Speaking of strain, just by looking at the man, I could feel the familiar irrational irritation bubbling up from the pit of my stomach like some noxious gas, but

I took a deep breath and pushed it back down. Once I felt in control again, I returned his gesture with a guarded smile.

For a few long, silent seconds we stood in place, smiling at each other like idiots, right until Melinda cleared her throat. It made the man flinch, but he collected himself and told me, "Oh, where did I leave my manners? Please, come in," in a surprisingly normal baritone voice.

I wanted to point out that technically I was already inside the room, but I decided not to, and instead I simply nodded and took a few steps towards him. He stepped forth as well, and once I got close enough, he extended his hand towards me.

"As you must've already figured out, I'm Abram Dracis, patriarch of the Dracis family."

I reached out and shook his hand. We were about the same height, so I had no trouble maintaining eye contact while doing so.

"Leonard Dunning. It's a pleasure to meet you," I presented myself with a voice that was just a teensy bit flatter than I intended. He didn't seem to mind, though, as after he let go of my hand, he gestured towards the sofas.

"The pleasure is mine. Come, let's sit down. I believe we have many things to discuss," he told me in a wooden voice, as if reading from a script.

"Do we?" the question inadvertently slipped out of my mouth, which made him pause in his tracks.

"Don't we?" he asked back, seemingly uncertain for a moment.

"Future young master is making things more awkward than strictly necessary," the chambermaid chimed in from beside the door.

"Ah! Right, that's what we were supposed to discuss," he stated, loudly, like he'd just discovered something profound. He pointed towards the sofa again and declared, "We should sit and talk about family business!"

"Such as?"

"Such as…!" he began with an enthusiastic voice, but then his brows furrowed and he glanced at Melinda.

"Such as the relationship between future young master, milady, and Miss Sennoma," the chambermaid provided the answer with a deferential bow.

"Yes, what she said!" Papa Dracis nodded with a dopey grin, and for a moment I could only blink at him as the realization set in.

I came here expecting a snobby aristocrat, and in his place, I got… this? And if this dude was running in the family… maybe Elly wasn't supposed to be an oujo after all, and I hadn't derailed her character. Maybe she'd inherited her personality from her father, and it simply came to the surface over time. That… kind of threw all my preconceptions about character tropes out the window, and if it wasn't for the large man urging me to sit down, I probably would have started taking notes on the spot. For now, I decided to file this new insight for later and sat down as instructed.

Papa Dracis followed suit, and after a short moment of silence, he loosened his tie and said, "So, Leonard…" he began, only to pause and hastily ask, "can I call you Leonard?"

"Sure, that's my name," I answered nonchalantly, and for some reason, he gave me a thoughtful nod in response.

"Good! It's a good name! Leonard Dracis has a good ring to it, too!" He nodded to himself repeatedly. Then he gave me a thumbs-up and a toothy grin and declared, "I approve!"

"Thank you… ?" I answered, but before I could say anything else, Melinda cleared her throat.

"Sir, shouldn't you hold your approval until after the discussion is over?"

The Dracis family patriarch flinched, then exclaimed, "Oh, right! So. Are you currently dating my daughter?" with the approximate bluntness of a sledgehammer to the face.

"Yes, as a matter of fact, I am," I said.

"Ah, so it's true!" he mused with a solemn nod. "You know, my daughter had told me a lot about you."

"Really?" I responded, suddenly feeling slightly bashful.

"Yes, yes!" he answered with another toothy grin. "I remember when she first mentioned you like it was yesterday! What did she call you back then? A *'handsome lecher,'* I think?"

"Heh," I snorted as I failed to stifle a chuckle. "That takes me back."

"I imagine!" Papa Dracis chuckled as well, then said, "My Elly has some of her mother's temper, so when I first heard her complain over the phone, I immediately had my suspicions, and by the next time we talked, you were a 'good friend.' Then before I knew it, she refused to even talk about you and called me a daddydiot for asking! It was around that time I figured out something was brewing between you two."

"*Daddydiot?*" I repeated after him in surprise, then grinned. "Did she really say that?"

"Yes, she did!" Abram answered with a smile mirroring my own. "Is my daughter cute or what?"

"The cutest," I answered with mock solemnity, at which point the large man let out a hearty laugh and gave me another thumbs-up. I couldn't help but chuckle along, finding myself caught up in his enthusiasm, and with every passing second, I felt more at ease.

"I will be honest with you, when my daughter told me she wanted to come to Critias to meet with her childhood friend, I was a little skeptical, but she was really insistent. I really didn't want to let her attend your school at first, but teenage daughters have their ways, and no father is immune to them."

"She sulked, didn't she?" I ventured a guess, and he confirmed it with a sagely nod.

"For three days straight!" he exclaimed in a loud, boisterous voice once again, which made me wonder if maybe he just didn't have an indoor voice. "She didn't talk to me, she refused to come out of her room, and she even refused to eat desserts!"

"That sounds… serious?" I said, my statement turning into a bewildered question, which earned me another laugh from the man.

"Yes, it was! So you can imagine how shocked I was when I heard that, instead of her childhood sweetheart, my daughter started dating someone else!" he told me, apparently finding the situation incredibly amusing. "Not that I was worried. My daughter always had great eyes for people, so I was sure that if she picked someone else so suddenly, he must be exceptional!" He abruptly paused and rubbed his chin as he looked me over. "Speaking of eyes, I like yours! Determined! Focused! Green! I can't wait to see them on my grandchildren!"

"Sir, you are getting ahead of yourself again," Melinda chimed in, and for once I could only nod in agreement.

"Like father, like daughter," I said under my breath, but Papa Dracis obviously overheard it, as he grinned bashfully.

"You think so?" he asked, followed by another hearty laugh. "My daughter wasn't the only one who talked about you. Can you guess who else?"

"Was it Sebastian?" I reckoned after a moment of thinking, still wondering if it was a trick question.

"Yes, it was him!" Abram slapped his thigh as if he just recalled a fun memory. "He was so angry, I could practically hear his blood boiling through the phone!"

"And that's a good thing?" I asked tentatively, slightly confused by his expression.

"Good? Maybe not, but really impressive! Angering the old man is not hard. He's been on a hair trigger for as long as I've known him, but I was truly impressed by the way you dared to do it over and over again! And you got away with it!" He let out another lively laugh. "I only really started to pay attention to you after Grandpa Seb told me he simultaneously wanted to strangle you and adopt you into the family."

"Wait, he actually said that?" I uttered in shock.

The Dracis patriarch beamed an impish smile.

"Of course he did! He was truly impressed, both by your courage, your wit, and especially your connections! Speaking of which!" He leaned closer before telling me, in a slightly more subdued but still loud voice, "I believe I never had the chance to thank you for the information you provided about the accursed Knights. By sharing it with our 'allies,' we not only managed to strike at several of their bases, but we put our 'friends' into our debt, as well."

I had a feeling that he was sure I already knew who these "friends" and "allies" were, even though I had no idea what he was talking about. Still, being in the dark never stopped me from playing along, so I gave him a slight nod and made a mental note to check the Hub for any recent changes in the Knights' situation.

"There's no need to thank me. It was part of a fair trade," I told him, and Papa Dracis leaned back on his sofa with a thoughtful expression.

"True. If I recall, you requested to enter our local library, didn't you?" My poor ears were just starting to feel comfortable again, when he raised his voice to exclaim, "Now that you mention it, Sebastian has also been singing the praises of little Miss Sennoma!"

"R-really?" I stuttered, thrown off balance by his sudden, upbeat shouting.

"Yes! I was told she rearranged and cataloged two hundred years' worth of records in just two weeks! She is an immensely talented young lady!"

"Yes, I'm well aware of that," I answered, mentally preparing myself for the inevitable question, and unfortunately, I didn't have to wait long.

"Speaking of which, you are also dating her, aren't you?" To my sincerest puzzlement, the man was looking at me with a mixture of expectation and… appreciation? Since I couldn't find the right words to say, I simply nodded with my most serious expression, at which point Daddy Dracis let out another window-shaking laugh. "Marvelous! You sure know how to pick them!"

If I wasn't confused already, this would have been the moment where I'd have tried to do the whole single-eyebrow-raise thing, but at this point, I was so past confusion, I was slowly entering a state where my higher thought processes were shutting down to allow me to just go with the flow. Still, I swam against the tide of bafflement threatening to wash me away, gathered what was left of my wits, and asked, "Are you… okay with that?"

"Why wouldn't I be?" Abram responded with a puzzled look of his own, then he let out a softer chuckle and told me, "You know about the marriage traditions of our household, right?"

"Of course?"

"Then you should know that I have four mothers and seven grand-mothers!" he told me like it was something to be proud of. Or… maybe he *was* proud of it?

"That's a lot," I managed to say.

For the following minute or so, Papa Dracis prattled about his extended female family members, while I just nodded, too numbed by trying to wrap my head around the situation to respond in any other fashion. No, scratch that; it wasn't just the casual discussion of polygamy or the fact that the Dracis patriarch was apparently a fervent supporter of it (even though he was in a monogamous relationship, go figure), but the implications of this whole discussion.

Let's wind back the clock a little and consider my previous theories about this world. I always considered that it had a certain setting or underlying genre to it. At first, I figured it was a school life romance narrative, then I thought it was a supernatural shounen battle narrative but, considering how accommodating this world seemed towards polygamy and polyamory…

Could it be that my jabs about Josh being a dense harem protagonist were more on the nose than I expected? Could it be that this was a straight up *"battle harem"* narrative? If that were the case… shit, I might even have to apologize to Judy for not taking her anti-harem measures seriously enough!

No, wait. Technically, the protagonist was still Josh, so he was the one who was supposed to get his battle harem of pretty, powerful action girls. Hell, even his unique power-up seemed to be tailor-made to get him into situations where he would exchange bodily fluids with multiple girls! But then, how had I gotten into a harem relationship while he was still single? Had I messed things up, or was this world this messed up from the beginning?

While I was silently pondering this, the Dracis patriarch finished listing the last of his "mothers" with, "… and so they all agreed to stay in touch, and they still play canasta every Saturday, even twenty years after my father died! Speaking of which, my daughter and Miss Sennoma are also in agreement, right?"

Violently thrown out of the window of my train of thought, I had to rewind the last few seconds in my head to figure out what the hell he was asking about. Then I quickly told him, "Yes, yes we all agreed on it."

"Great!" he exclaimed once again. "Both of you will be amazing addi-tions to the Dracis family!"

"A question, if I may?" I raised my hand to get the man's attention, and he gave me a gracious (and greatly amused) go-ahead gesture. "I was just wondering… if what I heard was correct, your family is very particular about maintaining your bloodline, right?"

"That's entirely correct!"

"So, why aren't you concerned about that?" He gave me an odd look, so I clarified, "I mean, shouldn't I be required to meet some kind of standard?"

"Oh, that?" The man let out a contented chuckle. "We've already tested you!"

I furrowed my brow.

"When?"

"While you were unconscious, obviously!" he declared, glancing towards the silent maid. "Melinda provided us with your blood sample!"

"Seriously?" I directed my frown at the chambermaid.

After a moment, she shrugged. "The future young master was spilling it everywhere, anyway, so I assumed you wouldn't mind."

Before I could respond, the patriarch loosed another boisterous laugh, which was getting a little grating, to be honest, and told me, "Leonard, you are a perfect match for my daughter! Your bloodline is more than compatible, you have talent, you come with a wonderful second wife, and you are a famed Chimera slayer! I would be a fool if I didn't try to snatch you up before someone else did." Then he sheepishly added, "Oh. And you are in love with each other. That's also important."

I gave the man skeptical look in my best impression of Josh, then flatly told him, "You are being a little overbearing, don't you think?" in my best impression of Judy, for an imitation one-two punch.

Papa Dracis glanced at the maid in the corner and asked, "Hey, Melinda? Am I overbearing?"

"Yes, sir, most certainly," she told him with a completely straight face. "Though I believe you can do even better."

"You are entirely correct!" the large man affirmed, and when he faced me again, he declared, "From now on, you must call me Dad!"

For a few long moments, I could only blink at the man in incomprehension, but eventually I let out a defeated groan and muttered, "What-the-heck-ever."

The Dracis patriarch laughed, elated by his victory. I, on the other hand, was feeling quite exhausted by this discussion. I mean, it turned out that my misgivings about running headlong into a tropey situation were off the mark by a huge margin, but at the same time, my self-appointed father-in-law was turning out to be way more high-maintenance than expected. On the bright side, by now the irrational irritation I'd felt had completely disappeared, only to be replaced by an entirely rational irritation. Yay?

Anyways, after my host stopped laughing, there was a natural lull in the conversation, which I decided to quickly exploit to ask a question that had been bothering me ever since I'd entered this room.

"So, I gather you like hunting?" I asked the man on the other sofa, but he only gave me an uncomprehending look in return, so I gestured towards the plaques on the walls and added, "These are your trophies, aren't they?"

"What?" he asked as he glanced around uncertainly. Then the light went on in his eyes, and he hurriedly said, "I mean, yes, of course! I just love hunting! It's a real man's hobby, don't you agree?"

It was time for me to apply my most skeptical gaze again, which made the patriarch conspicuously avert his gaze. I was once again surprised and a little disturbed by how similar his reactions were to my girlfriend's. I quickly shook off the impression and asked, "Do you really?"

Papa Dracis tried to pretend he didn't hear me, but he eventually slouched his shoulders and admitted, "No, I don't," in an almost sulky voice. "This is actually my late father's collection." He glanced up at me, and since I might've been showing the slightest smidgen of interest, he raised his voice into a boisterous thunder, telling me, "My father hunted prey all across Africa! Braved the jungles of the Amazon! He even wrestled with a narwhal! Unfortunately, he strained his back in the process, so he had to retire from adventuring, but we still have its horn to show!"

"I see," I nodded as I glanced around, but I couldn't see a single narwhal horn anywhere. I'd be lying if I said I wasn't a little disappointed, but I pushed on and asked, "Did you arrange the meeting here so that you could show off his collection?"

"Well, not exactly..." the grown man muttered like a little kid caught with his hand in the cookie jar. But then he bounced back and exclaimed, "Oh, to hell with it! We have already sealed the deal, so I might as well show you my vulnerable belly, am I right?"

The last bit was probably aimed at Melinda, as she let out a small sigh and answered something along the lines of, "As milord sees fit."

Now, there were many questions I would've liked to ask here, such as what exactly he meant by *sealing the deal*, or if showing his *vulnerable belly* was only an expression (I really, really hoped it was), but I didn't have the chance.

"I'll tell you now!" Papa Dracis began, but then, faltering, he leaned forward and gestured for me to do the same. I was a little wary at first, but I hoped he wasn't the type to yell into my ear for a cheap laugh, so I leaned in, too. "You see," he said with a somewhat uncomfortable expression, "I wanted to make a good first impression on my future son-in-law. I thought since you were a famous Chimera slayer and everything, meeting you here would… how do they put it? Build skinship?"

"It's *kinship*," I corrected him. "Also, please stop calling me that."

"Stop calling you what?"

"Chimera slayer. It's a dumb title, it's inaccurate, and it's embarrassing."

"You think so?" He stared at me like I was a white raven or something. "So… you didn't kill a Chimera?"

"I did, I just don't like it when people keep making a huge deal out of it," I admitted with a grumble.

"I see," Papa Dracis mumbled as he straightened his back, but then abruptly exclaimed, much to the lament of my poor ears, "Strong, handsome, resourceful, AND humble! Haha! If I didn't know better, I would think you are some kind of sneaky infiltrator designed to appear as my perfect son-in-law!"

"You forgot that I am also very tolerant of loud people," I muttered with just a hint of biting snark. But it was like throwing water on a duck's back, so I let it go and asked him, "Who would even try to infiltrate your home?"

"Take your pick!" Abram told me with a shrug. "The Celestials try to infiltrate everywhere on principle, the Magi also love to have informants planted around all our estates, and as for the accursed Knights, the less said is the better."

"I can't really argue with that," I replied, making another mental note about looking into any Celestial infiltrators on the Hub. Just in case.

Meanwhile, my self-appointed father-in-law's thoughts had returned to the previous conversation, as he added, "Actually, there was another reason why I wanted to meet you here. This is my favourite room in this mansion. When I was only a little older than you are now, my father and I always talked here, so I thought it would be a good place for us to talk. Bond. Build kinship. Those kinds of things," he finished with a grin. Then he added in a whisper, "Not to mention, my study is currently full of records, so we couldn't have been able to sit comfortably."

"Records?" I inquired by reflex the moment I heard the word. "What kind of records?"

"Er…" The patriarch gave me a classic deer-in-the-headlights look that once again reminded me of his daughter. "Mostly Dragon Prodigy, but there were a few boxes of El Drake, Jörmungandr, Wyrm Pride, plus a few dozen Níðhöggr albums—"

"Wait, hold on," I interrupted the man just as he began to count on his finger, an act that was infinitely cuter and less uncanny when performed by his daughter. "When you said *'records,'* you meant music records? As in, CDs?"

"Of course." Abram nodded like it was obvious. "I have no idea what's going on, but in the past couple of weeks, practically all music shops on the island reported that people stopped buying our products and keep asking about '*digital distribution*' and '*streaming*'! My top men are already looking into it, but for the time being, a lot of the excess records are being stored in my office."

"Hold on!" I raised my hand to stop him again. "You have a *record company?*"

"Well… yes! Yes, I do!" Papa Dracis declared with a mixture of pride and surprise. "You didn't know?"

"Can't say I did," I told him honestly.

"But you had access to our Library for weeks!"

"Yes, but Sebastian told us we weren't allowed to browse the parts that have current or confidential data that can compromise the security of the family," I told him matter-of-factly, and he once again looked at me like I was the last specimen of some species considered long extinct that had casually walked into his room.

"And you didn't look at them?"

"Of course not," I answered with a slightly irritated scoff. "First off, I have no interest in your finances. Secondly, Sebastian was always hovering around Judy when she came over, so of course she wouldn't try to read them even if we *were* interested. Thirdly, if God forbid something bad happened to any of you, I really didn't want to be put under suspicion."

"And that's why you didn't look at our finances or our holdings?"

"More or less."

To be fair, the other reason was that we were way more focused on researching the supernatural landscape of this world, plus I always had the Celestial Hub and its numerous informants to reach out to if I was really curious. Which I wasn't. Until now.

"So, what's the name of your label, again?" I asked as casually as I could manage.

"The family owns shares in all five major international music conglomerates, among many other industries, but I also personally own Dragonflame Records! Well, technically, I don't *personally* own the company, as it would leave a money trail. It would be more accurate to say I am its secret owner. In the shadows! Like a dangerous mob boss, except less dangerous and illegal!"

"I get it," I muttered, rubbing my temple. "So, your record label is called *Dragonflame,* and all your artists are either named after dragons or have the word in their name?"

"Yes! Ironic, isn't it?"

"Only if you mean it's ironic that you are trying to hide your involvement while broadcasting it to the world…"

"You hadn't realized it until now, though, and you are just about to marry into the family!"

"I…" I wanted to refute his words, but in the end, I decided to let it slide and only muttered a dispirited *"Touché,"* which only prompted him to laugh again. I decided to cut him short this time, so I threw him a curveball by asking, "So, if I get this right, you literally own a slice of the music industry? How come you cannot set Elly up as a singer again?"

"Oh, she told you about that?" Abram smiled at me for a moment, but then his countenance went grim. "To be frank, the accursed Knights are already aware of our involvement."

"They are?"

The patriarch nodded. "Fortunately for us, so long as we are not directly involved, they cannot really do anything to our businesses. It has something to do with their Oaths."

"Oaths?"

"One of their seven Oaths forbids them from hurting the innocent. *'Innocent'* essentially refers to people who are not aware of our existence or the other Old-Blooded Clans. If they break any of their Oaths, they lose a good chunk of their power, so they will always avoid doing so. So long as we keep our business partners at arm's length, they can't do anything to them, and by extension, us."

I was actually a little surprised by this new information. I was aware that the Knights took Oaths, but since nothing in the Celestial records indicated that they served any role other than chivalric role-play, I'd skimmed over them. I didn't expect to learn something this significant today, especially from the flaky individual before me, but hey, don't look the gift knowledge in the source.

I made yet another mental note on this, but in the meantime, I also asked, "What are the other Oaths?"

"We only learned of three through interrogation," the patriarch told me straightforwardly. "Don't hurt the innocent, don't abandon your allies, don't betray the other Knights."

"Fairly simple rules," I mused.

"Yes, yet if one of them breaks all their Oaths, they lose their qualification and their powers with it. My late father actually used that against them a number of times, but since we never learned all their Oaths, we could only exploit the first two."

"Food for thought," I muttered as I filed yet another mental note, but then I remembered where the topic started. "So, what you're saying is that if Elly became a performer under your label, it would give the Knights the excuse to attack your business?"

"Not only that, it would give them plenty of opportunities to attack my daughter!" He scowled. "Those accursed Knights never rest! I would bet my left wing there's at least one of them skulking around on this island even as we speak, looking for a chink in our armour to strike! They still fear the authority of the Magi, so they should not dare to attack us in the open, but you have to be ever vigilant! You hear me, Leonard?"

"Yes, yes, I hear you," I told the overly loud man before I let out a sigh. So, it was just as I figured. So long as the Knights were around, my girlfriend couldn't fulfill her dream. Oh well. I supposed, with all my other crazy long-term plans floating around, adding either *get rid of a centuries-old feud* or *get rid of one of the feuding sides altogether* wasn't going break the camel's back.

As such, I decided to focus on another part of the previous conversation, and asked, "You mentioned something about music records being sent back here?" Abram nodded, and while I wanted to inquire about how getting surplus merchandise delivered to his own study didn't contradict him being a "secret owner" of the business, I didn't want to get bogged down in another side topic, so instead I asked the main thing on my mind.

"What was that part about digital distribution, again?"

"Right! I don't even know what that means, but all the customers have been asking about it and none of them buy our records anymore!"

I nodded sagely, figuring it was yet another unforeseen consequence of the island's technology going through about two decades' worth of development in two months. Judy and I had already done a fair bit of research into the phenomenon, and it seemed to be an offshoot of the class of phenomena where the world interacts with observers and, in this case, their expectations. Through our experiments and repeated self-suggestion, we managed to bring technologies like social media and smart watches into existence. The fact that merely expecting something to exist was enough to bring it into the world was a scary, if exhilarating, thought.

To cut a long research entry short, apparently our careless meddling with the world's technological level created some unforeseen ripple effects, such as digital media displacing traditional physical media overnight. Now, while other people might have been horrified by this kind of careless, unconscious reality-warping, all I could feel at the moment was excitement over a sudden opportunity. If digital distribution didn't exist yet, but the placeholders were already clamoring for it, it meant I had a ginormous business opportunity on my hands, and the man who had the funds and manpower necessary to exploit it was sitting right in front of me.

I was just about to voice my proposal when we were suddenly and rudely interrupted by the chamber doors slamming open, followed by a surprisingly high-pitched yelp coming from Melinda as she jumped aside. Incidentally, we both sprang to our feet, though without any added noises.

"There you are!" declared an unfamiliar voice, and I glanced over to the doors... only to find myself staring at Elly's butt as she backed into the room. She was pulling something, which turned out to be a surprisingly sturdy-looking wheelchair.

As she finally got inside, she swung the chair around, so that both her and its occupant were facing us. The princess needed no introduction, and after just recently learning about her condition, the identity of the sitting woman didn't require too much brainpower to deduce, either.

Elly's mother sat ramrod straight in her chair. She wore a thick green gown and had a red-green tartan blanket covering her lap. She had long, wavy brown hair that was very similar to the princess's when she let her hair down, and the face her locks framed showed traces of Asian heritage, most visible in her almond-shaped eyes.

Speaking of eyes, at the moment she was staring daggers at her husband, and before he could've said anything, she asked him in an icy tone, "Dear, care to explain why you told the twins to distract our daughter while you kidnapped her friend?"

"I didn't kidnap anyone!" the patriarch defended himself with a raised voice, but the apologetic tone told me who was wearing the pants in this relationship. "I just thought that, as a father and a man, it was imperative that I had a serious discussion with my future son-in-law, just between the two of us!"

"Daaad!" Elly pouted from behind her mother's chair.

The lady of the house raised a curious brow as she looked at me and repeated, "Son-in-law?"

"I guess he's talking about me," I spoke with just a hint of embarrassment and gave her a nod. "I'm Leonard Dunning. I'm pleased to meet you."

"The pleasure is mine. Call me Emese," she told me in an almost robotic voice. Then she turned back to her husband and continued with a considerably more natural (and chilling) tone, "Dear, don't you think discussing your daughter's future shouldn't be done behind closed doors? Without her around? Or without *ME* around?"

"I just wanted to..." he began, but then we were all startled by a series of knocks on the doorframe. As I glanced up and over the two in the way, I saw Sebastian entering the chamber with my assistant in tow.

The old butler looked over the people gathered in the room and said, "It seems everyone is present. Marvelous. Dinner is ready, so I would advise we head over to the dining hall and continue whatever discussion you might have already begun before the food gets cold."

"Good idea!" the Dracis patriarch immediately agreed, and he skipped over to the wheelchair and all but yanked it out of Elly's hand before leaning down and whispering, in a still very audible voice, "Come on, Emmy! You're embarrassing me in front of the kids!"

"Don't you *Emmy* me right now, mister!" the lady in the chair countered in a hiss, and that was about as much as I could make out before Abram turned her around and they stormed out of the room together.

As I hastily followed, my two girlfriends naturally fell in line with me, and the moment she did so, Judy whispered, "Son-in-law?"

"Don't worry about it," I whispered back. "Elly's father is just being overbearing."

"I know, right? He's so cool!" Elly chimed in.

"Being overbearing is 'cool'?" Judy asked, and the princess nodded with all the confidence in the world. My assistant blinked at her for a moment, then she glanced up at me and stated, "Chief, with these people around, I worry about our future."

"So do I," I told her with a small groan, then hurried to catch up with the bickering couple and the silent butler while mentally preparing myself for yet another trope, the *awkward family dinner*.

PART 2

The dining hall of the Dracis mansion was, to my shock and disbelief, pretty cozy. After the flagrant displays of wealth so far, I expected to be led into a gigantic, lavishly decorated hall with a huge crystal chandelier hanging above a long-ass medieval dining table, with maybe a throne-sized chair at the upper end where the head of the household would preside.

What I got instead was a comparatively plain chamber, about the size of my own living room, with a medium-sized oval table in the middle. Maybe it was due to the contrast with the rest of the mansion's unifying theme, but the lack of decorations made the place feel surprisingly comfortable and, dare I say, homely.

However, what the surroundings lacked in lavishness, the menu made up for in droves. Most of the dishes were placed in the middle, within everyone's reach, and we had everything ranging from "simple" caviar to an honest-to-goodness turducken, and based on some of my host's stray comments, we still had a whole roasted suckling pig on the way.

Speaking of my hosts, Mr. and Mrs. Dracis sat together along one side of the oval table, while our little wholesome-threesome occupied the other, with Judy mechanically eating her meal on my left (it was probably her way of dealing with the tense atmosphere), while the princess on my other side blissfully munched on her own.

I was trying to enjoy the gastronomic wonders before me, but my efforts were considerably dampened by a certain noble lady in a wheelchair giving me the stink eye. I tried to ignore her to the best of my ability, though I would be lying if I said the awkward silence wasn't getting to me. On the other hand, I didn't seem to be the only one that thought so, as the uncomfortably fidgeting patriarch soon raised his voice in what I figured was his best attempt at small talk.

"So, Leonard! Have you tried the red sauce yet?"

Surprised by the sudden question, I replied with a tentative, "You mean that one?" while pointing at the small jar between the fried goods and the cold cuts.

"Yes, that one! I do declare it delicious."

"I second that!" the princess, well, seconded at my side. "It goes great with everything!"

"Really?" I muttered as I reached out and picked up the jar. I casually lifted the lid, and a strong, spicy aroma made me salivate with a single tingling whiff. "Well, it definitely smells great," I said with a small smile, only to get so startled a moment later that I almost dropped the whole jar.

"That's it!" Elly's mother exclaimed, pointing at me.

"That's what?" I asked back reflexively, at which point she gave me a triumphant smile.

"You smell weird," she told me matter-of-factly, earning her an odd look from her husband.

"Honey, you are being rude to our guest," Abram chided her, after which he took a few overt sniffs in my direction, he added, "And he smells perfectly fine!"

"No offense, darling, but we both know that your nose is about as keen as a wet sack of mice," Elly's mother retorted.

"That's a fun comparison," I stated absentmindedly.

"Why, thank you." The lady gave me a demure smile, but then, realizing who she was responding to, quickly forced her expression into an eerily familiar glare. "I meant to say, please be quiet. This doesn't concern you."

"Excuse me? Weren't you just talking about what I smell like? I think that concerns me plenty."

"He got you there, honey!" Papa Dracis exclaimed with a mirthful laugh before he reached out, gingerly picked up a tall wine glass, elegantly raised it to his mouth, then threw his head back and emptied it in one go.

"You are supposed to take my side!" the lady of the household retorted with an equally familiar pout. When she glanced at the giggling blonde at my side, she snapped, "And you! Stop laughing and help explain things to your father!"

"Mooom!" Elly whined, leaning towards me. "Stop bullying Leo!"

"But he smells weird!" Lady Emese doubled down while staring her daughter in the eye, at which Elly flippantly shrugged.

"It doesn't matter! It gives him character, and complaining about it to his face is really rude!"

"I remember you doing that a lot in the past," I grumbled. "In fact, you are kind of confirming what she says even now."

"Hush, Leo. I am defending you right now," the princess told me with a smug grin, then turned back to argue with her mother.

I let out a small sigh, then I leaned over to my other girlfriend and quietly asked her, "Hey, Judy? Do I actually smell?"

"I don't know, I don't care," she answered me quite bluntly. "I just want to finish my meal, go home, and steer clear of these weird people."

"They are not that weird..." I started, but then I noticed that Elly's father kept downing one glass of wine after the other like they were spirits, while the women of the household continued arguing about my odor. "Well, okay. Maybe a little weird."

"It doesn't matter whether you like it or not!" Elly's mother burst out, drawing my attention back to her just as she pointed at me, "He is still two-timing!"

"We are not!" Elly argued back. "It's a one-turn threesome!"

"One *true* threesome," Judy corrected her without even looking up from her food.

"Right, what she said!" the princess nodded so hard, it sent her hair cascading around her face, but then it returned into its previous, well-maintained shape.

Was that a Draconian or a simulation thing? I wondered, but not for long, as the lady of the house raised her voice again.

"What does that even mean?"

"It's a little complicated, but in short, it means that technically we are all in a single relationship," I tried to explain. "Technically, calling it an OTT is not entirely accurate, but for the sake of simplicity, you can think of it as each one of us being in some kind of relationship with the other two at the same time."

"Really?" Mama Dracis looked at me skeptically, and then glanced at Judy. "Does that mean that you are also in a relationship with my daughter?"

My assistant gave the lady a blank look, but then after I poked her in the thigh under the table, she shuddered, following which she told her, "If we follow the definition we were just given, then... yes?"

For a while, Elly's mother kept giving us weird glances, then she looked over at her husband, probably for support. Unfortunately for her, Papa Dracis seemed to be enjoying himself way too much, so he only grinned at her while a somewhat generic placeholder maid filled his wineglass once again. At last, the matriarch let out a disgruntled groan and then faced me again.

"So, let me see if I get this straight." She pointed at me, then at the princess. "You and you are dating." I nodded in the affirmative, and this time she pointed at me and Judy. "You and you are also dating." I nodded once again, so for the last round, she pointed at the two girls in turn. "And you two are also dating."

After a moment of hesitation, Elly adopted a determined expression and gave another big nod.

Her mother fell silent for a long moment, after which she asked, "How far have you gone?"

"Where?" I asked back while tilting my head to the side.

"Physically," she replied with a serious expression.

"Only kissing!" Elly hastily declared while going from determined to beet-red in a second.

"Same here," Judy said between bites, and while she tried to appear aloof, I could tell from the way she averted her eyes that she was more than a little uncomfortable, as well.

"With him?" Mama Dracis asked for clarity, and my girlfriends nodded in unison. "What about each other?"

"What about us?" Elly blurted out, and her mother immediately touched her own forehead with a defeated expression.

"You said you are in a relationship, as well. So, how far have you two gone?"

"Aaaaah..." The princess's face once again adopted a shade of crimson and she hastily declared, "We are not in *that* kind of relationship, Mom! It's more... erm..."

"I think the world you are looking for is 'platonic,'" I told her, and she immediately nodded.

"This is getting complicated," Judy noted without looking up from her food.

"Yes, platonic!" Elly nodded with a bafflingly confident expression. "We are still building skinship, but we are not doing *those* kinds of things!"

"Hah! I knew it was skinship and not kinship! I told you, son!" Papa Dracis exclaimed with a ginormous grin on his face.

His wife turned on him. "You were the one who planted all those ideas in our daughter's head in the first place! And don't call him son!"

"Why? It's practically a done deal at this point!" the patriarch answered jovially, followed by yet another hearty laugh that made the table dishes clatter.

Lady Emese opened and closed her mouth a couple of times, but in the end, she let out an exhausted groan and faced her daughter again, asking, "Are you sure you're fine with this?"

"Yes, Mom. This is for the best," Elly replied to her with a determined look. They silently gazed at each other, no doubt engaging in some kind of esoteric eye-contact-based form of arm wrestling until, to my sincerest surprise, the woman in the wheelchair let out a defeated sigh.

"Very well, I understand," she spoke, and Elly was just about to happily glom on to me, when she raised her voice again and said, "However, I want to ask the young man a few questions first!"

That stopped the princess in her tracks. She sat back down on her chair.

Her mother directed her piercing gaze at me again and asked, "Do you love my daughter?"

I didn't expect such a direct question, but I managed to squeeze out an adequately definite "Sure, I do."

Now, to be perfectly honest, those words didn't exactly come from the bottom of my heart, but I figured that saying *Well, I feel extremely deep affection towards your daughter, but I cannot truly ascertain whether my feelings would qualify under the traditional definition of love* would've been pretty counterproductive at this point.

Thankfully she didn't seem to pick up on my somewhat turbulent emotions, as she just gave me a nod and glanced over at the other girl by my side. "Do you also happen to love the young lady over there?"

"Yes," I answered, this time a little quicker due to no longer feeling like I was on the back foot.

"I see..." She nodded again, then she linked her fingers in her lap and asked me, "Which one of them do you love more?"

Aaaaand with that, I was back on the back foot again...

After a beat of entirely justified brain-freeze, I found myself involuntarily scowling at her, then, at last, I told her, "With all due respect, that is a pretty stupid question."

Mama Dracis's expression slackened, only to turn into one of annoyance a moment later when her husband let out another plate-rattling laugh.

"Fine, then let me ask you a hypothetical," she said after her pointed looks finally had an effect and Papa Dracis quieted down. She gave me a chilling stare and then, in a voice dripping with forced gravitas, said, "Let's say both of your girlfriends are in mortal danger, and you can only save one of them. Who do you choose?"

"Both."

Lady Emese's brows slowly knit together. "I think you misunderstood me. I said you can only save one of them."

"No, I heard you," I answered her without the slightest bit of pretense. "I just ignored that part because the question was silly."

"But... that was the point!" Mama Dracis exclaimed. "The whole point of this dilemma is that you can *only* save one of them!"

"Yes, and I'm telling you that it's stupid. If I can save one of them, I can save both. If I can save both, I will save both. End of moral dilemma."

"No, you still don't get it! The point is that, in this hypothetical scenario, *you are not able* to save both of them," Elly's mother explained with a voice bordering on desperation.

"No, *you* don't get it." I put my foot down and glared at the woman. "I know for a fact that if we ever encountered a life-or-death situation where both Judy and Elly were in danger, I can and will save them. You cannot dictate what I can and cannot do."

"Maybe, but the 'you' in *this scenario* cannot save both."

"If the person in your hypothetical scenario cannot save both, then it means I am not that person; therefore your hypothetical scenario is rubbish. End of discussion."

The woman kept gaping at me for a moment, then she threw her arms into the air in frustration and told me, "Fine! We are getting nowhere at this rate, so how about this—both of your girlfriends are in mortal danger. Who do you save *first?*"

"Oh, that's an easy question," I answered with a smile. "It would be Judy."

"You would save her first?" Elly blurted out.

"Of course. You are tough, so even if you were both in the same kind of mortal danger, it makes sense to get Judy out first, as you could probably hold out for a few seconds until I get you out, too."

"Oh, right. That makes sense," the princess nodded with an enlightened look on her face, then suddenly she asked, "You think I'm tough?"

"Of course you are," I told her honestly. "I mean, you have all those scales, and your horns, plus your Draconian physiology... You are the toughest person and/or thing I know this side of a Chimera."

"Boo! Don't compare me to a Chimera! Compare me to something cool!" Elly pouted.

"But I don't know any other tough things except for dragons, and comparing you to them would be redundant. Judy, do you have any ideas?"

"None, Chief," my assistant, who was incidentally the only person at the table with a nearly empty plate, answered me in the negative after wiping her mouth with a napkin.

"You see, even Judy doesn't know anything better."

"Boo!" Elly repeated while pointedly turning her face away from me, steadily entering into full-blown sulking mode.

"Okay, how about this... How about I say you are tougher than an '80s action star?"

"The ones that use machine guns with one hand and are too cool to look at explosions?" the Draconic girl asked with a strange sparkle in her eyes.

"Yup, them."

"I can live with that!" she finally smiled one of her smug little grins at me, and I couldn't help but reflexively rub the crown of her head, which quickly turned awkward when I remembered that we were still in front of her parents. She didn't seem to mind, but I still decided to cut the head pat short, earning me another *"Boo!"*

In the meantime, I faced the slack-jawed lady of the house and, after lightly clearing my throat, I cautiously asked her, "So... what were we talking about?"

She gave me a critical look in return, but then let out an enormous, resigned sigh and told me, with just the slightest edge, "Never mind. Let's say that, for the time being, I tentatively approve of your... what did you call it again?"

"Oh, I know now! A one true threesome!" Elly responded with a cheerful voice.

"If you really want to stick to that term, at least abbreviate it to OTT," I told my girlfriend, but she didn't pay me any heed. Honestly, I really wanted to come up with a better term for our relationship, but considering how attached Elly seemed to this one, I let it pass.

"Yes, that," Mama Dracis followed up with a considerably less cheerful tone.

I was about to agree, but then we were once again interrupted by the hearty chuckles of the patriarch.

"Great job, son!" the grown man at the table exclaimed. "You can go ahead and call her Mom now!"

"Most definitely not!" Elly's mother burst out, sending a scathing glare at her husband. "He may at most refer to me as *mother-in-law*!" she huffed, but since Abram only laughed in return, she suddenly reached out and grabbed hold of the man's ear. "Don't just try to laugh this off, mister! This whole predicament is because of you and the stupid traditions of your side of the family!"

"Ow! Honey, not in front of the kids!" the patriarch of the family exclaimed in… well, probably not in pain, but more in embarrassment.

I glanced over at Elly, who was happily munching on her food again, so I figured this must've been a fairly mundane occurrence to her. I decided to follow her example, but as I did so, my eyes skimmed over a particular jar, and it made an old question pop back up.

"Elly?"

"Hm?" she grunted, then quickly swallowed her mouthful and responded with a more intelligible, "Yes? What is it?"

"Since your parents seem to be busy, I decided to use the opportunity to ask this before I forget it again. Can you tell me about the whole *'smelling weird'* business again?"

"Oh, that?" Elly muttered as her cheeks visibly reddened. "I told you, you don't smell bad, just strange."

"Yes, and that's what I want to be clarified."

"I see." She raised a finger to her lips as she thought about it, then explained, "Mom and I can kind of—how should I put it?—smell mana, except not really. It's hard to explain. Not all Draconians can do it, but most of my relatives on my mother's side can."

"So, it's an extrasensory ability that is inherited in the maternal blood-line," Judy casually cut in between bites, earning her a frown from the princess.

"I can use big words too, you know! There is no reason to flex your vocabulary just because you can," she grumbled.

My assistant, unfazed as usual, shrugged.

"I'm not flexing. I'm just being precise."

"It doesn't matter either way," I came between them this time and told Elly, "So, when you sniff me using that ability, I have a weird smell?"

"It's not the smell that's weird," Elly said. "How should I put it…? It's like, every person has their own scent. But, when it comes to you, you just don't. Imagine that you pick up a flower and you sniff it. The first time it smells like chamomile, then pine, then roses, then freshly cut grass. None of those are bad, but when the same thing keeps smelling differently, it feels really… creepy. Do you understand what I'm trying to say?"

"I think I do," I told her with a theatrically downcast expression. "You are telling me I smell creepy. That makes me sad."

"That's not what I said!" the princess hastily denied on the brink of panic. "I told you I don't dislike it! In fact, I think I kind of like how you smell!"

That wasn't exactly the reaction I was expecting, but before I could say anything, Judy decided to throw some oil on the fire by innocently asking, "Smell fetish?"

"No!" I exclaimed in mock despair. "Where do you even learn about things like that?"

"The internet."

"Oh no! My girlfriend is being corrupted!"

"What's a *smell fetish*?" Elly inquired curiously over my shoulder.

"Oh no! My other girlfriend is also being corrupted!"

"Hush, Chief, you are being a nuisance," Judy chided me while reaching for a drink.

"I don't think we are bothering anyone. Those two are completely lost in their own little world," I told her, pointing at the bickering couple across the table, elbows-deep in an obvious lovers' quarrel.

"All the more reason we should quickly eat our dinner, thank them for their hospitality, and then leave before their weirdness rubs off on us."

"Yes. You are plenty weird already," Elly delivered a perfectly timed jab at my assistant, and before Judy could retort, Elly poked me in the side. "Hey, Leo? You still didn't tell me what a *smell fetish* is? Is it some kind of magical catalyst?"

I gave my surprisingly innocent Draconic girlfriend a flat look, then I told her, "I will tell you when you're older."

"Boo!" came the expected answer from her, but after a few head pats, I managed to placate her, and we all returned to our neglected plates.

I decided to sample everything, and while that might have been a little heavy on my stomach, I already had plans with Brang for the night, and I had a feeling that if I wanted to get everything done and sorted out by the time our weekend date rolled around, I needed all the energy I could stockpile. Also, for the record, it definitely had nothing to do with the red sauce being really, really good with everything. Overeating just because of that would've been silly, and we all know I never do silly things, right?

CHAPTER 11

PART 1

It was a beautiful Sunday morning. The picturesque blue sky was dotted with a herd of fluffy white clouds, there was absolutely no wind, and most importantly, the temperature sneakily climbed up by about ten degrees Celsius. It still wasn't exactly warm per se, but it was just balmy enough for a great outing with my girlfriends. Or wait… I think an outing was supposed to be the platonic version of a date, so this technically wasn't an outing anymore… but I've been using the word to refer to hanging out with Judy and/or Elly so much that the two words meant roughly the same at this point. Language drift in motion, huh?

"Chief, would you care to explain what's going on?"

I decided to put the capriciousness of our ever-changing vocabulary aside and face my dearest assistant. It was probably due to the special occasion, but she looked prettier than usual. She was not only wearing a surprisingly stylish ensemble, but she also had her hair done up (though it wasn't *that* different from her usual hairdo, really). She even had a hint of makeup on her face. We were currently in my living room, and while I had a distinct hunch about the subject of her question, I decided to play dumb for the moment.

"What exactly do you mean?" I asked with a mostly innocent expression, which elicited a small groan from her, following which she extended her index finger and swept her arm horizontally.

"I'm asking about them," she stated with an extra-deadpan expression. "Why are they here?"

"Oh, you mean the rest of the gang?" I mused as I glanced over at Josh, Angie, and the class rep awkwardly fidgeting on my couch. Well, at least Josh and Angie were. Ammy was mostly just giving me a silent, disapproving frown. Anyways, I flashed a smile at Judy and told her, "I invited them."

"Yes, I could figure that much out on my own," she grumbled. "I wanted you to tell me why you did that."

"I want to know, too!" Elly chimed in from the side. Just like Judy, she had made preparations for today's date, so she was not only wearing an expensive dress, white leggings, and knee boots, but her hair was once again in the familiar drills from the time we first met. Maybe it was because of that hairstyle, but she seemed to regain some of her recently tarnished outward dignity, as she appeared like a true noble lady elegantly holding a porcelain cup. Then, of course, she shattered the image by hunching over her drink to loudly blow on it.

"If it's too hot, I can use magic to cool it a little," Snowy offered with a modest smile.

"No need!" the princess declared, but then she continued to blow on her drink with renewed vigor.

"Are you sure? You're going to burn your tongue…" I told her, but she only shook her head.

"Nonsense! I am a descendant of dragons! We don't burn our tongues!" she huffed and, probably to prove the point, she took a sip from her cup, only to twitch and follow it up with an "Owowowowow!"

I failed to stifle my laughter at the sight, which naturally earned me a wounded glare from Elly, but instead of addressing me, she looked away, extended her cup, and muttered a sulky "Pwease…" towards Snowy, who waved her hands around the cup with a brilliant smile, apparently tremendously enjoying herself.

Before I knew it, the corners of my lips bent upwards, but before it could turn into an actual smile, I was shaken out of the moment by a certain subtly upset girl standing on her tiptoes and grabbing my ear to get my attention.

"Chief," Judy forcefully addressed me. "Stop trying to use her antics to sweep my question under the rug."

"I wasn't," I protested, but she didn't seem to care.

"Tell me why you invited everyone to our date," my assistant insisted with a visible frown, so I decided it was about time I stopped teasing her.

"Fine, fine," I mumbled as I gently removed her hand from my ear. Then I leaned closer and whispered, "I'm just trying to get ahead of the tropes for a change."

"Which trope?" she inquired, and her previous frown displaced by an intrigued expression.

"The date-stalking," I answered, still in a whisper. "It's likely that, since they know about our date, they would stalk us like the last time, so I figured I might as well invite them along. I'll pay for the tickets and snacks, and once we are at the date spots, we will break into two groups. This way we can have our date in peace, and they will have more fun, too." I paused here to let her digest my words, then I added, "Also, after the date, I was planning to show everyone the secret base, introduce Brang and company, and then do some preliminary combat tests to figure out everyone's strengths and weaknesses. It's simpler to do that if everyone is already with us."

"That… is unusually well thought out by your standards," she muttered. Then she reached out and grabbed my ear again. "Who are you, and what did you do to my Chief?"

"It's *our* Chief! I mean, *our Leo*!" Elly interrupted between two elegant sips from her newly cooled cup of tea.

Judy gave her a withering glance, by her standards, then she looked back at me with the largest "puppy eyes" I had ever seen on her and said, "Chieeeef. Eleanor ruined our skit. I'm devastated right now."

"Here, here," I playfully consoled her by patting her shoulder. "We have the whole day ahead of us. There will be a lot of opportunities to perform."

"But the first skit of the day is the most important of them all. Also, she'll ruin the rest, too. She has absolutely no sense of comedic timing."

"Hey!" Elly set down her cup. "I have a sense of humour!"

"Prove it," my assistant challenged her with a determined expression, which immediately threw my other girlfriend off-balance.

"Ve-very well!" the princess exclaimed. Then she fell silent for few seconds while her eyes scanned the room. At last, her gaze landed on her tea, at which point her face lit up. "So, I have a question! Why did the tea call the police?"

Elly waited expectantly.

"I don't know. Why did the tea call the police?"

"Because it was mugged!" Elly declared with a bombastic grin.

The room was dead silent.

Well, almost. Angie suppressed a giggle.

"Was that a dad joke just now?" I asked, fully expecting her to deflate, but instead she gave a giant nod.

"Yes, I learned it from Dad. How did you know?"

Judy looked at my other girlfriend like she couldn't decide how to react, then back at me and told me, with an entirely inappropriate amount of gravitas, "This is much worse than I expected. I must borrow Eleanor for a moment and fix this before her complete lack of comedy tears our relationship asunder."

"Um… you do that…" I agreed quite uncertainly, at which point Judy grabbed the confused dragon girl and dragged her into the kitchen before she even realized what was going on.

Once my girlfriends vacated the area, the atmosphere in the room became strangely tense, and as I glanced around, I noticed Josh waving a hand over his head to get my attention. Correction: I'd actually noticed it way before that; I was just ignoring him. Regrettably, that didn't seem to be an option anymore, so I faced my friend.

"Yes, Josh? Is there a problem?"

"Of course there's a problem!" he declared with a look in his eyes that was rapidly shifting between disgruntled, skeptical, and embarrassed. "Now that you're done flirting with your girlfriends, would you please address the elephant in the room?"

"I'm curious about your explanation, too," Ammy joined in, once again menacingly adjusting her glasses at me.

"You have to be more specific than that," I told them without a shred of shame, though I had a very good idea what they meant.

"It's Lili! What else could we be talking about?" Josh burst out, gesturing towards the girl standing by the coffee table with a gentle (if somewhat embarrassed) smile on her lips.

"Oh, riiiiight!" I exclaimed and theatrically slapped my forehead. "Thank you for reminding me. With all the commotion, it had almost slipped my mind. Do you remember how the class rep's grandpa dumped the responsibility of figuring out how to get a new identity for Snowy on us?"

I walked over to the Abyssal girl in question, all the while struggling to keep myself from breaking into laughter, and once I was beside her, I declared, "Well, it's done. Allow me to introduce you to Neige Liliam Inanna-Dunning!"

There was a very long moment of silence in the living room.

Angie tentatively asked, "You... married her?"

"What? No, of course not!" I denied it on the spot while giving the Celestial girl a stern look. "I adopted her! Well, technically, my parents adopted her, but that's only on paper. In practice, I'm her unofficial caregiver."

"Wait, hold on!" Ammy cut in. "You *actually* adopted her into *your* family?"

"Yes, that's what I just said," I answered with a nod.

"How come this is the first time I've heard of this?" came an unexpected question from the direction of the kitchen, where a certain blonde girl stuck her head through the door, but before I could answer her, she was dragged back inside by my assistant. It was weird, but then again, at this point, weird was becoming the new normal in my household, so I decided to ignore them for the time being and faced the incredulous trio on the couch again.

"Sooo..." Josh spoke up after he finally overcame his shock, "does that mean that Lili is your...?"

"My legal sister, yes," I answered with a grin while simultaneously tussling the hair of my newly minted little sister. Snowy let out an embarrassed noise, but to her credit, she stood tall and endured my overbearing big brother head pats like a champ.

"You still didn't explain how you arranged to adopt her into *your* family," Ammy reiterated her previous question, but I only shrugged at her insistent interrogation.

"It's not that big a deal. Snowy knew a guy who knew a guy, and I and the guy and the guy's guys met with the guy, and then we persuaded the guy to call a guy he knew to speed things up, and so Snowy is now my sis and her new ID card and other assorted papers should arrive in the mail in a week or so."

The couch trio still gave me skeptical looks, but at least Ammy was satisfied with my answer. Or at least she didn't pursue the topic anymore. To be honest, though, my explanation, meticulously detailed as it was, didn't perfectly reflect the events in their entirety.

For a start, while it was true that I had Brang lead me to the document forger, who turned out to be a fairly mundane middle-aged placeholder who worked at a government office, I didn't let the two of them meet. Since it was damn time I started reflecting on Judy's constant stream of complaints about my impulsive behaviour, I decided to put some extra thought into my affairs. I figured that if this guy was someone who already worked with the Abyssals, they might make contact with him in the future, so I decided to plant some misdirection in his head while I was there.

Since Brang was way too conspicuous with his size, limping, spear, and fancy armour, I decided to have him follow after me while using his cloaking ability (more on that later). I took the wolfish Faun with me to the meeting, and went ahead and disguised myself with a wig and a fake mustache I picked up in a costume shop on the way.

Once my preparations were complete, I introduced myself as an agent of the Nergals, another Abyssal family, and then I wove a long tale of conspiracy, where foisting Snowy on a certain Leonard Dunning was but step forty-two in a grand and elaborate plan to ruin the Inannas and take over their mana-well, and I told it with an appropriate amount of mustache-twirling. The document-forger had very little presence and was quite mechanical in his actions, even by placeholder standards, but I figured it was better to be safe than sorry, so I kept up the fake supernatural Mafioso act till the end. By the way, no matter what Brang says, I definitely wasn't having so much fun I forgot the time. Nor did I ramble. That Faun is a compulsive liar, I tell you.

Where was I? Ah, yes, the forger. So, after greasing the cogs of the system with a few wads of cash plus some highly descriptive threats, the man called his coworkers, and in just a few hours we managed to get our hands on a temporary ID. I was tempted to joke about how the illegal channels worked more efficiently than the actual government, but then I was informed that Snowy's records were slipped into the central system and that we would be receiving her new proper ID from them, so I wisely shut up.

Speaking of not talking, my friend on the couch was waving his hand high over his head, so I gestured for him to go ahead.

"Okay, guys," he said, glancing at the two girls beside him, "tell me if I'm wrong, but isn't Lili wearing a maid uniform?"

"Um… yes?" Angie agreed.

"Then why is it that none of you find it strange? I mean, it's strange, right?" Josh burst out, his eyes moving back and forth between Angie and Ammy, searching for validation.

"Ooooh?" I dramatically cracked my knuckles. "What did you say, punk? Did you just call my sister weird?"

"What? No!" Josh denied vehemently, waving his hands like an idiot. "It's the maid clothes! I mean, isn't it weird to dress up like a maid if you aren't one?"

"So, you're saying that my sister's hobby is weird?" I growled, trying to crack my knuckles again, though they didn't make much noise this time.

"No, not at all!" Josh denied once again, but before I could continue my act, it was interrupted by Snowy clinging to my arm.

"Don't fight!" she cried, stunning me for a moment. I let out a small sigh and once again placed my hand on the top of her head.

"We aren't fighting, silly," I chided her while ruffling her hair. "I'm just bantering with Josh."

"You sure?" Snowy asked with wide eyes.

"Of course. I was obviously just joking, right, guys?" I asked the trio.

Josh giving me a weird look was expected; the actual words coming from Ammy really surprised me.

"In fact, you looked like a violently overprotective brother just then."

"Really?" I asked back, at which point it was Angie's turn to repeatedly nod at me.

"Yeah, totally! It was kinda cool how it looked like you were just about to beat up Josh!"

"What's cool about that?" my friend protested, but his childhood friend completely ignored him in favor of giving me a sparkly-eyed gaze.

"Now I wanna have a big brother, too! Can you adopt me?" she asked with an impish smile that contrasted with her deadly serious eyes.

I let out an awkward cough. "No. You have perfectly fine adoptive parents already, don't you?"

"Wait, hold on!" Josh interrupted us. "You knew Angie was adopted?"

"Well, duh," I answered, shrugging. "She looks nothing like her mom and dad."

"Are you seriously telling me I was the only one who didn't notice?" Josh exclaimed in despair, while the Celestial girl gave me a sideways look.

"Leo, I don't think you've ever met my parents," she said.

As I readied a suitable excuse, a new deadpan voice joined the fray.

"You shouldn't point out the Chief's blunders like that," Judy declared while she came out of the kitchen, followed by a strangely unfocused princess. If we were in a cartoon, I was sure she would've had those weird, swirly eyes with large question marks over her head. While I observed her, Judy came up to me and continued, with complete seriousness, "That's my job." Saying so, she turned towards me and told me, with the same stern expression, "Chief, you've never met Angeline's parents."

"No, I haven't."

My girlfriend gave me a flat look (well, flatter than usual, at the least), and said, "No, Chief. This is the point where you're supposed to come up with a harebrained excuse so that we can have a back-and-forth skit and distract everyone from your slip of the tongue, and then Eleanor joins in to show off the results of our comedic training. It's common sense."

"Well, excuse me for not being able to read your mind," I huffed. "How was I supposed to know you made this elaborate plan?"

"People in a relationship are supposed to be on the same wavelength. You should know these things just by looking at me."

"Well, I'm looking at you right now, and I still don't see it. Are you sure you have your wavelengths tuned right?"

"Of course." Judy nodded so hard it looked like a small bow. "It's part of my morning routine. I brush my teeth, comb my hair, charge my internal batteries, and then I tune my built-in radio to your wavelength."

"Wait, are you using FM or AM?"

"AM, obviously."

"Well, there's your problem!" I exclaimed while gesturing with my hands. "I'm using FM. That's why we have a hard time communicating!"

"Oh, I see." Judy nodded twice, for emphasis, then puckered her lips. I was just about to ask what she was doing, when she started making some kind of wholly unconvincing whirring sounds and said, "Judy-bot's whistling update has been delayed, so Judy-bot set her broadcast to FM manually. Can you receive my feelings now?"

"As a matter of fact, I do," I told her with a smile, then I quickly leaned down, embraced her, and straightened myself up, lifting her into the air in the process, following which I whispered, "Are you back at that Judy-bot thing again? I thought we agreed that was a dead horse already. Stop beating it."

"You have no appreciation for the classics," she whispered back while her feet were still comically dangling above the floor, then she added aloud, "Beep-boop. Judy-bot's internal batteries are being recharged by the power of love. Judy-bot is pleased."

I was just about to respond with something about whether the power of love was a renewable energy source, but then we were interrupted by Ammy raising her voice.

"What are you talking about? Wavelengths? Batteries? What is going on? What even is this?"

Before either of us could say anything, the class rep's words seemed to have triggered something in Elly, as she suddenly shook off her stupor and exclaimed, "The Aristocrats!"

There were a good five seconds' worth of flabbergasted silence in the room, ultimately broken by my assistant letting out a defeated groan and muttering, "Still needs work. Lots of it…"

PART 2

"Where should we go next?" I asked, and even though it was pretty much just a rhetorical question, neither of my girlfriends sitting by my side offered up any ideas. While waiting for them, I took another sip from my large disposable drinking cup filled with cherry Coke (I felt experimental, and it wasn't terrible), but since they remained silent, I decided to ask, "How about the haunted house?"

"I wholeheartedly agree with your suggestion and consider it absolutely essential that we follow it post haste," Judy agreed between two bites from her crepe.

"You two are the worst," my other girlfriend fumed aloud while nibbling on her own thin pastry filled with all kinds of teeth-murdering goodness.

"Come on, princess. It was just a joke," I told her while putting my free arm around her shoulder. "We both know you are scared of that place, so we're just teasing you."

"I am not!" Elly denied with an offended huff and shook me off, but then Judy caught her in a pincer maneuver.

"So, you punched off the head of an animatronic because you weren't scared."

"No! I mean, yes, I might've overreacted a little, but it wasn't because I was scared!"

"Then prove it," Judy delivered her expected challenge.

The princess puffed her chest.

"All right! I will…" She jumped to her feet and struck a pose while pointing at my assistant, her image further accentuated by a fearless grin (made only slightly goofy by the crepe in her hand and the chocolate sauce on her lips), but then her expression froze. At first it changed into a thoughtful frown, then her eyes opened wide, following which she once again pointed her accusative finger at Judy and exclaimed, "Wait just a moment! I know what you are doing! You are trying to provoke me into making a fool out of myself in front of Leo so you can make fun of me! I'm on to you now!"

Judy clicked her tongue and turned to me.

"Chief, she is evolving," she told me with such a meaningful voice I had a feeling it was some kind of reference.

"Into what?" I asked, trying to figure out the allusion. Was it that dinosaur movie?

"Into something… unteasable," Judy concluded while giving me an expectant look.

Nope, that wasn't from the park with the featherless dinosaurs. Since I still had no idea what she was referencing (if she was doing so at all), I decided on a safe answer and jovially told her, "Nah, she is still pretty far from that. Right, honey?"

"H-h-honey?"

Elly was just about to sit back down, but upon hearing my words, she still managed to almost fall over with a luminescent blush on her face (metaphorically speaking, of course, as she didn't actually glow… I think), so I turned back to Judy and gestured with a *You see?* look.

"Chief used Unabashed Flirting," my assistant declared in a robotic voice. "It was super-effective."

"Ooooh, so it was that kind of reference!" I spoke with a knowing nod. She looked at me like she had no idea what I was talking about, so I continued, "It's that show about those games about those card games about those monsters where a bunch of kids run around the countryside and throw balls at small critters, and then they fight each other by going into a computer where those balls unfold into creatures and then they put them into attack positions and destroy their opponent's life points."

Judy gave me a long, flat look, then declared, "Chief used Intentionally Mashed-Up Pop Culture Reference. It wasn't very effective."

"Ouch," I hissed while grimacing. "Tough crowd tonight."

Judy was about to respond, when the princess burst out of her stupor and exclaimed, "This is too soon!"

"What is?" Judy inquired.

"The names! It's too soon!" Elly continued with gusto. "We have to start out slow. First, it should be just a first-name basis, then nicknames, and only after that can we move on to the really intimate pet names! You can't just jump to the heavy hitters when we are not engaged yet! It goes against tradition!"

"Your family traditions are weird as usual," I muttered with a slow shake of my head, and moved on from the pointless discussion by muttering, "Nicknames aside, we still didn't decide on our next stop." I paused on purpose here, and I very conspicuously stared at the huge roller coaster at our left. "How about—?"

"No!" my girlfriends declared in perfect unison, and I once again couldn't help but wonder at how they were so different yet somehow still on the same wavelength at the strangest of times.

By the way, I'm pretty sure it was abundantly clear by this point, but we were currently sitting on one of the benches surrounding the familiar sprinkler fountain inside the equally familiar amusement park where Judy and I had our first date by any other name. This time the place was slightly less packed, probably due to the changing seasons, but we still had dozens, if not hundreds of placeholders loitering around us, and unlike the last time, most of them were at the point where they could almost convince me they were regular people having a great time. If only they didn't act so even when they were picking up trash or waiting in lines, the illusion would've been... well, not perfect, but better.

Not that it really bothered us. Judy and I were already used to the placeholders' behaviours, while Elly and the gang still had some kind of perception filtering going on that let them seamlessly ignore the weird, wacky, and sometimes outright uncanny conduct of the people around them. Speaking of the rest of the group, as per my earlier plans, we did bring them along with the excuse of *"unwinding after the recent stressful events,"* and right now they were also somewhere in the amusement park, with *somewhere* being the key word.

We broke into two groups right after walking through the gates, and while Josh was less than thrilled by the idea, the last time I saw them, he was being happily dragged along by Angie and Snowy, while Ammy followed like an exasperated mother hen. In other words, everything was right in the world once again.

Maybe it was because I was already thinking about my brand-new little sister, but as I absentmindedly swept my gaze across the road, I noticed a pair of snow-white pigtails bobbing in and out of the crowd. Snowy wasn't wearing her maid costume anymore but one of the coats I'd bought her, yet she still stuck out like a sore thumb. On a closer look, she seemed to be searching for something. I figured it was most likely us, so I waved at her. It took her several seconds to notice, but then she perked up and dashed over to us.

It was only when she was already in plain view that I noticed that she had something unexpected in her hands, so once she got within arm's reach, I grinned and asked, "Hey, sis. Are you having fun?"

She hesitated, as if she didn't expect the question (or maybe she thought it was a tricky one), but then gave me an ear-to-ear grin and a huge nod.

"Yes! I love this place! Look what I just got!"

With that, Snowy presented the large penguin plushy in her hands. It was smaller than the polar bear I'd bought her, but this one was a brand-name product depicting one of the amusement park mascots. A young emperor penguin wearing a fancy little top hat and a monocle. It was pretty gosh darn cute, though the merry girl holding it gave it a run for its money.

"Wow, it's a nice one. Did you buy it?" I asked her, inspecting her spoils. I gave her a bit of pocket money, more than enough to pay for it, but Snowy shook her head.

"No. Josh won it for me."

"Won?" I repeated after her.

"There is this stand," she began, hugging the plushy tight with one arm and pointing behind her with the other. "You can win all kinds of souvenirs by shooting toy guns at yellow rubber duckies, and if you hit all of them, you get tickets that you can exchange for them."

"And Josh got this?" I asked, and Snowy nodded. "Just for you?" She nodded again.

"How did Amelia and Angeline react?" my assistant inquired while sneakily taking out her phone.

"What do you mean?" Snowy asked back with a pair of truly innocent eyes.

"Were they unhappy that only you got a gift?" Judy continued to grill her while typing.

"Maybe... a little..." Snowy muttered awkwardly, but then glanced up at me with an expression that said she'd just remembered something vitally important. "I almost forgot! I came to find you because Josh wanted me to ask you for a loan."

"A... loan?" I repeated.

"Yes," Snowy confirmed with an earnest nod. "He used up most of his pocket money to win my gift, and now he's trying to win the other mascots for Ammy and Angie, so he told me to ask you for a loan."

"Reeeeally?" I muttered, rubbing my chin.

"Pretty please?" My adopted sister struck me hard with the dreaded puppy-dog eyes.

"Ah, fine, fine!" I exclaimed, reaching for my wallet. I picked out a few banknotes of fairly high denominations and handed them to her with a frank smile. "Here you go. Tell Josh that whatever remains of this is yours, and we'll take care of his side of the bill later."

"That's… a lot of money," Snowy whispered while she gingerly took the notes. "Can I really keep the change?"

"Sure," I told her with a smile. "Consider it extra pocket money. Go buy yourself some snacks and enjoy yourself."

"You can buy a *lot* of snacks with that," Judy noted on the side. "You are spoiling her already."

"Hey, a big brother has to be magnanimous with his little sister," I answered with a toothy grin.

"She's been your sister for less than a day," Elly grumbled, her cheeks puffed up like a hamster's.

"My point still stands. Little sisters are made to be spoiled."

"Boo!" my princess exclaimed with an exaggerated pout. "Girlfriends need to be spoiled, too!"

"Huh? You want to be spoiled?"

"Yes!" she stated without a shred of reservation.

"At least she's honest," I mumbled. I faced the princess again. "Very well, your highness. How do you wish to be spoiled today?"

Elly flashed me one of those absurdly cute smug little smirks of hers (she must've realized I found them attractive, as she'd been doing them more often) and declared, "You should win me a plushy, too! And then you should take us to the lovers' tunnel!"

The first request was pretty much what I expected, but the second one prompted me to send a questioning glance towards Judy, as I was under the impression that it was on our schedule from the beginning. However, before I could voice my thoughts, Snowy of all people cut in by inquiring, "You also want to ride it at the same time?"

"Yes, that was the plan," I answered in Elly's stead, and the Abyssal girl shook her head.

"You can't," she told us while hugging her plushy with both arms. "We've already been there, and only two people can ride the gondola at the same time."

"What?" the princess raised her voice in a completely unwarranted, mortified cry. "How can this be? That ruins everything!"

"Don't be so overdramatic," I chided her while gesturing for her to calm down.

"I'm not being overdramatic! The tunnel is the most important part of this date, right, Judy?"

To my surprise, my assistant unreservedly agreed with her with a solemn nod and a slightly less solemn *"Mm!"*

"Oh please," I grunted. "In the worst-case scenario, I can just take two rides with you in turns."

"But that ruins the whole point!" Elly exclaimed, getting more and more worked up. "This just won't do!"

Before I could interject, she once again jumped to her feet, pointed an overbearing finger at the increasingly more confused Snowy, and called out, "Sister-in-law!"

The Abyssal girl blinked in surprise before she sheepishly pointed at herself and asked, "Me?" in an awkward voice.

"Of course I mean you!" the princess huffed before stepping up to her. "Guide me to the lovers' tunnel! I am going to have some stern words with the management!"

Snowy's mouth hung open before she sent me a helpless glance.

I let out a small sigh in turn and, seeing how motivated my girlfriend was at the moment, said, "Go ahead, but don't overdo it. Throw us a text message when you finished, and we'll meet you at the tunnel later."

Elly let out a satisfied grunt, and before I could say "supercalifragilistic-expialidocious," she dragged Snowy into the crowd. I looked at the girl at my side, still immersed in the process of typing on her phone.

"So, what did you find that requires so many notes?"

Judy finally peeked up at me and then, after a long moment of thinking, put her phone aside.

"I'm simply documenting your changing relationship with Neige," she told me frankly.

"What needs documenting about that?"

"Have you noticed how quickly everyone adapted to your adoption of her? Eleanor, for example, already considers her your sister."

"Well, I'd say it's because she *is*," I answered flatly, wondering where she was going with this.

"Legally, yes. However, a week ago, you not only had no relations with her, but she almost killed you." The way she said the last part made me wonder if she still bore a grudge, but before I could ask, she continued by saying, "Considering that, I find the way they immediately accepted her new role unnatural."

"Let me guess. Narrative influence, right?" Judy nodded, apparently not picking up the sarcasm in my words at all, so I rubbed my temple while adding, "You know, at this point, I'm starting to find your tendency of seeing shadows of narrative meddling everywhere a little worrying."

Judy apparently didn't find my concerns warranted, and gave me a disapproving look. "Chief, I'm being serious."

"So am I. Considering our current situation, with all the supernatural shenanigans, I think me adopting Snowy hardly counts as a big deal to freak out over."

"That brings us to the second point," Judy spoke up, completely glossing over my rebuttal. "I don't think you've adequately explained yet why you decided to adopt Neige."

"I am pretty sure I've already told you how it happened…"

"Yes, and your attempt at misdirection was a commendable step in the right direction. However, that wasn't what I asked about. You've yet to tell me why you adopted her into your family, in particular."

We locked gazes for a short while, and since she was entirely serious, I had no choice but to give her a straight answer.

"Before I start my explanation, are you familiar with the *imouto* archetype?" Judy gave me a nod, which wasn't surprising considering she probably had the whole trope website memorized, but I explained things anyway, just to be on the safe side. "To put it bluntly, I did it in another attempt to get ahead of the tropes. As you're probably well aware, the precocious little sister is one of the more prevalent archetypes in battle harem narratives. However, Josh doesn't have a sister, nor do any of the girls. Furthermore, the *'male friend,'* in this case referring to yours truly, having an eligible little sister as a potential love interest for the protagonist is also a common trope. Are you following me so far?"

"I think I do," Judy answered with a firm nod. "So, you directly invoked the trope to substitute Neige for your nonexistent little sister."

"Technically, we can't say for sure that I don't have one, considering my amnesia and all. That said, I decided that if I had the choice between Snowy and some as-of-yet unknown girl I don't remember, I'd pick the former, and doing so also serves as an experiment to see how the world reacts to this kind of substitution. This way Snowy gets a reliable big brother, I get a cute little sister while potentially avoiding an awkward meeting with a possible unknown variable in the future, and we all get some insight into the inner workings of the world. Everyone wins."

"I see," my assistant said, digesting my words. "That's actually fairly clever."

"Thanks," I responded with a smile, which was then immediately wiped off my face by her next sentence.

"So, you didn't adopt her just so that you could sneakily add her to your harem while not technically violating your promise to us."

"No, of course not. How many times do I have to tell you I don't want a harem?" I grumbled. "Not to mention, Snowy obviously likes Josh already."

"Eleanor did so, as well," my dear, if currently a little annoying, assistant pointed out. "At least before you seduced her."

"I didn't seduce her any more than I seduced you. Things just developed out of my control over time."

"Let's hope things won't 'develop out of control' this time, then," Judy quipped as she stood up and pocketed her phone.

"Where are you going?"

"Toilet," she responded curtly. "Don't go anywhere."

"I wasn't planning to."

The moment she got her answer, she turned on her heel and stormed off. Maybe she *really* needed to go to the toilet?

Anyways, since I had nothing better to do, I decided to practice my Far Sight 'roll call' routine. Since Judy was going to the restroom, I obviously didn't peek on her, so I started with my other girlfriend.

So, in order of observations: Elly was in the middle of heatedly making her case for why the three of us should be allowed to ride a certain gondola together, Snowy was with Josh's group at a nearby stand—the man himself collecting tickets for his entourage—while Sebastian, smiling creepily, was in the middle of assembling an ancient Egyptian puzzle made of gold, and Brang and Co. busily prepared the secret base for our planned afternoon activities. In short, nothing seemed to require my immediate attention.

Exiting Far Sight, I let out a deep breath, only for it to get trapped in my throat. I was glad I had already finished my drink, or I might've done a spit-take when my eyes unexpectedly landed on a certain woman in a familiar pantsuit, with a long object wrapped in purple cloth slung over her shoulder and a large ice cream cone in her hand. Needless to say, she was obviously the maybe-or-maybe-not-Knight visiting the island.

Worst of all, she was staring right back at me with an inscrutable expression.

No, scratch that! The worst part was that she started walking up to me! Like, what the hell?

She slipped between the oblivious placeholders with ease, and soon I found myself face-to-face with her. She was a fairly lithe, petite woman, no taller than the princess. Her jet-black hair was short, bordering on a boyish pixie cut, and if I had any doubts about her identity, the vivid red streak in it made it abundantly clear this was the same person. In fact, I kind of had to rely on that hairdo (and the purple object on her back) to identify her, as the images the arch-mage provided didn't capture her face well. She was fairly attractive, as expected, except for the fact that she had prominent dark circles under her eyes, giving her a slightly gaunt appearance. Speaking of eyes, her features were definitely East Asian, an impression that was further reinforced when she spoke to me with an accent full of strange intonations.

"Are you the Chimera Slayer?" she asked, putting me on the spot right away, not even bothering with introductions.

"Some people call me that, yes," I answered, obviously and justifiably on guard.

"We knew it!" the woman exclaimed with a wide and slightly disconcerting smile as she sidled closer to me. "We didn't expect to meet you here, but discovering a kindred spirit is always a pleasant surprise, no matter the circumstances!"

"A kindred spirit?" I repeated, slightly flabbergasted.

"Are we not?" she asked what felt like, from her perspective, a rhetorical question.

"Excuse me." I raised a hand, both to make her pause and to keep her at a distance. "Who are you, again?"

"We are..." she began, the corners of her lips drifting from an amicable smile to a full-blown slasher grin, "... a hunter of the dark underbelly of this world, like you are."

"I'm really not, though, and why are you using the royal *w*—?" I attempted to protest, but I was cut off as she leaned even closer, completely disregarding my outstretched palm.

"We should go on a hunt together! Come! Let us paint the streets of this sleepy city with the blood and offal of the monsters that prowl in the night! The slaughter... fufu... It will be *legendary*!"

For a good five seconds, I could only stare at the unhinged woman with a mixture of bafflement and apprehension, but fortunately I managed to collect my wits.

"I'm sorry. Your offer most definitely sounds tantalizing and not at all disturbing as hell, but I'm a little busy right now."

The broad grin on my abhorrent admirer withered, but not because she picked up on my extremely subtle sarcasm.

"Busy with what? Aren't we hunters, you and we?" she asked with an expression that reminded me of a confused kitten wondering where the laser pointer dot disappeared to. But then the cute image was shattered by her slasher-smile returning as she enthusiastically exclaimed, "We are the killers of the creatures that lurk in the shadows! Always ready for the hunt, eager for the sound of steel meeting bone, thirsty for the intoxicating stench of blood! What in the world could keep you from our ultimate calling?"

"Ultimate *what*?"

My brain was stuck in an uncomprehending loop, unable to formulate a response to her overly passionate tirade, so to gather some breathing room, I continued with an equally awkward, "Anyways, to answer your question about what I'm doing... we *are* in an amusement park. People usually come here to relax, you know?"

"What foolishness is this?" the eerie woman sternly responded. "The hunt never ends, and so a hunter never rests. It's common sense."

"Then why are you in an amusement park, eating ice cream?"

She stopped and gave me a look that said I'd just asked the stupidest thing she had ever heard in her entire life... Then she casually took a few licks from her ice cream.

"Nonsense," she declared and gestured broadly with her free hand. "We are preparing for the hunt even as we speak."

"By eating ice cream," I stated, channeling my inner Judy.

The woman shook her head.

"Okay, so you are *not* eating ice cream. Then what are you doing?"

"We are using the cold yin energy in this food to temper our body," she stated softly yet matter-of-factly as if she was explaining something to a child. "What other reason could there be?"

"Erm... people usually eat those on hot days to cool down," I answered on autopilot. I mean, just what the hell was going on with this conversation? Can you even call this thing we were doing a conversation? I don't think we had two sentences between the two of us that logically followed.

"That just proves that most people are foolish," she stated the obvious, at least from her point of view, then she continued to lecture me by explaining, "When it's hot outside, it's the best time to drink boiling sencha to temper your body with yang energy. That is self-evident."

"Don't you get heatstroke like that?"

"Heatstrokes are for the weak," she stated, then turned aside and loosed a high-pitched sneeze, no doubt due to the meddling of the invisible gods of comedic irony.

"What about catching a cold from eating ice cream in autumn?" I asked with fake civility, though she didn't seem to catch on to it.

"Nonsense," she emphasized with a scowl and another sweeping motion of her arm. "A true hunter never catches a cold. Colds are also for the weak."

"Whatever you say."

"We didn't say *whatever*, and whatever we said, it definitely wasn't whatever you think," she… protested, I think? Anyways, before I could attempt to disentangle her weird speech patterns, she did another of those sweeping motions. "We grow tired of this discussion of yin and yang, so we'll no longer think about it. Instead, tell us if you are ready for the hunt yet."

"Okay, first off," I raised my voice, getting a little tired of the conversation at this point. "Before I even entertain this proposal, I have a few questions for you."

She once again gave me a demeaning look, but then said, "Ask," in a patronizing tone.

"All right," I uttered with a relieved sigh, hoping that we could finally get somewhere. "First off, you still didn't tell me who you are."

That earned me yet another *Is this guy dense or what?* look from her, which annoyed the hell out of me.

"We told you already. We're a hunter of the dark underbelly of this world."

"I didn't ask what you were, but who you were," I pointed out, my patience steadily nearing its limit, but she only gave me a confused look in return.

I had no idea what this lady's deal was. By the looks of her, she was definitely important in the grand narrative scheme of things. Using our homebrew classification system, her hairdo alone would've landed her in the "side character" category at the very least, yet her repetitive, obnoxious behaviour put placeholders to shame. Also, I was still confused about the whole royal *we* thing she insisted on doing.

"A name. I'm asking for your name," I spelled it out at last, yet she was still as confused as ever.

"We only just met," she stated with a frown, and I nodded in return.

"Precisely. Normally people introduce themselves when they meet for the first time," I pointed out.

She scoffed. "Foolishness. We are not normal people, you and us. We are hunters!"

At this point I was ready to give up on this line of inquiry and decided to just mark her and figure out her name later through Far Sight. More importantly, I had to figure out if she was with the Knights of the Obnoxiously Lengthy Name, or a brand-new flavour of supernatural zaniness.

"Fine, we are hunters, then," I told her, receiving a nod in return. "Next question. What are we hunting?"

"The creature of the underworld," she stated like it was obvious. "It prowls the dark corners of this island even as we speak. We'll slaughter it and bathe in its blood."

"Literally?"

"Yes," she answered with a nod.

"Ooookay." I inched away from her, but she followed right after while keeping the same, uncomfortably close distance, so I gave up and threw my next question at her. "Is this *creature of the underworld* another Chimera?"

"I hope so," she responded as the slasher-smile crept on to her face. "I want to see the skills that felled a grand beast of the netherworld with my own eyes! I want to see you cut its skin, rend its flesh, and spill its crimson blood all over us! Blood, gushing like a geyser! Like this fountain! Like a—"

"I get it, I get it! Geez!" I interrupted her with my hands raised before she could get even more worked up. "Okay, so you're hunting a monster that may or may not be another Chimera." She nodded, so I breached my main topic by asking, "That means you are not after the Draconians."

The weird woman in front of me gave me another odd look and told me, "What business do we have with the half-bloods of the mountain deities?"

Now it was my turn to give her a long and slightly confused look, but since she didn't react, I answered, "I suppose... none?"

"Correct!" the huntress declared between two licks of her ice cream. I waited for her to finish eating it before asking my next question, but then she lit up and exclaimed, "We cannot bear this any longer! We can no longer restrain the boiling blood in our veins! Come, Chimera Slayer! Let's go on a hunt, right now!"

"As I said, I have a prior engagement," I answered with my best poker face, which was hard to keep up considering the circumstances. She was once again giving me that *What is wrong with this guy?* look, and since I had a feeling she wasn't going to accept my protest, I decided to approach the problem from a different angle and told her, "Not to mention, I... um... I normally hunt alone. And I don't want to do it with someone I don't know yet."

Whatever objection she had in mind at first, she swallowed it back down as she gave me a profound look (which made her slasher-smile even creepier, to be honest), and after a little while she replied with, "Yes... Yes! We see. You are certainly right. We are both hunters, kindred in spirit, yet we don't *know* each other yet. How could we acknowledge the other so easily?" She paused to cock her head to the side, as if listening to something in the distance. Then her eyes turned mirthful. "We know! We should hold a friendly competition!"

"Competition?" I repeated, once again whiplashed by the weird way this woman's thoughts operated.

"Yes! There are two of us, but only one prey. There is no better way to show our pride as hunters than to compete and see who can fell the mighty beast first! After that, there will be no choice but to acknowledge the other! We will be comrades in the hunt forever! There is no better way!"

"I'm fairly sure there are better ways to do that. A lot, actually," I tried to interject, but I might as well have been talking to a wall.

"Ah! Our blood is boiling again! Our blade thirsts! Fufu! We never felt so excited in our life! The massacre will be amazing!"

"I'm glad you are excited," I muttered. "Just don't slaughter anyone else on the way, okay?"

The moment I said that, she stopped chortling and glared, like I'd just thrown a bucket of cold water on her.

"That's a hard promise to make," she muttered with a strained expression. "Could *you* promise the same?"

"Yes, I can most certainly promise that," I told her flatly, though the effort was once again lost on her.

"You can?" She looked surprised, like not slaughtering innocent bystanders was weird. Still, after a moment, she gave me a big nod. "We don't have a choice then, do we? Very well! This will be a fair hunt. So long as you only spill the blood, tear the sinews, and spread the guts of the prey, we will also restrain ourselves."

"That's very reassuring," I answered woodenly, but then I realized that this was a great opportunity to mark her, so I quickly forced an amicable smile on my face, stood up, and extended a hand towards her. "Let's have a nice hunt, shall we?"

She looked at my outstretched hand like she was seeing a white raven for the first time, then she awkwardly switched the dripping cone over to her other hand and shook mine. Her gloved hand was really cold, but her grip was firm.

"Agreed. Let the competition begin!" she declared with gusto, accompanied by another sudden sweep of her arm… except she forgot that she had a cone in it.

The result was as comical as it was unique, as I don't think I'd ever seen ice cream fly for a good twenty meters on a ballistic trajectory and smack a random placeholder on his head before. As for the self-proclaimed huntress, she raised the empty cone to her eye level and let out a soft "Oh."

"Well, that was unexpected," I told her in a jovial voice, but then my amusement was quickly erased when my hand felt stuck. I glanced down and found her holding me like a vice.

"We've lost our tempering material," she stated, her eyes glued to her empty cone.

"I noticed," I told her as I tried to remove my hand, to no avail. "Why don't you buy another one?"

"We can't," she stated emphatically before taking a large, crunching bite out of the cone. "We must preserve our funds."

"Okay, then don't buy one."

She gave me a nod and continued to eat the empty cone without any apparent intention of letting me go.

I needed to do something, quick.

"How about I buy you a replacement to commemorate our meeting?"

She gave me a suspicious glance, but after a short while, she let me go, only to then hold her gloved hand out, palm waiting. I stifled a small sigh. Clearly, I needed to make a small sacrifice to get rid of her, lest Judy show up, misunderstand the situation, and then once again start pestering me about anti-harem countermeasures. So I took out my wallet and handed her a few bills. The moment I did so, the creepy huntress's eyes lit up with something approaching delight. She pocketed the money and gave me a small bow.

"We thank you, Chimera Slayer! With this, we can certainly finish tempering our body!"

"I'm glad to…"

I had to bite back the rest of my sentence, as she abruptly turned on her heel and dived back into the crowd, headed towards the fancy Italian sweets shop on the other side of the amusement park's central square. And not a moment too soon, as my dearest assistant showed up not a minute after.

"I'm back," she announced, only to stop in her tracks and give me a suspicious look. "Did something happen while I was away?"

I had no idea how she deduced that (maybe women's intuition was real?), but I had nothing to hide, so I told her, "Believe it or not, I ran into one of our leads."

Her suspicion melted into concern.

"The mad scientists, the presumed Chimera, or the presumed Knight?"

"The last one," I answered, followed by a tired groan. "She just showed up out of the blue a moment after you left. Speaking of which, let's get moving before she decides to come back."

My assistant glanced around, and then she stepped closer to me.

"Where is she now?"

"She's in the shop where we bought crepes this morning," I told her as we began walking towards Elly and the others.

Judy's previously guarded eyes flipped into skeptical mode. "What is she doing there?"

"Probably eating ice cream," I told her honestly, and since her eyes were still urging me to explain myself, I gave her an abridged description of my meeting with the weird woman.

"And then you bought her a sundae," she repeated after me when I reached the end of my tale.

"Yes," I confirmed.

Judy looked me in the eye for a few seconds with a complicated expression (which, once again, was by her standards, so for anyone else, she probably looked like her nose was a tad itchy), but finally let out a shallow sigh of her own.

"Did you at least probe her for information?"

"As much as I could. I mean, she was kinda nutty, but I think she wasn't a Knight, and I learned a… *few* things about her."

"What's her name?" Judy hit me on a sore spot right away.

"I have absolutely no idea," I admitted, earning me another sideways glance.

"Chief… you just had a chance meeting with a VIP, and you didn't even ask for her name."

"I did. She just refused to give me a straight answer. It doesn't matter, though. I marked her, so I will find her name out, sooner or…" My words trailed off as I noticed something, and a "Bloody hell" slipped through my lips.

"What? What happened?" Judy glanced around in alarm, so I quickly gestured for her to calm down while I tried using my Far Sight again, and… nope, still no reaction.

"So… as it turns out, I require skin contact to mark someone for Far Sight," I told her with a self-deprecating sigh. "On the bright side, at least we learned something new, huh?"

"We should go back and mark her while we have the chance," Judy told me, and I shook my head.

"No way. I'm happy I managed to get rid of her in the first place." My dear assistant wasn't happy about my dismissal, so I quickly grabbed her by the waist and led her along with the words, "Come on, Dormouse. Let's focus on our date. I'm sure there's going to be many contrived chances for me to mark her properly. Let's not let her ruin our day."

Unfortunately, my words alone weren't enough to completely placate her, so in the end I had to spend about half an hour trying to win a silly owl plushy just to get back in her good graces, and another thirty minutes more getting one for Elly. Needless to say, for nearly ruining my date, I unofficially added Miss Creepy Huntress to my list of personal persona non grata.

For the curious: she was right under Crowey and a notch above Lord Grandpa.

As for the rest of the names on that list, that is a tale for another time.

CHAPTER 12

PART 1

"All right, kids, gather round!" I called out to the gang scattered in my living room.

It was a little after 4 p.m. and, all things considered, our double date was a resounding success, even with the appearance of a certain creepy monster huntress. After the amusement park, we visited a nearby zoo (in fact, the two places were apparently run by the same company, explaining all the various animal mascots), and then we all had a hearty dinner at a fancy restaurant Elly suggested. We naturally had a lot of weird hijinks on the way, but for the sake of brevity, they will be omitted. Unfortunately, all good things must come to an end, so after we had our fun, we returned to my place as per our prior agreement.

"Uh-oh!" Angie exclaimed while sitting down. "Be careful, guys. Leo has that look again."

"What look?" I asked back with a strategically raised eyebrow.

"You know, the kind that you have whenever you are about to say something shocking. Or scary. Like when you told me my cover sucked."

"Or when you told us there were multiple prophecies," Snowy chipped in as she also sat down with a cup in her hands.

"Or that those prophecies were about me," Josh added in a grumble while already sitting on the couch between the aforementioned girls.

"Really? Do I have a specific look for that?" I directed the question towards my assistant, only to stop and give her a stern stare. "What exactly are you two doing?"

As far as I could tell, my two girlfriends were in the process of enacting some kind of miniature *kaiju* battle between their mascot plushies. But I decided to give them the benefit of the doubt.

"We aren't doing anything suspicious," Elly stressed while holding out her komodo dragon with a top hat (because *obviously* there was a komodo dragon plushy among the prizes) like she was restraining it.

"Indeed. We are discussing very mature and serious topics," Judy agreed, raising her own owl with a monocle up and down in a sweeping motion.

Well, as it turned out, that was my last bit of benefit of the doubt I had on hand, and they just wasted it, so I decided to ignore whatever silly new contest they had devised. At least they were getting along. Speaking of which, Ammy finally sat down, too, and while she was still giving me a hard look, I decided to push forward.

"Let's put aside my alleged looks for a moment. I told you that we were going to do some light exercise this afternoon, right?" The gang looked at me funny for a moment, but all nodded. "Good, good," I told them, doing my best impression of an all-knowing sage. "Did you all bring a change of clothes as we agreed?"

"I did," Angie confirmed, waving her PE bag.

"So did I," Josh seconded with considerably less enthusiasm, hefting a suspiciously similar-looking gym bag.

"I live here now, so my clothes are already here," Snowy muttered, seemingly embarrassed for some reason.

"I can use magic to change my clothes," Ammy finished the series of confirmations with a shrug.

"Oh, right! I can transform, too!" Angie once again exclaimed in revelation.

"Now that you mention it…" Snowy began, but I cut her off immediately.

"Oh, no, you won't," I told her. "We just got your wardrobe in order, and the last time I saw you transform, you literally exploded your clothes off your back."

"I will take my clothes off before I do that."

"Sure you could, but you shouldn't. I told you we couldn't get the heating working yet, and your Abyssal getup doesn't exactly cover a lot of skin."

"Hah!" Angie elbowed Josh in the side. "Look at that! He's been a big brother for just a day, and he is already trying to cover up his little sister!"

"Speaking of covering up!" I pointed straight at the Celestial girl. "Don't talk like your Celestial getup is even remotely winter-ready, young lady!"

"What?" She frowned. "Those are the standard Celestial battle garments!"

"It's literally an undersized bedsheet and a pair of boots."

"It's not a bedsheet! It also has a pair of bracers, too! And they're cool, right, Josh?"

"Um… sure?" my friend responded quite uncertainly, but it was enough for Angie to puff up her chest in victory.

"You see? I told you it's cool."

"I'd prefer if it was warm instead," I stated, my voice as flat as paper, earning me an unenthusiastic *"Oh snap"* from Judy on the side. I pointedly ignored her and continued with, "Do you even need to transform?"

"If you want me to show all of my abilities, then duh," Angie answered, rolling her eyes.

"Okay, so you *have* to put on your Celestial clothes… Can you at least put a jacket on top?"

"Nuh-uh." The Celestial girl shook her head defiantly at my proposed middle ground. "It would get torn off."

"It would?" I asked back for clarification, and it was the class rep who promptly provided it.

"Yes," she confirmed. "When the Winged Races unseal their suppressed powers, the excess mana forms a defensive layer over their skin. It tends to vaporize any mundane clothing."

"Then where do the new clothes come from?" Judy interjected, somehow typing on her phone with her left hand while still enacting a miniature monster battle with the owl in her other hand.

Multitasking, I was sure she'd call it.

"They are part of their transformation," Ammy stated offhandedly. "I don't know the details, though, as our outfits work differently. I'm directly transmuting my own clothes with a spell."

"Um… I have a question?" Josh interjected with a raised hand. "I don't remember my clothes vaporizing at any point last Sunday."

"To be fair, you weren't wearing much to begin with," I mumbled, then said louder, "Still, the question is valid. Does that mean that the whole exploding thing doesn't happen to Draconians?"

"That's correct," the class rep confirmed with another nod. "Draconians reinforce their bodies internally with the excess mana instead of creating a defensive barrier. They still have their scales, though, and those are usually more than enough to protect them."

"I see. So, instead of magical clothes, you get a power boost," I addressed the princess, only to immediately fall silent, my brows knitting themselves into a frown all on their own.

"Rawr!" Elly let out an admittedly pretty cute growl while pushing her plushy forward, only to stop when she noticed she was in the center of attention. Her face went red. I waited for her to freeze, or let out one of her classic strings of cutesy noises, yet instead she lightly cleared her throat and said, in an almost mechanical tone, "Excuse me, but could you repeat the question? I'm afraid I wasn't paying attention."

"Okay, time out." I raised my hands in a T towards the rest of the group before I addressed my girlfriends again. "You know what? I'll bite. Could you please tell me just what you two are doing?"

Elly blinked in surprise, then glanced over at Judy. It seemed like they were having a small conversation with their eyes for a second, after which she turned back at me and said, in a mousy voice, "We are playing with our plushies?"

"Yes, I can see that. But why?"

"B-because plushies are girly, right? So playing with them is girly too, right?"

I narrowed my eyes at her answer, then asked, "Is this another of those femininity-point-nonsense things you two were going on about last time?"

"That's correct," Judy answered in Elly's stead.

"But then why are you acting like your plushies are battling?"

"It's a reenactment of the finale of the famous sixteenth *King of Monsters* movie, aka, the best one," Judy told me like it was something self-evident.

I gave my dear assistant a skeptical look. "Okay, for the sake of my sanity, let's ignore *what* it is, and let's focus on *why* you are reenacting it with your plushies."

"For femininity points!" Elly declared, only to shrink back when I glanced back at her, and hastily add, "I-I mean... I didn't get it either at first, but Judy was really confident about it, and she said that if we kept it up, then you would get curious, and then it would be funny, though to be honest, it's actually pretty fun anyway, though I still don't understand what it has to do with femininity or points, but... do... do I make sense?"

I let the silence after her explanation linger, then I let out a dramatic sigh before facing Judy.

"Dormouse, I can't help but feel that you are a bad influence on Elly."

"That's just your opinion, Chief," she answered with an implied stuck-out tongue before she returned to their little reenactment, now all but confirmed to be an elaborate ploy to annoy me.

I turned back to the rest of the group.

"So, my occasionally weird girlfriends aside, where were we?"

"We were discussing a change of clothes, magical transformations, and things being vaporized," Josh reminded me with his face set in an odd mixture of empathy and schadenfreude.

"Right, that," I uttered with a knowing nod. Facing the class rep, I asked, "So, different folks do the transformation differently, right? Celestials and Abyssals explode their clothes and replace them with their fancy battle garbs or whatever, Draconians only transform their body, while you only transform your clothes. What about the Knights?"

"As I said, I don't know the details, but I think they actually have to manually put on their enchanted armours and charms," Ammy answered.

"Good to know. That means they should be easy to recognize ahead of time," I mused for a moment before snapping out of it and raising my voice. "All right, then! Everyone, grab your change of clothes, just to be on the safe side, and follow me."

"Where?" Ammy inquired with a curious glint in her eyes.

"We aren't going far, just to my magical closet," I told her while trying to keep my smile in check.

"Your magical what?" Josh exclaimed just a split second faster than Angie. In fact, everyone was equally surprised, save for Judy and Snowy, who were already in on the plan.

"Closet," I repeated while gesturing for them to follow.

Now, this likely requires some explanation. Judy and I spent a considerable amount of time debating how we should facilitate moving to and from our shiny new secret base without outright disclosing its location. I mean, if we did that, it wouldn't be a *secret* base anymore, now would it?

Jokes aside, the real issue was that, while we created a few false entries on the Hub discussing how the Magi had discovered several Celestial safe houses, with the abandoned shelter being just one of them, it still didn't mean that our base was completely off their radar. As such, I really didn't want to have any visible signs of use that could betray our presence.

That meant just hitching a ride on the bus to the mountainside was out of the question, which left us with utilizing my teleportation ability to ferry people as the most obvious solution. Unfortunately, said ability was also supposed to be a secret, leading to a long series of back-and-forths between the two of us resulting in the final compromise.

As Sun Tzu once said, in order to deceive your enemies, first you have to deceive your friends. Or at least, I think Sun Tzu said that. It's kind of vague, and I don't think it's from the Art of War, but it's kind of beside the point.

Anyhow, while I was pondering on the widespread misappropriation of various famous quotations, I reached the small closet under the stairs, and I waited for the rest of the gang to catch up to me before I put my hand on the doorknob and told them in a low, conspiratorial voice, "Listen up, guys, what I'm going to show you now is a huge secret. I expect everyone to keep it."

I waited until everyone, including my fellow accomplices, nodded, then after a satisfied grunt, I threw the door open, revealing... a fairly mundane coat closet, about one meter by two meters in dimensions and just high enough for me to enter without having to bend forward. At the moment, it had no clothes or any kind of lighting inside, and the latter in particular was because I removed the light bulb beforehand so that everyone could see the softly glowing circle of sigils on the floor.

The last bit was all thanks to Snowy. I asked her to make them visible for everyone, and although they were only a series of meaningless magical marks, I hoped they would look sufficiently authentic at first glance to convince, say, a grumpy mage girl that this was a genuine magic circle.

"That's not a magic circle," Ammy declared the moment she laid eyes on it.

"Like hell it isn't," I countered indignantly.

"Then why isn't it connected to the ley line? And where's its control array? Not to mention—"

"Hey, class rep? Would it actually kill you to listen to my explanation first?"

Ammy gave me a skeptical look but shrugged as if to say, *Be my guest.*

I let out a small breath, then pointed towards my closet again.

"So, as I was about to say before I got interrupted, this is my magical closet," I recited my preplanned explanation. "It cost me an arm and a leg and quite a few favors to set up, but it was a necessary investment."

I paused here on purpose, as this was the point where Judy was supposed to ask me about what the circle did, but instead it was Josh who voiced his question first by saying, "Hey, is this one of those teleport circles we talked about when meeting Ammy's grandfather?"

"Bingo!" I exclaimed and gave my friend a grateful thumbs-up.

"This? A teleport circle?" Ammy muttered while glancing between me and the glowing symbols on the floor.

"Yep," I confirmed with what I hoped was a confident smile.

"You're joking," she stated quite categorically. "That's not what a teleport circle looks like."

"Well, probably because this is kind of a special one," I replied with a coy smile as I stepped into my closet. "You see, this circle allows a maximum of two people to move between this place and our secret base."

"Wait a moment!" Josh cut in with a surprisingly enthusiastic voice. "You have a secret base? Really?"

"Yup," I told him, this time with 100 percent honesty. "It's a super-secret hideout I just recently obtained."

"A hideout? Like the ones in those spy movies?" Angie elbowed her way to the front to ask her questions. "With henchmen? And traps? And torture rooms?"

"Yes, yes, kinda, no, and hell no," I answered her in order. "Why would we even need a torture room? We are not the bad guys!"

"Oh, right," Angie whispered like she'd just realized that, but before she could say anything more, Ammy once again wedged herself into the conversation.

"So, you want to tell me that this garbled circle, unconnected to any ley line, is actually a long-range teleportation conduit?"

"Yes, that's exactly what I'm telling you, Miss Arbitrary Skeptic," I shot back at her.

"I don't believe you," she said outright, making the atmosphere a little tense for a moment.

"Okay, then I'll prove it," I told her while inviting her in. "Unfortunately, the circle is keyed to me, so you have to hitch a ride with me."

"Fine by me," Ammy huffed and stepped inside as well. "So?"

"Just a moment," I responded while sending a sneaky wink at the rest of the group, then closed the door on us.

"Why did you close the door?" the class rep asked, apparently quite startled by my sudden action.

"I told you, it's special," I answered with a grin, probably barely visible in the dim chamber. "It has a few inconvenient rules. First, it can only transport at most two people at a time. Secondly, it's keyed to me, so only I can use it. Thirdly, it also only works with the door closed. Finally, you should step a little closer."

"Why?" She sounded quite suspicious, but I only shrugged. Which she also most likely couldn't see.

"Because you need to be closer for the circle to register you."

With that, I extended a hand towards her shoulder and pulled her towards me, eliciting a tiny, surprised "Eep!" from her. Ignoring her protests, I wrapped my phantom limb around her waist in preparation.

Speaking of which, just when did things like wrapping phantom limbs around people become so normal for me? Was I getting weird? Metaphorically, I snorted at the thought and decided to worry about it later.

"Okay, this should work. Close your eyes for a second," I instructed my passenger, and while at first she gave me such an intense glare, I could feel it even in the dark, she still followed my directions faithfully, though not silently.

"I swear to God, Leo, if this is just some kind of prank, I'm going to charge you for harassment and—"

"All right, Amelia, we've arrived!" I raised my voice, cutting her tirade short and making her eyes pop right open in surprise. She glanced around and tried to step back, but I held on to her shoulder for the time being.

We were still in a small, dark compartment, though this one was slightly larger than my closet at home. To be perfectly honest, though, this was *also* a closet. A utility one, to be precise. I had the Fauns empty it out and then Snowy set up the same faux magic circle in it as she did back at my place.

Speaking of the Fauns...

"I will now open the door! Don't worry! There should be no one on the other side!" I exclaimed again, but I still grasped Ammy's shoulder and waited until I could hear a series of heavy footsteps followed by scraping metal noises coming from outside. Only then did I let out a small breath and unhanded the increasingly baffled class rep.

I wordlessly pushed the heavy steel door open, revealing a large, fairly bare concrete room on the other side. It used to be one of the smaller side rooms of the shelter, and based on the remaining furniture, it was most likely supposed to be a recreational or communal room. Not that anyone could tell that at this point, as I had the Faun, led by my enthusiastic little sister, completely empty it and it clean it up, too. I'm not going to lie; considering that they were literally designed to be terrifying, muscle-bound warriors and shock-troopers, I was shocked by how well they were doing as housekeepers.

None of them were around at this point, though, as having them wait just outside the "teleport room" was just a bloody incident waiting to happen, so, for the time being, I told them to remain in the central hall.

"Wow..." Ammy exclaimed. "Did we really teleport?"

"What does it look like?" I responded with a provocative smirk, but she didn't seem to notice.

"That's amazing... I didn't feel any disturbance in the ambient mana. I didn't even notice when you activated the circle..." Suddenly, she looked at me with a strangely fervent look in her eyes and took a heavy step forward, making me almost flinch in reflex. "Hey, Leo? Did we really use that circle? Did we?"

"Y-yes," I answered her a little less decisively than I wanted, still a smidgen off-balance by her sudden passion.

"Really? Can... can I study it?" she requested, turning bashful. "Please?"

"Um... no?" I told her, once again a little less decisively than I'd originally planned. Since I figured that wasn't enough to convince her, I proceeded to give her some of my pre-written excuses. "I mean, I told you it's a special one, right? It wasn't exactly cheap, and I have no way of replacing it."

"I'll be careful," she insisted. "I won't break it—I only want to look at it. And maybe take a few mana samples... and an imprint. No, two imprints!"

"I said no, and that's final." I stood my ground, not at all bothered or wary of her torrent of uncomfortably zealous gazes. "For now, stay inside this room until I get the others. Don't go outside yet."

"Can I look at the circle while you are gone?"

"No!" I exclaimed in exasperation, then I toned things back a little. "I mean, I need the door to be closed, so no."

"Aw," she sighed, sounding genuinely dejected.

Honestly, the longer I knew her, the less of a grasp I had on the class rep's character. Was she a shrinking violet? A strict honour student? An overburdened secretary? An easily excitable researcher type? None of these? All of the above?

Either way, I once again told her to stay put as I all but escaped into the "teleport room" and promptly returned to my closet. I let out a relieved sigh and opened the door, at which point the whole gang (or at least the ones not in on the scheme) let out a collective gasp. Were they holding their breaths until now?

"Wow! Ammy's really gone!" Angie exclaimed while sticking her head into the closet, then she faced me with a grin that revealed even her molars. "Awesome! I'm next!"

"Sorry, but nope," I said with a fake grin mirroring hers before gesturing for Snowy to step up. "You were supposed to be first, so let's get moving."

I wasn't lying. Originally, Snowy was supposed to serve as a gatekeeper of sorts, so that she would be on hand on the other side to mediate between the Faun and the gang in case something unexpected happened, but the class rep's challenge threw a minor monkey wrench into the works.

Snowy squeezed between the others to get into the closet, accompanied by a disappointed "Muh..." from Angie. After moving her over without any incident, I ferried the rest as well one by one, starting with the eager Celestial and concluding with Judy. As I came back from the last return trip, I found my assistant standing in front of the door with a conflicted expression.

"Chief?"

"Yes, Dormouse?"

"I was curious," she began as she glanced around. "If we both move over, how are we going to come back?"

I couldn't help but let out a deep and not at all ominous laugh I'd also prepared well in advance.

"I'm so glad you asked!" I gestured for her to follow me, which she did, though for some reason a bit reluctantly. Anyhow, I led her to the back door of the kitchen, which incidentally opened to the garage, and I knocked on it three times.

There was a short but meaningful pause, and then, just as my assistant was about to say something, the door opened, revealing a large, hairy shape on the other side.

"[Is it time, boss?]" Karukk, one of the friendlier members of Snowy's retinue, asked with an upbeat grin. Then he noticed Judy standing next to me, and quickly added, "Oh? To you, I say evening," in our native tongue.

His voice was incredibly deep, raspy, yet well defined, and his words were accompanied by a polite nod that made her shiver for some reason.

"[Aye, the time is nigh indeed,]" I answered while gesturing for him to come into the kitchen. "[I shall entrust my domicile to your care and vigilance. You may find various forms of nourishment in the frigid box yonder, though I warn you! You shall wash your hands, and wash them well, before reaching into its bowels. You also possess my permission to peruse the various channels of the device of audiovisual telegraphy within the lounge, and to do so in any manner you may find suitable for your tastes.]"

"[Got it, boss. When are you coming back?]"

"[That I cannot say, nor can I fathom. We shall return when our activities are finished, and no sooner.]"

"[Okay. Have fun.]" The Faun gave me a casual wave before hunching down in front of the fridge.

"You can't be serious," Judy complained behind me, and I only just noticed that she was hiding there the whole time.

"That's my line. And you're still acting like this is the first time you met Karukk. Or any other Faun, for that matter."

"It's because they are scary," Judy said with a huff. The Faun by the fridge glanced at her and she hid behind my back again.

"Come on, they're not *that* scary," I told her, patting her on the back to reassure her.

"Can we just get going?" she urged me with a pleading look so obvious, maybe someone else could've recognized it.

I couldn't help but wonder, though...

"You know that there are even more Fauns at the hideout, right?"

Judy gave me a conflicted look for a moment, but then she bravely (?) declared, "Don't worry about me. I'll just hide behind you again."

"You do that," I told her as I tried to grab her by the waist, but she stepped back. "What? Didn't you want to get going?"

"We are not in the magical closet," she stated while pointing towards the stairs.

"No, we aren't... but that was just part of the charade. We don't actually *have* to be there to teleport."

"I know," Judy huffed softly. "But Elly already got to hug you in a dark room, so now it's my turn."

"Are you serious?"

Instead of answering, Judy gingerly grabbed hold of my hand with just three fingers and began to pull me after her... well, *pull* was a strong word. *Attempting to lead* might've been a more accurate one. At any rate, I had no reason to resist, but as I followed after her, I glanced back and my eyes met with Karukk's.

The Faun, who just happened to have an entire salami in his hands, gave me a knowing smile and softly said, "[Women, am I right?]"

At first, I was quite surprised by his comment, but then I let out a small chuckle and answered, "[You most certainly are,]" before following after Judy for an unscheduled cuddling session. At least it seemed like she finally got over her grudge from before, so I decided to put on a stiff upper lip and endure her snuggling like a man.

Oh, the crosses I had to bear!

PART 2

"Hey, Leo! Leo!" Angie rushed up to me with sparkling eyes the moment I opened the door of the teleport closet, almost shoving me back in with her childlike fervor. "We're really underground, right? Right?"

"Um… Yes?" I answered after a moment of understandable hesitation.

"See, I told you!" the hyperactive Celestial girl flashed a victorious grin as she turned to the only other guy in the room. "It's a secret underground base! It's so cool!"

"I already told you that," Snowy sulked, apparently being ignored by the childhood friend duo. I found it my big brotherly duty to pat her on the head to reassure her… except a certain deadpan girl was just a step quicker than me. Judy ducked under my arm as she exited the closet, then she began to woodenly tussle the Abyssal girl's hair with an equally flat *Don't worry about it.*

I didn't have time to be bothered by her stealing my thunder, though. The moment I stepped forward, I was startled by a certain class representative abruptly popping out of my blind spot, asking, "Can I look at the circle now?"

"No!" I denied, a bit more vehemently than intended. "We have more important things to do."

"But… this could revolutionize transportation theory! If I could figure out how it works, I could even get a research grant from the Assembly!" Ammy pressed on, pleading with upturned eyes and clasped hands. "Come on, Leo! Just a tiny, little look! I will only take four… no, wait, seven! Seven samples. You already promised you would help me with my psychic research!"

"I don't remember ever doing that," I answered her after just the briefest of baffled pauses.

"Actually, you're right. You never helped me, so now's the perfect time to make up for that! Just nine samples, it's all I ask!"

"No, I meant I don't remember making a promise!"

"The number of samples also went up," Judy casually noted, still petting my new sister.

"Judy, please don't interrupt the negotiations," Ammy suddenly lapsed back into her strict authority persona, only to turn back at me to continue pleading. "Please, Leo! If I get a research grant, I can finally have my own workshop! Then I'll no longer have to do grandfather's paperwork! Speaking of which, you owe me this much for all the paperwork you've caused!"

"I thought we were over this already!" I groaned and took a step away from the class rep, but she followed right after me.

"Come on! Just ten samples!"

"The number of samples rose again," Judy helpfully informed me while not even trying to help. So typical.

"I said no, and that's final," I told the class rep. "I told you already. I cannot replace this circle, so if it's broken, we are screwed. No tinkering with it. Are we clear?"

If glares had weight, I would've been flat as a pancake under the one Amelia was sending my way, but after a fairly short stalemate, she finally relented with a dispirited, "Yes, we are clear."

I had the feeling that she would hold a grudge, so I wanted to give her an olive branch. Unfortunately, my efforts for upholding something even remotely resembling a coherent conversation were once again torpedoed, this time by the princess all but pushing Ammy to the side just to stand in front of me and declare, "Leo, this place smells weird!"

I gave my Draconian girlfriend a wry look (which was, I would like to stress, fairly low-key considering the circumstances), and after taking a huge breath, I courteously asked her, "Would you please elaborate?"

Elly scrunched up her nose as she took a few overt sniffs, then stated, "This whole place smells like Abyssals."

"Well, that's not surprising at all," I told her with an affectionate voice, as she just happened to accidentally hand me the cue required to move things forward. "You see, this place originally belonged to Crowey," I revealed our cover story with just the right amount of nonchalance to make it sound legitimate.

"It did?" Elly and Ammy leveled the same question at me almost simultaneously.

"It's true. Right, Snowy?" I threw the ball into the court of the Abyssal girl, and while her acting was quite wooden (to put it *very* mildly), she followed her script to the letter. Maybe even too closely...

"Y-yes. This abandoned u-underground facility was m-most certain a hidden hideout that my other older brother, who is not Leonard Dunning, ap-appro…" she paused here for a moment, then exclaimed, "Appropriated! That's the word!"

I gave my relieved sister an appreciative nod, then smoothly continued my explanation to the rest of the gang… although, technically it was only Ammy and Elly, as Judy and Snowy were already in on the gig, while Josh and Angie were too busy marveling at a pile of old tables in the corner to pay attention to us. Those two were weird.

Anyways, I began to confidently recite my own script, saying, "So, as she said, since Crowey is out of town, and we are not exactly on good terms anyway, I decided I might as well take this place and make it our little secret base where we can plan, train, and just generally hang out without any prying eyes hovering over our heads."

That last comment was mainly aimed at the class rep, but instead of responding to me, she faced Snowy and said, "Was this where you were hiding?"

"I… um…" Snowy stammered for a moment when faced with the unexpected question and sent me a helpless glance. I lightly shook my head, so she answered in kind. "No, I wasn't."

"And since when did you have this secret base on our island? Was House Inanna preparing to establish a foothold here? What was your plan?" came the next series of increasingly incriminating questions from Ammy.

"I… I don't know," Snowy muttered with round eyes, just about to cave under the pressure.

"Easy there, class rep," I said, gesturing *tone it back* with my hands. "You already know about Snowy's situation. You can't expect her to be privy to Crowey's plans."

"She's still his sister," Ammy countered.

"She was, and now she's mine, so I'd appreciate it if you stopped bullying her."

"I'm not bullying her. I'm asking perfectly legitimate and reasonable questions!" Amelia protested as she, for the first time in a while, reached up and tweaked her glasses in a strangely ominous fashion.

"Here, here…" I turned my back on her and reached for my visibly confused adopted sister's head and gently rubbed its crown, smiling my warmest smile. "Don't worry about the mean class rep. Your big bro won't let her bully you."

"I'm not bullying her!"

"You better not," I told her with a stern voice hiding my satisfaction.

Another day, another uncomfortable topic derailed.

Anyhow, after confirming that I still had my touch, I cleared my throat and raised the hand previously on Snowy's head over my own to get everyone's attention.

"Listen, guys! At this rate, we'll be stuck in this room till the cows come home, so how about we leave the legitimate and reasonable questions for later and focus on why we came here for once?"

"That reminds me, why did we come here again?" Josh inquired as he returned with Angie, who somehow already managed to get a giant smudge of dust on her face.

Judy also noticed it and was already taking care of it, so I decided to only focus on Joshua. Thus, I told him, "I think I already mentioned this, but just to be clear—we're here to experiment with our abilities and train for the possible dangers we might face in the near future."

"Train?" Elly, who was in something of a strange stupor while I was talking with Ammy, suddenly perked up at the mere mention of the word. "Are we going to work out?"

"Not really," I told her. "My plan was to dedicate the rest of this day discussing our abilities, testing any synergies, experimenting with Josh's transformations, and if we had the time, we would then do some light sparring to put things into practice."

"You want to spar here?" Elly looked around. "We don't have enough space."

Actually, the communal room we were standing in easily had an area of fifty square meters, minus the space that the furniture in the corner occupied. For normal people, that was probably more than enough room for exercise, but considering how the gaggle of supernatural scions I had around me were, the chamber did feel a little stifling.

"Well, it's a good thing we aren't going to be training here, then!" I responded with a toothy grin, and Elly's eyes opened wide for a moment, but then she averted them with a blush. I had no idea what I did to make her embarrassed like that, but I decided not to dwell on the mysteries of her mind. Instead, I raised my voice again to address everyone at once.

"Listen up! We are now going to move on to the main hall. I want to remind everyone that this place used to belong to Crowey. Everyone got that? Okay, then. I just want to warn you that the place came with staff, so don't get too surprised when we go over, okay?"

"Staff? What kind of staff?" Ammy latched on to the word, but for the time being, I only waved for her to follow.

"It'll be quicker to show you," I responded with a fairly clichéd (yet accurate) line and gestured for everyone to follow after me. I led the group to the steel blast door separating the two areas, and after some fiddling (I had Brang and Company oil the hinges, but they were still a little stiff), we found ourselves face-to-face with a row of Fauns.

Now, to be perfectly clear, I did not actually tell them to form an orderly line in front of the door, and while I did find their display imposing, at the moment it was pretty much the worst impression they could've picked to convey, as the surprised gasps behind my back testified.

"[General,]" I addressed the big bloke in the middle, who responded with a toothy grin that made the guys behind me audibly inhale once again. I held back a groan and instead told him, "[Your display is impeccable, yet entirely unwarranted.]"

If his expression was any indication, Brang obviously had some kind of fitting answer on the tip of his tongue, but before he could grace us (or, considering only I seemed to be fluent in Faunish here, just me) with its brilliance, we were once again interrupted by the class rep dryly asking, "Aren't these the Faun from last Sunday? Didn't they go back to the Abyss?"

"Why do you have to be so damn observant today?" I glanced over my shoulder in exasperation, only for Ammy to once again adjust her glasses and reply with a question of her own.

"I don't know. Why do you have to be so uncooperative today?"

My instincts told me to say *Touché*, but that would have been as good as admitting defeat, so we just stared daggers at each other for a few seconds. It didn't serve any purpose, though, as I couldn't come up with any snappy retorts, so I clicked my tongue and told her, "Yes, they are one and the same, but no, they are obviously not in the Abyss. You can think of them as Snowy's retinue."

"Are you sure they are not spies?" the Magi girl loudly questioned, and to his credit, Brang's only reaction to the accusation was his left ear swiveling in a curious manner.

"They are definitely not spies," I replied by filling my voice with so much conviction, I hoped it would browbeat her into compliance.

"Are they safe?" came the next question, this time from Angie, who was hiding behind Snowy of all people.

"Yes, they are," I answered. "They might seem scary, but they are nice guys." Saying so, I stepped forward and introduced the group, one by one. "This is Uncle Brang, ex-general and the current leader of this group. The others are, from left to right: Gram, Rabom, Hrul, Vurrok, and Pip."

Josh muttered, *"Pip? Seriously?"* in the back, but I ignored him and continued.

"They can understand you perfectly, but for some reason they can only speak in caveman-esq syntax. Don't ask why; nobody knows. Still, you should be able to communicate with each other well enough. If you hit a roadblock, call for me and I will translate."

"Actually, that reminds me. Since when can you speak their language?" came the next unwanted question from the class rep.

Judy must've realized I was getting quite fed up with her questions, as she stepped up to the plate and told her, "The Chief is a man of many talents. Linguistics is one of them."

"I think I've heard that before…" Josh pondered, but before anyone else could cut in again, I gestured for Brang to come closer.

"[I'm afraid our training excursion shall forever be akin to a fish aground so long as your kin is present. If I may be so presumptuous, might I request that you vacate the premises of this hall, if but temporarily?]"

The large Faun let out a subdued chuckle and gave me a small bow, much to my surprise.

"[Nay. There lies no presumption in thy words. We shall follow thy command.]"

I wanted to point out that it wasn't really a command per se, but I had a feeling his insistence most likely had to do with my adoption of Snowy and consecutively wedging myself into their hierarchy. I really wasn't in the mood to clear that up at the moment, so I let it slide and said, "[I shall require your aid shortly, so please equip yourself for battle and return to my side at your earliest convenience.]"

Instead of a proper answer, Brang and company gave me a salute, followed by another one aimed at their actual liege in the back, then they turned around and marched out of the main hall with a striking yet borderline comical lockstep. I waited for them to close the door behind them before I faced my friends again and clapped my hands to hype myself up, making them shudder so hard I was afraid some of them (read: the princess) might fall over.

I waited for the echo of my clap to die down, then told them, "All right, guys, I've had it with these distractions! I want you to change into your spare clothes and then we'll get started! The girls will change in that room; Josh and I will change here. Any questions?"

"Do I have to change?" Judy raised her hand, and I gave her a deadpan glance in return.

"Why would you?"

"Just checking," she answered unabashedly before grabbing Snowy and pulling her back into the room where we came from. They were just about to close the door behind themselves when I remembered something, and I quickly called out after them.

"Just a reminder—don't let the class rep mess with the magic circle!"

"Understood," my assistant responded, followed by some unwarranted protests from the Magi in question, cut mercifully short by the closing of the door, leaving Josh and me behind.

I glanced at my hapless friend, and I couldn't help but let out the mother of all groans. If I was already this tired before we even got started, I had to wonder just how busted I would be by the end of this day...

PART 3

"At last, some progress!" I exhaled in relief when the gang assembled in the main hall once again.

As per my previous request, my companions all changed into something more... well, I wanted to say *practical*, but considering Snowy was wearing her Abyssal outfit made of black leather strips held on by magic (or double-sided tape, one or the other), it probably wasn't the right word. *Comfortable*? No, it didn't look like that, either. How about *appropriate*? Well, she wore high-heeled boots on a transformation/uniform that existed (supposedly) for high-speed, high-stakes supernatural combat... I have to say, I really wanted to meet whoever designed it and give him a friendly pat on the back with a fireman's axe.

A broken-ankle-in-the-waiting and justified homicide aside, I'll get back to the story. We probably should start from the beginning. Or, in this particular case, from left to right.

First in line was the already discussed Abyssal sister of mine. She looked just like the last time I saw her transformed, with the fetish outfit, horns, and all else. On second thought, maybe not *all else*, as she didn't have her wings out. I didn't even know those were retractable.

Anyways, it was hard to tell if she was uncomfortable with the amount of skin she was showing or if she was simply feeling cold, but judging by the way she was sending bashful glances at Josh (who was conspicuously averting his eyes from her with a blush on his face), my money was on the former. Speaking of him, my friend was wearing his gym uniform, and would've probably stuck out of the group like a sore thumb, if not for Elly being dressed in the same manner... Which made *both of them* stick out of our group of impractically attired misfits.

Speaking of fancy and highly impractical clothes, the fourth person in the line was Angie in her white Celestial outfit, complete with her retractable bow-armguard-thingy. She didn't have her wings out, either. On the bright side, at least her footwear didn't have high heels. (I'll take my silver linings wherever I can find them.)

The one closing the line was naturally Ammy in her eminently frilly white and green dress. She didn't have her huge witch hat on, nor did she wield her staff, so as of now she only looked like an unusually brightly dressed gothic Lolita, which actually came across as fairly tame in this context. As they say, everything is relative, including supernatural fashion.

Our little group looked as eclectic as ever, and as ready as we were going to get. Time to get down to business.

"All right, everyone, let's get things on track! Judy, you are on record duty."

"On it," my assistant responded while lightly waving her phone.

"Good. First, let's discuss your transformations again. In particular, I want to know a bit more about that *barrier* you guys mentioned earlier." After saying so, I directly addressed the class rep, as she was the most knowledgeable about these subjects. "You said something about it forming upon transformation and shredding clothes. What else does it do?"

"It is in the name," Ammy stated the obvious.

"I want specifics. What does it protect against and how? Is it static, or can it be recharged? And more importantly, does it vaporize clothes even after the transformation?"

Our resident Magi gave me an intrigued look and contemplated that for a moment.

"It is a passive form of protection, so it naturally cannot be compared to active defenses."

"Like the one Neige's brother used," Judy spoke without glancing up from her notes.

"Precisely." Ammy confirmed with a nod. "It was a multilayered directional shield, as opposed to the Winged Ones' omnidirectional barrier."

"We saw it was pretty resilient. I guess the passive barrier is less so," I added while observing Angie to see if I could detect any trace of the subject of our discussion on her. Unfortunately, I couldn't see anything unusual beyond a very weak glow surrounding her. But then again, it might have been *exactly* what I was looking for.

"It depends on the individual, but it should be able to greatly reduce incoming physical impacts."

"Define *greatly reduce*," Judy chimed in again, causing our resident Magi to frown.

"As I said, it's different from person to person."

"All right, then. Let's particularize the question," I told her and then pointed at Angie. "Let's take her as our baseline. What would happen if Josh punched her?"

"Why am I getting punched?" Angie complained.

"The better question: why am I doing the punching?" Josh cut in with an equally displeased voice, but I ignored both of them and waited for Ammy to give her answer.

"Well..." she began while giving a furtive look to the Celestial girl. "Her barrier would absorb a lot of the force behind the blow, and then spread the rest over a larger area. In practice, it would reduce a violent punch into a stiff shove."

"I think I get it," Josh suddenly declared with an expression that said he'd just received a minor revelation. "Last Sunday, when I punched Lili's brother, it felt like I was hitting a bag of molasses. I thought it was because I had scaly hands and such, but it was probably this barrier thing you're talking about."

"Very likely," the class rep confirmed. "As a Lord of the Abyss and a powerful individual, Noire's passive barrier is likely leagues beyond Angie's. It is safe to say that the only one of us who did any damage to him was Eleanor."

"Oh, man." Josh slouched and then continued, with an exaggerated pout, "And I thought I was doing fairly well for myself back there."

"What if Josh had a weapon, like a knife?" I voiced the next logical question that came to mind. "Would the barrier protect Angie against cuts or stabs?"

"Why is it me again?" Angie grumbled, but she was summarily ignored by us.

"Depends, but passive barriers are slightly less effective against those than blunt force attacks," Ammy answered, this time a little uncertainly.

"Bullets?" came my next question.

"It's... fairly resistant to small caliber firearms, but it would still hurt a lot."

"Magical attacks?" Judy took the words out of my mouth, but I clarified after her all the same.

"Let's say we throw a fireball at Angie. What would happen?"

"That also depends on the person, but at a glance, Angie's barrier seems decently resistant against mystic phenomena. However—"

"Do barriers get weaker as they absorb damage?" Judy threw out.

"Naturally, yes."

"Hmm," my assistant grunted. "HP."

"My thoughts exactly. We'll discuss it later. But for now..." I turned to the increasingly befuddled Ammy. "Let's continue with the most important question: do they shred their clothes *after* the transformation is already done?"

"They shouldn't," Ammy answered with an expression that said she had no idea why I considered that so important.

"Unless the person gets attacked," Snowy quietly added. "It's as Amelia said. If you get struck by an attack while transformed, the barrier spreads out the damage, and if you are not wearing special clothes, it'll cause large tears."

"Chief," Judy called out to me while gesturing for me to lean closer. I was a little skeptical of her, considering her recent track record, but I decided to humour her for the time being and obliged. "People have HP, and now we have clothing damage," she whispered to me while pointing at her notes. "I believe… we live in an eroge RPG."

I gave my assistant a wry look. "Not now, Dormouse."

"It's a valid hypothesis," she pouted, but didn't press the issue.

I shook my head at my assistant's outburst of weird conclusions and faced Snowy again.

"So, if I understand this right, if you have your barrier up while wearing normal clothes, and then get hit, then the clothes get damaged." Snowy ruminated on my words for a moment, then nodded with conviction. "Okay, so if I turn that around, does that mean that if you *don't* get hit while your barrier is already up, the clothes *won't* get damaged?"

"I… suppose they won't," my sister confirmed my words, this time with less conviction.

"That's what I wanted to hear!" I exclaimed happily as I peeled myself out of my long black coat and draped it over Snowy's shoulders. Since it was about five sizes too big for her, she looked a tad ridiculous, especially with the lost look on her face, but it was better to look silly than to be cold. Or to look like a shy dominatrix. That's just too bizarre. In any case, I flashed her my brotherliest smile and told her, "I figured you were feeling chilly."

"I'm feeling cold, too," Angie muttered, but the target of her comment was too lost in his thoughts to notice.

"Me too," Elly added on with an even quieter mumble. Fortunately for her, I wasn't lost in my thoughts, so I gestured for her to come over.

"I don't have more coats, but I can keep you warm."

With a bashful smile, she pattered over to my side. I took her by the waist and pulled her closer. To be fair, with her draconic metabolism, it felt like she was the one keeping me warm, but she was happy enough, so I decided not to dwell on it too much (and ignore the annoyed whisper of "show-off" coming from a certain dense harem protagonist) and instead I turned to Snowy again.

"Okay, so we are clear on the wardrobe-shredding properties of your barriers now. I have two more questions. So, these barriers initially form upon transformation. Does that mean that, conversely, you don't have any such protection when you're not transformed?"

"That's correct," Snowy confirmed with a serious nod.

"That sucks, but it's good to know in case of an emergency," I declared solemnly. "My last question is this: can this barrier be recharged or replenished in any way?"

"Once again, it depends," Ammy stated while adjusting her glasses in a contemplative and yet peevish manner. "The strength of the barrier depends on the amount of mana released during the unsealing process. It's usually impossible to reinforce it after the fact, but it can slowly regain its peak strength over time."

"How much time are we talking about? Is it applicable in battle?"

"No." This time the answer came from Snowy. "The rate is too slow, at least for us."

"Now that you mention it…" I glanced at the silent Celestial girl in the back. "Hey, Angie? Come here for a moment."

"No," she replied and took a long step away from me instead.

"Um… is there a problem?" I asked her with a puzzled frown, but she only shook her head at me.

"No way!" she declared, crossing her arms. "I don't want to get stabbed!"

"Those were just hypotheticals," Judy told her, but the Celestial girl only shook her head again.

"No! You guys are scary!"

"Okay, then you don't have to come closer, just stop complaining and answer my question," I compromised, then to further emphasize the importance of this discussion, I added, "What we are talking now about can save your life one day."

She gave me the stink eye, but she finally relented and gestured for me to ask.

"I was curious if your barrier works differently from Snowy's."

Angie thought about it. "I don't know. Actually, a lot of this is news to me, too. The first time I ever got into a fight was last Sunday, so I have no experience with my barrier taking damage. Nor do I want any—so don't punch me!"

"I'm not going to punch you," I wearily told her before I focused on Ammy again. "Can you add anything on the topic?"

She deliberated, then told me, "As far as I know, Abyssal and Celestial barriers are similar in strength and utility, but there are great individual differences, so you cannot judge them without exchanging blows first."

"I see... So, I suppose the best way to make sure no one gets hurt is to avoid getting hit in the first place, but it's good to know that Snowy and Angie have some emergency defenses. Speaking of which, we already discussed how Draconians are tough even without a barrier, but what about the Magi? Do you have anything similar going on?"

"You could say," Ammy answered, gesturing at her clothes. "My conjured robes contain a few shielding enchantments that automatically trigger when I'm about to be injured."

"How does that work?" Judy inquired in my stead while I was busy reigning back the impulse to tell her that what she was wearing wasn't even in the same ballpark as a "robe."

"It's a form of reactive defense," Amelia said, patting her chest. "It possesses five charges, and when triggered, it deploys a directional shield that can neutralize most incoming attacks."

"I have a question," my assistant interjected with a raised hand. "Why didn't you use it against Neige's brother?"

The class rep gave her an odd look. "I was grabbed."

"Wait a moment," I cut in, alarmed. "I'm seeing a trend here. Do you mean to tell me that all of these defenses are *only* against getting hit? No protection against grappling whatsoever?"

"Isn't that obvious?" Ammy asked back like it really was, prompting me to groan aloud.

"Oh, that also makes sense now!" Josh exclaimed. "I remember putting Crowey or whatshisname into a scarf hold a few seconds after I threw him, and it actually worked! Then he sprouted wings and pushed me away, but... it still worked. For a while..."

I gestured towards Judy. "Dormouse, please make note of that. It should be one of our first priorities to do something about that."

"Grappling practice?"

"Exactly my thoughts."

"Understood."

I took a huge breath and used my free hand (the other one was still around Elly's waist) to massage my temple. Once I felt ready, I said, "I think I've got a good grasp on everyone's defensive capabilities now. Let's move on to individual skills." I looked at each of my friends in turn, only pausing when I landed on Josh. "You are a bit of a joker card right now, so we're going to come back to you later. For the time being, let's start with... you."

Angie blinked in surprise and pointed at herself. "Me?"

"Yes. I mean, we have to start with someone. Please explain your abilities to the rest of us."

Angie hesitated, then took a step forward and began with an unusually serious expression.

"Well, everyone knows already, but I'm a Celestial, so I can do a lot of Celestial stuff. So... I can fly?"

"Why was that a question?" Judy inquired, looking up from her phone.

"I mean, I *can* fly, I'm just not very experienced with it," Angie admitted, then exhaled hard. "More importantly, I can use harmonic magic to a degree. I was told I had a talent for healing hymns, so I practice those a lot."

"I'm very thankful for that," I said.

She grinned. "You're so very welcome! Where was I? Right, harmonics! So, I can also do utility stuff, like detection spells, but I'm not that great at those."

"Do you have any offensive spells?" the question surprisingly came from Ammy.

"Nah, I really suck at those." Angie puckered like she'd just bitten a lemon. Maybe she was reminded of a bad memory? It didn't last long, though, as she let out a pent-up breath and continued, "For offense, I mainly use this..." She waved her left hand back and forth, and the bracelet on her forearm unfurled into a pretty, if flimsy-looking, short bow. "It's a family heirloom. I got it in the mail together with my orientation kit when I turned twelve."

"Wait just a moment!" Josh said. "So back in middle school, you didn't get obsessed with archery because of that book series where a bunch of kids fight over food or something? It was because you got that as a birthday present?"

"A little bit of option A, a little bit of B," she replied with an impish smirk.

After saying that, Angie reached out and plucked at the glowing bowstring. It made a low yet strangely melodious sound, kind of like a harp note. Then it was abruptly silenced as she pulled the cord back, aiming at the ground. As she did, a softly glowing ethereal arrow materialized into existence, ready to be fired.

"Does that bow use ambient mana to form the arrow?"

The question once again came from the class rep. She looked intrigued and took a step forwards, leaning in to get a better look.

"Yes!" Angie confirmed with a proud grin, then slowly returned the string to its initial position without releasing the arrow, which dimmed until it completely disappeared. "Because of this, I have infinite ammo. It's a little hard to aim it because the weight of the arrow depends on how long I keep the bow fully drawn, but I think I'm a pretty good shot with it."

"You say it increases its 'weight,'" Elly spoke up, eyeing the bow. "Does it mean it hits harder the longer you aim?"

"Kinda. If I hold it too long, the arrow can get too dense and shatter on impact."

"Shatter? As in, explode?" Elly asked again.

"Well… you could say that."

"How big of an explosion are we talking about?"

"How should I put this…?" Angie poked Joshua in the side to get his attention. "Hey, Josh? Do you remember that old oak tree in our backyard?"

"The one that got hit by lightning last summer and split in two?"

"Precisely," Angie answered with a smug grin.

"I don't get it," Josh muttered, but then the proverbial light bulb lit up over his head and he hastily declared, "No, wait! I got it! I totally got that!"

I stealthily rolled my eyes at him, then patted Elly's waist to get her attention.

"Is there a problem with that bow?" I asked her after she looked up at me, and she seemed conflicted for a moment.

"It just reminds me of one of the Knightly weapons Sebastian told me about in the past."

"It had explosive arrows?"

She nodded.

"It could also make arrows out of thin air," she added before her pretty brows descended into a frown. "It is too much of a coincidence."

"It's not really a coincidence, though. The original weapons of the Knights with the unnecessarily long name were given to them by the Celestials, so it makes sense they'd be similar."

"Wait, what?" my draconic girlfriend's eyes opened wide in shock. "Is that true?"

"That's what my sources tell me," I answered a bit more carefully, realizing that this might not have been common knowledge.

In the meantime, Ammy continued to scrutinize the bow, muttering, "I noticed it was an unusual weapon before, but it might actually be relic-grade…" She looked its owner in the eye and requested, "Can I have a closer look at it later?"

"Um… sure?" Angie responded in the positive, even though her expression was more than a little skeptical of the prospect.

"Okay, I think we're done with Angie," I spoke to get their attention again, then addressed the class rep. "It's your turn now."

"All right!" she said. She faced me in particular, straightened her back, and looked me in the eye. "As a junior Magi of the Assembly, I am well versed in the theoretical aspects of most magical fields. As for the practical aspects, I am classified as a conjurer. I've studied the subject since I could read." While talking, Ammy extended her hand, and after a few flashes of magical light, she held a familiar silver staff in her grasp. Then she struck the end of the staff against the concrete floor and, with another flash of light, a bulky figure rose from the ground. Strangely enough, even though it looked like it literally clawed its way out of the concrete, once Ammy's golem stood straight, the floor under it looked untouched.

"This is my primary familiar." The class rep stepped forward and introduced us to her golem. "It is a variant of the standard Mahozan-patterned semi-autonomous artificial humanoid. Its base material is andesite with an etched brass core. It uses my staff as its summoning catalyst, which allows me to summon it repeatedly, so long as I can withdraw the necessary amount of mana from an accessible ley line." She finished her explanation by tapping her staff against the ground again. "And its name is Petra."

"Fitting," I told her with a smile. "So, aside from summoning this big guy, what else can you do?"

The class rep fell silent.

"You *have* other spells, right?"

"Of course I do!" she glared at me, angrily fiddling with her glasses. "I can use dozens of utility spells. I can also create magical lights! Like this!"

She waved her staff in the shape of an eight while quietly reciting something that sounded like mangled Latin. A soft, green light lit up on the tip of her staff.

"Very impressive," I told her without even the tiniest smidgen of ill will in any way, shape, or form. But not to Ammy.

"What?" she snapped. "Do you have a problem with my light spell?"

"None at all," I answered her on the back foot, but before I could add anything else in my defense, Ammy's shoulders drooped and she let out a sigh so depressed, it was almost physically painful to hear it.

"Fine, I admit it! I'm not very talented as a Magi! So what? That doesn't mean that all I'm good for is paperwork and helping with other people's research notes! Who needs fireballs? I don't! Petra alone is good enough!"

"If you say so," I told her diplomatically, making a mental note to stay away from this particular hornet's nest.

"What about defensive spells?" my dear assistant inquired with an egregious lack of tact.

Ammy's already flushed face turned an even deeper shade of red, so

I quickly came in between them and said, "Well, I think Petra is solid enough to take a few blows, so we can count it as a shield, right?"

"Yes! That is entirely correct!" Amelia declared with so much confidence, I was tempted to believe her.

"Great. I'm glad we're in agreement," I told her before swiftly moving on to my next subject. "All right, Snowy, since the class rep already showed us her trump card, that means you're next."

"Oh, o-okay," she responded a little uncertainly, no doubt due to Amelia's unexpected outburst. She took a deep breath and began with, "So... I can fly. Or rather, I can hover. I can use somatic magic, and I specialize in ice and frost. Aside from those... uhh... how should I put it... I'm... a Seducer from House Inanna, so... Well, our family is famous for its Seducers. I... used to think I was also good at it."

"As far as I understand, being a Seducer is kind of a constitution thing, right?" I asked a question that had been on my mind since I first read it on the Celestial Hub. "So when you say you are one, it means you were born with the ability to, you know, *seduce* people, right?"

"Yes," Snowy responded with an attentive look.

"So, I was just curious, but how does the whole 'seduction' thing work?"

"Um..." My sister blinked at me, then averted her eyes. "W-well, when it works, it's like... first, I create a link with someone. For some people, eye contact is enough, others need... um... physical contact. Then once I'm linked with them, I can use it to make them fascinated with me and then do what I tell them." She glanced back at me with a really embarrassed look on her face, probably because she was recalling our first encounter, and whispered, "It doesn't work on everyone."

I grinned. "I figured. Does that mean it requires conscious effort?"

"Yes." She nodded.

"So, it's not like you can accidentally seduce, say, Judy?"

"What?" my assistant glanced up from her notes, and I flashed a grin at her.

"Just making sure you're paying attention," I told her unabashedly before facing Snowy again, who was actually deeply contemplating my question.

"No. I don't think I could do it if I tried, either." She shook her head and added, "I mean, it's hard to create a link to someone who already holds a deep affection for someone else."

"So, it's not because you're both girls?" Instead of answering, Snowy averted her eyes again. I decided not to press the issue, so I got back on topic by asking, "All right. Seduction aside, what other powers do you have?"

"Well... I can create sigils."

"That's right," Ammy intruded into the conversation like her previous flustered outburst never happened. "You were the one who created the grand barrier inside the school grounds, right?"

"Y-yes."

"It was really impressive. Can I have a look at them later?"

"Um... sure," Snowy responded, mirroring Angie's earlier reaction to the same kind of question.

"So, what can your sigils do?" I moved the conversation forward by the next obvious inquiry.

"Many things," my sister told me with an unusually proud look. "Sigils are based on the old Celestial runes. They are like a magical alphabet, and if you know the right combination of words, you can get a lot of different effects. You can seal off an area, you can use them to dispel enchantments, you can hide things with them..." Then her mood deflated. "Unfortunately, it takes a long time to make a single sigil, so they can't be used freely."

"Just a moment," I said. "You mentioned hiding things. Does that also work on people?"

"Um... yes." Snowy nodded after a moment of thinking.

"Could it be that's how this guy and his fellows can turn invisible?" I asked while pointing at my side with my thumb, visibly confusing everyone else. They could see nothing more than thin air.

That changed a moment later, when a mirthfully chuckling Brang decloaked, startling everyone in general and my assistant in particular. In fact, she went so far as to wedge herself under my arm on the opposite side of Elly's.

"What the...!" Josh exclaimed, pushing Angie behind him. "Since when was he standing there?"

"For about five minutes," I told my surprised friend with a smirk on my face, then I turned to the Faun in question. "[Your mischief is unexpected yet amusing. I grant you my approval.]"

The ex-general smiled. Unlike the last time we met him, he was now wearing his full armour, cape and all, with two spears strapped on to his back. One of them was his usual weapon with its rhombus-shaped head, while the other was a blunt training spear I'd ordered online. I had to admit, with all that gear, he looked quite imposing... then he ruined the image by unbuckling his armour to show off his burly shoulder. He pointed at the magical mark on his skin under his spaulders.

"[Aye. My liege graced us with this power. I have also been granted—]"

"[Halt, general. No need to disrobe; we shall trust your words all the same,]" I interrupted him before he could take off the rest of his armour.

"What are you two growling about?" Judy whispered to me, sticking to my side like she was glued there.

"Brang just told me that he got his ability to turn invisible from Snowy. Also, he said he had something else."

Snowy muttered, *"Oh, right!"* then raised her voice and said, "Yes, I imprinted those on them! The others only have the one that hides their presence, but Uncle Brang has two more. You see, he let me use him to experiment with my sigils when I was learning, so they ended up very compatible with him. The second one lets him move quietly, and the third one lets him slow down his fall."

"That's pretty fitting for a scout-general," I mused, then I tempered my expectations and asked the most obvious question ever. "Do you think you can put those sigils on us?"

For some strange reason Snowy looked like she didn't expect the question at all, and it took her several seconds to respond.

"I... don't know. I only ever used them on the Fauns and myself, so I don't know if they will be compatible with anyone else..." She awkwardly glanced around, and after seeing the expectant looks we were giving her, she said, "I'll try."

"That's more than enough for me," I reassured her before glancing down at my draconic girlfriend. "What about you, Elly?"

"Huh?" She looked up, and after a moment of silence, she cleared her throat and said, "I mean... I'm not that complicated, really. In my Draconian form, I can use my claws, my scales can deflect both blades and bullets, and now I can breathe true dragon flame. That's about it."

"That's it?" I asked her to be sure, but she only nodded, and then subsequently she snuggled even closer to me. I let her, but not without a silent sigh. "If you say so. I suppose that leaves only me."

To my sincerest surprise, that actually got a huge reaction out of the rest of the gang.

"Really? Are you finally going to tell us about yourself?" Josh questioned me with a scarily intense look in his eyes.

"You already know about me as much as I do," I replied with a frown. "I'm only going to explain my abilities just like the others did."

"We're listening," Ammy declared, and I am not going to lie, the way she was staring at me without blinking got me a little unnerved.

"So, this might not come as a surprise to you, but I can see magic. Furthermore, if I can see it, I can dispel it by cutting it with my fingers."

"Like that time when you blocked brother's attack," Snowy noted, and I confirmed it with a nod.

"That's all?" Elly asked with a curiously cocked head.

After some hesitation, I decided I might as well reveal another card in my hand. Not completely, of course, but hey, at least I was making an effort.

I gestured for my girlfriends to let me go so that I could move around, after which I took a step forward and said, "Actually, there is one more trick up my sleeve."

I took a deep breath and leaned a little forward, like a sprinter who was waiting for the starting pistol. It was the first time I did this in reality, but I'd spent several hours practicing the motions with Brang using the multi-tasking support provided by doing Dominance, and so they felt completely natural. I sharply inhaled and lunged forward, but a second after I started to move, I teleported a couple of meters ahead, which put me just behind the group, where I came to an abrupt "stop."

I let out a deep breath and glanced over my shoulders, only to find the gang giving me completely amazed looks.

"What was that?" Angie exclaimed while glancing between my starting position and where I was standing now.

"Well," I began with a satisfied chuckle, following which I gave them the explanation I prepared with Judy, Snowy, and Brang. "I call this trick *Phasing*. It allows me to rapidly move in a straight line while ignoring any obstacles in the way."

"I knew it!" Ammy yelled out and rushed up to me. "This is what you used to escape from the gym storeroom when we got locked in last month!"

"Exactly," I agreed with my unwitting collaborator. "It's also what I used to outmaneuver the Chimera," I said, adding another white lie to the pile.

"How's the range?"

"A couple of meters."

"Can you really ignore anything in the way?"

"Most things."

"Does it have any restrictions?"

"I can only move in a straight line. I also can't use it repeatedly, because it strains my legs. Finally, if there is any obstruction at the endpoint, I can get hurt," I continued to deliver my pre-packaged deceptions with so much conviction even I was starting to believe them. "It's tricky to use, but it is a great skill for getting out of a pickle."

"Do you have any other hidden abilities?" Ammy asked with expectant eyes, but I let her down.

I shrugged. "Maaaaaaybe? Or maybe not." Pausing just for the dramatics, I turned towards the last member of our group and declared, "But enough about boring old me! It's time for today's main attraction!"

"Oh boy," Josh muttered with an apparent mixture of dread and expectation.

"Relax, I've things planned out for you," I attempted to reassure him, but when I reached into my back pocket, he still flinched.

I didn't comment on his reaction, but just pulled a cylindrical case from my pocket.

"What's that?" my friend asked nervously, hesitating between coming closer and taking a step away from me. In the end, curiosity must've won him over, as he walked up with a guarded expression.

"It's a blood lancet set," I explained as I opened up the case and showed off its contents. "It's usually used by diabetics for blood glucose testing, but it'll do for us, as well." I looked at each of our four supernatural girls in turn and asked, "Who wants to help with testing Josh's transformation?"

"I already did it once, so I pass," Elly mumbled while conspicuously looking away.

"I'm not good with needles," Angie pulled out of the race with another weak excuse, leaving only Snowy and Ammy.

"I... I will do it," Snowy declared with a flushed face.

"All right, then. Please come here and give me your hand," I instructed her, and she followed suit. I took her tiny hand into my own and began my explanation. "First, I'm going to disinfect your finger, like this. Then we take this lancet here. You see, it has a tiny little spring in it, so when I press it against your fingertip, like this..." I did as I said, and the thin needle in the lancet pricked the surprised Abyssal so fast she didn't have time to flinch. When I removed it, there was already a small bead of bright red blood growing on her white skin. "You see, it's already done."

I gave her a reassuring pat on the back, but Snowy just kept staring at her fingertip like she didn't understand what just happened. Then, after a few long seconds, she gave me one of those scared bunny looks and asked, "W-what now?"

"Now Josh is going to sample your blood, obviously," I told her, earning me a thoroughly petrified look in return.

"How exactly am I supposed to do that?" came the skeptical question from my friend, and I couldn't help but shake my head at his selective obliviousness.

"You suck on her finger, obviously," I told him while delicately taking hold of Snowy's hand once again and offering it to him.

"You can't be serious," he protested.

"Come on, man! Don't be a pansy and drink my sister's blood."

"You are just making this weirder than it already is!" he whined, shaking his head.

"Well, you either do this or you two kiss, and considering we already pricked her finger…"

The moment I mentioned kissing, Josh's face flushed crimson and he averted his eyes, then after a moment, he weakly nodded and said, "Fine, I'll take her blood."

Leave it up to the harem protagonist to get cold feet the moment a kiss is involved, am I right? Jokes aside, since Josh finally made up his mind, I once again offered up my self-conscious sister's finger.

"There you go. Bon appétit."

"And now you're making it *even weirder*," Josh grumbled, grabbing Snowy's hand. Then after an audible gulp, he whispered a limp, "Excuse me."

"It's okay," she replied with a bashful flutter of her eyelashes. Or maybe her eyelids were just cramping from the tension? Either way, Josh gulped again, closed his eyes, and then placed her finger in his mouth.

It took less than a second for the first change to occur. Josh's chest made a strange creaking noise, following which his body slowly swelled up to the point where he was almost as tall as me. His gym clothes, unfortunately, didn't survive the ordeal, and while they didn't quite get vaporized, by the end of his quick transformation, Josh was only wearing the patented Hulk-pants.

Overall, my friend's new appearance didn't look as drastically different as when he took Elly's blood, but it was still distinct enough to make it easy to realize he was an Abyssal now. Most glaring of all, his temples were adorned by a pair of horns the same colour as his hair, and the way they curled around his head made his face look wider. In fact, his face might've been wider, as now he had a much more defined jawline. Below the neck, though, the transformation was less pronounced. Sure, he got bigger and bulkier, but he didn't grow cloven feet or wings.

Anyhow, when he finally opened his mouth and let Snowy's hand go, his first words were, "Oh, for the love of…! This was my only PE uniform!"

"I'm glad to see you still have your priorities in order," I told him with a wry smile. "How do you feel?"

"I don't feel very different," he mumbled while glancing around. "Did you get smaller?"

"It's the other way around," I replied while gesturing towards Judy. "Start the timer."

"Started," my assistant responded.

"Good." I nodded in satisfaction before looking at Brang next. "[General, I request that you proceed as we agreed in advance.]"

The Faun let out a grunt in the affirmative, after which he stomped his feet against the ground, startling everyone for a moment. A hazy bubble spread out from him like a wave with him, and after it washed over us, we found ourselves standing in the same bare hall, except dressed in various shades of purple.

"All right, kids!" I exclaimed, startling everyone with a clap. "We don't know hold long this transformation will last, so..." I raised one hand to the side, and without any further prompting, Brang handed me the replica spear from his back. I took it, set its butt against the floor with a thud, and said, "Let's start the physical examination, shall we?"

CHAPTER 13

PART 1

"Ooow! Fuck!" Josh let out a rather undignified yelp as he rolled on the ground, cradling his shin, his horn clanking against the concrete floor with an oddly metallic noise.

"Oh please! I didn't even hit you hard that time!" I grumbled as I set my training spear against the ground and offered him a hand. "Come on, next round."

"I don't want to train anymore!" my friend whined as I dragged him to his feet with one mighty tug. "No, this isn't even training anymore! It's just an excuse for you to beat me up! What have I ever done to you to deserve this?"

"Don't be a baby." I dusted his shoulder. "I told you, this is for your own good."

"And now you're sounding like an abusive father! How do I get out of here!" Josh exclaimed in (what I hoped was) mock despair before he froze in his tracks.

"I think time's up," he called out to my assistant. At the moment she was sitting on a makeshift bench next to Angie, documenting their own little experiments using the class rep's golem as a glorified training dummy. She quickly entered something into her phone, probably something related to the giant freaking icicle sticking out of Petra's chest, before she gestured for Josh to repeat himself.

"I said, I think time's up!" he reiterated, and less than a second later, his body deflated. His solid muscles slowly shrank back into more human proportions while his curly horn swiftly retreated into his head, or at the very least that's what it looked like. If someone put a gun to my head and demanded I come up with an analogy for the sight, I probably would've said it gave me the same impression as watching one of those sped-up footages of plants growing, except in reverse. Then I would've grabbed the gun and kicked their butt, but that just might be the adrenaline-high talking.

Anyways, after Josh stopped being horny, Judy walked over and said, "Fourteen minutes and thirty seconds on the fifth transformation."

"So that means each transformation lasts about ten percent longer than the one before, right?"

"Precisely," Judy confirmed with a nod.

"If so, the next one should be around… let me see… Sixteen minutes, I think?" I ventured a guess after flexing my genius mind with some highly complex arithmetic.

"Roughly, yes," she agreed, but then just as I was about to call Snowy over, she quickly added, "You should take a short break."

"Why? I'm not tired."

"Maybe, but Joshua looks exhausted after all the bullying you put him through."

"Hey! Don't you get started, too! I'm not bullying him—this is training!"

My assistant looked entirely unconvinced by my protests.

"Ammy also needs to resummon Petra after our last test, so it should be a good opportunity for everyone to rest for a bit before we continue."

To be fair, I wasn't entirely against the idea, but on the other hand, I was kinda riding on an adrenaline-high at the moment, and I wanted to capitalize on it to test my limits… Though again, Josh wasn't exactly the best opponent for that.

Okay, let's be fair and objective for a moment. In his Abyssal form, Josh was granted a tremendous power boost, and he somehow had an instinctive understanding of magic that allowed him to pull off some neat tricks, yet he had little to no control.

Now, if this sounds familiar, I guess it's because that's pretty much the starting point for most battle-shounen protagonists. If I was forced to speculate (which I wasn't, since I had sources on the net to tell me, but I'm going to do so, anyway), it's so that there's a clear sense that they possess great potential, yet at the same time they have room to grow by mastering their powers and learning how to use them more skillfully. That description actually fit Josh like a glove, as he had access to a lot of raw strength, both physical and magical, but the only combat training he had was from a few judo classes in middle school.

If I'd have made these observations a couple days before, I would've brushed them off with a disinterested, *Well, that's a given*, but with my recent revelations about this world being closer to a genuine battle harem universe, they created a bit of incongruity.

Unlike battle shounen protagonists, one of the most common characteristics of battle harem protagonists (aside from being ungodly chick magnets) was that they were usually weak but very skilled. They also typically had unique abilities that were unassuming at first glance, often getting them constantly underestimated, but those same abilities would end up being game breaking in the long run. While Josh's ability to adopt the powered-up forms of other races was certainly unique, it lacked the finesse expected from a battle harem protagonist's power set. In short, shounen battle protagonists usually tended to be unskilled but strong, while battle harem protagonists tended to be weak but skilled, and for some reason, Josh didn't fit the new world-hypothesis I was developing.

But then again, maybe I was overthinking this. After all, this world was plenty complex, and I was in no position to declare it only adhered to the tropes of one genre or another. Maybe it didn't even adhere to any. Or maybe all of them.

Anyhow, let's put my ponderings on the meta-level aside and return to the previous topic: me kicking Josh's butt. To be perfectly transparent here, I was really, really tense before our first sparring match. I had no idea how powerful he'd be, so I felt no shame when I faced him with my full attention and a weapon in my hand. That quickly changed when it turned out Josh was… how should I put this gently? Let's go with "a total simpleton" when it came to combat.

Don't take me wrong, I'm not saying I'm some kind of heaven-sent melee genius or anything, but even without memories and only a single night's worth of intensive Dominance training with Brang, I was dancing circles around the guy. Granted, while I couldn't actually cause him any lasting harm (even though he was acting like a prima donna every time I smacked him with my training spear) because of his higher specs and barrier, I never even felt in danger from his advances. On one hand, this made me seem like a bully, but on the other hand, it vindicated my decision to have him spar with me instead of Elly or one of the Fauns. They would've completely destroyed him in seconds, and then I would've had to spend who knows how long nursing his wounded pride, not to mention possible actual injuries.

Ah, speaking of Elly and the Fauns…

"Hi-yah!" The princess let out a high-pitched cry as she lunged towards Brang. She was in her Draconian form, and I expected that she would utilize her claws in a fight, but instead she was using actual martial art stances and techniques. As far as I could gather from her stray comments, it was some kind of Chinese martial art designed to enhance "external techniques," whatever that meant in this context, and that she'd been practicing for years. She said she was still at a novice level, but based on her movements, I'd say she looked just like a bona fide expert to me. In fact, I kinda wanted to see her perform those moves in a traditional Chinese dress, just to crank the dissonance up a notch.

But back to the duel.

Elly dashed forward and her right arm lashed out in a straight line, her fingers curled inwards, presumably to deliver a strike with the heel of her hand. Brang held his trademark spear in both hands and waited until the last moment before he moved, pulling the shaft of his weapon into the trajectory of the incoming strike with practiced ease. The princess's palm and the spear met with a thunderous sound and an honest-to-goodness shock wave that tousled our hair even though we were standing a good ten meters away from them. That... was cool, but kind of silly at the same time.

A split second later, even before the first wave died down, Elly shifted her weight to her other leg and grabbed her spear. If the fierce grin on her face was any indication, she thought the Faun had fallen into her trap, and she hooked a punch with her left hand under the immobilized weapon. At least that was the plan, I presumed, but before the strike could connect, Brang twisted the spear around. Since the princess still had an iron grip on the shaft, this made her twist her arm with it, pulling her off balance.

With her stance broken, her left hook missed its mark by a mile, and before she had the time to regain her footing, Brang twisted his spear in the other direction, pulling her right along. Now she finally had the good sense to let go of the spear, but before she could pull back, Brang closed the distance into what looked like a shoulder tackle. I think if it was anyone else, I would've been worried for their safety because of the size difference alone, but considering it was the toughest girl of the gang we were talking about, I was only slightly pensive.

Instead of trying to tank the hit, Elly decided to evade it by moving just under the incoming tackle. Unfortunately for her, since her stance was still a mess, she overshot the dodge and had to soften her landing by a classic forward roll that should be familiar to anyone who ever played one of those games about souls. She was back on her feet in the blink of an eye, but in these kinds of close-combat scenarios, that kind of downtime was absolutely fatal.

Well, okay, maybe I was just a tad overdramatic just now. It wasn't actually fatal, only a huge damn opening any self-respecting fighter would immediately rush to exploit. Brang didn't fail to capitalize on the moment, either, as by the time Elly got ready to counterattack, he swung the butt of his spear with a smooth arc and hit her on her calf, just under the back of her knee. She let out a yelp that sounded more surprised than pained, and then she rapidly lost her balance as the spear continued onwards and completely swept her leg out from under her, followed by another squeak as she landed on her butt.

My description of the events might've made it sound complicated, but the whole exchange lasted for less than five seconds flat. So, yeah. While Elly might have looked like a martial arts expert in my eyes, Brang looked like a grandmaster schooling the younger generation with his superior kung fu. Or in this case, spear fu. Is that even a term?

My martial arts illiteracy aside, my draconic girlfriend grunted as she massaged her calf, only stopping when Brang leaned forward and reached out a hand towards her.

"Effort. Was good," he stated with an amicable smile, and Elly took his hand and rose to her feet.

"Thanks. You, too," she told him with an intensity that looked like the first sparks of a fiery rivalry.

We didn't have time for that, though, so I cleared my throat to get their attention and called out, "All right, everyone, we're going to have a short break. If you need to use the toilet, it's over there."

"Got it!" Angie replied with an urgent expression before she and the class rep both headed in the direction I indicated with my thumb.

In the meantime, Judy put away her phone for the first time in a while and declared, "I've got snacks."

"Wait, you do?" I couldn't help but ask as I glanced over, only to raise a surprised brow at what I saw. "Where did you get that lunch box?"

"It was in my backpack," she stated while opening said box.

"Okay, let me rephrase the question: where did you get the backpack?"

"It was on me all along," Judy answered as she handed me a sandwich.

"Seriously? I'm about ninety-five percent sure you didn't have one when we came over."

"And that five percent is where the magic happens," she told me coyly before adding, in a deadpan voice befitting her countenance, "Or you are just bad at paying attention to the small details."

"Maybe," I answered, and she pushed another sandwich into my hand.

I sent her a questioning look in return, and she explained, "You should treat Joshua."

"To a sandwich?"

"Among other things," she stated, and my expression must've looked at least half as dumb as I felt, as she let out a small sigh and elaborated. "You've been bullying him for the past half an hour, and he looks really down. You should advise him, encourage him, or at the very least act like you do, so that Neige and Angie can stop pestering me about your behaviour."

"I'm not bullying—"

Elly wedged herself between us. "Hey, Leo? Did you see my battle with the big guy?"

"I sure did," I answered her with a nod. "It was very impressive."

"Except the part where you lost," Judy added a completely unnecessary jab, which she softened by adding, "It was still a valiant effort."

"Well, someone has to lose during sparring, right? I also wasn't using my full power."

"Neither was he," my assistant commented, much to my curiosity.

"I noticed you have snacks," Elly said, finally revealing her reason for approaching us, eyeing the sandwiches in my hand.

"Are you a little peckish, by any chance?" I asked the obvious question, resulting in a huge grin on her part.

"A little bit, yes," she confirmed. "It's important to eat when you exercise, otherwise you won't build any muscles. Let's eat together!"

"Not now." Judy pulled on the princess's shirt at the waist and gestured for her to lean closer. She was confused at first, but complied, at which point Judy whispered, loud enough for me to hear, "The Chief's going to talk with Joshua now."

"Really?" She glanced over her shoulder towards my friend sitting morosely on one of the makeshift benches, then she joined in the conspiratorial whispering by asking, "About what?"

Judy glanced at me for some inexplicable reason, so I shrugged. She apparently interpreted that as *I leave it completely up to you how you deal with this situation*, which might've been a mistake. But the die was cast, so I held my breath and waited for her to speak.

"The Chief and Joshua are going to have a manly talk among men," Judy stated.

"A manly... talk? About what?"

"About manly things."

"I don't get it..." Elly admitted and looked to me for help, but she was once again diverted by my assistant grabbing her.

"I'll explain while we eat. Let's invite Neige, too."

"Oh? Okay then," she agreed while sending me a small smile, followed by Judy giving me a clumsy wink (which still didn't fill me with confidence), leaving me alone with two neatly wrapped sandwiches. I had a feeling this situation had some kind of profound meaning applicable to my life as a whole, but I couldn't be arsed to ponder that at the moment, so instead I turned on my heel and headed over to Josh. The guy was just as downcast from up close as he looked from a distance, and his disheveled hair (and only wearing his inexplicably intact pants and his jacket) gave him a wild look.

"Hey, pal," I said, sitting down beside him and extending my hand towards him with an amicable, "You hungry?"

"A bit," he answered, hesitating, then took the packet from my grasp. He unwrapped his sandwich, and after taking a few whiffs, he took a large bite out of it and chewed silently, a distant look in his eyes.

"So… what's eating you?" I initiated our alleged *"manly talk"* while unwrapping my own snack.

"It's a chicken breast sandwich, I think. It's good," he answered absent-mindedly, prompting me to sharply jab him in the side with my elbow.

"I didn't ask what you're eating, but what's eating *you*!"

Josh gave me an annoyed look, but after looking each other in the eye, he swallowed the rest of the first bite and let out a tired sigh.

"Do you really want to know?"

"That's why I'm here." I shrugged and took a small bite from my own sandwich, only to add in a mumble, "Wow, you weren't kidding. This is surprisingly good."

Josh didn't seem to mind my abrupt praise of my girlfriend's coo—… well, "cooking" might be inaccurate here, so let's go with *expert sandwich craftswomanship*. Instead, my friend let out another small sigh and spoke with the kind of tone you'd expect from a weary, burned-out middle-aged salaryman.

"You know, I actually thought this would be fun," he began, gesturing at our sparring area. "I mean, you already know how this whole *supernatural* and *close combat* stuff didn't sit well with me, but at the end of the day, I thought, *Hey, getting superpowers might be fun!*" Joshua sighed yet again and slouched even further. "The first time we sparred… it was sudden, and my clothes exploding? Yeah, that was awkward, and… you know, you could've warned me about that."

"We spent like ten minutes discussing what barriers do to clothes. I wash my hands," I replied between two bites.

"Still a dick move," he grumbled. He looked away. "So, as I was saying, I was actually considering that there could be some upside to all of this supernatural balderdash."

"Dude… did you just unironically use *balderdash* in a sentence?"

"Shut up, it's a proper word," Josh pouted, and I couldn't help but chuckle even harder. "Are you finished?"

"Yeah, sorry," I gave an apology I didn't really mean, then said, "So, we were at the part where you were getting excited about getting superpowers. What happened next?"

My friend gave me a critical look, then flatly stated, "You hit me over the head with a stick."

"A spear," I corrected him, but he only grunted.

"Same difference. The point is, I felt I had all of this power at my fingertips, and then I was smacked right down just as I was getting into it."

"Well, sorry for raining on your parade, but that's kind of the point of a sparring match."

"I know, I know," Josh relented, his words accompanied with yet another sigh. "Still, it was a bummer. So, I asked Lili for help."

"Oh, right… you *were* talking with Snowy a bit before we started round two. What did you learn?"

Josh paused again, the corners of his lips slowly lifting in a foolish little smirk before he caught himself and explained, "Since I got that transformation from her, I figured she could give me a few tips on how to use… it's magic, right?"

"Somatic magic, to be precise, but yes," I explained to him after swallowing the last bite of my sandwich.

"That," he agreed. "So, she was really helpful and taught me a lot of things in a short time. Like, she showed me how to do these simple hand gestures…" Josh gestured clumsily with his fingers. Of course, since he wasn't transformed just then, it didn't do anything, but he still repeated it a couple of times, as if fascinated with it. "I can't do them so well now," he admitted, "but when I was transformed, things just… clicked, I suppose."

"So, you learned that wind blast thing from Snowy? In just a couple of seconds?"

"Yeah." Josh nodded, his face once again softening before it shifted. He frowned and looked me in the eye. "Hey, Leo? Now that you've adopted Lili, are you going to live together?"

"That's the plan, yes," I answered, trying not to question the reason behind the sudden right turn in the otherwise pretty straightforward conversation.

"Lili is a very nice girl," Josh said, taking the conversation in another hairpin turn, and before I could react, he added, "She used to be a little weird at the beginning, but at heart, she's a really innocent, earnest girl."

"Um… yes, she is. I'm well aware."

"If so…" Josh's frown morphed into a determined glare, and he said, "If so, then you better not lay your hands on her just because you're living together."

It was at this point that I realized where he was going with this, and for a moment, I vacillated between facepalming or palming him upside his head. I ultimately decided on the former and let out an exasperated groan as I covered my eyes with my hand.

"Dude, you say the dumbest things sometimes," I mumbled.

"I'm serious," he emphasized, but it only earned him another groan from yours truly.

"Listen, Josh… just why the hell do you even think I would *lay my hands* on her in the first place?"

"Hey, you're the guy who couldn't be satisfied with just one girlfriend! I'm just being cautious," he told me with 100 percent honesty, which kind of threw me for a loop again.

"You can't be serious…" I muttered as I stifled the urge to palm my face again. "First off, don't pin my poly relationship on me alone. Secondly, I haven't even *laid my hands* on my girlfriends, let alone Snowy. Finally, and most importantly, she is my sister now, so if anyone should be worried about some guy *laying hands* on her, it should be me!"

"You've never touched Judy and Elly?" Josh asked with a baffled expression, masterfully skimming over the thinly veiled intent behind my third point.

"I've *touched* them, of course. In the literal sense, I mean. We even have sanctioned daily cuddling time, but we haven't gone any farther yet."

"Seriously?" My friend looked somehow more shocked than when I revealed that he was the subject of a full gamut of prophecies.

"Why are you looking at me like that? We've only been going out for a few days, for Pete's sake!"

"Well, yes, but… you always struck me as the kind of guy who would go… places."

"Do I even want to know what you mean by that?"

"I guess you… don't?" Josh replied with a steadily reddening face, his previous frown already a thing of the past.

"Why do you care, anyway? Are you interested in Snowy?" I threw out my most obvious conversation-derailing bait yet, and as per my expectation, my dear friend took it hook, line, and sinker.

"That's not why I was asking!" he denied on the spot, but then I guess he realized he was too definite and that I might tell Snowy about it, so he hastily added, "I mean, I'm not 'not interested,' but… it's just complicated, okay?"

"That was a double negative. In other words, you *are* interested."

By this point, he was red to the tip of his ears, which I found strangely cute, probably because it reminded me of the princess. Then he averted his eyes and muttered something along the lines of, "She's really nice and pretty and earnest."

"So is Angie," I threw out another bait just for the heck of it, but this time he didn't bite.

"Maybe, but she feels more like... I don't know... an annoying sister or cousin?"

"Why are you asking me? It's your preferences."

"I told you, it's complicated. Leave me alone."

"That's funny," I chuckled at my embarrassed friend's expense. "I can distinctly remember me saying the same thing when a certain friend of mine was pestering me about baseless accusations of two-timing. What a coincidence."

Josh remained silent for a while, either unwilling or unable to counter me. At last he quietly asked, "If I told you I'm sorry for doubting your character, could we drop this awful topic?"

"Sure. So... what were we talking about before this tangent? Something about you learning magic tricks from my sister?"

"Yeah, that," Josh started weakly, but then his voice gradually got firmer as he explained, "As I said, it's this move that lets me shoot a blast of compressed air. It's... kinda hard to explain how it feels, but each time I do it, it gives me a rush, so I thought, *Hey, that's pretty awesome! Maybe this whole supernatural crap isn't so bad.*"

"I know the feeling," I agreed, smiling. I remembered the first time I used my Phasing ability during my Dominance with Brang. Calling it a *rush* was a bit of an understatement.

"I figured," he told me flatly, then in a similar tone he added, "Then someone popped my wind blast spell thingie like it was a cheap party balloon and whacked me over the head with a stick. Again."

"Weren't we already over this? Also, I'm pretty sure you were there when we discussed my ability to disrupt magic, so you can only blame yourself for not paying attention and putting all your eggs into a single basket."

"Well, excuse me for failing to do something cool because I wasn't paying attention!" Josh huffed indignantly at my retort.

"Whoa, easy there, buddy!" I told him as I patted his back. "No one said it wasn't cool! I mean, it was actual magic, right? I wish I could do that!"

"You can do that Phasing thing, can't you?"

"It's not the same. Offensive magic is much cooler. You just need to practice how to use it. In fact, we all need practice. That's why we're here."

"Not all of us," Josh sulked unabated. "You don't seem to need any. In fact, to me, it looks like you have it easy."

"Do I?"

"Yeah." He nodded with conviction, completely oblivious to the troubled scowl I was directing his way. "You have two girlfriends who don't mind sharing you, you are rich, you have a secret base with minions, and you can kick people's ass, including mine. I, on the other hand, have to deal with all of this supernatural nonsense coming out of nowhere, being some kind of prophesized hero or messiah or whatever, put up with these silly transformations… and then when I finally start to feel like I am getting a grip, someone hits me on the head with a stick."

I waited for his outburst of complaints to end, and after letting him cool down a little, I simply asked, "Is that how things look to you?"

"Yeah?" he answered with a shrug, though his voice sounded uncertain.

I remained silent for a few seconds as we locked eyes with each other, but at last I exhaled a really, really long sigh and told him, "Listen, Josh. This is just between the two of us, so don't tell the girls about this, but things aren't exactly all sunshine and roses on my end, either." My friend was giving me a pensive look, and after a moment of hesitation, I decided to spill the beans. "I get you. I really do. On the surface, I probably look like I'm some kind of super-confident all-knowing badass with two awesome girlfriends and his own secret base and cool minions and being totally on top of things while you are still scrambling to figure out what's going on."

"Dude, are you complaining or bragging right now?" my friend blurted out with a single brow raised as high as it could possibly go.

"Please don't interrupt; I'm just getting to my point. The thing is, I don't blame you for thinking this, because it's the image I've cultivated, partially by choice and mostly by necessity. The truth is, I'm kind of in over my head right now and barely managing to keep afloat."

"You are?"

"Yep," I told him with a self-deprecating smile. "You know, it's at least partially my fault, but after what happened at the school last weekend, things just kind of developed in a way where everyone now thinks I'm more knowledgeable and resourceful than I actually am. On top of those expectations, I also picked up a few new responsibilities without thinking things through. Now I have to take care of Snowy, the Fauns… and of course, I have to look out for you, too." Josh let out a surprised hiccup, but I ignored him and continued with, "The thing is, as much as I didn't expect to end up in this pseudo-leadership position, now that I have, I've gotta at least try to keep things together, and it's not easy. I mean, disappointing the girls once they realize I'm not exactly some hyper-competent leader is one thing, but now I also have to be on the lookout for trouble and keep everyone safe."

"Oh, right. Your amnesia," my friend noted, and I gave him a tentative nod.

"Sure, among other things. In short, I acknowledge that you're having a hard time with all of this supernatural and prophecy business getting foisted on you, but you're not the only one who's having problems at the moment."

"I guess you're right…" Josh whispered a little sourly, following which we remained silent for close to a minute. Then he said, "You know, with how crazy everything's been lately, I totally forgot to consider your point of view." I blinked at him in surprise, and so he hastily added, "I mean, I've taken for granted the fact that you knew everything and had all of these resources, so I never really thought about how you managed to learn and do all of this without any memories and in such a short time. I'm not gonna lie, it kinda makes it even more impressive."

"To be honest, most of it was thanks to Judy's help. As for the rest, as much as I'd like to take credit, it's mostly the result of a chain of on-the-spot decisions that led to unexpected consequences and ultimately landed me here."

"It's impressive all the same," Josh reiterated with a small grunt. "I mean, if I was in your shoes, I can't imagine accomplishing a fraction of this. I'm just not cut out for making those on-the-spot decisions and going through with them."

"Nah. If anything, you'd probably make a better leader type. Or at least a more genuine one."

He shook his head. "Fat chance. I can't deal with pressure like you do."

"Hey, I'm bad with pressure, too!" I protested.

"Dude, you mounted and organized a rescue operation when I was kidnapped and saw it through even after falling off a roof and getting impaled. If I was in your shoes at the time, I would've freaked the heck out and hidden under my bed until Angie dragged me out."

"I was freaked out too, you know? I was just hiding it really well so that the others would remain calm."

"Isn't that exactly what it means to deal with pressure?"

I wanted to retort but had no words.

My friend flashed me a triumphant grin, then said, "I guess I have to try harder, too. Leaving everything up to you *is* a little unfair, now that I think about it. Also, I can't have you be the only cool guy in our group. I mean, I probably can't match you when it comes to resources or girlfriends, but I bet I can beat you in the coolness factor once I figure out how to properly use this transformation thing."

Well, I'll be damned. Somehow, I ended up motivating Josh just by venting. Could it be that I was really good at this inspiring leadership thing after all?

… Nah, who am I kidding? This was just another unexpected result of a whimsical, off-the-cuff decision. That said, maybe I could try to capitalize on the moment and motivate him even further.

"Considering you can already cast spells, it's only a matter of time before you'll become a bona fide badass. And that's just one transformation! You may get to fly, or breathe fire, or… do whatever mages do! You can learn all sorts of awesome stuff that I can't even dream to match. Just keep that in mind, and all the hard work and crazy crap flying around will feel much more bearable."

"To be fair, though, I'd really love to learn all that without getting smacked in the head with a stick."

I gave my friend a flat look and then promptly grabbed his noggin in a very friendly and in no way painful headlock.

"Would you stop complaining about it already?"

"O-ow! I get it, sorry!" Josh cried out in obvious fake distress, as there was no way my entirely friendly wrestling move, in which I didn't put any strength, I swear, could possibly have caused him any pain. Still, since he said he was sorry, I decided to let him go… after five more seconds.

Then I straightened my clothes and told him, "Just for the record, I'm not hitting you because I hate you, but because it's the only way you will learn how to do better."

"And now you're back to being an abusive father again!" my friend complained, massaging the back of his neck. "Is it too late to get another sparring partner?"

"Well…" I conspicuously glanced over the rest of the group, then faced Josh again and said, "Snowy and Angie have more of a ranged focus, so they are out of the question. Ammy only has her golem, and it's not exactly a martial artist, so… do you want to get wrecked by the princess or by Brang?"

"Why do you have to ask it like that?"

"Hey, you're the one who wanted a different sparring partner," I answered with a shrug.

Grumbling, Josh said, "I'll take my chances with Elly, thank you very much."

"Your funeral!" I jumped to my feet. "Come on, there's training to do."

My friend muttered under his breath, but he still took off his jacket and followed me. When she noticed our approach, Elly stood up and awaited our arrival with a suspiciously curious expression.

"Hey, Leo? Did you really talk about manly things?"

"Um… kinda, I suppose," I answered, a little taken aback by the way she was looking at me.

"Really?" She scrutinized my face, then she let out a low grunt and told me, with a familiar finger pointed at my nose, "You shouldn't talk about girls' b-breasts behind their backs! It's rude, and it's lewd!"

It only took me half a moment to figure out what was going on, so I asked, "Was that Judy's explanation of what a 'manly talk' was about?"

Elly nodded.

"Go figure."

With that, I flicked my assistant's forehead with extreme prejudice.

"Ow," she stated, unsurprised.

I turned to the princess. "Let's put your misinformation aside for now. Josh wants to train with you for a change. So, I was thinking, could you teach him some basic techniques first? Footwork, the proper way to break a fall and roll, that kind of stuff."

"Sure!" she beamed at me. I figured she was happy to be relied on.

"If Joshua trains with Eleanor, what are you going to do?" Judy inquired, one hand still on her forehead while she used the other to fish her phone out of her coat pocket.

"I was actually thinking about testing my limits a little, so…" I turned around and sent a challenging look towards the Faun standing a dozen or so meters away from our group, probably as a courtesy (and to put Judy at ease), and I told him, "[I appeal for the cooperation of you and your warrior kin, general. I have certain… group tactic drills in mind.]"

PART 2

"Ready, set, it's round four!" I declared aloud as I raised my spear in the purple-tinted training area.

"[I'll catch you this time!]" Hrul lunged forwards with an excited battle cry, not showing any hesitation whatsoever. He had a slightly lighter build than his comrades, which resulted in marginally faster movements, though they were always predictable. His weapon, a training long sword I'd bought with that spear, looked small in his hand, but I knew very well that trying to block it was a bad idea, as he had all of his considerable weight behind it. However, dodging to the side was also out of the question, as I could already see another Faun, Rabom by the looks of it, moving to intercept me.

As such, I stepped forth and right into the trajectory of my first opponent's assault. I used the superior reach of my weapon to strike at his exposed shoulder with a swift jab. Hrul naturally flinched at my aggressive counter and tried to evade, creating a gap that allowed me to slip just under his raised arms. From the blind spot behind his bulk emerged another Faun in the form of the wolf-headed Pip, wielding two swords and twirling them in an unnecessarily flashy flourish, granting me ample time to use my momentum and evade them by simply shifting left. Right after I slipped under his wooden blades, I slapped him with my spear and declared, "Tag!"

Pip's eyes opened wide as saucers. He started to say something, but before he could, I rushed past him. As I did so, my dodging instincts screamed out in warning. Planting my spear against the ground, I changed my trajectory just in time to avoid a body blow from Gram. Unlike the rest of the Faun, he was unarmed, and his entire strategy revolved around trying to grapple me. Considering the guy had tree trunks for arms, getting in his reach was a bad idea.

Because of my sudden change in direction, he barreled past the spot where I was supposed to be. He was trying his best to come to a halt, but by the time he did, I raised my weapon once again and, using the blunt end, jabbed his abdomen. He used his vambraces to block the stab, but since he was off-balance, he didn't quite manage to stop the second, and the third one landed cleanly, resulting in me declaring, "Tag!" once more.

Two down, three to go.

In the meantime the remaining Fauns—Rabom, Hrul, and Vurrok—attempted to encircle me. Unfortunately, while they might've had a chance when there were five of them, a circle with just three members wasn't viable. Especially when I could use my fake "Phasing" ability to move right behind Vurrok.

He must have expected I'd try something like that, as the moment I arrived, I ducked under a heavy slash he delivered by hastily spinning around. Impressive… but I still tapped my spear on his shin and exclaimed, "Tag!"

After the first surprise, the Faun warrior growled a long string of colourful expletives I shall omit here. Anyhow, after whittling down their numbers like that, it only took a couple of seconds to mop up the remainders. I caught Rabom off guard by parrying his stab with his own spear and using the same momentum to hit him on his head. Then I humoured Hrul by engaging in a little back-and-forth dueling against him before I exploited him overreaching with one of his swings, allowing me to step in and tap his neck, resulting in the last shout of "Tag!" for the day.

Five morose Fauns stood around me, their pride wounded. To be fair, though, the rules of our little training exercise were in my favor, but the fact they couldn't manage to touch me in four rounds weighed heavily on them. Be that as it may, they agreed to those rules at the beginning, so they couldn't complain aloud, yet their eyes spoke volumes.

Now, one might ask what I was doing fighting Snowy's retinue all by myself in the first place, but as always, there was a method to my madness. Footwork and other forms of basic training were infinitely more efficient in Dominance, as demonstrated by the last-minute practice I did with Brang the night before, yet it had two major flaws.

The first one was the obvious fact that only I could do it in our group. No, not even Josh could enter into Dominance with the Fauns during his Abyssal transformation, which meant this was probably related to one of my weird secondary abilities.

The second problem was the fact that it was a contest between two Fauns (or in this case, one Faun and one… whatever-I-was). This was great for dueling practice, but it precluded any kind of training related to acting as a group—or in my case, dealing with multiple opponents at once. In order to remedy this situation, I devised this improvised little contest, where I would face off against all the Fauns (save for Brang and Karukk, for obvious reasons). This method, unfortunately, involved a high chance of injury, but since I figured it might help me develop both my dodging and my awareness in battle, I decided it was worth the risk, with the added rule that if I managed to land a clean hit on any of my opponents, they would be "out" for the remainder of the round, as a way to give me a little advantage.

In retrospect, I didn't really need it. While individually each of the Fauns were formidable, and I often needed to utilize my supernatural dodging and other abilities to deal with them, as far as group combat was concerned… How should I put this gently? Let's just say that Brang's subordinates were really, *really* bad at teamwork, and leave it at that. Now, I had two separate hypotheses as to why this was the case, an in-universe one and a meta-explanation.

The first one relied on the same idea as to why we were having this asymmetrical group battle to begin with. If I presumed that they were only training via Dominance, it would mean they were naturally really experienced with dueling an opponent of similar stature and strength, but since the same limitation of one-on-one fighting applied there, it meant they had way less experience when it came to acting as a unit in battle.

Now, this hypothesis of mine had only one glaring flaw: the fact that they *were* well-trained professionals capable of executing complex actions based on hand signals alone, so it didn't make sense that they would lose all cohesion the moment they entered into actual combat. This was a discrepancy that was unfortunately explained, if a little crudely, by a single meta-observation: the Fauns were mooks.

What are mooks? It's the informal term for the standard-issue, disposable minions of the bad guys, specifically designed to appear threatening yet be incompetent enough to be easily dispatched by the heroes when the need arises. Sound familiar?

This interpretation would also perfectly explain why, despite outnumbering and outgunning the girls (at least as far as sheer size and strength were concerned), they managed to completely fail to hinder them from roaming the school building and reaching the rooftop during the incident a week before. They certainly looked imposing—I had to admit they were a little scary when they all rushed at me during the first round—but at the end of the day, their skill levels were just a notch above Josh's and not even in the same ballpark as, say, Brang.

Speaking of which, if I concluded that the Fauns were the *mooks* to the Abyssals' *antagonists*, then what did that make Brang? I mean, he was obviously on a completely different level than the rest, so... was he an *elite mook*? Or maybe a mid-boss? Judy and I had discussed this topic in the past, and if our ad hoc theory about the school incident being an arc-ending climax was correct, would Brang have been the *dragon* to Crowey? I don't mean the literal kind but the *literary* kind—the powerful second-in-command in service of the villain. It would fit him, but...

No, scratch that. That role was probably supposed to be Snowy's, so... maybe he *was* supposed to be an "elite mook." But if so...

I glanced over at the other side of the training hall, where Brang stood with his spear against the ground, his face set in a profound frown and his eyes gazing into the infinite distance. He was the perfect image of a lonely expert standing at the peak of attainment. It was a great image, slightly tarnished by a certain friend of mine rolling on the ground, cradling his shin.

"Why! Why do they both keep going for the goddamn legs?" he protested quite loudly, so I decided to leave the petulant atmosphere surrounding the defeated Fauns behind and instead bask in the petulant atmosphere surrounding the victorious Faun.

Just as I did group training, I asked Brang to be the opponent of the rest of the gang. I hoped he could impart some of his experience to them so that they could, with some luck, learn how to work as a team against a single, powerful opponent. The results were as follows: Josh, currently in an Abyssal transformation, was still rolling on the floor. Elly sat leaning against the nearest wall, with an exhausted Angie healing some scratches on her legs. Ammy was dismally staring at the pile of rubble on the floor, no doubt the remains of the late Petra. Meanwhile, Snowy was... awkwardly standing in front of Brang, obviously not knowing what to do. Since she was his liege, he didn't want to hurt her, and since he was her "Uncle Brang," she didn't want to chuck ice spears at him. Instead Snowy tried to support the others, and once they were defeated, she didn't know what else to do.

Because I couldn't bear to watch her fidget any longer, I walked over to her side and patted her on the back.

"So, are you finished, too?"

"Yes," Brang responded curtly in our language, probably realizing along the way that talking in Faunish in front of the gang was kinda rude. Anyhow, he looked over the sulking group of Fauns on the other side of the hall and let out an ominous chuckle. "Lost? Need training."

"They sure do," I agreed as my eyes skimmed over my equally dejected friends. "So do they, now that I think about it. We should make these training sessions a regular thing."

"Agreed." Brang nodded. "Good experience."

"Also fun," I egged him on.

"Also agreed," he, well, agreed with a toothy grin.

From the ground, Josh wailed, "No wonder these two are getting along! They're both fiends!"

I rolled my eyes and offered him a hand. "You're being a baby again. Get up already."

Josh continued to grouch, but to his credit, he took my hand and got to his feet, though not without theatrically groaning and hissing. I'm not going to lie, though; after he took some basic footwork lessons from the princess, I'd expected him to do better. After all, he did manage to hold his own against Crowey, if only briefly.

Maybe he couldn't tap into his full potential unless it was a serious life-or-death situation? Or, considering he was the hero, maybe he had to work himself up into a hot-blooded state for his powers to shine? Or, hell, it might just be the power of friendship was missing. I mean, Judy had been pestering me about narrative influence this and narrative influence that ever since I'd awakened, so who knew? Maybe the Narrative did power him up as the situation demanded it.

Speaking of which, these kinds of situational power-ups were the reason why I'd decided against trying to come up with an unofficial power-ranking where I could slot people into ranks and whatnot. I mean, Brang here already showed that there was a difference of earth and sky between one Faun and another. Not to mention, power levels were just silly.

"Hey, Chief?"

Judy jolted me out of my momentary stupor by grabbing my sleeve.

"Yes?" I responded and was momentarily taken aback by the eager light in her eyes.

"I have finished compiling all my observations about your training today, and I think I have everyone's power levels figured out."

"Dormouse. You're killing me."

"No, I'm not," she replied, either completely oblivious to my exasperation or uninterested in it.

"I still don't care," I told her wearily. "Send it to me in an email later."

For the next five seconds, my assistant gave me a look that said I would pay for ruining her fun like that, but in the end, she just let out a small "spoilsport" under her breath.

"Did someone just say 'power levels'?"

Angie poked her head between us with a curious expression, followed by the disheveled princess. On a sidenote, she completely nailed the whole "unkempt beauty" aesthetic.

"No, nobody said anything like that," I lied before turning to the blonde girl. "Are you okay? I think I saw you being thrown across the room at one point."

"I'm fine," she responded with a scowl, then quickly added, "I'll get him next time!"

Brang's ears swiveled in response to her declaration, and he let out a mirthful little chuckle that didn't help my girlfriend's mood one bit.

In the meantime, Josh gasped as his transformation came to an end, and as it did, his whole body shuddered.

"Can we go home already? I'm tired, I'm cold, and I'm really, really hungry."

"Oh, that's probably because of your transformation," Snowy explained. "I also get hungry after it."

It was the perfect moment for someone's stomach to growl, and to my sincerest surprise, it was my own. Hello, trope!

"Well, I suppose that means I'm hungry, too," I stated.

"Does that mean we are calling it a day?" Josh asked in a hopeful voice, and when I nodded, he almost did a fist pump. "Finally! I can put some clothes on."

"Yeah, sure, whatever," I mumbled as I stretched my back and looked around. In retrospect, invoking the Purple Zone was a bit of an overkill as, contrary to my expectations, the sparring matches didn't cause much collateral damage. It was still better to be safe than sorry, and I don't think anyone can blame me after seeing what Snowy and Elly did to the school grounds the first time I saw them transform.

Anyhow, since there was absolutely no need for it anymore, I turned to Brang and asked him, "[If it is within your means to end the existence of this Area of Violet Colours, might I request you do so?]"

The ex-general gave me an odd look at first, but when he finally figured out what I was talking about, and he raised his spear off the ground, only to hit its butt against the floor so hard, I was afraid the concrete would fracture. Then it did—or at least that's what it looked like as hundreds of hairline cracks spread across the hall with Brang in their center, following which the entire room shook. A few short seconds later, we were back in normal space.

I did my best to ignore how overly elaborate our exit from the Purple Zone was, and instead I picked up my coat. I had a whole speech prepared for the occasion, waxing lyrical about how we'd all explored our strengths and weaknesses and whatnot, but I decided to leave it all for after we were back home. Speaking of which, it was high time I did a quick check on Karukk. I'd done so every once in a while during our training, and each time he was either snacking or watching my TV in the living room, but I figured it wouldn't hurt to see what he was doing one last time before I started ferrying the others over. As it turned out, it was very, very fortunate I did that.

What I saw through Far Sight made my blood run cold. It took all my presence of mind not to teleport over right away, but I remembered that I had a pretense to uphold, so I hastily threw my coat on my back as I exclaimed, "Training's over!" and added a curt, "[Stay alert!]" for Brang in particular before I dashed into the adjacent room housing the local magic closet, slamming the door shut behind me with a loud bang. By the time the sound would have died down, I was in my living room.

What I saw was, in short, complete and utter chaos. My sofa was turned over, and it had a large gash on its side, through which I could even see the springs. My coffee table was broken right in half, and my carpets were scattered around the floor and stained by a spray of blood. There, right in the middle of this whole horrible spectacle, was an injured Faun holding up a broken dining chair in defense, kind of like an animal trainer in a circus ring, while opposite him stood a very familiar and dangerous woman.

Miss Creepy Huntress had her patented slasher grin plastered on her face, and she was standing in a low stance. She gripped her weapon high, drawn back next to her ear, and her whole body was tense like a bow-string, prepared for a lunging stab. Said weapon, by the way, was one of those Japanese swords. I wanted to say "katana," but it seemed too long and straight for that. Maybe some kind of fantasy variant?

More importantly, the whole blade of her sword was purple, with only its edge a slightly lighter shade, closer to pink. The purple cloth in which it was originally wrapped was now attached to the end of the handle, and for some reason it billowed in a nonexistent wind. The way it moved was also just a wee bit unnatural, like poor CGI.

Now, while I would've loved to discuss real special effect failures in detail, and if Judy was around, it was guaranteed to turn into a skit, at the moment, I had to ignore the topic in favor of asking the most obvious question.

"What the bloody hell is going on here?"

Suddenly aware of my presence, Karukk twitched as he glanced at me in surprise, while Miss Huntress shuddered so hard, her stance practically collapsed.

I was still in the dark about what happened here, but my brain, probably because it was still in a higher gear after the sparring matches, immediately categorized the situation as an opportunity, and so I instinctively moved to capitalize on it by looking over the carnage with my best theatrical show of dismay.

I exclaimed, "What have you done to my living room?" closely followed by a dramatic groan, the latter of which I used as a handy way to disguise my Faunish directed at the frozen Karukk. "[Cease standing around akin to an imbecile of the highest order and vacate my domicile while I distract her!]"

The stupid look on the Faun's face thankfully only lasted for a moment. Then he let out a gut-shaking battle cry that actually translated to, "[G-got it, boss! I'll go and hide!]"

Declaring so, Karukk jumped away from the crazy huntress and towards me, and in order to keep in line with the hasty script I threw together in my head, I helpfully grabbed hold of his uninjured shoulder and used his momentum to throw him towards the open door leading to the street. After a series of panicked noises, the big guy rolled to break his fall, and then he sprang to his feet and rushed right through the door which, as I just noticed, was also broken. The moment he was through, he activated his cloaking sigil and dashed into the early evening twilight. Now I turned my attention towards the only remaining person in the house... who was looking at me like a little kid whose toy was taken away.

"It's gone," she muttered with a dejected expression, all her menace gone.

I rolled my eyes. *This woman.*

As a prelude to my verbal assault, I once again observed the sorry state of the living room, and then I leveled my first question at my unwanted guest.

"What exactly are you doing here?"

Miss Huntress gave me one of her trademarked *What a dumb question* looks before simply stating, "We came to pay you a visit."

"Why?"

"Because we were patrolling the neighbourhood," she answered like it was the most obvious thing in the world.

"So you decided to break down my door."

"There was a creature of the underworld in your home," she explained as if I didn't know. "When we found it, we couldn't restrain the unquenchable hunger of our blade, so we—"

"I don't care!" I cut her off and then pointed at her weapon. "Also, stop waving your sword around. It's dangerous."

She gave me an irritated frown, then she extended the hand holding her weapon towards me as if to show it off, saying, "Look. Onikiri still thirsts for blood."

"I told you, I don't care."

She looked at me, then down at the sword, then back at me, her expression growing more and more puzzled.

"But it's the rule that we must drench her blade in blood before she can be sheathed."

"This is my house. Here, I set the rules, and one of the rules is that you are not allowed to wave an unsheathed weapon around in my bloody living room."

"Really? Let us see what Onikiri says." She closed her eyes for a moment, and when she opened them again, her confusion had evaporated. "Onikiri says it's important for an effective hunter to observe the inferior and silly customs of the natives when on a hunt abroad."

A talking sword? How come I wasn't even surprised anymore?

"Natives, huh?" I muttered, but in truth, it was just the kind of segue I'd been waiting for. "I already figured you weren't from around here, but where are you from?"

Before she answered, my oblivious home invader held her sword vertically, with the blade pointing at the floor. When she did that, the unnaturally billowing shroud trailing from its end came to a halt, only to suddenly come alive again and tightly wrap itself around the whole sword like some kind of textile boa constrictor. Seconds later, the familiar bead chain reappeared.

Only after her weapon was hidden in plain sight again did the huntress let out a sigh and answer, "We come from the East."

"Anything more specific?"

"Japan," she stated dourly, apparently annoyed by my insistent inquiry. Oh boy, if only she knew this was just the beginning…

"I see," I whispered, though "I figured" would have been more fitting. The not-katana was kind of a giveaway. "You came a long way just to trash my living room."

"Preposterous," she huffed at my accusation. Then she slung her bundled-up sword across her shoulder and declared, "Our intervention just revealed a cowardly ambush the despicable creatures of the world's darkest corners schemed against you. We demand appreciation."

"Oh, yes, I greatly appreciate what you've done to my house. I love the new décor, especially the bloodstains on the floor. Very art deco."

"No, you are supposed to appreciate our intervention," she told me like she was explaining dinner etiquette to a kindergartner, prompting me to groan in frustration.

"It's called sarcasm, woman! Learn to recognize it!" I paused here for a second and then decided to throw in a few technical truths to get the conversation rolling again by saying, "I've been fighting a small horde of Fauns for the past hour, and I already knew one was here. There was no reason to 'intervene' and break my stuff."

"You have been hunting, as well?" my unwanted guest's eyes opened wide and the corners of her lips drifted into a familiar grin. "We understand now!"

"Pray tell, what do you understand?" I asked her wearily, which unfortunately prompted her smile to completely shift into slasher mode.

"We didn't understand why you appeared so aloof and weak the last time, but now we have a full understanding of your strategy. Instead of searching the land for worthy prey, you created a trap with yourself as the bait! You made the creatures of the underworld think you were vulnerable, only to close the iron jaws of your cruel trap around them from the inside. A truly unique way to hunt!"

Now it was my turn to award her a *What the bloody hell is this person blabbering about?* look, but then I decided to just go with it. "I'm glad you finally realized why breaking into my house was unnecessary."

"We should've been more perceptive. Accept our apologies!" She bowed to me, but before I could respond, she straightened herself and gave me a brilliant, yet just as unnerving smile. "We are glad you take our contest so seriously."

"Contest?" I whispered to myself in surprise, but then I remembered that she did get me one-sidedly involved in one. Speaking of which, since she had a better impression of me this time around, I figured this was the best time for me to draw some further information out of her regarding her target... But then she stalked towards the front door. "Wha... ? Where are you going?"

"Our pride as a hunter cannot allow us to stay idle while our rival is one step ahead! We shall—"

"Hold on a moment! Don't just leave a conversation whenever you please!"

Miss Creepy Huntress gave me an odd look and asked, "We don't think there is anything else for us to discuss."

"Yes, there is!" I countered, getting steadily fed up with her. "You haven't even told me your name, for example."

"We have not?"

"No, you haven't."

She paused for a few seconds, as if searching her memories. Then she crossed her hands in front of her chest, conspicuously averted her eyes, and muttered, "The rules of our clan forbid us to share our name with outsiders... but we are fellow hunters of the darkness... and you are our rival..."

She kept on muttering, and while I really wanted to point out that I was not, under any traditional or sane definition, her rival, I was afraid it would throw her thoughts onto another tangent and we wouldn't get anywhere. At last, she let out a sharp breath and looked me in the eye again.

"We decided to grant you the knowledge of our name!"

"Um... thanks?" I responded a little weakly, but she didn't seem to mind.

"You may address us as *Onikiri no Tsukaite Rinne*."

"That's obviously not your name but some kind of title, isn't it?"

"It is our name," she emphasized with a frown. "It is how we are addressed by our clan and family! I demand that you be grateful for allowing you use of it."

"Oh, I'm sooo grateful right now," I told her rolling my eyes. "It's long, though. Can I just call you Rinne?"

All of a sudden, my unwanted home invader's face flushed crimson in anger and she hastily declared, while grabbing the wrapped-up sword on her back, "Most certainly not! Even if we are fellows in the hunt, such informality is beyond shameless!"

"Fine, forget I asked!" I told her with my hands raised.

"We shall leave now! The hunt awaits, and Onikiri still thirsts for blood! We shall—"

"Before you go," I quickly called out to her again, partially to interrupt her once again before she could gather steam, but also because I still had one thing I absolutely had to do before she left. I took a step closer to her, my palms open and showing no foul play, and once I was in arm's reach, I slowly raised my hand up to her cheek. "You have—" I tried to say, but before I could get the words out, my instincts told me to dodge, and I immediately complied. A second later, her sword, still in its cloth wrap, cut through the space where my torso used to be.

"What are you doing?" I exclaimed in alarm.

"That's our question to ask!" she exclaimed back with a scary expression on her face.

"You had a bit of blood, on your cheek, so I thought I'd be nice and wipe it off for you," I told her while poking at my own face for reference. Of course, there was no blood on her, but as I recently discovered, I needed actual skin contact to tag someone for Far Sight, and since she was wearing gloves, her face was the only exposed surface I could use.

She kept looking at me with a furious scowl, but when I didn't make any further moves, she hastily raised her arm to her face and rubbed both her cheeks with her suit's sleeve.

"It's gone now," she stated while gripping her bundled blade.

"Actually, you still have a bit over there. Just let me help you and…" I attempted to step closer, but she jumped back and simultaneously swung at me once more, forcing me to dodge again. "Hey, stop that! It's dangerous!" I reprimanded her, but in the blink of an eye, she was already under the doorframe of the entrance.

"We know what you're doing!" she yelled, gripping her weapon with both hands. "You are trying to use your devious ways to confuse our minds and hinder our hunt! We shall not fall into your trap! No matter how you attempt to approach us, you will not distract us away from our calling any longer!"

"I have no idea what you—" I tried to say, but she'd already dashed out of my house. I briefly entertained the thought of chasing after her with my teleportation ability just so that I could tag her, but the moment she reached the sidewalk, she leaped ten meters into the air and disappeared behind the next row of houses. I guess she didn't skip leg day, huh?

Thus concluded our second meeting, and I still hadn't managed to tag her. Furthermore, she was now on guard against me, so any further attempts would just lead to more resistance. Why did all the women I knew have to be so difficult?

Speaking of which, what was up with her behaviour at the end there? Did she have androphobia? No, she was starting to act weird even before that. I mean, weird compared to her previous conduct. Was it around the time I called her by her name that she…?

"Oh, fuck me," I uttered when the realization finally dawned. She was from Japan. There is a Japanese trope about being on a "first-name basis," where the only people who are supposed to call others by their first name were family, very close friends, and lovers. I'd inadvertently done just that, and she seemed furious, but… what if she was embarrassed instead? And then I'd tried to touch her and she had an overt reaction. But while she had swung her sword at me, it was still wrapped up and lacked any clear intent to injure me.

Q.E.D.: "I really need to ask Judy to let me in on those anti-harem countermeasures before things get out of hand."

I let out another sigh and decided to look on the bright side of things. If I somehow managed to accidentally make her develop some form of affection towards me, then at least it meant she'd be less of a possible threat towards me and my friends. Unless she was a *yandere*, in which case I was screwed either way.

While I was pondering about these things, I noticed that there were some shuffling sounds coming from outside my door. I walked up to the ruined doorframe and looked outside, and it didn't take me long to notice Karukk hiding behind the tree in the front yard. His hazy outlines told me that he was still cloaked while pressing a hand against his left shoulder, so I gestured for him to come in.

He did just that, and since my door was off its hinges, I set it against the frame the best I could before turning towards him and asking, "[Is your injury a threat to your continued existence?]"

"[It is but a flesh wound,]" Karukk replied with a wince. "[It could still use some field dressing.]"

"[If so, I shall request my companion of the empyrean race to treat your wound later. For now, please enlighten me of the highly improbable excrement that transpired within these walls.]"

"[It is a short story,]" he answered, grimacing in pain. "[I was minding the place when the doorbell rang. I went up to the door to see who it was when this crazy broad stabbed me right through the door, then she kicked it down and tried to cut me to ribbons.]"

"[She obviously failed in her endeavour.]"

"[Not for lack of trying,]" the Faun told me with a strained smile, then added, "[If you had not shown up when you did, I would be dead right now. I barely managed to hold my own for ten seconds.]"

"[Restrain your equines. This thorough desecration of my abode occurred in ten breaths' time?]"

"[Roughly,]" he confirmed with a nod. "[Sorry, boss. She caught me off guard.]"

"You weren't the only one," I muttered, then gestured for him to sit down. "[Rest, lest you aggravate your wounds. I shall bring aid within the minute.]"

"[Thanks, boss.]" Karukk lightly bowed to me with a strained smile before sitting down.

This time I didn't bother going to the magical closet, but just I teleported straight over to the secret base. As my vision blurred, I couldn't help but feel that, contrary to my previous words, this day was far from over.

CHAPTER 14

PART 1

"Are we clear on this?" I asked in a grave tone befitting the situation as I raised the photos I received from the arch-mage and flashed them in everyone's direction. "If you see this woman, don't talk to her, don't fight with her... actually, just don't engage her in any way, period. Any questions?"

"I've got one," Josh spoke up a touch hesitantly. "What if she 'engages' us?" he asked, complete with air quotes.

"You run away and call me. If that's impossible, stall her and call me," I stated matter-of-factly. "Anything else?" For a second or five, the gang crowding my ravaged living room kept glancing at each other, but then all shook their heads. "Good. I'm glad we're on the same page."

I was just about to continue, but a car beeped outside.

"The taxi arrived," Judy informed me.

"About time," I grumbled, checking the clock on my phone. It was 7:30 p.m., meaning I'd spent roughly thirty minutes explaining what just happened to my living room to my exhausted friends.

After I ferried Angie over to give emergency first aid to Karukk, I took him back to the shelter and carried the rest of the team over here for an emergency meeting. Technically I could've done the same thing at the base, but that would've left no one here at home to teleport back to, so I decided to focus on explaining things to the gang first. Then I'd have a separate meeting with Snowy's retinue, as they were the ones in actual, imminent danger.

Not that I felt my friends were perfectly safe, mind you. So, instead of letting them walk home, I arranged rides for all of them, despite their protests.

"Let's not make the driver wait too long," I began as I headed towards my front door, which Ammy had restored using some kind of utility spell, and the entire group followed after me. "This was a long day with some unforeseen ups and downs, wasn't it?"

Opening the door, I was hit by an unexpected sense of déjà vu.

I walked up to the cab parked in front of my curiously well-kept lawn (evidently the ninja maids were also into gardening). It was only when the cabbie rolled down the window that I recognized the source of the peculiar sensation from a few moments before.

"I knew your voice sounded familiar! I never forget a tipping customer," the cabbie told me with a wide grin accentuated by a missing eyetooth, his accent still as thick yet completely unidentifiable as the last time I met him. I'd sent Snowy home with him over a month before, but he was hard to forget. By the looks of it, I'd left an impression on him, too. "Hah. It's a small world, ain't it?"

"You have no idea how right you are," I responded dourly.

I mean, what were the chances of running into the same taxi driver twice in a row like this? Not high, I'd reckon. However, even during my first encounter with the man, I could tell that he was not just a run-of-the-mill placeholder. If the Narrative couldn't be bothered to make our classmates into anything resembling normal, just what were the chances of this guy being a random, onetime encounter? As far as I knew, he was the only cab driver in this entire city, poised to respond to us whenever we needed a ride. Hey, it wouldn't be the weirdest thing I've seen in this "small world."

Anyhow, the driver shrugged and said, probably as an attempt at small talk, "I see the little missy got over her rebellious phase."

I didn't quite get what he meant at first, but then I followed his gaze, which led me to Snowy awkwardly standing by the entrance. After finally realizing what he was hinting at, I let out a small chuckle and told him, "Yes. Let's just say I managed to remove the negative influences from her environment." I probably sounded just a tad ominous, as the cab guy became visibly guarded towards me. I handed him a hundred Jen bill. "Long story short: some unsavory types tried to break into my house. I'm a little worried about my friends, so I'd like you to take them home. This should cover it. Keep the change."

"If you say so," he replied, pocketing the bill. "What's the address again?"

"They'll tell you," I answered him while gesturing the Josh-Angie-Ammy trio to come over. "Now, if you'll excuse me, I have other business to take care of."

Saying so, I stepped away from the car and looked left, just in time to see a large, black luxury sedan turn the corner and glide up to the taxi in front of me. Of course, the reason I knew it was coming had nothing to with the playful spirits of convenient timing playing into my hands, but the fact that I had a mark on its driver.

"I still think I should stay here." Elly stepped up beside me and declared with just a pout.

"And I think you shouldn't," I answered without missing a beat, causing her pout to intensify by about 35 percent, give or take.

After learning about what happened to my living room, she was very insistent about sleeping over, ostensibly "to be on the safe side." While the notion of her being this worried about my safety was really, really sweet of her, it conflicted with the fact that I was also worried for *her* safety, and the safest place for her to be was inside her family mansion. It took a bit of coaxing to have her agree to call Sebastian over, but based on her sulky expression, I figured I wasn't entirely successful.

"Then stay in our guest room," she offered while earnestly looking me in the eye.

I shook my head.

"Can't do. I have to look after Snowy."

"She can stay, too!"

"My answer is still no," I told her, and after some hesitation, I gently wrapped my hand around her waist and pulled her to my chest. Then I whispered, "I told you, I don't think she poses a threat to me. Just go home, relax, and we'll pick you up on our way to school first thing tomorrow morning."

"You promise?"

"Sure," I told her with a smile. I almost gave her a peck on the forehead for emphasis, but then I became aware of a certain irritating butler frowning in my general direction, so I abstained for the time being and instead told her, "How about you say goodbye to the others? I have a feeling your steward wants to talk with me."

She gave me a disappointed "Boo," in return (which kinda made me want to kiss her, anyway), but she obediently walked over to Judy and Snowy. Meanwhile, I turned my attention to the foppish old butler walking towards me, frowning disapprovingly.

"It appears the head of the family wasn't joking about your relationship with the young lady. Oh, how far our noble lineage has fallen," he lamented, shaking his head.

"Very cute, old man, but I'm really not in the mood right now."

"Oh, are you not?" he inquired with a mocking little tilt of his head, but I took a deep breath and ignored his obvious provocation.

"No," I spoke with extra emphasis, then continued by telling him, "Please convey my apology to Mr. Dracis. I'm afraid I won't be able to visit him tonight. If you are there, please ask him when he will be available to finish up our business negotiations."

"You two are having business negotiations?" he questioned me again, this time in an audibly staler tone, as if he couldn't understand what I was saying.

"Yes," I confirmed with a sigh, not at all amused by his insistent provocations. "It's about creating a digital music distribution service platform, and no, I have neither the time nor the patience to explain what that means right now. Ask him if you're curious. Meanwhile"—I showed him one of the photos of a certain Japanese creeper—"be on the lookout for her."

The butler frowned at the image, then said, "I guess I might as well bite the bait, considering you went through all the trouble to secure my attention." He snatched the Polaroid out of my hand and held it up. "Who is this?"

"I'm still working on the particulars, but in short: she is an erratic Japanese monster hunter with a talking sword and a weird obsession with slaughter." I waited for the old man to stop staring at the picture and look back at me again, and when he did, I added, "I'm fairly certain she isn't one of the Knights. She's more than a little obsessed with anything related to the Abyss, and shows little to no interest in your extended family. Still, she's entirely unpredictable, so I'd recommend you keep your distance for now."

Sebastian gave me a doubtful look, but then it quickly morphed into a mocking smirk.

"Are you worried about my safety, boy?"

"Are you getting senile with age, old man?" I snatched the photo away from him. "If I'm worried about anything, it's collateral damage. This is someone who kicked down my front door and trashed my living room in the name of 'helping.' Who knows what kind of damage she could cause if she gets worked up again?"

"Is that so? I'm glad to see that even you are capable of showing a spark of intellect every once in a while."

"Can it, you lousy old lizard. I told you, I'm not in the mood."

I put the photo back into my coat pocket, yet for some strange and uncomfortable reason, Sebastian kept staring at me with eyes that appeared alarmingly curious. I ignored him, and we quietly waited for the princess to say her goodbyes to the rest of the gang.

Soon the other half of our group squeezed themselves into the taxi, and the cab rolled away. Once they were out of sight, the princess stopped delaying the inevitable and walked over. However, instead of heading for the sedan right away, she sidled up to me first.

"Stay safe, okay?" she asked, though it felt more like a command coming from her.

"That's the plan," I answered with what I hoped was a reassuring smile.

My girlfriend gave me a hard look. Then her eyes softened, and she rose on her tiptoes to plant a chaste and quite unexpected kiss on my lips.

"You better," she whispered after our lips parted. Then she added, with extra emphasis, "If she tries to break into your house again, call me."

"You can be such a worrywart sometimes," I said and reached to tussle the crown of her head, the smile on my face feeling light and easy. Then, remembering the gloomy old man beside me, I glanced at Sebastian.

"What?" I spoke in a cold tone. Not to hide my embarrassment, but just because I felt like it. That's all.

The old butler stared at me with an odd expression, but then shook his head with an amused smirk.

"Nothing," he stated in a tone that certainly meant the opposite, but he probably found it more amusing to let me come up with my own interpretations behind his word. I, naturally, didn't play along with his game, so I ignored his smiling eyes and gestured towards the car.

Still reluctant, Elly climbed into the limo and let the annoying butler drive her away. With a sigh, I headed inside, where I could hear Judy and Snowy moving around in the kitchen.

"Hot cocoa or tea?" Snowy leveled the question at me the moment I looked inside the room, and it took me an embarrassingly long moment to interpret it and answer.

"Tea, please," I told her, and she responded with a huge nod.

"On it!"

While my sister was busy with that, I walked over to Judy, who was in the process of packing a familiar lunch box with equally familiar sandwich bundles.

"Lunch for tomorrow," she answered my unasked question, stuffing even more food into the small box with expert-level Tetris skill.

Watching the two of them busy themselves made me feel like the odd man out, so I headed back to the living room. The place was still a disaster zone. After assessing the damage one more time, I piled up the unsalvageable causalities first.

Said pile consisted of two blood-splattered carpets, a broken chair, and ripped drapes. The coffee table also seemed to be a goner at first, but after I tried putting it back together, it turned out nothing was really broken, so I decided to keep it. As for the sofa, I was torn on the issue, pun intended. The large gash on its side was unsightly, but Ammy swore she had a spell that could fix it. Speaking of which, she had fixed my lock once when I was unconscious, and she also restored my broken door into a semblance of integrity. Perhaps the class rep had a future in the maintenance industry?

Jokes aside, I was genuinely impressed by how she could restore broken objects with just a few waves of her staff and some eerie faux-Latin chanting, yet when I tried to tell her that, she got really defensive all of a sudden. Maybe she did have a complex about only being able to use utility spells and her golem? I decided I should focus on her a bit more during our next training session, as I smelled great untapped potential in those so-called utility spells.

It was just about when my living room finally returned to a semblance of normalcy when the two girls came out of the kitchen, Snowy carrying a familiar tray with three gently steaming mugs on it. We sat down around my newly restored coffee table and sipped our beverages. It was… honestly, surprisingly cozy considering the circumstances.

But *someone* had to break the comfortable silence, so I did it by clearing my throat and addressing my girlfriend first.

"How long are you staying today?"

"I have permission until nine," she answered between sips.

"Good. If we don't finish, I suppose we'll continue on the phone as usual."

"Yes."

"Doing what?" came the awkward interjection from Snowy. She seemed genuinely curious about what we were talking about.

"Research stuff. It's just a thing we do," I told her, then after some contemplation, I continued with a question. "Can I ask you for a favor?"

"Yes!" Snowy agreed, without even bothering to listen to my request first.

"I'm glad to see you're eager," I told her with an appropriately brotherly smile, then I pointed at the doorway. "Considering today's events, I really think I should invest in some heavy-duty security measures, and I couldn't help but recall those fancy barriers you set up around the school. Could you put something similar around this house?"

Snowy looked weirdly surprised by my request, but after glancing around the room, she answered, "I… I don't think I can do that."

"You can't?" Judy asked, and my sister shook her head.

"I-it's not that I don't want to, but I really can't! That kind of barrier… I could only make it work at the School because it's built on top of a junction of mana veins, so there was an abundance of ambient mana to draw on, and there's nothing like that under this house. A-also, it was designed to only work for a few hours, and making it permanent would be… I don't think I can do it."

"By mana vein, you mean a ley line, right?"

Snowy nodded, and I couldn't help but groan. Not because my house lacked that power source, but because the more I learned about the supernatural elements of this world, the more it felt like there were no unified naming conventions for them. What a pain in the neck.

Snowy shrank back in her seat, so I quickly told her, "Don't worry, sis, I don't want you to do the impossible. If you say it cannot be done, I believe you. Still, can't you do something similar? I don't need it to be impenetrable, just solid enough to prevent someone from waltzing into my living room and making a mess again."

"You mean, like… area denial wards?" she asked in an awkward voice, and after I gave her a tentative nod, her eyes lit up and she declared, "I can do that!"

In fact, she was so enthusiastic, I was afraid she'd jump to her feet and start working right away, so I hastily gestured for her to stay put and said, "Great! Let's discuss the particulars tomorrow. I was only curious if it could be done."

"Oh, okay," she agreed with a smile, and so we returned to the comfortable silence once again. This time it only lasted until Snowy finished up her drink, at which point she let out a satisfied sigh, set her empty mug on the table, and then addressed me with a soft, "Leo?"

"Yes?"

"Can I… also ask for a favor in return?"

"Well, sure, but let's not have a this-for-that thing. If you need help, just ask."

"I understand. So… could you take me to see Karukk? I'm worried about him."

I shrugged. "I think Angie fixed him up well enough, but I can see where you're coming from. Do you want to go right now?" She nodded eagerly, so I told her, "Okay then. Call me when you're ready to leave."

"Thank you!"

With that, she jumped up and headed towards the entrance, probably to get her shoes.

While she was out of earshot, I glanced at Judy and told her, in a low voice, "I'll meet you in my room. We have a lot of things to talk about."

My assistant raised her brows at that, which I interpreted as agreement. Snowy reappeared, so we both left for the secret base, putting this short but much needed downtime behind us.

PART 2

"I'm back," I announced as I reappeared in front of my swivel chair and dropped into it. To her credit, my girlfriend sitting on my bed was only mildly startled by my unforeseen arrival. In fact, she looked more annoyed than anything else.

"You're late," she told me in her usual expressionless tone while dramatically checking the time on her phone.

"I thought that if I was over there, anyway, I might as well brief Brang and the rest of the Fauns. They… unfortunately took what happened here as a challenge, but I convinced them to stay away from the crazy huntress for now."

Disinterested in my explanation, Judy kept swiping on her phone until she found what she was looking for.

"Speaking of *her*," she began, her voice flatter than usual, "did you manage to draw any new information out of her this time around?"

"Not as much as I would've liked," I admitted with an exasperated sigh in tow. I leaned forward and clarified, "I mentioned most of this to the others already, but just to reiterate, she's some kind of monster hunter from Japan. She has a hate-boner for anything Abyssal-related, and she has a talking Japanese sword." I waited for Judy to stop typing, then once I had her full attention again, I said, "The keywords we should look into are *Onikiri*, *Rinne*, *clans*, and *sentient weapons*."

"Which one of them is her name?" Judy asked a pointed question.

"The second one, I think."

"You think."

"I'm about ninety percent sure, but I'm still not convinced that what she gave me wasn't some kind of ceremonial title."

"I see…" my assistant began typing again, while I took a deep breath and prepared to broach the main topic. I just had to decide from which direction I should approach it.

"Judy, listen to me for a moment please."

"I'm always listening," she responded and finally looked up at me. I must've had a strange expression on my face, because she cocked her head and asked, "Is there a problem?"

"You could call it that, yes," I answered as I closed my eyes for a moment. Then, steeling my nerves, I looked her in the eye and said, "Well, I might have, by a complete accident, left an… unnecessarily good impression on her."

All of a sudden, my girlfriend's face got so frosty, I could swear I was looking at a glacier. A *scary* glacier, with blank yet chilling eyes, and a cute little frown, aaand my analogy kinda breaks down here, doesn't it?

"Please elaborate," she spoke softly, though her gaze made sure I realized it wasn't just a polite request but a demand. I rolled my eyes at her theatrics but did as she said.

"In short, I called her by what I presume is her first name without realizing it was a cultural faux pas, she got flustered, then I tried to touch her, at which point she got *really* flustered, and then she left in a hurry."

"You tried to touch her?"

"Yes. For Far Sight," I spelled out in a hurry.

"Oh, I see… So? Did you mark her?"

"Unfortunately, no. As I said, she literally ran away."

"I see," she responded a tad morosely before summarizing things by saying, "So, you flirted with the woman who broke into your house, she was receptive, and now you don't know what to do. Is that the gist of it?"

"I wasn't flirting with her per se, but, yes, that's about it."

My assistant gave me a sideways glance, then looked away and let out a truly exhausted groan.

"I really can't let you out of my sight even just for five minutes…" she muttered, and while normally I would've protested, this time I decided it would have been counterproductive… but then she just had to add, "Please tell me you're not interested in her."

Now *that* was a comment I couldn't jolly well leave alone without any protests.

"Dormouse, would you please take this seriously? Would I talk to you about this if I was?"

"You talked about 'letting Eleanor down gently' in the past, and yet look where we are," she countered with a petulant edge to her words, and for a second or two, I was lost for words.

"Apples and oranges," I responded with a nonanswer, in place of anything better. "Also, we are veering off topic. Listen, the point I'm trying to make is that, dumb as it might sound, I might be in need of some anti-harem countermeasures."

"Oh?" Judy's eyebrows rose in surprise (just a little), and she looked me over from head to toe like I was a rare black sheep or something. "So, you've finally recognized that your constant flirting is a problem. Good, that's a step in the right direction."

"I don't think I'm flirting with anyone but you and Elly, but that's a point we are going to come back to later," I told her a smidgen indignantly. "No, the reason I ask is because I think we have to reevaluate the world's genre again."

"Again? I suppose you have a new hypothesis."

"Yes," I confirmed with a slightly more serious expression. "I believe we are living in a supernatural harem battle school life setting."

"Isn't that something we already concluded?"

"Yes, but no," I told her, straightening in my seat. "The key is in the order of terms, and the word *harem* in particular. Previously I thought it was the generic, extended love triangle kind, where everyone pines for the same guy without entering into a relationship. I also thought that the harem shenanigans were just a carryover from the early school life period. However, in light of recent developments, I realized that this world is just a wee bit too accommodating for straight up polyamorous relationships for that to be the case."

"By recent developments, do you mean Eleanor's family?"

"Precisely." I nodded in agreement. "I originally thought their family tradition was just a quirk, but it might actually be an intentional precedent for polyamory."

"And by polyamory, you mean…?"

"The 'real' harem kind, where one person, in our case probably Josh, is supposed to be in a relationship with multiple love interests at once."

"So, it's what you're doing."

"Yes, but on a bigger scale."

"I think I see what you mean," Judy mused while poking at her phone. "If we presume that this world had planned a narrative that involved some form of polyamory, then it would explain why baking such a tradition into the Dracis family's backstory would exist—to support such a real harem, as you call it. It's a thought worth entertaining."

"Thank you, though I think you are being a bit too much of a reductionist again."

"It's my job," Judy said, puffing out her chest. "Lately you've been trying to avoid looking at things from a meta-narrative standpoint, so I took it upon myself to do it for you. That's what I was hired for in the first place. "

"I'm not trying to avoid it, I'm just too busy with the surface stuff to worry about the meta at the moment," I grumbled. But I closed my eyes and let out a deep breath. "We are getting off topic again. Whether there is a grand, pre-written plan to this world that pigeonholes me in, or it comes about just from personal relations and random chance, I still need to be sure not to accidentally attract annoying people."

"Fair enough," Judy said with a nod. "Self-awareness is the first step in self-improvement. How can I help?"

"First off, I want you to teach me how to be unattractive," I told her as unambiguously as I could, yet for some reason, she scowled. Hard.

"Chief, you are really lucky I'm a generous person and I decided *not* to interpret your words as, *You are unattractive; show me how to be more like you.*"

It took me an embarrassingly long time to respond to that, but when I did, I rolled my eyes so hard, it almost made me dizzy.

"Come on, Dormouse! Weren't we over this already? You know you are plenty attractive, so why would you even think that?"

"Am I?" She gave me an unusually sardonic look, then asked, "If so, then can you name my most attractive attribute?" I didn't even have time to open my mouth, but she already cut me off by raising a hand and declaring, "And you cannot say 'your brain.' You've already used that card once."

"Oh please! Can we just stay on topic?" Her expression said she was serious about this, so I gave up and told her, "Fine! It's your voice."

"My voice," she repeated after me, and I'd go as far as to say she was surprised by my response.

"Yes, it's your voice. It's soothing and I like it."

"Really?"

"Yup," I told her with a reassuring smile. "So, can we go back to the anti-harem talk?"

"Might as well," she answered with a shrug, though I couldn't help but notice a tiny little smirk at the corner of her lips, so I figured everything was fine. "Where do you want to start?"

"First things first, I want to know what you think constitutes as 'flirting,' so that I can hopefully stop accidentally doing it."

"Hm," Judy let out a thoughtful sound and raised the corner of her phone to her lips. "To begin with, the biggest problem is that you have no sense of personal boundaries."

"I don't?"

"You don't. You don't possess a shred of reservation towards the opposite sex. That kind of overly confident and casual attitude comes off as you hitting on someone."

"Wait, hold on!" I stopped her in her tracks with my palm held up. "You want to tell me that just being unreserved equals to flirting around these parts?"

"In your case? Yes," she told me with another nod. "You are tall, fit, and handsome. If you walk up to a girl, make eye contact, and engage her in small talk, anyone would think that you're hitting on them."

"Hold your horses again!" I stopped her once more, this time while massaging my temple. "So you want to tell me that, just because I'm conventionally attractive and not socially awkward, every time I talk to a member of the opposite sex, it could be interpreted as flirting?"

"It also has a lot to do with your informal attitude, but yes, that's the gist of it."

"I'm pretty sure that kind of mindset is some kind of *-ist*, you know?"

"I don't know what you are talking about. Also, you asked for my advice, so don't complain."

"Ugh, fine." I slouched in defeat. "Anything else?"

"You are also way too direct with physical contact." Judy dealt me another blow with a tone that said it was self-evident. "For example, you said you tried to touch this 'Rinne' woman?"

"Yes, I did."

"Did you ask for her permission first?"

"Well… no, not explicitly," I admitted, scratching the base of my neck.

"Can you explain to me what happened, in detail?"

"Erm… So, I need skin contact to mark someone for Far Sight. We know that, right? So, since she was wearing gloves, with only her face exposed, I had to touch her there without appearing as some kind of creep, so I thought I would do that thing where I casually step up to her and wipe a stain off her cheek, like in the movies, but when I tried to do that, she got really flustered and she ran away." In response to my explanation, my assistant gave a look flatter than the Maldives, forcing me to prompt her with a tentative, "What?"

"You said it out loud, and yet you still don't understand?" she asked me with a face filled to the brim with disbelief (full by Judy standards, I mean). "Chief, what you did sounds just like a cheesy scene from a *shoujo* manga."

"No, it doesn't," I denied on the spot.

"Yes, it does," she doubled down with a frown. "Imagine this from the point of view of the person on the receiving end." She paused here for a moment and continued with a low, husky voice, "Imagine that you are alone with a tall, handsome stranger in a room. Then, without any warning, he takes a step towards you. He looks you in the eye, and there is no threat or reservation in them, putting you at ease. Then he smiles and gently reaches his hand out towards you and tries to touch your face while whispering sweet nothings…" At this point, she fell silent, shuddered, and then added, in her usual voice, "It sounds like a romance manga cliché, doesn't it?"

"When you put it like that, of course it does!" I protested as all my suppressed indignation bubbled to the surface. "Since when are you an expert on shoujo manga tropes, anyway?"

My assistant conspicuously averted her eyes and stated, "Research," with a suspicious amount of emphasis, then hid behind her phone and continued with, "Don't change the subject. The real issue here is that you have no concept of personal space and, combined with how overly familiar you are, it can make people think you are coming on to them."

My skepticism was wider and deeper than the Pacific Ocean, but I also knew that there was no point in arguing this one, so I soon gave up and concluded with, "Long story short, the first step in my anti-harem measures should be trying to be more conscious of women's personal space."

"Other than mine or Elly's, obviously," Judy corrected me.

"Obviously," I agreed. "That's for future encounters. What do I do with someone who may or may not have already developed an unwarranted infatuation on me?"

"I'd like to say you should just reject them outright, but considering your track record, that doesn't seem to work." I wanted to object, but then I thought about it and decided it wasn't a hill worth dying on. In the meantime, Judy was in deep thought, resulting in her suggesting, "How about passing her on to Joshua?"

"That... is certainly something that could work, but I don't think he would appreciate it."

"Then find someone else," she stated like it was an easy solution.

"Honestly, I'd be happy even if she would just leave the island. Some things about her just don't add up, and it bothers me." Judy looked curious, so I elaborated by telling her, "For example, she knew my face, and she even knew where I lived."

"I noticed that, too. Do you think she stalked you?"

"No." I shook my head without even entertaining the thought. "I think someone's pulling the strings from behind the stage and set her up to meet me."

"Who?"

"My money's on Lord Grandpa, but I have no evidence yet... More on that later. For now, let's focus on this Rinne woman."

"If you just want her to leave, you could try to resolve her subplot," Judy posited. "In my opinion, the Narrative introduced her as part of a subplot related to the stray Chimera on the island. If you find it and get rid of it, then it would conclude the plot, and she will leave the island."

"While that's hypothetically sound, we still don't know enough about how the Narrative works and how much it influences things," I countered. "It's just as likely that removing her reason to be on the island would cause another reason to pop up to keep her around." I paused here for a second, and a small grunt later I added, "Not to mention, I think this entire 'subplot' you are talking about is probably all tied to Lord Grandpa, and going after the Chimera just to get rid of her makes me feel like I'm playing into the old man's hand..."

"Do what you want, so long as it doesn't result in another girlfriend. Or sister."

"Ouch, Dormouse," I whined. "You're really grumpy this evening, you know that?"

She stuck her tongue out at me, which was both kind of cute and uncanny at the same time, because the rest of her face stayed as deadpan as usual, and I couldn't help but stifle an amused little chuckle. I glanced up at the clock and noted that we still had a lot of time left before Judy would have had to go home, so I asked her, "Do you have anything else to add to this topic?"

"There's a lot to be said about potential subplots and the narrative, but those aren't for now," she spoke half-heartedly, but her fingers suddenly picked up pace as she began flipping through her notes. Then her eyes flashed with what I presumed to be excitement and she declared, "I have another topic we should discuss, though."

"Really? What is it?"

My assistant turned her phone my way, showing off some kind of diagram, and then she explained, "I have compiled a preliminary power-level ranking."

"You were serious," I muttered with a deadpan voice, and she gave me a firm nod in return. To be perfectly honest, I wasn't in the mood for this, but for some inexplicable reason she seemed to be really excited about the subject, so I let out a small sigh and gestured for her to speak up. "Very well, you have my attention for now."

"Since I had nothing better to do while you had your fun bullying Joshua and the Fauns, I decided to interview everyone and try to figure out the combat rankings of the people we know, for future reference." She fell silent, and a moment later, my phone buzzed. I picked it up from the computer desk and found a new email with an attachment in my inbox. Unsurprisingly enough, it was the same diagram she'd just showed me. In the meantime she got up and stood beside my chair while she waited for me to open it, then she said, "The rankings you see here are based on the interviews, my own observations, and my educated estimates of how much each of the participants was holding back during the sparring matches. You can also find yourself on the list."

"I see..." I began and then immediately raised a single, surprised brow at the name on the top of her list. "Snowy is number one?"

"Yes," she confirmed with a smirk, apparently amused by my reaction. "If you tap on her name, you can see that she has very high scores in mobility, offensive capabilities, and utility. Her skill score is also above average, with only her defense being subpar."

I gave her a skeptical glance, but went ahead and tapped on Snowy's name. A page popped up with one of those hexagonal skill diagrams you would see on a game character's wiki page.

"I would be lying if I said that I wasn't impressed by this, but... when did you even make it?" I asked the obvious question, but it was like water rolling off a duck's back.

"If we consider her sigils and the general combat performance she showed during her battle with Eleanor and at the School, there is no doubt she is currently our strongest combat asset."

"You are using words that are scaring me a little," I whispered as I closed the pop-up page and looked at the second place, and it made me raise my bafflement-brow once again. "Elly is the second?"

"You sound surprised," Judy said as she leaned even closer, as if to get a better look at me. "Did you expect you would be second?"

"No, actually. I expected Brang would be."

"Not a chance," my assistant honest-to-goodness scoffed at my response. "Eleanor is leagues above him."

"I can't help but recall her getting her shapely posterior consistently handed to her by Brang, though," I murmured, earning me another scoff.

"You should not consider the results of a sparring match as a clear indicator of power levels. Eleanor was holding back a lot during today's training in order not to cause any harm to your Faun friend. She never used her claws or her beam attack, and after interviewing her, I'm fairly certain she would also win in a contest of raw strength if she was serious."

"Really?" I glanced between Judy and my phone a few times, and she responded with a satisfied grunt. I scrolled down, reading, and my eyebrows shot up. "And what am I doing at the third place?"

"Is there a problem with that?"

"Yes! I mean..." I scrolled down the list and back up again before I explained to her, "I kinda get why Josh is at rock bottom. Angie being above the class rep, I can also understand, with her combination of healing and ranged firepower. I also get why Brang is above them on the rankings, but why am I above him?"

"Look at your stats," she prompted me, and I did so. "Your mobility is excellent, you have high scores both in skill and utility, and, most importantly, the Faun said you are better than him."

"He did?! Wait, when did you even ask him? I thought you were afraid of him."

The corner of Judy's left eye twitched in a very, very conspicuous display of... something, and then she told me, "I asked Neige to be the messenger between us. My point still stands."

"No, it doesn't," I protested while closing the unnecessarily detailed diagrams.

"You realize that you took on the entire Faun squad and won, right?"

"That doesn't count," I grumbled as I waved in dismissal. "They are mooks."

"Come again?"

"Mooks? You know—minions, goons, henchmen, small fry—"

"That's not an argument," Judy huffed. "Also, according to both Eleanor and Neige, they wouldn't have been able to defeat them as easily as you did. In fact, I believe that if you had a real weapon, and didn't try to fight your opponent head-on, you are potentially the most dangerous person in our group."

"And I think you are just biased."

"No, I'm not," Judy denied with an imperceptibly puffed-out cheek. "Listen, Chief, you might not have Eleanor's raw power or Neige's spells and abilities, but you have a unique, out-of-context power set. Your ability to freely teleport and your precognition might look unassuming at first glance, but they are incredibly effective. All you need is a way to deal damage, and you—"

"Wait, wait! Hold on for a second!" I cut her short as her monologue suddenly reminded me of something. "So... you are saying that I have a game-breaking set of powers that is easy to underestimate because they are not flashy?"

"Yes. Just like how you underestimate yourself," my assistant confirmed my words, defiantly crossing her arms in the process.

"And apparently I'm attractive and my natural behaviour somehow appears seductive to the opposite sex."

"I don't know how it relates to the previous question, but yes."

"Oh my God..." The words slipped out of my mouth before I knew it. "Judy, you might want to sit down before you hear this."

"Okay," my assistant responded by sitting on my lap. Normally I would've pointed out that I didn't mean it quite so literally, but I decided to let her have her way, and instead I took a deep breath.

"Judy..." I began, my voice exactly as grave as my recent revelation demanded, "I think I might be turning into a battle harem protagonist..."

PART 3

"Do you have your school supplies?" I asked my newly minted little sister as we stepped through my front door.

"Yes," Snowy replied and hefted her bag on her shoulder.

"Spare key?"

"Got it," she declared after taking a keyring out of her coat pocket and playfully jangling it in front of me.

"Emergency app?"

She blinked at me, then she hurriedly put away her keys and fished her phone out of another pocket. Less than three seconds later, there was a loud notification blaring from my phone.

Last night, after I took Judy home, I downloaded one of those stranger danger apps on to her phone. With a press of a single virtual button, the application would send an emergency signal to the parent app on my phone with the ID and GPS location of the sender. The latter was useless to me, but it was still an essential safety net I planned to install on everyone's phones.

I turned off the alarm and pocketed my phone with a supremely satisfied grunt, then I locked the front door and we headed towards the first stop of our morning commute. We were actually a little early, but Snowy turned out to be an early riser, and since I promised I would pick Elly up on the way, I figured heading out a little ahead of schedule was the prudent thing to do.

Our first destination wasn't the Dracis estate, though, but Judy's place down the street around the corner. Snowy was in high spirits and walked beside me with a spring in her steps. We reached my assistant's doorstep in record time. Even so, we didn't have to wait long, as Judy walked through the front door just a few seconds after we arrived, followed by her familiar, absurdly youthful mother.

"Good morning, Dormouse," I greeted her, then I flashed a smile in the other woman's direction and added, "Good morning, Mrs. Sennoma. You look great as usual."

Hearing my comment, my embarrassed girlfriend ineffectually elbowed me in the side, but I only chuckled at her expense. Serves her right for making fun of my dramatic revelations the day before.

In the meantime, Mrs. Sennoma let out a charmingly girlish giggle and told me, "Oh, you flatterer!" while dismissively waving a pasta spoon in my direction. "I've heard you were sick, Leonard. Do you feel better now?"

"Thank you for the concern, ma'am, but as you can see, I'm fit as a fiddle," I answered her coyly while striking a silly bodybuilder pose, which earned me another poke in the side and a stream of tinkling laughter from Judy's mom. Then she noticed the white-haired girl quietly standing beside me.

"Oh? Who's the cutie?" she asked while leaning forward with her hands on her knees, which inadvertently emphasized her rather generous bust. I wasn't looking or anything, but Judy still elbowed me in the side for the third time. Speaking of her, I had no idea why my dearest assistant was so conscious of her appearance. If she inherited just half her genes from her mother (which was kind of a given, now that I thought about it), she should turn into quite the looker in a few short years.

Future expectations aside, I was asked a question, so I gently pulled the hapless Abyssal girl to the front and replied, "I believe you haven't met my sister yet. Her name is Neige." I pushed her forward a bit more and added, "Come on, Snowy, say hello."

"U-um…" she stuttered for a moment, and I was afraid that she might accidentally lapse into her vamp persona, but thankfully she collected herself and said, "G-good morning… uh… Miss?"

"Aaaaw!" Judy's mom cooed with a dopey smile, but before she could say anything else, my assistant pushed her back into the house by her shoulders.

"Stop bothering them, Mom. We have to go or we'll be late for school."

"Oh, okay," she agreed, slightly disappointed, but then she bounced back and graced us with a fittingly motherly smile and said, "Have fun!" while waving at us with her random cooking utensil still in hand.

We returned the gesture (though in our case without any props) and after exchanging a few more pleasantries we were on our way again, with Snowy on my left and Judy on my right.

"Let's pick up the princess next," I suggested, earning me a disinterested shrug from Judy. I figured she might be pouting, so I grabbed hold of her waist, pulled her closer, and whispered, "Guess what? The ninja maids worked overtime last night," right into her ear.

My assistant looked puzzled at first, but then she gave me an extra deadpan look and replied, "Is that really all you wanted to tell me right now?"

"More or less," I answered with a grin as I let her go.

It wasn't a joke, though. While the damaged furniture remained unchanged, all the bloodstains and dirt were cleaned off both the floor and the carpets I initially threw aside. I kind of hoped that the ninja maids were also into furniture renovation, but I suppose it was too much to ask for.

While I explained this to my still peevish girlfriend—and made her download the aforementioned emergency app—we reached the Dracis mansion's neighbourhood, and even from a distance, I could see the princess impatiently pacing up and down before the gates. She wasn't alone.

"Son!" Papa Dracis boisterously greeted me, and his wheelchair-bound wife rolled her eyes at his exclamation. Not only were they there, but Sebastian, Melinda, and even the two weird twin maids were crowding in front of the driveway. I felt a headache coming, but I returned his greetings—albeit with slightly less gusto.

"Good morning," I addressed them at once as my eyes swept over the group. "I'll be honest here: I'm feeling kind of weirded out by this reception. What's going on?"

The Dracis patriarch let out a hearty chuckle. "Our princess spent the entire morning tense as a piano wire waiting for you, so we decided to look after her to make sure she doesn't snap!"

"Daaad!" Elly protested, but her father only let out another deep, affectionate chuckle in response.

In the meantime, Melinda rolled the sharp-eyed mother of the household over to my side, and she immediately shot me the question, "Did someone really break into your house?"

"News travel fast, it seems," I muttered, sending a meaningful glance at the princess. "Yes, they did. My living room got turned over, but no one got hurt."

"Was it one of those accursed Knights?"

"I'm not one hundred percent sure yet, but I personally don't think so. I'm running a background check on her, just to be safe, and once I've got a definite answer, I'll inform you."

"Good man," she… approved, I think? Anyhow, after nodding to herself, she pointedly glanced at Snowy, who was for some reason hiding behind my back, and she curiously asked, "And who might she be? She smells… like the Abyss?"

"She's my sister," I told her with my most harmless smile, and when she raised a critical brow in return, I hastily added, "Freshly adopted."

Lady Emese looked like she really wanted to say something, but she didn't get the chance, as all our attention was drawn to a certain blonde dragon girl stomping her feet and loudly declaring, "Daddy, you… you nincompoop!" with a beet-red face.

After delivering this most serious of insults, Elly turned on her heel with a huff, linked her arm with mine, and began to forcefully drag me away.

"Er… goodbye and have a nice day, I guess?" I mumbled and waving with my free hand, which must have looked really comical, as Papa Dracis loosed a hearty guffaw. After the initial confusion, Judy and Snowy followed after me, but it wasn't until we were out of the mansion's view that the princess finally stopped pulling me, though she didn't let go of my arm.

"My dad can be such an idiot," she grumbled, making me raise a puzzled brow. I admit, I wasn't really paying attention to the two of them after her mother engaged me, but I didn't remember anything coming out of her father's mouth that warranted such a response. I was tempted to ask, but my train of thought was quickly derailed by Judy stepping up and grabbing hold of my other arm.

More amusingly, since both of my sides were quite literally taken, Snowy was momentarily flustered and unable to decide where to walk, ultimately settling with falling in line next to my assistant. It felt a little weird to walk like this, but it definitely wasn't unpleasant.

We were already in the neighbourhood of the school by the time I found Josh and Angie on the road. I would've liked to wave, but my hands were occupied. Snowy got their attention in my stead by raising her hand high over her head and calling out, "Moooooorning!" in a chirping voice.

What can I say? Apparently little sisters aren't just cute, they are also really convenient.

Jokes aside, once they noticed us, the childhood friend duo hurried over.

"Hi, Lili. Hi, Judy. Hi, Elly," Josh greeted each of the girls in turn, then he looked at me and added, in a decidedly wooden voice, "Good morning, Casanova."

I let out a tiny scoff and told my friend, "Sorry, pal, but I *do* have two pretty girls clinging to me. You really need to up your ribbing game if you want to get a rise out of me now."

Josh grimaced like he'd just bitten the world's sourest lemon, a picture made even funnier by Angie barely managing to stifle her giggles at his side.

"Morning, guys," the Celestial girl greeted us at last, her eyes still smiling with schadenfreude.

"Hi, Angie. Did you sleep well?"

"So-so," she responded while twisting her hand back and forth, then she and Josh fell in line beside us as we all continued our commute as usual.

"This is weird," Joshua suddenly spoke up with a conflicted expression on his face.

"What? Walking in a line like this?" Angie spoke while looking over our group, but Josh quickly shook his head.

"No, I mean…" he paused, seemingly lost for words as he looked at the steadily approaching school grounds, then said, "In the past week, I was almost kidnapped, I learned that I have superpowers, and I trained in how to use those superpowers against a scary goat-man… and now I am walking to school like everything's normal. Isn't that weird?"

"Not really, no," I answered him, then nodded at the always dependable (and frowning) armband guy. "You shouldn't compare your boring, peaceful days against the crazy ones. You should just savor them while they last."

"Savor them?" Josh repeated, as if he'd just heard something really profound. I wondered what he was thinking about for a second, but decided it probably wasn't important.

And just like that, we began yet another boring, peaceful, blissful school day, and I, for one, intended to follow my own advice to the letter.

CHAPTER 15

PART 1

My morning within the walls of the familiar classroom was decidedly normal, as far as such a word could be applied to the weird little world I lived in. Our classes were all held by Mrs. Applebottom, as usual, and the curriculum was mind-numbingly boring, also as usual.

If there was one thing that might have changed, it was that the placeholders seemed to be just a tiny bit less vacuous than before, but considering that I have already seen a similar development in the average passersby on the streets, it was by no ways surprising. It wasn't until the brunch break (which, as the designated snack time, was a few minutes longer than the rest of the breaks) that things started to proceed down a pretty weird path.

Right at the beginning of the break, the princess and Judy conspicuously left the classroom to discuss something between the two of them. If I had to make an educated guess, it was probably Judy laying the foundations to the anti-harem countermeasures we'd discussed the day before. Or rather, the parts we managed to agree on before I got fed up with her making fun of the threat of me being squeezed into the template of a battle harem protagonist and chased her home.

Josh also left the place with Angie in tow, ostensibly to see how Snowy was doing. I didn't really see the point, as I'd already entrusted Ammy to deal with the paperwork on the school's side of things the day before, and as for the social side, since she had the same cover story as us about catching a nasty flu, I didn't see how him checking on her would affect that in any way, shape, or form. But then again, Josh seemed to favor her over the other members of his entourage, so maybe it was just an excuse to see her again?

Speaking of Ammy, though, she was apparently forced to "take a day off" (her words, not mine) to rest, on her grandfather's orders. Despite my assurances that the paperwork wasn't particularly time-sensitive, she worked on it late into the night. Maybe she was a bit of a workaholic? Anyways, that explained why she wasn't there that morning. I hoped she would get some actual rest and be slightly less cranky by the next time we met.

Anyhow, I was just about to put my English books away and take out the science ones in preparation of the next, no doubt absolutely riveting lesson, when I became aware of the fact that someone was standing by my chair. In actual fact, there were multiple someones. A grand total of four of them, to be precise. I straightened my back in my chair, a little apprehensive of the fact that I was suddenly surrounded by a small mob.

Placeholders, all of them. Four guys with almost identical builds and simple haircuts denoting that they weren't particularly important in this world's grand scheme of things. Seeing them gathering around me like that was highly unusual, so after the first surprise wore off, I cautiously asked, "Can I help you with anything?"

"Say, Leo?" the guy on my right with unkempt, slightly greenish hair asked me in a very familiar tone, though for the life of me I couldn't remember if I ever talked to him in the past.

Still, after a bit of consideration, I prompted him to continue with a cautious, "Yes?"

The guys shared somewhat nervous glances, which incidentally managed to get *me* nervous as well, until the same dude took a shallow breath and asked, "Are you and the new girl, like... an item?"

For the longest moment, I could only blink at them in baffled silence, but at last my brain rebooted from its incredulity-induced blue screen of death, and I answered with a flat, "If by 'the new girl,' you mean Elly, then yes, we are."

"You see, I told you," another of the guys, this one sporting a brownish bowl cut, elbowed his comrade in the side with a robotic jab.

His friend's lips bent in a smile that didn't really reach his eyes, and he muttered, "You did."

To be frank, I was getting really, really freaked out by this blatant deviation from placeholder behaviour, but I kept my expression in check and only awarded them what I called a *Single Eyebrow Raised in an Intrigued Manner; ver. 0.7.2.* In the meantime, another member of the group, this one with a short crew cut, grabbed an empty chair and pulled it over so that he could sit down next to me.

"You lucky son of a bitch," he told me with a toothy yet wooden grin. "I can't believe you managed to nab one of the school's four goddesses."

"Five goddesses," the last member of the troupe, a guy with short, spiky hair, interjected.

"Oh, right, she's there, too," Mr. Crew Cut agreed.

"Hold on for a moment," I awkwardly wedged myself into the budding conversation. "What exactly are we talking about again?"

"You don't know about the four goddesses?" Mr. Bedhair asked me as if I was the weird one.

"Five," Mr. Spiky corrected him.

"Everybody knows who the goddesses are!" Mr. Bowl Cut asserted with rock-solid conviction. "As we all know, the members of the photography club and the journalism club create the monthly rankings of the most popular girls of our school."

"Yes," Mr. Crew Cut agreed while mechanically nodding over and over again.

"It is common knowledge," Mr. Bowl Cut continued, "that after collecting the votes, they are handed over to the dependable and entirely unbiased analytics club, who then hand the final results back to the journalism club. Any of the girls whose popularity reaches the threshold of forty-five point three two six percent amongst the male population are considered to be an official Blue Cherry High goddess."

"Indeed," Mr. Crew Cut agreed again.

It took me about this long to realize that I was on the receiving end of an honest-to-goodness infodump about the dumbest thing I have ever heard in my... well, maybe not life, but the last couple of days, I'd reckon. Anyhow, since this gaggle of placeholders went out of their way to share this vital and not at all banal information with me, I decided I might as well humour them.

"Sorry, but I wasn't really keeping up with this... um... ranking-thing? You mean to tell me Elly is on it?"

"Of course she is," Mr. Bedhair confirmed with unenthusiastic fervor.

"And who are the rest?" I probed, mostly out of a sense of bile fascination.

"As we all know," Mr. Bowl Cut started again while counting on his fingers, "We have the new girl, Eleanor, who took the rankings by storm and propelled herself to the top in record time! Her natural beauty, her demure temperament, and her high-class upbringing is a definitive hit with the voters."

I wondered just when the situation turned into a sales pitch, but for the time being I decided to go with the flow.

"The next one would be Angeline," Mr. Spiky asserted himself with a still wooden grin. "Her natural, tomboyish charm and upbeat personality is a definite hit with the target demographic."

"Then we have Amelia," Mr. Bowl Cut spoke without leaving even a second of breathing space in their explanation. "She single-handedly brought the academic type back into popularity with her outstanding beauty and shy temperament. She is also popular with the crowd in love with the levelheaded, sisterly type."

I wanted to point out that she wasn't particularly shy or sisterly, but before I could, they dropped a minor bombshell.

"The fourth goddess is naturally Mrs. Applebottom," Mr. Crew Cut stated like it was obvious.

"Really?" the incredulous question slipped out of my mouth before I knew it, and the gaggle of sentient haircuts around me nodded in unison.

"Of course!" Mr. Spiky exclaimed with something best described as dull indignation.

"Yes," Mr. Bowl Cut seconded. "Her mature charm and the excitement of a forbidden student-teacher affair propels her straight to the top amongst the goddesses."

"And as for the fifth goddess," Mr. Spiky cut in before I could voice my nuanced opinion on the matter, "she is naturally no other than the true rising star of our school, the one and only Neige from class 1-A! She took the rankings by storm and propelled herself to the top in record time!"

Under normal circumstances this would have been the point where I injected a snide comment about them using the exact same words to describe Elly, but considering it was a group of unusually animate placeholders we were talking about here, I decided not to waste my breath.

He continued, "Her pure, innocent charm and her natural grace and beauty immediately stole the hearts of all of her classmates, and the number of her fans swells by the day! Even if you don't pay attention to the rankings, you must have heard about her."

"Actually," I elbowed my way back into the conversation, "she's my sister."

"Really?" Mr. Crew Cut asked in an astonished voice that didn't show on his face at all. "You are a lucky man! You are not only dating one of the goddesses, but you can also bask in the glory of another! How enviable!"

"Truer words have never been spoken," Mr. Bedhair said in a, dare I say, profound voice before he let out a theatrical sigh. "Alas, once we also considered ourselves lucky, by being in the same class as three of the goddesses and taught by the fourth one. Oh, the folly of youth!"

"Okay, let's put the community theater dramatics aside and just tell me what happened," I cut in, spinning my finger to move them along.

"Joshua Bernstein happened!" Mr. Bedhair told me with a still needlessly theatrical scowl. "He single-handedly monopolized two of the goddesses from the very beginning, and rumors say that he already sank his fangs into the innocent flesh of Neige, as well! He is the enemy of every single warm-blooded boy in our school!"

I gave the disturbingly enthusiastic *warm-blooded boy* a Judy™ deadpan look and asked, in a strained but polite voice, "You are aware that I am friends with Josh, right?"

"Of course," Mr. Spiky confirmed. "That's why we want you to become our ally!"

"Your what again?"

"Our ally," Mr. Bowl Cut repeated with a meaningful nod. "Since you are close to the fire, metaphorically speaking, we want you to ensure that Joshua doesn't monopolize all our goddesses by himself."

"By that same logic, shouldn't you also dislike me for going out with Elly?" I asked the obvious question, but the four of them only shook their heads in unison.

"That is different. We are not so petty as to stand in the way of true love," Mr. Bedhair explained.

"Everyone could see that you two had a thing for each other from the beginning," Mr. Spiky added without eliciting any reaction from the previous speaker. "So long as you do not intend to hog all the other goddesses, too, you are okay in our book."

"If you do, then you are going to become the next number one public enemy of all boys in the school," Mr. Crew Cut added offhandedly.

"Think about it," Mr. Spiky concluded, and all of them seemed to agree with him, as they unceremoniously scattered without as much as a "bye" or something, leaving me sitting all alone and more than a little confused by the entire encounter.

PART 2

"So, that just happened," I concluded my retelling of the brunch break's events to Judy with a tired shrug, and she handed me a neatly wrapped sandwich in return. It was lunch break o'clock, and while the others went to the cafeteria, Judy and I were having a separate meal on the rooftop. At first, I was curious why Elly didn't insist on joining us, but as it turned out, it was all part of some kind of rotation my two girlfriends agreed upon beforehand, and I was just the last to know.

"I have a hypothesis," my dear assistant stated while unwrapping her own food.

"Don't you always?" I jested with a smile, but gestured for her to speak it all the same.

"I believe we might have been mistaken about our initial assessment regarding the school's importance in the broader narrative," she told me while gesturing for me to come closer on the bench, so I did just that.

Unsatisfied, she slid over until our shoulders and hips both met. Then she continued.

"We have already noted that the student body of the school is composed almost entirely of placeholders. In my opinion, this serves as a strong indicator towards the school itself not being considered a crucial element by the Narrative."

"So, if I understand your reasoning right," I mused between two bites, "since Josh's school life wasn't supposed to be super-important, the world didn't spend the effort to populate this place with anything other than rudimentary placeholders and annoying school nurses."

"In a nutshell," she confirmed.

"So the reason why the placeholders are suddenly making creepy lists about pretty girls in the school is because…?"

"Most likely, the Narrative has just raised the importance of the school, and with it, the placeholders began to develop."

"So, it's similar to our previous hypothesis about the simulation adapting to our presence by increasing the complexity of its visible parts," I mused, only to pause when I noticed that Judy had an *I really want to ask Leo a bothersome question* look on her face. And, since I noticed it, I was pretty much obliged to ask, "Is there a problem?"

With an unusually intense look, she asked, "Was I on the list?"

"Not that I know of, no," I told her honestly, and when she puffed her cheeks, I hastily added, "Come on, Dormouse! Why do you even care about some silly list put together by horndog placeholders? On my list, you are already number one."

"Oh?" her expression momentarily brightened, only for it to return to its usual deadpan glory when she questioned, "What about Eleanor?"

"She is also number one, obviously," I told her with a wink before taking a large bite from the sandwich in my hand.

"That's a cop-out."

"But true," I riposted with a smile, which seemed to put the topic at rest. "I wonder if our experiments with placeholder memory have anything to do with this sudden development?" I pondered in order to bring the conversation back to its roots.

"Almost certainly," Judy affirmed with a nod. "We have already established that if you pay a lot of attention to a placeholder, they stop being one and become your girlfriend."

I gave her a pointed look and then pinched her side, which made her jump in surprise.

"Stay focused on the topic."

"I am," she protested and pinched my side in turn, though as usual, her attempt at physical violence only tickled. "I am the walking, talking proof that if you interact with someone long enough, they stop being generic placeholders and rapidly develop a personality. Unlike Joshua, who is still blinded by some form of perception filtering, we have been actively interacting with the placeholder population. After all the stimuli we provided, it makes perfect sense that they would develop their own personalities and quirks, as well."

"I think making lists about their 'goddesses' is a little bit beyond something I would call a simple 'quirk'."

"It could be worse," Judy told me with a shrug. "They could be convinced that we live in a simulation and try to investigate it."

"Touché," I muttered while wiping my mouth with the napkin provided by my thoughtful assistant, and after a few seconds of silence, I decided to break the ice on a certain topic that we couldn't resolve the day before. "So, speaking of roles and meta-stuff, did you have any idea about how I could avoid turning into a protagonist?"

Judy gave me an odd look.

"Why are you so fixated on that?"

"I can't help it," I answered with my earnestest gaze. "Whether it's because of the designs of your pet narrative theory, or just due to the tropey laws of this universe, at this rate, if I'm not careful, I could end up usurping Josh's rightful place as the main character."

"I still don't see why you're making such a huge fuss about the prospect," Judy said, seemingly disinterested, and she took out a thermos from her bag.

"For a start, it would be an enormous pain in the arse," I grumbled. "For example, all the bad guys would want a piece of me."

"Don't they already do that?"

"Well, I suppose Crowey would, but that's a special case." I dismissed her objection with a wave. "I am talking about prospective antagonists and villains and other assorted miscreants who would inevitably show up to complicate the protagonist's life."

"What would you do if they showed up to complicate Joshua's life?" Judy asked, taking me aback.

"Um... well, I would probably try to deal with them before they could cause major trouble," I answered truthfully, earning me a triumphant "A-ha!" from my girlfriend.

"Then it doesn't make much of a difference, now, does it?"

"Yes, it does!" I protested, albeit more feebly than I'd have liked, so I picked another approach, one towards which I hoped she'd show more of a reaction. "Bad guys aside, if I get shoehorned into the role of a battle harem protagonist, I will also have to deal with a constant stream of prospective harem members showing up to further complicate my life!"

"Once again, it doesn't sound too different from your current situation."

"Then why don't you stop being cheeky about it and instead try to help me?" I finally snapped.

Judy once again sent me an odd glance, but at last she shrugged with an expression that said *Might as well.*

"Might as well," she whispered, and I almost told her she was being redundant, but I managed to stay silent. I patiently waited for her to say her piece, which came in the form of the question, "What is the definition of a protagonist?"

"Uh… the main character of a story?" I guessed, but she shook her head.

"I mean the etymological definition. The protagonist is the 'first mover' in a play or tale. They, by definition, move the plot forward." She paused here and dramatically pointed at my face. "That person is you."

"Er…" I stammered, lost for words.

Since I couldn't find them in time, she continued.

"Ever since you woke up last week, you grabbed the reins of the situation and never let it go. You set up a relationship, made yourself leader of our group, struck a deal with the most important person in town, secured a secret base and rescued a group of fugitive warriors, you adopted someone, and then you made contact with a monster hunter who invited you to a hunt. Then you flirted with her." She paused here again, probably waiting for my reaction, but I only rolled my eyes at her last point, so she added, "In the same time span, Joshua, our alleged harem protagonist, didn't advance his relationships, got dragged around by you, and didn't really accomplish anything beyond learning about the rules and elements of the setting, most of which was also provided by you."

"Well, sure, if you compare things so directly like that, then it's obvious that I would appear to *move the plot* more than Josh, but this should be only temporary," I countered with a frown. "If anything, I am running him through the express boot camp specifically so that he can assume his role as the protagonist as quickly and as safely as possible."

"Intentions don't change the facts," Judy said with a small shake of her head.

"Fine, fine," I grudgingly relented. "Let's say I grant you all of that. Do you have any advice for me?"

"Of course I do," she answered with startling confidence, and after poking at her phone, said, "It is very simple, actually. You just have to stop moving the plot forward."

"And how do I do that? No, scratch that! How would I even know if I *was* moving the plot forward without knowing what it is or even whether it exists?"

"I see two options," she said, holding up her fingers. "First, you could completely remove yourself from Joshua's circle and become an independent observer."

"That's not likely to happen," I told her frankly. I had already gone above and beyond the duty of a simple friend in order to keep everyone safe and working together, so completely abandoning them would've been the equivalent of flushing all my hard work down the drain. Not to mention, since Snowy was my sister at this point, and she was firmly entrenched in Josh's entourage, cutting ties would've meant abandoning the family.

"In that case, the second option," Judy began, then paused as she tried to bend only her middle finger. For some weird reason she couldn't seem to manage, so she used her other hand to bend it and then continued like nothing happened by saying, "The second option is that you let others, in this case Joshua in particular, move the plot in your stead. This alternative only requires that you loosen your iron grip on Joshua and the others."

"Wait, what?" I muttered as my brows involuntarily descended into a frown. "You are saying that like I'm some sort of tyrant…"

"No, not a tyrant," Judy acknowledged. "You are more like a mother hen."

"That's… not much better."

"If you don't allow them to progress the plot on their own, you cannot expect them to shoulder protagonist duties in your stead."

"True," I grudgingly admitted. I mean, I still didn't think I had an "iron grip" on the group, but at the same time letting them run free before I thought they were ready simply made me too worried for their safety, so… maybe I was acting like a mother hen after all? Damn.

"If you pick option two and want to shed your prospects of becoming the protagonist, I recommend you decide upon another role in the group, with a fitting character archetype to go along with it. I believe the 'idiot friend' position is still open."

"Ha. Ha. Ha. Very funny."

"Thank you, I'm trying," Judy answered with a teeny-weeny little smirk. "If that's out of the question, how about becoming a mentor?"

"No good." I shook my head. "They have a nasty habit of coming down with a sudden case of deathinitis."

"Are you sure?" She cocked her head to the side. "You are already fulfilling most of the criteria."

"I'm fairly sure that I'm not nearly old enough to become a mentor character," I retorted.

"I said 'most' of the criteria. Also, it's not a problem a fake beard couldn't fix. And I have a handy list of pithy yet profound last words I can mail over to you if you are interested."

"Thanks, but no thanks," I told her bluntly. "Also, hold your horses for a moment. Do I really have to try to adhere to some kind of character trope? Can't I just be myself?"

"You are yourself right now, and that's why you are worried you will turn into a protagonist," Judy answered while she unscrewed the top of the thermos and poured tea for us.

"Yes, but… do I *really* have to change up how I act? I mean, we already discussed how I should change my behaviour around the opposite sex to avoid further romantic complications, but this sounds uncomfortably more… comprehensive."

"Either that or, if you cannot stop yourself from meddling, you should do it more covertly and in a way that from the outside you wouldn't seem to be in the center of attention," she mused as she handed me a cup.

"Thank you," I spoke with a grateful smile, and took a sip from the warm beverage. "Getting out of the spotlight sounds way more reasonable."

"In that case, you should aim to become a Hypercompetent Sidekick."

"A sidekick to whom?"

"Joshua, obviously." She took a big sip from her tea and let out a satisfied sigh. Then she added, "Or if you want to be less obvious about it, you can always become an Almighty Janitor."

I gave my girlfriend a flat look. "I rue the day I introduced that trope site to you."

"No point crying over spilled milk," she told me coyly. "So, what will you be?"

I shook my head and groaned. "You know how much I hate considering people as walking character archetypes. Do you really think I want to purposefully become one?"

"You don't need to *become* one, only act like one in public. For example, you have already built up a reputation as an information broker. Use that as an excuse to stay back, support the others from the background, and let them deal with the villain of the week."

"For that to work, we will have to get Josh to the point where he could actually deal with something like that on his own."

Judy frowned. "You also need to put a stop to your Chronic Hero Syndrome."

I rolled my eyes at that. "Yeesh. That's way too much trope talk for one day."

Judy stuck out her tongue at me, the rest of her face completely aloof as usual, then she leaned closer to me and rested her head… well, not on my shoulder, but more against my upper arm, really.

"Fine. If you don't want further advice, I will proceed to our next order of business."

"Cuddling?" I asked, slightly apprehensive.

"Yes," she answered, rubbing her head against me. "We skipped the sanctioned cuddling time yesterday, so we should at least try to catch up to our quota."

"Be my guest, then," I yielded with a small chuckle, finding her unusual way of showing affection strangely amusing.

While I wasn't exactly satisfied with the results of this conversation, I had to admit that Judy's viewpoint was once again a valuable one. I didn't think I had something as silly as a "chronic hero syndrome" going on, but it was hard to deny that, in my mad scramble to ensure everyone's safety, I probably overdid things a little. Maybe toning back my efforts to maintain a semblance of control over the unfolding situation wasn't such a bad idea.

In fact, as much as I hated to admit it, Judy's suggestion of being an Almighty Janitor held a kind of juvenile attraction for me. I mean, who wouldn't want to be an underestimated, hidden badass who would show up in the nick of time to save the protagonist? Not to mention, it came with the benefit of, by definition, not being the protagonist. A win-win for me.

As to how to accomplish this, or at least pretend to be one… that was a question for another time.

Unfortunately, our tranquil little moment didn't last long, as the single roof access door was suddenly (and borderline violently) pushed open.

"There you are!" an exhausted and visibly irate class rep, dressed in her casual clothes, declared the moment she laid her eyes on us. Which, considering we were sitting on the bench right in front of the exit, wasn't a tough feat.

"Hi, class rep," I greeted her with a purposefully wooden expression.

"Don't *hi* me!" Ammy fumed as she stomped over. "Why are you here?"

That question made me glance at Judy, but she seemed to be as lost as I was, so I answered by stating the obvious.

"We're having lunch. Speaking of which, what are *you* doing here? I thought you had the day off."

"I would have, if someone would've just picked up his phone!" Ammy declared with a scowl aimed at me. I reached into my pocket to get my phone, and lo and behold, it indeed had about half a dozen missed calls on it.

"Oh? Sorry, I have my phone automatically muted during school hours. It's regulation, you know?"

"I know," the class rep fumed while placing her hands on her hips. "What I also want to know is why you are eating outside in the cold instead of in the cafeteria, like normal people!"

"It's not *that* cold, right, Judy?"

"I don't know, I'm being warmed," she responded by pointedly rubbing her head against my arms.

"You guys are very cute, but it doesn't change the fact that I had to run over the entire school to find you," Ammy continued to gripe, crossing her arms in front of her chest.

"Fine, I'm listening," I told her. "Why were you looking for us?"

"I wasn't the one looking for you," she denied immediately, much to my surprise. "Mr. Peabody wanted to see you for a medical examination."

"And he sent you to talk to me?"

"No, he told Grandfather, and *he* sent me to talk to you."

"Seriously? Are you the only person in the entire school than can be entrusted with any task?"

"Don't get me started!" Ammy began to fume once again as she sat down next to me, and complaints spilled out of her like smoke from a chimney. I glanced at Judy again, but she didn't seem to mind, so I listened to her woes. It didn't cost anything but time, and since it was our unscheduled cuddling time, anyway, it wasn't like I had anything better to do.

PART 3

The sound of the last bell of the day filled me with, of all things, trepidation, all thanks to a certain workaholic class representative. This might come off as a surprise, but I really, really didn't want to meet the weird school nurse with his annoying laugh and stupid mallet. Unfortunately for me, Ammy spent an uncomfortable amount of time nagging me about how I had to go there first thing after school before she left.

It might have been an exercise in delaying the inevitable, but I waited until Mrs. Applebottom left the classroom before I managed to will myself to my feet.

"Are we going to have another meeting at 'your place'?" Joshua asked me while packing his bag with one hand and making air quotes with the other.

"Yes," I told him.

"Are we going there right away?" Angie asked, hefting her own bag. "I have my spare clothes ready."

"No, I have to visit with someone first. Let's meet up at my house later."

"Really?" The Celestial girl leaned forward with an impish grin. "Are you having a clandestine meeting behind your girlfriends' backs already?"

My first reaction was to flick her forehead in retaliation, but then I recalled what I discussed with Judy about being way too casual about physical contact with girls. But then again, do forehead flicks actually count as physical contact? Not to mention, it was Angie we were talking about here. It wasn't as if a small gesture like that could be somehow misconstrued as flirting, right? In fact, considering our association was of the "good friends" variety, *not doing it* would have been more conspicuous than doing it!

Like that, I finally reasoned myself into inflicting light corporeal punishment on the nosy girl, but unfortunately getting there took so long I lost the opportunity to do so. One of my aforementioned girlfriends suddenly leaned into my field of vision, asking, "What were you talking about? Some kind of meeting?"

"Yeah," I answered the curious Elly with a smile, and since I had no reason to be reserved with her, I repurposed my flicking-finger into a poking one and I gently nudged her nose with it. "Don't worry; I'm only visiting the school nurse."

"Shouldn't that make me more worried?" She tilted her head to the side.

"Nah." I shook my own and told her, "It's probably something silly, like the last time."

"When was the last time?" Came the next question, though this time from my dear assistant, who made her way over to us in the meantime.

"It was... I think it was just around the time Elly transferred in."

"Now that I think about it," Josh mused while thoughtfully rubbing his chin. "The last time I saw him was when Judy got sick and had to be taken to the infirmary. I don't think I've met him ever since."

"Me, neither," Angie echoed his sentiment while mimicking his chin-rubbing, prompting Josh to poke her in the side. See? I wasn't the only one who wasn't reserved about physical contact! But then again, this was *Josh* we were talking about here, so if I wanted to avoid being a harem protagonist, maybe following his lead wasn't prudent.

Anyways, while the childhood friends entered into a silly little slap fight (which was cute and all, but when I looked at them, I could kind of understand why the haircut troupe considered him their rival), I shrugged and told no one in particular, "The school nurse is a rare and cautious animal. You are unlikely to meet it in the wild unless you walk into its lair."

Elly gave me a blank stare, but Judy just rolled her eyes, leaned closer to the draconic girl and whispered, "The Chief is doing a skit now. This is the point where you are supposed to either give a punch line or provide him with something he can follow up on to get to a punch line."

"Oooooh!" The princess's eyes opened wide in revelation. Then she glanced at me, then back at Judy, and asked, "So… what am I supposed to say now?"

"Something that fits," my assistant told her, nudging her forward. "Just say whatever comes to your mind, as we practiced."

I'd be lying if I said I wasn't curious about what Judy meant by "practice," but I decided not to interrupt. After a few seconds of hesitation, Elly finally looked me in the eye and asked, "So… um… is he… endangered?"

"Unfortunately, no," I answered without missing a beat. "School nurses are rare simply because they are very territorial, you see. So long as ours is here, no other would dare enter his territory."

"Then how do they breed?" Judy kept the ball rolling.

"Ah, I'm glad you asked," I told her with my best professorial smile. "You see, young lady, like all species of the Healthcareus Workeriensis genus, the School Nurse does all its breeding during a period colloquially referred to as 'college.' After they grow out of the college years and establish their territory, the common School Nurse is a rather solitary creature."

"Fascinating," Judy concluded with a profound nod.

Elly, on the other hand, only looked at us funny. "I just can't keep up with you two."

"You just need practice," Judy encouraged her with a few mechanical pats on the back, which was a surprisingly heartwarming sight.

In the meantime, the childhood friend duo also stopped bickering, so I turned to them and said, "In conclusion, I'll be visiting the nurse. I don't know how long it will take, so I want to ask you a favor."

"Ooookay," Josh answered in the positive, yet for some reason he seemed really guarded, as if he was expecting some kind of trick. "What is it?"

"Can I ask you guys to escort Snowy home?"

"Sure! We are going to your place, anyway," Angie answered in Josh's stead.

"Thanks. Just remember—if you catch even a whiff of an annoying monster huntress, press the button."

"Ugh," Josh groaned, rolling his eyes. "You have been repeating that line so many times it's going to show up in my dreams."

"Even if she only shows up in your dreams, you should still press the button," I told him with a smirk. I picked up my bag and added, "I will catch up to you guys as soon as I'm finished. Judy has my spare keys, so you should be able to get in."

"Since when do you have a key?" Elly questioned my assistant as I walked out, and I could hear the beginning of her explanation concerning how it was necessary because a certain someone broke my lock in the past. After I exited the classroom, I headed towards the nurse's office, weaving between the torrent of placeholders filling the familiar hallways.

At first, I didn't exactly know why, but as I walked, I started feeling something similar to déjà vu, and it took me a while to figure out what it was about. I recalled my first day in school, right after I woke up in this weird, terrifying, yet strangely interesting world, and how I just "followed my legs" and let them take me wherever I was supposed to go. Funnily enough, I realized I was doing something similar again, but this time not because I was lost and strangely compelled. Quite the opposite, really. I was walking on autopilot precisely because I was so familiar with the school at this point. It made me feel… happy wasn't the right word. Content? Maybe. It was a strange yet not at all unpleasant feeling of realizing that I had a familiar place where I felt grounded.

While pondering this, I reached the nurse's office before long, and for a few seconds, I lingered before the door, weighing my options. I had to admit I was honestly curious about what the annoying nurse wanted from me, but at the same time I was more than a little apprehensive about it, too. But as they say, nothing ventured, nothing gained!

Though again, they also say curiosity killed the cat…

I knocked on the door and soon heard a familiar voice from the other side.

"O-ho-ho. Come on in, it's open!"

"Oh great. I'm not even in yet, and I'm already annoyed," I quietly griped as I cautiously entered the infirmary.

The place was… exactly the same as the last time I came by. The portly man sitting by his desk was the same. He glanced over his shoulder when he heard the door open and gave me the same welcoming smile, then stood up and straightened his white coat.

"O-ho-ho. The dean said you would be coming over, but I didn't expect you would show up so early. What a pleasant surprise."

His mention of the dean gave me pause. Was the good nurse actually a mage under Lord Grandpa's payroll or just an ordinary school employee? I knew that the student council was apparently in on the whole masquerade, but I never asked the class rep about the man in front of me. Maybe it was time I poked him a little…

"Really? Did he get his door fixed yet?"

"Pardon?" Mr. Peabody muttered as he looked upon me with confusion. At least it wasn't a thousand-yard stare as in the past.

"I meant his underground study's big fancy door. I... heard someone might have accidentally broken it."

"Underground study?" The man's eyes went wide under his bushy eyebrows, then he let out another grating laugh and told me, "O-ho-ho. What a peculiar thing to say! Could it be your memories are still missing? But wait, even if they are, you should know that his office is on the first floor. Truly peculiar!"

His short outburst made me come to a dead halt as a cold shiver of recognition ran down my spine. After recollecting myself, I took a deep breath and tentatively asked him, "Now that you mention it, I told you about my amnesia, didn't I?"

"O-ho-ho. You most certainly did, and I most certainly didn't forget!" Mr. Peabody tapped his temple with his index finger and smiled affectionately. "Indeed, such an uncommon ailment is hard to forget."

"Did you tell Lo... I mean, did you tell the dean about it?"

The nurse gave me an odd look, then told me, with a deadly serious expression, "Young man! How could you think I would break my oath of medical confidentiality!"

"What oath?"

The nurse huffed. "The Hippocratic oath, of course. It is the most fundamental oath all health care providers must adhere to, and I will do so, as well. Wait, could it be that you didn't know because of you amne—?"

"No, not that," I cut him off. "I just thought it was some more specific oath instead of the Hippocratic one because you made it sound like it was a huge deal."

"O-ho-ho! But it is a big deal, isn't it? Do you think I want to be hunted down by the Brotherhood of Hippocrates for my breach of the oath?"

"Wait, what?" I blurted out.

Mr. Peabody looked me in the eye with a dead serious expression... for about a second. Then he burst into an especially high-pitched version of his signature grating laughter.

"O-HO-HO! I'm only joking, young man! Don't worry, there is no chance such an organization would—"

"Stop right there!" I exclaimed while pointing at him, visibly startling him. "Don't deny it outright because that's just tempting fate. Don't talk about it, either, because that just increases the chances that it'll become real. Just keep silent, move on, and pretend you never even made that joke. Are we clear?"

I must have looked at least half as hysterically angry as I felt at the moment, because the nurse immediately nodded in the affirmative. Good. The last thing I needed to complicate this world (and my life by extension) was a secret brotherhood of assassin doctors running around.

Once I recollected my nerves into a semblance of stability, I took a deep breath and asked, "So, why did you want to see me?"

"Well, to be perfectly honest, while I did want to talk with you, I didn't expect you would show up so soon," the still slightly apprehensive nurse explained while gesturing for me to take a seat. "However, Mr. Amadeus said that I should conduct a comprehensive medical survey if you were to come here, so why don't we do just that?"

"Is that really necessary?"

"O-ho-ho. I was told you suffered some injuries not too long ago. Is that right?"

"Well, yes…"

"O-ho-ho. And I was also told you didn't visit the hospital, right?"

"No, I didn't…"

"Oh-ho-ho. Then I would say it is very, very necessary."

Letting out a defeated sigh, I complied by taking a seat on the bed. Peabody let out another, supremely grating chuckle and rummaged through the various cabinets in the room, retrieving all kinds of tool and medical instruments, and piled them on his desk.

Right. So, he wasn't joking when he said he wanted to do a *full* checkup. The process, which started rather innocently by measuring my height and weight, escalated until I found myself lying half naked on the bed with a series of wires with suction cups attached to me, and the alleged medical professional making profound humming noises while fiddling with an EKG machine. Under normal circumstances, I might have questioned why on God's green earth a high school infirmary would have an EKG machine, but by now, I felt that pointing out such mundane idiosyncrasies was beneath me.

Anyhow, the whole medical survey lasted about an hour, and after we were done, Peabody finally took off the electrodes and allowed me to stand up and get dressed.

"How fascinating," he murmured while looking over the page where he was collecting my results. I had a feeling that he was speaking up just to prompt me to ask, but since I was tired of dealing with him, I decided not to try to engage in any mind games and addressed him right away.

"How are my results?"

"Outstanding," he told me straightaway. "Are you part of the track club, by any chance?"

"No, I'm not."

"Really? O-ho-ho. How curious. Your records are like that of a professional athlete, so I thought you must have practiced regularly."

"Well, I do my fair share of push-ups every day, but I'm certainly not an athlete," I told him just as I finished dressing up. "I gather there were no problems with my vitals."

"O-ho-ho. None at all," he reassured me and glanced over me one more time. "Both your physical condition and your parameters seem to be perfect. Those old scars bother me a little, but there isn't much we can do about them. Although, on second thought, I believe I could introduce you to a great plastic surgeon."

"Thanks, but no thanks. If everything is fine, can I go now?"

Peabody took another look at my results and nodded.

"Certainly. If not for the dean's insistence, I would have never thought you were injured." He paused, then asked, "Were you?"

"It wasn't a big deal," I answered dismissively. I even meant it, since if he thought my injuries from a week ago were old and his biggest concern was about how they looked, I felt entirely justified in calling them flesh wounds. Speaking of which, why is it a "flesh" wound? Wouldn't that mean that the injury cut into one's, well, flesh? That sounds serious, so why is it used to *dismiss* injuries?

My random irritation at silly phrases aside, I decided it was high time I left, so I said my goodbyes and left before the good nurse suddenly recalled another test to perform. My stay in the infirmary lasted longer than I'd expected, but shorter than I feared, and now I was reassured that the secret of my amnesia was being kept confidential.

Nah, who am I kidding? While he was ever so slightly less annoying than the last time I met him, I wouldn't trust the nurse as far as I could throw him. And considering how fat he was, that wasn't far. Since most of the tests required some amount of physical contact, I naturally marked him for Far Sight and planned to keep tabs on his activities in the near future, just to be on the safe side.

Once I left the good nurse's company, I took my sweet time getting to the shoe lockers, most of which was actually spent wondering just why we even had them. It wasn't like the island had a custom for taking one's shoes off indoors, so having to switch shoes in school actually stood out quite a bit.

As far as I knew, this was a Japanese thing, or at the very least it was most commonly seen in Japanese school life settings, so maybe the custom existed here just because of that. Not to mention, the whole *love letter in the shoe locker* cliché, of which I was already on the receiving end more than once (though neither notes were actual love letters, now that I thought about it), just wouldn't work without an *actual shoe locker.*

But then again, didn't Judy recently theorize that the school itself was largely unimportant in the grand scheme of things? If so, then why would the Narrative go out of its way to include lockers? Just to facilitate the cliché? Or maybe there was some other reason?

...

Wow. Look at me now, seriously considering the existence and intentions of the nebulous Narrative... Judy's insistence must have begun to rub off on me.

Anyhow, I finished putting on my outdoor shoes and I was just about to walk through the main entrance when my musings were interrupted with dramatic abruptness by a siren. I twitched in surprise, but managed to regain my cool and take out my phone.

"Crap. I didn't expect it would be so soon," I muttered, attempting to keep my rising anxiety in check. "The ID is... number three, so... Judy?"

That was ever so slightly shocking, but I didn't dwell on it and—while refusing to give a flying Fudgsicle about the fact that I was standing in a doorway with placeholders giving me odd looks—I jumped into Far Sight. After a very short, and by now not even particularly disorienting, change of scenery, I found myself looking at my somewhat disheveled assistant accompanied by an equally scruffy Angie. They were half-hidden in the back of a shopping district alley that I recognized from our daily commute. Even more troublingly, I couldn't see anyone else.

My first instinct was to immediately transfer over there, but I reined in the impulse and instead I turned on my heel and dashed into the nearest toilet on the ground floor. This also turned a few placeholder heads, but considering the circumstances, I am sure they would understand why I didn't give a bloody damn about them.

Once inside a stall, I used Far Sight again, and a moment later, I reappeared not too far from the two of them. I briefly contemplated doing something flashy, like appearing right behind them, or on a nearby rooftop from whence I could swoop down like a certain nocturnal echo-locating flying mammal man, but I quickly discarded the idea, or rather I shelved it for a less uncertain occasion.

"What's the situation?" I asked in a calm yet stern voice that didn't reflect my actual state of mind at all, my eyes covertly scanning the perimeter for any signs of the monster huntress.

"Oh, my Deus!" Angie exclaimed in a borderline shriek as she shoved Judy behind her back. Now that I looked at her in person, I realized that she wasn't wearing her school uniform anymore but a set of gym clothes.

Now, I wasn't a detective or anything, but even a cursory observation like that told me a few things. First off, it meant she probably had to transform to her combat gear in a hurry, vaporized her school uniform, and then she had to change into her spare outfit afterwards. That meant she'd been in a combat situation until not too long ago, but the fact that she had the time and leisure to undo the transformation and then change her clothes meant that the crisis was already over. Furthermore, while she looked a little rattled (though I had no idea how much of that had to do with my unexpected appearance), she was unharmed, so I reckoned that whatever incident must have happened, it wasn't the life-threatening kind. After concluding my deduction with that, I let the tension seep out of my shoulders… right until I was startled by a certain Celestial girl.

"Where did you come from? We just called you!" Angie exclaimed with a glower and a foot stomp. "You scared me so bad, I almost transformed!"

"Sorry. I was already on my way," I told her before glancing around again, pointedly ignoring her tantrum. "Where are the others?"

"Inside the Restricted Space," Judy informed me while swiping her phone. I paused for a moment, and true enough, a quick immersion into Far Sight told me that the others were indeed nearby, except not really.

"I gather there was a battle, then. Did she attack you?" I asked a question I thought was fairly obvious, but to my surprise, she shook her head. "What? Then what happened?"

"It's hard to describe," Angie told me after she finally calmed down a tad, though she still cautiously glanced around. "We were going to your house when we were pulled into a Restricted Space. There was an entire group waiting for us there and they ambushed us."

"What kind of group?"

"About twenty identical robots led by this man," Judy answered, showing me her phone screen. Truth be told, I couldn't decide whether I should praise my girlfriend's mental fortitude for staying collected and taking a snapshot of the attackers, or chide her for mismatched priorities while in danger.

In the end, I decided both praises and reproaches had to wait, and instead I focused on the photo on the screen. In the middle of the image, there was a fairly short, slender man. He was wearing a white lab coat strategically torn at its edges so that it would appear wild instead of just sloppy. He also had a shaggy mane of black hair, and his face was entirely covered by… well, the closest thing I could liken it to was a welding mask, except instead of the single rectangular visor in the middle, it had two circular holes on it with what looked like a pair of swirly party goggles set in them.

That was weird enough, even by the recent standards of this world, but then I noticed the alleged robots in the background. Let's just say that if I was drinking just then, I would have done a spit-take, cliché be damned.

"Okay, I have to see this in person," I stated before I vanished and reappeared in the same alley, except it was all purple. I did so in Angie's view, but I already knew that moving in and out of the Purple Zone was similar to my teleportation, so I felt confident in excusing myself to her. Anyhow, I walked out on to the street, and I found myself face-to-face with a startling amount of destruction. Practically all the storefronts on my left were wrecked with glass scattered all over the ripped-up sidewalk paving stones. The road ahead of me had actual craters on it, and just on my left, I could see the bent remains of a streetlamp torn from the ground. Furthermore, all over the place, both in the ground and in the walls, were dozens of long, translucent ice spears that somehow, against all the laws of physics, managed to embed themselves into solid concrete and brick walls like they were made of play dough.

I would have continued to drink in the scenery, oddly fascinated by its savaged state, but I was stopped in my tracks when I laid eyes on a certain *thing*. It looked exactly the same as in the picture Judy showed me, except ice spears pinned to a wall like the ugliest butterfly in someone's bug collection.

The robot, to use Judy's terminology, was humanoid in shape. It was also covered in lime green spandex from head to toe, except for what looked like a large, stylized cogwheel on its chest. It also had a matching pair of black leather boots and gloves, reaching up to its knees and elbows, respectively, and decorated with a series of silver spikes. Its head had no eyes; instead, it was covered with something like a motorcycle helmet with a black and blue decoration that, at a cursory glance, looked kind of like the zodiac sign for Pisces. Moreover, it was grasping a large, weirdly proportioned butcher's knife in one of its hands, its gloved fingers still holding it tightly even after its obvious demise.

Now, I wasn't one to jump to conclusions, but after some preliminary observations, I had to conclude that it looked, without a shadow of a doubt, incredibly stupid. More alarmingly, it looked eerily familiar, though I couldn't remember why.

I didn't have much time to think, though, as my attention was drawn to a small group huddled around one of the slightly less wrecked parts of the scenery. It didn't take them long to notice me, either, and when they did, Elly rushed towards me so hard, I was afraid she'd tackle me off my feet.

Thankfully, she managed to stop her momentum just in time, and instead she exclaimed, "Leo! You won't believe what just happened!"

"Won't I?" I jested as the rest of the group also made their way over to me. Elly was no longer transformed, yet the damage to her clothes showed that she probably hadn't shied away from whatever combat had unfolded here. Snowy, on the other hand, was still in her Abyssal form. If I had to guess, I would have said it was because she also transformed in a hurry like Angie, except she didn't have any spare clothes to change into. She also looked unusually sheepish, but I couldn't spare the time to ask her about it. More importantly, both of them seemed to be entirely uninjured.

The same could not be said about the last member of the group. Josh was also still transformed, into his own Abyssal form, and he was only wearing his inexplicably vaporization-proof Hulk pants. He also didn't have any major injuries, but based on the number of scrapes and bruises on his skin, he was obviously worse off than the girls.

"I gather this had nothing to do with the monster huntress?" I asked them.

"No." Snowy promptly shook her head.

"So, it really is a brand-new flavour of what-the-hell. Lovely," I muttered, ending it with a groan. "Can you tell me what just happened?"

What followed my question was several minutes of disjointed, often-times contradictory testimonies, including some overly dramatic battle descriptions, replete with sound effects. After they finished, I took another huge breath, held it in for a moment, and then let it out in the mother of all sighs.

"So, just to summarize," I began while absentmindedly rubbing my temple. "You got dragged into the purple zone. You got challenged by some guy calling himself 'Dr. Robatto' and his minions called the 'Sprockets.' Then he said he had something really important to do and left without telling you *why* he challenged you. Then you fought his minions, who were waving butcher knives but never managed to hit any of you, until there were none left standing. Is that the gist of it?"

"Yes," Josh approved my summary. "We also tried to look for Dr. Robatto after the fight, but he was gone."

"He probably left the Restricted Space very early on," Snowy theorized.

"Two questions," I raised my hand with two fingers outstretched. "First off, why didn't you call me right away?"

"You cannot call people on the outside while you're in a Restricted Space, silly!" the princess explained with a cheeky smile and wrapped her arms around me. I had a hunch that she was unusually giddy because she was still riding on the adrenaline high after the battle, so I didn't protest. Instead, I just clicked my tongue as I realized this was another blind spot I hadn't considered before, which made my clever solution with the emergency app significantly less useful than I'd hoped.

"The second question," I asked grumpily while dramatically bending one of my fingers. "Why are you still in here?"

"We don't have spare clothes," Josh told me with a shrug. He was surprisingly less upset than I'd expected, but I figured it wasn't exactly a bad thing.

"We told Judy and Angie to go out and call you and bring us something to wear," Snowy elaborated, earning her a small nod from me.

"I see," I began, only to be immediately interrupted by a high-pitched sneeze from the girl still embracing me. I glanced at her and then said, "I suppose I better do that before you all catch a cold."

"To be honest, I don't really feel it," Josh stated absentmindedly, only for his body to abruptly shudder and shrink as his transformation ended. He gave me a wide-eyed look for a second, then he amended, "Actually, never mind what I just said. I would really appreciate some clothes after all," his words accented by his teeth chattering.

I gently unwrapped Elly's arms from around my waist.

"All right, I'll be quick. Stay put and keep each other warm."

I ignored the easily misinterpretable nature of my comment and hastily walked back into the alley, where I immediately and unceremoniously teleported behind Angie and Judy again.

"Dormouse, walk with me," I instructed her while conveniently ignoring the startled Celestial girl giving me the evil eye. Or rather I would have, but then I remembered I needed someone to be on teleport anchor duty, so I told her, "Angie, please hold the fort. We are going to be back in a few minutes."

"Whatever," she pouted in response while folding her arms. I really wasn't in the mood for this, so I added, in lieu of the proverbial carrot, "Once everyone's dressed, let's go and have some snacks to let the events sink in a little. You pick the place."

"Really?" Her eyes sparkled, her previous grudge all but forgotten.

"Sure," I told her with a nod before gesturing for Judy to follow, and we hurried away.

Once we were out of sight, I cleared my throat and told her, with my calmest voice, "Judy, I hope you are aware that what just happened means war."

My dear assistant sent me a surprised glance and stated, "You probably don't mean a war against Dr. Robatto."

"No, of course not," I scoffed. "I meant a war against your Narrative."

Judy's eyes opened wide, and she said, deadpan yet astonished, "You are serious."

"Of course I am," I answered through gritted teeth. "Say what you will about harem shenanigans and shounen battles—at least those I can stomach. But look at what we've got here! A stupid-looking villain leading an army of equally stupid-looking and ineffectual goons that get defeated in minutes by a group of overbearing and emotional teenagers. Does that ring any bells?"

"Is it that series with the morphing time and the annoying robot?"

"Yeah," I growled. "And I'll be damned before I just roll over and allow this world to *genre shift us into a bloody* sentai!"

CHAPTER 16

PART 1

A simple thrust down on the right, then a sharp swing back up and diagonally to the left. Keep up the momentum by spinning the spear overhead once and cut down diagonally from the other side. Pull back with a half-step and level the shaft with the ground, bend the knees, and jab forward. Pull back before it becomes a full lunge and parry counterclockwise, then chain that into a low stab. Use the momentum to sidestep left while pulling the spear back overhead. Feint a high stab, then change it up in the last second into a horizontal swipe.

Swish. Swish. Swish. My battered yet reliable training spear made a soft whistling noise every time it cut empty air. There was no profound technique behind my movements. In fact, there wasn't much in terms of rhyme or reason in them to begin with. I wasn't fighting an imaginary opponent, either; I simply moved for the sake of moving my body, chaining one strike into another based on nothing but instinct and how comfortable the movement felt at the moment. There was nothing deep about it; neither was I in some kind of meditative trance or anything. I was simply exercising to let off some steam, and ho boy, did I have a lot of pent-up steam to work out!

At last, after about fifteen minutes of intense sparring with thin air, I finished my impromptu training session by setting the butt of the spear against the concrete floor with a *thud*. I wiped my forehead with the sleeve of my sweater and, fittingly enough, I was sweating so much, I looked like I'd just run a marathon in the Sahara Desert.

"[The form of thy spearmanship is remarkable as ever, Blackcloak,]" Brang grunted and handed me a clean towel with the nonchalant familiarity of a local gym trainer looking after the newbie. I graciously received it and this time I wiped my whole face. While I did that, the Faun ex-general continued to play his role by reminding me, "[I beseech thee to rest, or thy body will suffer.]"

"I know," I answered, handing the towel back to him. "I'm just about done."

He gave me a small nod, and while his expression didn't change, his eyes were strangely affectionate. Was this what people called 'smiling eyes'? When he looked at me like that, I could kind of understand why Snowy called him her uncle. Under all the fur and muscle and creepy ram features, he was kind of grandfatherly… if you squinted hard enough.

But enough of that. I set the spear against the wall by the improvised weapon storage the Faun constructed from some spare lockers. Speaking of them, I turned on my heel and looked over the mook squad, who were also training in the spacious main hall inside the shelter.

"[I request your presence! Come forth at once!]"

The Faun all stopped in their tracks (though, since most of them were doing Dominance training, they weren't moving around much to begin with) and sent me some questioning glances. But soon they joined Brang in a tidy line right in front of me. By the expectant looks in their eyes, I had a feeling they knew what I wanted to tell them.

Adopting my best drill sergeant impression, I said, "[Hear me, and hear me well! Aware as you are, I shall echo the events of the not so distant past, for their weight is one that we shall bear for a long while. My kindred suffered the perils of an ambush most craven, right within the heart of our home of concrete and steel.]" I paused for a moment, and after some hesitation, I decided to go with the third explanation I came up with during my exercise. "[The governors of our land, the wingless leeches of the veins of the silver essence, act as a gaggle of incompetent buffoons at best, or may not even be feigning at worst. Thus, we shall not entrust our safety into their hands.]"

"[Wingless what of what?]" Hrul muttered, and Rabom shrugged.

"[Leeches, I think. I didn't get the second half, eith—]" he whispered back, only to freeze up when he noticed I was looking at him.

"[Hold thy tongue and heed my words,]" I warned him with a frown, and he averted his eyes with an almost bashful expression. "[As you are absconders in the eyes of the loathsome vassals of the raven-haired one, I have long wished to conceal your presence from the ever-prying eyes of the outside world, yet the irksome state of affairs surrounding us leave me with nary a choice but to set your wings free in the night.]"

"[What is thy command, Lord Blackcloak?]" Brang cut in eagerly. He placed his clenched right fist against his broad chest in a salute, a gesture the rest of the group followed, if a little less quickly. As for me, I couldn't help but employ the tried and tested combination of an eye roll and groan to express just how bloody annoyed I was about all this.

"[For times uncountable and more, cease your incessant attempts to hang yet more superfluous titles upon my person!]"

Brang didn't respond with words, but merely gave me an amused smile, obviously not taking my protest seriously at all. I suppressed my indignation and made a mental note to give him an earful after this briefing was over, following which I turned towards the rest again.

"[Let us return to the true substance of our discussion. A request, nay, a *mandate*, I do possess. Faun of the House Inanna, I—]"

"[Inanna-Dunning,]" Karukk corrected me in such an innocently helpful tone, then added, "[We are serving the young lady, and she now has your name, so technically we are—]"

"[Cease thine interruptions, or you shall oblige me to insert my hind limb into thy hole of excretion so deep, it shall take you weeks to wash the taste of boot leather from out of thy mouth!]"

Karukk shot me a comical look, and in retrospect, I realized that my words might have been a smidgen more graphic than I originally intended, so I hastily cleared my throat.

"[Those words you shall not mind. In their stead, heed my words once more, for I shall call to a halt the superfluous walloping of the vicinity of the shrubbery! You shall all scour the lands surrounding my home with prejudice of the most excessive variety. I require you to seek any and all traces of the eastern slayer of phantasmal beings, the furtive creature she seeks, or the preposterous lifeless constructs in lemony colours menacing my kin. For this purpose, you shall be allowed to leave the walls of this subterranean fortress at your own discretion. If you possess inquires, voice them now.]"

"[What do we do if we find any of them?]" Pip asked.

"[Observe, track, report. If discovered, elude pursuit.]"

I glanced over the group, but they didn't seem to have any other questions. I hoped it was because they were professional enough that my instructions were sufficient. Anyhow, I exhaled a long breath and told them, "[I leave your methods up to your preference,]" as my way of ending the briefing before turning around and heading towards the far corner of the hall, or more specifically to the makeshift bench over there. It had a set of empty lunch boxes on it, which incidentally used to contain my dinner. At first, I wanted to teleport back home right away, but on second thought, I decided to sit down for a moment first.

The reason why I was all alone (save for the Fauns) was fairly simple: I needed some time by myself to calm down a little. I was simply too restless to think straight.

After the most recent incident was definitely over, I gathered a change of clothes for Josh, Snowy, and Elly. Strangely enough, even though they were just recently ambushed, they insisted I uphold my promise with Angie and take them out to the local sweets shop.

That was taking things in stride a little too easily, if you asked me, but then it turned out that Josh himself was, I kid you not, completely hyped up by the whole ordeal. It probably had something to do with him trashing a couple of those Sprocket things, at least according to Snowy's description of the events. Ugh, just remembering those atrocities against good taste and competent minion design made me shake with barely restrained indignation.

Anyhow, over the span of our stay at the confectionery, it became blindingly apparent that the people who were actually ambushed were not shaken by the ordeal at all, while I, the person who wasn't even in the same neighbourhood at the time, was feeling dangerously stressed out by the events. Because of this, after we all returned home and they recounted the incident one more time, I excused myself and hopped over to the secret base to... well, I actually told them I did it because I had to think by myself, but it was honestly to do that exact opposite.

I emptied my head, immersed myself in swinging my spear, and let out some steam. And it worked. But while I was no longer a bundle of nerves, I was still far from being the next incarnation of the Buddha. It must've shown on my face, as before I knew it, I had everyone's favourite Faun ex-general walking towards me with a curious yet somewhat worried expression.

I know it's not exactly the best moment to point it out, but just why the hell were Faun faces so expressive, anyway? You'd think that a genetically engineered race of hyper-muscular goat/ram/whatever hybrid shock troopers would be completely stern and unreadable, but instead they were walking, talking open books. Though again, apparently only Snowy and I could read them so well, so maybe it had more to do with our aptitude than their expressiveness. I was tempted to believe it was more of a mix of the two. Still, after a while it was hard to take them seriously as proud and honourable warriors when even their leader kept making goofy faces.

Brang studied me in silence for a couple of seconds and then let out a shallow growl.

"[What burdens thy shoulders, Blackcloak?]"

I was tempted to just explode in the guy's face, but after taking a *painfully* deep breath, I managed to keep my calm. If he hadn't gotten the memo about the whole "Blackcloak" moniker being my very own berserk button yet, I figured explaining it to him in a quiet and not at all raving mad manner one more time wouldn't do it, either.

Just let it go, I told myself. Then, letting out the breath that threatened to burst my lungs (why did I even think this was a good idea?), I told him, "It's complicated."

"[Are you troubled by the unforeseen assailants?]" he guessed.

I shrugged. "You could say that, yes."

"[Vigilance is a matter of great importance, yet I must confess, by the heiress's recounting, her ambushers posed but the feeblest threat to her and her company.]"

I gave the big, friendly creature of campfire scare tales a sidelong glance, then told him, "Not all threats are physical. This one poses more of a… metaphysical problem."

Brang's ears swiveled in obvious perplexity, so I explained.

"What I wanted to say was that, even if those bloody ridiculous-looking robot things posed absolutely no threat to us, the mere fact that they exist in the first place is causing me a lot of headaches."

"[I understand,]" Brang grunted, though his tone implied he still had no idea what I was talking about and wasn't invested enough in the conversation to pry any further. "[I advise you not to let such pains of thy head sap thy vitality. Nay, if I may be so presumptuous, I shall urge you to take good care of thy health, for as regent, thy wellness of being is the wellness of the House Inanna-Dunning.]"

After he finished speaking, for a couple of long seconds, I stared at him in deafening silence. He didn't seem to get the clue, though he must have realized there was something wrong, as his ears kept swiveling left and right.

I closed my eyes, took a deep breath, and after looking him in the eyes again, I asked him, in my most discreet voice, "Excuse me, but could you repeat that? Specifically the last part?"

Brang tilted his head, his face set in a mixture of incomprehension and curiosity, and repeated, "[Thou art the regent of House Inanna-Dunning, indeed.]"

"Since when?" I asked back sharply.

"[Thou hast taken custody of our young heiress, and she adopted thy name in return. After arrangements such as these, the conferral of regency until the young heiress comes of age is all but a formality. I knew the surface of thy mind, Blackcloak, and so I reckoned thou eschewed to observe the ceremonies of old, yet I never for a heartbeat doubted thy legitimacy. Were my deliberations in error?]"

I gave the befuddled Faun a long, hard, critical look, yet he seemed to be in earnest.

"So, the reason why you called me 'Lord' before was because…?" I nudged him a little.

"[While I'm aware that you do not ascribe much weight to the traditional approach of leadership we are familiar with, my age and experience both tell me that some modicum of hierarchy must be maintained for the younger ones to fulfill their duties with the vigor and dedication expected of them.]"

"I see…" I muttered as my hand reached for my temple practically on its own. I could feel another, not-so-literal headache coming. "How about we come back to this discussion later? Preferably when Snowy is also with us?"

"[As you wish,]" Brang answered with a small bow.

Taking this as my cue to call it a day, I stood back up and limbered up my shoulders.

"I think I'll get going now. Please do as we just discussed. Make the huntress your first priority, then the ambushers, and then the stray Chimera."

The big Faun flashed a toothy grin and gave me a vigorous salute.

"[As you command.]"

I rolled my eyes at his theatrics and, without any further ado, I left the secret base the usual way.

"I'm back," I greeted Judy after reappearing in my living room. It was a testament to her adaptability that she barely batted an eye at my unexpected arrival.

"Welcome home, Chief." She glanced up from her notes (as in, actual dead-tree-pulp-based ones for a change) and greeted me back, only for her to stop and look me over. "You're sweaty. Go take a shower."

"That's the plan," I responded while stretching my back. "When did the others leave?" I asked more out of courtesy than actual curiosity, as I kept tabs on them via Far Sight and saw them leave.

"About an hour ago," she responded offhandedly while holding a stack of pages vertically and hitting the edge against the tabletop. "Eleanor wanted to wait for you, but I kicked her out."

"That's a rude thing to do."

"But necessary," she countered while organizing another bundle… of empty papers. It made sense that she didn't need to write a lot of things down, considering her excellent memory, but then why did she even bother? Maybe it was just to create the right atmosphere? Sometimes my assistant's thought processes felt completely impenetrable.

In the end, I shrugged and headed upstairs. After a quick and refreshing shower, I changed into a fresh set of clothes and walked back downstairs with a towel thrown over my head.

"That's better," Judy stated after laying eyes on me. She gestured for me to sit beside her. I graciously declined the offer and instead took a seat on my usual, if slightly battered, comfy chair. In my opinion, it was more productive to have discussions face-to-face.

"I hereby open today's emergency meeting," I stated a little dourly.

"Present." Judy raised her hand as she responded.

"Are you prepared?" I asked her as my eyes conspicuously scanned over the stacks of mostly empty pages in front of her, and she nodded. "Very well. As we agreed beforehand, you're in charge of the Doylist side of things, as usual, while I will focus on the Watsonian explanations, also as usual."

Judy nodded in agreement, and I took a deep breath in preparation.

Now, some might be curious about what the heck we actually agreed on just now. In short, after the world threatened to flip its setting upside down on my head, I concluded that, if I wanted to keep up, I'd have to compromise my stance on the meta-narrative.

I still wasn't ready to jump headlong into subversive, meta-knowledge exploiting shenanigans yet, so for the time being I proposed a new way to analyze our surroundings and the events. Since she already had an affinity for it, I tasked Judy with proposing meta-analysis, while I would stick to the more common sense explanations.

As for the terminology, it actually comes from Sir Arthur Conan Doyle's *Sherlock Holmes* stories, and they are usually invoked to explain plot holes and inconsistencies. To give a concise explanation, let's try an example.

Sherlock Holmes is a great detective. He is smart, knowledgeable, intuitive, a habitual pipe smoker, and a bit of a smug douche, but that last part is not relevant in this example.

Let's say our super-detective walks into a crime scene. A poor bloke is dead all over the dinner table. Our dear Holmes then looks over the scene and picks up the half empty (or half full, if you are an optimist) wine glass from the table, and just by taking one whiff, he deduces its brand and year based on its aroma alone, much to the awe and wonder of a certain Watson who tends to hang around the guy. So far, so clichéd.

Then, a few chapters later, after interrogating a bunch of people (even though if he was as smart as he thinks he is, he would know that the butler did it, because it's *always* the butler) and some misadventures (during which he may or may not get high as a kite), he figures out that the hapless victim was assassinated by cyanide in his wine, a compound that has a distinct smell similar to almonds, and one that a super-duper-the-best-thing-since-sliced-bread detective would surely notice... or would he? How does one reconcile these two seemingly contradictory elements?

The Watsonian explanation would use in-universe elements to explain away the inconsistency, just as a character in the story, say, a certain Dr. Watson would do. The idea is that, if you asked him the question, *Hey, did Holmes just screw the pooch?* then the poor, psychologically conditioned tagalong would obviously try to excuse him with all his might.

For a start, he could say that the aroma of the wine was so strong it masked the smell of the cyanide. Sure, that's plausible. Then, alternatively, he could point at an earlier scene where Holmes sneezed as he walked into the building, proposing that he had a stuffy nose and in fact couldn't smell anything, meaning his grand deduction was just a show he put on for the onlookers, and he actually knew the vintage of the wine by recognizing the open bottle on the same table, the cheating git.

On the other end of the spectrum, we have the Doylist explanation, which is based not on the story and its elements, but the author and the quirks of storytelling.

In this interpretation, Holmes didn't make note of the faint scent of almonds because the author himself wasn't aware of the fact that the poison has a characteristic smell to it. Alternatively, he was aware, but he wanted to have a specific scene where Holmes amazes his onlookers with his all-encompassing knowledge and decided to fudge this small detail, hoping his readers would skim over it and it wouldn't impact the overall experience. And then, of course, one could even argue for authorial genius by noting that cyanide actually smells like *bitter almonds*, so Holmes's inability to smell and/or recognize it is actually just the author showing off their research in a roundabout way only the *true connoisseurs* of the literary arts could appreciate.

In other words, one method was concerned with explaining events and inconsistencies using available in-universe evidence, while the other invoked authorial intent and narrative devices to do the same. It sounds complicated, but it's actually pretty straightforward.

That said, I took a huge breath and began.

"Let's start from the very beginning and open with a topic we already partially discussed."

"Namely?"

"The big conflict with Crowey at the school," I clarified.

"I presume that we are in agreement that it was the climax," Judy proposed.

"More or less, though the question of 'the climax of what' is still not clear."

"In my perspective, it was for the school life period of the narrative," Judy told me with confidence. "It existed to violently expose Joshua to the supernatural elements of the setting. It was also a contrived situation designed so that only our group could resolve it."

"You say 'contrived,' but all of the elements that lead to the situation make internal sense," I countered. "They kidnapped Josh because they were privy to his significance in the prophecy. It took place at the school and at a time when no one was around to stop him because Crowey was flexing his 'genius' scheming abilities and chose the time and place in advance on purpose. All of this makes sense in context."

"True," Judy conceded the point. But then she said, "However, it is also true that all the major supernatural players conveniently vacated the island on the same night, as if just to allow him free rein, and Neige's suspicious activities were ignored both by the mages and us."

"Please don't say narrative influence," I muttered, though I was already certain of her answer.

"But that is the most obvious explanation," she told me with a tiny frown. "Why do you keep denying it?"

"Because it is such a broad term that if I accepted it at face value, it would mean literally every single one of our actions could be the result of it."

"In that case, let's narrow it down," my assistant compromised. "We already theorized that people are subject to a certain level of perception filtering regarding the more obvious peculiarities of the world, such as placeholder behaviour. Let us presume that it also applies to us to some degree."

"So, the idea is that any time we realize something that would drastically change some predetermined event, our perception would be compromised to keep us in the dark," I mused aloud, and then, after a short but meaningful silence, I continued, "So, theoretically speaking, let's say I would've taken Snowy's odd behaviour seriously and investigated it. What would've happened?"

Now it was Judy's turn to fall silent as she considered things in earnest.

"You would've stopped her preparations for the barrier. Without the barrier in place, Noire would've had to abort his plans, meaning Joshua wouldn't have been initiated into the supernatural elements of the setting, meaning the whole scenario would've been set back at best or completely ruined at worst."

"So, your hypothesis is that narrative influence isn't random, but a subtle form of railroading?"

"Please define your terms," Judy cut in with a prompt she occasionally used in the past whenever I spoke about unfamiliar tropes.

"Railroading is a term originating from tabletop role-playing games, where one participant takes up the role of the storyteller responsible for creating a scenario for the rest. When the players go too far out of the bounds of the plot the storyteller devised, they might try to put them back on the right track by force if necessary. Say, if the ragtag, low-level adventurers wanted to go left at an intersection, but the game master wanted them to go right, he might subtly influence them to go in the *correct direction* by, for example, dropping a hydra on them and having it chase them there."

"Thank you, that was very informative." She showed her appreciation with a small smile, but then reverted to serious mode. "But back to the original topic: if we grant that, would it mean that any occurrence of such perception filtering would serve as a strong indication that the event or situation that triggered it is crucial for the Narrative's progression?"

"That's an interesting idea," I pondered for a moment. "Would that mean that, so long as we could reliably detect them as they occur instead of in retrospect, we could use them to get a handle on our elusive Narrative?"

"Possibly. We should devise a testing protocol for that. We are already behind our monthly testing quota."

I didn't respond right away, but when I did, my brows skyrocketed. "Wait, since when do we have a quota? I don't remember explicitly agreeing on one."

"I had one from the very beginning, because at least one of us had to take things seriously," Judy told me with just a hint of smugness. "It was on hold until now because of your injury and the incidents since then."

"Really? Then I guess we have some catching up to do," I told her while rubbing my chin, then I used the same hand to lightly point at her and added, "Also, that was as good a segue as any, so we might as well discuss the recent events." I leaned forward in my seat and asked, "How would you categorize the current situation from a meta-perspective?"

"I'm not entirely sure," Judy replied thoughtfully, "but based on how the incidents progressed, there seem to be at least two main plot threads running in parallel."

"What are you thinking of when you say 'plot'?"

"A preplanned, interrelated sequence of events that leads or drags us towards the next plot point."

"I can work with that," I told her. "And I presume the two main plotlines you are talking about are related to the monster huntress and the ambushers."

"Indeed. Both are external elements that came into existence just to create a conflict. If I had to make an educated guess, I'd say the reason behind the two separate plots is you." Judy paused here for a while, and it took me an embarrassingly long time to gesture for her to continue. She gave me an odd look but nevertheless proceeded to elaborate. "As you've previously deduced, your actions during the climax of the previous story arc, in conjunction with your general attitude and behaviour, designated you as a 'protagonist.' Due to that, the Narrative, or whoever is in control of it, created a plotline for you. Dr. Robatto and his Sprockets most likely exist as low-threat introductory antagonists to ease Joshua into combat scenarios, while the hunter woman and her prey exist for you to follow up on and solidify your status as a monster slayer." She paused again, then after a few short seconds, she asked, "Any objections?"

"Um… None at all, for now," I answered, slightly disoriented. "So, I gather that is your Doylist analysis?" She nodded, so I inhaled deeply and said, "I have an objection, though."

"You just said you had no objections…" my dear assistant stated flatly, and in response I playfully wagged my finger in her direction.

"I also said, 'for now.'"

"Thirteen seconds ago," she continued her deadpan assault on my flawless reasoning.

"But what an insightful thirteen seconds it has been!" I exclaimed with a dramatic sigh and then, seeing that she wasn't receptive, I said, "Jokes aside, I do think there's one blind spot in your theory, the involvement of an ethereal, unverified manipulating force notwithstanding."

"I'm listening."

"It's Lord Grandpa, obviously," I told her without bothering to beat around the bush. "Not only that, but in my interpretation of the events, there is only one 'plot' here, and he is responsible for it."

"Oh?" Judy let out an intrigued little noise. "Now you have my full attention."

"Really? How much of your attention did I have before?"

"About two-thirds."

"Neat," I answered with a poker face matching hers. "Where was I? Right, Lord Grandpa."

"You said he is responsible for the Narrative."

"No, not the *Narrative*," I denied with a shake of my head. "When I said 'plot,' I meant the other definition of the word. I'm fairly sure this is all some kind of huge, overly elaborate, inefficient scheme he is weaving."

"Do you have any evidence to support your hypothesis?"

"Thank you for asking!" I flashed a grin at my assistant and assumed my best "inscrutable erudite" impression by linking my fingers and straightening my back. "While I currently only have circumstantial evidence, all of it points in his direction. First off, we have the three leads he foisted on me. Since we already discussed their idiosyncrasies, I won't repeat myself.

The second hint was how Rinne, who apparently just arrived on the island, already knew my face and address. Someone had to clue her in, and I'd bet my pancreas that it was the old man. Thirdly, today's incident was all kinds of fishy."

I took a deep breath and began to count the ways.

"First and foremost, remember how Ammy turned half the school upside down to find me and tell me to go to the nurse's?"

Judy nodded.

"She said Peabody told her grandfather he wanted to see me, and he, in turn, told her to get me. However, when I got there, Peabody was surprised I showed up, and it almost sounded like *he* was also told by the arch-mage that I'd be coming over to visit him. Not only that, but the ambush on you guys *coincidentally* happened just when I was occupied elsewhere, and I wouldn't have been so if not for a certain old badger pulling some strings to get me to show up in the infirmary. Oh, and also note that Ammy was also *coincidentally* told to take a break from school, but at the same time, she was still used as a messenger by her grandfather. It's almost as if *someone* wanted to keep me and his granddaughter away from the battle."

"Or it could be that the Narrative made sure you were engaged elsewhere so that you wouldn't interfere with Joshua's plotline," Judy posited.

"Possibly, but I still find it more reasonable that Lord Grandpa set the whole thing up."

"Wouldn't that mean that he could control Dr. Robatto?"

I sent my assistant a flat look and told her, in no uncertain terms, "Stop using that stupid name. Even Stevie Wonder could see that it was the Research Society, and he doesn't even know about the supernatural!"

"True, but irrelevant," Judy countered with a slight pout on her lips. "We don't actually know the name of the person behind the mask, so Dr. Robatto is a perfectly fine designation for him."

"Suit yourself then, but I still won't call him that," I compromised. "Anyhow, you have to admit that the timing was simply too perfect, and I still think it was because I was set up."

"Very well, let's entertain the thought," Judy compromised as well and stole my pose by linking her fingers and leaning back. "Let's presume that Lord Amadeus purposefully misdirected you, and then he leaked this information to Dr. Robatto so that he could attack the rest of us. Do you have any motive?"

"Aside from general animosity, no, I don't," I admitted. "However, we also don't have a reasonable motive for why the masked guy with the stupid name wanted to attack the gang, either. We don't know why, or even *if,* he was after Josh."

"I grant you that. He started to give some kind of speech, but then Neige transformed, and he ran away."

"There was a speech? The others didn't say anything about a speech. What did he say?"

"He said, 'Aaaah! I, Dr. Robatto, have reawakened after ten thousand years! It's time to conquer Earth!' Then, after Neige transformed, he said, 'My head hurts! Sprockets, take care of them!' and he left."

"Wow," I muttered as I was caught in a moment of stupor. "That guy is truly fearless. He didn't just steal the aesthetics; he even ripped off the catch phrases! Maybe he has amazing copyright lawyers."

"I don't get it," Judy told me with an uncomprehending frown on her brow.

"Never mind," I dismissed the topic with a wave of my hand. "The actual point is that he didn't really give you any reason why he attacked you. As far as we know, he might've been set up by the old man, as well."

"Chief… are you sure your theories are not influenced by the irrational animosity you feel towards Lord Amadeus?"

"No, Dormouse," I said while emphatically shaking my head. "I assure you, my hatred towards the old coot is entirely rational."

"Putting rationality aside, you still didn't produce a reasonable motive for Lord Amadeus to… Chief, why do you keep spacing out?"

"Huh?" I blinked a few times in surprise, then I told her, "I'm listening. I was just checking on Ammy."

Judy's expression subtly swung between bafflement and peevishness, ultimately settling decidedly in the latter category, and she stated, "We've only been dating for a few days, and you are already openly ogling other girls while we are talking with each other. Is the flame already gone?"

"Not funny," I reproached her before I let out a shallow sigh and explained, "Since phones don't work in and out of the Purple Zone, I decided to keep closer tabs on the important people in my life so that I wouldn't be caught with my pants down like today. It just so happened that I was looking at Ammy when you called me out."

"What is she doing?"

"You can have three guesses," I said in a bleak tone, which I figured was enough for her to figure it out.

"Paperwork?"

"Bingo," I answered, then I closed my eyes and shook my head. "At this rate, we'll have to organize an intervention for her."

"What about Noire?" Judy suddenly asked, completely skimming over my previous comment.

"Who...? Oh, wait, you meant Crowey, didn't you?" I paused for a moment while I switched my attention to his dot, and I told her. "Nothing much. He's still recuperating. Why do you ask?"

"I think it's prudent to keep the man who wanted to kidnap your friend and kill you under surveillance."

"Hey, I *am* keeping him under surveillance! It's just that nothing's happening around the guy. I've been peeking on him three or four times every day, but for the past three days, he was just lying in his bed and staring at the ceiling. Not exactly riveting to watch. Not to mention, the number of people I have to routinely check on keeps increasing all the time. For example, just today I marked the..."

"You marked who?" Judy inquired with audible apprehension in her voice.

"The nurse, and I have to go," I told her in a hurry as I jumped to my feet, only to realize that I was still in just a shirt and sweatpants after my recent shower, so I rushed over to the hangers by the entrance and pulled out one of my identical coats.

"Is there an emergency?" Judy asked.

"No, it's more of an *opportunity*. Don't go anywhere. I don't know when I'll be back. Let's continue this conversation later."

Judy was obviously about to object, but by then I'd already put on my sneakers and disappeared from the room. I had a feeling I'd get an earful for that later, but I decided I'd avoid that bridge when I got there.

PART 2

I took a shallow breath the moment I arrived at my destination, held it in, and quickly hid in a dark little cranny I'd chosen ahead of time by the nearest door. I was in a poorly lit concrete corridor, and the familiar smell of heavy and slightly stale air told me that I was underground. I couldn't see too far in either direction, since the only source of light in the hallway was coming from the open door by my side. By the looks of the slightly arched ceiling and the various metal pipes running by the walls, I figured it was probably some kind of service tunnel, if a fairly prim and clean one. No surprise there. The ninja maids were ever-present and very meticulous, after all.

After making sure there was no one in sight (I already looked around once during Far Sight, just in case there was any magical or mundane surveillance in the tunnel, but hey, looking twice never hurt anyone), I inched forward and set my back against the wall before using my Far Sight again.

I squinted for a moment while my incorporeal eyes got accustomed to the cold, blue neon light coming from the various light fixtures in the room. It was a medium-sized chamber, about five-by-five meters, with white walls and even whiter furniture. On the left side, stacks of books and papers covered the desks, and the workbenches were crammed—glass tubes, round flasks, beaked alembics, and other containers filled with liquids of various colours and consistencies, some of them violently bubbling, others letting off copious amounts of dangerous-looking white vapors, filled every empty space. On the right, the situation was mostly the same, except instead of stereotypical chemistry sets, every surface was packed full of large devices filled with exposed tesla coils, metal boxes with lots of buttons and switches, and small round screens that reminded me of old analog oscilloscopes.

In short, the place looked just like the ominous lair of a cackling mad scientist type. Cue…

"Ki-hi-hi!"

No, I wasn't surprised. The aforementioned laughter came from one of the three people inside the room. The first one was obviously Mr. Peabody, who had just finished putting his coat on a hanger by the entrance, still close enough to the wall so that I could transfer to the other side without anyone being the wiser. His presence was quite self-evident, as without him being here, I wouldn't have had an anchor for Far Sight to target. The other two figures, on the other hand, were considerably less obvious.

First off, there was the fairly short source of the cackling. I'm not going to mince my words here; he was obviously Dr. Robatto, though this time he wasn't wearing his ridiculous getup. Since he was looking at the nurse, and thus roughly in the direction of the door, I could get a good look at his face (though again, since I could freely change my point of view in a small radius around Peabody, it was more or less incidental).

He had a pair of round, thick-rimmed glasses sitting on a small nose, and overall I'd go as far as to say that he was deceptively handsome even with the disheveled hair and the dark circles under his eyes. Actually, wasn't there even a character archetype for this kind of appearance? I think it was for shoujo manga male love interests—something about being handsome but sickly and frail to create a contrast and trigger maternal feelings or something. I decided to ask Judy about it when I get back, since she seemed to have made herself an expert on the subject.

But back to the description: he was also pretty young, probably in spitting distance to twenty by the looks of it, and while this time he wasn't wearing the silly mask, he was still sporting the same frayed lab coat from the picture. All things considered, while he didn't look exceedingly weird at the moment, if I was lost in a bad neighbourhood, I sure as hell wouldn't ask him for directions.

However, if we wanted to talk about weird, the woman standing beside him definitely provided enough of it for the both of them. She was almost a head taller than the guy, with her long, purple hair in a ponytail that reached down to her waist. She had a full hourglass figure, which was put on full display by her dark green, honeycomb-patterned bodysuit. As if that wasn't enough to show off all her "goods," her outfit had a neckline that plunged right down to her navel, revealing a generous amount of cleavage in the process. On top of all that, she was wearing thick, heavy-looking boots and gauntlets covered in complex, circuitry-like golden filigree, with equally well-decorated golden shoulder pads and a thick, angular single-piece diadem with a freaking unicorn horn in its middle. Furthermore, where the woman's ears were supposed to be, a pair of sleek metal *somethings* with green lights on them stuck out of her head like giant, high-tech earphones.

While I was observing the two, Peabody made his way over to them and said, "O-ho-ho. How did the operation go?" his characteristic laughter made even more grating by the slight echo provided by hearing him both with my ears and through Far Sight at the same time. On a sidenote, though, it was good to know that he wasn't doing the silly laughter just to annoy me.

Anyway, the younger guy let out a grating chuckle of his own and said, in a high-pitched voice, "Ki-hi-hi! It went exactly as I expected! All the first-generation foot soldiers got wiped out, but I got a lot of tasty, succulent data out of the encounter!" He paused for a moment, then added, "I wasn't expecting the Abyssal, though. She was scary," in a considerably less manic voice, only to flare up again by saying, "Also, very scantily clad! It was weird, right, Galatea?"

"I wasn't there, master," the woman mechanically stated. As in, her voice sounded synthesized. The guy let out a surprised grunt, then he grabbed his chin and looked her over from head to toe.

"It had to be an attempt at psychological warfare—to distract the opponents and make them hesitate! Ki-hi-hi! Too bad such shameless tactics didn't work on my Sprockets!"

"They still got wrecked in minutes, though," the woman stated.

"I told you, it was all within my calculations!" the presumed mad scientist huffed before he looked the woman over one more time and said, "Ki-hi-hi! Hey, Galatea?"

"Yes, master?"

"How about we take a page from their books and try to apply some of that psychological warfare ourselves?"

"A brilliant idea as always, Master," she answered with a robotic nod. "I will now proceed to browse Speedos in master's size on the internet. I'm certain master will do a great job at distracting the opponents."

"Halt! Halt, I tell you! I wasn't talking about me, but you!" the man protested while frantically waving his hands.

"Error," she stated while repeatedly blinking. "My visual receptors have been fortified against such tactics, so my cogitation core cannot compute a scenario where Master's naked body would distract me. Please clarify your query and try again."

"O-ho-ho! I see you are still getting along like you are attached at the hip," Peabody cut between the two of them with a few jovial steps.

"Error. Such attachment would greatly reduce my operation efficiency. Please reconsider."

"Ki-hi-hi! Don't pay attention to Galatea, Uncle," the guy in the lab coat told the nurse with a dismissive shrug. "She's just in a difficult phase."

"O-ho-ho! I see, I see…"

I had no idea what he was seeing, but as for me, I was getting more and more confused by the scene. Still, I bided my time and waited, hoping that they might accidentally drop some tasty bits of information. Such as this one.

"What are the plans for next time?" Peabody inquired, further solidifying his status as an accomplice.

"I plan on doing the same thing, but with more Sprockets!" Lab Coat Guy declared with his arms akimbo. Then he quickly added, "Oh, and I will also mix in a few MkII models to see how they perform in a group." At this point, there was a long pause in the conversation, during which he awkwardly tried to decide whether to keep his hands on his hips or cross them in front of his chest, but eventually, he pocketed them and paced up and down beside the chemistry sets. "Ki-hi-hi! If my calculations are correct, then four or five such tests should yield enough usable data to upgrade them to MkIII!"

"O-ho-ho? Won't you run out of robots? I thought you were short on funds."

"Ki-hi-hi! Don't worry, Uncle! I calculated everything, including the budget! Even then, if the Sprockets won't be enough, I will just release one of the Biomechanical Gigants!"

"Correction," the woman cut in with an unchanging serious expression. "The precise term is *Biomechanical Kernels*. They only become beings of unusual size after they are injected with the growth hormone formula, and their rapid transformation is triggered by the predetermined embarrassing code phrase Master came up with."

"Thank you, Galatea, that was very helpful," Peabody told the woman with a jovial voice, though her "master" rolled his eyes and continued pacing.

"Uncle, don't encourage her! She's getting worse ever since I let her browse the internet unsupervised..." The nurse only let out a soft "O-ho-ho!" in response, so the mad scientist cosplayer rolled his eyes at him and continued. "I still need some time to work out some of the kinks with the MkII Sprockets, but they should be ready by tomorrow if I pull an all-nighter. When the time comes, could you stall the Chimera Slayer again? Oh, and the Abyssal girl, too, if possible. If the Sprockets are destroyed too fast and his agent cannot intervene in time, then our sponsor's going to be really mad at us."

"O-ho-ho. My boy, you are asking too much from these old bones," the nurse answered while theatrically stretching his back. "If not for Endymonion's cooperation, I doubt I could've even gotten him to come to the infirmary. He is a very willful young man."

"Really? That's a right pickle! Ki-hi-hi! I might have to roll out the Gigants for him to play with," the guy in the lab coat muttered before turning around and facing his "uncle" again. "You said he was in the infirmary. Did you find his weakness?"

"My boy, I told you not to ask about confidential details. I don't want to break my Hippocratic oath," the nurse ominously said.

"Yes, yes, because then the Brotherhood of Hippocrates would hunt you down. You've been telling me that since I was five years old!"

"O-ho-ho! You are right! I can remember it like it was yesterday! You've grown so much since then!"

"Master has indeed grown in many ways, except for his height," the woman stated, earning her a glare from the younger man.

"Shut up, Galatea," he hissed between clenched teeth, "or I'll have you clean the waste disposal chute again, and this time you won't be allowed to turn off your olfactory sensors."

"If I'm on cleaning duty, can I change out of this outfit?"

"No."

"Processing... processing... I conclude that I must stay silent."

"Good," he stated with a huff before turning back to the nurse again. "Okay, so the same trick cannot be used twice to stall him. What about the Abyssal? Can you at least pull her aside with some excuses?"

"I'll think of something," Peabody relented, prompting the other man to rub his hands together.

"Ki-hi-hi! Good, very good! I can't wait to get my hands on all that juicy data! Then, our funding will be stabilized, and we can finally focus on the important things! Like taking over the world... of SCIENCE! Ka-ha-ha-haaaa!" After he finished cackling maniacally, there was a long moment of awkward silence in the chamber, only for him to clear his throat and add, "Speaking of funding, I think we need to reconsider our quarterly budget after all."

What followed were several minutes of mind-numbingly boring finance numbers being thrown back and forth between the two of them, so I used the time to organize what I'd learned.

One: this guy was running some kind of workshop where he was making artificial life-forms. Two: while they never said it outright, I'd bet my head that he was part of the Research Society. Three: Peabody was in cahoots with him, and it was possible that he also worked for the Research Society. Four: they apparently worked with Lord Grandpa, or at the very least he was helping them out, though their exact relationship was never stated. Five: he had a freaking fembot! I mean, that's really obvious, right? Not only that, it was a snarky, deadpan fembot! I had a feeling that if my dear Judybot heard about it, she'd either suffer another existential crisis or threaten to sue someone.

Jokes aside, it still meant that, if they had the tech for something like her, then our weird little world had advanced magitech at best, or straight up mad super-science at worst.

Anyhow, I wasn't going to learn anything important just by sitting still. In fact, if I only wanted to listen in on their conversation, I didn't even need to teleport over. My actual goal in coming here was pretty simple: since I literally couldn't keep a constant eye on all of my friends all the time, just in case this *sentai* rip-off showed his not particularly ugly mug, I figured that I could mark and keep an eye on him instead, avoiding a lot of hassle in the process.

Unfortunately, getting there wasn't entirely hassle-free, as tagging the guy was easier said than done. I'd hoped that maybe he'd leave through the door, or even just get close enough for me to sneakily touch him, but the three of them seemed to be rooted in their spots and refused to budge. I also considered just teleporting on top of him, but he was constantly looked over by the fembot, and I had no idea of her capabilities, I didn't dare to risk it.

If only my phantom limb could tag people... Actually, if it could, I wouldn't have had any problem marking the huntress, either, but that would be too easy, wouldn't it? One would think that, since it was crucial for taking people along when teleporting, and my ability to mark people and to teleport seemed to be closely linked, my invisible extra appendage would naturally be able to mark people, too. Yet after a few quick tests, it became obvious it wouldn't work. I swear, sometimes I felt like there was no consistency in the metaphysical rules governing the supernatural of this world. Or maybe it was just my powers that were all kinds of screwy? Either way, it was a pain in the neck.

I couldn't just sit tight and wait forever, either, so after some consideration, I decided to try my luck with some tried-and-true distraction tactics. I pulled out my phone and went into the clock menu to set an alarm, choosing an especially jaunty tone from the list. I cranked up the volume to the max and set the phone down next to the open door.

The plan was simple and straightforward: First, wait for the alarm to sound. The people in the room would, hopefully, all look towards the door to see what was going on, and during that window of opportunity, I'd teleport behind them and tag the guy, and immediately leave the premises.

Not only that, but if the situation was absolutely perfect, I figured I might as well try to grab my target and teleport him with me. In that case, I naturally wouldn't go home right away, but would teleport right next to Brang instead, so that he could help me to apprehend the guy. That was, of course, the best-case scenario, but hey, it didn't hurt to be optimistic every once in a while.

As such, I prepared myself by taking a huge breath, calmed my nerves, observed the frantic pacing of Lab Coat Guy, aaaaand... alarm!

The moment Tchaikovsky's *1812 Overture* began to blare out of the small yet surprisingly impressive speakers on my phone, the three people inside the room all shuddered in apprehension.

"W-what's that?" Lab Coat Guy yelled out with equal measures of fright and confusion as he jumped behind his fembot.

At the same time, the previously expressionless woman's face also crunched up in a glare and she exclaimed, "Master, step back!" while extending her right hand towards my location. Peabody, on the other hand, was completely shocked silly by the developments and was standing still like a statue with his mouth agape.

While all of this was going on, I wasn't sitting on my laurels, either. I considered my options, and after a moment of hesitation, I discarded my covert kidnapping idea as too risky, since my target was clinging on to his android's back almost as tightly as her outfit. Instead, I focused on my main objective, so without any further hesitation, I teleported right behind the hapless mad scientist and delivered a single, precise karate-chop right at the base of his neck.

The short man let out a high-pitched yelp. I knew that it was going to draw the others' attention right away, so I teleported right back to my starting position. To be honest, the rapid back and forth transportation was playing havoc with my head, but it was a small price to pay. I held back the momentary vertigo by sheer force of will and reached out for my phone, only to be hit by an unexpected and quite chilling sense of dread.

Time itself came to crawl as my probably supernatural sense of danger told me that I was currently in some serious jeopardy, and I should dodge and flee right away. At the same time, a more rational part of my brain told me that I should not leave behind any evidence.

While these thoughts battled it out in my head, the wall I was touching began to violently tremble. To be frank, I wasn't entirely sure about how I managed to do it in a split second, but I entered into Far Sight, threw myself to the side, found Judy, reached out and grabbed the phone mid-roll, and teleported out of danger.

Unfortunately for me, because of the way my ability conserved momentum, as soon as I appeared back in my living room, I immediately toppled over. No, scratch that. I actually had so much momentum that I was sent tumbling back, rolling on the floor before ending up on my back, staring at the ceiling in a sort of startled stupor.

"Chief, are you all right?" Judy appeared out of thin air—though, in retrospect, I probably just blanked out for a second or two while she rushed over.

After taking a few deep breaths to reorient myself, I raised the hand that wasn't still clutching my phone up to my temple and muttered, "I'm fine, I think..."

I didn't feel fine at all.

"You are bleeding," my assistant gasped while she propped me up so that I could sit.

"Where?" I asked as I absentmindedly touched my face. My fingers came away wet, immediately answering my question. I stared at the red liquid on my fingertips, and after letting out a surprised grunt, I asked, "Hey, Judy... did I get one of those cool scars or an ugly one?"

"Stop joking and get up! We need to clean those wounds! And why is your phone still playing music at a time like this?" Judy complained while dragging me to my feet, just in time for Snowy to show up at the top of the stairs.

"What's going on? Did something happen...?" My sister trailed off into a stunned silence, then exclaimed, "I'm getting the first aid kit!" and disappeared into the bathroom. Wow, I must've looked much worse than how I actually felt, and considering I felt like crap at the moment, that didn't bode well.

Meanwhile, Judy continued to drag me towards the washroom, interrogating me the whole time. "Where did you go? What happened?"

"I paid a visit to that Robatto guy," I answered her honestly. "As for what happened… give me a second," I told her as we stopped just in front of the stairs, and I quickly entered into Far Sight again. A split second later, I was back in the mad scientist's workshop, now filled with concrete dust and the sound of coughing.

"What the hell, Galatea? What's wrong with you?" Lab Coat Guy yelled out between coughs.

Once the dust settled, in this case quite literally, I glanced around from my disembodied vantage point and found Peabody hiding under one of the tables. The fembot, on the other hand, was standing still in the middle of the room. Her right hand was literally hanging off the bottom of her vambraces, as if on a hinge, and from the stump extended a short barrel still glowing after its discharge. When I followed the direction where she was pointing at, I realized that the section of the wall behind which I was hiding just seconds before was completely gone, replaced by a circular hole, its edges still glowing like burning coals.

While I was inspecting said hole, the fembot's arm cannon retracted back into her forearm with a series of metallic clicks, and her hand swung back into its natural place. She moved her fingers one by one, probably to make sure they were functioning right before she turned to her "master."

"I detected an intruder, Master. I neutralized them."

"With your Plasma Disintegrator?"

"Yes," she responded like it was the most natural thing in the world. "Master, my batteries are low. I request permission to recharge."

"You wouldn't need to recharge if you showed just a little restraint! Look at that hole! You probably vaporized whoever was on the other side!"

"Affirmative. That is what the Plasma Disintegrator is for."

The two of them continued to bicker, and in the meantime the chamber was quickly flooded by a combination of seemingly identical, ugly as sin Sprocket bots, probably in response to the noise.

Overall, while I might've made a mess, and had made a risky call at the end, I couldn't help but smile, for there was a brand-new red dot on my Far Seeing radar.

"All right, so I was apparently attacked by something called a Plasma Disintegrator," I told Judy, and she immediately began to pull me along again.

"You can tell me about it later. First, we need to remove all of this concrete shrapnel from your side."

"Sure, I'll tell you in great detail," I answered her while still grinning to myself, only to pause and tentatively ask, "Wait… did you just say 'shrapnel'…?"

CHAPTER 17

PART 1

"Ouch!" My entire upper body jerked back as a hiss escaped my mouth against my will, much to my eternal (or at the very least momentary) shame.

"Sorry," Snowy yanked back her hand as if she'd just touched a hot stove, nearly dropping the swab of cotton wool in it.

"I'm fine, don't worry about it," I reassured her and gestured for her to continue. She smiled apologetically and, after a moment of hesitation, she resumed her basic but much-needed treatment of my wounds, which quickly managed to draw another pained hiss out of me.

"No matter how much you play it up, I'm not going to feel sorry for you," Judy grumbled nearby, prompting me to send her an annoyed glance.

We were all in my room, and my dear assistant was sitting on my bed with one of our first aid kits on her lap, and yes, I did use the plural there. I bought half a dozen of them the moment I realized we were in a battle-shounen setting. Getting hurt was inevitable.

Speaking of wounds, while Judy's initial description of my condition painted a grim picture, I actually only suffered small cuts, albeit quite a number of them. Whatever a "Plasma Disintegrator" was, it apparently turned solid objects into tons of small fragments moving at high speed, but with little penetrative power. Either that, or I made my departure just in the nick of time and managed to avoid all but the first wave of the shrapnel sprayed out by the exploding wall.

Speaking of shrapnel... well, I did have a few pieces of sharp concrete fragments stuck in my face and my right shoulder, but they barely pierced past my skin, so it was easy (if not exactly pleasant) to extract them with a pair of tweezers.

Anyway, I sent a reproachful glance at Judy and told her in an especially neutral and in no way whiny voice, "I'm not hissing for attention. When something hurts, it hurts."

"Such cutting insight," she responded sourly while raising a bundle of bandages to her eye level and inspecting it like she hadn't seen one in her life. It was probably her way of showing her dissatisfaction by pointedly refusing to look at me. In the meantime, Snowy began disinfecting another scrape on my cheek, so I let out a silent hiss that somehow still didn't escape her notice, prompting my assistant to let out a soft huff that I could easily translate as a snappy *Serves you right.*

After rolling my eyes, I turned in my swivel chair so that I was facing her (which also forced Snowy to move, but she didn't seem to mind), and I grumpily told her, "You know, Dormouse, you're being so grouchy, one would think *you* were the one who almost got blasted by a murderbot."

Judy shot me a sharp look, after which she put the bandages back in the box and put the first aid kit on the bed beside her. Only then did she answer.

"Yes, Chief, I'm angry. With you, in particular." Her straightforward confirmation took me aback for a moment, but before I could formulate a proper response, she continued, "I thought we agreed that our safety, which incidentally includes yours, was very important, yet you went ahead and got yourself injured. Again."

"Hey! I didn't go over there with the express purpose of getting injured," I objected with a forceful wave of my hand. Snowy, in the meantime, completely avoided both our argument and my hand and continued to treat the smaller scrapes on my shoulder and chest. My little sister was such a trooper.

Judy kept giving me the same cold look, so I explained to her, "Listen, Dormouse, I told you I only went over to tag the mad scientist guy while the rare window of opportunity presented itself. It was a once-in-a-lifetime deal!"

"You still should've been more cautious about it," she retorted with the same disapproving look on her face... which actually didn't look all that different from her normal expression, but trust me, it was so scathing it could intimidate water into boiling at room temperature.

"I was careful!" I objected maybe a smidgen louder than strictly necessary. "I made sure to hide, and I distracted them and everything! How was I supposed to know his android had a buster cannon and that she wasn't three laws compliant?"

"If you didn't know her capabilities, then that's all the more reason to be careful and not rush things," she countered. "You should've waited until they were separated."

"But I had no way of knowing if they would! Did you expect me to stake them out for hours just on the off-chance that they might separate for a moment?"

"No, I didn't, because you didn't tell me where you disappeared to."

I had a snappy comeback on the tip of my tongue, but then I thought things over, and settled on, "Well, okay, I admit that's true, but it was a sudden opportunity. If I didn't act right away, then I might've never gotten another one."

"Or you might have calmed down, thought things through, avoided running headlong into danger, and we wouldn't be having this conversation."

"Oh, please! I told you, I was simply blindsided! It happens to everyone! I was simply a victim of the circumstances."

"If you are a victim, then why do you keep defending yourself so vehemently? Could it be you have a guilty conscience?"

"No, I obviously don't," I fumed. "What about being innocent until proven guilty? Where is my attorney? Can I at least get my phone call before anything else?"

"Stop doing that," Judy grumbled. Then her eyes suddenly sparkled with some kind of realization, and she turned to Snowy and told her, "See? Whenever he knows he cannot win an argument, he derails the conversation. You should really keep an eye on that if you plan on living in the same household with him."

"Hey!" I interrupted before Snowy could respond to my assistant's attempt at character assassination. "Don't try to turn my sister against me!"

"I'm not turning her against you; I'm simply delivering some important advice regarding her reckless, irresponsible adoptive brother."

"No, you're not!" I continued my protests. "You're the one who cannot prove that I was careless and not just a victim of blind chance, so you are trying to get me to back down by using peer pressure!"

"I am not," Judy denied, then she pointed at the hapless girl glancing back and forth between the two of us and proposed, "Why don't you ask her whether she thinks you are a careful person or someone who refuses to take responsibility for his reckless actions?"

"You know what? I will do just that!" I answered defiantly before facing Snowy and asking her, at point-blank range, "So, sis? Do you have anything to add to our discussion?"

Snowy was obviously taken aback by how she was suddenly thrust into the spotlight, but after a short moment of fidgeting, she glanced between us one more time, and then she told me, "I... I'm sure Leo wanted to be careful and didn't put himself at risk for no reason." At this point I wanted to direct a giddy grin at my grumpy girlfriend, but before it could materialize on my face, Snowy continued by saying, "But... I think you should be even more careful. I mean... um... I really don't want to sound selfish, and I'm sure you are doing your best, but if you made a mistake and something really, really bad happened to you, I... I really don't know what I would do, or where I could go. So... um..." She paused again, sent one helpless glance at each of us in turn, and then she blurted out, "So, please take care of yourself?"

For a moment, there was a strange silence in the air as Judy and I glanced at each other. I figured Snowy's reaction wasn't exactly what either of us was expecting, but it was my brotherly duty to break the ice, so I carefully placed my hand on my fidgeting sister's head and began to rub it.

"If you put it like that, I can't really argue, now, can I?" I spoke with a gentle smile to put her at ease. "I promise I'll be even more careful in the future, all right?"

"O-okay." Snowy awkwardly nodded, and we were just about to have the inkling of a cozy atmosphere when Judy butted in.

"How come when I tell you the same thing, you argue tooth and nail, but when Neige does it, you immediately fold and agree?"

"What can I say? It's the power of a little sister. I'm helpless against it," I replied with a suitably brotherly grin.

Judy's eyes told me she was still peeved, but for the moment, she remained silent. I considered that to be a tacit admission of defeat, a conclusion that was entirely reasonable and in no way a convenient interpretation of the situation. No, sir.

Anyhow, I reluctantly stopped petting Snowy, and while drawing back my arm, I also limbered up my shoulder a little.

"So, how's my treatment? Are we finished?" I asked in a fairly transparent attempt at directing the conversation into a more neutral direction.

"I think I did what I could," Snowy began, but stopped in surprise when Judy sidled closer to her and began stroking her head in turn, probably as a show of her competitive spirit. Either that, or maybe seeing me doing the same simply got her in the mood. Either way, after a brief spell of confusion, my sister continued, "None of your wounds were deep, but you should have Angie take a look at them tomorrow."

"I'll do just that. Thanks," I told her with a smile before I rose to my feet and checked out my Band-Aid-covered right side. All in all, while my fresh collection of scrapes and cuts stung quite a bit, they didn't hinder my movements. Bearing in mind our unpredictable and oftentimes dangerous circumstances, my mobility was vital, especially since I'd just promised Snowy that I'd be really careful. If nothing else, now I felt reasonably certain I'd still be able to get out of the way of another stray Plasma Disintegrator blast coming my way.

"Before that, you should try avoiding getting attacked in the first place," Judy warned me with a strained frown, which she no doubt found hard to maintain due to the amazing soul-mending effects of petting a little sister.

I tell you, if they didn't exist, we'd have to invent them… which, now that I thought about it (and considering our unusual familiar circumstances), I kind of did.

Anyhow, I gave my assistant an odd look and asked, "Did you just read my mind?"

"No, I simply extrapolated that from the *I feel tubular! I'm gonna totes avoid any gnarly men in grey suits next time! Mondo cool!* look on your face."

"Wait… why does my inner monologue sound like surfer lingo?"

My dearest assistant only shrugged, as if I was the silly one for even asking, and I felt that if I continued with my questions, we'd either get bogged down in another argument, or end up in another of Judy's skits. I wasn't in the mood for either, so I simply ignored her and addressed Snowy again.

"Thanks for dressing my wounds, sis, I owe you one. That said, if I don't need any more treatment, I think you should go and finish your homework. It's getting late."

Snowy hesitated, but when Judy removed her hand from her head, she yielded and got up, too.

"You're right. I've got a lot of catching up to do."

She headed over to the door, but after opening it, she glanced back and quietly said, "Don't fight," before quickly walking out.

After the first moment of surprise passed, I couldn't help but let out a mirthful little chuckle. I sat back down on my chair and told my sulky assistant, "You know, I think adopting Snowy was the second-best decision I've ever made."

"What was the first?" she asked back without batting an eye.

"I'm not telling," I replied with a positively impudent grin.

"That does it," Judy responded as she crossed her arms. "If only you said it outright, I would've let you sweep your previous faux pas under the rug. Now I'll have to—"

"Later, Dormouse. Later," I cut her off in a considerably more serious voice. "We have more important things to discuss first."

She gave me a long, hard, critical look, but at last she sighed and said, "I'm listening."

"You do that," I replied as I moved to a more comfortable position in my seat, after which I began by explaining, "Since I didn't have the chance to clarify what just happened while I was away, I think I'm going to start with that. I don't want to bore you with the nitty-gritty details so, in a nutshell: The nurse works with the guy who ambushed you. Using him as an anchor point, I teleported over to their base. The guy had a hilariously dressed fembot. I overheard that they are working with Lord Grandpa, that they are planning further ambushes, and that they are wary of me and Snowy. After learning all of this, I set up a diversion and managed to mark the guy, but his fembot blew up a wall and I got hit by the debris. You know the rest. Any questions?"

"Where is their base?" came the first one right away.

"Somewhere underground. I don't know its exact location yet, but I should be able to figure it out soon enough."

"How exactly is Mr. Peabody related to Dr. Robatto?"

"He called the nurse 'uncle,' so probably familial, though I can't be sure yet. Also, stop calling him Robatto; it's obviously a fake name."

"Do you know his real name, then?"

"No, I still don't know, but I should learn it any time now."

"In that case, since the only name by which we know Dr. Robatto is Dr. Robatto, I will keep calling Dr. Robatto Dr. Robatto until we learn the alleged true name of Dr. Robatto."

Initially, I wondered if she was serious, and since it seemed like she was, I let out a tiny little groan.

"You know, I think I won't even ask if you're doing it on purpose, because you didn't even bother to be subtle about it. Instead I'll just ask you to stop it."

"I'll stop it if you stop being reckless," Judy responded sharply.

"Ugh. Not this again… I wasn't reckless. Everything was perfectly under control."

"Until a wall exploded."

"Well, yes, I admit that wasn't in my calculations, but only because it is hard to account for something so randomly over the top. By the same logic, you might as well say that walking outside is reckless because a random, unexpected thunderbolt could hit me at any time."

"No, Chief." Judy shook her head hard as her expression grew frostier by the second. "The reckless part would be going out in a thunderstorm while yelling at the sky and calling Zeus a pansy who couldn't hit the broad side of a barn."

"Ooookay, I kinda lost the tail end of that analogy, but I'm pretty sure I didn't do that," I responded a little awkwardly, but then I forcefully inhaled and firmly stated, "We are getting so off topic, I'm afraid soon we'll make a full circle and get on topic again by accident."

Judy's expression was still colder than the tundras, so I let out an exasperated breath and decided to try a slightly less confrontational approach by softly pleading, "Come on, Dormouse, cut me some slack already. If you want me to apologize for scaring you, then I will. I'll even apologize for leaving without telling you where I was teleporting to. However, I still think that I did the objectively right thing in the situation. I've successfully infiltrated an enemy base, gained critical intel, and marked the leader for surveillance. Was a few scratches really such a bad deal in exchange for all of that?"

"There was a four-centimeters-long piece of jagged concrete in your shoulder," Judy countered with a flat voice that told me she was fed up with the argument. She wasn't alone, but I tried my best to keep things civil.

"Yes, but it only stuck a centimeter in. You're making it sound like a bigger deal than it was."

My assistant was still giving me a disapproving look, but after a short while, the tension seemed to seep out of her shoulders, followed by a small sigh.

"Listen, Leo," she began, and I'm not going to lie, just the fact that she was using my actual name made me twitch in apprehension. "Since you are incredibly dense about this, I'm going to spell it out for you so that there's no way you can misunderstand or make a joke out of this... Neige is not the only one who is relying on you. If something were to happen to you, I would be just as lost. Actually, no, I would be even worse off. She's a major part of this world. Even if you disappeared, she would have Joshua and her own importance in the narrative to fall back to. Me? Chief, if it wasn't for your influence, the 'me' you are talking to right now wouldn't even exist." She looked me in the eye, probably to gauge my reaction, and she must have found it lacking, as she soon added, "You have to understand, I'm not worried about you just because I love you. I am also worried because if something were to happen to you, I would lose the literal reason for my existence."

"Oh please, Dormouse," I cajoled her as I rose from my seat again and sat by her side instead. "I'd be lying if I said that I didn't feel unduly flattered by the fact that you find me so important in your life, even if the way you express your concern is a little naggy, but we both know that's a straight up hyperbole." She wasn't too receptive to my words, so I changed my approach. "Okay then, how about we put all that aside for a moment and instead we address the proverbial elephant in this room?"

"Which is?" Judy obediently prompted me.

"It's obviously the fact that you are laboring under the false impression that I'm some kind of daredevil taking risks left and right," I clarified with just a hint of indignation. "It's almost like you think I'm seeking dangerous situations on purpose, but it's the exact opposite! Everything I do is to reduce the amount of danger all of us, including myself, are exposed to. I scouted out the enemy, discovered some of their plans, and I successfully marked my target so that I could find out their future plans, as well, and best of all, they are none the wiser about my involvement. No matter how we look at this, it was a rousing success that will ensure that we can stay one step ahead and avoid any future dangers from that front."

"And that is your excuse for willingly putting yourself in harm's way," Judy stated with an edge of vitriol in her voice, but I could still feel that I had a foot in the door.

"No," I responded while putting an arm around her waist. "I feel like a broken record, but it seems like I have to repeat this again: This was a covert operation. I didn't go there to pick a fight, and the only reason things got even remotely dangerous was because the fembot decided to blow up a wall for practically no reason. However, even if we say that my injuries weren't just the result of an unreasonable reaction by an unpredictable android-person-thing but a risk I took, I'd still say it was better to expose myself to a small risk now than to be in the dark about a much bigger danger in the future."

"Fine, I understand." It appeared Judy had finally thrown up the white flag. She leaned against me a little before she continued. "I think... I *know* that I'm irrational right now, but—"

"I get it," I interrupted her as I squeezed her a little closer. "You were scared when I showed up covered in blood and bits of concrete. It turned into anxiety, and then you pestered me out of frustration. You just explained that to me."

My girlfriend glanced up at me and her previously thawing expression froze over once again.

"Chief, are you picking a fight with me?"

"No, I'm not. I'm just summing things up on no uncertain terms so that we can both move on and have make-up-snuggles," I responded. After a short but intense standoff, Judy sighed and rested her head against my shoulder, and my hand automatically reached around her waist to hold her even closer.

"I understand that you can't help taking some risks. I also understand that you don't do it on purpose. However, I want you to understand something, as well. If something like this were to happen again, and you return covered in blood, I'm going to get Elly, Neige, and everyone else, and we are going to do an intervention so traumatic, you won't even dare to think about being reckless for the rest of your life. Are we clear on that?"

"Crystal," I told her with a chuckle that she didn't seem to appreciate at the moment, as she immediately slipped out of my embrace and put a nominal distance between us.

"Very well. So, since we buried the hatchet for the time being, could you put on some clothes?"

"What?" The question fell out of my mouth in surprise. I looked myself over. "Is there a problem?"

My dear assistant gave me an *Is this guy serious?* look (which was admittedly still vastly preferable to her subzero frowns from before), but since I still couldn't decipher her precise meaning, she explained, "While I don't feel strongly for or against bandages, I have to admit that they give you a rugged look that is somewhat… distracting."

Even after that, it took me several long seconds to figure out what she was getting at, but when I did, I couldn't help but grin mischievously.

"Oooooh? I get it now," I said, and while my instincts told me to tease her for a while, I figured that since we just reached a common ground, doing so would've been counterproductive. Instead, I stood up and proceeded to put on a clean T-shirt and a sweater before I sat down by her side again. The atmosphere was a little tense, in a different way from just a few minutes before, but I decided to simply ignore it.

"So, where were we before you got distracted by me?"

"We were discussing your recklessness," Judy supplied the wrong answer with a straight face.

"No, I meant before that," I clarified.

"Marking Dr. Robatto."

"Right, that." After a moment of thinking, I said, "So, the plan, for the time being, is fairly simple: I keep an eye on the guy and foil future ambushes. I also have a bit of a side plan, so to speak, inspired by our discussion on the rooftop."

"About avoiding being a protagonist?"

"Precisely," I answered with a nod. "I plan to set Josh up to capture the guy. This way we can hit kill two birds with one stone—we can put an end to the sentai shenanigans, and at the same time, we can have Josh take a more active role and reassert himself as the protagonist."

Judy looked at me oddly for a while, then she eventually asked me, "Chief, just why are you so against sentai?"

"Was that a serious question?" I asked back with a suspiciously raised brow.

"Yes. I did a little research while you were gone, and to be honest with you, if we really are experiencing a genre shift, we could do a lot worse than that." She saw that I was far from convinced, so she clarified, "According to what I found, sentai narratives appear to be less bloody and have fewer competent antagonists than harem-battle or shounen narratives. Their main plots are also simpler and more predictable, which would help with setting up controlled scenarios for testing narrative hypotheses."

"Is that all?" I inquired after waiting for a few seconds to see if she wanted to add anything else.

She suddenly perked up. "Actually, mentors seem to have a very high survival rate in sentai, so you might want to consider that role for the future."

I sneakily rolled my eyes at her remark and reiterated my previous question.

"Anything else?"

"I only had a few minutes to look it up, so that's all I have for now," my assistant admitted a little uncomfortably. Whether that was because she felt bashful about her lack of knowledge or because of my blunt mannerisms, I didn't know.

"I see," I muttered under my breath with a sagely nod before I raised my right hand (ignoring the stinging pain in my shoulder) and showed her three fingers. "I can give you exactly three reasons why genre shifting into a sentai would be absolutely horrible." I curled two fingers and shook the remaining one for emphasis. "First and foremost, it's this little thing called 'villain of the week.' I think you should be familiar with the term." Judy nodded in confirmation, so I didn't bother to explain it. Instead I went into what it implied. "Imagine that we collectively must deal with a new mustache-twirling villain or monster showing up at regular intervals, only for them to get defeated and never mentioned again. And then another. And then another. Rinse and repeat, ad nauseam."

"I don't think our current situation is dissimilar," she offered the counterpoint without missing a beat. "A week after Noire, we had the monster hunter and Dr. Robatto appear in quick succession."

"Precisely. Imagine if this kept happening all the time, except with mostly unremarkable fodder opponents. It would be one unremarkable fight after another, day in, day out."

"Wouldn't that be a good way to train Joshua and the others?" Judy proposed.

"That's…" I wanted to dismiss the idea out of hand, but I did give it some thought. "I mean, it's not a horrible idea, especially now that I can track our 'villain' and make arrangements before his ambushes to make sure they would turn out well for us, but I feel it would be simply too much work."

"You're probably right," Judy readily conceded the point, much to my surprise. "We already spend too much time dealing with these diversions, and we are behind on our experimentation schedule by a country mile."

"That's true. We haven't really had the time and opportunity to focus on studying the world as of late," I mused for a moment, but then I quickly added, "Although, now that I think about it, trying to prevent a genre shift would certainly qualify as a grand experiment, wouldn't it?"

"I suppose." Judy shrugged in a decidedly noncommittal way. But she also took out her phone and began taking notes and encouraged me to continue by stating, "You said you had two more reasons to stop the genre shift."

"Yes, I had," I confirmed as I raised my hand again, this time with two fingers extended. "The second serious problem is about secret identities. In a sentai series, the main characters, which would be us, would always fight the big evil doughnut-monster-in-space or whatever while keeping incognito. That, of course, means silly costumes and even sillier transformation sequences. I think we have our hands full with the already existing masquerade and keeping Josh's status as the prophesized chosen-one-of-everyone a secret. We don't need alternate superhero identities to further complicate things on top of that."

My dear assistant faithfully typed what I said into her notes.

"I suppose that is a valid concern, after all. What was your third point?"

"It's silly," I answered right away.

"Your point?"

"No!" I answered with a huff. "Sentai. It's silly."

My girlfriend's fingers stopped mid-tap and she glanced up at me with an extra-deadpan expression.

"Is that really your capstone argument?"

"Actually, yes. Yes, it is," I doubled down without a moment's hesitation. "If you want to know why, just take my previous two points, and add the fact that instead of not-demons and shape-shifting monsters, we would be dealing with ridiculous-looking robots and stuff like bulky, mechanical, half-aardvark-half-elephant-half-octopus creatures with giant stop-signs on their backs doing martial arts and ninja flips."

"That would be certainly weird," Judy concurred.

"Precisely. And, in the immortal words of a certain spiky-haired person whose name eludes me at the moment, *If everything is bloody weird, nothing is bloody weird.*"

"Was that a real quotation?"

"I might've been paraphrasing a little, but the sentiment is the same," I responded with a confident nod. "We've been trying to catch the coattails of the rules that run this world by picking at things that conflict with our common sense. If we genre shift into a sentai, it follows that space alien invasions that no one notices and apocalyptic battles that somehow cause zero collateral damage are going to become a norm. If that happens, then common sense goes out the window. If it goes out the window, our research is screwed. It's like when we discovered the supernatural, but ten times worse."

"That objection was actually considerably more nuanced than I expected from the initial premise. Good job, Chief."

"Thank you, I'm trying," I answered with a modest smile. "So, as I said, we really need to avoid this scenario. I'm personally in favor of setting things up so that Josh deals with Lab Coat Guy himself while we are still in the battle harem genre, and then quickly disassemble his operation to prevent any resurgence of the sentai shenanigans."

My dear assistant remained silent for a second, not even typing, and ultimately asked, "How is calling him Lab Coat Guy better than Dr. Robatto?"

"It's in the principle, my dear," I told her with fake condescension before switching back to normal and asking, "Do you have anything else to add?"

"I still think we should consider exploiting them at first," Judy proposed. "If Dr. Robatto and his group really serve as ineffectual introductory villains who exist to give free group combat experience to Joshua and his love interests, then it logically follows that such experience would be required by the Narrative for later events and antagonists. Depriving them of it might cause more harm than good in the long run."

"That's true, but only if we presume that it is their Doylist 'purpose,'" I countered. "If we consider them in the Watsonian context, they could easily be just cogs in a bigger plan."

"Are you still convinced that the arch-mage is behind everything?"

"More or less, yes. Now we know the Masked Science Bandit is working with him, and since I have him marked, it's only a question of time before I'll catch him red-handed and we learn all the juicy details."

Judy sent me a flat look and then she, unexpectedly enough, began to straight up plead with me.

"Chief, could you *please* just call him Dr. Robatto?"

"No, never, not a chance," I answered her firmly. "Seriously though, based on what they said, I think they might serve as some kind of distraction."

"For what?"

"I'll be damned if I knew, but that's also something I should be able to find out soon-ish," I paused here and gave my assistant a cocky little grin.

"You see? Marking Mr. Panda-Eyes McSpikyhair opened up so many new avenues to approach the current situation."

"I'm not even going to comment on the new name," Judy grumbled loud enough for me to hear.

I stifled a chuckle and absentmindedly added, "I should try to mark Lord Grandpa next. The moment I do that, we should be able to unravel this whole plot like an ugly knitted sweater."

"You should also mark the huntress," my assistant added. "Preferably without any flirting in the process."

"I know, I know," I muttered. Then I had an idea. "Now that we're talking about this, give me a second to check my marks."

Judy shrugged nonchalantly but still looked apprehensive after what happened last time.

"So, let's start with Crowey. He is staring at the ceiling. Not particularly riveting. And... nothing with Josh. Nothing is going on over at Angie's place, either. Ammy is still doing paperwork, so same old, same old. The sentai wannabes are currently... filing for insurance over the wall. How oddly mundane. The Fauns are currently..."

"Don't you dare...!" Judy hissed when I jumped to my feet. She hastily rose from the side of the bed, as well.

"They found her," I told her curtly, untangling my slightly damaged coat from the back of my swivel chair.

"You are injured," she insisted and tried to take my coat away, but I wouldn't let her.

"Only a little, and this is important," I argued back. "I'm not going there to fight anyone. I'll just get in, mark her, and get out."

Judy didn't say anything right away, only glared at me, but at last she let out a shallow sigh and told me, "If there is even the slightest hint of danger, you are coming home, right away."

"I promise," I responded with a smile.

"I'm serious. If there's a single new scratch on you when you return, I can't promise I won't strangle you."

"Then I'd better return unscratched," I told her, and then I quickly followed it up by leaned over and planting a small kiss on her mouth. "I'll be super-safe. Love you, xoxo."

And with that, I teleported away.

This time I had to be very thorough, both in terms of safety and anti-harem countermeasures, lest Judy declare a cold war on me right after we'd made up. But then again, with my recent track record, that might happen, anyway, no matter how careful I was. Oh well, I decided I'd swim under that bridge when I got there, and instead I focused on accomplishing my new self-imposed mission while staying safe. I had a feeling it was easier said than done, but such was my life.

PART 2

I appeared on a rooftop somewhere in the urban center of Timaeus. It was a cold, cloudy evening, so I was definitely glad I brought my coat. It was only when I buttoned up that I realized I'd forgotten to bring my phone with me. I didn't plan to stay for long, so I decided it wasn't worth going back just to pick it up.

I glanced to my right, towards the rooftop's edge, and after making sure my footing was secure, I made my way over to the Faun crouching nearby like a certain flying mammal–themed superhero. He was covered in a thin layer of rippling orange light, which meant he was magically camouflaged. That meant he couldn't be seen even though he was leaning over the edge, but since I wasn't stealthed, I stopped well out of sight from the ground and softly called out to him.

"[Hrul.]"

Despite my best efforts to stay low-key, the ram-headed muscleman let out a startled gasp and spun around on the spot so hard, I was afraid he would slip and fall. Luckily, his sense of balance proved unexpectedly impeccable, and he managed to face me without any complications. Small mercy.

After he recognized me, the Faun's ears drooped in a mixture of relief and perplexity. "[Oh, it's you… sir,]" Hrul muttered with polite embarrassment (or embarrassed politeness, one or the other) while scratching the base of his neck.

"[Leave off your pleasantries.]" I gestured towards the spot he'd been staring at. "[I was made aware that your path intersected with the slayer of phantasmal beasts. Am I correct?]"

"[Yes, sir,]" he answered, then sneakily glanced over his shoulder, as if to make sure that she was still where he'd left her. He let out a relieved breath and told me, "[I encountered her only a few minutes ago, after I broke off from the main group in the suburbs. She was tracking something, so I kept my distance and observed her, as per your orders.]"

"[I acknowledge your words,]" I grunted, then inched towards the edge and took a peek down the street. Sure enough, Rinne was crouching in an alley behind a restaurant, exactly where I'd spotted her while making the Far Sight roll call.

On a sidenote, I was in an unfamiliar corner of the city, which wasn't *that* surprising considering it was pretty big, and I rarely had the time to just stroll around the place outside of our usual commuting and hanging out routes. What *was* surprising was the fact that the architecture and décor dominating the surrounding streets were all stereotypically Chinese. I mean it—colourful tiled roofs with those odd ornaments at the corners; pagoda-style multi-story buildings; and large, lavishly decorated pavilion gates. Also, if that didn't make things blatant enough, the bright neon signs of the storefronts and eateries on both sides of the road made perfectly clear the cultural heritage of the inhabitants with their complex, often stylized logograms.

Does Timaeus have its very own Chinatown? I wondered.

This, of course, also meant that the target of my attention was skulking in an alley behind a reasonably high-class Chinese restaurant. She was wearing the exact same clothes she wore the last time I saw her.

Does she even have another outfit? Or maybe she's one of those boring people who has several sets of clothes and wears them in a rotation...

My somewhat unnecessary pondering about the huntress's wardrobe was soon interrupted when I noticed the Faun closely inspecting me.

"[Sir Blackcloak... are you injured?]" he asked.

I sneakily rolled my eyes at the question and explained to him, "[My flesh was lightly cut upon the volatile dispersal of an internal partition.]"

"[The vola... did you mean *exploding*? As in, an exploding wall?]" he paraphrased after me. "[How did that happen?]"

"[I discovered and intruded upon the lair of my kin's ambushers, after which excrement occurred, and a partition of man-made stone shattered due to a collision with a crumbler of matter composed of lightning-infused gaseous substances. It was nothing spectacular,]" I impatiently told him.

In response to my words, the Faun mumbled to himself for a few seconds, his expression growing more and more befuddled, until his ears drooped in resignation.

"[Erm... sir, I'm afraid I couldn't understand most of what you just said.]"

I sent the ram-man a long, slightly withering glance, then let out a shallow sigh and whispered, "I said I found the bad guy's base, and when I infiltrated it, a nearby wall was blasted by a plasma disintegrator, and I got hit by the debris."

"[Oh!]" Hrul's eyes lit up, but I couldn't help but shake my head.

"You know, I was speaking in Faunish precisely so that we can avoid miscommunication, but it seems like my efforts were in vain," I grumbled and glanced over the edge of the roof. Rinne hadn't moved an inch, so I turned back to the Faun at my side, and to my surprise, I found him awkwardly fidgeting like a schoolboy who'd just gotten scolded by the principal.

"[I'm sorry, sir,]" Hrul apologized in earnest the moment our eyes met. "[It's not your fault. It's simply that your words are...]" At this point he paused, obviously looking for the word, and then he muttered, "[Old?]"

"Old," I repeated after him. "Do you mean old-fashioned?"

"[No, no,]" he denied on the spot, but then after a moment of thinking he told me, "[Or maybe yes? Your words are very...]" He paused, again. Then his eyes lit up and he exclaimed, "[Archaic! That's the word I was looking for.]"

"I'm glad you found it, but keep it down before she notices us," I warned him, and he fell silent. Thankfully, our target of observation was none the wiser, as she was still crouching in the alleyway while occasionally hitting her wrapped-up sword against the nearby wall. I had no idea what that was about, but for the moment, I was a bit more curious about the interesting little morsel my companion just dropped.

"Just for the record, how archaic are we talking about?"

The Faun warrior considered that. "[It's hard to say. The words that you use and the way you string them together are both very, very old.]"

"Older than Brang?" I asked absentmindedly while keeping one eye on the irrational huntress seemingly arguing with her sword.

"[The general is from the sixth generation,]" Hrul replied while rubbing his nose with one oversized thumb. "[I never asked him about his age, and I don't think he's keeping track of it anymore, but he should be over nine hundred years old.]"

"What? Really?" I whispered in surprise, and the Faun nodded.

"[Yes. He is one of the oldest Faun in the entire Abyss. Compared to us of the fourteenth generation, he is a living ancestor.]"

"Wow... Nine hundred years? Really?" I muttered in disbelief. It was really hard to wrap my head around such a huge number. Wouldn't that mean that Snowy's somewhat goofy Faun "uncle" predated the modern English language? Hell, maybe even Middle English! No wonder he spoke funny. But more importantly...

"Wait, you're saying that the Faun dialect I use is actually older than nine hundred years? Seriously?"

"[I think so,]" he confirmed with a nod. "[I recommend you ask the general. He could probably tell you more.]"

"I think I'll do that. Thanks," I concluded the discussion, and turned around to study the erratic huntress in the alleyway.

Hrul also joined me, and the two of us proceeded to spend the next couple of minutes wordlessly staring at a grown woman muttering to herself while occasionally glaring at her sword. It wasn't exactly the most riveting spectacle, but I didn't have much choice for entertainment.

"[So… are we just going to watch her?]" Hrul inquired. I glanced at him and, after some thinking, shook my head.

"No. I actually plan to get close enough to touch her."

"[To… touch her?]" the Faun wondered.

"I meant that literally. It's a trick that lets me track people."

"[I see,]" my companion stated with a knowing nod, after which we both fell silent once again. The silence didn't last long though, as a couple of short seconds later, he asked, "[So… why aren't you going down to lay your hand on her?]"

I decided to ignore his random (and probably unintentional) innuendo and told him, "I'm thinking about how to approach her as safely as possible. I mean, I just got a tiny bit injured, and Judy got angry at me over it. I might've left in a hurry, as well. So if I return with even one scratch on me, she just might beat me up."

"[She would? I didn't think she was the violent type.]"

"Not *literally*," I grumbled under my breath before deciding to continue my observations. "What do you think she's doing now?" I asked absent-mindedly while subtly nodding towards the alley.

Hrul followed the direction of my gesture and, after a bit of consideration, he guessed, "[Maybe she's waiting for something? When I first saw her, she acted like she was tracking something. Maybe she found where the trail ended, and now she is waiting for her game to come out of its nest?]"

"Maybe…" I granted him an ambivalent response and then fell silent again.

All things considered, it appeared Rinne wasn't going anywhere. At least not for the time being. As such, I went through my options.

First, I could use some distraction tactics again. For example, I could ask Hrul to jump down and scare her a little, then while she was focusing on him, I would use the Faun as an anchor to teleport behind her and… well, maybe not karate-chop her, but at least mark her in some way. Maybe a light tap on the top of her head?

The more I thought about that, the less confident I became about this idea. I mean, while I arguably made an unnecessary deep impression on her, it didn't mean that she wouldn't cut my hand off if I startled her, and if I came home with an arm missing, Judy might literally strangle me, after all. What other options did I have?

Well, I could try to kidnap her… which sounded really creepy, but it wasn't, I swear! It would be similar to my Plan B with Lab Coat Guy. Jump in, grab her, jump next to a Brang and Company, and then subdue her, tie her up, gag her, and…

Okay, screw it, even I'm starting to think this is creepy. Never mind.

On a more serious note, the reason why it wouldn't have worked was fairly prosaic: since I told them to scout the city, the Fauns were literally all over the place, so even if I teleported her away, we would be in the exact same scenario with one me, one creepy huntress, and one Faun. In short, ambush strategies were out of the question.

So, what options did I have left? I could always just shadow her from a distance, I supposed. Maybe I could follow her to where she was staying, wait until she fell asleep, and then teleport into her room and touch her. I mean, that still sounded super-creepy, but it was definitely the safest method at my disposal, and today "Safety" was my middle name. Leonard S. Dunning. It didn't even sound bad.

I also had one more option, which was the simplest but at the same time the least predictable.

Hop down into that alleyway and have a friendly chat with her. As in, walk up to her, have some small talk about the weather or something, and then when I got her guard sufficiently lowered, bam! I sneakily poke her to make my mark and beat a hasty retreat. Simple, and still "reasonably safe."

Unfortunately, Leonard R. S. Dunning didn't have the same ring to it. Maybe L. R. S. Dunning? That kind of made me sound like some big shot author. Okay, I'm sold—"reasonably safe," it is!

Jokes aside, it was pretty much my best bet for placing a mark and getting home before Judy got herself worked up again. As such, I steeled my nerves, took a deep breath, and told my Faun companion, "I'm going in. Be on the lookout."

"[Understood,]" Hrul solemnly nodded and gave me a short salute.

Anyhow, I looked at the irritating huntress and put together a path of approach in my mind. The ground was too far down, so instead I Phased over to a nearby rooftop, startling Hrul in the process. By the way, I'd been thinking a lot about this recently, and I decided that I'd officially christen my teleportation ability as "Phasing." It was technically inaccurate to call it that, but since it was my cover name for it, anyway, it never hurt to keep my terminology consistent so that I wouldn't trip up during a conversation with the others. Also, it just sounded nice.

I Phased over to another roof on the other side of the street, then to an elaborately ornamented balcony covered with numerous bright neon signs on the outside. From there, I managed to reach one of those external fire escape stairways, and only there did I finally land on the ground.

Now, there's a funny little thing I must admit here: If I'd really wanted to, I could've Phased down to the ground from my initial vantage point, as the maximum range of my ability seemed to be about ten meters. However, the farther I moved, the more disoriented and nauseous I'd be after arrival, so the practical range was closer to five meters. During the recent training sessions with the Faun, I'd discovered that if I kept the jumping distance under that, it would greatly reduce the vertigo and other annoying side effects of Phasing. Thus, covering the same distance over five short Phase jumps left me in much better shape than doing it in one long one. As for why, I had no idea whatsoever, but when life gives you a free broken ability, it's common courtesy not to look it in the mouth.

Either way, I finally arrived at my chosen destination, which was near the entrance of the alley Rinne was staking out. I limbered up my every-thing, took a deep breath to calm myself, pocketed my hands, and then casually rounded the corner and headed right towards my target with a friendly (but in no way flirty) smile on my face.

"Oh? Good evening," I casually greeted the woman skulking in the shadows, followed by a strategically deployed, laid-back wave. I was going for a "jovial, good-natured neighbour" kind of air, but the creepy huntress stared at me like I was some kind of scary wraith that had materialized before her. Quite rude, I must say!

After a couple long seconds of heavy silence, she jolted out of her stupor and exclaimed, "What are you…? We mean, good—No, we mean, why are you here?"

I shrugged then spread my arms in the universal *I mean no harm—please don't freak out* gesture.

It didn't seem to work so well, so I let out a shallow sigh and told her, "I was just taking a stroll and noticed you were in there, so I thought I'd say hi."

"Really?" Her guarded expression eased, but then she glanced down at the wrapped-up sword in her hands and forcefully shook her head.

"Right, that's too convenient! You must have been stalking us!" she exclaimed.

She looked me in the eye, and after a second or two, her lips stretched into a familiar, but no less disturbing, slasher smile… except not really. Her grin was a bit strained, and on top of that, her cheeks were flushed.

"Usually we are the ones doing the stalking," she began with an equally familiar, unsettling voice… except it was also off-key and a bit stuttery. "It's a… new experience."

"No, I'm not stalking you," I told her while hiding my rapidly rising exasperation as well as I could. "This meeting is entirely coincidental, and I thought that since we ran into each other like this, I'd say hi and ask how you're doing. Not a shred of stalking was involved."

"Can we believe you?" she asked in a considerably more normal voice, then after deliberating, she shook her head. "No, Onikiri says we can't trust you."

"She said that?" I asked with only partially feigned interest as I took one step closer to her. "What else is your sword saying about me?"

She gave me a strange look, almost as if she didn't expect I'd take her comments about a talking weapon seriously, but since I looked earnest enough (or at least I hoped I did, as I was doing my best to do so), she decided to tell me.

"Onikiri says you're the kind of man who uses all sorts of dirty tricks to get ahead in the hunt."

"Really?"

She gave me a firm nod. "She says you would deceive us, trample on our innocent maidenly heart, and then discard us and revel in the catharsis of the slaughter all by yourself. She also says you are a male vixen and a female dog." She abruptly paused here, as if she couldn't understand what she'd just said and asked me, "Are you really a female dog?"

I gave her a skeptical look in return, but since she turned out to be entirely serious, I pointedly glared at the bundled blade in her hand and told her/them, "No, I'm not, but you are one rude ass sword."

"So, you're not," she (Rinne, not her foul-mouthed sword) stated. "Nevertheless, we cannot trust you. We are hunters in kind, so you should know that the only pleasure of the flesh we seek is parting the viscera of a worthy foe and the sight of their crimson lifeblood—"

"Yes, yes, I get it," I interrupted her. "I'm not lying, though. I swear," I lied to her like a champ.

"You do?" she perked up. "That changes things," she declared as she switched her grip on her sword so that she held it by the cloth covering it just below the guard. Then she held it out horizontally between the two of us.

For a while, we silently stared at each other without moving a finger, right until I couldn't take it any longer and asked, "So… now what?"

"You said you would swear," she told me matter-of-factly. "If you swear on Onikiri, she will immediately know if you are lying."

"Seriously?" I responded to her claim with a skeptically raised brow.

"Yes. Any oath sworn on Onikiri cannot be broken."

For a moment, I wanted to ask, *Wait, isn't it Odin's Gungnir that does all that?* But I decided against it. In fact, I was a little wary of the whole "unbreakable vow" thing, so I asked the obvious question.

"How exactly does that work?"

Rinne gave me an *Is this guy messing with me or is he really a natural-born simpleton?* kind of look and explained, "It's simple. You will touch the shroud of Onikiri, then swear upon Onikiri that you will only tell the truth, and then so long as you hold on to Onikiri, you won't be able to tell a lie. Even a child could do it."

"After you explain it to them, sure," I quipped back before asking for clarification. "So, does that mean that the whole 'unbreakable oath' thing only works so long as I'm touching the sword?"

"The shroud of Onikiri," she corrected me, "but yes."

"So... once I let go, I'll able to break an oath that was made on your sword."

"Yes." She nodded like it made perfect sense.

"But then it's not an 'unbreakable' oath," I flatly told her, at which point she gave me another *Is this guy dense or what?* glance.

"It is unbreakable because if you break it, we will cut you down with Onikiri," she clarified with a foreboding smile.

"That... still doesn't make it unbreakable. It just means you punish the person breaking the oath, and frankly speaking, you're not giving me a lot of incentives to do this."

"Incentive?" she muttered while tilting her head to the side a little. "Doing it would earn our trust. Is that not an incentive?"

"Yeah, but... to be honest, I think the possibility of getting cut down is a little disproportionate in comparison."

The creepy huntress gave me a curious look, and after some vacillation, she ultimately stated, "Onikiri is now curious about you. If you cooperate with the oath, and you are not found wanting, we will grant you a request." A second after saying that, she blushed, and she hastily added, "Onikiri wants you to know that if you make a lecherous request, she will cut you, anyway."

"Good to know," I muttered, but at the same time the gears in my head had already begun to turn. Sure, there was a tiny bit of risk involved, but if I played my cards right, I could potentially ask her to let me touch her, and... that would get me cut down. Okay, so I'll have to be careful about how I word it, but it would still be doable, and it would be much less awkward and weird than some kind of convoluted plot to sneakily poke her.

As such, after much deliberation, I decided to say, "All right. I'll swear upon Onikiri, if you agree to shake my hand afterwards." Since she didn't answer and only blinked at me in confusion, I clarified, "I mean, a proper handshake to signify that we acknowledge each other. Without gloves."

She still looked befuddled, but then her eyes cleared up and she asked me, "Onikiri is curious to know if you are a degenerate manswine who derives carnal pleasure from vulgarly fondling a pure young woman's delicate hand?"

For a second or five, all I could muster in response was a look flatter than a roadkill skunk after a steamroller parade, but at last I gathered my wits and replied, "No, and now you are only the second most insufferable person in this alleyway. Congratulations."

"Thank you," she responded with perfect seriousness before she waved her still horizontal sword in my direction. I only hesitated for a moment before I decided to just go with the flow and grab it. "Now what?"

"Make the oath," she told me like it was absolutely obvious.

I let out a tiny little groan on principle and said, "Okay, let's try it. How about, I solemnly swear that I will not lie while I am holding this sword? That shou—"

I got cut off by a strange, slightly numbing sensation around my nape. It was a little disconcerting, but it wasn't bad enough to warrant running away while screaming like a little girl, so I decided to bear with it for the time being.

"Did it work?" I asked tentatively, and Rinne nodded in confirmation. "Okay, so let me try this first. *My name is Leonard Dunning.*"

Nothing happened.

"Okay, so I'm in the green with that one. How about, *I did not follow after you.*"

There was still no reaction, which told me that technical truths were also fine. That actually took a pretty big load off my mind. After all, technical, half-, and metaphorical truths were my bread and butter. Still, just to be on the safe side, I also tried a full-out, context-appropriate lie.

"*I fought against a group of Faun and got injured.*"

To my surprise, that also didn't trigger anything, though the numbing sensation became considerably more unpleasant. Maybe it was all about context? Or in this case, the lack thereof? I mean, I did fight against Karukk and the rest during training, and I did get injured today, so the two parts of the statement weren't categorically false, per se.

At last, I decided to go balls to the wall and said, "Okay, how about this: *I ate a—*"

I wanted to say *a whole semitruck for dinner*, but when I tried to do that, the previous slight numbness at the back of my neck became... well, not exactly painful, but kind of uncomfortable. It also somehow suppressed my ability to say the words in my head, which was even more uncomfortable. It didn't last long, though, as something sparked in my mind, a strong sense of indignation about something trying to restrict what I could do or say. It might've been a preconditioned reflex that came to be because of all the "narrative influence" discussions I'd had with Judy in the past week, and the moment I let it loose, it was like a torrent of raging water that completely washed away whatever mental binds tried to hold me down, and I uttered, "—*truck for dinner,*" managing to completely surprise myself.

The shock I felt probably couldn't compare to what the woman in front of me felt, as her jaw pretty much hit the floor.

"Y-you broke the oath," she stuttered. "Why did you break the oath? How did you break the oath?"

"It's... kind of hard to explain," I told her tentatively. "Though in my defense, I didn't really break the actual oath, just the magical binding thingie that came with the oath," I argued while reaffirming my grip on the sword. "Let's try again. This time, I promise I won't accidentally break anything."

She remained silent for a little while, apparently listening to her sword, but at last she said, "Onikiri says something is weird about you, and we should cut you into tiny ribbons of flesh writhing in agony... but we're okay with giving it another try first."

"How gracious of you," I muttered before flashing a totally genuine smile and reiterating, "So, again, I swear upon this here sword that I will not speak a single lie while I hold it."

After a second or so, I could once again feel the uncanny numbness, meaning that the oath had taken hold again.

I let out a shallow breath and told her, "Okay, let me get started. As I said, I didn't stalk you. I tracked a Faun, and we met after I left him behind."

"I see. So, you fought one of the lesser creatures of the underworld?"

"I've been fighting Fauns a lot as of late," I gave her an out-of-context truth, but she didn't seem to mind or notice.

"So, the creatures of the underworld are your sworn enemies, as well."

I paused for a second. Technically speaking, the "creatures of the underworld" would probably cover both the Faun and the Chimera. Since Crowey and I obviously had bad blood between us, and he commanded way more Fauns than our ragtag group of dissenters, it was accurate to say that the vast majority of them were my sworn enemies, so I responded, "Yes, they indeed are."

"Did you get injured during your battle against the lesser creature?" came the next question as she gestured at the Band-Aid on my face.

"No, I was injured when I infiltrated the secret hideout of the enemy," I replied confidently.

"The creatures of the underworld have a secret hideout?"

"Yes, they do," I answered her, this time 100 percent honestly.

"We didn't know that," she muttered. But then she paused and added, "Onikiri says we are getting sidetracked. She says you are a duplicitous shark and we shouldn't let you lead the conversation or you will trap us in a web of false truths until you can ravage my body and mind."

This time, I directed my disapproving look at the sword, but since it didn't react (not that it could), I glanced back to Rinne and told her, "I'm not going to ravage you."

"You won't?" she responded in surprise, as if what I said was some kind of shocking revelation, then after another brief pause, she said, "Onikiri told me we should ask you if you want to play with my maidenly heart, wring us dry, and then laugh at our misery."

Grimacing, I said, "Your sword has issues, but no, I don't want to do that."

"You don't?" She once again seemed shocked to the core. "She also told us to ask if you are only after our body."

"I'm..." I wanted to say "no" right away, but then I could once again feel the magical restriction stopping me from continuing. I took a deep breath and calmed my nerves before I could accidentally undo the bindings again, and instead I thought about my options. Since I wanted to mark her, and I needed to touch her skin for that, I supposed it was true that I was after her body in a sense, just not in the way she was thinking. However, that meant I wasn't after her *whole* body, only her skin. So...

"I'm... not really after your body, per se?"

"Not even that?" she acted shocked for the third time in a row.

"No, not even that," I stressed, feeling a little awkward. "Is there anything else you wanted to ask, or are your doubts cleared up?"

She didn't answer for a long time, perhaps because she was silently arguing with her sword. When she did speak up, it was almost like she deflated.

"Yes. We trust you now," she told me in a dour, almost dejected voice.

I immediately let go of her weapon and used the same hand to scratch the back of my neck until the numbness went away.

"Okay then, so, now that we are trusting each other in earnest and all that jazz, can we get on with the handshake? It's getting cold, and I'm not dressed for staying out in the open."

"Oh, right. There was that," she muttered as she offered a hand.

"Without the glove," I warned her, and after some hesitation, she began to grudgingly take it off… only to freeze midway as her eyes opened wide as saucers.

At the same time, my danger sense spiked and, with little conscious input, my body immediately hunched over and I literally rolled to the side. And not a millisecond too soon. Even from my tumbling point of view, I could see the creepy huntress swinging her rapidly unwrapping sword towards the exact spot where my head used to be.

Then there was a strange, squelching sound followed by a high-pitched screech, and the moment I landed on my feet, my entire right side was sprinkled with a warm, slightly viscous liquid, forcing me to stagger in surprise. When I finally came to a halt, I also registered the fact that something, or rather two somethings, had landed close by.

I exhaled hard and quickly took in the scenery. Rinne was, for some reason, maintaining the exact same position, with her blade held in both hands, its swing stopped right at the zenith of its arc, the purple cloth billowing behind her in a nonexistent windstorm. More importantly, on the ground beside her, I saw a rapidly bleeding out creature, in two parts.

"Is that what I think it is?" I asked her, pointing at the corpse.

"It's the spawn of the creature of the underworld," she stated as she finally dropped her pose and, after getting the blood off the blade by doing a few swings, her sword rewrapped itself in an instant. "Your reflexes are great as expected from a fellow hunter of the dark corners of this earth," she complimented me, but I summarily ignored her, and instead I focused on the bisected thing on the ground.

At first glance, it looked a lot like the four-legged version of the Chimera I encountered in the school. The two biggest differences were its uncannily long hind legs, which kind of reminded me of a frog's, and the fact that, if I put the two halves back together, the whole creature would be roughly the size of a pug.

"Did you say 'spawn'?" I questioned her, observing the twitching remains in front of me.

"Yes," she responded with disinterest. "This creature is cunning, sending its spawn out to forage food while the true body stays hidden. As devious as it is irritating. These small ones provide no challenge."

"I think I get it," I responded as I faced her. "You staked out the back of the restaurant to see if one of these spawns showed up, and then you wanted to follow it back to the main body."

"Precisely. Except your presence foiled my plans."

"To be fair, I think we all got carried away with the whole oath business, so I'm not taking full responsibility for this."

Rinne gave me a peeved look, but at last she said, "Onikiri wants us to tell you that this is the first time the spawned attacked someone first, which just confirms that your very presence is so aggravating that even mindless beasts cannot tolerate you."

I rolled my eyes at her comment. "Your sword is the most obnoxious thing I've met in a while. How do you even live with something like that?"

The usually creepy huntress suddenly gave me a startlingly vulnerable, almost helpless look, and she whispered, "Not by choice." Then she shook her head and added, in a much more forceful tone, "Onikiri is right. Your presence seems to drive the spawns into a frenzy. It's a good thing."

"I'm a little afraid to ask, but how so?"

My mostly unwanted conversationalist gave me another of those rude looks that I didn't even want to decipher, after which she told me, "Our plan was as you said. However, your presence creates a new possibility. Were you to patrol with us, we could draw out the spawns of the creature. Once enough of them perish, it would have no chance but to come into the open and face us in battle!"

"So, you want me to be your bait?" I asked, and she shamelessly nodded. "Ooookay, but didn't you want to make this into a contest or something?"

"Contest?" she asked back with an expression that said this was the first time she'd heard of it, but then her eyes lit up and she repeatedly shook her head. "Nonsense! We trust each other now, so there is no need for the contest anymore. Since we trust each other, it is time that we join hands in our efforts to eradicate the creatures of the underworld! As hunters who trust each other! We should not ignore the call to slaughter for such a petty thing as a contest!"

"Sure, whatever. Let's say I agreed. What's your exact plan?"

"We'll hunt the spawn of the creature night after night by visiting various parts of the city. We should focus on areas where discarded food is readily available, such as the malls, shopping streets, restaurants, and the parks."

"So... let me see if I get this straight," I spoke up while gently massaging my temple. "You want us to meet every evening, and then stroll around the various recreational areas of the city, just the two of us, and wait for these spawn things to attack me?"

"Yes."

"Okay… but what if they don't attack me? What if this was just a fluke?"

"We must still try. It's of the utmost importance," she told me with such conviction I was tempted to nod along.

I pondered my options but eventually decided to play along.

"All right, it's worth a try."

"Great!" Rinne suddenly flashed me a surprisingly normal smile, which honestly took me aback for a moment. Unfortunately (or maybe fortunately, depending on one's point of view), said smile quickly warped into a much more typical slasher one as she continued to mutter, "We shall walk the twilight, slay the insulting brood of the cunning beast hiding in the shadows, and once it shows itself, only *then* will the *true* slaughter begin! The blood and viscera will—"

"Sorry to interrupt," I interrupted without being sorry at all, "but could we get on with things? I'm feeling really cold, and I still have some errands to run tonight."

"Get on with what?"

"You still owe me a handshake," I pointed out, and for some reason the annoying huntress's face got flushed again. Normally I would have considered this a warning sign and might have even deployed some anti-harem countermeasures, but to be frank, I just wanted to get things over with and finally mark her before something else got in the way.

At last she took a deep breath and removed her right glove with timid motions, then after some further unspoken qualms, she finally offered me her hand.

"Finally," I whispered, and without further ado, I grabbed hold of her hand, eliciting a surprised gasp from her. As I did so, I quickly checked with Far Sight, and I noted with no small amount of satisfaction that I had a brand-new red dot on my radar.

"Onikiri is curious," Rinne suddenly interrupted my happy moment. "She told us to ask you how you can live with yourself as a lecherous freak with such a nonsensical fetish like that."

I took a deep breath, glanced down at the sword in question, and simply said, "I'll answer her if she can explain to me how a piece of metal can become such an insufferable wanker."

"She says you are a son of a female dog," Rinne replied, slightly confused by the words coming out of her own mouth again.

"Still better than being a chunk of sharpened pig iron with delusions of grandeur."

She fell silent for a long moment, during which her expression clouded and then cleared up.

"Onikiri doesn't make any sense. She's saying something about your mother, but I can't make heads or tails of it."

"It's best you don't even try," I told her and finally let go of her hand. "Also, I think this is a good spot to close this meeting. I'm already getting pretty chilled."

"A true hunter shouldn't feel the cold," she told me like it was self-evident.

"Yeah, sure, whatever," I dismissed her as I quickly turned on my heels and strode out of the alleyway before her sword regained her composure.

… Did I really just use her sword regained her composure *in a sentence, and it actually made sense? Damn, my life is weird.*

Anyhow, I gave her a small wave when I reached the corner of the alley, and she returned the gesture in an uncharacteristically subdued fashion. The moment I was out of sight, I focused my Far Sight on Judy and found her in Snowy's room. The two of them were diligently going through her homework and what she missed over the week we were absent from school. I didn't want to disturb their study session, but I didn't have any other choice, and I really did feel a little cold, so after picking a spot beside the bed, I Phased right back into my house.

"I'm back," I declared a little wearily, feeling drained after interacting with Rinne for so long.

Unexpectedly enough, there was little to no reaction upon my arrival. I glanced over to Judy, and I found both her and my sister staring at me with eyes wide open. For a moment, I had no idea why they were so mortified, but then I glanced over myself and noticed that I was still covered in the aftermath of the Chimera spawn dissection.

"Um…" I quickly raised my palms and told them, "It's not my blood!"

In retrospect, I should've probably said something along the lines of *Please don't strangle me!* But hindsight is always twenty-twenty.

CHAPTER 18

PART 1

It was a little after midnight. The only light in my room came from my PC monitor, and my glowing face probably looked pretty spooky as I frowned at it in dissatisfaction.

Ugh, fine. I might as well be honest here and admit that I wasn't really frowning at the screen. I'd been doing that for a while even before I turned on the PC. The reason behind my sour mood was actually quite simple, and it was related to a certain lovely yet decidedly naggy girlfriend of mine. She was pretty angry at me when I returned covered in blood, but after I cleaned up and I let her confirm that I was unharmed (or at the very least I had no more injuries than before I left), she calmed down a little.

That calm before the storm lasted precisely until the moment I explained to her that I would be accompanying the weird huntress and her even weirder sword on starlit strolls through the most scenic and romantic parts of the city every night from now on. Her words, not mine, and from that it was easy to understand why I was currently feeling more than a little blue. Some might say it was our first outright lovers' quarrel, but from the way she left, it felt more like a lovers' cold war, which was not nearly as benign or amusing.

Anyhow, I shook my head and put the topic aside for the moment. I was sure I'd have to come back to it when I tried to convince Judy that my interest in Rinne was about as far from romantic as Proxima Centauri, but for the time being, I had more important things to do. Such as replying to the message right in front of me.

"Admin: Are you serious? No Research Society activity whatsoever?"

After I typed that into the chatbox, it took less than three seconds for someone to respond.

"MoroseMoose: I was surprised, too."

"W1NG3D N1NJ4: THEY MUST BE AFRAID OF THE ARCHMAGE OF THE ISLAND TOO! \\(° □ ° l||l)/"

"W1NG3D N1NJ4: I WOULD KNOW, I LIVE HERE! HE IS SCAAAAAARY!!! (≧Д≦)"

"MoroseMoose: Yeah, I know. The man has a reputation for not tolerating anyone else on his territory."

"Admin: Are you sure we are talking about the same guy?"

"MoroseMoose: Pretty sure? The post of the arch-mage is one for life."

"Admin: That still makes no sense. His 'territory' has a mansion full of Draconians in it, and he was making sneaky deals with the Abyssals."

"Admin: Plus, I've heard from a firsthand source that the Research Society was not only on the island, but he's in contact with them."

"W1NG3D N1NJ4: WUT MATE!? SERIOUSLY!!!??? ∑(O_O')"

"MoroseMoose: I'm a little skeptical, too. I've never read anything about that on the forums."

"Admin: You must've heard of the incident at the School a few weeks ago."

"MoroseMoose: … Yes?"

"Admin: Did you think the Abyssals causing a ruckus materialized out of nowhere?"

"W1NG3D N1NJ4: HE GOT YOU THERE! (—‿—)"

"MoroseMoose: To be fair, the mages clamped down on the island pretty hard after the incident, so it's obvious I would be out of the loop. I'm not even on Critias."

"W1NG3D N1NJ4: BUT I AM! I AM RIGHT HERE! (Oω<)~☆""

"Admin: And you didn't provide a single report to the database about what happened."

"W1NG3D N1NJ4: SOWWWY… /(/•/ω/•//)/"

"MoroseMoose: Actually, how do YOU know about what happened over there?"

"Admin: I just told you, I have an informant with firsthand information on the events."

"MoroseMoose: One of ours?"

"MoroseMoose: I've read there was an asset involved in what happened."

"Admin: No, not her. Let's just say it's a third party not directly affili-ated with us."

"MoroseMoose: … Is that safe?"

"W1NG3D N1NJ4: YEAH!! BE CAREFUL, ADMIN!!!!!!!"

"W1NG3D N1NJ4: THE HIGHER-UPS ARE ALLERGIC TO OUTSIDERS! (ò‿ó)"

"Admin: Don't worry; my source of information is about as reliable and confidential as I am."

"MoroseMoose: Then why didn't you add the info you got from them to the database yet?"

"Admin: Because first I have to come up with a reasonable explanation for how I received the intel in the first place."

"Admin: I don't want to appear compromised to the higher-ups, either."

"W1NG3D N1NJ4: DON'T WORRY BOSS-MAN!!!!"

"W1NG3D N1NJ4: IF YOU GET BUSTED, I WILL TAKE CARE OF YOUR ASSISTANT FOR YOU!!! (♥ω♥)"

"Admin: I won't be, but even if I somehow was busted, you better not."

"W1NG3D N1NJ4: (｡T ω T｡)"

I let out a small sigh and readjusted my posture in my seat, and after some hesitation, I also patted down and lightly massaged my injured side. It didn't really hurt, per se, but it was itching like crazy, and I didn't dare to actually scratch it lest I accidentally tear off some scabs and ruin all of Snowy's hard work. The kneading didn't help a lot, so I diverted my attention back to the screen instead.

"Admin: That aside, have you guys found anything related to my other query?"

"MoroseMoose: About the woman with the Japanese sword?"

"MoroseMoose: I tried to PM some guys I know, but they didn't answer yet. Nothing on my end, sorry."

"W1NG3D N1NJ4: OH! OH! I ACTUALLY HAVE SOMETHING FOR YOU!!! (′｡• ω •｡‵)"

"W1NG3D N1NJ4: I FOUND THIS IN THE ARCHIVED POSTS! I'M SENDING IT OVER!!!! ⊂(•∀•) 彡=￣ ⊠"

A few seconds after he wrote that, there was a new notification about a message in my PM box. I opened it, and it contained a single link pointing at one of the archived forum threads of the Hub's slightly more public section, where the average Celestial users, plus some of the more socially active agents, congregated.

I quickly skimmed what was written there, and it turned out to be a fairly straightforward back-and-forth discussion between a handful of users about an encounter one of them had in the past. It was in that user's posts where the keyword Onikiri appeared in relation to… wait for it… a secret clan of demon-hunting ninjas. Yes, I'm dead serious.

From what little information the posts provided, it appeared that they were an offshoot of some kind of minor, neutral supernatural faction based in the Far East. There was no mention of sentient swords in the discussion, but Onikiri was mentioned as some kind of sacred weapon used for hunting demons, youkai, and whatever other supernatural nasties they came across. Apparently, the clan mainly consisted of a handful of individuals centered around the current generation's wielder of Onikiri, and when they ran out of monsters to slay in the area they currently occupied, the entire clan would move on to greener pastures.

In conclusion, they were nomadic, monster-exterminating, highly visible ninjas. At least that was new. It would also explain what Rinne was doing here. Or rather, it would clarify some of her motivations, as I already knew she was here to hunt the stray Chimera. Speaking of which, I made a mental note to ask her about where she learned about the Chimera in the first place, as unless this clan of hers had some pretty amazing intelligence network, she showed up too fast for my liking. My bet was on the arch-mage once again, but I decided to give him the benefit of the doubt and ask, anyway. Not that he deserved it.

Anyhow, since it was just a short discussion with some dead links strewn in for good measure, I didn't learn a lot, but it was still better than nothing.

"Admin: It's secondhand information, but it seems trustworthy enough to act as a starting point."

"W1NG3D N1NJ4: HE-HE-HE! DON'T WORRY ADMIN! I ALREADY HAVE ANOTHER LEAD!! (￣ω￣)"

"MoroseMoose: You do?"

"W1NG3D N1NJ4: YUP! I KNOW A GUY WHO KNOWS A GAL WHO KNOWS A GUY WHO SHOULD KNOW AAAAAAALL ABOUT THEM!!!"

"W1NG3D N1NJ4: I WILL ASK MY CONTACT TO INTRODUCE ME, AND THEN I WILL INTERROGATE HIM ALL SECRET AGENT LIKE! COOL, HUH? o(>ω<)o"

"Admin: Yes, yes, very cool. Good luck with that, and thank you for your hard work."

"W1NG3D N1NJ4: I WAS PRAISED!! YAY!!!! ୧(୨˙ω˙)୨✧"

I let out a shallow sigh and stretched my back. Maybe it was because of my superficial injuries that were not a big deal at all in any way, but I was already feeling uncomfortably numb in my seat, even though it had been less than an hour since I sat down. Because of that, and since it didn't seem like they could show me anything new, I typed:

"Admin: I suppose that's it for today. Thanks for the help, guys."

"MoroseMoose: You're welcome, though I couldn't help much."

"W1NG3D N1NJ4: YOU ARE WELCOME, ADMIN!!"

"W1NG3D N1NJ4: I WILL GO TO BED NOW. I HAVE LECTURES IN THE MORNING. BYE-BYE!!! (￣ρ￣)...zzZZ"

"Admin: Sleep well."

"MoroseMoose: Good night. I also should hit the sack. I had a long day at work."

"Admin: Do that. Admin, out."

"MoroseMoose: Bye."

With that brief exchange of farewells over, I closed the Celestial Hub and immediately stood up. It only took a few seconds for my vertical orientation to get my blood to flow all nice and proper, and once my joints were no longer stiff, I decided I might as well go for the whole mile and do some light exercises.

I did just that, starting with a few push-ups, but I was always an avid advocate of multitasking, so I didn't let my mind stay idle while my body was moving. For a start, I decided to check on Rinne. I'd gone through a lot of trouble to mark her, so I figured it was about time I capitalized on my efforts. I used my Far Sight without any further delay, but much to my disappointment, I found her quietly sleeping under a pile of blankets in what looked like a modest motel bedroom.

In retrospect, I don't even know what I was expecting; it was well after midnight, after all. Nonetheless, being cautious was my current motto, so I observed her for a short while, just to be sure, before I moved on to the others on my roll call list. The members of our merry little gang were also all in dreamland, so there was nothing to see or say on that front, either.

As such, I moved on to our irritating antagonists, starting with everyone's favourite asshole Abyssal lord... who was still lying in his bed doing his best dead herring impression. Every time I looked at him like this, I was tempted to hop over and liven up his life a little. I wasn't thinking of anything major, just some silly little pranks to get him to stop staring at the ceiling with those glassy eyes. Maybe replace all of his medicine with industrial-strength laxatives. Or release a herd of feral skunks into his bedchamber. Pop a pipe bomb filled with sneezing powder. And shrapnel. But mostly sneezing powder.

Unfortunately, my recent agreement with Judy prohibited me from engaging in such activities, as traveling into the heart of the Abyss for "silly" reasons was deemed "unsafe," so I had no choice but to cancel my order for a pack of skunks from the local animal shelter. You wouldn't believe how easy it is to order even the weirdest things over the internet...

But I'm kidding, of course. I wasn't so evil as to trap those poor creatures in the same room as Crowey. That would have been just straight up animal abuse! Anyways, since the pranks were off the table, I proceeded to observe him for a few minutes, just on the off chance that some of his minions would conveniently show up to give him a report. Unfortunately, nothing of the sort happened, so I switched over to doing sit-ups and then moved on to my next target.

Said target was, of course, no one else but Dr. Lab Coat Guy! I'd actually observed his activities during the evening, and I had a good grasp on his plans and affiliations, but I figured it never hurt to take one more look, just in case.

Once my vision settled, I immediately tried to close my eyes because of the sudden, sharp light coming from the workbench right in front of me. That was, of course, quite impossible, considering there were no eyes or eyelids involved in the process of observing the scenery, but biological habits die hard.

Once I overcame my initial surprise, I took a closer look at my unfamiliar environment. It was similar to the underground room where I'd marked Mr. Lab Coat, except about half the size, and most of the space was taken up by various metalworking tools and equipment. In fact, the place was so cluttered, I wondered how anyone could safely work there.

"Ki-hi-hi! Almost done!" the person actually working there exclaimed in a voice muffled by the large welder's mask. Lab Coat Guy stood in front of a large vice attached to one of the workbenches, a welding torch in one hand and a metal brush in the other. In the aforementioned vice, there was a weirdly shaped angular piece of metal with a large hole in the middle, and the man was apparently putting the finishing touches on it.

"My assessment remains unchanged," a second voice chimed in, and when I swiveled my point of view in its direction, I noticed the ridiculously dressed fembot sitting on her heels while facing the corner.

"Silence, Galatea! You are in the time-out corner until you properly reflect on your behaviour," the guy retorted after raising his welding mask, but since she didn't reply, he turned back to the thing in the vice, let his mask back down, and then he continued to weld… well, *something* on it. To be honest, I still had no idea what it was supposed to be. Maybe a postmodern sculpture?

Anyhow, soon he raised the mask again. Then he used the metal brush to clean off the slag from the welding area before he let out a satisfied grunt. He placed his tools on the bench, and after struggling with the crank, he successfully removed the object he produced from the grasp of the vice.

"Ki-hi-hi-hi! Look, Galatea! It's finished!" he called out in an excited voice while raising the thing over his head like a certain elven purveyor of master swords and green tunics.

"Negative. Master told me to sit in the corner until I am done reflecting. According to the progress bar, my reflection is only sixty-eight percent complete," the fembot answered with an understandably mechanical headshake.

"Stop being obstinate and look over here already!" Saying so, Lab Coat Guy swiftly stuck his head through the hole in the object he held, and only then did I realize what it was…!

Well, okay, I admit I still didn't know *what* the actual name of the thing was supposed to be, but, roughly, it looked like a rigid combination of a pair of shoulder pads, a chest plate that didn't even reach down to the guy's abdomen, and a tall neck guard that was more like an oversized shirt collar. All of that was a single metal piece, with no articulation or any moving parts, and on the surface, it appeared to be a collection of welded metal triangles, kind of like a low polygon model from an old video game.

Once he had it over his shoulders, the guy chuckled and called out, "You don't have to reflect on things anymore, so turn around already!"

The fembot in the corner released a series of mechanical noises (though I was about 90 percent sure she was making them with her mouth) and replied, "Negative. I believe it is for my own good that I continue to run reflection.exe to completion."

"Stop being obstinate!" Lab Coat Guy griped as he walked over with a weird gait, probably because of the extra weight on his shoulders, and gingerly nudged the android with his feet. "Come on already!"

The absurdly dressed mechanical woman let out a deep sigh and finally stood up and turned around.

"Analyzing new equipment," she stated in a mechanical voice while looking over her master, after which she added, "Impractical to the highest degree," in a truly authoritative tone that managed to bleed through even her synthesized voice.

"It's not impractical!" Lab Coat Guy cried. "Look! It has neck protection for any future sneak attacks!"

"Error. No sneak attacks necessitating such protection have been found," the fembot countered.

"I told you already! Someone hit me in the back of the neck!" Hilariously enough, he tried to point at the affected area, but because of the construction of his "protective gear," he couldn't raise his arm high enough, so after some struggling, he simply crossed his arms in front of his chest... which was also foiled by the points and edges on the chest plate segment. At last, he let out a defeated sigh and whispered, "MkI suffers from some design flaws. I should work them out in MkII..."

In the meantime, the android looked over her master one more time.

"Master?"

"Hm? Yes?"

"Do you intend to wear this tomorrow?"

Lab Coat Guy didn't answer right away. Instead, he glanced over to the large clock on the wall.

"It's getting late, so I won't be able to make the MkII version today, which means I'll have to."

"Understood." She nodded and extended her hands towards him. "Please hand over the protective equipment. I will perform the final adjustment so that Master can go to bed."

"You want to do that?" he inquired with a faint hint of suspicion in his voice.

"Affirmative. Sleep deprivation may negatively affect tomorrow's operation."

"You're not wrong about that..." he muttered as he awkwardly lifted the completely impractical spaulder/neck guard hybrid over his head. "Can I really leave this to you?"

"Affirmative," she repeated with a firm nod, and after just a bit more hesitation, he handed it over to her.

"All right. To be honest, I'm feeling a little drowsy, and I have to be in my best condition for tomorrow!" As he said that, the corners of Lab Coat Guy's lips curled into an eager smile, and he rubbed his palms together in a very dastardly display. "Tomorrow Endymonion's granddaughter will be there, as well! Ki-hi-hi! I shall be sure to leave an impression!"

"I'm sure Master will leave a very deep one," she encouraged him, though I could, probably due to spending so much time with my own dead-pan companion, detect a distinct sarcastic edge in her words.

"Very well! I'm going to bed now! See you in the morning!"

"Good night, Master," the fembot replied with a small nod, and the moment her master turned around and headed towards the exit, she walked over to the cabinet in the corner filled with various brightly coloured painting cans.

I had a good idea of what she was planning, but since Lab Coat Guy was steadily getting out of range, I decided to cut my strategic observation of them for the day. As it happened, this also coincided with the moment I finished with my light workout routine. I actually felt strangely refreshed, and even my wounds didn't itch so much anymore.

I looked over myself, and after a brief hesitation, I decided that, while it meant I would have to change some of my bandages, it was best I cleaned myself up a little. After that... well, today was incredibly long and hectic, so I figured I'd try to relax a little, at least as much as I could. Not being able to sleep had its downsides from time to time...

PART 2

"Good morning!"

I was greeted by a sunny smile as I approached the gates of the Dracis mansion in the silent company of Judy and Snowy. The princess skipped over to me and gave me a rib cage-creaking hug made only marginally more bearable by her unreservedly pressing her squishier bits against me, completely disregarding the fact that the entire household was watching her. I'm not going to lie, the whole *being greeted by a small crowd in front of the gates during our morning commute* thing gave me a serious case of déjà vu, but I ignored the sentiment and just smiled at my unusually eager girlfriend.

"Good morning," I responded to her, then turned to the entire extended family and asked, "Is there a problem?"

Mama and Papa Dracis glanced at each other very meaningfully, but it was the annoying butler standing by their side that eventually spoke up and gave me an answer.

"The young lady told us she had a rather 'peculiar' encounter yesterday," he told me while making honest-to-goodness air quotes around the world *peculiar.* "We were curious if you wanted to comment on the events."

I rewarded Sebastian's forthcoming attitude with a curiously raised brow, and after a moment of consideration, I gently separated myself from the girl still hugging my waist and told him, "You mean the guy in the lab coat and the stupid robots, right? Don't worry, I already got them in my palm."

"You do?" Elly blurted out in surprise.

"Yup," I told her with a wink and a totally charming smile, if I do say myself.

She must've appreciated the effort (not that I practiced it in the mirror this morning or anything), as her cheeks actually became a bit flushed, but this time they were more rosy than her usual beet-redness. It was a pretty cute reaction, all things considered.

"Are they a threat?" Mama Dracis interrupted in a stern voice, which kind of ruined our moment.

"Do you want me to be frank?" It was a rhetorical question, but she gave me a pretty intense nod, so I told her, "They probably pose more threat to themselves than to us. For the time being, they can be safely left alone. If they become an actual hazard to any of us, including you, I'll contact you and we can just smash their base at our convenience."

Lady Emese blinked in surprise, then stated, "So, they really are in the palm of your hands."

"Would I lie about this?" I responded with a tiny little smirk.

"What about the swordswoman?" she said, continuing her impromptu interrogation.

"Oh, I've got her under control, too," I told her maybe a smidgen too cheekily, as my silent assistant let out an irritated huff behind me. "I made contact with her yesterday, and now I'm sure she is not affiliated with the Knights. She is more of a nomadic monster-slaying ninja. I'm still working on the particulars, but the important thing is that I'm keeping her under close surveillance, and she doesn't seem to pose a threat to any of you."

The lady of the household gave me a long, hard look as if she were trying to determine whether she could trust my word, but she eventually let out a long breath and told me, "I see you've been working hard."

"Of course he has!" Papa Dracis cut in, accompanied by a hearty chuckle. "I told you there's nothing to worry about!"

"I believe you should actually worry a bit more about this young man's motives and capabilities," Sebastian chimed in while pointedly shaking his head.

"Oh, Sebastian, don't be so negative!" the Dracis patriarch exclaimed while thumping the old butler on the back. In fact, he did it so hard, I was pretty sure a normal person would've fallen on their face from the impact, but the old butler endured it without flinching, like an annoying, snooty boulder. "If you cannot trust your own family, then who can you trust?"

"He is not part of our family yet," Mama Dracis countered with a frown, but her husband completely ignored her and he turned to me instead.

"Speaking of which! Son, when are you coming over for dinner? I had my top men put together one of those fancy-pants website things you proposed, and I want to see what you think about it before we make it live!" He stopped here for a very meaningful pause, and then coyly added, "It's your project, after all!"

"Project?"

"What project?"

Elly and her mother both blurted out their surprise. Since Abram was too busy chuckling to himself to answer, I decided to do it in his stead.

"After your father complained about how the record company's sales are down, I offered him a business proposal and invested some of my money into an online music distribution service."

"You invested in our business?" Lady Emese inquired with a somewhat dazed expression.

"Yes. It was the majority of my savings, but I think it's better to invest my money than to just let it collect dust in my account." Now it was my turn to pause meaningfully here, during which I flashed Papa Dracis a confident smile and finished with, "And what better place is there to invest but in the family business?"

It was at this point that my self-proclaimed father-in-law stopped chuckling and began straight up hooting with laughter as he walked back to his wife's wheelchair and placed one large hand on her shoulder.

"I told you, honey! Our daughter has an amazing eye for men! She must have inherited it from you!"

"I don't know about that," Lady Emese grumbled as she pointedly looked the other way, but at the same time, she gently placed her own hand on top of her husband's.

Why do I have the feeling these two used to be one of those absurdly adorable clumsy couples when they were younger? I thought.

Anyhow, I shrugged and told Abram, "I'll be busy after school, but I think I should be able to come over tonight."

"Great!" he exclaimed with a toothy grin. "Sebastian? Tell the staff to prepare a feast!"

I left the Dracis family to their impromptu dinner preparations and said my goodbyes, following which our little group turned around and happily continued on our merry way to school… for about half a minute. Then the princess tugged my sleeve.

"Hey, Leo? Why's Judy mad at you?" she inquired with all the care of a toddler driving a pickup truck through a china shop.

"What makes you think she is mad at me?" I asked back.

"She looks like it. She isn't speaking to you. Did you do something to make her angry?"

"Maybe?" I replied a little sheepishly as I theatrically scratched the back of my neck.

"Not maybe, definitely," Judy, walking a couple of paces ahead of us with Snowy, finally spoke up without looking our way, her voice about as icy as it was the day before. "Why don't you tell her what happened yesterday?"

"I might as well," I told her with a cheery grin, even though she couldn't see it. "Listen, princess, I actually found the base of the guys who attacked you yesterday on the way home."

"Don't forget to mention that you got severely injured in the process," my assistant chimed in again while still looking the other way.

"You were?" Elly's voice rose a pitch in alarm as she looked me over and took note of the scuffs on my face.

"Yes, but not *severely*. These are just scrapes. I'll have Angie cast a healing spell on me and I'll be as good as new."

"Oh, that's good," the princess deflated with a sigh of relief. "But then why is she angry with you?"

"It's because of the next part," Judy fumed.

"Right. After that, I made contact with the huntress we talked about before."

"And?" Judy prompted me.

"And I resolved our differences."

"And?"

I let out an exasperated sigh and finally admitted, "And then I agreed to hunt the stray Chimera with her."

"And that is why I'm mad," my dear assistant concluded before she glanced over to Elly and added, "And you should be, too."

"Why? You don't want him to hunt the Chimera?" she asked back, genuinely confused, before she looked at me. "Is it going to be dangerous? Do you need help?"

"That's not the problem," Judy grumbled as she slowed down and fell in line next to the two of us. Then she grabbed the princess and told her, "The Chief arranged to have clandestine meetings with the hunter woman from now on."

"Wouldn't the fact that I just told you about it mean that they're not clandestine?" I asked while showing off my slowly advancing mastery of raising only a single incredulous eyebrow.

"Hush, Chief, I'm incriminating you."

"I noticed. That's why I'm interrupting you."

Judy finally looked at me, and when I told her I wasn't going to budge on the issue by wiggling my brows a bit more, she relented and told Elly, "Fine. The Chief is having non-clandestine dates with the hunter woman from now on."

"They are not dates, either," I protested once again.

"A man and a woman setting an appointment for going into town together. What do you call that?"

"By our recently developed standards, that would be an 'outing,' but in this particular case, it's closer to a hunting trip," I told her straightaway.

"You're just playing with words now," my assistant huffed before she turned to my other girlfriend. "What do you think? It's a date, no matter how we look at it."

"Don't answer your own question," I chided her, but in the meantime, Elly put some thought into her reply.

"Are you attracted to her?" she leveled the question at me, and I immediately shook my head.

"No. There is a slight chance that she is interested in me, but I mainly find her annoying and want her gone. That's why I'm trying to help her hunt down the Chimera, so she'll go away."

"And you're not going to do anything... um... lewd with her, right?" she asked the next question, this time a little more hesitantly.

"Definitely not. Even we haven't done any lewding. Why would I even think about doing it with someone else?"

"That's still not a word," Judy whispered beside us, but she was summarily ignored by the dragon girl in our midst.

"It's okay then," Elly stated with a relieved smile.

"It's okay?" my assistant repeated after her with an extra wooden voice.

"Yes." She gave a huge nod. "Leo already promised that he is not interested in anyone else, and he is not physically attracted to her, either. I trust his word, so I'm certain he won't cheat on us."

I gave the beaming blonde girl a surprised look, and after I overcame it, I turned to the other girl and told her, "You see, Judy? Elly trusts me. Why can't you do the same?"

"Because..." she began to answer, but her words, probably due to the crossfire of our gazes, got lost somewhere along the way, and they came out as a heavy sigh instead.

I decided to capitalize on the moment, so I carefully pulled Elly away, wedged myself between the two of them, and grabbed hold of Judy's hand.

"Come on, Dormouse. I already told you I don't care about other girls. We are going to hunt some Chimera spawn, and once we're done, she'll be out of our collective hair for good. There's absolutely nothing romantic or adulterous in our arrangement. Please stop being jealous for no reason and just give me the benefit of the doubt already."

"That's right," Elly unexpectedly backed me up. "You have to trust your partner. Mother always said that a stable relationship is built upon mutual trust, so you have to trust your partner even if he is a good-for-nothing oaf who cannot read the mood even if it kills him!"

"Wait a sec, she actually said that?" I muttered in surprise, and she responded with a huge nod.

"Yes, word for word!" the princess declared rather proudly. "She also told me that for skirt chasers, it is best to give them boundless trust, no matter the situation, until they feel too guilty to even look at other women, let alone marry them using their family's stupid customs for justification."

"Wow," I exhaled with a mix of awe and dread. "Your mother is a formidable woman."

"Women have to be formidable to hold on to a formidable man," she told me with that smug little smirk of hers.

"You see, Judy? You should follow Elly's mother's example and trust me."

My dear assistant turned to me with conflicted eyes, but at last she squeezed my hand and said, "No flirting during the dates."

"They are not dates, and no, I won't be flirting at all. I won't even buy her a snack this time."

"This time?" Elly cut in, dismayed. "You bought her snacks?"

"Yeah. It was to distract her so that I could get away when I first met her."

"Oh, I see," she muttered in relief.

Hey, weren't you the one who said you'd trust me no matter what? I thought. *Why do you sound like you're doubting me right away?*

"You are only going to track the Chimera," Judy wrestled my attention back by making another statement.

"Yes. No dillydallying around the city, just tracking some monsters. All business, no fun whatsoever."

"And you are going to stay safe."

"Yes, perfectly. I'll let the creepy woman and her stupid crazy sword do all the dirty work, and I'll stay completely out of the fighting. Scout's honour."

It was blindingly obvious that Judy wasn't 100 percent satisfied with my heartfelt promises, but after a long moment of silence, she sidled close and entwined her arm with mine.

"Fine," she said with just a tiny hint of sulking still infused in her voice. "I decided I'll trust you one last time."

"You say that like I've betrayed your trust before..."

"You told me you would be careful, and yet you came back home covered in blood," she retorted, and I couldn't help but glance away.

"Um... Yeah. I really should've thought that through before I entered the room like that. I'm sorry for scaring you guys... But on the other hand, I wasn't actually hurt, so does it actually count?"

"Yes, it does," Judy stressed, squeezing my hand even harder.

"Okay, then I'll make sure not to get bloodied and come back home looking like a horror show, either."

"You better," she still grumbled, but I had a hunch that we were over the roughest part of our quarrel. I momentarily considered using the opportunity to tease her a little, but then my attention was quite literally grabbed by the princess taking hold of my free arm.

"Today I have the right side," she declared with a smile, which made me wonder. Did they ration out who grabbed which of my arms? Wasn't that going a little too far?

I didn't have the opportunity to ponder that either, though, as once she noticed we were huddled together, Snowy also slowed her pace and let us catch up to her.

"Is everything all right now?" she timidly asked as she looked us over.

"Did you go ahead to give us some space to talk?" I ventured an educated guess, and she nodded without hesitation.

"I shouldn't have?"

"No, you did good," I reassured her with my brotherliest smile. "Remind me to give you a head pat once my hands aren't occupied."

"Y-you don't have to…" she protested, though a little feebly, prompting me to turn my single-eyebrow-raising technique on her.

"You don't like it?"

"It's not that… It's just embarrassing…" she muttered while refusing to meet my eyes.

I let out a merry little chuckle and told her, "Okay, then you will get a private head pat for being such a good little sister."

"You are spoiling her," Judy told me in a flat, almost disinterested voice that told me she was probably picking a fight just to get my attention.

"I told you, little sisters exist to be spoiled," I responded to her with an irreverent smirk. "You should know. You're probably giving her more head pats than I am."

"Should I give it a try, too?" the princess wondered aloud, bringing our developing rapport to a screeching halt. When she noticed we were giving her blank looks, she hastily clarified, "I mean, she is going to be my sister-in-law soon, right? If Judy is already petting her all the time, shouldn't I do it, too? Otherwise, it wouldn't be fair."

"So, you want to pet my sister?"

"Yes," she confirmed.

"Weren't you the one who repeatedly tried to tackle her and chase her away just a few months ago?" I teased her, and my draconic girlfriend's face immediately flushed in a familiar shade of crimson.

"That was a long time ago, and it doesn't matter! We are family now, so the situation is completely different!"

"We are technically not a family yet," Judy objected, using a familiar set of words, probably out of habit.

"But we're almost, and that makes building skinship even more important."

"Kinship," I corrected her.

"That, too." She nodded without getting a clue.

I let out a shallow breath and asked my sister, "What do you say?"

"Uh…" Snowy hesitated, but after looking eye to eye with Elly for a few seconds, she said, "I… I think it's going be really awkward, but I don't mind."

"Good!" the princess declared with gusto, and she immediately reached out for my sister's head, but Snowy skillfully dodged her hand.

"N-not in public!" she cried out, but as she did so, my overly enthusiastic draconic girlfriend let go of me and chased after her.

I stifled my chuckles and, along with my other girlfriend muttering something along the lines of "So noisy so early in the morning," I continued on towards yet another day that promised to be just as eventful as the day before, but with one crucial difference: this time, I was prepared for… well, maybe not anything, but close enough.

PART 3

"Morning," I greeted Josh when I reached my desk.

"Hi," he returned the greeting with a lazy wave, not even bothering to change his slacker posture in his seat. "You're late."

"I had to pick up the girls on the way, and we kind of lost track of time," I explained myself as I put my bag down on the desk.

"Go ahead and explode, you normie," he told with an annoying grin plastered on his face, and I automatically rolled my eyes.

"That was not only a tired old meme, but it also isn't even applicable to me. F minus, see me after class."

My friend let out a mild, noncommittal chuckle and deflected by asking me, "Speaking of your girlfriends," he said while putting an obnoxious amount of emphasis on the *s* at the end of the word, "where are they? I didn't see them come in."

"Judy said she had to go to the toilet. As for Elly, she's probably still pestering my sister."

"Pestering?" He raised a rather elegant skeptical brow, as if just to mock my own efforts in the field of eyebrow-raisiology, but I refused to let it bother me. "Are they fighting again?"

"Nah. If anything, they are too friendly." Josh still looked skeptical, so I dismissed him with a quiet "you will get it when you see it" whispered under my breath as I sat down. "What about Angie and the class rep? I'm not seeing them anywhere," I inquired while deliberately glancing around.

"They left to get some papers for the teacher," he said as he slouched even lower in his chair. "Something about a questionnaire for the cultural festival before Christmas, I think."

"Wait, we have cultural festivals?" I blurted out a surprised question the moment it surfaced in my mind, and Josh responded with a firm nod.

"Yeah, it's before winter break," he clarified while finally returning into a more sensible sitting position. "If it goes like last year, then first we'll have an open day on Thursday, where the parents sit in during classes. Then the actual cultural festival happens on Friday, where every class has to set up a stall or an attraction. And then on Saturday evening, we're going to have the Christmas ball."

"Really? Sounds like a busy weekend."

"Yeah," Josh spoke with a tired sigh. "Last year we had a haunted house in the classroom. It was okay. I only had to move the sets with the other guys," he reminisced with a nostalgic smile. Then his expression quickly clouded over and he added, "I had sore muscles all over and could barely move the next morning, and Angie got mad at me because I couldn't accompany her to the Christmas ball."

"So, it's like a prom?"

"Something like that." Josh shrugged.

"And Angie invited you to it?"

"Yeah. She said she couldn't bear the thought of her childhood friend being a wallflower at the ball, so she'd sacrifice herself and accompany me even if it would completely mess up her plans for the evening. Then, when I couldn't go because I could barely walk, she refused to talk to me for a week. Girls can be weird sometimes."

"Yeah, sure, whatever," I wrote off my friend's denseness-induced misconceptions with a slow shake of my head, but then I fell silent as I ruminated on an idea. "Say, Josh? Now that we're talking about girls being angry at us and whatnot, can I ask you for a bit of advice?"

Granted, asking him of all people about women-troubles might have sounded monumentally dumb, probably because it was, but I had to consider my options, and since my only other male "friends," by a loose definition of the word, were a giant half-ram muscleman and the father of one of my girlfriends, said options were rather limited for this kind of discussion. As such, I decided to bite the bullet and ask Josh, sink or swim. I mean, even a dense clock is right twice a day, so it was at least worth a shot.

"Sure," he answered without hesitation. "If I can help, I will." He paused, then added, "However, I cannot promise I won't make fun of you in the process."

"How gracious of you to warn me ahead of time," I grumbled aloud, yet my friend only gave me a toothy smile in return. I let out a small sigh. "So, here's the deal. Yesterday, I went out and tracked down the guys who ambushed you in the afternoon, during which I got a tiny bit injured. Nothing major."

"Oh." Josh responded by once again raising a supremely executed, curiously raised eyebrow. "I was meaning to ask about the Band-Aid on your face."

"Yeah, I'll have Angie take care of that..." I muttered. Then, after a pause, I added in a tired whisper, "Geez, just how many times have I repeated this explanation already...?"

"Excuse me?"

"Nah, I'm just grumbling," I told Josh while shaking my head. "Where were we?"

"The point where you got injured."

"Right, there. Okay, so here's the thing: After I came back home, Judy got really mad at me. As in, *genuinely* angry. We made up, I think, but it still bothers me." Josh gave me a look that told me he still didn't get my point, so I decided to be blunt. "To put it simply, I get her reasons. She doesn't want me to get hurt. I can see her point, as I don't want me to get hurt, either. I mean, duh, right?"

"Right." Josh nodded, though he still seemed a little lost.

"So, now that we're clear on that, I also get why she was mad at me. I think it's something called 'anger born of worry' or some such. You might've heard about it? Anyhow, I really don't want Judy to be angry with me, but I already know that I'll inevitably have to take risks in the future, which means she will get angry over it. However, if I don't take such risks, then we might get blindsided by even bigger threats, and if I get hurt *then*, she'll be just as angry with me, made even worse by the fact that others can also get hurt on top of that. It's a total catch-22, I tell you."

"And how exactly can I help you with this?" Josh cut in, and based on his still confounded expression, my explanation of the problem had been less than stellar.

I took a deep breath, tried to reiterate my point, but in the end, I just deflated and told him, "Honestly, I don't know. I'm open to any and all suggestions."

"Hm," Josh let out a low noise and he pondered for a couple of seconds. "You said that you'll inevitably have to take risks. Are you sure about that?"

"Let's just say that there are things only I can do, meaning I must do them myself," I told him a tad cryptically.

"Okay, then why don't you try to keep it a secret from her?"

I gave my friend a cutting glare and replied, "That's just a recipe for a disaster. Don't even joke about it."

"Fine, fine! No need to bite my head off, geez…" Josh had an annoyed grimace on his face, but it only lasted for a second, soon to be replaced by a contemplative expression more fitting our discussion. "So, you can't hide it and you can't avoid it. Can't you at least lessen the risk of whatever this thing is that only you can do?" I gestured for him to continue this train of thought, and after taking in a shallow breath, he leaned closer and told me in a whisper, "For example, when we were ambushed yesterday, the girls told me to stay safe, but I couldn't just sit still while they fought those Sprocket bots. I didn't want to get in their way, since they are obviously way more experienced in this kind of situation than I am. So in the end, I stayed back and only used the wind blast spell that Lili taught me to support them as much as I could."

"And how exactly is that applicable to my situation?" I asked the million-Jen question.

"I can't put it into words well," he muttered, scratching the back of his neck. "What I'm trying to say, I think, is that if you already know that you'll be in danger, and others want to keep you out of it, but you can't afford to do so, then you should show her that you are trying to lessen it with your actions. Like, if you know you are going to be in a situation where you might get injured, then get some padded clothes or armour or something to show that you are aware of the danger and you are doing your best to mitigate it. That way Judy will be less worried, and even if you do get injured, you can point at it to prove that you tried your best to avoid it."

"That's… actually some really good advice," I mumbled as I digested his words.

"Is it?" he asked back a little sheepishly. "I still don't think I managed to put my ideas into words properly."

"No, I understand your point perfectly," I reassured him with a genuine smile. "Thanks, man. I owe you one."

"Don't mention it," he replied with an honest smile of his own, but then it immediately turned mischievous when he added, "But if you really want to thank me, you could always treat me to some foie gras."

That was the point where my smile vanished faster than a toupee in a hurricane.

"Don't tell me we actually have that in the cafeteria…"

"We sure do!" he told me with a toothy grin. "How about we have lunch there for a change?"

"We can't," a new voice denied his suggestion, and quite harshly at that, making Josh jump in his seat in surprise.

"Hi, class rep," I casually greeted the sneaky newcomer. "Are you sure you are a mage and not a ninja?"

The class rep glanced around and then reprimanded me with a low, "We are in public."

"Nobody is paying attention to us. Also, let's backtrack a bit. Why can't we eat in the cafeteria, again?"

"It's not about food," she told me firmly. "We need to meet on the rooftop during lunch break. I have important things to discuss."

"Such as?" Josh asked back with a glint of curiosity in his eyes.

"Not here. Too many onlookers," Ammy told us in a hushed voice. "Let me repeat this, just to be clear—don't go to the cafeteria. We must all meet up on the roof."

Her insistence was a little suspicious, but at the same time she sounded sincere enough, so after a moment of hesitation (which she obviously noticed), I gave her a big nod.

"All right. Lunch on the roof, then," I confirmed, and only then did she stop frowning at me.

"Also, stop talking about things you should *not* talk about in public, *while* in public," she warned me, and then she turned around and headed for her desk. I followed her with my eyes, then I let out a deep breath and glanced over my shoulder back at Josh.

"What are you doing?" I inquired after taking in the sight of my friend looking into the invisible distance with sorrow in his eyes.

"I really wanted to try foie gras," he answered despondently.

I groaned. "I'm happy to see you are back to normal after all that happened recently, but I didn't miss your obsessions with using me to pay for your overpriced food."

"It's not overpriced!" Josh vehemently denied. "Authentic foie gras is made from the livers of French Mulard ducks specifically bred for this purpose and fattened up by gavage! It's one of the world's foremost delicacies!"

"Just one question," I interrupted, my hands held up to keep Josh at bay. "What the hell is a *gavage*?"

"Oh, that's just the French word for force-feeding the ducks with a feeding tube," he explained as matter-of-factly as if it were common trivia.

"Isn't that animal abuse?"

"I suppose," he admitted, albeit a little reluctantly. "I've heard it's illegal to make it at most places, and that's why it costs so much to import foie gras."

"In other words, its supply is low, so it's overpriced," I concluded, and Josh gave me such a hurt look in return that I couldn't help but shake my head and add, "Fine. I will buy you some artificially fattened mallard liver. Are you happy now?"

"It's Mulard, but yes," he told me with a shit-eating grin.

I let out an only ever so slightly exasperated sigh and turned away from Josh. As they say, the more things change, the more they remain the same…

PART 4

"The weather is surprisingly mild today," I noted to no one in particular as we walked under the metal doorframe of the rooftop access and into the open.

"I'm still a little cold," Judy told me as she deliberately shortened the distance between us while we walked side by side. I knew what that meant, so I stifled a low chuckle and gently wrapped my arm around her waist, pulling her even closer. She let me do so without any complaints, and she might've even breathed out a comfortable little sigh in the process as well.

"Does this mean you are officially no longer angry with me?" I playfully asked her, and my dearest assistant let out a huff.

"It just means I'm colder than I am angry right now," she retorted and pointedly turned her face away from me.

"Dooooormooouse…?" I cajoled her, but since she only huffed in indignation made entirely transparent by the fact she was still sticking to me like my shadow, I continued with, "I already promised I'll be a good boy. Can you forgive me, please?"

My girlfriend glanced up at me and was immediately taken (or shocked, one or the other) by my best puppy-dog impression and, at last, she relented.

"Fine. You are on probation until further notice. Just stop giving me the bedroom eyes."

"What? These are not bedroom eyes!" I protested with all the righteous indignation of the falsely accused.

"So, you are telling me you are not interested in me? Probation extended."

"Aw, come on. Not this again…"

Fortunately, it was around this time that Angie and Elly also exited the roof access and so I quickly greeted them before my dear probation officer could find more reasons to roast me. However, before I could get a word in, the princess suddenly pointed a familiar (and lately rather rare) accusatory finger at the girl clinging to me.

"Hey! We agreed that today's my turn!" she exclaimed as she made her way over to me and grabbed hold of my free hand, a process which was made slightly more complicated than necessary by the large, multilayered lunch box she held.

"The early bird catches the Chief," my assistant stated with the verbal equivalent of a disinterested shrug.

"But I couldn't get here earlier because I had to bring our lunch!" My draconic girlfriend's protests were further emphasized by her waving the large box around like it was weightless.

"Oh, right. In that case, I suppose you are entitled to your share of cuddling," Judy declared as if it was obvious.

"So? Why aren't you letting go of Leo's right side yet?"

"It's cold," she stated again as she nuzzled even closer to me.

"It's not! It's actually…" Elly began, but then a moment later her eyes lit up and she declared in high spirits, "I mean, yes, it's obviously cold! Brrr! Leo, warm me up, too!"

With that, she flung herself at my chest, almost throwing all of us off-balance. Thankfully, my well-honed girl-catching reflexes didn't let me down, and I managed to grab hold of her and pull her into a one-handed embrace.

"Careful there. If you want to snuggle, just say so. I'm big enough for two."

It was at this point that my ears picked up nearby snickers, and I glanced up towards their source.

"Awww… you guys are so cute together!" Angie teased us with her usual wild abandon that knew not the face of mercy, her sharp words cutting into my fragile emotions like not particularly sharp things cutting into not particularly solid stuff. Long story short, my face may or may not have gotten a tiny bit flushed. Thankfully, there was no photographic evidence, so I could easily deny it to my grave.

Anyhow, I glanced around the empty rooftop, with only our slowly swelling group on it, and I couldn't help but wonder aloud.

"Where is the class rep? Wasn't she the one who really wanted us to come here?"

"Last I saw her, she was going down to the basement," the princess told me with her head still buried in my chest. "I saw her through the first floor window," she hastily clarified, though she didn't really need to.

"And what about the others?"

"Josh went down the stairs to get Neige. They should be here any moment," Angie answered my question while glancing over her shoulder, and lo and behold, that was the moment when the two missing sheep returned to the flock.

"Hi guys," Josh greeted us as if we hadn't seen each other in a while. "Hey, Leo? Did you know that the cafeteria offers packaged meals that we can take home? Even for premium menus? Just sayin'."

He accentuated his last sentence by a frankly cheesy wink.

Groaning, I said, "You will get your stupid up-marked duck liver, okay? Stop pestering me already!"

"It's not stupid." Josh's retort was lacking in impact, and for the better, I'd say, as I really didn't want to get into another argument about his culinary tastes at the moment. Afterwards, he glanced around and asked, "Where's Ammy?"

"Good question," I replied under my breath.

In the meantime, Elly finally slipped out of my embrace and she, along with Snowy, began to unpack her lunch boxes on a nearby bench. The morning bonding session apparently worked unexpectedly well, as the two of them were getting along swimmingly.

We spent the next couple of minutes with inconsequential small talk about schoolwork and other mundane things, carefully avoiding anything related to the supernatural zaniness suffusing our lives as of late. I'm not going to lie; it felt really nice to just chat about random stuff instead of any heavy topics. But then, of course, such a nice, cozy atmosphere couldn't have lasted long, as just around the time when we were about to sit down and start snacking from the lunch boxes (they were big, but not big enough for six meals for six people), the access door abruptly opened, revealing an entirely expected face in the process.

"Why is the roof so high?" The first words coming out of the heaving class rep's mouth were somewhat baffling, but not as much as the large, matte silver briefcase she was carrying using both of her arms. It was the kind that you would see in one of those tacky TV game shows, the ones that would stand in for money, with big numbers written on them. Anyhow, it looked pretty heavy, and I was about to walk over and help her carry it, but Josh beat me to the punch.

She gave the guy a shy, appreciative smile. It was an expression she hadn't shown me for ages, and I was entirely happy about that. I could do with a little less scowling, though. Anyhow, she took out a large key, and she promptly locked the only door to the roof, which inevitably raised a few eyebrows, including mine.

"Everyone's here. Good." Her eyes swept across our group clustered around the bench, and it looked like she was about to continue when her gaze snapped back and she muttered a confused, "What are you doing?"

"Are you talking to me?" Elly asked while using one hand to point at herself. Her other hand, at the moment, was occupied petting a certain younger sister of mine.

"Of course I'm talking to you," Ammy stressed with an expression that hovered in the borderlands between baffled and exasperated. "Why are you… why are you stroking her head?"

"Oh, that? It's for building kinship," she stated like it was the most natural thing in the world. "You should try it, it's amazing! When you do it, it's like all your worries in the world melt away!"

"Really?" Angie chimed in, her eyes sparkling with interest. "Can I try it, too?"

Elly sent me a questioning gaze, so I told them, "Don't look at me. Ask Snowy if she minds or not."

"Uhh…" My little sister was apparently in a tight spot for a moment, but at last she nodded, and without any further ado, the Celestial girl trotted over to her side and began tousling her hair, prompting her to let out another soft sound.

"You have to be gentler," Elly chided her as she moved Angie's hand away and straightened Snowy's hair. "You have to do it like this," she instructed her, and after following her lead, the resident hyperactive girl giggled.

"You are right—it's strangely calming!"

"It's the magic of little sisters," I told them with a sagely nod.

"Hey, Josh! You have to try this!" Angie prompted her somewhat uncomfortable childhood friend, but before he could do or say anything, the class rep harrumphed so loud, I was afraid she'd hurt herself in the process.

"Please stop that and pay attention to me. This is important."

After she gained everyone's attention (with maybe the exception of Angie, who continued rubbing my sister's head), Ammy dramatically pushed her glasses up the bridge of her nose and stated, "Just yesterday, you were attacked by an unknown group!"

For a few seconds, there was a kind of awkward silence hanging in the air, but since everyone seemed too confused to say anything, I decided to break the ice.

"So?"

Ammy glanced at me while doing that thing where she somehow managed to adjust her glasses in a way it felt more menacing than staring a Faun in the eye and said, "How can you all be *this* carefree just a day after the fact?"

"It wasn't that big a deal, though," Elly muttered, casually plucking a piece of fried fish from one of the boxes. "Not to mention, Leo already has them in his palm."

"Figuratively speaking," I added.

The class rep shot me a withering frown.

"Stop joking around. Whoever these people are, they pose a real threat. Just the fact that they managed to operate on the island without our School's knowledge means they must be well-organized and dangerous, and they are probably after Joshua."

I had my objections on the tip of my tongue, but after some consideration, I swallowed them back down. I was curious about where she was going with this, so I subtly prompted her to continue. For some odd reason, she kept eyeing me in a blatantly suspicious manner, but when I didn't say anything, she resolved herself to continue.

"So, as I was saying, we are facing an unknown threat that could strike us at any moment. I talked with Grandfather about this, and he said while we cannot afford to spare any School personnel to guard you twenty-four/seven, he allowed me to use the resources of the artificer department."

"You mean those weird guys with the glowing orb?" Josh cut in, and for once his dreaded critical brow of skeptical incredulity was pointed at someone else other than me.

Now as I thought about it, the last (and only) time we visited the School under the school, the rest of the gang took a guided tour of the facilities while I was having my discussion with a certain smug arch-mage in his chambers. I had Judy describe the place, and the most vivid part of her report concerned a huge chamber with a giant floating blue orb in the middle, surrounded by concentric circles of workbenches. Her description sounded strangely sci-fi, and so it left a bit of an impression on me.

Anyhow, Ammy turned to Josh and countered his eyebrow with her patented glasses adjustment, and she stated, "They are not weird. They are very nice people. And they are very passionate about their work."

"Yes, but they talked weird, and they wanted to take Lili's blood and did take all kinds of measurements," Josh continued his argument unabated.

"Indeed." The class rep nodded as if she was waiting for him to say that, and she picked up the metal briefcase by her feet. "It was for this." Saying so, she clumsily undid the simple locks and opened the case's lid.

The inside was padded with spongy black material, and embedded in it were five small objects. At first glance, they looked like oversized toy wristwatches made of cheap plastic, and each device was coloured differently and... and...

"Oh no..." I whispered under my breath, but no one heard me.

"We've already discussed the inconvenience that barriers pose when transforming in the past," the class rep spoke to the group, completely disregarding my probably quite shocked appearance.

"Exploding clothes?" Josh ventured a guess, and she nodded with approval.

"Precisely. Since we could be attacked at any moment, it's important that you're be able to respond immediately without having to worry about your modesty being compromised."

"So, you brought us watches?" Elly inquired as she leaned forward to inspect the items in question.

"They are not watches." Ammy walked over and set the briefcase on the bench beside the lunch box. "They are minor artifacts enchanted by the best of our artificers."

"Really?" Angie peeked over her shoulders and let out a soft "Ooooh!"

"What do they do?" Josh asked next and, following his lead, the rest of the group also crowded around the bench... well, except for me and Judy, that is.

"To put simply, they are specialized summoning tools. Upon activation, they remove all clothing items worn by the user and store them in a specialized pocket space while simultaneously summoning a full suit of defensive gear tailor-made for the user and enchanted with various protective wards. It is similar to my own combat garment, except without any customization."

"What exactly does that mean?" came the next question from Angie, her body language clearly broadcasting that she really, really wanted to try out the new toy in front of her.

"The artificers already had to work overtime to finish them so quickly, so right now they should look very simple. According to the description they gave me, it should be a formfitting, one-piece bodysuit with protective wards, and designed not to interfere with natural barriers, allowing the users to use their abilities without fully transforming. They also have handy helmets with face masks, in case you are in public and you need to hide your identities."

"Oh nooo…" I whispered, but only Judy paid any attention to me, and that only briefly.

In the meantime, the class rep took out one of the non-watches and handed it to Elly.

"Be careful. Each and every suit was made using your individual measurements for a perfect fit, so make sure you don't accidentally mix them up. Thankfully, the artificers had the foresight to colour-code each of the artifacts." I was just about to let out another big no, but then the class rep added, "Also, the suits themselves are colour-coded, as well," so I decided to go with a huge no instead.

"Nooooo…"

"Chief, stop that. It's annoying," Judy reproached me, but I only gave her a curt "No," so she rolled her eyes as if to say she didn't know why she bothered trying.

Meanwhile, everyone picked up an article of their own, including the class rep. At this point, she turned to the two of us with a remorseful expression.

"Sorry, but we couldn't make suits for you two. We didn't have Leo's measurements for the fitting, and as for you, Judy, since the triggering mechanism requires some form of magical input, it would be useless for you." She paused here for a long moment, and then hastily added, in a voice reminiscent of the old, slightly awkward class rep, "B-but don't worry! I asked some people for passive protective talismans—they just take longer to make! I didn't forget about you, I swear!"

"It's okay, I believe you," Judy told her, though her words still felt like they had a hidden edge to them.

But Ammy didn't notice. She let out a relieved breath and faced the rest of the group again, who wasted no time and all had their new toys on their wrists already. Speaking of which, just what the heck were these things called again?

Judy must've read my mind, as the moment the question popped in my brain, she voiced it.

"What are these artifacts called?"

The class rep glanced back at her and told us, without the slightest bit of reservation, "The artificers called them 'Transmorphers.'"

I glanced down at my girlfriend and whispered, "Well, that's it, then. We're screwed."

"Chief, could you please stop being so overdramatic?" she whispered back.

I thought about it and decided to reply in the only way that fit the situation.

"Noooooooooooooooooo…"

CHAPTER 19

PART 1

I could already see it in my mind's eye. I could literally see it. Well, not literally *literally*, but literally in the figurative sense… Language drift is messed up, isn't it? Anyways, the important part is that I could totally picture it both literally and figuratively, dictionaries be damned!

Somewhere, in a very public and well-lit parking lot, Lab Coat Guy appears out of thin air flanked by a small army of ridiculous robots randomly waving their limbs around. On the other side of the parking lot, Josh, Elly, Angie, Snowy, and Ammy dash into the frame, only to come to an awkward halt as the camera zooms in on their surprised faces.

Then Josh, as the hero, exclaims something along the lines of, *It's Doctor Robatto! We must stop him for great justice!*

When he hears that, Lab Coat Guy lets out a shrill laugh and says, *Ki-hi-hi! Look at that! Five overbearing and overly emotional teenagers! Your do-gooder antics end here!*

To which Josh replies, *Die, monster, you do not belong in this world!*

Lab Coat Guy answers, *What is man but a miserable pile of SCIENCE! But enough! Have at you!* and then he transforms into a giant bat and… wait, wait… wrong franchise.

It's *Josh* who then transforms. Or maybe Angie? I mean, if someone put a gun to my head and demanded that I tell them who was the one amongst our little group who'd be the most likely to engage in the typical sentai brand of limb-flailing-fu and related tomfoolery, I would've named Angie in a heartbeat. She'd also have a huge grin on her face all the while.

But back to the scene.

At Josh's command, they all strike a weird but strangely dynamic pose, pull out their cheap off-brand morphers—the camera zooming in and out as if the cinematographer was attacked by a swarm of angry bees and can't decide what to do—and then, finally, at last, in the very end, ultimately…

"Okay, time out! Time the bloody hell out!" I yelled out with my hands in a *T*, visibly startling the gang who was in the middle of discussing the finer details of their shiny, new, and totally-not-copyrighted toys.

"What do you mean by *time out*?" Ammy responded, her brows descending into a frown of the most critical variety.

"It means I can't deal with *this* right now, so…" I walked over to the briefcase on the bench with firm steps and picked it up before anyone (read: a certain class representative) could get in my way. "For the moment, I'm going to confiscate these for a safety inspection. Please put yours back into the case."

"Oh? Okay," Elly complied without even a hint of objection. It was probably because of her prompt agreement that the others followed suit and obediently placed their magic gadgets back into the case. Everyone, except for the class rep, of course, and she didn't bother to hide her misgivings.

"Why? Do you think I would hand these out if I thought they were dangerous?"

"No, of course not. I'm only doing this because everyone's safety is paramount."

"Since when do you care about safety?" my dear assistant threw a sulky jab, and I responded by flashing a toothy grin.

"I've always cared about safety! What do you think the 'S' in my middle name stands for?"

"Wait, you have a middle name?" Josh blurted out in surprise.

"Well, maybe not legally, but in spirit. Leonard S. Dunning sounds pretty good, doesn't it?"

"Does the 'S' stand for 'seducer'?" Judy wrestled my attention back to her with an outrageous proposition.

"No! It's *safety*!" I retorted indignantly before facing Amelia again. "Since I'm all about safety now, it's only natural that I should double-check these artifacts or what have you. Better to be safe than sorry, don't you agree?"

"And how exactly are you going to do this 'safety inspection'?" she pressed on with her inquiry without letting go of the thingie in her hand, though the glance that accompanied said question was much less hostile than I originally expected.

"Trade secret," I answered her while forcing out a wink, for which I really wasn't in the mood, but I had to because the situation demanded it. She was obviously less than thrilled by that, so I quickly amended, "Trust me, I know what I'm doing."

Of course, I really didn't, and I was just doing my best to create some breathing space for myself at the moment, but she didn't need to know that. Or maybe she already did, as she looked quite skeptical. But then she let go of her "Transmorpher" with a grunt and a warning of, "Don't break them."

"Thanks," I said with a smile I deemed reasonably genuine, especially considering the circumstances, and snapped the lid shut. "All right, I'm now going to study these awhile, let's say… over there! I'll be right back, so you can eat your lunch—no need to wait for me."

With that, I gestured for Judy to follow and we hastily made our way over to the other end of the roof.

"Chief, what are you doing?" my assistant inquired once we were out of earshot.

"Isn't it obvious?" I responded with an equal measure of relief and exasperation. "This is our ground zero. If these things really do what Ammy described and in the way she described it, then the moment I allow them to transform into brightly coloured bodysuits, we are irrevocably going to be locked into a sentai universe with no way out. We can't have that."

"So, you're stalling," she stated, and I confirmed her deduction with a nod.

"Yes. Even if it's just a few minutes. We need to figure out how to defuse this situation. Any ideas?"

"Depends. First, let's pinpoint the problem before we start looking for a solution."

"The problem?" I repeated after her with my brows set to 100 percent incredulity. "The problem is that these things don't make any sense in context," I blurted out while shaking the container in my hand, but since the items inside were secured, it didn't make any noise.

"Please elaborate," my dear assistant prompted me, and after taking a deep breath, I did just that.

"Okay, let's start from the beginning. We've already established that we are on the cusp of a genre shift, right?"

"Yes, like the time when Eleanor and Neige fought."

"No!" I exclaimed while pointing at her, which apparently startled her a little, so I quickly toned it back with an apologetic smile. "Sorry. What I meant to say was that we didn't genre shift back then. This world was always on the shounen battle harem spectrum. It just wasn't readily apparent because we were also fooled into thinking this was a mundane school life harem dramedy or whatever setting. We saw the clues, but because we didn't have the full context yet, we didn't realize that they were clues at the time."

"You were also in denial."

"Yes. I was in denial. Thank you for always reminding me of my foibles," I told her politely, and I swear my words weren't dripping with sarcasm at all.

"You're welcome."

"Yeah, anyhow, the point is, this time around I wasn't in denial. The reason why we're on the precipice of a genuine genre shift is because all the sentai elements came out of bloody nowhere and they are taking over. There were no clues, no hints, nor any of the staples of the genre present before Lab Coat Guy showed up out of the blue with his stupid spiky hair and inane cackling."

"To be fair, our group does possess five suitable teenagers with elemental affinities who fit right into the mold."

"Elemental affinities?" the question slipped out of my mouth before I could catch it.

"Yes," Judy nodded as she glanced over to the rest of our group chatting around the lunch boxes and she began to stealthily point at them one by one. "Eleanor is fire because she is related to dragons, so she's red. Neige has ice magic, so she's blue. Amelia has her golem, which is earth, so she's green. Angeline can fly, so she is air, which means she is white."

"What does that make Josh?" I asked, mostly out of bile fascination.

"He is the heart of the team, so he is obviously the pink one. Obviously." After stressing that, she glanced back at me, looking straight up smug. "You have to admit it, Chief, it fits."

"Yeah, and by the same logic, we could receive magical rings from the goddess of the planet at any moment and then be sent on a wild goose chase to stop some mustache-twirling rich guy from polluting the environment for shits and giggles. Face it—these elemental tropes are too common to be called clues for the world being intended to be a sentai from the beginning. Hell, I'm pretty sure that full elemental coverage is just as common in battle harem narratives."

"Point taken," Judy relented, but only to turn around and say, "Do you think that this time it's the Narrative forcing the genre shift?"

"Precisely," I told her with a firm nod, and for a few seconds, she looked at me as if I told her I was the second coming of Elvis and I needed to borrow her vuvuzela to fix my spaceship.

"You actually mean that," she stated after looking me in the eye.

"Of course. Things like these," I shook the briefcase in my hand again for emphasis, "don't just randomly come to be. Someone or something had to consciously design our current scenario to push us towards sentai."

"Hold on, I need to process this." Judy theatrically crossed her arms. "All this time, you pushed back against me whenever I advocated the Narrative hypothesis, and now you are just accepting it as if it were obvious all along. What gives?"

"Because it *was* obvious. The tropes, the genre conventions, the prophecies being possible routes—they all point at there being a preplanned plot in the works. It is also obvious that said Narrative is now, for some reason, trying to twist the genre of the world. It has to be an outside force. The only possible Watsonian explanation I have for all of this is that it could still be part of Lord Grandpa's secret master plan, but I sincerely doubt that he would even know what sentai *is*, let alone put all of this together based on it."

"So, you accept the existence of the narrative influence now?"

I had no idea why my assistant looked so expectant, but I had to let her down by shaking my head.

"No, not that. It is one thing to accept the existence of a grand conductor that creates and forces various events on us, but an intangible force that's constantly influencing our actions and thoughts is another thing entirely. That said, we are getting grossly off topic. We should focus on how to screw the literal plot devices for now."

"Oh. I see what you did there," Judy stated while giving me a thumbs-up, though I wasn't entirely certain how serious she was because her face stayed even more expressionless than usual.

"Thank you. So, any ideas?"

"Let's get the obvious one out of the way first: do we really *have* to avoid this genre shift?"

"I think we've already discussed this in detail, but to reiterate: yes. We really want to avoid ending up in a sentai, as it would negatively affect both our day-to-day lives and our long-term research."

"And these transforming artifacts would directly lead to that?"

"Precisely."

"So, leaving them alone is not an option." She paused for a long moment, and then at last she proposed, "I am against property damage on principle, but you could always just break them. They are magical artifacts, so your anti-magic skills could theoretically work on them."

"Yes, theoretically..." I repeated after her, albeit a little uncertainly. "There's regrettably a serious problem with that idea."

"Is there?"

"Yeah. Let's disregard the genre shifting implications of these morphing thingies for a moment, and look at what they are: they are magical armour. Silly and made of spandex, but armour all the same."

"Ah. I suppose breaking them wouldn't be a good idea when the people using them could be in danger at any moment."

"To be fair, they wouldn't be in a *lot* of danger either way, but yeah, robbing them of their armour would kinda be a dick move, especially under the current circumstances."

"So, we are back to square one."

"Indeed."

I must have sounded quite disheartened, as Judy fell silent alongside me, and for a couple of seconds neither of us said anything.

No matter how I looked at it, I had to get rid of these things, but getting rid of them could potentially increase the threat of injury Josh and company would face, including my sister and girlfriend. No matter which option I would choose, I would have to make a major compromise.

Okay, let's approach this from another direction, I thought. *Breaking the morphers and not breaking them are both bad, but which is the lesser of two evils? If I don't break them, then the cat's going to be out of the bag for good, and no matter how hard I try to avert it, it's guaranteed we'll get dragged more and more deeply into sentai shenanigans.*

Breaking them would indirectly harm my friends, and could result in the class rep getting really angry with me, but it would at least temporarily alleviate the threat of sentai, and I could actually take some countermeasures to keep them safe by using my surveillance on Lab Coat Guy.

In short, if we looked at this objectively, disabling them was definitely the better option.

"Okay, breaking it is," I whispered while exhaling a long breath. "It should buy us some time, and then we'll use it to get rid of the problem at its roots by taking down Lab Coat Guy, so they wouldn't be needed, anyway. Any objections?"

"None on my part," my dear assistant agreed with me, which made me feel a little less unsure about my decision. There was only one small matter…

"Can I even break these?"

Judy didn't respond to my mutters, and after an exceedingly long instant of hesitation, I put down the case and opened it. I looked over the five oversized wristwatches and decided to pick up the green one that belonged to Ammy. To my surprise, it was a bit more substantial than I expected, and while it looked like it was made of cheap plastic, the actual material felt really solid. Some kind of ceramic or glass, I reckoned. Now that I had it in my hand, I took note of a few smaller details, such as instead of a dial, the front of the watch had an etched insignia of the school on it. As in, Blue Cherry High's, not the Magi School's. It was probably some sort of disguise, I ventured.

I raised the morpher to eye level to see if there was any trace of the characteristic magical glow on them. When I squinted really hard, I could actually see a faint corona of bluish light around the edges, but nothing as overly visible as, say, the needlessly bright spear in Sebastian's office. Still, magic is magic, so I wrapped my hand around it and tried squeezing it.

"How is it?" Judy inquired while doing a horrible job of hiding her interest.

"Nothing," I admitted after giving it a few more squeezes. I poked the thing in my hand and mused, "Maybe the actual enchantments are on the inside? If I can't touch them, I can't dispel them."

"Can you take it apart?" my assistant inquired, standing on her tippy-toes to take a closer look.

"I don't see any screw holes or assembly marks..."

"So, it's a no, then," she stated and let her heels touch the ground again.

"Well... I cannot take it apart, but that doesn't mean I cannot get inside," I told her maybe a smidgen mischievously. It took her only a second to figure out what I was hinting at.

"Your phantom limb," she stated as if it was entirely self-evident. Well, maybe it was in retrospect, but I still expected at least a tiny bit of enthusiasm.

"Yes, my phantom limb," I followed up by poking her nose with it, but since she couldn't see or feel it, my actions naturally had no effect.

This extra, invisible limb of mine was definitely my most underutilized supernatural ability, but for a good reason. It was necessary for Phasing with others in tow, and it could also be used to dispel all sorts of magical odds and ends, yet it didn't really have much use outside of those circumstances. If it could pick up things or even just mark people, it would've made my life infinitely easier, but instead I didn't dare to let it carelessly touch anything or anyone lest I once again make acquaintance with the mother of all headaches.

Anyhow, after I had my fun poking her, I sharply exhaled and focused on the thing in my hand. My phantom limb, still as jointless and tentacular as ever (though I wasn't sure if the latter was a real word), was poised over the morpher.

Frankly, I had my fair share of misgivings about utilizing it, as the memories of the last time I tried to directly use it on an object were burned into my mind in vivid detail, but I hoped a quick poke was probably not going to hurt too much. That said, I figured it was better to err on the side of caution when it came to this particular ability of mine, so I sat down on the nearest bench first.

"Listen, Judy," I addressed my covertly fidgeting girlfriend while tapping the spot beside me for her to sit down. "Hopefully this won't become a repeat of the last time I tried to reach inside an object, but please be on the lookout in case I have a seizure. If it looks like something went wrong, yank the stupid thing out of my hand. I mean, I'm sure that nothing bad will happen, because I'll be really cautious, but just in case, okay?"

"You are already jinxing it," my dearest assistant grumbled as she sat beside me, but she didn't actually make a serious objection, which I decided to interpret as her silent approval of my plan.

"Nah, I'm just being super-prudent and careful right now. Please remember to praise me later."

My girlfriend rolled her eyes, and with that as the signal, I held out the device on my palm, poised my invisible extra limb right on top of it, and after holding my breath in for a moment, I used its tip to stab down into it.

I really hoped I would experience nothing more than the characteristic tinkling sound of the magic breaking. That was my best-case scenario, and I missed it by a country mile. Of course, I also missed my worst-case scenario by the same margin. That was supposed to be reassuring, and it might've been, if not for the sight in front of me.

How should I even describe this? The sensation was similar to when I'd "interacted" with my mug, except subtly different. It was like I was disembodied and floating inside a vast space, yet at the same time, it felt suffocatingly tiny. What would be a good analogy to illustrate the sensation? Let's say… it was as if I were floating inside an enormous ocean, with all of its weight pushing me down, but also shoved inside a single teaspoon's worth of water. It felt considerably more manageable. But restrictive.

I tried to look around, and maybe I even managed to do so, but I had no way to tell because there was no left or right or up or down in the space I beheld. Not just that, but I also felt that the mere concept of spatial directions was an alien notion here. Strangely enough, I was oddly calm, considering the circumstances. This… felt right somehow. I wondered if this was what being asleep felt like.

Putting such philosophical questions aside, I had to wonder what exactly was going on. However, even before the notion of being curious could take root, I was shocked to realize that I knew the exact answer to that question.

I was, for lack of better words, linked up with the morpher, or rather, the enchantment inside it. Wait, no. Even that wasn't entirely correct. What I was interfacing with was the underlying structure that supported the phenomenon that manifested as an enchantment on the surface. I had no bloody idea how that worked or what exactly it meant, but the whole thing felt so intuitive that I decided to question it later, when I was in a slightly less bizarre situation.

Oh, but speaking of intuitive, I somehow also knew that this imaginary space was something of an... interface? Menu? No, nothing as crude as some kind of transparent panel with buttons. It was more organic. For example, let's say you imagine a person. Now, imagine that person, but with their head twice the original size. You didn't have to open up some menu and pull a slider or write in some large numbers into the *head size* field. It just happens naturally, because that's how imagination works. This place felt like that—the inside of my head, except more tangible and less prone to stray thoughts messing things up.

So, for example, I imagined the morpher that was supposed to be in my palm, and *pop*, it was floating in front of me... except not really, because I was somehow looking at it from all possible angles at the same time, so... would it have been more accurate to say it was inside of me? This was all kinds of screwy, but at the same time it all felt entirely self-evident, which only made it all the weirder.

Anyways, since I already had it in front... inside... whatever! The point is, since the morpher was here, I began to digest it. Digest? I wanted to say analyze, though that sounded fancier than what was actually going on. Semantics aside, it took me an indeterminate amount of time, which was neither especially short nor particularly long, to completely understand the structure of the device, except I didn't understand it at all. Except I did, on an intuitive level.

Okay, I think it's analogy-o-clock again, because there was no way in hell I could properly explain this. So, my current familiarity with the device was akin to moving a part of my body, such as picking up something with my hand. You don't control every single individual muscle, nor are you even consciously aware of most of them, yet you still have full control over your movements and can pick things up without a second thought. It's like... your conscious mind makes the decision to move, and your motor cortex takes care of all the minutia involved with the action. It wasn't a perfect analogy, but it was close enough.

Back to the morpher. I now knew it as well as the back, front, and everything in between of my hand. Because of this, I already knew that Ammy's description of the thing was mostly correct. It used a fairly complex procedure to remove anything designated as "clothes" from the person using it and to replace them with the suit stored in its... well, I wanted to say "memory," but that wasn't the right word. I didn't know what the right word was, so memory would do.

Where was I? Ah, right, the transformation.

As I thought about it, the image of the device twisted and I found myself face-to-face with the full bodysuit stretched out on an anatomically correct but invisible mannequin. It looked just as campy as I feared, and let that suffice as a description for now.

I spent only a short while observing the suit, but I had to note that the class rep was apparently even better developed in the chest department than I thought. What was the measurement unit for these things? D cup, I think? I had to admit, the skintight suit put quite a bit of an emphasis on her assets. Not only that, but when I proceeded to further observe her measurements, the fabric seemed to tuck in even closer to her skin, which was both hilariously random and a major revelation at the same time.

If I could tweak the appearance of the outfit just by paying a little too much attention to Ammy's secondary sexual characteristics, then what was stopping me from changing the design of the outfit? Or even switch it out for something else entirely!

If I had a mouth at the moment, I would've been grinning like Archimedes in his bathtub as I tried to change the outfit and found it fairly simple to do. Well, at least as simple as rearranging the complex molecular structure of a macro-object, but that was something for my motor-cortex-analog to worry about. For a trial run, I imagined the class rep as I saw her just a couple of minutes before, and in a matter of seconds, the garish green jumpsuit metamorphosed into our school's standard female uniform. The whole process was so simple and straightforward that I was almost disappointed, but not really, because getting rid of the sentai suit filled me with such bliss, there was no place for any other emotion.

With the trial run over, I considered what the final form of her armour should be, but then I paused and thought things through. Did the transformation actually have to "transform" anything? What if I left it as their school uniform? That way, they could wear it all day long without anyone being the wiser, and even during battle, they wouldn't look nearly as silly.

I looked into the idea, and by that I meant I rapidly deepened my understanding of the suit and the morpher by... well, I'll be damned if I knew, but it almost didn't feel like learning but recalling something I already knew. Once I considered the feasibility of my idea in light of that knowledge, I couldn't help but be a little disappointed.

First off, these things apparently ran on the user's mana reserves, which could be substituted by tapping into their barrier. Quite a clever design, I had to admit, but it had a few downsides. While it allowed the user to fight without their "natural" transformation, doing so consumed much less magical stamina. In exchange, their specs were considerably lower than when they were fully transformed, but due to the combination of natural barriers and the passive and active defenses the suits themselves provided, the users would still end up incredibly tough. In other words, using the suits exchanged offense for defense, but since the members of our group had already outgunned what Lab Coat Guy threw at them, I figured this evened the playing field a little.

Unfortunately for me, it was also readily apparent that there was no way to make the outfits permanent, since they imposed a constant magical drain on the user. Whatever laws magic had in this universe, it was still operating under some variation of the law of conservation of energy, and although changing the design of these outfits was bafflingly easy, there were things I couldn't change.

Or... could I? Because I wasn't really operating on the enchantment itself, but more on the underlying reality that housed the magic... I think? It's complicated. Anyhow, what exactly was stopping me from changing the principal effects so that the suits would have an infinite battery? Or to take away all their negatives and make the users invincible?

Although it was intended as a rhetorical question, something in me instinctively shrunk back by the mere mention of the idea. It was weird, so I tried to focus on the source of my doubts. It wasn't exactly a fully formed thought or idea, more like a series of disjointed, fragmented flashes of insight. I spent a few minutes assembling them, and while I had a hard time contextualizing most of them, I managed to "recall" something from them.

There was a kind of gut reflex embedded in those thought fragments, something similar to a fight-or-flight response. It told me that I should be wary and that I was only able to act as freely as I could because I was tampering with the insides of a... gland? Sack? It was probably supposed to be a container. Maybe it referred to the morpher device?

It also told me that I should not, under any circumstances, try to muck with the underlying principles of the... something-something. It was not really a word, but more of an abstract idea, like the sound of the colour blue. It was something that *they* created, and I didn't want *them* to learn of my existence.

I naturally had no idea what any of that meant, but if fragments of my own psyche and memories were telling me to stop messing with things I didn't understand, I had no choice but to oblige. I mean, if I couldn't trust myself, who could I trust?

With that, I gave up on trying to create a magical perpetuum mobile and instead focused on other, more practical things. For example, I decided that I'd stick to the school uniform, as it was not only unassuming, but a big *screw you* to the genre shift, as well. However, since I was already at it,

I decided I might as well let my creativity free frolic on the blank canvas of the class rep's outfit first.

That was a mistake.

After the third failed experiment resulted in a maid outfit, I decided that my creativity needed to be sent to a dark corner for the time being so that it could learn discipline, and I returned the outfit to its school uniform roots. I contemplated tweaking it a little further, but in the end, all I added were a few *Tron*-style glowing lines around the sleeves and lapels, mainly so that it could be distinguished from the regular uniform at a glance.

I also, maybe against my better judgment, tweaked the enchantments a little. Not too much, just to give the wearer more of an edge, only stopping whenever I was warned by a sense of apprehension that I was pushing things too far. Oh, right, and I also erased two tracking spells and a sound recording charm thing. Lord Grandpa was nothing if not consistent.

Overall, when I finished, I was quite satisfied with my handiwork... though if someone asked what I did or how I did it, I could only shrug and make weird, confused noises.

With that said, I proceeded to withdraw my phantom limb, and when I did so, I found myself on the rooftop. Unlike when I was Phasing, the transition was instantaneous, and while it didn't cause any nausea, the sudden change in my range of senses left me disoriented.

"Chief? Is everything all right?"

I glanced over at the worried girl at my side. "No problem. Just a little dizzy. How long was I in?"

"In?" she repeated after me while curiously tilting her head to the side. "If by that you meant to ask how long you were staring at the artifact in your hand without blinking, it was a little over three minutes."

"Really? It felt a lot longer," I muttered while I loosened up my neck. "Though that does explain why my eyes sting."

"So? Did you manage to break it?" Judy inquired in a whisper after checking that the others were still out of hearing range, and I couldn't help but grin in response.

"No, I did one better. I hacked it."

"How?"

"With my 133t hacking skills." My irreverent answer (or the fact that I actually wrote out the numbers in "133t") seemed to confuse her, so I sheepishly added, "With my phantom limb. It turns out it is unexpectedly *handy*."

This time Judy outright rolled her eyes, but I didn't sweat it. I'd just successfully counterattacked the genre shift, simultaneously figured out a way to interact with a deeper layer of this world, and I didn't even get a migraine in the process. I think I deserved a dad joke or two.

PART 2

I reappeared on the rooftop and dashed over to the closest bench and more or less fell onto it, butt first, in my hurry. Once I was seated, I opened the silver briefcase on my lap, removed a morpher, and raised it to my eye level with a suitably profound expression forced on my face. My setup was done not a second too soon, as a moment later, the access door opened and Amelia stepped out with a disapproving expression.

"Careful, class rep. If you keep frowning like that, you're going to get wrinkles."

"You really skipped afternoon classes up here," she stated.

I shrugged as I placed the modified morpher back into the case and told her, "I told you I would, didn't I? I hope you covered for me."

"I did!" Elly wedged herself into our conversation by pushing Ammy forward and skipping up to my side in one breath. "I told the teacher you had stomach problems and had to go home. I also took notes for you."

"Thanks, princess, you're a gem."

"You're welcome," she replied with a grin and grabbed hold of my free hand. Then her expression quickly changed into a puzzled one. "Your hand is warm."

"Thank you?" I told her, a little puzzled myself.

"I thought you'd be cold after staying up here since noon, but your hand is really warm," she reiterated while holding my hand in both of hers.

"Well, I was working hard, so my hands didn't have time to cool down," I told her a little white lie with the practiced ease of a seasoned professional.

It was only natural that my hands hadn't gotten cold, as I'd only just gotten on the roof. Once I recognized the insane possibilities of this new and unexpected discovery, I convinced the others that I needed some time to finish examining the artifacts, and so I stayed behind on the roof after the lunch break. However, once they left, I immediately Phased over to the secret base (much to Brang's surprise) and spent the school day experimenting with our new toys.

To say that the implications of what I discovered were staggering was an understatement, and it was the first real breakthrough in the nature of this world since... well, it might've been the very first one, actually. I couldn't decide if this was more hilarious or infuriating, but the fact that I'd stumbled onto something so absurdly significant by accident was remarkable.

I felt like I could spend days just poking the magical innards of these artifacts, but at the same time, I didn't forget to keep an eye on the gang with Far Sight, if only so that I could come back the moment school was over. I never thought I'd say this, but I was actually a little reluctant to part with them, though I didn't have much of a choice in the matter. I went through all the trouble to tweak and fix them, so it would've been a waste not to let the guys use them. It was also the most beautiful way to give the middle finger to the genre shift, and that was enough to lessen the pain of separation, a tad.

That said, I made a mental note to ask the class rep if she could set me up with their artificers in the future. Getting access to more devices like these would probably allow me to penetrate the systems governing this world even deeper. But then again, the fact that I tweaked the morpher options would probably put Lord Grandpa on guard, so maybe I shouldn't. After all, I still had my self-appointed in-laws to exploit. They likely hoarded piles of magical gadgets and gizmos, as dragons tend to do, and I'd have the perfect opportunity to ask Abram about them during dinner that evening. Speaking of which, the irritating butler certainly had a lot of fun toys in his study. Maybe I should try to poke around there, as well... pun intended.

But that was for later. Back to the current situation.

The gang assembled on the rooftop, with Judy being the last to arrive and closing the door behind her. I looked over our little group and cleared my throat.

"Listen up, guys, I've got some news," I told them using my best salesman smile.

"News?" Angie at the front tilted her head to the side and gestured for me to continue.

"Good news, actually," I reiterated while holding up the briefcase for emphasis. "I checked these things, and they should be perfectly safe. I've done some modifications as well, though they should be self-explanatory."

"Wait! What kind of modifications?" the class rep interrupted my explanation, so I sent her an annoyed glance, and she actually backed down.

"As I said, they should be fairly evident when you try them out. I also removed the magical bugs on them while I was at it." At this point, I paused on purpose and sent Ammy another pointed glance. "Speaking of which, please tell your grandfather to stop trying to be clever with his surveillance, or I'll be forced to take direct action."

"Hold on, Leo! You can't do that!"

The objection, much to my surprise, came from the princess.

"I can't do what?"

"You can't just threaten the arch-mage of the island," she exclaimed, her arms akimbo. She was also glaring at me, but for some reason I found that kind of cute instead of annoying like in the past. Weird.

Anyhow, I told her, "It wasn't a threat, per se. It was just a reminder that I already warned him not to try to spy on us. So if, say, one day he woke up to find all of his liqueur stolen and his beard dyed neon pink, he would have only himself to blame." At this point in the conversation, I turned to Ammy again and added, "By the way, you can tell him what I just said, verbatim."

"Grandfather doesn't really appreciate jokes like that."

"It's not a joke. I already bought the hair dye. You know, just in case?" The class rep also didn't seem to appreciate my definitely-not-a-joke, so I quickly changed the direction of the conversation by lightly shaking the case in my hands. "Never mind that—let's just see if these puppies work as advertised! Who wants to be the first lab rat?"

"Volunteer, Chief. Volunteer," Judy corrected me, and I gave her an expression that roughly said, *Isn't that the same thing?*

She was oddly adamant about my terminology, so I gave up.

"Fine, let's go with 'volunteer,' then. Anyone?"

"Me! Let me try it first!" Angie raised her hand high over her head, her boundless enthusiasm about as vibrant as it was predictable.

"Come over," I told her as I retrieved one of the devices and handed it over to her. "Yours is the white one."

"Can I try it out?" she asked me, her eyes sparkling with excitement, and based on the expectant looks from the rest of the group (with maybe the exception of Judy, who was busy taking notes), she wasn't the only one.

"You have to put it on your wrist like this," Ammy abruptly took the lead and helped the Celestial girl out with the arduous task of putting on a glorified wristwatch, but since she was just trying to be helpful, I decided not to complain. However, I had to butt in after she began to explain, "You have to hold your arms like this and then recite the activation phrase to—"

"Actually, no," I cut her off before she could put any silly ideas into Angie's head, like *posing*. I put the case aside and stepped up to the two in order to explain.

"I took the liberty to streamline a few things while I was investigating the internal workings of these transmorphers. There's no need for any complicated activation sequences. You just have to press the top and insert a trace amount of magic into the device, and bam, you're done."

"Really?"

"Try it, if you don't believe it. It should be super-intuitive."

The Celestial girl looked just a smidgen skeptical, but I urged her to try, and she did. There were no flashing multicoloured lights, nor any silly robotic spirit animals swooping in for dramatic effect. I made sure to remove anything even remotely resembling a sentai morphing sequence, with extreme prejudice, so all that really happened was a brief gust of wind rustling Angie's hair as the enchantment displaced her clothes and replaced them with a more or less identical-looking set of enchanted garbs.

"Did anything happen? Did I miss it?" Josh muttered while looking understandably confused.

"Wow... this is so weird..." Angie muttered as she dramatically stretched her arms.

"This doesn't look right," came the next confused comment from the class rep as she looked over our volunteer.

"This is amazing!" Angie exclaimed, completely disregarding Ammy's comment. "I have my barrier, and yet these clothes don't explode! Look, Josh! I can even get my wings out without fully transforming!"

"This looks waaaay more convenient than I feared it would be," Joshua mused aloud as he looked her over, from head to toe. "Can you use your bow, too?"

"Let me try... Wow, look! I can! This is almost as good as my Celestial transformation!"

"And it covers more skin, too," Josh said with a sagely nod.

"And why is that a problem?" The Celestial's girl's eyes narrowed into suspicious slits.

"It's not a problem, it's just... you know?"

While the two childhood friends were having their awkward discussion about the distracting effects of stripperific transformations, Amelia hijacked my attention by grabbing hold of my jacket. Not in a cute, romantic way. More like a Mafia enforcer getting hold of her mark before the beating commenced.

"Care to explain what's going on?"

While that might've sounded like a request on the surface, the class rep's tone made it blindingly obvious she wouldn't take "no" for an answer. First things first. I carefully pried her off me, and only then did I respond.

"I told you I made some minor tweaks, didn't I?" It was easy to see that my coy answer wasn't to her liking, so I exhaled sharply through my nose and proceeded to give her a slightly more nuanced explanation. I mean, poking her every once in a while was fairly amusing, but I didn't want to antagonize her for no reason. "You told me that your artificers put these together in a crunch, right? Since I was already poking around in the insides of their work, I decided to patch up some of the corners they cut to finish the devices on time. The look of the suits was one of them, so I fixed that."

"Since when can you do that?"

"What can I say? I'm a man of many talents," I told her with a humble little smile.

"That's my line," Judy abruptly cut in while simultaneously stepping on my toes.

I flashed my dear assistant my best toothpaste-commercial smile and told her, "Yes, and it's a good one. That's why I borrowed it."

"It's not borrowing if you don't ask for permission. It's copyright infringement."

"So? Are you going to sue me?"

"I might do just that," Judy huffed with faux indignation. Or, at the very least, I sincerely hoped she was just pretending.

"Want me to introduce you to a good copyright lawyer?" the princess piped up, throwing us both for a loop. When we didn't respond, she added, "W-what? Father works in the record industry! It's only natural that I know a lawyer or two!"

I sighed. "That's not really the issue—"

"I will take you up on your offer," Judy said. "Let's sue the Chief and split the profits, sixty-forty."

"Hmm." Elly tapped her lips as she considered the offer, then nodded. "It's a little on the low side, but very well, I'll take sixty percent."

Judy blinked.

"Did you hear that, Chief? Prepare to be served." She employed a dramatic pause here, then added, "Of course, we can always settle out of court, so long as you are willing to pay the appropriate compensation for your heinous wrongdoing."

"Since when did copyright infringement become a 'heinous' crime?" I asked.

"Chief, you have to keep up with the times. Copyright infringement is the worst thing you can do to someone. It's worse than kicking their dog."

"Truly?"

"Definitely." Elly snapped a frighteningly intense nod.

"Woe is me, then. How can I ever pay for such terrible crimes staining my once pure soul?"

"You can start by making reparations," Judy proposed.

"In what? More sandwiches?"

My dear assistant shook her head and told me, in her usual deadpan voice, "Sandwiches are a defunct currency, Chief. Now we only take payments in kisses."

"But you are already getting a lot of those..."

"Not enough."

"You can never have enough," Elly agreed with another huge nod that made her hair cascade back and forth, always returning to her previous tidy hairdo afterwards.

"Fine! You have a deal," I grumbled with mock reluctance as I offered a hand, and Judy shook it.

"It's been a pleasure doing business with you," my assistant chirped, and I was just about to roll my eyes when I noticed that the princess was uncharacteristically fidgety at our side.

"Is there a problem?"

"Was... this a skit?" she asked.

"Yes," Judy confirmed with a slight nod. "You participated well. We are making progress."

"Thank you, I think, but... if that was a skit, does that mean we aren't actually getting extra kisses?"

"That's a salient question if I've ever heard one." Judy turned back to me with an expectant, "Chief?"

"What? You seriously want me to pamper you even more?"

"Little sisters are for spoiling; girlfriends are for pampering," Judy stated in a way that made her words sound profound, even though they were anything but.

"Oh fine," I gave up without much of a fight, though I did add a quiet, "You make it sound like I'm frigid or something..."

"Are you quite finished?"

The class rep looked about as far from pleased as was humanly possible, so I deemed it was time to stop playing around, ignore my girlfriends giving each other a high five for some strange and wholly incomprehensible reason, and instead focus on addressing whatever questions Ammy had.

"Yes. Sorry for the intermezzo. Where were we?"

"You still haven't told me since when you can modify enchantments," Ammy answered while readjusting her glasses. She looked like she thought I was still keeping secrets from her... which was true, of course, but this one really wasn't one of them, as I was also unaware of my phantom limb's extra capabilities until just a few hours ago.

"It's a skill I developed recently," I told her with all the confidence and authenticity only a technical truth can provide.

"How recently are we talking about?"

"I learned how to do it within the last two weeks."

"You can't learn how to make artifacts in two weeks," Ammy emphatically stated while looking me right in the eye. She was probably trying to put pressure on me to see if I would slip up.

"Hold up. I didn't learn how to make these things," I clarified while I picked the green morpher out of the case. "I can only tinker with stuff that's already present. By the way, here is yours, give it a try."

She still looked more skeptical than a NASA engineer at a flat Earth conference, but at long last she took her device.

"I still don't understand why you changed how the outfit looks," she grumbled as she buckled the morpher on to her wrist, and while it might have been a rhetorical question, it didn't mean I couldn't answer it.

"Okay, class rep, let's be serious here for a moment. Did you actually look at those original suits?"

She pursed her lips. "No," she admitted.

"In that case, let me explain to you why I changed things in meticulous detail. First and foremost, the original suits were conspicuous as all hell. They couldn't be used in emergencies because they would draw all the attention to us. The closed helmets, while providing some extra protection by serving as binding-points for more defensive enchantments, were actually very restrictive and would prove more of a hindrance than help in a high-speed close combat situation. Most importantly, though, they just looked silly and really uncomfortable."

"If you say so."

Ammy's response to my explanation was fairly noncommittal, but at the same time she didn't object, either, so I figured she gave up the argument. I was just about to say something when she activated her morpher and... well, to say that she "transformed" wasn't exactly correct. Which reminded me—I needed to come up with another name for these gizmos. Something that better reflected what they did. Maybe "Quick Change Systems" or "Dress Alternators" or something similarly removed from anything even remotely related to sentai.

I'll workshop that later with Judy and Elly, I decided. For the time being, I focused my attention on Amelia, who was in the middle of very carefully inspecting her sleeve with her other hand on one of the temples of her glasses.

"The wards seem to be intact. No looping or leaking, either. The performance is..." She left off fiddling with her glasses and slapped her sleeve, hard. The impact let out a soft crackling noise. She hissed and shook her hand. "It seems there is no problem with the wards' reaction times or output, either."

"You could've tested it in a better way, you know?"

She disregarded my criticism and instead did a couple of warm-up stretches. I'm not going to lie, I was a tiny bit confused, but I figured she must've been doing it for a reason, even if I couldn't think of one. I wondered if that's how the others felt whenever I used "refuge in audacity" to bullshit my way out of a situation, but before I could get too deeply absorbed in that, she abruptly addressed me.

"The performance of these suits seems to be even higher than I hoped for. It's not as good as my personalized robes, but closer than I thought. I only have two questions."

"Shoot."

She raised her arm and pointed at her sleeve.

"What are these green lines for?"

"Fashion."

She didn't seem to appreciate the joke.

"It's so that you can tell it apart from your regular school uniform. You can turn off the glow with the switch inside your lapel, in case you want to be sneaky and don't want to glow in the dark."

"Can we try it out now?"

I turned to the source of the question and found an unusually impatient Josh flanked by Snowy. I glanced back to the class rep (though it wasn't like I needed her permission or anything), and once she nodded, I handed the devices out to their owners.

"Listen, Josh, just a bit of a heads-up," I called out to my friend before he could put on the no-longer-morpher. "Your device is slightly special. Since you have no mana on your own without first transforming, I tweaked the settings so that it would activate as you transform. As a side effect, it suppresses your physical changes, but on the bright side, at least you no longer have to run around in just your pants whenever you do that. Oh, and on the same note, make sure that you only transform into an Abyssal for the time being."

"No problem. I am the most comfortable with that one, anyway," Josh told me with a childish grin betraying his excitement. It was weird how much he resembled Angie sometimes.

Are all childhood friends this similar? I wondered. *Or only the tropey ones?*

Anyhow, I handed Snowy her own device, as well, and Josh dragged her away, no doubt so that he could transform and try out his new gadget.

"Can I ask my second question now?"

"Yeah, sure," I answered as I turned back to the class rep and saw that she was awkwardly pointing behind her back. Or rather, *at* her back.

"What is the ward on the back? Around... here...?" she struggled to reach behind her, until she noticed Angie standing nearby. Before the hapless Celestial girl could get a word of objection in, Ammy had dragged her over, turned her around, and pointed a finger at the area just under her clavicles. "Here! What does this one do?"

"Thank you for asking," I replied while handing out the last device to my draconic girlfriend. "Remember how we discussed that barriers had no protection against grappling?"

Ammy nodded.

"I figured, while I was at it, I might as well try to do something about it. So if, for example, someone grabs you and puts you in a full nelson..."

To illustrate my point, I carefully grabbed hold of the princess and she obediently let me put her into the hold, though she did make some nostalgic noises of embarrassment in the process. I naturally ignored them and continued on.

"As I was saying, if someone puts you in a full nelson, or some other kind of hold from the back, all you have to do is to snap your fingers three times in succession, like this." I let go of Elly to illustrate my explanation by snapping, though since I wasn't wearing a magical uniform, nothing happened. "When you do this, it creates a strong concussive blast from the area you were pointing at. I didn't have any way to test it, but unless I forgot to carry the two when I did my calculations, it should be about as strong as a solid uppercut from the average heavyweight boxer. Not enough to kill someone, but more than enough to make the person behind your back rethink their life decisions."

"How did you do that? I thought the wards on the suits were all defensive ones."

"What makes you think it's not a defensive ward?" I responded to the class rep's question with a coy question of my own. "It's actually a repeller array, except with its area reduced to the minimum, its output cranked up to eleven, and with a manual trigger added on top. Nothing fancy."

"Can I try it out now?" Angie asked me with a suitably angelic look on her face, but I firmly shook my head.

"No. You will have the opportunity to play around with it on your way home. Speaking of which..." I cleared my throat and raised my voice to get everyone's attention. "Gather up, guys, I have an important announcement to make."

"An important announcement?" Snowy repeated after me as she and Josh came back.

"An announcement? Sounds official," Joshua mused while rubbing his chin. "Did you get engaged?"

"No, not that kind of announcement." I rolled my eyes and then proclaimed, "Listen up. I want you guys to stay in your new magic uniforms." The moment I said that out loud, I realized it sounded kind of silly, so I hastily whispered to Judy, "Remind me to come up with a snappy new name for these things."

"Roger."

"Naming aside, the reason why I want you to keep them on is that, on your way home, you're going to be ambushed again."

"We are?" Ammy blurted out in surprise. In fact, she was so surprised that her glasses slid down to the tip of her nose. She quickly shoved them up again and said, "Are you certain?"

"One hundred percent." My response, coupled with my firmest nod, still didn't seem to ease her doubts, so I decided to elaborate. "To be more specific, once you leave the school, you are going to be pulled into a purple zone... let's see... around the crossroads with the antique store and the shop with the big fat fisherman logo."

"How do you know?" came the next question from the incredulous magi.

"I put surveillance on Lab Coat Guy." It appeared my casual answer confused her a bit, so I let out a small sigh and told her, "The guy who ambushed the group the last time."

"This sounds serious," Elly muttered, and Ammy fervently agreed.

"Yes, it is! Why didn't you warn us sooner? Ugh, I'll have to tell Grandfather about this."

"Don't bother. He already knows."

My words stopped her in her tracks, and she looked at me with a genuine sense of appreciation for the first time in a while.

"Have you already contacted him? Good."

"No, you misunderstand me. You don't need to tell him because he masterminded the ambushes."

Aaaaaand her appreciation immediately switched over to suspicion and annoyance again. Oh well, it was nice while it lasted.

"Ammy's grandpa is behind the attack? Seriously?"

"Yeah, I find it hard to believe, too," Josh agreed with his childhood friend's objection, and both of them looked at me expectantly to see how I would react.

"Trust me, I'm about eighty-nine percent sure he had a hand in every single headache we've had in the past couple of days. Plus or minus twelve percent."

"You can't be serious," Ammy whispered in denial, so I addressed her directly.

"Okay, then if you don't believe me, just do what I say. All of you, go home together and go to the crossroad I talked about."

"You *want* us to get ambushed?" Josh spoke up with his critical brow raised sky-high.

"Since you know about it ahead of time, it won't really be an ambush anymore, but yes, that's exactly what I want you to do." He looked less than convinced, so I argued, "You all probably noticed, but those idiotic robot things are not exactly a mortal threat to any of you. Lab Coat Guy is going to bring along a few improved models as well this time around, but as far as I could gather, 'improved' only means they have a different colour scheme and don't make clanking noises while they wave their arms like a bunch of imbeciles. This should be a good opportunity for you to familiarize your-selves with the uniforms' capabilities and, maybe most importantly, you don't even have to wreck the robots. You just have to play around with them for a good ten or so minutes, maybe even pretend to be struggling, and then Armband Guy will swoop in to heroically rescue you and chase away Lab Coat Guy."

"Armband who…?" Ammy uttered, but then her eyes opened wide and she exclaimed, "Wait, do you mean Pascal?"

"Yes, I obviously meant him," I affirmed, the statement drawing a small sigh from my assistant.

"Chief, you should really stop giving nicknames to everyone and just use their names instead. You can be really confusing sometimes."

"Hush, Dormouse, we are discussing serious things here. We have no time to argue about nicknames. Right, princess?"

"Umm… Sure?" Elly agreed, though based on her surprised visage, she probably didn't know exactly *what* she was agreeing with.

"You see? So, back to the topic. Armband Guy is going to chase off Lab Coat Guy. When they leave, the robots will become disorganized and ripe for you to beat them up. Just as you finish, Armband Guy will come back and tell you that his target got away, and he was under orders from Lord Grandpa to look after you. He will also tell you that you should reconsider joining the School, which you shouldn't do. Everyone following me so far?"

"Barely," Josh griped.

I turned to Ammy. "So, here is my proposal. Please go ahead and let yourself be 'ambushed' and 'rescued.'" When I said that, I involuntarily made air quotes with my fingers, a bad habit I probably picked up from Sebastian. It was definitely his fault. "My evidence of your grandfather's involvement is the script I just described."

"You're telling me that if things will happen as you said, it proves he is conspiring against us?" she reiterated, and I could only nod, since it was literally what I just said.

"Precisely."

"But... why would Grandfather do something like this?" Ammy blurted out in a confused, almost pained voice. That took me aback for a moment. I thought she would argue against me, defending her grandfather to the bitter end, and I even prepared a few additional responses just for that, but based on her reaction, it seemed like she already more or less believed me. Maybe she trusted me way more than I thought?

Either way, I quickly explained, "I still don't have enough intel to explain his motivations for choosing such a roundabout and, frankly, silly method, but I can say that Lab Coat Guy is more or less just a glorified scarecrow. He is supposed to harass us, and Josh in particular, to the point where we would take his offer and join the School as affiliates. They are being a good sport about it, though. Lab Coat Guy is not allowed to target any of you individually, he can only attack you inside Purple Zones, and he cannot take hostages or even cause distress to anyone else but you guys. Just more proof that he is supposed to be loud, startling, but mostly harmless. It's the main reason why I'm still only at the stage where I'm warning your gramps about the dangers of pink hair dye."

That, and the fact that I didn't really have the leverage yet to casually kick down his door. But one thing at a time.

"Where did you learn all this?" came the next question, and for a moment I couldn't help but pause. I naturally couldn't tell her that I had Lab Coat Guy under almost constant Far Sight surveillance, and so I'd overheard their entire plan for today's surprise attack, but since I didn't want to reveal my cards just yet...

"Another trade secret," I answered, holding my finger to my lips. "But I can tell you that my information is about as trustworthy as if I'd heard it with my own two ears."

"Let me guess," Josh spoke up, crossing his arms in front of his chest, his face plastered with a cocky grin that didn't quite reach his eyes. "You said you got injured last night while infiltrating Robatto's lab. I bet you overheard all of this back then. No, wait! I'd bet my left leg you even bugged the place and that's how you know all this!"

"Maaaaaaaybe?" I responded while flashing him a roguish grin. "Putting my source of information aside, all you have to know is that it's credible. So, I want you guys to leave school as a group, like everything is fine, and get totally surprised by the oh-so-unexpected-and-absolutely-shocking ambush, then go wild! Get familiar with your gear, test its limits, and just let out some steam until Armband Guy shows up to gallantly save the day. And as for you, class rep..."

I turned to the conflicted girl in the middle of our group and told her, "You should go along and see if things proceed as I described. All I ask is that, whether you believe me about your old man's involvement or not, please do not confront him about it for the time being. If I may be honest with you guys, I'm still fairly early in my investigation of his motives, and I don't want to poke the hornet's nest until I'm sure I have a long enough pole."

"All right." Amelia once again proved unexpectedly docile. "I'll go and see it with my own eyes."

I decided not to look the gift agreement in the clause, so I just smiled and said, "Great! You guys get going! Don't want to keep your dastardly attacker waiting."

"You're not coming with us?" Snowy spoke up for maybe the first time since she'd arrived, and she immediately pinpointed the crux of the situation. Just as I expected from my little sister.

"No, I have a prior appointment. You were supposed to go to the school nurse for a checkup, but since you are unfortunately preoccupied with something else, as your big brother, it falls on my shoulders to go and have a long, long chat with a certain annoying old man. Speaking of which, why are there so many annoying old guys in my life?"

No one seemed to want to answer my rhetorical question, nor would they have the opportunity, as the class rep immediately followed up by saying, "Okay, how do you know *that*? Mr. Peabody told me just last break to have Neige visit him." She looked me in the eye, but when it became obvious that I wouldn't answer to her satisfaction, she let out a shallow groan and said, "Let me guess? Is it another trade secret?"

"Bingo!"

She didn't seem to appreciate my irreverent grin, and turned on her heel. Following her example, the others also headed towards the roof access, except for my two girlfriends, of course.

"Do I have to go home alone again?" the princess nagged with the pout to end all pouts, and in response I chuckled and rubbed the crown of her head.

"Sorry, but I really have to stay back. If it makes it any better, I can go to your place a little earlier and we can cuddle a bit before dinner?"

"Ah, right!" The pout, which looked as firm as basalt on her face, melted away into a sunny smile. "I almost forgot you were coming over! I have to make sure everything's prepared right!" With that, she rose on her tippy-toes and pecked my left cheek, then dashed after the rest, passing by Ammy on the way.

"I don't get you, Leo," Ammy told me when the only three people left on the roof were us plus my dear assistant. "I don't know how you can do so many things. But one day, I swear, I'll get to the bottom of you."

Saying so, she turned around and left through the door. When it was finally only Judy and me, I glanced down at her.

"That sounded mildly ominous. Do you think I should be worried?"

"You'd better be," she mumbled while stepping closer until our shoulders met. "If I learn that you let any girl lay her hand on your bottom, other than us, I'll kick it."

"Her hand or my bottom?"

My girlfriend glanced up at me with an odd intensity in her eyes.

"Yes."

CHAPTER 20

PART 1

"Oh? You're already done?"

Judy looked visibly surprised (by her standards) when I left the infirmary just a few short minutes after entering it.

"I told you I'd be quick," I responded as I threw my bag over my shoulder.

"I thought that you were going to drill Peabody about his involvement with Robatto."

"Nah, it's too early to put direct pressure on him. Not to mention, I don't want him to put Lab Coat Guy on guard just yet."

After I told her that, I beckoned for her to follow me. It wasn't exactly prudent to discuss things like this right in front of the man's door, even if Far Sight told me he wasn't eavesdropping now. Speaking of which, I Far Glanced over to the rest of our group, and after observing them a little, I said, "It seems things are wrapping up on the others' side, as well. No injuries, though the class rep is pretty down. I guess she's disheartened by how accurate my script was."

"She'll get over it."

"I'm sure she will," I responded a little absentmindedly just around the time we reached the shoe lockers.

"Do you want to go and meet up with them?" Judy questioned me as she headed for her own locker.

"Nah. Didn't we talk about how we should let Josh act independently every once in a while? He's doing good, too. He is passive-aggressively heckling Armband Guy like a pro."

My dear assistant gave me an odd look and said, "I will now graciously avoid the question of why you consider picking fights with vastly more powerful people a good thing, and instead ask why Joshua did so."

"I wouldn't call him 'vastly' more powerful..."

"Chief, please focus on the actual question."

"Right. To answer your query, I'd say it's probably because my description of the conspiracy and him playing along with it left a bad impression on Josh. Either that, or he is miffed by the dude acting so familiar with the class rep."

"You mean to say he is jealous."

I pondered how to answer that as I watched her put on her left shoe while hopping on the other foot.

"Maybe? I mean, it can be pretty hard to follow the thought processes of a harem protagonist."

"I can attest to that," she threw an obvious bait my way, but I decided to ignore it, and quickly slipped into my own outdoor shoes.

"Either way, Josh and company are fine, so let's discuss my newest discovery instead."

"Your phantom limb's ability to modify enchantments," Judy stated what she thought was obvious, but I shook my head.

"No, Dormouse. That's just the tip of the iceberg."

"Really?"

That comment piqued her interest all right, but before saying anything else, I waved for her to follow.

"I'll tell you on the way home."

Saying so, I left the school building, with Judy following close behind me, and I only hit up the conversation again once we were already walking downhill.

"Okay, so, do you want to review what we thought my extra limb could do, at the risk of being redundant, or do you want me to cut to the chase and tell you the big discovery I made?"

"The latter."

"Too bad—I'm still going to do it. Do you remember what happened the last time I tried to use my phantom limb to experiment on my mug?"

"You scared me pretty badly," came the morose answer in return.

"Maybe, but that's not what I'm talking about now. Remember what I told you? About the overlapping mugs and the psychedelic experience surrounding it?"

"Yes," she said, though it was little more than a verbal prompt for me to continue.

"I think I figured out what happened back then. You see, this invisible appendage of mine," I said while waving it in front of me, though she still couldn't see it. "I still don't know where it came from, why I have it, or how it works, but now I know *what* it does. It is, for lack of better terms, something that lets me interact with the World."

"Chief, that's literally what arms are for," she stated, her voice flat as an ironing board.

There was a snappy comeback right on the tip of my tongue, but I swallowed it back down and instead I said, "Sorry, I suppose I wasn't clear enough. I meant the word *World* with a capital *W*. As in, the simulation or whatever it is that we live in."

"Are you serious?"

I nodded, and Judy immediately took out her phone, no doubt in preparation for taking notes, but I snagged her hand.

"Dormouse… just how many times do we have to repeat this conversation? Please don't take notes while we are walking. It's dangerous. When you're not paying attention, you can easily stumble into something or someone."

"Such as those people?"

"What people?"

I followed her eyes, and as I did that, I recognized the silhouettes of a familiar trio.

"Crap!" the shortest member of the Goldfish Poop Gang let out a low hiss the moment our eyes met. "It's him! It's the bully!"

"What do we do, boss? I think he noticed us…"

"Shut up, you scaredy-cats!" the big guy with the pompadour-to-end-all-pompadours stage-whispered back. "Just hold yer heads up and stick to the plan. And remember, don't make eye contact!"

"I think I already did…"

"Then don't do it again! And act casual!"

With that, the three of them formed an orderly line and proceeded to… walk by us without even glancing our way.

We stood in place as they passed us by, and the moment they were behind us, they quickened their pace and soon disappeared around a nearby corner.

"What was that about?" my girlfriend asked.

"Damned if I know," I replied, similarly baffled.

"One of them said you were a bully," she noted with a hint of unwelcome curiosity in her eyes.

"Must have confused me with someone else," I forcefully stated before pointedly clearing my throat. "Anyhow, let's return to the previous topic, shall we?"

Something told me she was still really curious about what just happened, but she obediently nodded and put her phone away before she asked the pivotal question of the day.

"In that case, please elaborate on how you interacted with the capital *W*."

"At once," I replied before taking a deep breath to collect my thoughts. I had actually spent quite a bit of time thinking about how to put my experiences into words even as I was experimenting with the artifacts, yet I still found the prospect exceedingly hard. "Okay, let's start with the basics. As I said, the phantom limb allowed me to peek behind the veil and see things as they are."

"Was there an old man who tried to convince you to ignore the man behind the curtain?"

"No, but I almost wish there was."

"Really?"

"No."

"Are you sure the *S* in your nonexistent middle name doesn't stand for *spoilsport*?"

"Yes, I am. Also, please focus. Okay, here's a disclaimer first... Please don't ask about *how* certain things work or how I figured out what I'm about to explain, because I'd bloody well like to know that, as well. That said, here's some of what I gathered. First off, let's put one of our old questions to bed—this world is certainly artificial, and more importantly, it is a constructed one."

"Constructed," Judy repeated the word after me. "I suppose that means it was constructed by someone."

"Most likely."

"Could the creator of the world be the source of the Narrative?"

"No idea. It could be them, or an autonomous self-correcting system. I don't know yet."

"You said *them* just now," Judy pointed out my slip of the tongue with the precision of a trained bloodhound. Or rather, an adorable puppy. Doggy analogies aside, I let out a sharp breath before I answered her.

"As I said, don't ask me why, but I have something of a hunch that there are multiple people or beings or whatever running the show from the backstage."

"How many?"

"I dunno... Let's say, more than three but less than five?"

"So, four."

"Maybe? I mean, it could be three-point-one-four, as far as I know." At this point, I took another huge, dramatic breath and emphatically stated, "Anyways, we are getting off topic. As I said, I've gained some insight into this world."

"I'm listening," my assistant prompted me, and I obliged.

"First and foremost, this is a world of natural physics, or at least 'natural' in the sense of what you would find in a textbook. Also, on that note, while I cannot rule out the hypothesis that all of this is a simulation in the traditional sense of the word, my foray into reality hacking made me realize that the 'resolution' of *everything* is insane. It might even actually go down to the atomic level, though I cannot be sure because I had a hard time conceptualizing changes on that scale in motion."

"So, you're saying that even if this world really is a simulation of some sort, on a physical level, it's indistinguishable from a non-simulated world."

"Yes, though to be fair, that is a statement philosophers debating the nature of reality could probably argue about for days. Unfortunately, we don't really have the time for that."

"Unfortunately? Does that mean that if we had the time, you would like to talk about it for days?"

"You know what I meant."

"Understood." Judy's response made me wonder what it was that she 'understood,' but she continued by saying, "So, if this world is practically indistinguishable from reality on a physical level, then how can we explain placeholder behaviour?"

"Beats me," I admitted. "Maybe simulating consciousness is harder? Or it could be that the world wasn't designed with simulating people in mind. Or people with minds. Or there could be a completely unrelated reason."

"In short, we don't have enough data to come to a definite conclusion yet."

"Exactly," I agreed with a small nod. "But back to the beginning of our discussion: you remember how I had an adverse reaction to interacting with my cup?"

"To put it mildly," Judy grumbled.

"The reason it happened was because changing something directly causes the World to push back. Let me give you an analogy. Imagine you are at the bottom of a swimming pool."

"Okay."

"Let's say you put your hands together so that you have a ball of water which you want to replace with another ball of water. Are you following me so far?"

"I'm trying to."

"Okay, so, let's say you're really, really fast. Like, Superman-on-methamphetamine kind of fast. Yet, when you remove the original ball, it naturally leaves behind an empty space. Since it's empty, the water pressure in the pool immediately tries to fill up the space, no matter how fast you are. Do you understand what I'm getting at?"

My girlfriend looked at me oddly for a second. "Chief... I don't want to hurt your feelings, but I think you're horrible at analogies."

"Nonsense," I dismissed her out of hand. "Okay, let's try this more directly. The swimming pool is the World. The ball of water is the mug. When I interacted with it, I unknowingly attempted to replace it with another piece of glazed pottery. While both of them are technically the same, the act of changing things disturbs the fabric of the World, and it doesn't like it when that happens, not one bit. It's doesn't consciously dislike it, though. It's more like how water immediately fills in a hole you try to create in it because of surface tension and pressure. The water doesn't do it to spite your efforts; it's just how water works. So, to stay with my analogy, in order to replace the water ball, I must first separate it from the rest of the swimming pool, and while the process lasts, I have to keep the water from pouring in and mixing stuff, because if that happens, it creates waves that others can notice."

"By *waves*, you mean the three-point-one-four creators," Judy stated with her tongue set in her cheek so hard it almost poked through.

"Yes, I mean them."

"And that would be bad."

"Probably."

Judy let out a soft grunt that I decided to interpret as agreement.

"So, in short," I continued, "using this arm of mine to hack reality is not entirely feasible. I think it can be done, in theory, but it's hard, dangerous, and it makes my head hurt something fierce."

My assistant looked at me expectantly, most likely waiting for me to continue, but when I didn't, she rolled her eyes and said, "All right, I will ask the obvious question. If using your immaterial limb to change objects is unfeasible, then what did you do to the morphers?"

"Thank you for asking!" I responded with gusto. "But... before I tell you, remind me to come up for a new name of those gizmos later."

"Noted."

"Thanks. Now, as for what I did, it all ties back to my description of how the World seems to adhere to natural laws. In fact, the World seems to have multiple 'layers,' so to speak. Surface one is what we see and interact with on a daily basis. It follows the laws of physics. Then there is the second stratum underneath it that is for the operation of anything supernatural. Spells, enchantments, transformations, and such are all embedded into this stratum, and when they are invoked, they get superimposed upon the first layer, and thus they manifest in the 'real world.'"

"So, instead of modifying the morpher directly, you modified the substrate that housed the information of what the enchantment was supposed to do."

"Bingo!" I confirmed with a big nod. I knew she would get it. This is why smart people are awesome.

"So, it's a loophole."

"Kind of," I told her a little less enthusiastically before adding, "There's also a third stratum I haven't mentioned yet. It seems to be under both the natural and the supernatural layer. To come up with an analogy..."

"Please don't."

"Too late, already have one," I responded with a smirk. "It's like a firmware, and the world is like an operating system sitting on top of that."

"So, what are we? Programs?"

"I dunno. I didn't think so far," I admitted, a teensy bit embarrassed.

"Figures," Judy mumbled before exhaling sharply and telling me, "Putting your analogies aside, do you think you could get a better understanding of the world by exploiting your newly discovered ability?"

"Certainly. I think I only scratched the surface of the system that runs this place."

"Then we need to experiment," Judy stated with the gravitas of an especially venerable patriarch making a declaration. The kind that's so authoritative it gets into important books and people follow them even though they're silly, just because they were said by a very confident guy. Of course, it wasn't a great parallel, because what she said actually made perfect sense.

"Agreed," I, well, agreed with my sageliest of sagely nods. "To do that, we first have to establish a supply of magical doodads and whatchamacallits to experiment on."

"You sound like you already have a source in mind."

"Two, actually," I responded with a modest smile. "The obvious one is the magical workshop under the school. They should have a lot of fun toys to play with, but getting them could pose a bit of a problem."

"Unless you can convince Amelia to smuggle some artifacts for you, I doubt they would be willing to hand their things over to you."

"I wouldn't bet on the odds of convincing her, but it's an option," I told her noncommittally before I outlined my second proposal. "I also had the idea of asking my proposed father-in-law if their dragon hoard might have a few trinkets I could borrow."

"Borrow, just like you did my catchphrase?"

"It wasn't your catchphrase, and please don't needlessly derail the conversation."

My dear assistant tsk-tsked, which I ignored with the firmness of a mountain made of frozen Jell-O.

Speaking of which, I was getting peckish. I wondered what we would be having for dinner, but I quickly shook away my salivating guesses, and instead I told Judy, "Do you think asking the irritating butler if I could play around in his study would be a bad idea?"

"Yes."

"I thought so, too. I'll do it, anyway."

"Then why did you ask for my opinion?" Judy asked back with the tiniest of irritated frowns forming on her brows.

"Force of habit," I answered with my fourth iteration of the "roguish smile" I may or may not have practiced in advance. It didn't seem to have too much of an effect, so I figured it was time to go back to the drawing board. Or rather, the mirror. Where I may or may not practice facial expressions when I get bored during the long nights. Please don't judge.

"Have you thought about the Hub?"

Judy's abrupt question threw me, as I had no idea about how it related to my smile, but then I managed to collect myself and requested her to clarify.

"What I was trying to say," she began with a frustrated huff, "is that if you want to have ensorcelled objects to study, you could use your black market connections to purchase some."

"Wait... I have black market connections?"

"You do. Not as Leonard S. Dunning, but as Admin of the Celestial Hub." After a pause, my dear assistant innocently asked, "By the way, does the *S* stand for *scatterbrained*?"

"No..."

My answer was actually closer to a groan of exasperation than the actual word, but let's not split hairs about it. Judy certainly didn't do so, as she continued the conversation as if her jab against my very collected and thoughtful personage was just a figment of my overactive imagination.

"I believe there are no less than three black market vendors on the forums. You should ask them if they have anything you could use. Failing that, you could ask the regulars if they have any spare tools or leads on unguarded artifacts you could borrow."

"It's worth a shot," I agreed a little half-heartedly while simultaneously ignoring the air quotes she was making when she said the last word. "There are still some other minor hypotheses I have regarding the strata and my interactions with them, but let's save the in-depth discussion until I have some empirical evidence to back them up."

"If you say so," Judy responded with some degree of disinterest, but then she sidled closer to me and linked her arm with mine using practiced motions before asking, "Can I stay over tomorrow?"

The question came out of the blue, but after some consideration, I nodded in the affirmative.

"Sure. If I can get my hands on some magical thingamabobs, we might as well do some tests."

"I was thinking about something else," she stated with upturned eyes.

"Can I ask for some clarification? I could interpret your proposition in a lot of different ways…"

My dearest assistant rolled her eyes as she tightened her grip on me and asked, "What are you going to do with Eleanor today?"

I wondered if that was a trick question, but she looked straightforward enough, so after some consideration, I honestly told her, "Well, I guess we're going to have dinner, and then we're going to cuddle? I might have a separate discussion with Abram and the frustrating butler, but aside from that, I don't have any big plans."

"I plan to do the same," Judy told me quite categorically. "Not the discussion parts, but the first half." I might have looked a little puzzled by her words, for she soon elaborated by telling me, "We have been going out for more than a week, but we have barely acted like a couple. I don't like it."

"Soooo… in short, you want to just sit back, watch a movie, and chill while we cuddle?"

"Something along those lines."

"I can do that," I told her in conjunction with the fifth iteration of my roguish smile. "Any requests on the movie front?"

"Anything goes, so long as it's not a sappy romantic comedy."

"Roger."

With that decided, we walked in silence for about ten seconds before Judy uttered, "You're going to get the sappiest romantic comedy on the planet just to mess with me, aren't you?"

"I cannot confirm or deny such accusations. Please direct your inquiries to my attorney."

"Just you wait, Chief," my usually deadpan girlfriend pouted in a rare, clear display of emotion. "Do it, and I swear I'll start to hate you."

"Yes, sure, if you say so…" I muttered, and I couldn't help but let out a soft chuckle as we continued on.

It should be a little tricky to squeeze an evening of chilling out into my timetable, but then again, I was the one who declared that I would utilize my sleepless nights to have the time to cater to two girlfriends' worth of needs. I just had to put the determination into practice now! Oh, the crosses I had to bear!

PART 2

"Hi, princess, I'm—" I greeted my girlfriend in the doorway of her room, but before I could finish, I was grabbed by the hand and dragged inside.

"You're late!" Elly exclaimed and slammed the door shut behind us.

"I'm sorry, I couldn't help it."

My attempt to placate the sulking resident was less than successful, a fact that she made quite blindingly obvious with a soft yet decidedly angry grunt.

"You promised it would only take a few minutes," she grumbled as she dragged me even farther and forced me to sit on her bed. Then she stood in front of me and continued by directing her patented brand of accusative finger at me. "You even promised you'd come over a little earlier so that we could spend some time alone!"

"In my defense, I *did* come over early. It was your mother who kidnapped me the moment I stepped through the main entrance."

"That's right," the princess huffed. Then she redoubled her finger-pointing efforts. "Why did it take you so long to discuss things with my mother, anyway?"

"You ask it like I had much of a choice in the matter," I protested and gave a tired sigh. "I didn't expect she would be so mad about allowing you to play around with the brainless robots."

"Aren't all robots brainless?" she asked, genuinely curious. But then she quickly remembered that she was supposed to be angry with me. "I mean, it's true, Mom can be a little overbearing sometimes, but you are smart! You were supposed to come up with a smart excuse and come over right away!"

"I am glad you think so highly of me, but it's hard to come up with a 'smart excuse' when your mother refused to even entertain the thought that the mostly harmless, brightly coloured robots that were programmed not to harm you were, in fact, not a big deal." I paused here, extended a finger of my own, and gently pushed hers aside before asking, "I mean, they weren't a big deal, right?"

"Not at all," my girlfriend agreed, swatting away my finger and pointing at me again.

I picked up the slack and pulled back my finger before stabbing towards her hand again. She skillfully parried my extremely dangerous attack while she absentmindedly added, "There was one small problem, now that I think about it."

"Really? What is it?" I inquired while feinting and aiming a devious finger at her unprotected belly.

My girlfriend didn't get flustered and blocked it with a well-timed swipe of her own.

"To be honest, the Magiform was a little uncomfortable," she stated while changing her center of mass and attempting a low stab to slip under my guard.

"*Magiform?*" I echoed the word, raising an intrigued brow and parrying her incoming finger.

"It's a name I came up with, with the help of Josh and Angie," she told me with a small smirk that suggested she was probably taking more of the credit than duly deserved, but I naturally didn't call her out on my suspicion. "It's because they are magical, and they are uniforms."

"So, Magiforms," I concluded while launching a counterattack towards her upper arm, which she dodged before initiating her own riposte. I met her strike halfway.

"Yes," she confirmed with a beaming smile made somewhat strained by our fingers being locked in a contest of strength. I hate to admit it, but she was winning. It was probably because she was standing and I was sitting. Leverage and stuff. Obviously.

Anyhow, I couldn't allow my pride and honour to be besmirched by losing in an absolutely serious and downright momentous match of physical prowess, so I did the only reasonable thing under the circumstances... and cheated like the AI in a strategy game on hard mode by opening my hand, grabbing hold of my worked-up girlfriend, and pulling her towards me with one mighty (yet careful) tug.

The princess tried to resist for a moment, but this time leverage was working for me, and in a moment, she all but tumbled into me. Fortunately, and in no small part thanks to my well-honed girl-catching reflexes, I managed to guide her landing safely to my lap.

"Aw!" she let out a dissatisfied noise the moment she gathered her wits, and she glanced at me over her shoulder. "That's not fair! I was winning!"

"Maybe, but... why were we finger-fencing in the first place?" I asked the fuming girl sitting on me, and my question gave her a pause.

"I... don't really know." She visibly deflated upon admitting it, but then a moment later she perked up again as she clumsily turned one hundred and eighty degrees on my lap until she straddled my hips with her face just inches from mine. She looked me in the eye and declared, "It doesn't matter, either. What does is that you still owe me a bunch of kisses."

"I do?" I asked back by reflex.

Speaking of reflexes, my sixth sense suddenly warned me of incoming danger, and I hastily put my hand in front of my face, just in time to hold back the princess's forehead before she could accidentally headbutt me by nodding so close.

"Yes," she stated emphatically, not caring at all that she'd just sandwiched my poor hand between our heads. "You promised me on the roof."

"Now that I think about it… I did, didn't I?"

Elly tried to nod again, but since we were already deadlocked, all she could do was grunt.

Well, I was a man of my word, and since she was already in reach, I figured I might as well start fulfilling my promise right away. I took a shallow breath and, just by angling my face a little, I successfully got our lips to touch.

I expected her to stiffen for a moment, but instead she leaned into the kiss with a blissful little snicker. Because of this, what I originally intended to be just a quick peck ended up quite unnecessarily passionate. For a moment, I even entertained the thought of attempting some of that tongue stuff people considered an integral part of the experience, but then I decided that it was a little early. I also wasn't entirely confident about the prospect. I mean, I obviously had no experience in the field, and although I'd naturally researched the topic in detail, it wasn't exactly something one could practice in front of the mirror.

We stayed connected for a good couple of seconds before she finally pulled back, but only so she could take a deep breath, after which she locked on to my lips once again. If my mouth wasn't otherwise occupied, I would have probably complained about excess and whatnot, but since I had already promised her and everything, I decided I might as well spoil her a little. I mean, it wasn't like it was some kind of ordeal I had to put up with. While it didn't make my head swim or light fireworks behind my eyelids, as some might have described it, kissing my girlfriend was still a pleasant little experience. I definitely wasn't against her indulgence in the act.

And indulge she did, as it took almost five minutes before she had her fill. She separated from me for the last time, her face glowing with satisfaction, and I couldn't help but say the thing that had been on my mind for quite a while.

"You know, princess, you've changed a lot."

My mostly cute girlfriend cocked her head to the side, and while she looked curious for a moment, it didn't stick. Her expression almost immediately bounced back into a contented one, even as she asked, "How so?"

"Well," I began as I put my hands on her waist and began to gently coax her to sit by my side instead of on me. "Not so long ago, you would've glared at me and made funny noises if I so much as just touched you." I suddenly felt a little mischievous, so I tried to tickle her a little, and she let out a pretty cute yelp in response, so I smugly added, "Exactly like that."

"Stop it," Elly reproached me while she pried my fingers off her sides and took a seat beside me with an indignant huff. "It was precisely because of things like this!"

"I don't remember tickling you when we first met."

"No, but you were just as impudent," she countered, but then a moment later, she reconsidered and added, "In retrospect, I have to admit that I don't entirely dislike this side of you, though."

"In retrospect," I repeated after her, and she nodded like it was a profound statement, and then she exhaled a shallow sigh.

"It's strange, isn't it? When I came to this island, I never thought things would end up like this."

"You came to this island to seduce a boy you last met when you were in kindergarten, so yes, I can see your point."

"Uh… Don't put it like that! It makes me sound like a creepy stalker!"

Elly punctuated her argument with a playful yet fairly solid punch to my shoulder, so I figured it was in my best interest to cede the argument to her.

"Got it. No creepy business at all."

"That's right," she declared with a huge nod, and for a few seconds, we both fell silent.

"Now that I think about it," I broke the momentary lull in the conversation by absentmindedly uttering another question that had been sitting in the back of my mind for a while. "It really is weird how we ended up like this."

My statement wasn't just idle small talk. As I looked back at our time together, it was hard to pinpoint why we ended up in a relationship. Early on, I even mistakenly thought that I was the "protagonist" of the story, and Elly was the classic high school romance love interest for me. I even consciously attempted to avoid any romantic development with her, yet here we were.

"Hey, Elly?" I addressed my spaced-out girlfriend, and she turned a questioning eye towards me. "When exactly did you start to like me?"

My somewhat strange question was little more than a whim on my part, yet the princess seemed to consider it with the utmost seriousness.

"When did I start to like you?" she reiterated while raising a finger to her lips. Her face became a little flushed, probably from remembering an embarrassing memory (we'd had many), but at last she told me, "I think it was since that time we met on the roof."

"Really? Since Snowy started attending the school?" I wanted to tell her that she started crushing on me a lot earlier than I expected, but the princess quickly shook her head, much to my confusion. "No? Then the time after that?"

"No, *before* that," she clarified, and it took me several seconds to figure out what she meant.

"Wait a moment. The only time we met on the roof, just the two of us, was on the day you transferred."

She gave me a small nod, confusing me even further.

"Wait, hold on... So, you say you've liked me since the day we met?"

"Yes," she answered with just the barest hint of hesitation. "I think I didn't really realize it back then, but looking back on it, it's obvious I liked you since then and there... and I had no idea how to deal with it." After she said that, her previously rosy cheeks gradually began to pale until she finally uttered, "I... have been acting really weird and stupid, haven't I?"

"Weird, yes. Stupid, nah." I slipped my arm around her shoulder and pulled her close. "But it's strange. I don't remember doing anything back then that would warrant you to fall for me. I mean, you technically fell *on* me at the time, but I don't think that counts."

"It does," Elly enlightened me as she nuzzled closer, though to be honest, I was actually feeling more confused. "You caught me. You did it twice, in fact. You also took me to the infirmary and looked after me without complaining. You were really gallant."

"I was?" I asked back with a considerable amount of incredulity, but she just nodded at me with such a genuine smile that I had no choice but to believe her. "Weird. I don't remember doing anything special."

"And that's why you're cool," she heaped more unwarranted praise upon me, and I could barely manage to suppress a bitter smile forming on my lips. I wanted to say something in denial, but before I could open my mouth, Elly said, "Now it's your turn."

"My turn at what?"

"I told you when I fell for you. Now it's your turn."

I am not going to lie; I actually froze up for a good five seconds, blue screen of death and everything. My stupor thankfully broke, and once I gathered my wits, I repeated, "When I fell for you?"

"Yes. Now it's your turn," the princess stressed it, for the third time, and she nuzzled even closer to me like a kitten, probably thinking that I was teasing her and needed some direct application of cuteness to loosen my tongue.

Unfortunately for her, I was genuinely on the cusp of a mild panic attack. I mean… when *did* I start liking her? I don't think I'd ever had a proper, dictionary definition *crush* on her, and while I found her attractive and seven flavours of amusing since pretty much the beginning, I never really fell for her, per se. And as for love… I still wasn't sure I had a grasp on the emotion, let alone applying it to people close to me.

However, I had to say something, so after some thinking, I decided to go with, "Honestly, there wasn't a definitive point. I think you just gradually grew on me."

"That's a cop-out," she stated in a voice that, swear to God, channeled Judy to such a degree, I was spooked.

"No, not really," I continued to excuse myself. "I just liked to tease you, and then I liked to be in your company, and now I just like you. It was a gradual process. There wasn't any one moment where I realized I liked you; I just did before I knew it."

"Uh… that sounds so unsatisfying," my girlfriend grumbled and her brows descended into a frown. "It almost sounds like you never fell in love at all."

"Does it?" I uttered, trying to ignore the cold sweat breaking out on my back like a tiny, immensely mortifying tsunami. Elly looked taken aback by my ambivalent response, so in a panic, I continued, "To be honest with you, I am really inexperienced with this whole 'love' business. I mean, you know I have amnesia, right?" She nodded, her expression clearly showing that she was curious where I was going with this. "What I am trying to get at is that I have nothing to compare my current feelings to." She had no adverse reaction to my words so far, and after some hesitation, I decided that if I'd already opened the mouth of the bag, I might as well let the cat out of it and be done with it.

"Okay, so what I am currently trying to clumsily convey is that, while you are truly dear to me, I love spending time with you, miss you when we are apart, and I would be happy to spend the rest of eternity in your company, what I feel just doesn't seem 'passionate' enough for me to confidently call it love."

"What about Judy?" she asked the obvious question, and I promptly shook my head.

"The same. I like her a lot as well, and I tremendously enjoy her company, but even if you put a gun to my head, I wouldn't dare to confidently call what I feel 'love.' I might not be the most sincere person in this world, but telling someone I love them without being completely certain is a low even I wouldn't stoop to. Do you understand what I am trying to say?"

The princess stayed silent for a short while, her face slowly twisting into an odd expression, before she muttered, "Leo, you're really weird."

"Am I?" I asked a little hesitantly, and my question was answered by a hearty nod.

"Yes!" she stated with the kind of gusto that reminded me of her father. "You're weird! You're capable of saying something as embarrassing as 'spend the rest of eternity together,' and yet you still don't feel confident enough to say the word 'love'! That's weird!"

"I... think you're right?" I muttered in response as I replayed the words I just said in my head. "I mean... I did say that, didn't I?"

"You sure did," she confirmed with a somewhat giddy look in her eyes.

"It totally sounded like a proposal, didn't it?"

"It sure did," she reiterated with an impish little smirk. "And I'm going to hold you to it!" I couldn't help but smile at her confident declaration, and when she saw that, she quickly added, "Leo, you are overcomplicating this. 'Love' is just a word. You obviously think it's a very important one, but when you can say embarrassing lines like that with a straight face, I don't need you to say the word to believe in your feelings. If you cannot believe in your feelings, then believe in me, who believes in you!"

Once again, for the umpteenth time, there was a long pause in our conversation, and while she was looking at me with eyes as clear as the conscience of a goldfish, I couldn't hold myself back from asking the obvious question that demanded to be asked.

"Was that a reference?"

And like that, the serious atmosphere evaporated like a soap bubble on the surface of the sunny side of Mercury.

"What?" Elly uttered in confusion, her head cocked in a cute blonde tilt.

"That last line? Was that a reference to the series with the drilling robots?"

The princess punched me in the shoulder, this time so hard enough, I almost fell off the bed in surprise.

"Damn it, Leo! Why do you always have to ruin the moment? We were having a really good mood and everything, and you just had to throw in one of your stupid jokes!"

"Ow... I wasn't joking," I objected, rubbing my aching shoulder. "I really thought it was a reference, and the question just kind of slipped out."

"That's not an excuse," my girlfriend fumed and defiantly crossed her arms.

"Sorry, I didn't mean to do that," I readily apologized, and after taking a deep breath, I told her, "Nevertheless, I think I understand what you were trying to say. If you are willing to believe in my feelings even when I'm not sure myself…" I paused here, and after some thinking, I decided to say something unusually sappy. "Let me say this: I am fairly sure I love you, but just in case I'm not, I promise I will make sure to properly fall in love with you as soon as possible."

Elly stared at me for a good ten seconds, as if to further fray my nerves, but in the end, she failed to stifle her laughter and she told me, between chuckles, "That… was the sweetest and most awkward thing you have ever said! I'm dying from secondhand embarrassment here!"

"Why, you little—!" I exclaimed and grabbed her waist again, prompting a surprised squeak from her. "I am doing my best to open my heart to you, and you laugh at me! I shall have my vengeance! To the tickle dungeon with thee!"

"No, wait! Stop!"

She tried to twist herself out of my grasp, but I held on tight, and in the scuffle, we fell over and sprawled out on the bed. That was no reason to stop my assault, though, and I kept tickling her until she ran out of breath and I no longer felt embarrassed, both of which took quite a while.

At last, we both lay across the bed, panting, and somehow she ended up nestled up to me and holding on to my back. Heaving and disheveled, we stayed still and silent for about a minute before I exhaled hard and told her, with renewed seriousness, "I meant what I said."

There was a moment of pause, after which she responded by telling me, "So did I."

"Good," I concluded, and we drifted back into silence. It was a comfortable kind of silence, which made me appreciate just how much worse our previous discussion could have gone, and as I thought about it, I abruptly sat up, startling Elly in the process.

"What? Did something happen?"

"No, I just remembered something," I replied and pointed at the device on her wrist. "Before we completely went off the rails, you mentioned something about the uniform being uncomfortable."

"Oh, that's right." She also sat up and after quickly fixing her hair (and I do mean *quick*; it was back to normal in a matter of seconds), she began to explain her problem. "When I use it, it feels a little tight, or stifling. It's like when you put on some old clothes that you grew out of already."

"I think I get what you're trying to say," I mused while trying to disregard how my girlfriend was already back to normal, as if the previous critical conversation about our love life didn't even happen. But back to the issue: "The… what did you call them? Magiforms?"

"Yes."

"Okay then. So, remember when I told Josh that the Magiformer would inhibit the physical changes when he turned into an Abyssal? The same goes for yours, as well, and since most of your draconic abilities come from your physique, restraining it would obviously feel really restrictive."

"Can you fix it?" She held out her wrist to me.

"I… um… I can't. I mean, suppressing the transformation and providing an alternative is the whole point of the device."

"But I don't like it."

"I know, but I can't help it."

Elly turned a disapproving eye towards the Magiformer, then back at me, and then she let out an angry "Hmph!" and pointedly looked away.

"Oh, come on, princess! Don't sulk!"

"I'm not sulking," she replied while pouting so hard, it was comical.

"But you totally are. Don't be like that."

My high-maintenance girlfriend didn't respond at first, but soon let out a forced groan and turned back to me.

"All right. I'm willing to forgive you under one circumstance."

"Forgive me for what? I told you, I cannot—"

"I'll let it go if you say something romantic."

"Romantic?" I blurted out in surprise, and she nodded quite vehemently.

"Yes. Something nice, like the last one about spending an eternity together."

"Do I really have to?" I tried to ask, but then she reentered pouting mode, so I hastily sputtered out, "Er… how about… when you are not around, I… er… I miss you so much that one hour feels like sixty minutes!"

"That's," she began as her visage brightened, but then she frowned and said, "th-that's the same thing!"

"I'm sorry, but what did you expect when you put me on the spot like that?" I excused myself maybe a tiny bit more indignantly than strictly necessary, but she just shrugged and nestled closer to me again.

"Oh well. I give you a pass for trying."

Saying so, she rubbed her head against my shoulder with a tiny little giggle, and somehow I couldn't stay mad at her.

"How gracious of you."

"You are welcome," she answered with a playful little smirk before she resumed nuzzling me. It didn't last long, though, as she looked up and said, "It's still an hour until dinner. What should we do?"

"I thought you wanted to cuddle?"

"I meant after that. Obviously."

"I don't know," I replied with a shrug before looking around in her room. Elly's eclectic bedroom had no television, so watching something on it was out of the question. She didn't have a PC, either, so browsing the net for cute cat videos or something was also out. In fact, her room was fairly barebones when it came to entertainment, so much so that I couldn't help but ask her about it. "Say, princess? What do you usually do after school?"

She looked a little confused by my question, but after some thinking, she told me, "Not much. I either study for school, study business, or spend time with Mom and Dad. Why?"

"I just noticed you don't really have anything in your room we could use to kill time here."

"I suppose not..." She sounded a little disheartened. Maybe she took my words as criticism? I was just about to clarify my point, but I never got the chance, as her eyes lit up and she grabbed my hand. "Hey, Leo? Do you want to see my singing room?"

Now, there were many questions I could have asked here. What is a singing room? Was it literally a room for singing, or was that just some kind of euphemism? Why did she suddenly mention it? Why did she even have one?

I could have asked any of those, and more, but when I saw how excited she was, the only words that came out of my mouth were, "Sure, I'd love to."

CHAPTER 21

PART 1

"This way, future young master."

I sneakily rolled my eyes at the braided maid's words and told her, "Yes, I know. This is not my first time." While I might have grumbled, I still followed after her before adding, "Also, I asked you already, but please stop calling me that."

"What could future young master be referring to?"

"Do you really intend to keep going? Is this some kind of passive-aggressive power play?"

"Please forgive me, but this lowly servant still cannot understand what future young master is talking about."

It was at this point I could no longer hold my exasperation at bay, and I let out a groan that made my throat sound like it was made of sandpaper.

"Fine, do whatever you want."

My words, which were not an admission of defeat, by the way, made the chambermaid brighten and she said, "I shall endeavour to do so."

I decided to leave it at that, and for a while, we silently walked through the corridors of the mansion. To be honest, I was feeling a little tired at the moment.

It might sound obvious, but even if you love spending time with your significant other, devoting your full attention to them for an extended period of time can be a little exhausting. Considering I followed that up with a family dinner with my self-proclaimed in-laws and then a business discussion with Abram, it was no wonder I was feeling tuckered out.

However, there was one more item on the table for today's agenda, and I was heading right towards it, which only added to my enervation. Needless to say, I blame all of the above for the fact that I was caught completely flat-footed by Melinda's next words.

"Does future young master's sister enjoy the uniform?"

"Pardon?" I blurted out in a surprised and uncomfortably high-pitched voice.

The chambermaid looked at me like I was an alien or something, and it took me several long seconds to realize she wasn't talking about the magical uniforms.

"Oh, you meant the maid costumes!" I exclaimed and theatrically slapped my forehead. "Yes, she liked them very much. Thanks for giving them away."

"The uniforms technically belong to the estate, so please direct your gratitude towards Lady Eleanor."

"Yes, I know, but you were the one who was using them, so it's only fair that I thank you, too. Anyhow, Snowy doesn't have many chances to wear a maid uniform during the day, but she dresses up every evening when we make dinner and wash the dishes."

"Is that so?"

"Yes. I think she even customized one of them a little by adding more ruffles to the edges and the headpiece. Oh, and now that I think about it, she only wears stockings with the other one. She even made a lacy garter for that. I never would've figured, but she is surprisingly handy with the needle."

"Shocking."

"Isn't it? You would think as the ex-heiress of an Abyssal House, she'd be pampered, but instead it turned out she's unexpectedly self-reliant. Though again, since her brother is an asshole, I guess it might not be that surprising after all... I mean her biological brother, not me."

"Naturally."

"Anyhow, the important part is that she really likes the uniforms, she made them cuter, and she looks cute in them. That's all that matters."

"I'm glad to hear that."

That's what she said, though she sounded quite unenthusiastic. But who knows, maybe she did mean it? Maybe there was a form of unspoken camaraderie between maids and maid-enthusiasts and she was just shy about sounding excited about it in front of a relative stranger. It wouldn't have been the strangest personality quirk I'd seen. Not by a long shot.

Anyhow, while we kept noncommittally chatting about maid stuff, we arrived at a certain annoying butler's study.

"Thank you for your guidance. I'll take it from here."

My words were little more than a formality, yet Melinda acknowledged them with a graceful curtsy. She held the pose, and I had the uncomfortable feeling that I was supposed to do or say something in response, but before I could figure out what, she straightened and wordlessly walked away. That was weird, but I had no time to ruminate upon its implications, as I already stood at the doorstep of the lion's den. Though again, maybe calling it the dragon's den would have been more accurate. Or was that too on the nose?

Semantics aside, I took a deep breath to prepare myself and knocked on the fancy hardwood door in front of me.

"Come in, it's open," came the surprisingly neutral response from inside. I wasn't shy enough to just meekly stand in front of the door even without permission, but since I was invited in, I had even less of a reservation about throwing it wide open.

"Good evening!" I greeted the startled old man sitting at the heavy desk at the other side of the room, my upbeat tone further reinforced by a shit-eating grin so wide, it made my mouth hurt.

"Oh. It's you." Sebastian accentuated his dour response by pointedly setting the porcelain cup he was cleaning down with a *clank*. "I was told you would be paying me a visit, but I didn't expect you to arrive so soon."

"What can I say? Visiting you is like pulling a tooth. The sooner it's done and over with, the better."

"You are charming, as always."

"Thank you, I'm trying."

Saying so, I closed the door behind me and took a slow, meticulous look around the study.

It wasn't the first time I was here, but the thick, slightly moldy scent of history still tickled my nose with every breath. More importantly, though, maybe because now I was just a teensy bit more acclimated to the magical sub-layer of the world, I couldn't help but marvel at the various, softly glowing curios lining the walls and filling the shelves. I couldn't wait to get my hands on them, but as much as I wanted to just rummage around, I was still in my girlfriend's home. A certain amount of tact was required.

"So? Why exactly are you here?" the bothersome butler raised the obvious question.

I promptly told him, "I came over to play with your toys!"

Hey, I said *a certain amount* of tact, not a *lot*.

Still, Sebastian looked unduly surprised by my response, so I amended, "And by that, I mean I came over to study some of your artifacts. Didn't Abram tell you about it?"

The old man heaved a tired sigh.

"No, he didn't. It appears the family head hasn't grown out of his mischievous phase. Still a child in every manner but his stature."

"Are you sure it's okay for you to say things like that about the family patriarch?" I teased him a little as I walked closer to his desk, and he invariably rolled his eyes.

"Don't feign idiocy, boy. You know of my identity, so you should be well aware that if there is a person on this island who may call the esteemed head of the Dracis family the child he is, it is I."

"Got it, Great-Great-Great-Grandpa. Just checking."

He obviously found my stellar wit too much to deal with, as he let out a defeated sigh and stood up with an excessive display of weariness.

"So, you wish to 'study' my collection. I never imagined you as an admirer of antiques."

"Nah, I'm more interested in their enchantments than the items themselves," I admitted freely.

"Really? Do you perhaps fancy yourself as a fledgling artificer, boy?"

"It's a recent interest of mine, old man," I said with an absolutely genuine smile.

"Normally I wouldn't tolerate the idea of allowing your grubby hands to lay a single finger on my possessions, but as it was a request by the family head, I'm willing to make an exception under one condition."

"Which is?" I asked, ignoring the devious way the old man was angling his brows.

"It is quite simple." He slowly walked around the desk, one hand slowly and methodically stroking his beard. I had to give credit where it's due—the guy had the "diabolical mastermind" look down pat. "I only require you to ask. Humbly."

"That's all?" I inquired a little suspiciously, and Sebastian nodded.

Was that really the whole breadth and depth of his demands? That was... kind of adorable, actually.

"Okay then," I responded absentmindedly before I took a deep breath and put on my most innocent face. "Sir Steward? I humbly request your permission to study the magical properties and enchantments of your prestigious collection. May I have it?"

The antiquated butler looked at me like I was a white raven riding on a black sheep for a couple of seconds before he let out a supremely baffled "huh."

"I am not going to lie, boy. I thought your pride wouldn't allow you to agree to my request so easily."

"Oh please. Why would I have a problem with something like this? They're just words, nothing more. Kind of like your idle death threats."

Sebastian's eyes narrowed into annoyed slits and he vehemently started, "I assure you, my boy, my threats are anything but idle."

"And if you can honestly believe that, I bet you can also believe that my previous words were sincere." The skunk-striped butler let out a groan that sounded like it came from the bottom of his soul (or at the very least his pancreas), which I naturally disregarded, and instead I asked, "So? Can I start?"

Sebastian gave me a look that said that he could drown me in a spoonful of vinegar (in other words, slightly more agreeable than usual) and stated, "Whatever piques your interest. But be warned; I'll be watching you."

"Naturally," I responded before I carefully swept the whole room with my eyes, looking for my first object of interest.

There was a plethora of attention-grabbing items on display, but none more prominent than the spear in the corner. In fact, it was practically impossible to miss, as the bloody thing glowed as bright as a neon sign. I even found myself subconsciously filtering out its light so I could see the other enchantments, and while it was tempting to go for it right away, I was afraid picking up the dragon-slaying lance first in the dragon's lair might lead to a misunderstanding.

As such, my first "victim" was the creepy Japanese doll sitting on the shelf by the doorway.

"I'll start with this," I told my observer while lightly shaking the doll, which earned me a curiously raised brow.

"An odd choice," Sebastian mused under his breath, but I ignored his comment and used my phantom limb to peek inside the enchantment on the creepy little thing, and it didn't take me long to furrow my brows.

"Hey, old man?"

"Have I told you that I disapprove of your disrespectful conduct?"

"Not today, but that's beside the point." I shook the doll again. "Did you know that this thing is cursed?"

"Cursed," he repeated after me, his voice more than a little baffled. "How so?"

"It's obvious! I mean, you could tell just by looking at it. It's a creepy doll straight out of a cheap horror flick. Furthermore, if you put it into the right circumstances, which is, if I 'read' this right, a high school classroom after midnight, it will cause people in a large radius to become paranoid and hallucinate all kinds of nasty things and then try to murder each other while thinking that everyone else is a monster." We both fell silent after my explanation, but as I looked at it one more time, I couldn't help but let the bubbling indignation trapped in my belly out by loudly asking, "By the way, just who in their right mind would even make something like this? And on a related note, why would *you* have it?"

"Regardless of the nature of its enchantment, it is still a unique, one-of-a-kind item," Sebastian stated a tad defensively.

"I hope so!" I exclaimed while indignantly shaking the thing in my hand. Again. "Having just one creepy doll from a cheap Japanese horror story is bad enough; I don't want to live in a world where there are more of them!" It took several deep breaths to regain some of my cool, after which I asked, "I hope you don't mind if I'd take apart the enchantment on this thing."

"I absolutely would!" Sebastian responded rather indignantly. "Studying my collection is one thing, but I never granted you permission to—"

"Oh, come on! This thing is *literally* cursed!" I interrupted him, waving the object of our argument in front of his nose. "Why in the nine layers of hell would you want to keep a curse on a doll?"

"It's a *collector's item*!" He tried to snatch it out of my hand, but I was just a smidgen faster and managed to evade him.

"Okay, calm down!" I stressed hard while keeping the doll away from him with one hand and holding him back with the other. "How about a compromise?"

"What kind of compromise?" the old man eyed me suspiciously, no doubt weighing his options. I really hoped one of them wasn't about whether turning me into a pile of ash on the floor was a reasonable response.

"Simple. I'm not going to destroy the enchantment. Instead, I'll modify the trigger mechanism. Say, I add a few more conditions, so it would only activate under needlessly convoluted circumstances. Say, only after midnight, in a high school classroom, with a single person present, and only if said person is dressed as a clown. You can keep your stupid curse, but at the same time the activation trigger will be so unlikely, it might as well not even exist. Think of it as removing the firing pin from a gun in a museum. It's for safety."

The owner of the doll kept eyeing me suspiciously.

"Are you able to make it so?"

"I'm fairly sure I can." My words didn't project enough confidence, at least according to the skeptical look Sebastian was giving me, so I amended, "I mean, modifying the framework of an enchantment is somewhat more involved than tweaking just the effect, but it's doable."

The old man ruminated on the idea but eventually gave me a nod, though his expression said he could not believe he was doing it.

"You are correct in your assertion that removing the trigger of a cursed item is the prudent thing to do. However, if you damage my property, I swear I will make you pay."

"There you go with the threats of violence again..." I shook my head, but the man only scoffed at my comment.

"No, my boy, not that. But once our family lawyers drag you to civil court over property damages, you'll wish for corporal punishment."

"Scary," I stated while channeling my inner Judy. Then I pointed at a nearby antique sofa. "May I sit down?"

"Of course." The annoying butler indicated where I should sit with a courteous wave, though considering the context, he was probably being sarcastic. It didn't stop me from responding with a polite nod that was about as sincere as a presidential campaign speech, after which I casually plopped down on his vintage furniture.

Now, to be perfectly honest, what I was going to do didn't require me to sit. In fact, aside from the middle stage of the process, it didn't even require much concentration. I didn't lie when I said that the modification I was attempting was "involved," but it wasn't particularly complicated, either. How should I put it?

How about this—in essence, an enchantment can be broken down into multiple, interlocking functional parts. For example, the Magiformers were designed to remove clothes from the wearer, store them, and then replace them with another, preset outfit. The first part was essential for its functionality, as it was impossible to put a full set of clothes on a person without removing the one they were already wearing. The second part was slightly less rigid, as, for example, instead of storing the clothes, it could vaporize them to make space for the new ones. As for the "preset outfit" part, it was by far the easiest to modify, as the whole framework was designed with that option in mind.

Now, the enchantment I literally had in my hands was slightly different. Since it was a curse in the broad sense of the word, it wasn't designed with post hoc modifications in mind. It only had two main components: a detection mechanism tied to the trigger, and the "curse," which was an ongoing perception manipulating spell. There were also some miscellaneous parts, such as the mana accumulation and storage elements that allowed the whole thing to work, but those weren't important right now.

What *wasn't* is the fact that, since the curse/enchantment wasn't meant to be changed after the fact, it was like a giant clockwork filled with interlocking gears that were already in motion, and moving any one of them would wreck the whole thing until it collapsed in on itself. In retrospect, I figured my anti-magical abilities probably worked on a similar, implody principle, but that's beside the point now.

So, back to the enchantment. To modify it, first I had to isolate which of the gear-analogs belonged to which of the various parts that made it up. Funnily enough, this was the easiest part, as I could tell them apart at a single glance. I had a feeling it was supposed to be a lot harder, but I decided that it was something to think about later.

As for the second step, it was... how should I put it...? I would like to say I had to unravel the enchantment, but I already went with the clockwork analogy, so... let's say that I had to take the gears and... so, it's like the gears were made of plasticine, but they were frozen solid, so before I could do anything with them, I had to thaw them, but before I could thaw them, I had to make them stop spinning, and once they became pliable, I had to...

Damn. Maybe Judy was right. Maybe my analogies *are* horrible.

Or maybe it's the system that was horribly counterintuitive and complicated.

Actually, it was probably the latter. Definitely.

Arriving at that conclusion, I took a deep breath and began the process, which was... not particularly riveting. I mean, what I was doing at the moment was... hard to describe without another analogy that may or may not backfire on me, so let's just say it was simple, repetitive, and unfortunately absolutely crucial. So, I did it in silence for about a solid minute... right until the moment when I ran out of patience with the butler intensely staring at my face.

"Is there a problem?" I inquired with a single brow raised high, and Sebastian sharply shook his head in return.

"No. I was just observing what you are doing." He paused here to lean forward and stroke his beard. "It doesn't look particularly impressive so far."

"I'm laying the groundwork as we speak," I told him a little bit indignantly, and it was his turn to raise an intrigued brow.

"Then why are you talking to me instead of focusing on your task?"

"It's not particularly hard, so I can pay attention to other things, as well."

"Really?" Sebastian straightened his back again and mused, "I thought paying attention to two things at once was only something women could do."

"Nah, I think it's one of those pop-science generalizations that people just believe because it sounds nice. I personally think the individual differences dwarf the general trends."

"I see," the old man responded a little absentmindedly before he finally sat down on the nearby divan. "It can be hard to keep up with the shape of the ever-billowing cloud of human knowledge."

"That's a needlessly fancy way to say it, but yes, I agree. I guess it must be even harder for someone like you."

"Someone like me?" he repeated after me with a critical edge to his voice, so I proceeded to clarify my statement.

"I meant someone as old as you are. I imagine it is hard to keep up with modern minutiae, such as whether or not women are better at multitasking, when you were born before they were even allowed to vote. Or rather, before democratic votes were even a thing."

"My boy, I might be old, but I assure you that ancient Athens was before even my time," Sebastian emphasized a touch indignantly, and I couldn't help but roll my eyes.

"You know that I meant modern democracy; don't be a pedant."

My incensed host let out a grunt, which I could interpret in a myriad of ways, so I naturally picked the one where it meant he was ashamed of himself and his heckling ways. Hey, I didn't say I picked the most likely one, did I?

Anyhow, the silence in the room was getting heavy again, so after making sure things with the enchantment were progressing smoothly, I cleared my throat and turned a cordial smile towards my grumpy host.

"So, staying on the topic of you being an old geezer..."

"Rude as always," he whispered.

"... can you tell me a story?"

"What kind of story?" he said, apparently baffled by my suggestion.

"An old one?" came my clarification in the company of an innocent smile. "For example, how about you tell me about your romantic escapades? I bet you've accumulated quite a number of them over the years," I posited harmlessly before I added, "Or if that's too personal, you can always tell me about your collection here, like how it came to be and such."

My request was very much on the nose, but it wasn't without reason. As a wise man once said, asking your enemy a question without an ulterior motive is a breath wasted. I'd like to add that, if you're already asking, having just one ulterior motive is inefficient. As such, I found it quite respectable that I managed to squeeze no less than three motives into one request.

The most obvious one was naturally how I might sneakily learn something about relationships from the old man. I mean, he should have quite a lot of experience, and even if it turned out his history with women (or men, I won't judge fire-breathing flying lizards) was an absolute royal mess... hey, a bad example is still an example! However, if he decided he didn't want to share his love history with me, by providing him a second option to talk about, he would most likely pick it before even recognizing he had other alternatives, like talking about his old pet turtle called Perry or something.

However, my request also had a third layer to it. Here's the thing: at this point, I had more or less concluded, without a shadow of a doubt, that this was a constructed, artificial world. That meant someone made it, which meant that it had to be "finished" and "turned on" at some point. In other words, this world had a beginning. My question was: when?

I had two hypotheses at the moment. According to the first one, the world we lived in began recently, maybe as recently as the day I first woke up, while the second hypothesis said that the world had been around for a long time and it was only the "plot" that picked up not too long ago. In some ways, the two options were a microcosm of the whole young-Earth versus Big Bang debate, but I digress.

Let's look at the options in turn: if the world was young, it would explain why everything is clean and brand-new, why placeholders would be under-developed, and why things had been rapidly adapting to our expectations, at least on the technological front. On the other hand, it meant that all the memories of the people around me were also artificial and had been already in place the moment the simulation started, or they were retroactively cre-ated when the framework at the bottom stratum of the world decided they needed fleshing out.

While this option sounded fairly reasonable, and it fit a number of our previous observations, such as how placeholders developed, it left a bad taste in my mouth. I mean, if this was true, it would make Judy and Elly less than two months old, and that would make me a bloody toddlercon!

… By the way, don't look up the definition of that term. Just don't. The internet is the final frontier, and it's a scary, inhospitable, and oftentimes rather squicky place.

Anyhow, let's focus on the second option, which thankfully solved the whole underage issue, but it regrettably did much worse when it came to explaining the other problems this World threw at me. In this scenario, the World itself wasn't brand-new, and it had been running for some time, which would allow the ages and elaborate, independently verified memories of my friends to be true, but in exchange, it did little for resolving the ques-tions of the brand-new world or placeholder behaviour.

And so, we were back in the present situation. As the oldest living person I know, followed by Brang, probing Sebastian for his early memories, however insignificant they might've seemed, could help us shed some light on the timescale of the world and refine our current hypotheses. He was especially useful in this regard as, unlike my self-appointed Faun subordi-nate, the Dracis steward was likely much more involved in human affairs and history, and thus his memories might be cross-referenced with records.

Now, granted, there was no way for me to know whether those records would be "real" or generated in real time to fit his memories and keep the world consistent. But if I kept suspecting that every single memory, record, and element of the world might be subject to retroactive continuity, I might as well hang up the proverbial brainy specs, because then there was no way to ever gain any reliable information about anything ever. And yes, I just said "ever" twice, because it's that big a deal.

As such, for the time being, I decided to shake the tree and see what fell, because the alternative was an existential nightmare where I couldn't even be sure that there was a tree in the first place. Speaking of which, my idiomatical woody perennial plant let out a soft grunt and seemed to come to a conclusion of some sort.

"You wish to hear a tale of romance? How peculiar." He silently stroked his beard in the deliberate motions of a hard thinker, or failing that, someone with an itchy chin. "Very well. I might as well indulge your curiosity."

"You would?" I exclaimed in surprise, and Sebastian seemed to wring an uncomfortable amount of joy out of my expression as he replied with an almost grandfatherly smile that didn't look right on his eminently annoying mug at all.

"Certainly. For you see, my habit of collecting rare memorabilia is intrinsically linked to my last companion. Oh, but I'm getting ahead of myself, aren't I?" Sebastian let out a mild chuckle that was so natural, for a moment I almost believed he didn't do it just to annoy me. In the meantime, he rested his back against the divan and, after a wistful sigh, he began to speak in a clear, somewhat melancholic voice. "I have lived a long life, yet I only ever loved three women. Do you find that hard to believe?"

"Not at all," I answered, mostly just to keep the conversation rolling.

"Is that so?" He sounded genuinely surprised, but it didn't last long, as he immediately proceeded to continue his tale. "My first lover... she was one of my kind. She was older than me when we first met—not by much, just about a century or so—yet she captivated me the moment I laid my eyes on her."

"I guess she must have been beautiful."

"Beauty... such a thing means little to my kind," Sebastian shook his head with an amused little smirk and continued as if he was explaining things to a child. Well, to be fair, from his perspective I was one, so there should've been no hard feelings, but it was still annoying. "We are radiant beings, not this crude flesh and bone."

It took all my willpower to stop myself from asking if he was making a thinly veiled reference, but after my recent blunder with the princess, I managed to keep the question down. It must have been just a coincidence.

"If she so chose, she could make herself the most gorgeous woman in a king's court or an old crone selling apples in a market. She was a free soul, and no place or identity could hold her for long. I adored her for it, and wherever the wind took her, I followed. Our courtship lasted for well over two decades."

I wanted to point out that following someone around for twenty years sounded incredibly stalker-ish, but I figured the jab wasn't worth breaking the current peaceful atmosphere, so I only muttered, "That's a long time."

"Indeed it was," the butler agreed with me, much to my surprise. I would've thought he would have a different outlook on time, but based on the self-deprecating chuckle he followed his words up with, I figured he was aware of how weird his situation was. "Our hearts could not connect with ease. It wasn't her fault, but mine. In my youth, I used to be brash and oftentimes quite irascible. It led to… complications."

"In your youth?" I couldn't help asking.

"Yes. If I was as short-tempered as I was back then, you would be but a scorch mark on my floor."

"Point taken," I relented a little reluctantly before clearing my throat and asking, "So, if you pursued her for twenty years, I imagine you were madly in love with her."

"Yes," the old man readily admitted in the clear way only old men could. "I can still remember the feeling—the constant, burning yearning in my chest; the deep, immaterial pain of separation whenever I couldn't meet her; the sweet bliss of speaking with her again."

"Sounds intense."

"In a way you couldn't imagine."

"I think we can agree on that," I admitted, and paused to tweak the enchantment a little. When I was done, I turned back to Sebastian and stated the obvious. "So, after two decades, the two of you finally became lovers."

"Yes," he confirmed with a nod and a nostalgic look in his eyes. "We shared our lives for three centuries. We never stayed in one place for long, and we saw much of the world, from the throne room of Charlemagne to the gardens of the Song dynasty emperors. We sailed on the boats of the Viking to the cold north and visited the Empire of Ghana in the heat of Africa. There was no land on this world our feet didn't touch."

"Wow. I'm not going to lie, that actually sounds kind of awesome."

"We had all the time in the world… or so we have thought."

Suddenly Sebastian's tone took a sharp left turn into melancholy-country, and for a moment I was tempted to just outright ask what happened to her, but I decided I might as well not poke at some millennium-old wounds. In its stead, I inquired about another thing that was on my mind.

"Did you have any kids?"

The irritating butler's expression turned on a dime and he frowned at me as if he wasn't sure if I was serious.

"No, of course not. It is well known that we cannot have children amongst ourselves."

"What? Really? I didn't know that."

"Are you serious?"

Sebastian looked exceptionally skeptical, so I gave him an enormous nod to emphasize my words.

"Yes, I really didn't know. But if you cannot, you know, procreate, then where did you come from?"

"The mountains," he stated matter-of-factly, but he must have recognized the puzzled look on my face, as after a tired sigh, he proceeded to explain. "We are born from nature itself, much like the other phantasmal beings of the land. Leviathans of the seas, behemoths of the rivers, rocs of the skies…"

"… dragons of the mountains," I finished his sentence for him, and he nodded in acknowledgment. "Wow. So, does that mean you don't lay eggs?"

"Even if we laid them, *I* obviously wouldn't," Sebastian scoffed at my question. I didn't mind it, though, as this was brand-new info, or at the very least I didn't remember reading about this anywhere. Though again, considering how surprised Sebastian was about my lack of knowledge about the subject, maybe I should ask Judy first, just in case it was already in our notes and I'd skimmed over it.

Anyways, that was for later, as I already had another question on the tip of my tongue.

"So, you cannot reproduce with each other, but you can with humans?"

"After taking a human form, obviously."

"Yes, obviously. If you couldn't, there would be no Dracis family."

"Correct."

"The same goes for the other… what did you call them?… Phantasmal beings?"

"No. Unlike us, the *others* were far more territorial and less inclined to mingle in human society. Because of this, they didn't leave behind many offspring of mixed heritage, if any. Quite unlike my more infamous kin."

"Please don't tell me you are referring to the whole 'dragons kidnapping princesses' thing…"

"No, of course not." It wasn't particularly surprising, but my host sounded almost offended by the concept. "That was done by first- and second-generation Draconians hoping to preserve the strength of their bloodline by choosing what they considered to be outstanding partners. It was a reasonable assumption at the time, considering nobody had any idea about genetics and inbreeding." He paused here, only to awkwardly scratch his chin and add, "I may have also engaged in the practice a few times, but only for sport. It was a phase."

"I'm not questioning that part," I cut in, completely disregarding the way he downplayed this "phase" that, if my sources are to be believed, lasted for well over a century, and focused on the more important point. "If it's not the kidnapping, then who were you referring to when you said 'infamous'?"

"Zeus."

"Pardon?" I responded, so surprised that I almost botched my enchantment manipulation. After making sure I didn't mess it up, I let out a relieved breath and inquired, this time a little more calmly, "Excuse me, but did you just say 'Zeus'? As in, the Greek god Zeus?"

"Among other things," Sebastian told me in an awkward fashion, as if he was talking about an embarrassing uncle. "My older kin have developed certain, somewhat unsightly habits over the centuries. Posing as the gods of fledgling human civilizations and taking advantage of them was but one."

"Wait, hold on a bloody moment! Are you telling me that the Greek gods were dragons?"

"Some of them."

"What about the other pantheons?"

"The same. I mean that literally. Unlike your ancestors, mine had access to wings and could travel around the continents. One of them could be Zeus on Monday, Donar on Thursday, and on the weekend, he could be Indra."

"And all of the demigods are…?"

"First- and second-generation Draconians, though it is likely even they weren't aware of their true origins. After all, in ancient times, there weren't any theologians to debate the nature and definition of gods, so as far as they were concerned, their deities and my kin were not fundamentally different."

"Wow… So, I guess if even just a fraction of those legends are true, there were hundreds… no, rather *thousands* of Draconians all around the world."

"You are most likely correct."

I'm not going to lie, I was floored by this discussion. I expected that I would hear some supernatural tidbits about the world, interwoven into the old man's romantic endeavours, but I didn't expect that it would all go back to ancient Greece and the Greco-Roman pantheon! Thankfully, I quickly recovered when I realized that the enchantment had finished "thawing," so I quickly did all the necessary modifications while I could. Truth be told, I felt like there was an easier way to do all of this, without all the extra steps, but I figured it was important to get a solid foundation via practice before I started experimenting.

Sebastian must have realized what I was doing, as he also fell silent and watched me work, though he probably couldn't see anything of the actual process. Subjectively, the recalibrating of the enchantment's trigger took about ten minutes, but if the time dilation effect stayed the same as before, about a minute should have passed on the outside. At last, I let out a pent-up breath and, after shaking the doll a little on principle, I handed it back to the elderly steward.

"There you go. It should be relatively safe now."

He reached out and gingerly took it from me, and after a few seconds of intense scrutiny, including actually smelling the damn creepy thing, he stated, "I can't say I can discern any changes."

"What kind of changes did you expect? I simply altered the trigger conditions, nothing else."

"If so, then how can I be certain you did anything at all?"

"It's simple," I answered with a wide grin. "Take the doll to a high school after midnight. Nothing should happen. Then put on a clown outfit, and then you should get cursed, proving that I changed the trigger. It's simple as that."

At the outset, the Dracis ancestor looked at me funny, but after I met his gaze for a few seconds, he exhaled a defeated sigh and told me, "I shall take you on your word, then."

Saying so, he stood up and walked over to the shelf from where I took the doll in the first place. In the meantime, I stretched my back, followed by a small groan, prompting the old man to send me a curious glance.

"Do you want to take a break?"

"Maybe?" I answered, a little uncertainly, and after a soft grunt, the room's denizen walked over to a cabinet.

"Do you drink tea?"

That question also threw me for a loop, but after inspecting it from every angle for some kind of trap, I tentatively nodded.

"Earl Grey, English Afternoon Blend, or Russian Caravan Tea?"

"Um... Surprise me?"

That was apparently enough for my suspiciously amiable host, as he began to methodically prepare something in a large, vintage metal kettle. Meanwhile, I stood up and began looking through the shelves for my second victim.

After some consideration, I decided on the small fertility idol that caught my interest the first time I came to this study. I carefully poked its insides with the phantom limb, and after less than a second, my facial muscles cramped up in indecision over whether I should look intrigued, incredulous, or just baffled.

"… Must be a fluke," I muttered.

I set the idol down and picked up a small, blunt knife—maybe a letter opener of some sort?

Anyhow, after a short inspection, my facial muscles got even more indecisive, so I hastily put the item back down and moved over to a nearby cabinet, where I chose a large metal brooch. It was quite eye-catching, as it was in the shape of a large fly or cicada, with gems in place of its eyes. I held it up and went through the whole routine again, and this time all the tiny muscles in my face reached an agreement, a supremely exasperated one.

"So, Sebastian?" I called out to my host, who was in the middle of sorting out various tea leaves in waxy brown paper bags.

"Yes, my boy?" he looked at me over his shoulder with a somewhat apprehensive look in his eyes, but I completely disregarded his body language and showed him the item in my hand.

"I'm curious. Can I ask you a question?"

"About that fibula?"

"It's called a 'fibula'?" I mused as I was momentarily tossed off my tracks, but I hurriedly recovered by shaking my head and telling him, "No, actually, I was curious if there is an item in your collection that *isn't cursed*?"

PART 2

"I think I figured it out," I stated just a hint cryptically before taking another sip from the best damned cup of tea I'd ever had.

"And, pray tell, just what did you discover?" Sebastian prompted me with an exhausted yet at the same time inexplicably smug expression, so he was… smughausted? That sounds about right.

Putting my impromptu wordsmithery aside for a moment, I took a deep breath and said, "I think I figured out your plan."

The old butler gave me a look that hovered somewhere between curious and exasperated, but at last he set his own cup on the table and said, "My plan. What plan?"

"Your plan to ruin any future teas I drink by treating me to one that would make all of them taste like lukewarm water by comparison, thus ruining my favourite drink forever! Absolutely diabolical!"

My elderly host gave me a strange look that turned straight up funny when I took another sip from my cup. Then he groaned and asked me, "Was that your attempt at a backhanded compliment, my boy?"

"Definitely not," I defiantly stated as I sloshed the spoonful of tea remaining in my cup, and then begrudgingly extended it towards him.

He glanced at my outstretched cup, then back at me, and after another roll of his eyes, he graciously gave me a refill while muttering something about how there should be a limit to how difficult someone could be. Since it was not only obvious but entirely reasonable to conclude that he was talking about himself, I silently applauded his ability to self-reflect.

Putting my own rationalization aside, I took another sip and savored the frighteningly rich taste for a moment before I set my drink aside for the time being and focused on the eclectic array of curios lined up on the table in front of me.

As it turned out, the old man's collection could be sharply divided into three categories. The first one contained all the unenchanted things, like the lion trophy on the wall and the various porcelain tea sets. The second category was for all the cursed items. The third category was the spear.

Yes, that actually meant that every single enchanted item in the room, aside from the eyesore in the corner, was cursed in one way or another. Now granted, none of them were as nasty as the Japanese *denpa* horror doll, and a lot of them weren't necessarily "cursed" based on the context, but still...

For an example, let's look at the fertility idol. According to its history, which Sebastian explained to me in excruciating detail while he brewed his tea, it originated in an old African empire most people have never even heard about. It was a wedding gift from one particularly influential noble family to another, and while it was entirely functional in its intended role, it was actually part of a devious ploy.

You see, while the enchantment would, in simple terms, strengthen the sperm cells of the man if placed on the bedside during horizontal gene transfer, it would do so in a very specific way. I don't want to go into the particular mechanics of this thing, as I didn't fully understand them during my quick once-over, but the idea was that it would actively kill off about half of them, and in return make the remaining half super-hardy.

Now, here comes the twist: that 50 percent it eradicates? That's all the sperm cells with a Y chromosome, leaving (and strengthening) only the X chromosome ones, raising the overall rate of conception, but in return guaranteeing that the resulting child would always be a girl. How is this a curse, you might ask? It's not one for an average person living in a modern society, obviously. In fact, if I ever wanted to have a daughter in the future,

I would be tempted to borrow this thing, because it was just that straight-forward and handy.

However, the gifter and the giftee were not average modern people, but aristocrats living in an olden kingdom with primogeniture as their preferred system of inheritance. For them, having at least one, preferably more, male heirs to inherit the family land and titles was paramount, and so this fairly innocent-sounding "curse" was nothing less than the complete sabotage of their future. Heck, according to Sebastian, it eventually led to the downfall of their entire nation. I have no idea how that happened, and to be honest, considering how long-winded Sebastian's original explanation was, I didn't dare to ask, lest he talk my poor ears off.

As for the other cursed items, some of them were nonfunctional, such as the letter opener that would inflict any wound caused by it on to the wielder, as well... except it was completely blunt with a tiny decorative handle that was impossible to hold properly, and thus it was entirely unsuitable to be used as a weapon. Then there were the objects with utterly banal curses, such as the ornate, jewel-encrusted golden chalice that would make the drinker flatulent, or the fancy military medal that gave the bearer male-pattern baldness.

So... I already asked this with the doll, but I have to ask it again... Just who in their right mind would come up with this kind of stuff? And just how unlucky did this old man have to be to amass such a huge collection of oddball artifacts? On the other hand, though, since most of them either had a very narrow "application" or unlikely trigger conditions, he was incredibly unlikely to trigger any of them. So, in some way, gathering all of these in one place, he'd inadvertently saved people from getting cursed. That was pretty lucky.

Putting my musings about the nature of fortune aside, I regretfully emptied my cup and, after sufficiently savoring the last drops, I put it aside and faced the elderly butler.

"Break time's over. Let's get started." Saying so, I gestured at the items in front of me and told him, "None of these are terribly dangerous, but all of them are still cursed. Are you sure I cannot just disable them?"

"I believe I've already told you about my stance on vandalizing my property," he responded with an annoyed frown.

"I told you, it's not vandalism. It's prudence! Why would you want to have dangerous cursed items in your study?"

"I believe you just said that none of them posed a hazard."

I shook my head. "No, I said none of them are 'terribly' dangerous. As in, they wouldn't hurt you, but they could still cause problems. Like this one."

I picked up the old fountain pen case I'd set aside and showed it to him.

"It's a gift I received from the previous family head," he told me while looking more than a little skeptical.

"Well, I have no idea where he got it from, but I would advise against leaving it alone for long."

"Is it cursed as well?"

"Of course it's cursed! I wouldn't be talking about it otherwise!" I scoffed. "It's a literal bomb."

"A bomb," he repeated after me, still unconvinced.

"More or less. It's set up so that if a certain person used it to write a certain number of letters, it would explode. It might've been a novelty assassination tool or something."

"A certain person? Is it me?"

"No," I replied with a shake of my head. "I don't know who the original target was, but based on the way the pen accumulates mana for the explosion, my money is on a Magi."

"In that case, the previous family head might've received it as a gift from one of his associates amongst the Wingless Lords."

"Wait, do you also mean the Magi?" I interrupted him, and he nodded with an implied *why?* in his eyes. "I'm just asking because I've never heard them referred to that way." Also, while I didn't mention it, the term was still oddly familiar.

"It is an old expression, no longer in common use," Sebastian nonchalantly explained before falling silent. Then he leveled the question, "But if its target was a Magi, then why does it require intervention?" at me.

"Because whoever originally owned the pen already filled it up to about halfway," I said. "Sure, that's not enough to cause too big of a *kaboom*, but it should be still as mean as a box of firecrackers, and while the enchantment should hold up for a couple more decades, considering your lifespan, I think it would be better to get ahead of the trouble before one day you wake up in the middle of the night to find your study radically rearranged."

"Point taken," Sebastian relented, much to my secret satisfaction.

"So, can I get started?"

"Be my guest."

"I already am," I replied as I put the pen down and picked up a handle. It looked like it originally belonged to a European sword with the blade snapped off at the base. It also had one of the more baffling curses, as it would make the wielder smell like rotten eggs, but only to members of the opposite sex. I couldn't decide if that was silly or pathetic, but either way, it was going to be removed. I mean, Elly already gave me a lot of flak for my magical smell, so I could totally understand how troubling it could be and how big of a dick the person who cursed this item was.

Once I began to do the groundwork, I looked Sebastian in the eye and asked, "So? Where were we before the tea break?"

"I believe we were discussing my kin's habit of posing as deities," he helpfully provided the answer, but I shook my head.

"No, that was more of a tangent… But since you already brought it up, can I ask another related question?"

He nodded.

"So, if I get this right, dragons took the identities of local gods. What about the Abrahamic one?"

"What about him?" my host asked back with a somewhat puzzled expression.

"I mean, I don't think anyone really cares about whether someone pretended to be Zeus, because most rational people don't believe he exists, but then what about the Judeo-Christian God? Was he also impersonated by dragons?"

"Not that I know of, no," Sebastian replied in a tone that told me his answer was much less certain than what the wording implied. "I'm afraid I can't say for sure, as I was born well after the times of the Old Testament, but I've never heard of anyone in the older generation who had done so."

"I see. What about the Celestials?"

"What about them?"

"Please stop answering my questions with questions! It's obvious what I'm asking!" I burst out a little indignantly in the face of him playing dumb. "The Celestials bear more than a passing resemblance to angels, and their leader was literally called Deus. You can't blame me for thinking that they might've also taken a page from your book."

"It's not impossible," Sebastian admitted with an expression that said it was a novel idea he never in a million years would have thought up on his own, even though it was blindingly obvious. But then again, depending on the nature and the intensity of the proposed perception filtering, it might actually be the case, so I cut him some slack.

"I suppose I'll have to ask my sources about it," I mentioned offhandedly before I forcefully grabbed hold of the horns of the conversation and yanked it into a different direction, lest I accidentally make the annoying butler meta-aware. "Anyways, I think before we went on the whole deity-masquerade tangent, you were telling me about your tumultuous love life."

"I don't remember ever calling it 'tumultuous,' albeit I admit, my years with my first companion were undeniably eventful."

"Right, the dragon lady. I never asked, but were you actually married?"

The elderly man before me gave me a funny look, as if I'd just asked something unexpectedly naïve, and answered, "No. Marriage was and is a human invention, for linking families and sharing property. What use would it have had for the two of us?"

"If you put it that way…" I admitted and, after a deep breath to punctuate the discussion, I did what I always do and steered the conversation into yet another direction. "That said, what actually happened to her? Was it the Knights?"

Now granted, in retrospect, that might not have been the best direction, but hey, I was improvising.

To my eminent surprise, Sebastian let out a wistful sigh and slowly shook his head.

"No. In the beginning, the accursed Knights were more concerned about the Lords of the Abyss and their secret war against the Lords of Providence."

"Whoa, there! You are throwing old terminology at me again," I stopped him, my brows already in a frown. "Who are these 'Lords of Providence,' again? The Celestials?"

"Precisely."

"And they fought a war with the Abyssals. I get it so far. So, were the Knights on the side of the Celestials in this war?"

"Were they?"

"I just told you to stop throwing my own questions back at me! It's annoying!" I objected, but the old man didn't seem fazed by my outburst at all. I paused for a long moment, and after mulling it over a little, I decided I might as well tell him a bit of my conjecture. I mean, I'd already told Elly a part of it, and knowing how bad she was at keeping secrets, I wouldn't have been surprised if the old steward caught wind of it soon, anyway. "Fine, I'll tell you. You said the Knights were fighting against the Abyssals, right?"

"That is correct."

"And I presume they had all their fancy weapons and enchanted armour on them."

"That is also correct."

"Those came from the Celestials."

If this was a sitcom, this would've been the point where we had a blaring *Dun-dun-DUN!* on the soundtrack, coupled with gasps from the studio audience. Instead of any of that, all I got was a skeptically raised eyebrow.

"That's a bold accusation, my boy."

"It's not an accusation; it's a fact. The Celestials supplied them with all their enchanted gear, and they stopped doing so relatively recently, at least if my sources are to be believed. Also, while diplomatic relations are nonexistent now, the Knights must have taken orders from them at one point or the other, because they are routinely referred to as 'rebels,' 'failures,' and 'oathbreakers,' which, considering that they seem to be pretty big on oaths, had to be the result of a fairly big incident."

Sebastian listened to my rudimentary explanation, and after a few seconds of mulling things over, he told me, "What you just said is… hard to believe."

"If you don't believe me, just take it up with the Celestials. Oh, but not Angie."

"Who?" he responded a little absentmindedly, as if this was the first time he'd heard her name.

"Celestial girl, fun and energetic, our friend, something of a sleeper agent, knows considerably less about Celestial affairs than I do," I gave him a CliffsNotes description of Angeline, but for some reason he seemed more confused than before.

"And from where exactly does *your* knowledge of 'Celestial affairs' originate?"

Overcoming my annoyance at his sarcastic air quotes, I flashed him a business smile. "Trade secret."

Then, moving the conversation along before he could start nagging me, I theatrically set down the item in my hand and picked up another one.

"Okay, I'm finished with that one. On that note, why don't we finish this topic and move on to what happened to your first lover?"

Sebastian was obviously a little grumpy about my refusal to elaborate, but he regained his cool and told me, "Very well. You have provided me with new knowledge, so courtesy dictates that I must return the favor… but mark my words. One day I shall draw out all your secrets."

"But that day's not today," I told him maybe a smidgen more cheekily than I originally intended, but the slightly-less-annoying-than-usual butler took it in stride.

"Don't judge the day until it's over," he warned me before shifting his pose in his seat and continuing his tale. "My first companion fell in the war between the Lords of the Abyss and the… and the Celestials of old. I had no ties with either side. She, on the other hand, had numerous associates amongst the Celestials, so when they called for her aid, she readily provided it."

"So, she went to war on her own," I concluded in a neutral tone, and he nodded in confirmation.

"She was free to do so, and over the centuries, I often wondered what could have been if I had tried to stop her. But alas, it was not my place to restrain her, and at the time, the war seemed to be nothing but a series of quick skirmishes leading to a certain victory."

"That sounds familiar," I muttered idly, and I wanted to leave it at that, but my elderly conversational partner seemed oddly curious, so I elaborated by telling him, "You know, the First World War? Everyone thought it would be a slam-dunk victory for their side, but then more and more nations joined in. Before long, it became a long, drawn out war of attrition. You should know; you lived through it."

"To be precise, I didn't live 'through' it," the once-again-slightly-more-annoying butler corrected me with his patented air quotes, which he was probably doing just to get on my nerves. "I didn't involve myself in the great war at all. That said, your comparison is truly apt, except that instead of nations, it was an unprecedented number of my kin who joined the fray. Some, like my beloved, joined the side of the Celestial Lords, while others of my kin aided the Lords of the Abyss. It was not out of loyalty, but due to family ties."

Right, Abyssals are actually hybrids of dragons and Celestials, so it made sense that they would throw down on the side of one or the other, probably depending on whether they had Celestial spouses or Abyssal children.

"So, it was the biggest family feud in the history of ever," I concluded.

"And my companion was one of the first causalities." There was not a small amount of disapproval in his voice, so I hastily mumbled a "Sorry, my condolences," which was enough to calm the old man down, and he continued, "After her death, I was tempted to join the conflict myself, but I ultimately refrained from doing so."

"Really? I thought the young, hotheaded you would've immediately embarked on a roaring rampage of revenge," I mused as I finished with one artifact and moved on to the next.

"My boy, you are labouring under a misconception," Sebastian told me with a smile that didn't reach his cold, vicious eyes. "I'll let you know, I personally gutted every single individual, be they mortals or my kin, who had anything to do with my companion's demise, and I did it slowly."

"Ah, I get it. You went on a vengeance spree, just didn't join either of the sides."

"Yes, that is precisely what I just described."

"Oh. Sorry for interrupting, then. Please carry on."

Sebastian changed his sitting posture once again, and as he did so, the coiling tension in his body language slowly dissipated, crescendoing in yet another nostalgic sigh.

"For two centuries after that, I lived alone, wandering continental Europe and never staying in one place for too long. It was during my years as a vagabond that I became known to humankind, and there might have been a ballad or two written featuring me."

I rolled my eyes at the old man's humble-bragging, but he didn't notice.

"It was during my stay in Paris when I met the second woman I ever loved."

"Meeting her in the city of love. How fitting."

"Don't be daft, my boy. This was ages before that city reinvented itself in such a manner. Not that it matters. I met her when I was passing through the town. Our meeting was rife with coincidence and unlikely circumstances, yet once the dust settled, I found myself traveling in her company."

"That was pretty vague…"

"Do you wish me to share every excruciating detail of our encounter?"

"Well, no, but a little context would help."

My host released a deep sigh.

"She was a young Celestial. After their war against the Abyss was over, her kind became an increasingly rare sight, as they hid themselves amongst the populace."

"So… kind of what they are doing to this day?"

"Indeed. It was also the time when the Wingless Lords became more and more prominent, and they were hostile towards both my kin and hers. As a matter of fact, she was chased by a group of their enforcers, which was the spark that ignited my curiosity."

"Oh, wait, let me guess—it was a rescue romance! You saved her, and she fell for you on the spot."

"Quite the contrary," he told me with a pained grimace, as if I just poked an old wound. "I indeed rescued her from her pursuers, and she became my traveling companion, but as for her affection… gaining it was truly an uphill battle."

"Come on, old man! Stop dragging your feet and tell me what happened."

I was rewarded with an annoyed glance and a subdued groan on one hand, but on the other hand, I finally got a proper answer.

"She was the sweetest person I ever knew. Every single pore of hers radiated warmth, and her blue eyes were infinitely deep wellsprings of kindness. Once a man fell into them, he could never hope to escape. It was the same for me."

"Love at first sight, but only for you?"

"More or less," Sebastian responded curtly, probably out of embarrassment.

Honestly, I really wished he'd stop showing me more sides of himself, as it made it really hard to hate his guts. Very inconsiderate of him.

"She also had an uncanny penchant for attracting trouble wherever we went, and even decades after I first met her, she remained the same naïve, eternally positive girl inside."

At this point, there was a long pause in the conversation as Sebastian waited for me to switch to another cursed item, and then he continued with, "Unfortunately, while she could capture a man's heart with a single glance, to the point where I had to employ constant vigilance lest she gather unwanted admirers in every country we visited, her own heart was quite impenetrable. Worse yet, due to her childlike innocence, I never managed to resolve myself to employ more… 'direct' methods to express my fondness for her. As such, it took me nearly five years to get her to recognize my feelings."

I stifled a chuckle at the old man's expense, and while I could kind of understand his situation, I never thought dense protagonist types were a thing so far back in history. I was about to gesture him to continue, but then something clicked inside my head.

"Okay, so just to reiterate," I started, "she was an impossibly beautiful and sweet young woman who immediately wrapped you around her little finger, tagged along on your adventures, and she had numerous suitors that you had to fend off, yet she was completely unaware of any of this. Does my description sound right?"

"I would say it's adequately accurate."

"Damn," I whispered under my breath, which he seemed to take as a tacit acknowledgment of his troubles. To be fair, he wasn't entirely wrong about that, but the main reason why I was really shocked was due to the fact that what he'd just described to me sounded waaaaaay too reminiscent of a shoujo manga protagonist's attributes and escapades. It was easy to see how this information would have insane ramifications if my conjecture was even in the ballpark of being correct. But for the moment, I decided I'd consult with Judy first before I tried to poke the elderly butler for more information on this topic.

Speaking of which, Sebastian continued to narrate his tale, completely disregarding my momentary daze.

"It took years, but once my feelings for her were successfully acknowledged, we found ourselves a quiet corner of the countryside and settled down. We did not have any children, though not for lack of trying, and while the peaceful and modest life we led was something I found stifling at the time, looking back through the lens of age, I have to admit that the few decades I have spent in her pleasant company were some of the happiest years of my life."

"It might be just me, but wasn't the way you loved her very different from the case of your first love?" I probed him a little, never forgetting to keep in mind my three initial ulterior motives.

"Indeed," he readily admitted, but no matter how long I waited for him to elaborate, he remained stubbornly silent. As such, I was forced to ask the next obvious question.

"I'm kind of dreading to ask, but what happened to her?"

"Old age," Sebastian softly said. "We lived a long, quiet life, and it ended just as quietly. There wasn't much else to say about the years we shared under the sun."

"You stayed with her until the end."

"Until the very end," he confirmed with a solemn nod. "She left me in her sleep, and I buried her on my mountain." The old man seemed genuinely dispirited as he mused, "It's such a strange thing. My first companion and I were equals, and my love for her burns even to this day, yet the one I miss the most is my second love. I miss her smile, her voice, her touch... but maybe more than anything, I miss those serene days we shared."

After saying that, he fell silent for a long time, and I was tempted to say something to move things along, but before I could, he suddenly added, "Mark my words, my boy. Be it a love of true companionship, a love of quiet tranquility, or a love of burning passion, you must treasure them. Nothing in this world lasts forever; only the memories remain. Therefore make as many of them as you can with those you love. A life well-lived is the most wonderful thing you can share, both with those who leave and the ones who remain."

... God dammit, old man! Stop looking so pained and gentle and kindly! Stop being so sympathetic and making it harder to hate you! It's not fair!

Putting my gripes with my host's unnervingly benignant behaviour aside, I said, "I presume the 'love of burning passion' refers to your third lover."

"You are once again correct in your deduction," he answered with a level voice, his nostalgic melancholy seemingly losing its grip on him. I may or may not have looked more expectant than I thought, as Sebastian let out a gratingly grandfatherly chuckle and told me, "After I buried my second love, I couldn't bear to stay in our empty home, so I once again began to roam around the whole world. Not a lot had changed since I removed myself from human affairs, and no place could tie me down for long before my wanderlust would urge me on the road again. In the following centuries, humanity began to develop by leaps and bounds, and observing them from afar kept me from becoming bored for a long, long time. I also witnessed the acts of the Knights, the Wingless Lords, the exiled Abyssals, and others, but I never involved myself with their affairs, either. I thought I would be content to just stay an eternal wanderer, until a fateful day in Vienna."

"I figure that is where you met your third lover?"

"Yes," the old butler answered in the company of a soft yet delighted chuckle, which was certainly yet another of his attempts to lower my guard by acting all nice and likable. Fortunately, I knew better than that, so I only smiled in return. Warmly. For a few seconds. Because I have principles, dammit. Anyhow, he continued by telling me, "She was one of the Habsburgs living in the city, and I met her during a birthday ball I attended on a whim."

"Hold on for just a second. Wasn't the Habsburg dynasty kind of a big deal? I mean, I don't know exactly which century we are talking about right now, but I'm fairly sure they were big shots for most of European history."

"I can tell you exactly when we met," the aged steward declared with a proud smile. "It was the fifth of March in 1870."

"So, it was in the late nineteenth century... That means it was the time of the Austrian Empire, led by the Habsburgs, which means your lover was... an actual princess?"

"An archduchess, to be precise, but yes," he replied, and somehow I couldn't help but feel that his smile went from proud to smug in the blink of an eye. "I remember the date well, for it was her fifteenth birthday, and it was her birthday ball I unknowingly attended."

"I see. Was it love at first sight again?"

"In a manner of speaking..." When he said that, the smile withered off the man's face and he let out a tired sigh. "She was quite a splendid young lady. Unfortunately, as the first daughter of the emperor, she might have been pampered more than strictly necessary, so her personality was... how should I put it? She was sweet yet passionate. Very passionate. She was also stubborn, easily embarrassed, yet at the same time often incredibly blunt and unladylike."

"So... kind of like Elly?"

"Precisely like her," Sebastian agreed. "In truth, even their appearances are strikingly similar."

"So, it's in the blood, huh?"

"You could certainly say that," he replied with an uncertain shrug.

At this point, there was another pause in the conversation as I finished up yet another cursed item on my to-do list.

"Done. So, where were we? The ball, I think?"

"Yes. At the time, I was posing as a successful merchant, and I was invited by one of the nobles I'd helped to procure some rare items using the connections I'd made over the years. I did not expect that when she arrived at the ball, out of all the hundreds of people in the grand hall, she would single me out. Her attention was very... ardent."

"So, she fell in love with you at your first meeting?"

"Yes. Furthermore, over my stay in the capital, she fabricated countless excuses to allow her to meet me again. She was incredibly persistent."

"Well, considering the present situation, I figure she must have grown on you."

"In a manner of speaking," Sebastian stated a bit awkwardly. "I never disliked her, but she was simply too young, and I imagined that the passion of her first love would abate once we were separated. As such, I prepared to leave not only the city, but the whole continent for the time being, yet I felt it would've been cruel to leave without a word. Because of this, I quietly visited her on the evening before my departure and told her not only that I would be leaving, but about my own nature. I told her that if she still felt the same way after my return, I would not turn her away."

"How did she take it?"

The old man let out another deep sigh and told me, in an obviously embarrassed voice, "To cut a long tale short, she forced me to elope with her."

"Forced you?" I repeated with my Joshua-brand raised eyebrow, and Sebastian responded by awkwardly clearing his throat.

"She was really, *really* passionate, and she somehow grabbed hold of the conversation and never let it go. Thus, before I knew what happened, we were on a boat heading for the Americas."

"Wow, that's..." I wanted to say something snappy in response, but when I thought about how my own effort to 'let Elly down gently' ended up, all I could muster was a flat, "... entirely too familiar."

The look in the aged butler's eyes felt grossly sympathetic, and he continued his story, destroying my opportunity to justifiably tell him off.

"My relationship with her was both eventful and bountiful, as you could most likely gather from the existence of my descendants. It was also her who introduced me to the joy of collecting rare memorabilia. As she put it, since I would inevitably outlive her, she wanted me to have something to remember her by. That, of course, was wholly unnecessary, as her memory lived on within all our progeny, but I humoured her. Mainly because she was really persistent."

"I imagine," I muttered as I just finished modifying the last item and exhaled a satisfied breath. "But wait, does that mean that these are items you two collected?"

"Don't be silly, my boy." Sebastian shook his head with a smile that said I once again asked something amusingly naïve. "These are but a part of my private collection. I keep all the important mementos in a safe place only I can access. Well, all of them, except this one." Saying so, he reached into the breast pocket of his uniform and retrieved a small silver locket. "This was her first gift to me, so I always keep it close to my heart."

"That's sweet…" I began as I vacillated on whether I should address the elephant in the room. At last, I exhaled hard and decided to just do it, sink or swim. "Speaking of safety and access, don't you think that keeping that anti-dragon spear out in the open is a little dangerous?"

I could tell by the way the atmosphere in the room suddenly tensed up that its owner instinctively wanted to ask me how I knew it was the dragon-slaying spear, but before he could do so, his eyes sparkled with realization.

He wearily asked me, "Did the young lady tell you about it?"

I nodded.

He groaned. "I should've known. That said, the spear is perfectly safe here."

"Yeah, it's safe right now, when you are in the room, but what if you were away?"

"I would take it with me."

"What if you had to leave in a hurry?" Sebastian looked decently intrigued, so I elaborated on the idea by telling him, "For example, if I was a wily Knightly type and I learned that the anti-dragon MacGuffin was here, I wouldn't try to get it head-on. I'd do something devious—say, stage a bomb threat or a hostage situation—to draw you out. Then when the place was undefended, I'd swoop in and steal the spear, maniacally cackling all the way home."

For some ungodly reason, Sebastian kept eyeing me suspiciously before he finally asked, "Then tell me, my boy, what do you propose we do about the weapon?"

"Throw it into a volcano," I replied on the spot without any need to think about it. "We have a perfectly good one right here. Or if outright destroying it is not an option because of some esoteric reason, like say, there can be only one super-duper dragon-slaying weapon, and they can't make another unless you get rid of this…"

I paused and sent my host a glance that asked, *Is there?*

He shook his head.

"… Anyhow, if you don't want to just break it, cast it into concrete and drop the slab into the Mariana Trench. Problem solved. It also works for immortals and really persistent tax collectors."

"Neither of those options is tenable."

"How so?" I asked, surprised by his hard denial.

Sebastian closed his eyes and inhaled sharply through his nose before giving me an answer.

"It is the weapon that inflicted Lady Emese's wound. We are in contract with numerous artificers with the purpose of lifting its effects on her body, and for that, we must have it easily accessible for them."

"Oh? Artificers, you say?" I mused with my words coated by gallons of industrial-strength sarcasm. "Have any of them noticed that you were surrounded by cursed items?"

"No," Sebastian responded a little sheepishly. "Though, in their defense, I never let them study the items of my personal collection."

"Not a good excuse," I told him flatly before glancing at the eyesore in the corner. "Would you mind if I took a look?"

My host was oddly wary of my proposition. He mulled it over for several seconds before he stood up, removed the weapon from the hand of the mannequin wearing the damaged full plate armour, and he gingerly placed it on the table in front of me. He didn't say anything during the whole process, but it was easy to guess that I had his tacit agreement, so I carefully extended my hand towards the spear.

It was a fairly simple weapon, not too long, but not too short, either. It had a smooth, undecorated wooden shaft with a rounded metal cap at the butt end and a simple, leaf-shaped spearhead on the other. The blade of the spear was fairly narrow with an elegant curve in it, and at the base of the edges, there was a small, rectangular crossbar. All the metal parts were made of a matte, bluish material, and they bore no decoration whatsoever. The whole thing was also impeccably clean, but that no longer surprised me anymore.

I tried to touch the spearhead, but the moment I did that, it felt like there was a mild electric current running through my fingertip. I jerked my hand back, much to the butler's surprise.

"Ouch," I hissed and shook my hand. Then, after an awkward silence, I whispered, "I think this thing doesn't like me."

Sebastian kept silent, so I took a determined breath and attempted to grab the weapon again. This time I was prepared, and while holding the thing still felt incredibly uncomfortable, I managed to pick it up from the table and take a closer look. Of course, observing it from the outside was not particularly constructive, so after I sufficiently prepared myself, I poked it with my phantom limb to see what made it tick.

The actual enchantment was, oddly enough, not exceptionally complex. In fact, its internal structure felt quite familiar, and after a few seconds spent comprehending it, I turned to Sebastian and told him, "Okay. I have only done a preliminary inspection so far, but correct me if I am wrong—this thing works by messing with the injured Draconian's ability to transform and heal, right?"

"That is correct."

"In other words, it causes an ongoing negative effect to affect the target of the enchantment."

"Yes," he spoke in a mixture of uncertainty and suspicion.

"Do you know what that means?"

"Enlighten me."

"It means," I declared, unable to keep the smirk off my face, "that literally every single enchanted item in your collection is cursed! How do you even do that?"

My host only gave me a flat look, and after a short standoff, he groaned aloud and stated, "This is not the time for joking."

"I'm not joking. A spear that causes wounds that cannot heal is an archetypal cursed item. I think it was a gáe-something-or-the-other? It's from Celtic mythology, I think. Have you heard of it?" Sebastian was giving me the cold shoulder, so I shrugged my own and concluded with, "Whatever, it's not important."

"Neither is your harangue about cursed items," he spoke so sourly, he could make limes jealous. "Can you actually do something about it?"

"Let me take another look."

With that, I once again delved into the enchantment on the spear, and my first assessment turned out to be completely accurate. While the actual surface enchantment was insanely complex, most of it was grandiose gibberish. Multiple invocation phrases, multistage unsealing, particle effects up the wazoo, performance enhancers that boosted the user, the works. However, by observing it from a lower stratum, I could peel away all the special effects and presentation, which left me with a very simple conditional curse that only activated if the target happened to possess the *essence of dragons*. It sounded fancy, but in reality, it was just something of a tag used by the supernatural layer of the world.

Anyhow, once I located the core, I was about to tweak it when the actual part of me that seemed to instinctively understand what was going on began to freak out, stopping me in my tracks. It took me a subjectively long time to figure out what the problem was, but after analyzing it from every angle, my conclusion was that I really shouldn't mess with this enchantment because it was "important."

Important to whom? That was a tall order to figure out, but after a few more minutes of pondering, I came to a startling conclusion—it wasn't *whom*. It was *what*. As in, it was important to the narrative. This spear was supposed to play some part or another in a grand design, and messing with it could have all sorts of nasty consequences. More surprisingly, my aversion seemed to only cover tweaking with it using my phantom limb, as I never had any negative reaction to the idea of throwing the bloody thing into a volcano.

Could it be because changing the enchantments my way was considered unnatural by the system that was running this world, while physically enacting the same thing wasn't? And how come every time I made a discovery, it only led to more questions?

"So?"

I was jolted out of my revelation-induced stupor. I glanced at Sebastian, thought hard, and then told him, "I have bad news. I don't think can disable this thing; it seems to be immune to my kind of tinkering."

"Is that so?"

"Yes. Howeeeeever…" I drew out the words to pique his interest, and when he seemed expectant enough, I explained to him, "while *I* can't change it, I believe I could give some decent pointers to whatever artificers you were in contact with."

"You think so?"

"Sure. My approach is somewhat unorthodox, but it should still help them."

Sebastian thought long and hard about my proposal, resulting in a shallow nod.

"I will discuss the matter with the family."

"Oh! And while you're at that," I said, putting down the spear, "since the curse has a continuous magical effect, I might be able to do something about my prospective mother-in-law's injury. I mean, I can't promise anything yet, as I might run into the same roadblock as I did with the main enchantment, but if it's possible, I'll help."

"I will convey your words," he said as he placed the spear back.

I stood up and stretched out my limbs. For some reason, I felt really tired even though I'd been sitting in place the whole time. Of course, since I had no frame of reference, as far as I knew, I might've been doing seven different kinds of impossible things that would have made your average artificer's head explode, so getting a little tired over it probably wasn't that bad. Speaking of which, I glanced over the neat pile of miscellaneous odds and ends on the table, following which I addressed their owner.

"Thanks for letting me play with your toys. It was very educational."

"You are welcome." Sebastian's reply was a little odd, as if he didn't really have his full attention on me. In fact, it felt like he was internally debating over something. Suddenly, he said, "Since you have already 'played' with all the enchantments in this room, I'm afraid I have nothing left to show you *here*."

The last word had an odd emphasis, so I asked, "What about somewhere else?"

"Well, of course. Did you believe this was the whole breadth of my collection? For example, the items I have left in our mansion in Berlin are not only more numerous, but I can also assure you that none of them are cursed." He paused, as if waiting for me to ask something, but when I didn't, he cleared his throat and added, "That said, if you do not believe me, I can arrange them to be carried here so you may see them with your own eyes."

"Can you?"

"Certainly. You need but ask. Nicely."

I couldn't decide whether I should laugh or cry, but I soon settled for a wry look and an absolutely unconvincing, "Pretty please?"

"If you insist," my host replied with a borderline mischievous smile, and... honestly, I didn't like it.

"Hey, Sebastian?" I called out. "Can I ask you something else?"

"Depends on the request."

"Well, this might sound weird, but could you get really snobby with me?"

"Pardon?"

"Okay, how should I explain this... Think of it as an experiment. I want you to act like the first time we met. You know? Annoyed, hostile, demeaning? That kind of thing."

"Why?"

"I just told you, it's an experiment."

He looked both puzzled and unconvinced by my words, but he still played along by setting his mouth in a thin line, giving me an annoyed frown, and then stating, "My boy, your request makes absolutely no sense, and it makes me wonder about your mental faculties."

I looked him in the eyes, aaaand... nothing. Not a whiff of unnatural irritation.

"... Okay, this doesn't work. Let's try this again, but this time, can you use some kind of mystical intimidation tactic?"

"*Mystical intimidation tactic*," he repeated after me, getting more confused by the second.

"Don't you have anything like that?"

"I can't say I do."

"Aw, man," I grumbled as I shook my head. "This is bad."

"What's bad?"

"The fact that I almost don't find you annoying anymore. It's a troubling development."

"My boy, you really need to stop hiding your true thoughts behind wordplay."

"I'm not, and we are going to get back to this at a later date, when I won't feel so tired. Maybe that's what's throwing me off. In fact, I should go now. I promised the princess I'd listen to her sing some more after I'm done here, and it's getting late. I should go to her before it's curfew-o-clock."

"In that case, I recommend you don't make her wait."

"I won't." With that, I headed towards the door, but before I could leave, Sebastian somehow got ahead of me and opened it for me. It was like he was a real butler or something. I gave the man my best nonplussed look and, after a momentary stalemate, I muttered, "Goodbye."

"I wish you a nice evening," he returned the gesture, and after I left the room, he closed the door behind me.

Well, that was awkward. Still, while I did find it mildly disquieting that Sebastian was no longer just *that annoying old coot* in my mind, I shrugged it off and headed down the hall. My promise to Elly wasn't just an excuse, so I Far Saw her and found her still practicing in her singing room. I was about to take a shortcut and just Phase over, but before I could get to it, a new thought stopped me in my tracks.

I'd learned a lot of things. Most of them, like the stuff about Sebastian's love life, was, while not strictly applicable to my situation, at least mildly edifying. My slowly broadening horizons regarding enchantments in particular and the magical substrate in general were also promising. However, there was one bit of information that was vital enough that I figured I should share it right away.

As such, I took out my phone, dialed the first number on my contact list, and after just a few rings the line connected.

"Good evening, Chief," my dear assistant spoke in a way that sounded like she was yawning at the same time.

"Hi, Dormouse!" I spoke with only slightly forced enthusiasm and a not at all forced grin. "Guess what? I just found a plot device!"

CHAPTER 22

PART 1

It was just a little after 9 p.m. My room was, unusually enough, lit by the ceiling lamp instead of the customary PC monitor lighting, and while it hurt my eyes a little, it was unfortunately necessary. Why, you might reasonably ask? It was so that Snowy could easily move around while she was taking care of me.

Speaking of which, I let out another soft groan, which made my maid… or little sister… let's go with maidster… twitch in apprehension, but I gestured for her not to mind me. Hesitating, she continued changing my bedsheets. Meanwhile, I pulled the blanket over my shoulders even tighter around me and tried to sit straight on my chair, but my body refused to obey my clear and concise commands. I slouched back in the chair.

Just as I was feeling a bit more comfortable, my phone on the computer desk lit up, followed by a jaunty little tune. I was a little startled at first, as I was fairly sure that wasn't my ringtone, but after a few seconds spent rummaging through the messy memory-cabinets of my brain, I remembered that I'd changed it during my sneaky operation at Lab Coat Guy's place and forgotten to change it back. That was one mystery solved.

"Uh… Aren't you going to pick it up?" Snowy asked me from beside my bed, and after forcing my addled brain to process the question, I responded with a grunt.

"I… guess I should?"

I reached for the ringing device. After spending an uncomfortably long time fiddling with the screen lock, I read the caller ID, and after taking a deep breath, I raised the phone to my ear.

"Hi, Dormouse…"

"Eleanor called me a few minutes ago," my dear assistant cut to the chase without even bothering to greet me. "She said you were sick but refused to stay over."

"It's nothing serious," I responded while trying to put enough strength into my voice to sound in the ballpark of normal. "I think I just overworked myself a little."

"What did you do?" Judy leveled the question at me with the kind of verbal intensity she only showed through the phone for some reason.

"Oh, you know? Stuff?" My brilliantly descriptive answer obviously didn't satiate her curiosity, so I reluctantly told her, "When I got into Sebastian's toy box, I may have overexerted myself a bit. Apparently mucking around with enchantments is hard on your head-stuffing. Who knew? Well, I didn't until I finished tweaking all his artifacts, and now here we are."

"Was this before or after you called me to tell me about plot devices and *otome* protagonists?"

"Before that, obviously."

"You didn't make a lot of sense back then."

"Yeah… in retrospect, I was probably a little bit feverish and I just hadn't realized it yet. Adrenaline high and stuff."

"So, you had a fever. What else?"

"Fatigue, muscle pains, mild nausea, headache, enervation…"

"The first and the last one are the same," Judy told me in her usual monotone, which was made uncanny by the fact that she usually wasn't so flat on the phone. "Do you still have a fever?"

"A little."

"Give me numbers."

"Thirty-nine point six."

"Celsius?"

"No, it's obviously Kelvin. Fevers are well known for almost reaching absolute zero." There was a long stretch of silence filled with a distinct sense of displeasure coming from the other end of the line, so I hastily cleared my throat and added, "Sorry, I'm kinda snappy because I feel sick. What I meant to say was that it was indeed Celsius."

"That's not *a little* fever. I'm coming over."

At first, I could only blink in surprise at my girlfriend's categorical declaration, but once I overcame the initial shock, I hurriedly told her, "Wait, Dormouse! There is no need for you to come over this late."

"You are obviously sick, so I am going."

"For what? I told you I just overexerted myself a little, so it's not something you can help with, and Snowy is already servicing me enough as is. I don't need…"

It was only at this point that I realized I'd let an uncomfortable and equally unnecessary detail slip out of my mouth, so I immediately clamped it shut.

Too late.

"She is *servicing* you," Judy stated a little incredulously, and since the cat was already out of the bag, I decided to just tell her what was going on, if for nothing else than to get ahead of any future misunderstandings.

"Yeah. She's in her maid outfit and cleaned my room, changed my bed-sheets… she even made me chamomile tea! I'm positively pampered right now!" After saying all that, I paused, realizing that I was getting worked up over something silly again, so I took a deep breath and quietly added, "I'm not going to lie; I think she's actually enjoying the situation more than strictly necessary."

"Is she there with you?"

"Not right now, no," I replied while glancing around. "She went down-stairs not long after you called. I think she is making some kind of porridge with milk and cinnamon and… Oh, speak of the Abyssal—I think she's coming back."

Snowy entered my room right after I said that, carrying a wooden tray I was pretty sure I'd never seen in any of my kitchen cupboards. On it sat a medium-sized plate with a milky white porridge in it, topped by a fine layer of brown powder. It smelled surprisingly nice.

"Is something wrong?" my still fairly new little sister questioned me a tiny bit uncomfortably, and I shook my head.

"Nah, Judy was just curious about what you were doing and—"

It was at this point that my dearest assistant interrupted me by point-edly clearing her throat.

"I gather she is in the room now. Can I talk to her?"

"Er… Sure?" I responded and gestured Snowy over. She placed the tray on the desk next to me, and after some extra gesticulating, she gingerly took the phone from my hand.

"Hello?"

She took a step back before she spoke up, so I couldn't hear the other side of the conversation, but based on how serious she looked, they must have been discussing something important. Like me.

Jokes aside, I decided to use this opportunity to haul myself up into a more comfortable dining position, and once I accomplished that, I picked up the spoon before Snowy tried to feed me, as well. I mean, being pam-pered was nice and all, but there are limits to everything.

That said, the cinnamony porridge she made was surprisingly good. It had a smoother consistency than I expected, and it was really sweet. As I absentmindedly ate, I also continued to observe this side of the phone con-versation, and while it wasn't exactly riveting, the way Snowy kept seriously nodding to whatever Judy was saying was actually a little amusing.

Before I knew it, I finished up my late-evening meal, and as per the unwritten rules of convenient timing, the conversation on the phone ended right around the same time. I mean, I really hope it was an 'unwritten rule,' since if it wasn't, it not only meant that Judy's interpretation of the Narrative was true, but it had way too much time on its hands to spend on silly stuff, such as conveniently timing completely trivial events like this.

While I was ruminating about that, Snowy carefully handed me my phone and I immediately raised it to my ear again.

"So?"

"We reached an agreement," Judy stated. "I won't go over tonight and I will leave you in Neige's care. Listen to everything she says like it's me telling you."

"Are you my girlfriend or my mother?"

"Your concerned girlfriend who is getting tired of you getting into trouble the moment she takes her eyes off you," she snapped back, and for once, I had nothing in return.

"Got it."

"Good. Now rest up. I'll see you the first thing tomorrow morning."

"Okay then. Good night, Dormouse." I waited for her to say her good-byes as well, but then on a whim, I added, "I love you."

For some odd reason, there was a long pause on the line. I was just about to ask if everything was all right when my dear assistant blurted out, "Chief, could you repeat what you just said?"

"I said I love you," I did as I was told, if maybe a little more awkwardly than the first time, resulting in another unnecessarily long bout of silence.

"Chief, I might need to go over, after all. I think you might be delirious."

"Oh, ha-ha!" My reply came packaged with an annoyed roll of the eye, which she naturally couldn't see, so I narrated. "Just so you know, I am rolling my eyes so hard, they kinda hurt."

"Then stop it."

"I already did," I responded while rubbing my aching ocular organs. "But, anyways, what's wrong with me telling my girlfriend I love her? Is this that toxic masculinity thing I keep hearing about?"

"Political joke, abort at once," Judy warned me, and then she explained, "I honestly didn't expect you to say that. Did something happen at Eleanor's place?"

"A few things. I'll tell you in detail tomorrow."

"Did it involve lewding?"

"I'm pretty sure we both agreed that's not a word, but even if it was, no, it didn't."

"Good." I could totally picture her resolutely nodding to herself as she said that, an image that easily managed to bring a small smile to my tired face.

"Let's try this again: See you tomorrow, Dormouse. Sleep well."

"Good night, Chief," Judy said her farewells and cut the line, and I involuntarily let out a pent-up breath when she did so. Cruel as it might have sounded, I felt really exhausted already, so I didn't want her to come over. No matter how much she would try to take care of me, at the end of the day, I would not be able to keep myself from playing around with her, which was not beneficial to recovery of any kind.

Speaking of which, I turned to my patiently waiting sister.

"So, what *exactly* did you two agree upon?"

"Judy told me to make sure you don't go anywhere, that you drink plenty of fluids, and that you rest without any disturbance," she said without the barest hint of reservation.

"That's... surprisingly normal," I mused while deliberately narrowing my eyes in my best impression of a suspicious detective probing a witness. "Are you sure there wasn't anything more specific than that?"

"Uh..." After letting out a hesitant noise, followed by a short but intense bout of fidgeting, my dear sister quietly told me, "She said I shouldn't let you meet with the swordswoman."

"Meet with the swo—Hold on!" I exclaimed in a mixture of realization and alarm. "Dammit, I totally forgot that I was supposed to go out hunting with her tonight!"

"You can't!" Snowy declared in a rare moment of steadfast determination, which I, unfortunately, made a little redundant by immediately agreeing with her.

"Of course I can't! I feel like a particularly worn-out washcloth at the moment. I am in no shape to go out and hunt for tiny shape-shifting monsters."

"That's... that's right! So, don't even think about it!" Snowy doubled down with what remained of her previous gusto, though instead seeming determined, now she felt more like an angry puppy. An angry puppy in a maid outfit. Who was also my adopted sister. I think if I could squeeze just one more random fetish in there, I could make the whole concept completely collapse on itself, but I couldn't be arsed to do it at the moment.

Nor could I let it show that I wasn't taking her seriously, so I acted reasonably cowed and told her, "I'm not thinking about it, I swear! I promise I won't even leave the room."

"That's good," Snowy declared and proudly puffed up her chest, kind of like a puffin, but even cuter. On an unrelated note, why was I so fixated on animal comparisons just then? It must have been the fever.

Unfortunately she quickly deflated when she noticed I already ate all the gruel she brought.

"Why are you looking at me like that?" The question inadvertently escaped my mouth. "I obviously didn't need feeding, so I ate it while it was warm."

"Was it good?" my dear sister asked while twiddling her thumbs.

"Of course, it was. I wouldn't have eaten it otherwise."

"Are you sure? I thought you were the type who would eat it even if it was bad and tell me it was good so that you wouldn't hurt my feelings."

"What a silly notion," I scoffed at her completely incorrect and borderline slanderous assumptions, but for some reason she only giggled as she nimbly packed my empty plate and utensils, no doubt about to head out and do something maid-y, like washing dishes.

I decided not to bother her while she worked, so instead I obediently headed over to my bed and sat down on it while making sure that I still had my blanket tightly wrapped around me. I had cranked up the thermostat already, but I still felt cold. Fevers suck, amirite?

Since I had nothing better to do, I decided to do a Far Sight roll call, just to see if I could catch something important happening. First, I leafed through the rest of the posse. Snowy needed no look-over, as she'd just left the room. Nor did Judy, as we'd just talked, so I switched my perspective over to Elly, who was actually studying in her room. How diligent.

Since I was already in the mansion (I wasn't really, but you get the point), I glanced in on Sebastian and the Dracis parents, too. The former was having a night snack in the kitchen by the looks of it, while the latter were... um... they were *busy*. With the birds and the bees, if you get my meaning. I was no voyeur, so I quickly left and gave them some privacy.

Moving on, I checked Amelia, and, to my shock and surprise, she wasn't doing paperwork! A real bombshell, I know! As for what she *was* doing, it appeared she was having a discussion with a group of distinctly placeholder-looking older men. I had a hunch they might have been the rumored artificers, if for nothing else than because all of them were wearing those odd jeweler's monocles with multiple lenses strapped to their heads. I think they're called "loops" or "loupes" or "lopezes" or something.

No matter what their official name was, each of the balding, bearded men wore one either over their eyes or pulled up to their foreheads. I only listened to their conversation in passing, but they were apparently discussing how hard modifying an already placed enchantment was without specialist tools. Yup, that was totally going to bite me in the ass when the class rep inevitably interrogated me about it the next day. At least I had advance warning, so now I had a whole night to come up with reasonably plausible excuses.

Moving on again, this time I checked on Angie and Josh. To my surprise, the hyperactive Celestial was already in dreamland even though it was barely half-past nine. Maybe that was the secret of her boundless energy? How did the idiom go again? "Early to bed, early to rise, makes a young girl hyper and nice"? Yeah, that sounds about right.

Josh's turn. I found him… hunched over his desk and writing in a diary? That was unexpected enough to tickle my interest, so I… well, I suppose *floated over* would be the right term to use… and took a closer look. It didn't take me long to realize that what he was writing was nothing as mundane as a common diary.

The visible pages of the standard A4 spiral notebook on his desk, the same kind we used for schoolwork, were completely filled with tiny letters interspersed with odd diagrams and arrows pointing every which way. It took me a little while to figure out what all of that was about, but the longer I looked at it, the more it reminded me of those game plans you sometimes see in movies and games about American football (or, as people of culture like to call it, *handegg*), and then it finally clicked with me: I was looking at battle plans!

Well, okay, maybe not "plans," but considering some of the circles representing people had our little collection of supernatural misfits' initials in them, I figured Josh was either documenting and analyzing the battle that took place earlier that day, or he was making up tactics in advance. Both options were equally surprising, and I had to admit that I didn't think Josh had an interest in this kind of stuff, yet judging by his notes, he was doing an admirably good job pinpointing the strengths and weaknesses of the people in our group.

Oh, speaking of which, I just noticed that he had notes on me, too! It said I was… *unpredictable*? Well, okay, I can live with that, but what's that under it? *Shady*! And *stingy*? What does that even have to do with combat roles?

If I'd had a head in my disembodied viewpoint mode, I would've shaken it. Some people…

Anyhow, I decided to leave Josh to whatever he was doing and move on to the bad guys. Well, okay, not all of them were "bad" or "guys," but my first target definitely qualified for both, as it was Crowey. He was… catatonic, as usual.

I'd been wondering about this for a while. The more time passed, the fewer things seemed to happen around him. I joked about him being catatonic, but in reality, he seemed to be in much better shape than he was right after our altercation. Yet nowadays, all he did was eat, sleep, and stare at the ceiling. It got progressively worse to the point where I wondered if whatever underlying system was running this world simply put him on "low priority" to save resources because he was "out of sight" at the moment, and I was only half-joking about that.

In short, there was nothing going on with everyone's favourite Abyssal, so I promptly moved on to my next target.

Lab Coat Guy. To my shock and confusion, I found him not in his hidey-hole, but just in the process of leaving Lord Grandpa's office! My first reaction was to curse out loud for missing such a great opportunity to catch them red-handed, but then I realized something—the old man was actually leading him out! And they were still in front of the door of the study! This was the perfect opportunity to Phase over and rummage through the old man's stuff while he was away. Who knew what kind of juicy blackmail mater— *cough* I mean, *vital information* I could find there? And it was just a quick jump away. So I... immediately slapped some sense into myself.

"No! Bad brain! No ideas about going outside! Bad!" I whispered and shook my head. I'd just promised Snowy I wouldn't go anywhere, so I obviously wasn't going to teleport away and make her sad. But then again, this was a rare opportunity with just a small window to exploit it, so maybe... "No! Very bad brain! Stop thinking bad things!"

"Is there a problem?"

I shuddered in surprise and hastily looked around, only to realize Snowy was already back in the room.

"Um... nothing?" I told her a little weakly, hoping that she didn't hear me muttering to myself, but if her awkward expression was any indication, she sure as hell did. But then again, Snowy was often awkward even if there was no weirdo whispering stupid things in the room, so I decided to try to sweep things under the carpet by changing topics.

For example, to the tray in her hands. I pointed right at it.

"What's that?"

"Ah, this?" My little sister angled the tray in question so I could see it better and told me, "I didn't want to throw this out, so I thought I'd ask you if you wanted seconds."

"Well, I'm mostly full, but I guess I have space for one more bowl."

My reply pleased her more than it had any right to, and she pattered over to my side with an unusual spring in her steps. I flashed her my Brotherly Smile™ v0.8, which she also seemed to appreciate, so I figured I could take it out of open beta soon.

While I considered that, she put the second helping on my lap, tray and all, and then took a step back, continuing to stand ramrod straight, attentive to my every move. It was the most maid-like behaviour I'd ever seen, and considering that I was actually on a first-name basis with a genuine chambermaid, that said something.

"Is it just me, or are you actually enjoying yourself?" I leveled the question that was on the tip of my tongue for a good while at her, and unexpectedly enough she immediately nodded in confirmation.

"My brother never got sick, so I never had the opportunity to take care of someone. I always wanted to try it once... Am I doing it right?"

"You are doing great," I reassured her with Brotherly Smile™ v.0.8.1 (the difference was in the angle of my head), and she let out a breath of relief.

"That's good. I think I have done everything on the list."

"You have a list?" I was prompted to ask, and she nodded with her usual innocent sincerity.

"Yes. I made chamomile tea, I changed the sheets, I made porridge, I moisturized the air..." She counted each one on her fingers until she came to a stop, paused, and then added, "I hope I didn't forget anything."

"I don't think there is much else you could do," I told her just to keep the conversation going, but then her words reminded me of something, and I clicked my tongue in frustration. "I, on the other hand, have forgotten something. Give me a minute."

My request startled Snowy, but she dutifully took her *attentive maid* posture again and waited for me to finish my business. Speaking of which, I quickly Far Glanced over to Lab Coat Guy and, regrettably, he was already on his way back to his super-secret mad scientist lair. Peculiarly enough, instead of some kind of oddball transportation method befitting his aesthetics, he was riding in a simple family sedan driven by the trigger-happy android (who was dressed much more sensibly this time around).

I waited awhile, just to see if they would drop something relevant to my interests, but they staunchly refused to discuss anything more riveting than what they would have for dinner. Not particularly riveting. I was just about to return to my room when I belatedly realized that there was one more elephant in the room I'd consistently ignored ever since Snowy brought it to my attention.

Oh well. There was no sense in delaying the inevitable. I decided to just bite the bullet and look into Rinne's whereabouts. In fact, it felt like she was fairly close by, so I quickly found her and... wait. Is that my...?

"Snowy! Open the window, now!"

Okay, I know this is an unexpectedly tense moment and all, but if I may go on a tangent, I wanted to mention one of the many reasons why I (platonically) loved my new little sister. Most people, when they were suddenly yelled at in a situation like this, would have frozen up. Maybe they would quickly glance around, and say something like *What?* or *Why?* or even just *Okay…?* wasting precious seconds in the process.

Not Snowy.

The moment I exclaimed, she leaped over to the window and threw it open. It felt so nice to be in the company of someone who followed instructions even under pressure.

That tangent aside, let's get back to the present situation. The window was open, and the cold air coming in sent a chill down my sweaty back, but at first nothing happened. This time the rules of convenient timing must have been out of lockstep, as the two of us had to stare at the window for several long, awkward seconds before anything happened.

But then, in the span of a blink of an eye, there was a sudden gust of wind, followed by a dark figure soaring through the open window before landing on my floor, rolling forward, and coming to a standing halt.

Needless to say, the shady figure was none other than everyone's least favourite monster huntress, who then proceeded to spend several seconds staring at the wall right in front of her nose, as if in a trance.

"What the hell is wrong with you?" I burst out, making the other people in the room jolt in surprise.

Rinne turned on her heel and looked at me with a neutral, almost disinterested expression.

"We have found you, Leonard of Clan Dunning," she stated as she took a step forward, her weapon drawn. In an uncharacteristic display of common sense, she followed the direction of my eyes. She let out a noncommittal grunt and wrapped up her weapon, after which she forcefully cleared her throat and said, "Good evening."

"Don't you *good evening* me!" I exclaimed and wildly gestured towards the open window. "What the hell were you doing flying through the air towards my room?"

"We used a combination of *shunpo* and *kage no—*"

"I didn't ask *how* you did it! I asked you *why!*"

"Oh." My unwanted guest sounded disappointed. "Since you didn't come to participate in the hunt, we resolved to seek you out ourselves. Upon our arrival, we found your house's entrance warded by some form of *omyodo*, so we concluded that if we wished to employ your assistance in the efficacious slaughtering of the creatures of the underworld, we must enter into your lodge by other means." Then she glanced down at her sword, nodded, and turned back to me. "Onikiri wishes to know why you have sealed off the main entrance of your lodge."

"Because someone broke down my door and destroyed my furniture a few days ago," I snapped, and she once again proved her complete lack of self-awareness by giving me a shallow nod in return.

"So, it was to prevent the spawn of the underworld infiltrating your territory again. We understand. Very sensible of you. Onikiri agrees. She says even a dead timekeeper tells the correct time twice." She paused, again, and after wrinkling her brows, she added, "We do not understand how a dead person who keeps the time can say anything, but Onikiri is wise, so she must be correct."

I opened my mouth to respond, but I simply couldn't find the words to adequately describe the way I felt about her answer, so instead I just closed it again and proceeded to rub my temples. In the meantime, Rinne looked around the room and noticed Snowy.

"Who is that?" she asked me with the bluntness of a falling ACME anvil.

"She is my sister. Her name is Snowy."

My flying home invader stepped up to her and looked her over from head to toe.

"Uh… Hello?" my sister awkwardly greeted her, but the creepy huntress completely ignored her in favor of continuing to be creepy. At last, she turned back to me.

"She has a funny name," she stated with an odd smile that was neither genuine nor one of her slasher grins. "Onikiri says she likes her clothes. We might like her."

"Weird. But I'm still happy to hear it."

"Are we also taking her with us into the blackest night to quench our thirst for the hunt in the blood-drenched cadavers of our prey?"

"No."

My categorical denial apparently took her aback, but she quickly shrugged it off. "In that case, let us embark on the warpath on our own!"

"No," I repeated, in the exact same manner.

That stopped her in her tracks for a bit longer than just a moment, but she bounced back all the same with a disappointed, almost whiny, "Whyyy? Do you not want to shed the crimson essence of the monsters that lurk in the deep dark corners of the city with me anymore? Was Onikiri right about you? Are you really a male version of a small female dog?"

"Would you please stay silent for a moment?" I asked her, though considering I was already running a deficit on my available fucks to give, my voice was considerably more commanding than I originally intended.

"I can't go with you because I am sick. I cannot hunt for tiny Chimeras like this."

"Sick, you say?" Rinne's expression changed into a curious one, and she extended a gloved hand towards my face, stopping about a finger's width away from my forehead.

"What are you doing?"

"We're affirming your justification by examining whether you have a feverous condition," she replied while waving her hand in front of my face again.

"So?"

"We can't say we feel anything."

"Maybe… you should take the gloves off?" Snowy suggested from the sidelines, and Rinne grunted in approval.

"The little sister is right. I am in error." Saying so, she flung her sword over her shoulder and began to take off her glove, but then she abruptly paused halfway, glanced between the two of us and added, "Onikiri suspects that you two might be working in nefarious tandem for the sake of tricking us into touching your disgusting manflesh with our tender fingers to satisfy your depraved hand fetishism." There was a long, incongruous beat of silence in the room, during which she cocked her head to the side in a display that might have even been cute if it was on anyone else, after which she asked, "Are you?"

"Obviously not." My barely restrained indignation might have bled through my words a little, as she took them at face value without any further malarkey and she gingerly touched my forehead.

"It appears you indeed possess a feverous constitution," she commented, pulling her glove back on. "It must be a sickness of the most vile variety to cause harm to one such as you."

"I don't know about that," I stated after a dog-tired sigh. "I'm pretty sure I just accidentally overworked myself."

"What an unbecomingly silly notion," scoffed the annoying huntress. "The obviousness of the fact that you have unknowingly fallen victim to the malicious machinations of the vile denizens of the underworld is downright blinding."

"Is it?"

"Certainly," she responded with a huge nod. Then she turned to Snowy and told her, "Pay attention, little sister! Your older brother was most likely poisoned by the abhorrent dwellers of the underworld. It must be part of yet another wicked plan to stop us from clearing their filthy existence out of this land by righteous slaughter. Were they to attack now, it will fall upon your shoulders to protect your kin! Are you prepared?"

"Uh…" Completely overwhelmed by Rinne's fervor, Snowy sent me pleading glances for help, so I gestured for her to just agree with whatever she says. "Y-yes?"

"Good." After affirming her answer, my unwelcome guest faced me again and told me, "They must be waiting for you to weaken even further so they can slay you when you are most vulnerable. But fret not! We shall find them and strike them down as they approach, paint the city streets in the red of roses with their blood! Rest in peace knowing that even if the venom of their hidden blades may cut the thread of your life short, we will give them a death to remember in kind."

"How are they supposed to remember something if you…?" I wanted to ask her, but before I could finish, Rinne took a running start and dived right out through the window without saying anything else, leaving us behind in a decidedly confounded silence.

Finally, Snowy broke the ice by awkwardly pointing at the still open window and asking, "Was… that really the monster hunter?"

I nodded.

"She is rather… odd."

"That is by far the most diplomatic way you could have described how balls-to-the-wall cuckoo-for-cocoa-puffs she is."

"If you say so…" my sister muttered. Then she looked me in the eye. "What do we do now?"

"Well, there are a couple of things to consider," I mused as I glanced at my lukewarm food. "I think we can both agree the most important thing at the moment would be to ward the windows…"

PART 2

"It's about time," I thought aloud as I interlinked my fingers and stretched my arms over my head. I have no idea why that felt so satisfying, but it did, so I did it a second time, just for good measure. Once the blood rush died down a little, I shook my hands and quickly closed my useless Celestial Hub browser tabs.

I was still a little miffed about that. I'd spent several long hours browsing the Hub and interviewing the regulars, and after all that, I had to close my inquiries on whether or not Celestials had anything to do with the Abrahamic religions with a resounding *Who knows?* It was damn irritating.

But enough about that—I was about to have visitors, so I had to prepare.

With that thought, I jumped to my feet… or rather, since I was still sore all over, I carefully rose to my feet, slipped into my slippers, and I put my PC into standby mode, after which I had a quick shower. The water felt only warm even though it was the same temperature as usual, so I figured I still had a fever. I'd taken some medicine that morning, so there wasn't much else I could do about it. Hence, after I finished washing up, I quickly got dressed, walked down to the ground floor, filled the water heater, prepared a couple of mugs and a box of tea bags, and then I waited.

Fortunately, I didn't have to do so for long, and I didn't even need to use my Far Sight to figure out that the gang arrived, as they made enough noise to wake the dead. I consequently turned the heater off, walked over to the front door, and casually opened it just as my dear assistant was about to insert her key into the lock.

The unexpected, slightly uncomfortable silence that followed hung in the air for only a few seconds, as Judy slowly let her hand down and spoke up in a flat and yet at the same time distinctly disapproving voice.

"Why aren't you in bed?"

"Hi, Dormouse, I'm happy to see you, too." I flashed a toothy grin and gestured for the group to come inside.

My non-draconic girlfriend might have huffed and puffed, but did obediently cross the threshold, if only so that the others could follow without having to push her out of the way. My friends all looked quite cold, so I didn't blame them for trying to get inside in a hurry; it was late autumn, after all, and the weather was especially chilly that morning. There was also another reason why they were all flushed, but I wasn't supposed to know about it yet, so I didn't mention it and simply directed them towards the living room.

In order of arrival, we had Josh, who was in strangely high spirits; then Elly, who sidled up to me with the excuse to check my temperature (even though Judy was already doing the same, but I digress); then the ever-tired class rep, followed by Snowy and an unusually downcast Angie.

"Hi, Leo..."

My impression was further solidified when the Celestial girl only gave me a shallow greeting, followed by a depressed sigh. Not only that, but Snowy seemed to be in the process of consoling her. Considering she was completely fine when I last spied *cough* I mean, *observed* her, her behaviour was pretty suspicious. So, while the others were putting their coats on the racks, I waved her over and casually asked, "Why the long face?"

"Nothing..." she replied in the same dour voice as she crammed her beanie into the sleeve of her coat. I waited for a bit, just in case she would add something else, but instead she just exhaled another sigh and silently headed into the living room after the rest of the girls.

Now *that* was disconcerting. I subtly gestured Josh over. By then, my girlfriends had already left to prepare drinks for everyone, so I picked a slightly more secluded spot (which wasn't an easy task considering my home wasn't *that* spacious), which was pretty much just the corner by the coat rack.

"Is there a problem?" Josh asked before I could get a word in, and while I wanted to just shake my head, I had to shrug.

"That's what I wanted to ask. Angie seems unusually down," I broached the question right away, and to my sincere surprise, my friend's face instantly twisted as if he'd bitten a lemon.

"Oh, you mean *that*," he said, and his shoulders fell. "Where do I even begin?"

"At the beginning?" I proposed.

"Okay, here goes. So, you were sick and didn't come to school. When Elly told us it was for real and you had a fever, Angie had the idea to buy you some get-well cakes on the way home."

"*Get-well cakes?*" I repeated after him with a skeptical brow raised for emphasis.

He nodded. "I think she just recently learned that there was a new kind of Jaffa cake available in our favourite sweets shop, and she just wanted an excuse to try them. Anyways, we took a detour there on our way here, and she bought a whole box of them, but then right after that, we were ambushed by Doctor Robatto."

"I hope nothing serious happened," I said out of courtesy, though I was already well aware of the recent event that could be generously called a "battle."

"Nah, nothing. There were a bit more of the yellow Sprockets, but we mopped the floor with them." Josh sounded almost proud, but he quickly caught himself and continued in a more neutral tone. "The point I was getting at is that in the commotion, Angie lost the cakes. We would have been here a good ten minutes ago if we didn't have to look for them, but they were completely gone."

"Maybe Lab Coat Guy took them?"

"Who knows?" Joshua shrugged. "Angie was pretty mad about it at first, but by the time we got here, she calmed down a bit."

"She still seems pretty downcast to me."

"Don't worry, she'll bounce back in no time," my friend reassured me.

Just as if to prove his point, Angie poked her head through the doorway, and the moment our eyes met, her lips curved into a giant grin.

"Hey, Leo? Neige let me look through the kitchen, and I found three full boxes of cat's tongue biscuits! Can I have some? Pretty please?"

At first, I gave the suddenly energetic Celestial girl a blank look, but I told her, "Sure. You already know where you can find the milk and the instant cocoa, right?"

"Of course! Thanks!"

After beaming at me one more time, she disappeared into the kitchen, with my friend giving me a somewhat smug *See? I told you* look. I graciously ignored him and was just about to tell him to follow me into the living room when the princess peeked through the doorway.

"What are you two doing over there?"

"Oh, nothing. Just discussing our diabolical plans for world domination as usual, right, Josh?"

He only looked at me funny, so I elbowed my friend. He spoke in a staggered, mechanical voice, "Yes, plans. About what he said. Domination and stuff. Very diabolical."

Josh's acting was so stilted, it would give wader birds a run for their money, but my girlfriend didn't seem to mind.

She walked over, grabbed my hand, and proceeded to more or less drag me along while telling me, "Stop joking around and come inside. It's cold here in the entryway, and you are still sick."

"Maybe, but it's not because of the cold…" I protested, but my words fell on deaf ears as she pulled me into the living room and practically forced me to sit on my slightly battered comfy chair.

"There!" she declared with a satisfied huff. Then she turned towards the kitchen and called out, "Is the tea ready yet?"

"Just a moment!" came the instant answer from Snowy, and a few short seconds later, she emerged from the kitchen with a tray carrying a single steaming mug. Even more inexplicably, she somehow managed to find the opportunity to put on her maid outfit between the time she arrived and the time I came back to the living room. Her dedication to her hobby was admirable yet baffling. "One mug of herbal tea, as requested."

Saying so, she placed the suspiciously dark cup of liquid in front of me, but before I could voice my qualms about it, I noticed Judy tottering down the stairs with a staggeringly large pile of pillows and blankets. I was just about to get up to help her, but the princess beat me to the punch. She took about half of them before they both came back down and began to wordlessly cushion me into my sofa.

"Is this really necessary?" I asked maybe a little less intensely than the situation demanded. Judy immediately rebuked me by placing a blanket on my lap.

"You are sick, and since you are horrible at taking care of yourself, we have to do it."

"Yes, but… I mean, no, I am perfectly capable of… Princess! I do not need another pillow behind my back!"

"Better to be safe than sorry!" she told me with an irreverent smirk before attempting to wedge another pillow under me.

"Speaking of sickness," the class rep intruded into our domestic horse-play, accompanied by her customary adjustment of her glasses. "I don't believe we have been told what happened to you yet."

"There's not much to explain, really," I attempted to deflect the question, but it was unable to redirect her attention, so at the end of the day I told her, "Oh, fine! So, you remember how I tweaked the Magiformers yesterday so that you guys wouldn't look absolutely ridiculous while using them?"

"You actually use the name we came up with! Yay!" a certain Celestial interjected at the most inappropriate of times, only to turn to the guy on her side and exclaim, "High five!"

Josh immediately raised his right hand, as if by muscle reflex, and their palms met midway with a satisfyingly sharp sound. Putting the childhood friends doing their childhood friend things aside, I shook my head and turned back to the increasingly impatient Amelia.

"So, as I was saying, I revised the enchantments a little—" I could see that Ammy was just about to cut in to ask about that, so I raised my voice and continued with, "NOW, as you might imagine, modifying an already placed enchantment without any specialized tools is pretty damn hard, but in my excitement, I managed it, but I might have overexerted myself a little. You can see the results with your own eyes."

The class rep opened her mouth to respond, but after some hesitation, she closed it, looking both conflicted and maybe just a tiny bit suspicious. I would have liked to chalk this up as a victory for myself, but whatever satisfaction I could derive from the verbal sparring was disrupted by Elly shoving the mug of a strange-smelling concoction under my nose.

"If you are overworked, then it's all the more reason you should drink this! It's the ultimate herbal remedy my great-grandfather learned from an Indian yogi. It's great for colds, joint pains, sore throats, and receding hairlines!"

"That last one has nothing to do with the rest, and even then…" I began, but I was interrupted by Judy coming back to pile yet another blanket on me. "Oh, come on, Dormouse! At this point, it's starting to look like I'm sitting inside a cushion fortress!"

My reprimands fell on deaf ears, as my girlfriend proceeded to tuck me in, anyway, an experience that already was embarrassing, but then it was made a hundred times worse by the fact that I had an audience watching… though, to be fair, they were having fairly odd reactions to my plight.

Ammy was mostly disinterested, though I could swear I saw some schadenfreude in her eyes. Angie, on the other hand, was beaming, with a bunch of elongated of biscuits in one hand and an open jar of peanut butter in the other, and she was giving me a revoltingly warm gaze, as if my situation was *cozy* or *heartwarming* or, heaven forbid, *wholesome*. Ugh.

Well, at least Josh was on my side… Right? Maybe. It didn't take long for me to realize that there was more than sympathy in his eye.

"Do you want to say something, Joshua?"

My ever so tactful prompt was quickly answered by my friend awkwardly scratching his chin and telling me, "Well, you know… I was just thinking that you are *living the life*, being pampered by three girls and all."

In return for his forthcoming answer, I awarded him the flattest look three-dimensional space could possibly represent before exhaling a shallow groan and turning to my sister instead.

"Did you hear that, Snowy? Josh is disappointed because I'm the only one who is being *pampered*? Why don't you go over and *pamper* him a bit."

"I didn't say that," Josh called out in alarm.

"Now, now, don't be modest. After all, it's a maid's duty to entertain guests, isn't it?"

"I… I think you are right?" my sister responded and turned to Josh, her cheeks maybe a tad rosier than usual.

"Wait, Lili! You don't actually have to take everything that Leo says seriously!" Josh tried to avoid the coming embarrassing shenanigans, but it was too late! I had already used the magic word, so it was inevitable that our resident maid-enthusiast would heed the call without fail…!

Or, at the very least she would have, if not for a certain class representative clearing her throat in the most pointed of fashions.

"I'm glad to see you are all full of energy, but can we actually address the reason why we all gathered here in the first place?"

"To visit Leo and wish him a swift recovery?" Angie suggested, her reasonable words only slightly undermined by the fact that she had peanut butter on her nose.

"Well… certainly, I admit that was the original plan," Ammy acknowledged in an unusually flustered display before our eyes met again. After adjusting her glasses, she swiftly declared, "However, as you can see, he seems perfectly okay, doesn't he?"

"I guess?" Angie muttered while she dunked another biscuit into the jar. "But then why are Judy and Elly piling so many blankets on him?"

"That is a really good question!" I burst out, only for Ammy to shake her head at me.

"Doesn't really matter. What does is the fact that we were attacked, once again!"

"I've heard," I responded just a smidgen begrudgingly as I tried to ignore Elly's insistent attempts to make me drink her family's suspicious "traditional herbal tea mix." "So?"

"So?" she indignantly repeated.

"Yes, that's what I just said. I said that because I have no control over whether or not Lab Coat Guy harasses you."

"I never implied you did. I brought it up because it's a threat we have to deal with!"

"Do we?" I asked. "Shouldn't you ask your grandfather to deal with him? After all, it is his *territory*."

I must have hit the nail on the head, as she visibly reeled back, if only for a moment, before admitting, "I… tried to ask Grandfather about it."

"You did?"

That was mildly surprising. Now, I admittedly didn't have the capability of keeping tabs on everyone 24/7, but I was pretty sure I never saw her in the vicinity of the old man yesterday. But the class rep nodded and began to tell me what happened in a dour voice.

"I called him over to discuss the threat these attacks posed to us and the people of the city. I… I didn't tell him about your claims. I thought I should first confirm his reaction before accusing him."

"And? What happened?" came the prompt from an inexplicably attentive Josh.

Ammy let out a defeated sigh.

"He was evasive and claimed that the School couldn't afford to divert resources on a wild goose chase, right after the incident with the Abyssals."

"Even though you were also in 'danger'?" I inquired, earning me a dispirited nod.

"He didn't seem to care about my safety, either," the class rep muttered.

"Or rather, he knows that there is no danger, so he is not worried about you, at all."

"Maybe," she granted me.

"Oh? Does that mean you actually believe me?" I asked her with a barely restrained grin, and she gave me a weak nod in return.

"Maybe," she repeated, this time a little more firmly.

There was a short spell of silence in the room, which I used to organize my thoughts. As a matter of fact, the old man's behaviour felt fairly odd to me. He flagrantly ignored the 'threat' the Research Society posed, even in front of his own granddaughter. If it was me, I would have at least attempted to make a show of combating their flamboyant menace, even if just on the surface, but instead he just dismissed it.

No matter how I tried, I couldn't make heads or tails of the old man's motivations. Maybe it was some sort of test? Like, was he actually dropping clues for us to figure out it was him behind it all, waiting for us to kick down his door only to reveal it was just an elaborate ruse to see if we were worthy of joining the School? Or was it Judy's version of the Narrative making him act stupid, just to create clues that point at him as the current antagonist so that they could be claimed as foreshadowing once we reach some kind of climactic reveal? Complicated.

"All right then, let's discuss Lab Coat Guy after all," I declared, earning me a few curious looks from the gang. "What? You said you wanted to talk about his attacks, so here we go." After I said that, I got my hands out from under the blankets and linked my fingers in my trademarked "diabolical mastermind" pose before I continued. "So, as far as I can see, we have three options. First, we could try to avoid further confrontations."

"Can we do that?" came the doubtful question from Josh.

I gave him a solid nod.

"Certainly. I have my eyes on the guy, in more ways than one, so while it would be a little tricky, I could probably give you advance notice whenever he tries to ambush you. Since he is contractually obligated to use the Purple Zone to attack you, and considering that those have a limit to their sizes, you can simply avoid those on your way home and leave him fiddling his thumbs inside."

"That sounds reasonable," Josh mumbled.

"The second option is that we attack the problem at its root by storming Lab Coat Guy's hideout and putting an end to his mustache-twirling antics once and for all."

"Can we actually do that?" Judy asked me, just as she finally gave up on trying to pile another blanket on me (at this point I was pretty sure she was only doing it for the attention), and I nodded in the affirmative.

"Sure. I have the location, we have both our group and Brang's Fauns, and I'm fairly sure we could rush their base and *blitzkrieg* them before they could put up too much of a resistance."

"It still sounds dangerous," my assistant commented.

"Well, it would be more or less a paramilitary operation, so of course things could get dicey. That said, we also have one more option left."

"Which is?" Elly urged me on.

"To do nothing."

The gang looked confused.

"By that I mean we would simply allow the ambushes to continue, with maybe one or two emergency plans in place. As you have probably noticed, Lab Coat Guy and his cronies do not actually pose a serious threat; however, they do serve as great punching bags. We might actually run into real threats in the future, so I think it would be beneficial for you to gain some combat experience this way and learn how to support each other and work together as a group."

"I agree." Everyone turned towards the unexpected source of agreement, and Joshua visibly flinched from all the sudden attention. He quickly collected himself and explained, "I mean, I do think that Leo is right. If we are ever going to run into a situation like when I was almost kidnapped, we need to learn how to efficiently work together, and these attacks are providing a great opportunity to do that."

"There is one more option you are ignoring," Judy cut in. "We could also directly confront Lord Endymonion about his involvement."

"True," I agreed. "Unfortunately, I don't think we have enough presentable evidence yet to put him in a corner."

"So, you think we should allow Doctor Robatto to continue his operations in order to gather more evidence," my assistant stated as if she was reading my mind.

"More or less."

"Also, it's not like we can't do the whole 'storm the enemy's secret hideout' thing later, right?" Angie commented between bites, earning her a nod from me.

"Sure. If playing around with the silly robots gets out of hand, the other options still remain perfectly viable."

"I'm in favor," came the next baffling vote of agreement, this time from Amelia of all people. "If Grandfather is truly responsible for Robatto's actions, he must have a good reason. I want to learn why he is doing this."

"Let's hope you have the opportunity," I responded before looking at the group. "All right, let's put this to vote. All who are in favor of exploiting our attackers, raise your hands."

I raised mine, followed by Josh and the class rep. Judy and Snowy followed suit, the latter probably because she was just deferring to my decision.

"I don't mind either way, but I am kind of curious about what a *biomechanical gigant* is, so count me in!" the resident Celestial declared as she raised a hand.

"What *is* a 'biomechanical gigant,' anyway?" Elly mused as she belatedly raised her hand.

"I don't know, but Robatto said he was going to *'strike fear into our feeble hearts'* with them, and their name sounds kind of cool, right, Josh?"

"I suppose," my friend tentatively agreed, and Angie giggled.

"All right, then," I said. "I suppose we are finished with this topic. What now? You guys said you wanted to come over to see how I was doing. Did you really have no plans beyond that?"

"We had snacks, but they disappeared," Angie told me with a sad sigh, only to bounce back and declare, "But Leo is right! Since we are all gathered here, it's the perfect time for some group activity! All we've been doing for the past couple of days are sparring matches and serious discussions upon discussions! I'm sick of it!"

"Okay then, group activity it is," I responded with a smile. "What do you have in mind?"

"Well, I… um… Do you have any board games?"

"I can't say I do," I told her, though considering how many unexpected things I'd found in the house already, it wasn't entirely out of the question.

"How about card games?" Elly proposed, earning her a curious raised brow from yours truly.

"Such as?"

"Dad plays poker a lot, and he occasionally let me join in. It's a fun game," the princess insisted, but I could only shake my head.

"I'm sorry, but I don't think we have cards, either."

"No problem! I will call Melinda and ask her to bring our spare set over. It has a mat and tokens and everything."

"That sounds really nice, but… Do any of us know how to play poker?" I raised my next objection, only for Elly to flash me a grin in return.

"Don't worry—I'll teach you!"

"Oh well, then. Any objections?"

Everyone seemed to be fine with the idea, so the princess fished out her phone and made the call.

In the meantime, I had to admit that maybe playing around like this every once in a while wasn't such a bad idea. Maybe after all the recent stressful events, a few friendly rounds of cards were all we needed to unwind.

Yes, a *friendly* card game where *everyone* had the *same* chance of winning. Yeees.

"No cheating," Judy warned me, her eyes already set in a suspicious squint.

But I must say, I had absolutely no idea what she was talking about. Not one bit.

ABOUT THE AUTHOR

Gábor Horváth is a Hungarian social worker employed in a nursery home for the elderly. He studied archaeology but, due to a financial crisis in the family, was obliged to withdraw from university and enter the workforce. Also known as Egathentale, Horváth has been writing for his own amusement ever since high school and started publishing his work online at the encouragement of friends.